THIS BROKEN WORLD

BAEN BOOKS by CHARLES E. GANNON

The Terran Republic Series
Fire with Fire
Trial by Fire
Raising Caine
Caine's Mutiny
Marque of Caine
Endangered Species (forthcoming)
Protected Species (forthcoming)

The Vortex of Worlds Series
This Broken World
Into the Vortex (forthcoming)
Toward the Maw (forthcoming)

The Ring of Fire Series
(with Eric Flint)
1635: The Papal Stakes
1636: Commander Cantrell in the West Indies
1636: The Vatican Sanction
1637: No Peace Beyond the Line
1636: Calabar's War (with Robert E. Waters)

The Black Tide Rising Series
(created by John Ringo)
At the End of the World
At the End of the Journey

The Starfire Series
(with Steve White)
Extremis
Imperative
Oblivion

To purchase any of these titles in e-book form,
please go to www.baen.com.

THIS BROKEN WORLD

BOOK ONE OF THE VORTEX OF WORLDS

CHARLES E. GANNON

A Baen Books Original

Baen Publishing Enterprises
P.O. Box 1403
Riverdale, NY 10471
www.baen.com

ISBN: 978-1-9821-2571-4

Cover art by Kurt Miller
Maps by Rhys Davies

First printing, November 2021

Distributed by Simon & Schuster
1230 Avenue of the Americas
New York, NY 10020

Library of Congress Control Number: 2021042030

Pages by Joy Freeman (www.pagesbyjoy.com)
Printed in the United States of America
10 9 8 7 6 5 4 3 2 1

To my late mother, Cecilia Klemm Gannon,
who encouraged my imagination at every turn
and whose advice for happiness became both the
wisdom and watch-words by which I've lived my life:

Make your avocation your occupation.

THE WORLD of ARRDANC

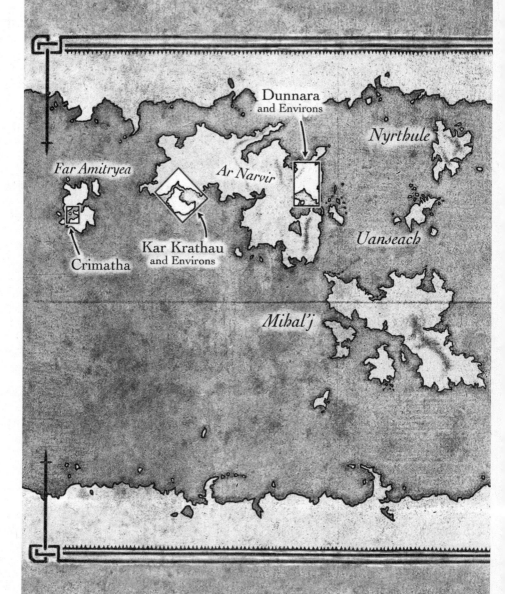

Far Amitryea

Crimatha

Dunnara
and Environs

Nyrthule

Ar Narvir

Kar Krathau
and Environs

Uanseach

Mihal'j

(POST CATACLYSM)

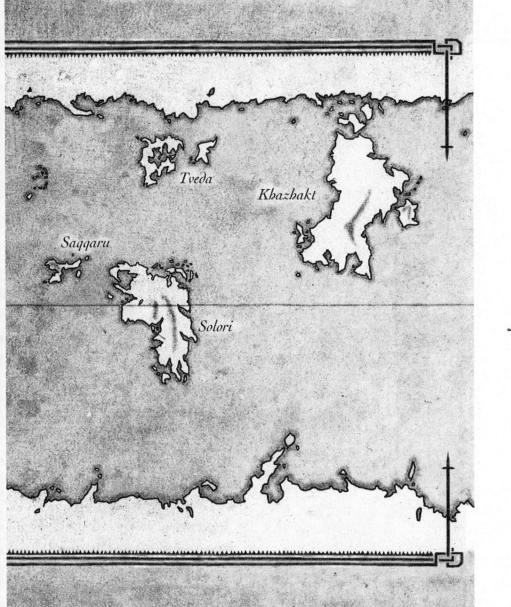

Tveda

Khazhakt

Saqqaru

Solori

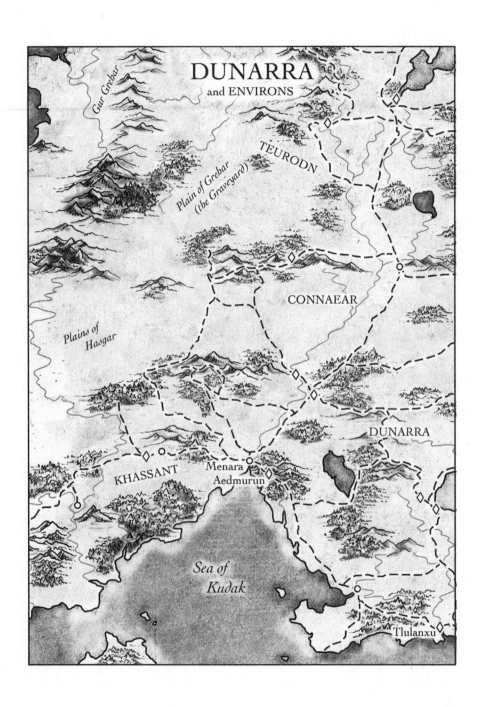

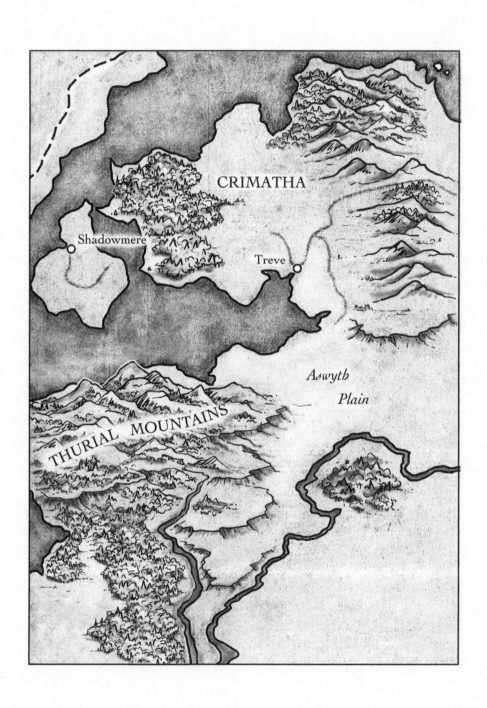

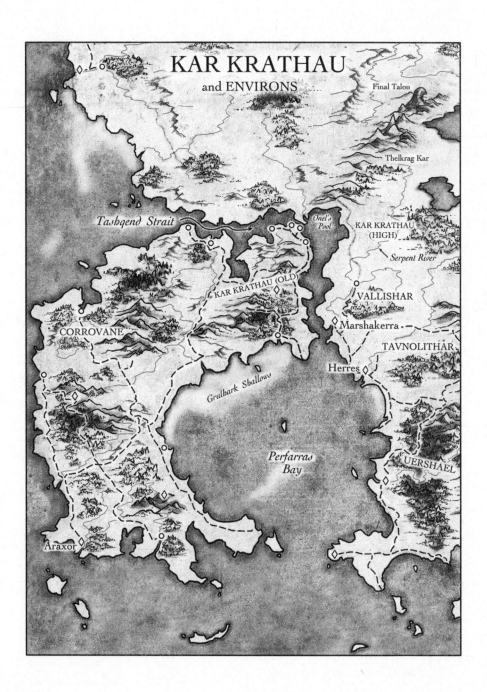

KAR KRATHAU
and ENVIRONS

Final Talon

Thelkrag Kar

Tashgend Strait

Onel's Pool

KAR KRATHAU (HIGH)

Serpent River

KAR KRATHAU (OLD)

VALLISHAR

Marshakerra

CORROVANE

TAVNOLITHAR

Herres

Grulbark Shallows

UERSHAEL

Perfarras Bay

Araxor

PART ONE

FIRST LESSONS

Journal Entry 1
8th of Running Deer, 1783 S.C.

This is the ~~jernel~~ jurnal of Druadaen u'Tarthenex. I am nine years old this past Adamant. I am keeping this ~~jernel~~ jurnal because my father said it would be a good idea. He says he wishes that he could go back and read what he did and thought when he was my age. Also, he ~~encurrejjed~~ ~~encuorjed~~ urged me to start now, since I will want to remember what I see and hear during my first trip to a big city!

We are leaving for Aedmurun tomorrow. Mother says it is not as big as the capital at Tlulanxu, but it is still one of Dunarra's most importent cities. The ~~juorney~~ trip will take a week, maybe more. It depends on how we travel there. If we take an omni, we will go faster but will also have to stop each night, so we will spend less time moving. The barge goes more slowly, but since we would stay aboard, we will cover more leagues since we will only have to change the team of titandrays twice a day. Of course, if we were on the wallway itself, we might reach Aedmurun even faster, despite the overnight stops. But my parents say the wall-ways are mostly reserved for official bisiness.

My friend Heyna thinks we might be allowed to travel on the wallways anyway. Even tho we live beyond the Dunarran border, she says she knows more than I do about such things. Even more than Dunarran adults. I'm not sure about that, but Heyna is almost twelve and is certain about many things. Even things that happen in other countries.

Heyna's older brother and sister (their mother is Connæaran, so their family is very large) didn't seem to believe her. When she spoke about the wallway, they just rolled their eyes and kept working with my parents. They are learning how to take care of our farm while we are gone. I don't know how my parents can afford it. The other farmers nearby call us "the gardners," since we grow so few crops. But I think father and mother earn a lot of billon when they go back over the border to the closest wallway tower every month. I ask questions about what they do there, but they always change the topic. I act like I do not notice when they do that. But I know that they are trying to distract me. I also know that if they could tell me, they would.

I think whatever work they do at the wallway tower may be the reason we have been invited to the big gathering—or "progress"—that will take place in Aedmurun. Honestly, the farmers who live near us are right: we make just enough food for ourselves, and neither father or mother are very good at growing it. But we seem to have money when we need it and new books to read when we finish the ones borrowed from their friends back in Dunarra.

I'm just excited to see a real city, although I will miss our mastiff Grip and all our cats. And Shoulders, our draft horse, and Mama has told me to snuff out the candle, that we have a long day of travel ahead of us, and that if I'm tired, I might miss all sorts of things. So I am putting out the candle right away.

But I'm not sure I will sleep. I'm still too excited.

CHAPTER ONE

Druadaen had to lean backwards to see the parapet at the top of the lookout spire. Rising up from one of the wallway towers, the slender stone needle seemed poised to chase the day's sparse white clouds higher into the bright blue sky.

His mother leaned down close to his ear. "From the top," she whispered, "you can see all the way to the bay."

Whereas just a year ago, Druadaen might have become wide-eyed in surprise at such a claim, he buried that reflex under a doubting sideways glance. "Mama—Mother: that's almost fifteen leagues."

His father shrugged. "A bit more, actually. But you can indeed see the bay and well out into the Sea of Kudak."

"So, have *you* been up there?"

His father's eyebrows raised in what began as genuine surprise and then became feigned injury. "Son! You don't believe me? I am cut to the quick!"

Druadaen smiled. "Still, Papa, you didn't answer the question: Have you been on top of the spire?"

His mother wrapped her arms around him from behind. "You are as stubborn as your father!"

Who smiled ruefully. "I prefer the term 'persistent,' dear wife."

Her answering laugh sparked Druadaen's own. His father's smile widened. So did his arms as he reached out and gathered them close. It was a fine feeling, being in that family embrace, looking out upon the ships coming up the river as they stood on the wallwalk, cool in the wide shadow of this particularly squat wallway tower.

None of the wallway's many towers were *exactly* alike, but seen from the barge that had brought them almost a hundred leagues south into Dunarra, their outlines were identical. But this tower also served as the spire's foundation, and so was very different. "I wish we *could* go up there," Druadaen said, pointing overhead. "I would like to see the bay!"

By way of answer, his father swung him up to his broad shoulders and pointed to where the river wound through forests to the west.

Druadaen hugged his father's forehead with both arms. "Thanks, Papa...but I *still* can't see the bay."

His father tilted his head to smile up at him. "Your mother's right. You *are* stubborn."

"Persistent," she amended with a smile.

Druadaen was still staring at the top of the spire. "That's a lot of stairs. It must take an hour to climb them all." He considered. "Is there a faster way up? In case of emergencies?"

His mother smiled. "Yes, and that's a very good question."

"So how do they do it?"

His father hitched him up a little higher on his shoulders and Druadaen could hear the grin in his voice. "Maybe *you* can tell *us*."

Druadaen sighed. He usually enjoyed answering his father's real-world riddles. Except when they didn't come with any clues. Like this one. Besides, Druadaen just wanted to watch what was happening down in the port, look at all the different ships pulled up along the wharves, all the different peoples working in and around them, all the different cargos...

Cargos...

Druadaen glanced back at a ship that was off-loading a very heavy crate but without any stevedores manning the block and tackle. Instead, there were only two Dunarrans standing by. The one on the deck of the ship signaled that the crate was secure. The one waiting on the dock nodded, but rather than hauling on the pulley lines, he simply reached down and released a lever that protruded from between the wharf's granite blocks. After taking a moment to make sure that the load wasn't swaying, he pushed a second, longer lever.

The large crate rose slowly, the cables groaning but without anyone straining at the ropes. Druadaen stared. Was Dunarra so wealthy and powerful that it used mancery just to off-load cargo ships?

But that made no sense; mantics did not agree to use their powers for day-to-day tasks. So Druadaen looked more closely—and discovered that the main cable from the block and tackle was not wrapped around what he'd thought was a take-up drum. Instead, it was simply passing over a roller which guided it down through another gap in the wharf's stonework.

As Druadaen wondered what was lifting the crate, he was distracted by motion up at the bow of the ship; a work gang was slowly turning a windlass to retrieve the anchor. He flinched at what felt like a bright flash in the middle of his mind: sudden understanding of how the crate was being lifted, which also revealed how people could move up and down the tower so quickly.

"It's machines," he blurted out, the ideas coming much faster than he could find words. "It's like the anchor's windlass. The power is stored. Like in a spring. In a machine built under the wharf; that's what's lifting the crate." He pointed at the top of the tower. "And something like that must be used to move people up and down the spire."

"Yes, 'Dae." his mother murmured through a pleased smile. "The machinery is in the tower. It raises and lowers an enclosed platform, rather like a coach, called a funicular. That, and the weight of the spire, is why this tower is so much larger than the others along the wallway."

Druadaen laughed, not because it was funny, but out of sheer joy at solving the puzzle. Until he realized there was a potential problem with the solution. "Still," he said, "it would take a lot of people to wind the spring, or the ropes, for the elevator."

"That's true," his father agreed. "So I wonder: Are there other ways to get those gears turning and store that power?" But rather than looking at Druadaen, his eyes had begun to follow along the river's upstream course. It ran close against the outer edge of the city wall, where, at regular intervals, small, fortified mills dipped their waterwheels into the swift current.

Except, Druadaen realized, those weren't mills at all. He

pointed. "It's those. They're doing the work. Instead of people or animals."

His father's arms tightened briefly, imparting a fond hug to both legs. "That's right, lad."

But Druadaen wasn't done. "And the mills—uh, wheels: they're all the same. Like the walltowers. Like...like almost everything here!"

Again, he was almost drowned under a sudden rush of ideas and concepts for which he had no words. But he knew what he wanted to say, and what it meant about Dunarra. So much of what was built here was nearly identical, as if it had been cast from molds like they used back home when making candles and loaves. But here the tools, and wagons, and ships, and machines, and even most of the buildings had been formed that way, too.

His stuttering struggle to find the right words wasn't necessary. His father patted his thigh in a way that said, *Yes, son. You are correct.*

It was everywhere, Druadaen realized, as Aedmurun transmogrified before his eyes. The weapons of the guards, their armor, the tack of the horses and titandrays, the streets, the lights that lined them, even the clothes of the people going about their business: they weren't exactly alike, but they all had the appearance of having been shaped and finished in the same fashion. "How... why...?" he said hoarsely, mostly to himself.

By way of answer, his father turned slightly. Now Druadaen was facing directly over the wall into the trade quarter: the maze of market stalls where foreign merchants came to barter, buy, and sell.

Again, the setting transformed. What Druadaen had beheld just minutes before with both delight and wonder—all the different people with different languages and gestures and dress—was now a scene of desperation and want. Most of the outlanders were not so much fit as wiry; many were underfed. Their clothes, while varied, were as much made from patches as original materials. Swarms of young children—far younger than Druadaen—were hard at work alongside their parents. And many of the adults were so wrinkled that he couldn't be sure whether they were parents or grandparents.

Druadaen swallowed. "So many of them are old...and still they work? After all the years they had to save?"

His mother's voice was quiet. "Most outlanders age much more quickly than us and have more children to feed."

"But isn't it harder to raise and feed so many?"

"It is, but in most nations, children must help so that the family can fulfill its obligations."

"Obligations? You mean, like your work tithes?"

His father's voice was dark. "No, 'Dae. Most of those people must give a part of everything they make, or grow, or earn to a ruler who also decides how much they must give."

"But if their lives are nothing but work, then how do they learn to read or—?"

His mother put a finger against his lips. "The world is very different beyond the borders of Dunarra, dear son."

He rarely heard sadness in her voice, but it was there now. He also heard something similar to . . . fear? "Our emperor doesn't treat people that way . . . does he?"

"Dunarra has a Propretor Princeps, 'Dae, not an emperor."

"But if this is an empire, shouldn't it have an emperor?"

His mother shook her head. "Dunarra isn't an empire. It's a Consentium." She frowned. "Who told you it was an empire?"

"Heyna. She says that Dunarra is an empire with an emperor and that it used to rule the world."

His mother smiled the way she did when she was being extremely patient. "Heyna is a young lady with very strong opinions."

Druadaen shrugged. "Yes. And sometimes I think she tries to make me feel stupid."

His father leaned his head back and smiled up at Druadaen. "That's because she likes you."

"That's a strange way of showing it."

"Yes," his mother explained, "but sometimes that's what young girls and boys do when they are embarrassed about . . . liking someone."

Druadaen heard the evasive tone. "You mean she likes me *that* way? But I'm nine, and Heyna's—"

"Why, she's almost a grand old lady of twelve," exclaimed his father. "Three whole years older than you!"

Druadaen did his best not to sound surly. "Well, only *two and a half* years older."

His father swung him down and rested a hand gently on his

head. "'Dae, you're so big for your age, I think *all* of us have a hard time remembering you are not quite as old as you look."

"Heyna says that, too. And she says I'm too serious. Like her parents."

Druadaen's mother had that expression she got when she was about to roll her eyes but stopped herself at the last moment. "Yes. And I can imagine just how she sounded when she said that."

Druadaen was about to nod but was distracted by a faint odor of grilled *something* that wafted up from the stalls down near the docks. His stomach growled in response.

One of his father's eyebrows rose. "Sounds like someone is hungry."

Druadaen was about to deny it when a woman's voice answered before he could: "Well, of course 'someone' is hungry. You'll all starve to death up here!"

His father glanced over his head, smiled at whoever he saw there. "We'd starve to death anywhere, if we were waiting for *you*," he answered with a broad smile.

Druadaen turned. The woman who had spoken was considerably older than the two people who were approaching with her and smiling more broadly with every step. The next moment, Druadaen was caught in the middle of five adults welcoming each other with nods, embraces, and clasping of forearms. He tried to step back from the scrum of camaraderie but didn't make it out in time.

The woman who had spoken to his father looked down at him. "And is this young master Druadaen?" He nodded. She nodded back, smiling, but her eyes were intent. Or maybe they just seemed that way because they were staring out of a well-seamed face framed by silver hair.

Which gave Druadaen a moment's pause as he realized, *She's very old, for a Dunarran.* So formal address was wanted. "I am honored to meet you—" And he stopped. *By what title should I call her?* "Elder" would be appropriate, but she might be insulted—

Her smile became wry and she waved away his confusion of courtesies. "You may call me Shaananca if I may call you Druadaen. Would that be acceptable?"

The words left him a relieved rush: "Yes, please! Thank you, kind Lady!"

Shaananca's smile slipped from wry to rueful. "I am not of high birth," she murmured. "No one is, here."

Druadaen's mother put an arm around his shoulders. "And these two people with Shaananca are our friends, Indryllis and Varcaxtan."

Druadaen bowed slightly as they nodded and smiled. His eyes were on Indryllis' unusual...robe? gown? habit? It had what appeared to be fine silver threads woven into its length. "Are you a priestess, Mistress Indryllis?"

Her eyebrows rose, as did the corners of her mouth. "In a manner of speaking. I am what is called a Guide."

Druadaen frowned. "A guide? I have not heard of temples with 'guides.'"

Indryllis nodded. "You are correct. I serve in no temple."

"But then—?"

His mother hugged him. "Plenty of time for questions, later, 'Dae."

Varcaxtan, a heavily built and muscular man in a tanned tunic and breeches, nodded. "No mysteries to solve in my case, young Druadaen. Your father and I were comrades, years ago."

"So, you, too, are a mariner?" But his garb was not like any mariner Druadaen had ever seen or heard of.

Varcaxtan's quick glance at Druadaen's parents did not escape his notice. "A mariner? Sometimes. We served together on land, as well."

"I should like to do that, too. Very much," Druadaen said more loudly than he had intended.

"Well," the large man answered with a serious nod and assessing gaze, "you certainly look big enough for it! How old are you? Eleven? Twelve, maybe?"

"No! I am only nine, but everyone says I look older, and that I'm very big and strong for my age!"

"Well, well: you certainly are that!"

"And so you are hoping to become a mariner, too?" Indryllis asked.

Druadaen looked at her in surprise. "No. I will serve in the Legions once I grow up. And become a general!"

All the adult eyes around him widened. "That is quite an ambition," Shaananca said with a somber nod.

"It is," Druadaen answered with a frown. "But I am working to be worthy of it. I exercise and run every day, that I might be the best recruit there has ever been."

Shaananca was peering at him oddly. "You may be the size of a twelve-year-old, young master Druadaen, but your dedication is that of a still older person."

"A person of, well, fourteen, do you think?"

Shaananca's answering smile was both amused and rueful. "At least," she murmured. "But how will your parents tend to the farm without you when you are a Legior?"

"Oh, they won't be alone." Again he was ringed by perplexed adult stares. "By then, I will have a brother or sister. Actually, by this winter, I suspect."

What happened next struck Druadaen as very odd. The adults not only became silent but became very still. Varcaxtan's and Indryllis' eyes were wide and lips tightly closed.

However, Shaananca was looking over Druadaen's head at his parents. She, too, appeared surprised, but she also seemed to be concerned. Or angry. Or maybe fearful?

His father leaned closer. "How long have you known, 'Dae?"

Druadaen shrugged. "Maybe a month." When his father's eyebrows rose, he explained, "Mother doesn't run as much or walk as fast. Your walks have become slower and longer. And Grip always sticks close to her now. He even chases off the rooster." He shrugged again. "It's not so different from how Heyna's mother acts when she is with child. It's just happening more slowly with Ma—Mother."

Shaananca's gaze had shifted to him, but when he fell silent, her eyes returned to Druadaen's parents. "This news is most unexpected."

Druadaen's father stood straighter. "We had intended to share it while here."

"And not earlier? *Much* earlier?"

Indryllis stepped forward. "Certainly, questions can wait, and surprise should not keep us from honoring so happy an occasion." She bowed slightly toward Druadaen's mother. "Your joy is a blessing upon us," she intoned ritually.

Varcaxtan and Shaananca murmured the same phrase and copied the bow, but there was still something wrong. Druadaen was sure that Varcaxtan and Indryllis would rather have been somewhere—anywhere—else, now.

A long, silvery trumpet peal sounded down near the docks. Shaananca straightened. "She has arrived."

"Who?"

"The Lady of the Mirror," Druadaen's mother murmured.

"The one making a progress through Dunarra?" Druadaen was happy for something to break the awkwardness he'd caused by referring to his mother's pregnancy.

"Yes," answered Shaananca. "It is why I suggested we meet here." A genuine smile came back to her face. "So that you might see her arrival." She pointed over the parapet of the wallway.

A large ship, flying several different standards and long, streaming silver pennants, had drawn up to the wharf. As its mooring lines were tied off around the bollards, a broad gangway was run out to its side, where a large group was gathering, preparing to debark.

Druadaen stared. It was the strangest entourage he had ever seen. Granted, he hadn't seen many. However, every year, at least one or two went past on the road near their farm, and they all had one thing in common: almost everyone traveling with it wore livery that matched the house or league colors of the person whom they were escorting.

Not so this group. All of them wore tunics and robes of different colors and cuts. Of those in armor, no two wore the same kind, just as no two had the same helmet. The mix of field plate, mail, boiled leather, and two form-fitting Iavan sheath suits created a restless collage of contending shapes, angles, and colors. The weapons were no less distinctive and disparate.

"Tell me, Druadaen," Shaananca asked from over his shoulder, "what is that you find so interesting about the Lady's traveling companions?"

"They are all dressed—and equipped—so differently."

Shaananca nodded. "That is because the Lady has no retinue of her own."

"Why?"

Shaananca's eyes twinkled. "You should ask her yourself."

"But . . . how would I do that?"

"Why, when you meet her. Come: we'll have to start now if we mean to make sure that you get some food!"

CHAPTER TWO

They moved from the wallway to a network of flyover footbridges that not only joined various roofs but provided Aedmurun with an almost fanciful skyline. However, Druadaen did not miss that those graceful arches also provided excellent vantage points upon the neatly cobbled streets below.

The journey ended when they crossed a drawbridge to the fortified roof of a stately columned building. Its imposing stairs led down to a vast square, bordered by a broad expanse of trees and green sweetgrass on the other side. Water jetted upward from a wide fountain at the nexus of radial walkways that cut the greenery into tidy, well-manicured sections. Druadaen watched the spray fall back into the smooth marble basin with a sound like raindrops becoming musical notes, and he wondered: *Is that mancery or not?*

His father's voice pulled him out of the trance. "She's coming!" He pointed down toward the base of the stairs.

The entourage that Druadaen had seen debarking at the dock was already arrayed to ascend the steps. Seen more closely, the wild diversity of the Lady's guard was even more pronounced. The silks and loose cotton tunics common in the southern lands known as Mihal'j were comfortably draped upon the limbs and necks of many of those attending her. An equal number, obviously from the regions of Nyrthule, were at pains to be quit of the fur capes and trims typical of their homelands.

The individuals wearing the sheath armor were indeed Iavarain. He had only seen two of that race before and it was sometimes difficult to distinguish the men from the women; they were equally lithe and sure in their movements, like dancers who were also athletes. This pair was no different. They stood apart from the others, conversing only with a large, powerful man whose square-cut white hair ended in a jet-black fringe, wherever it hung free.

It was he who held up a hand that stilled the restless movement and mutters among the entourage.

The Lady emerged from their ranks and began ascending the steps without any fanfare or ceremony. If she had arrived in a carriage or a palanquin, Druadaen could not see it. Even amongst the equality-minded Dunarrans, it was odd that she had not been provided with *some* kind of conveyance, if for no other reason than to show respect.

But she looked neither road-worn nor insulted. Instead, she smiled freely as she mounted the stairs: an expression without any of the careful reserve that Druadaen had often observed upon the faces of persons of high stature. But ironically, it was her relaxed gait and unhurried acknowledgement of well-wishers on either side of the stairs that made her seem so profoundly out of place.

It was wonderfully refreshing, in one way: people of her station rarely took the time to acknowledge individual greetings. But it was not solely a product of aloofness; rather, it was a convention born of simple necessity. If a noble guest responded to but a fraction of such expressions of respect and honor, the event itself would never end. Even at the far less formal affairs back in Connæar, the endless courtesies and receiving lines made Druadaen long to be back home, mucking out the livestock pens. Though, come to think of it, there were some points in common between those two experiences.

Once the Lady reached the top of the stairs, she took a moment to rearrange her flowing raiment and passed into the building directly beneath Druadaen. "Where is she going?" he asked.

Shaananca both looked and sounded relieved. "To a formal greeting by Dunarra's leaders."

"I thought the empire's leaders were in Tlulanxu."

Varcaxtan smiled. "The *Consentium's* leaders meet there," he corrected gently, "but they have traveled here for the Conferral of Dignities." Seeing Druadaen's perplexity, he added, "It's similar to the way that rulers who visit another land are shown special honors when they arrive."

"How is this, uh...this *Conferral* different?"

Indryllis crouched down next to him. "The Lady isn't royalty. She isn't even noble. But she's very important. There's no one else in the world like her, really."

Druadaen swallowed. "It sounds as though she must be very old. But she looks young."

Shaananca nodded. "And so she is. She is still relatively new."

"New to what?"

"To her station. Come, Druadaen; if we are to meet the Lady, we must do so before the pretors and councilors get a hold of her!"

Druadaen was not fond of being a child; most adults did not listen to, let alone heed, anything nine-year-olds said. But on this occasion, their lack of attention was an unexpected boon. They were so focused on situating themselves where the Lady was likely to pass that he went totally unnoticed. Even his parents and their friends did little more than ensure that he didn't become separated from them in the crowd.

At first, that is. As their attention waned, he lagged further and further behind until, with a sideways step, he was able to slip away and observe what interested him the most: the Lady.

In some ways, her behaviors were very like those of the Dunarrans. She did not use nor expect proud-sounding titles and seemed to possess a great deal of knowledge about, and familiarity with, even the most unusual of their devices. But on the other hand, her guards were routinely frustrated by her incautious movements, and she often appeared uncertain when commencing one of the ritual introductory exchanges with nobles from different lands.

As Druadaen watched her complete yet another intricate set of diplomatic courtesies, a sizeable crowd passed by, blocking his view. When it cleared, the Lady was gone. He craned his neck, trying to catch a glimpse of her but to no avail. He rose up on his toes to get a better look...

"I'm right here," said an amused voice behind him.

Druadaen turned and found himself staring up at the Lady herself. He swallowed, made his best bow. "My Lady," he said.

She laughed easily. "One of my guards thought you might be a sly assassin disguised as a boy"—Druadaen tried not to let his shoulders or face fall in dejection—"but the only danger I perceive is that you might kill me with courtesy. So, since you are clearly not an *almost* full-grown assassin"—he stood straighter at that—"to what do I owe the intensity of your attention?"

Druadaen strove after the kind of answer that stuffy adults would have called "seemly." But no such words came to him, so instead, the truth jumped out of his mouth: "I'm curious, my lady."

Her smile became quizzical. "Curious? About what?"

"Why, about you!"

She laughed. It was a silver sound. "There's very little to tell. I have come from Far Amitryea, at the invitation of the Propretoriate of the Dunarran Consentium, to be formally recognized."

"As what?"

The voice that answered came from behind him. "As the locator of lost children, evidently." Shaananca drew alongside him. "In addition to her other roles." She sounded cheery, but when adults used that tone, it often meant they intended to scold a child in private later on. But instead, she glanced sideways at him and winked so quickly that he wondered if he'd imagined it.

The Lady laughed again. "Actually, Senior Archivist Shaananca, I didn't find this young fellow so much as he found me." She looked over Druadaen's head, smiling at whoever had come up behind him. "Which, I gather, is what the rest of you were trying to do. He simply succeeded first."

"He is quite resourceful," his father's voice said with hints of both irony and pride. He rested his hands gently on Druadaen's shoulders.

His mother stepped forward. "We are his parents, Mressenë and Tarthenex."

"Of Dunarra?" she asked.

"We dwell in Connæar," his father answered.

That spawned a quick exchange of glances, the kind that went back and forth between adults who were uncertain of what to say next, if anything. It was Shaananca who broke the silence as Varcaxtan and Indryllis arrived to either side of her. "They have a long history with the Consentium and would be welcome within our borders. But the current arrangement in Connæar was deemed more suitable."

The Lady's frown deepened, and she nodded. "I see." Her tone said that she did not but understood that it would be awkward for her to inquire further. She straightened and brightened. "And will you be attending the Conferral of Dignities?" she asked Druadaen.

"Yes, I hope so!" He looked at his father and mother. "I mean, if we are permitted."

The Lady laughed again. "You are not merely permitted but invited. And I would be sad not to see you among those who attend."

Shaananca reached out and put not merely a gentle, but almost uncertain, hand upon his head, as if she were touching an animal that might prove to be snappish. "And I'm sure that he will be quite pleased to sample the refreshments laid out in your honor."

The Lady bowed and they responded in kind. "I shall look forward to seeing you there. And learning more about you and your family, young master . . . ?"

"Druadaen!" he supplied proudly.

She nodded, smiled, and walked on. Her retinue quickly formed a palisade of armored and ready shoulders around her.

"So," asked Shaananca as the formation withdrew, "how did you like the Lady? Is she what you expected?"

Druadaen shook his head. "I did not expect anything. But I like her. I think."

"You 'think'?" exclaimed his mother.

Druadaen looked after the Lady's retreating retinue. "She spoke very kind words to me, and I believe her smile shows what is in her heart. And yet, having met her, she seems more a mystery than before."

Shaananca patted his head once. "Perceptive, indeed," she said. "Come. If you are to have any food, we must not be stuck at the rear of the hall during the ceremony. And then we must make a quick exit; there is much to see in this city, and you haven't much time to see it."

"But we'll be here for days!"

"Trust me," Shaananca said, smiling down at him, "they will pass all too quickly."

Shaananca had been right. The days in Aedmurun passed all too quickly, and nothing reinforced that feeling so much as the utter dullness of their return to the Connæaran countryside. Having seen all the sights on the barge to Dunarra, the trip back offered no surprises or novelties.

On their first day back at the farm, Druadaen awoke to the

normal round of chores. Nothing had changed except that now, merely being there at all felt . . . well, it felt peculiar. Having seen his parents so lively and engaged—youthful!—in Aedmurun, he now had to wonder why they were on a Connæaran farm at all. As ever, they struggled for mere adequacy in the many requisite skills that came naturally to their neighbors. And although they were diligent, they did not evince the same intense concern over the state of the weather, the crops, or the thousand other factors that were portents of plenty or privations, come harvesttime.

All told, the first day was a wearying reminder of just how exhausting and repetitious the work was. After supper, none of them had the energy to immediately set about cleaning up, but instead, sat half-collapsed around the table. Druadaen, slumped down in his chair, surprised himself by saying, "I wish we lived in the city."

His parents exchanged glances.

"Couldn't we move there?" Druadaen asked. "You don't seem to like the farm, or at least the farming. And there's so much to do in Aedmurun. And so much to see. And so much to learn."

His father folded his hands and nodded slowly. "Maybe we shall do that, one day. We will certainly talk about it." He smiled. "It doesn't seem like you have any interest in becoming a farmer."

Druadaen cocked an eyebrow as his father often did, only realizing the mimicry after doing so. "No, I don't want to be a farmer. But Father, Mother, you don't seem to want to be farmers, either. Even for a small family, we don't raise many crops or keep many animals." Druadaen paused, but his parents had no reply. Instead, they were watching him with strange looks on their faces: part surprise, part resignation, and maybe some pride. Undeterred, he continued. "It's the coin you earn at the walltower that keeps us alive, isn't it?" More silence. "But what do you do there, that the Dunarrans would pay you so much for only a few days every other moonphase?"

His mother sat slightly straighter. "Your father and I are—we work with books. With ideas."

Since leaving Aedmurun, Druadaen had imagined them on brief but urgent riverine adventures or on secret missions with Varcaxtan and Indryllis. Something exciting, at any rate. But . . . books? He frowned. "So, you are archivists then?" It was a term that he'd heard often during their few days in Dunarra. In neighboring lands, even here in the countryside of Connæar, the closest equivalent was "scribe"—but that just meant someone who made their living by writing and, sometimes, reading. But in Dunarra, where literacy was almost universal, the term archivist took on a meaning closer to "scholar" or even "researcher."

His father answered slowly. "Our work is often similar to that."

Druadaen didn't miss the measured, even careful, nature of his father's response. Something else to find out about—but later. "Then why are we living on a farm at all? Why don't we live near the walltower that you go to? Or near the sea? I would much rather live as you did: a mariner traveling the world! Like you and Varcaxtan." Druadaen looked at his mother. "And, maybe, like you and Indryllis."

His parents exchanged glances again. There was a hint of surprise, but only a hint.

Druadaen shook his head. "I just don't understand why we're all up here, instead of down there near them. And all the interesting things in Aedmurun." He looked up. "I think you'd be happier there. I know I would be."

His mother had come up behind him; she put her hands on his shoulders. "I can see that we have a lot to talk about. I also see that the sun will be touching the horizon in an hour."

Druadaen frowned. "But we *will* talk about...all of this?"

As his mother sat down next to him, his father nodded. "We promise." After a long silent second, he smiled and picked up a just-washed pumpkin that was sitting at the center of the table, drying. "But before you're ready to go to the city and learn everything there, there are still some lessons you can learn here."

Druadaen couldn't keep a dubious tone out of his voice: "Lessons about...pumpkins?"

His father's smile broadened. "No, about the world." He rose and took down one of the two lanterns framing the hearth, lit it, and slid the bullseye cover down over the glass. The broad wash of light was suddenly choked down into an intense beam.

Druadaen glanced out the window. "We won't need a light for at least an hour, Papa."

"True."

"Then why have you lit the lantern?"

"To illuminate the truth of the world," his father answered, his smile a little more serious.

"By shining it on the pumpkin?" Druadaen asked.

"By shining it on the pumpkin," his father affirmed. Mischief wrinkled his smile.

Druadaen wondered if maybe, despite his strength, his father had worked a little too hard during this first day back on the farm. But if he saw Druadaen's dubious stare, he gave no sign of it. Instead, he put the pumpkin in his son's hands and brought the lantern close so that the beam from the bull's-eye aperture brightened one side of the pumpkin. "Imagine that this light is the sun and that the pumpkin is our world."

"So the world *is* round!" Druadaen exclaimed triumphantly.

"Why, yes," his father answered, startled. "Of course it is. Who told you otherwise?"

Druadaen's mother grumbled from over his shoulder. "Let me guess: Heyna."

"Well," Druadaen admitted, "actually, it was Heyna's mother. I'm not sure Heyna believed her, either."

His father shrugged. "So as I was saying, imagine this lantern is the sun. The pumpkin is our world. And if we are right here"—he put his finger on a slight dimple in the side of the pumpkin facing the light—"then how is it that the sun comes up to the east of us and goes down in the west?"

Druadaen would never say so, but for a moment, his father's question seemed, well, like nonsense. Why would one even need to know such things? "Well," Druadaen started, "at dawn, this point of the pumpkin"—he poked his finger into the dimple—"has to begin in darkness. So you need to move the light to the other side of the, er, world." His father moved left. As he did, the beam moved similarly. The line of shadow advanced from the right side of the orange sphere until the dimple was fully in darkness.

"And now?" his father asked.

"Now, move to the right."

His father nodded and complied. The circle of light on the pumpkin crept back to the right until its rim touched the dimple. "There," Druadaen said, "that is dawn." He nodded for his father to resume moving.

The beam inched further to the right until the dimple was in the center of the illuminated half of the pumpkin. "Now it is noon." His father nodded, smiling, and kept walking until the left edge of the light passed the dimple, plunging it into darkness. "And now, nightfall." Druadaen smiled. "That wasn't so hard."

His father cocked his head. "No, it wasn't," he agreed. "But tell me, what about the stars? Do all of them move the way the sun does, but at night? Is that why we see them track across the heavens?"

Druadaen frowned. "What do you mean?"

"Well," his father said with a shrug, "Do the stars *all* circle around us, too?"

Druadaen felt the frown return, deeper this time. It was tempting to say "yes," but something about that didn't make sense. Particularly not since Arrdanc's three moons (which some said were other planets) did not obey the orderly pattern of the sun and the stars. Although it was clear that they, too, followed in some strange dance around Arrdanc, they did so in a pattern—a "moonphase"—that repeated every fourteen nights.

So, if they did not revolve evenly around Arrdanc, then how could it be the center of *all* things? And if not, then why presume it was at the center of *any*thing?

However, the hieronoms and sacrists of every temple insisted that their world was the locus of the universe, and it was unwise—and thus, uncommon—to question those who were in direct communication with the gods. Still, every time Druadaen listened to temple consecrants explain how creation was arranged so that Arrdanc was always at its center, there came a point where he could no longer follow the logic. But the older he grew, the more he began wondering if their explanations weren't, well, just a little *too* complicated. More than once he had thought that there had to be a simpler answer, something that didn't involve so many exceptions and special details and rules in order to work.

He looked at the bull's-eye lantern in his father's hand. Then at the pumpkin. And then at the dimple which was still in darkness. Restless, he changed position...and the pattern of light shifted upon it.

Druadaen stopped seeing the lantern or the pumpkin... because the shape of the whole universe changed in the course of his one surprised blink. It was a sensation at once disorienting, wonderful, and arresting. It was like the time he'd seen drawings in a book that tricked the eye into believing it saw something other than what was actually there.

Maybe the universe did the same thing.

Druadaen rotated the pumpkin so that the dimple was once

again just beyond the edge of the circle of light. Then he started turning it slowly in his lap.

This time, the bright circle itself did not move, but as the pumpkin turned, the edge of the light advanced, revealing the new surface that rotated toward it, just as the part rotating away was swallowed by darkness. And as that slow process continued, the dimple smoothly went through the same three points it had when the light, not the pumpkin, had been moving: dawn, mid-day, night.

Druadaen sat looking at the round orange world in his hands. "That's how it works." He seemed to hear himself say it from a great distance. "That's how all of it works. That's why the stars turn." He frowned, looked up. "But the moons don't do that."

His mother and father were smiling quietly. She nodded. "You're right, 'Daen. The moons move in a very different pattern. There are many people who argue over how that can be and what it means."

His father sat and leaned closer. "But in Tlulanxu, you just might find the answer. If the question interests you enough."

Druadaen nodded. "It does."

And at that moment, he realized that his mother and father never meant to be on the farm forever. Which explained why they hadn't been determined to excel at the tasks and management of it the way they excelled at everything else. The farm was a temporary home while they pursued some other purpose—whatever that might be.

"So, we were going to leave anyway," Druadaen said. He had initially intended it as a question; by the time it came out of his mouth, it was a statement. "But then why come here at all?"

"Another good question," his mother said softly. "And another day coming in which we may answer it."

His father smiled and gently tousled his hair. His mother hugged him from behind. And then he had the most unexpected realization of all: *I will be sorry to leave this place, this house where we have been together for as long as I can remember.*

His mother hugged him more tightly. "Time to clean up. And then to bed, my darling son."

✦   ✦   ✦

Druadaen woke with the sun full in his face. Which meant he'd overslept. Except...

His bed did not face east.

He raised his hand to shield his eyes, discovered he was more weary than when he'd gone to sleep, smelled sweat—

"Druadaen," a gentle voice murmured. A woman's voice. But not his mother's.

He sat bolt upright, looked around quickly.

A vast chamber of white stone, with windows that ran from the floor to the sharply peaked ceiling. The intense yellow sunbeams shooting through them were so bright and sharp-edged that they looked solid. Muted sounds of movement and speech echoed up into the groined vaulting high above him, returned down as indistinct murmurs. And standing nearby, looking down with smiles more mournful than any expression of grief he had ever seen, were Indryllis and Varcaxtan.

Druadaen knew why they were here, even before he could choke out the words, "Where are my—?"

"Your parents cannot be here," Indryllis whispered, sitting swiftly on the edge of his bed—which stank of sweat. His sweat. "I know they would wish to be, but—"

"Where are they? Where am I?" Druadaen tried to hold in the fear, the rising anguish. But even as he strangled back the sobs pushing to escape his throat, he felt tears flooding down his cheeks.

"Your mother—" Indryllis started, and then her voice faltered, halted; her eyes were liquid bright.

"Your mother has passed," said Varcaxtan, kneeling down beside the sick bed. "But we—"

"Mother is...? What about Papa? Is he still alive?" The sudden, aching rush of hope was wild, brutal: Druadaen would have tossed his own life aside without a thought if that would have bought the "yes" he so desperately needed to hear. But which he knew he would not.

However, fate had an even crueler answer in store, apparently. His parents' friends glanced at each other, mouths opening uncertainly.

"Is Papa alive?" Druadaen screamed, his words ringing back down from the stones of the ceiling.

Shaking, Indryllis closed her eyes, her tightening eyelids squeezing out a flood of tears. "Not entirely."

PART TWO

YOUTH

Journal Entry 27
12th of Green Passing, 1788 S.C.
Tlulanxu

Tomorrow I will at last be allowed to enter an epiphanium and become a follower of Amarseker. My many false starts may finally be made right and whole. I hope that once I am welcomed into a deity's community that I will at last bask in its creedlands as I sleep, that I will be able to recall most of my dreams, and that I will discover why the ones I do recall have always been so disturbing. And perhaps I will learn if the reason I have been unable to recall my other dreams is somehow related to why I still cannot recall what happened the night I lost my parents, now five years past.

Although I am late come to the knowledge of Amarseker, the dreamguide says that will not be held against me. Amarseker is one of the least followed Helpers and his consecrants do not proselytize. In fact, the sacrist who is to be my dreamguide says it actually may be auspicious that I am late come to awareness of him and his creed. Amarseker is said to be a solemn god, and so, is quiet—until he has something of import to convey. So it may be with his accepting me as an epiphane.

It was easier to believe I would find the right creed when I began my search just after I turned eleven. Most of the other children were raised with the words of one or more creeds always in their ears. It gave them comfort, so they were ready when they became old enough for epiphanesis.

But my parents were not only gone but had never spoken of creeds or gods. Only the Being. Well, just "Being." They did not use that word as if it referred to an entity, but more like a state of mind.

Still, it came as a surprise when the dreamguide at the first temple I approached—Adrah's—sadly informed me that I had not been accepted as an epiphane, that the door to his deities' creedland would not be opened for me. It was not unusual, he assured me, for a child's first attempt to be frustrated: dreamguides have no power over whether we are made epiphanes or not. It is the deities themselves that discern whether their creed is right for any given supplicant.

But after being turned away six more times, it is hard to believe that this long wandering will ever come to an end. Every dreamguide I approached seemed to have heard of me, since no one in living memory has ever been refused entry to the epiphanium so many times. And I can see that makes them uneasy, upsets their orderly views of an orderly universe. I suspect some wonder if this is retribution for misdeeds of my unknown forebears.

And maybe they are right. Maybe it is evidence of a judgment against me or my kin. Maybe that is why I cannot recall what happened the night that I lost my parents. Maybe that is why my father remains where he is. Maybe my memories—and my father—will only be restored to me once a deity has accepted me into their creedland. It hardly seems possible that so many strange circumstances could all stem from separate causes.

But I shall not think of it further. Tomorrow, when I enter the epiphanium and am shown into the Creedlands of Amarseker, I can begin to seek the memories and answers of what happened to my parents as I slept through that fateful night. And just maybe, once in the creedlands, I will even see their smiles again, at long last.

CHAPTER THREE

Druadaen knew exactly what path, and what time, it was best to run to the patientium. He had learned, during his five years in Tlulanxu, that early on summer mornings the stevedores in the trade quarter would have already finished unloading the cargo of ships that arrived late on the preceding day. That way, those who meant to depart swiftly had empty holds ready for lading shortly after dawn.

As a result, beyond the meandering wall that separated those docks from the city proper, the streets were already filled with jostling draught animals, pushcarts, ostlers and sutlers, all trying to out-shout and out-curse each other. So Druadaen had hit upon a shortcut that also kept him too busy to dwell on the misgivings that arose before his visits to the patientium: he ran across the ramshackle roofs of the trade quarter.

The tricky course had him running along the tops of walls, scrambling up this roof, leaping over that eave. It was excellent conditioning for service in the Legion, and also, was too exacting to give his mind enough time to linger upon things he'd rather it didn't.

As he jumped down to and then raced along the roof peak of the trade quarter's largest inn, a Basakayn-accented voice called up to him. "*Ai*, boy! You will fall to death of you!"

Druadaen smiled; he not only recognized the creaky voice,

but also the lame grammar and easy jollity. "No time to worry, Pozhup! Back to sea, soon?"

"Hey-ah, boy! Before noon. You no fall! Or I scold you ghost!"

Druadaen laughed and ran swiftly on his way before his fears could catch up with him.

Still, he knew his footing so well that he did catch occasional glimpses of the bazaar. This day, it was mostly wares from the lands of Mihal'j. Embroidered bolts of white Basakayn etamine were being unrolled, their red and yellow arabesques moving in the ocean breeze as if reluctantly emerging from slumber. Lajantpuri merchants were hanging robes, sashes, and capes of foulard, their intricate silken designs shining wherever the sun caught them. Amidst loose ranks of rickety stalls marked by billowing sheets of Azhkanti homespun, Druadaen saw a table laden with brass chandlery from Athaericos, where a bright wink caught his eye. Nestled among the nautical hardware were pieces of sea-green murrhine glassware, each piece featuring a scene made from actual marine life frozen forever inside. He almost slipped trying to make out the details of one of those tableaux, but then righted himself and sprinted on before the aroma of grilled Lirhyzi mutton could pull him back.

At the end of his shortcut, he leaped back up to the city wall and flashed his student token at the two closest guards, who stared before they recognized and waved him on. He nodded his thanks and ran faster still, trying to reach his father before the weight of this fateful day could bring him, crush him, down.

Once in the patientium, Druadaen sat beside his father, as close as when he'd been a little boy, sharing thoughts and questions he hid from every other person, even his beloved mother.

"I'm scared Papa." He whispered the affectionate pet name self-consciously, even though the tiny patientium held only the two of them. "The borders of Amarseker's Creedland have still not appeared to me in my sleep. And the dreamguides say you usually see it at least once between becoming an epiphane and the day of your epiphanesis."

He ground his palms together. "My dreams have been getting stranger. They are a jumble of scenes that make no sense. Some show things and places I know, but others are of places I don't recognize, and which I doubt could exist. Some repeat, some do not. But they are never, ever peaceful."

He looked at his father's face. He always hoped for a response, but the only one he ever saw was a slow, glimmering trickle out of the corner of a closed eye. He thought of it as a tear, though the physicians insisted it was simply a reaction to the sound or movement of another person.

He put his head in his hands. "I'm afraid that this is what goes on in the minds of the insane. I'm afraid that on the night that you and Mama..." He couldn't complete that sentence. "I'm afraid that the rat-bite fever I contracted that night damaged my brain in some way that not even physicians or sacrists can detect."

He tightened his jaw against another surge of the fear and grief that arose with every visit to the patientium. It was as if he was living through the loss and the mourning all over again. At least with his mother, there had been an end to the grieving; she was ashes out upon the sea, in accord with Dunarran custom.

But that begged the old, unanswered question. "So," he asked his father's motionless body, "if you and mother really were Dunarrans, where are your parents? Your siblings? Any family at all?" In a nation where lifespans were three or four times those lived in other countries, it was wildly improbable that any one disaster or war could have wiped them all out, let alone erase all record of their existence.

And yet, to all appearances, that was what had happened. Long before Druadaen had awakened from his fever, both Connæaran and Dunarran officials had begun searching for the identities and whereabouts of his relatives. None were found, nor any records of them. Those Dunarrans who had known his mother and father, even Indryllis and Varcaxtan, explained that the topic of family rarely came up with Tarthenex and Mressenë, and that they had never been particularly forthcoming when it did.

Even Shaananca's researches proved fruitless. Once Druadaen had been placed under her combined tutelage and care, she had shown him the personal inquiries she had sent. Indryllis and Varcaxtan did no less before being called away to their far-flung duties. By the time Druadaen knew enough to ask more detailed and informed questions, their returns to Dunarra had become infrequent and never brought them to the capital. To his way of thinking all he had left of his earlier life was his determination to become a part of the Legion.

But even that had changed. It was no longer fueled by youthful desires to perform great deeds and accrue great acclaim. Now, his quest to join the Legion was both a memorial to his father and a cherished vestige of the minutes and musings they had shared together.

Druadaen leaned back, wiped his eyes. "I wish I wasn't so rushed today, father, or so tired." He sighed. "I wanted to get to sleep early, but I was so worried, I couldn't keep my eyes closed." He stared at his father's inert body, realized the irony in his complaint. "Whereas you can't wake up. Not even to eat. Not even to care for yourself. And somehow, you remain alive. But how?"

It made no sense at all...but not in the way that all mancery or divine power defies practical explanation. The mystery in this case was why such a power was being exerted at all. But, now that Druadaen thought about it, maybe there *was* a way to find the answer to that question, along with others about the attack that had killed his parents.

He rose. "When Amarseker allows me to pass into the epiphanium, Father, and when I have dreamwalked to his Creedland, I will find out what has been invoked to keep you here. And why." He placed a slow kiss on his father's forehead. "I swear to you: I shall get those answers or become an outcast trying."

Druadaen strode out of the patientium, glad to leave with a purpose rather than lingering on in his grief.

As he did far too often.

CHAPTER FOUR

Druadaen was only vaguely aware of approaching the steps to the cupola atop the Great Archive and wondered if he had heard or only imagined the welcome from the guards at the bottom of the stairs. They were all that had stood between him and the small dome's brass funicular which led down into the welcoming dark of the tube that was the sole means of ingress or egress for the library's most restricted section: the Archive Recondite. Once there, he would finally be spared having to see the skyline of Tlulanxu and the bay that rolled outward into the wide world beyond. From having to pretend it was a pleasant place to be. From having to meet its inhabitants. Instead, he could finally be alone, at least for the few minutes it took to descend.

But as he reached the bronze doors of the cupola, he heard two muted voices approaching from its far side. One was Shaananca's. The other was not immediately recognizable, but still vaguely familiar.

Druadaen moved slowly, keeping the cupola between him and them. Not because he wanted to hide—not exactly—but because the last thing he wanted to do on this day was to come face to face with Shaananca and, worse still, some visitor to the Archives. Any visitor escorted by Shaananca was sure to be a person of importance. That meant courtesies and patient, gracious answers to their questions, as well as equally gracious attentiveness to their opinions or reflections. On any other day, that would have been fine, but on this day, he would have gladly spent three hours hauling bricks if that meant he could avoid three minutes of playacting at interest and amiability.

The women's voices neared, but then became fainter. He peeked around the curve of the cupola; Shaananca and a taller, younger woman had not stopped at the doors to the funicular, but had continued toward the stairs he'd just ascended. As they slowed and prepared to say their farewells, he ducked back. Shaananca's title might be Master Archivist, but her senses, her alertness, and her scarred forearms suggested that her prior service to Dunarra had been of a far more active nature. Druadaen allowed that he would be lucky if she hadn't already seen him.

A moment later, the soft pad of her sandals reapproached the cupola. They entered and, soon after, the low moan of the unspooling cable told him that one of the funicular's two cars had started down.

After the cable finally groaned to a stop, he heard the familiar *clank* of the second, waiting car locking into place. He circled back toward the doors and the promise of the sheltering darkness behind them.

"Druadaen?"

He was so startled he almost dropped the radial vellum scroll he'd just finished refolding. Shaananca was standing within arm's reach. *How can she get so close without being seen or heard?* "Yes, Master Archivist?"

Shaananca flapped a long, heavily veined hand at the central area of the upper reading room. It was empty. "We are alone. No need for titles."

He nodded. Her pause and steady gaze confirmed Druadaen's worst fear: that she had sought him out not arising from his responsibilities as one of the Archive's assistants, but on a personal matter.

She sighed, folded her hands. "Unless my memory is going along with my knees, you went to the epiphanium this morning."

He nodded slowly. *As if it could have slipped* your *mind.* And if Shaananca's knees were getting stiff or creaky, Druadaen had seen no sign of it.

But as maddening as Shaananca could be sometimes, she did

not do what most other adults would have done: pretend that his subdued manner had escaped her notice, or what it might signify regarding the outcome of his epiphanesis. Instead, she nodded back at him, eyes never leaving his face. "I would hear what happened," she said simply.

It was not an order, not even a request . . . which was why his resolve to remain silent evaporated like morning fog in sunshine. "Nothing happened."

Her expression became skeptical. "I doubt that."

He shook his head. "No, Shaananca. I mean it literally; nothing happened. There was no epiphanesis. I did not enter Amarseker's Creedland." He closed his eyes, resolved not to cry in front of her. "I never even saw it."

She frowned. "Forgive me, Druadaen, but I am not even sure what you mean by that."

He nodded, eyes still shut tightly. "I went to the epiphanium. I met my dreamguide in the antechamber. He asked the ritual questions and was surprised that Amarseker had still not shown me his creedlands in my dreams. But he said that happens, some-times. We went in and I laid down in the godpalm. He covered me with the robe of souls and gave me a sip from the cup of creed. And I waited to enter the waking dream."

"All in accordance with the ritual," Shaananca nodded.

Druadaen felt like he might throw up. "But it didn't work. The dreamguide flinched a few times, looked surprised, and shook his head. He told me that my epiphanesis wasn't to be. That Amarseker had shown him that I didn't belong there. And that I never would."

Shaananca put a hand on his arm. "Druadaen, I know it is painful, but think carefully: Are you sure the dreamguide said you 'didn't belong there'? Are those his *exact* words?"

Annoyance at Shaananca's apparently insensitive attention to pointless details gave way to realization that her question did not arise from idle curiosity. Druadaen closed his eyes again, tried to remember.

He recalled the dreamguide putting out a gentle hand to help him up from the slightly concave *supinial* of the godpalm. "I am sorry. I . . . I have been shown that you are unable to enter Amarseker's Creedlands. Neither in your sleep nor when you die."

"B-but," Druadaen had stammered, "how can this be? If

Amarseker knew I was not worthy, then why did he consent to my becoming an epiphane?" He did not add, *after I have spent years being turned away from so many others!*

The dreamguide looked not only perplexed but shaken. "I have no answer that would be meaningful to you. Or even to me."

Druadaen had to concentrate hard; that was the point at which the rejection, and what it meant, had descended upon him so heavily that he had ceased to become fully aware of his surroundings.

"I can only tell you this," the dreamguide continued. "Amarseker intended that you come here today, to the brink of epiphanesis. But to what end, I cannot say. To my knowledge, this has never happened before." The dreamguide extended his dark brown hand a little farther, looked as miserable as Druadaen felt. "Come. We must leave the epiphanium."

Shaananca's eyes were narrow as he finished. "Being 'unable' to enter Amarseker's Creedland is very different from 'not belonging' there."

Druadaen felt too hollow to care, but he asked anyway: "Then what *does* it mean?"

"I am not sure, but I mean to find out." Shaananca looked annoyed, but with herself. Or maybe the world. She put her free hand on his other arm. She held him hard, almost fiercely; it was probably her expression of love, he realized. "Young Druadaen, when a god neither wishes nor welcomes your devotions, the god is *not* indecisive or subtle. You would never have been made an epiphane."

Druadaen shrugged. "Then maybe it was my fault."

Shaananca frowned. "How could that be?"

"Today, when I went to the patientium, I realized I'd be willing to devote myself to *any* deity, if that would allow me to speak to my parents. Or to find out what had happened to them. Maybe that's what Amarseker sensed: that I hadn't petitioned him because of his creed, but because it was a means to an end."

Shaananca folded her hands. "Tell me, Druadaen, why did you choose Amarseker? And why was he not your first choice?"

"Because as I grew older, I discovered that the gods I first petitioned—of Goodness, of Light, of Mercy, others—didn't fit with what was inside of me. Their creeds had nothing to do with what I wanted to do in *this* world."

"So you want vengeance?"

Druadaen shook his head; Shaananca *had* to know better than that. "Amarseker is *not* the god of vengeance; he is the patron for avengers of wrongs. And his correct title is the God of Justice."

Shaananca raised an eyebrow. "Unless things have changed a great deal, Torm is the God of Justice."

Druadaen sighed. "Torm is the god of *divine* justice, either among the gods or in their interactions with the world. Amarseker is the god of *mundane* justice, of our affairs with each other." He stared at her. "Which you already knew."

Shaananca nodded. "Naturally. And now that you have reminded yourself who and what Amarseker is, do you really believe such an entity would bring you to the very brink of your epiphanesis out of spite?"

"Maybe not, but then why did he do it?"

Shaananca sighed, released his arms. "Most of the motives and actions of gods are mysteries to us mortals, and the more complex the god, the more confounding their ways and deeds." She looked carefully into his face. "But it is not just the rejection that troubles you, is it?"

Druadaen looked away again, shook his head. "It's the dreams." He closed his eyes. "I am afraid that I am insa—that my mind is damaged."

He heard a small smile in Shaananca's voice. "Trust me, Druadaen; you are not insane."

He opened one eye and looked at her. "Then what causes these chaotic dreams? And why only in me?"

"Firstly, my boy, many other people have dreams such as yours."

He momentarily forgot his terror, discovered he'd opened his other eye. "If that's true, then why hasn't anyone told me?"

Shaananca sighed and closed her own eyes. "The ways of temples are sometimes as puzzling as the gods they serve. In this case, I suspect it is because they do not want others speaking too much about the Wildscape."

He blinked at the unfamiliar term. "What is that?"

Shaananca shrugged. "A space like the creedlands, but without any order or any deity presiding over it. The dreams there are not fashioned for a purpose and they are as often distressing as they are reassuring. Often they are simply strange, unfamiliar, surreal."

He nodded vigorously. "Yes! That's what it's like!" *If only I'd known to ask...!*

In response to that thought, anger brewed up hot and fast from his gut, rose into his head. "So because the temples do not want anyone talking about the Wildscape, they allowed me to go on fearing that I was insane?"

Shaananca slowly reached out and touched his cheek. "I allowed you to think it, too, Druadaen."

The heat behind his forehead became ice. "Why?"

"Because the lands seen in dreams are the province of the temples—*only* them. And they believe that it is their duty to guide people to the creedlands that would make them the happiest. So they do not speak of Wildscape simply because it points to the existence of other dreamlands. Besides, to be fair to them, very, very few people ever experience the Wildscape. Very few *can* experience it."

"So because not many people experience the Wildscape, the temples decide not to at least explain what it is to those who must live with it? How is it that any god tolerates such consecrants? They are monsters!"

Shaananca shook her head. "Always bear this in mind, Druadaen: you walk without a god. So take care in your speech. If you hold the gods in contempt, do not share that opinion except with the most trusted of friends." She sighed, looked tired. "And even then..."

Druadaen nodded. "I understand." He had calmed enough to remember he was holding the velum scroll; he put it back within its granite arkalith. "Still, if just one of the temples had told me, at the start, that I could never enter a creedland, I wouldn't have spent all this time trying and hoping and thinking it was because of some transgression. I wouldn't have tortured myself with the possibility of seeing my parents again, and maybe remembering what happened to them. To us." He shrugged. "So if I can't do it through a creedland, then I suppose I must petition the consecrants to enact that miracle on my behalf."

Shaananca gestured toward a table. As they sat, she murmured, "You must be aware, Druadaen, that speaking with those who have died is deemed a solemn and serious act—a bestowal, they call such things. It is not something the temples do lightly. And it carries a significant cost of service."

"Or coin, I've been told."

Shaananca shrugged. "Most of the gods you have approached

do not buy and sell their powers. For them, there is no connection between wealth and either worthiness or devotion. The rest are not much different. If they were, then the rich would be more likely to receive the favor of the gods than the poor."

Druadaen shrugged back. "Then I would have pledged service to a temple."

She smiled. "The few hours that remain in your day after your studies are concluded are already dedicated here. And they earn you the stipend that keeps you housed, clothed, and fed."

Druadaen bit his lip. No matter how Shaananca's point galled him, it was also the truth. And as a ward of the state, he had little to complain about. His existence was in no way grand, but it was also more than adequate in every particular. "I would have found some way. Promising future service, maybe."

She softened her tone. "I know you miss your parents. I see it every day you are here, and at every meal we take together. But that will not move a sacrist to trouble their deity. If it did, the lines of those who would pay any price to speak to their loved ones again would stretch into the hills. How is your need any different than theirs?"

"How many of them have a father who is stuck between worlds?" he shot back. "Not fully gone from this one, but not completely in the next. I thought that, maybe, if I could talk to Amarseker, to any of the Helper deities—"

Shaananca was shaking her head. "Druadaen, my dear boy. You are clever and you have learned so much, both in your classes and here. But it is hopeless to petition a god to intervene on behalf of your father."

Druadaen looked up sharply. "I don't understand what you mean."

She studied him, as if reading what lay behind his eyes. "Yes, you *do*. Tell me: Do you think mancery, of any kind, could preserve your father in his current condition for five years?"

Druadaen felt his lip quiver. "No. It would require too much mastery, too much power to be maintained at a distance—if at all."

Shaananca nodded. "So, by process of elimination—"

"—the power must be divine." He shut his eyes, seeing where that led. "And if it *is*, then for any other god to undo it is a blatant challenge. And the greater the undoing, the more serious the challenge."

Shaananca patted his knee. "And that is why there is no petition you could have made, no service you could have offered, which would have changed your father's state. They will not risk going to war over this matter, no matter how unjust it might be."

Druadaen nodded, tried to keep his grief over his parents separate from his resentment of the gods—all the gods. Which became anger over his weakness, his limitations, his failure to find a way to free his father or at least find answers...

Druadaen felt a hand cup his chin, lift his head. He found himself looking into Shaananca's deep blue eyes. "You cannot— you *must* not—blame yourself for any of this."

"How can I not?" He almost sniffled. "I was there when my parents died. And I didn't do a thing to help."

"And what do you think you could have done?"

Druadaen looked away. "I don't know. Fought."

"And you would have died." She peered closely into his face. "Tell me, child, what is the last thing you remember from that day?"

He sighed. "Father was the first who heard something, went to see what it was. There was fighting. Mother went to help him but barely got out of the house.

"Father fell outside. Mother made it back into the house. They couldn't win. The house was burned. There was almost nothing left."

"And who attacked them?"

Druadaen shrugged. "No one knows. And no one knows why, either."

Shaananca shook her head. "That is what you were *told*, shortly after you recovered from the rat-bite fever. I asked what you *remember*. What did you see and hear that day?"

Druadaen tried to recall images, concentrating so hard that he thought he could feel his pulse hammering in his temples. When he'd awakened from the fever, he'd tried to recall what happened, cried for days when he couldn't, eventually consoled himself with reliving the happiness of the last minutes he *did* remember: his parents promising that they would talk about why they were on the farm and also, why the time had come to leave it. He'd been so excited...

But then nothing. They must have cleaned up the supper plates and peppered the food they had not finished. And then he must have prepared for bed. He did recall being very tired. "I remember going to sleep." He frowned. "I think."

"Do you remember going to sleep *that* night? Are you sure it wasn't some other night you remember?"

"Uh, well…no, I'm not *sure*. I don't feel that sure of anything, right now."

Shaananca nodded. "You're tired. Rest a moment."

He did. The day was barely half over but he was already exhausted. He felt like he'd been pulled in five different directions by wild horses.

"That's right," Shaananca murmured. "Rest your head on your arms. Good. Now, tell me everything you remember about that day. But slowly."

Druadaen thought back, but instead of becoming tense, he relaxed. He felt safe with Shaananca nearby. He even felt himself becoming drowsy, felt his awareness of the last five years slip away as he fell into living that day again.

Fell past the point where his memories ended…

CHAPTER FIVE

The pumpkin that had represented all of Arrdanc was back at the center of the table as they brought their supper plates to the steaming pot of dishwater by the hearth. Normally a time made lively by chatter and perhaps a bit of teasing, today was more quiet. The mood from the meal-end conversation on the nature of the world and the end of their time on the farm was too serious for a quick transition into jocularity. But Druadaen did not miss it. Instead, the promise of new possibilities left him feeling quietly eager, lighter: the way he did after they aired the house out in spring.

His father had lit the second lantern in anticipation of the approaching dusk and was bringing it to the table when he stopped and listened.

Druadaen did too... and heard a distant, furious snorting and then a whinny that sounded more like a scream.

His mother rose. "That's Shoulders."

His father nodded as he put the lantern next to the pumpkin and headed for the door. Once there, he paused, then reached up and took down the sword that Druadaen had rarely seen out of its sheath. It was long and sharp and too unique to have been issued by the Legions. "Stay here," his father muttered as he opened the door and stepped outside.

"I will not!" Druadaen's mother snapped as she rushed toward her small dresser. In the instant that her focus shifted fully to the contents of the bottom—and forbidden—drawer, he darted through the doorway, eager to see what was happening.

Druadaen stopped just a few steps beyond the threshold, so bewildered by the scene that, for a moment, he could only stare.

Their various animals had somehow gotten loose and were acting oddly. Their cats were trying to run to the house despite spasms wracking their bodies. Their two cows were lowing, trembling, and rolling their eyes as if they'd gotten into madweed. The goats were butting each other, the side of the barn, and apparently, phantoms in midair. The chickens were flying at each other in general fury.

And beyond that scene of rabid madness, Druadaen could see more animals coming: birds from the surrounding copses as well as two foxes. Even three of Heyna's cats were stumbling toward the house, hissing at each other and the empty air.

Without looking around, Druadaen's father said, "Back in the house." He drew the sword and added, "Bar the door," then ran toward the paddock that ran all the way to the stream that marked the eastern limit of their farm.

Still too surprised to react, Druadaen stared after his father, saw what he was sprinting toward: Shoulders. The big, gentle draft horse was stamping, twitching, and bolting in sudden, frenetic starts like a colt with a nervous affliction. Then it stopped, eyes rolling wide and white, as if in terror of fire, before it ran again. Shoulders' movements became even more erratic and desperate as Druadaen's father approached, whinny-screaming as if he were a pack of wolves. Teeth showing, the horse made ready to charge... but then swung unsteadily away, as if straining against a heavy chain.

Which seemed to break: Shoulders wheeled. Still running with a strange, broken gait—like a puppet fighting against its puppeteer—the draft horse charged up the hillock on which they'd built the shed that covered their root cellar. Druadaen's father yelled for Shoulders to stop.

The horse's immense head turned back once and, with a look at once sorrowful and insane, he redoubled his speed—which carried him up the last furlong of sloping grass and then over the small cliff perched above the rock-strewn stream below.

That was the moment that the chaos began to coalesce upon

Druadaen and his family. Shoulders' screams drove nails of ice into Druadaen's marrow. His mother sprinted out of the house, yanked him back, and yelled a warning at his father: one of the cows had broken through the paddock's light fence.

As the cow stumble-charged forward, Druadaen's father raised the sword in his right hand, seemed to be balancing with his left as he walked slowly toward it. As if confused by the human's stance and approach, the cow slowed, shook its head, legs growing wobbly—just as his father sprinted at it and drove the sword into its head. The long blade went in so swiftly that it had either been a lucky poke through an eye socket or an exquisitely precise thrust at the end of a long, running step.

Suddenly the air around Druadaen was filled with their chickens: flapping, pecking, furious, but hampered by sudden jerks and starts. The goats were in mid-charge when Grip, the family's mastiff, appeared around the corner of the house and moved to intercept them. But his ears were down and quivering and his legs were oddly stiff, laboring forward as if a millstone was tied to each one.

"Lock yourself in!" his mother screamed as she ran out, spinning on the ball of one foot to give Druadaen a quick push back toward the doorway. Then she headed toward his father, drawing two long, but very different, daggers.

Druadaen felt the reflex to obey his parents pulling him into the house at the same instant his desire to help them pushed him to run after his mother. For a long second, he just blinked; the division—and the struggle—in both his heart and mind left him motionless.

His father began running back to the house, waving for his mother to turn around. Distracted, she almost failed to hear a fox streaming low over the ground toward her, but at the last moment she turned and slashed—left, then right—as it leapt. What fell was silent and half-gutted.

Bloodied, Grip limped past the open door, the now-hamstrung goats bleating insanely after him. Moving even more slowly, the dog angled toward the second cow which charged in from the direction of the barn, its head streaming red from where it had butted open the door. Jerking, frothing green, it seemed startled to discover Druadaen staring at it, and veered in his direction.

"'Daen!" his mother screamed, too far away to help.

But Grip managed to get between him and the cow—and took a hoof in the haunches, unable to dodge in time. The cow swung back, head bobbling obscenely, searching.

But the sharp kick that had knocked Grip aside had cleared Druadaen's head just as sharply. Whether he meant to shelter or fight, he'd have to go back to the house, either to hide or get his father's Legion-issue shortsword out of its hiding place. With ravens arrowing in like black daggers, he turned and ran the three steps it took to get back through the doorway, his mother right behind him.

And the cow was right behind her, horns lowering...before it let out a bellow of rage and pain: Grip, one leg dragging uselessly, had its tail in his viselike jaws.

Druadaen's mother turned as she came through the doorway, daggers ready to hold off any creature that might reach it before her husband could dart through. Past her, the cow shifted and Druadaen saw Grip's unflinchingly loyal eyes locked on his own—just before they were blotted out by a massive, muddy hoof.

The cow's kick struck the dog square in the snout. With a crack like wind-snapped green wood, the mastiff's head went back at an angle that would not be possible if its spine were still intact.

Choking back a sob, Druadaen dove under the table, immediately crawling toward the far side of it—and the armoire that stood out from the east wall.

His mother was screaming for his father, who did not answer. Smaller animals came at her—chickens, another fox, a racoon, a small goat—which she dispatched almost as afterthoughts. "Druadaen?" she shouted.

"Yes, Mama?"

Her head swiveled in his direction. "What are you doing?"

"Getting the sword from behind the armoire!"

She checked over her shoulder, ran toward him. He thought she was coming to scold or pull him away, but instead, she heaved on the armoire—and it shuddered forward just far enough for Druadaen to get half his body behind it and reach up to the bracket that held the shortsword to its rear.

The moment he got the hilt in his hand, he heard a scramble and a hiss at the other end of the narrow gap behind the armoire: one of Heyna's cats. Spittle flying out of its mouth, it launched itself at him—just as he got the sword out.

The tomcat hit the blade head-on. It yowled hysterically, head shaking, blood flying on the wall, the armoire, and Druadaen. As it writhed and tried to regain its feet, he cut downward, putting an end to the threat and to its struggles.

He pulled himself out from behind the armoire, slashed at a crow that was plummeting toward him—but it was simply falling, already killed by his mother. "Get out of there! We have to bar the door until—" And then she was suddenly silent, her eyes flicking toward the arm with which she had pulled the armoire.

An asp, teeth embedded in her upper forearm, was hanging there by its fangs, curling and coiling in a frenzy. She cut through it with a single slice of the dagger in her right hand, then swept the head off with a slower, closer sweep along that arm. She took a step, staggered, grunted, "Go. Out. No good here." Druadaen had never seen his mother drunk, but she was starting to sound that way.

He bolted toward the door, shortsword raised. He heard his mother stumbling along behind him, yelling, "Go, go, go!" As he plunged out the doorway, he readied the sword against any and all attackers—and discovered the cow charging straight at him. He dove aside and stumbled along the wall of the house, falling behind a now-ruined wheelbarrow which had been thrown against it in the chaos.

Either the cow lost track of his movement or didn't care; she slammed into the doorway at full speed. Her already damaged left horn tore away as it ripped that side of the doorjamb off the wall. Blood sprayed as the animal pressed on into the middle of their house. From inside, his mother shouted, "Druadaen: the cellar! Run! I'm right behind you. I'll be—"

Then he couldn't hear anything over the smashing of wood and bellowing of the cow. The table was flung over and the lantern shattered; a sudden rush of smoke obscured the desperate struggles inside. Animals crowded to push through the blood-smeared doorway, despite the orange flame-tongues that winked and flickered through the growing gloom.

Weeping silently, Druadaen wriggled out from behind the wreckage of the wheelbarrow and sprinted up the slope toward the small shed they'd built over the root cellar.

Birds screamed after him, but they were small ones. He shielded his eyes, barely felt their savage pecking at his arms and cheeks. He looked around for his father, saw him motionless on the ground at the far end of the paddock. Apparently, several neighbors' dogs had joined the insanity and he had met them head-on. They lay scattered around him. Whether he was dead or not, Druadaen couldn't tell.

And did not have time to look more closely. He hit the shed's door at full sprint, stumbled and fell on the dirt floor. He started to rise—which became a leap backward and straight to his feet; two rats were in front of him. They were unusually large, bigger than cats.

One had been staggered when the opening door smacked it in the face. But the other was hunched in readiness, its black-bead eyes glistening as it started unsteadily toward Druadaen—who jumped forward and kicked it as hard as he could.

It soared over the barrels of meal and salt lining the north wall. Which it hit with a meaty thump. It emitted an abbreviated squeak and fell behind the casks.

Druadaen was too busy snatching a jute bag off the top of a crate to see what became of it. He got the rough cloth wadded around his left hand just before the second rat doubled up and then uncoiled into a leap, gnashing furiously.

Druadaen got his hand in the way just as the rat's long dive put it in range. The animal's teeth dug into the fabric, chewed fast and hard. But as it did, he managed to shift his hand so as to grasp the back of its boring, biting head. He swiped his sword horizontally, just below where he had hold of it.

The cut was both imbalanced and crooked, but it still took off a rear leg and opened the rodent's gut. He flung it away, but the moment it hit the floor, it rolled over and began dragging itself toward him on its three remaining legs, squealing in a horrible mix of rage, pain, and madness. But at the rate it was losing blood, it would never—

He blinked as something flew down into his face, claws raking. A bat, probably one that had wriggled through the gap beneath the eaves. He grabbed it with his burlap-wrapped left hand, felt it squirm around, trying to bite...but not before he smashed the hilt of the shortsword into its body. With a sound like kindling being crushed inside a tearing leather bag, the bat went limp.

He flung it away. Paused to breathe and look—and through the narrow doorway saw the roof of the house go up in a sheet of flame.

He didn't think to be silent, might not have been willing or able to even if he had: "Mama!"

Creatures, once as familiar and welcome as pets, turned wide, quivering eyes toward him: chickens, a goat, another cat. He heard the bellowing of yet another cow coming in across the fields.

He could not survive them all by fighting. He had to escape. And there was only one way to do that.

He rolled a barrel of quicklime away from the north wall: the trapdoor beneath it was just big enough for an adult, but an easy fit for him. He grabbed the nearby pry bar, jammed its beveled end into the access notch, and stamped down on its handle. The door popped open, revealing the steep, lightless shaft down to the root cellar. He scattered lime around the opening, dove inside, turned, and drove home the bolt—just as his father and mother had taught him.

He grabbed the flint striker off the wall, checked that its spring was cocked, and turned back to light the pitch-soaked hay in the iron cresset near the top of the shaft—at the very moment a snake came squirming down through the trapdoor's access notch.

He should have been terrified, but he wasn't. It happened too quickly. One moment, he was face to face with a young asp, the next it was striking and he was sweeping the shortsword at it.

No neat decapitation, but as it flew away, the arc of its body looked broken and it was hissing wildly.

He triggered the lighter. The shower of sparks from the flint striker caught the pitch-treated tinder. The sudden burst of firelight revealed the asp, its blood-blackened and half-severed body coiling to strike. But too slowly. He chopped at it. Then again, and again, and again.

He might never have stopped except for the pain that flared in his left calf. He looked down, expecting to see that some of the burning tinder had dislodged and fallen on him.

But his eyes and the second hot flash of pain told him a different story: the rat he'd kicked, the one he'd presumed dead, was sinking its yellowed teeth into his leg a second time with manic ferocity and speed.

Again he didn't think; he acted. He thrust the sword straight into the rat, not considering the strong chance he'd slice into himself instead. But for once, he struck true: the point of the sword split the rodent's skull right down its center.

He scrambled away from it, feeling sudden exhaustion—and then a lance of pain in his shoulder.

He looked over, saw a swinging, sinuous form: another snake had followed the first halfway down through the access notch. He felt an icy flame spreading into his shoulder, saw the narrow wedge of the serpent's head start to rear back, and hoped his father would have approved of the fight he'd put up. His limbs were already heavy and his vision blurry as the snake became motionless for an instant: the pause that was the prelude to the strike.

But instead of shooting forward, the asp was suddenly moving the other direction, thumping roughly against the sides of the notch as it was pulled back up and out of sight. A moment later, a square of late daylight appeared where the root-cellar door had been, and through it, he saw a cured leather gauntlet clutching the writhing snake. Both disappeared as the wearer of the gauntlet shouted, "No you don't, you bastard!" A savage stomping began, a dull sound against the earthen floor of the shed above.

Then a woman was standing in the light. The silhouette was like—

"Mama! Mama? Are you—?"

"Shhhh..." wept a different voice, and suddenly—as if the world had gone black for a long moment—the face of Indryllis was very close to his. "You shall be well, Druadaen. I know what to do, I will..."

But her words seemed to fade and fuse together into distorted gibberish. Her face went away, swallowed by strange darkness, which, when it lifted, seemed to carry him along into the light. He was in someone's wide, powerful arms, being carried aloft toward the orange glow of sunset. He looked up, tried to see across the impossibly great distance of a few inches....

Varcaxtan's tear-stained face was looking down into his. He said in a voice gentler than Druadaen had ever heard, "You are safe now, child."

And then, from over his shoulder, he heard a ghostly addition from Indryllis' spectral shadow, even though she whispered it into Varcaxtan's ear: "As safe as fate allows."

Druadaen's head snapped up so quickly from where it was resting on his arms that he experienced a moment of vertigo.

Through the spinning, he saw Shaananca, and shouted, "What did you do? Unlock my—my memories?"

She sat back calmly. "No. It was more like drawing aside a curtain. You yourself could have brushed it away at any time your inner mind was willing. Which would have happened soon enough." She frowned. "And no, I did *not* keep your memories from you out of some foolish combination of mercy and arrogance! How dare you think such a thing, you insolent pup! I did what had to be done to save your life."

The sharpness of Shaananca's rebuke told Druadaen that she was not dissembling. "You mean, the memories could have killed me?"

Her face changed from stern to somber. "When you first arrived here you were so weak that—well, you were close to discovering whatever lies beyond your particular mortal coil. The venom had weakened you, enough for the rat-bite fever to take firm hold in your body. That is why you were in danger for so long; since you could not sleep, you could not gather the strength to throw off the infection."

"Because I dreamt of what had happened on the farm."

She nodded. "As your body was fighting to overcome the fever, your nightmares kept waking you up. You never slept more than two or three hours. So, I drew a curtain across those memories. Not a block, just a change of emphasis."

Druadaen stared.

Shaananca explained. "Think of a landscape painting. Some of the figures and trees are in the foreground, others in the midground, others further and further in the background until they fade away. I invited your mind to store the dangerous memories as part of the distant background. But your mind went a step further and put them in a vault. I knew that might occur, but it was a risk that had to be taken. After that . . . well, your own mind was the best measure of when you should remember them."

"But you didn't wait for my mind to do that. You pulled them back up."

"Dear boy, I bade you rest because I could tell that the memories were ready to emerge. To process the reversals and shocks of this day, your mind now requires the context of those suppressed memories. But had they arisen at night when you were alone, or in your dreams—well, that was a pain and a danger that I did not want you to have to face alone."

Druadaen was vaguely aware of her words. "All those animals that attacked us...What would cause that? Was it the work of a faunamancer?"

Shaananca shrugged. "We do not know; it could have been. However, there are other arts that could achieve much the same effect that our sentinels observed."

"Sentinels? You mean Varcaxtan and Indryllis?"

Shaananca nodded. "And others who...watch." Her tone shifted into musing. "I had a discussion about such matters with a visitor today."

"I saw you escort her as she was leaving the Archive," Druadaen commented, hoping to surprise Shaananca; doing so was a rare victory.

"Yes." Shaananca nodded. "I know."

"But...you did not see me!"

"Are you so very sure of that?" Shaananca's smile became wry. "Perhaps you should pay more attention to your *own* powers of observation."

"What do you mean?" Druadaen asked.

"Did you not recognize the dignitary?" When he shook his head, Shaananca explained. "It was the Lady." She emphasized the final word.

"Yes, I know the dignitary was a lady, but—" Druadaen stopped. "You mean *the* Lady? The one from five years ago, in Aedmurun?"

"The very same," Shaananca said.

"And did she also know I was there watching?"

"She did not say." Shaananca smiled. "But I would not be surprised if she did."

"Why was—is—she here?"

"Research. And discussion."

Druadaen frowned. "It must be very important research for her to travel here all the way from Far Amitryea."

Shaananca schooled her face and voice to patience. "Far Amitryea. Am-*it*-ree-yuh, not Am-it-*ray*-uh," she corrected. "As to the urgency of her researches?" Shaananca shrugged. "This Lady, and those who came before her, keep their affairs largely to themselves. Out of necessity, I suspect."

"And will she be back tomorrow?"

Shaananca shook her head. "She intends to depart today. But I believe she had some final business to finish."

"Where would I go to see her?"

"She will depart directly by ship," Shaananca said. "However, I would not be surprised if her business will compel her to take the long route to the harbor. Through the Temple District."

Druadaen rose quickly. "Master Archivist, I respectfully request a brief—"

Shaananca waved her hand. "Go. You are wasting time."

Druadaen sprinted along the stretch of wall that took him closest to the Temple District and scanned the arching walkways ahead. Nothing to be seen. Maybe she was gone already...

No: there she was, appearing much as she had five years ago. She was walking quickly, already leaving the Temple District for the bay. Evidently, she had finished her business—but what had it been?

He scanned back along her path, quickly identified the cluster of buildings from which she had just emerged...and felt as though his heart stopped for a moment. He was probably mistaken, or maybe it was just coincidence...but on a whim, he headed in that direction, rather than after her.

Just to make sure.

Druadaen reached the broad alabaster stairs, streaming sweat. Wet hair hanging over his forehead, he doubled his pace as he started up the risers two at a time, sometimes three.

The guards turned to stare, but knowing him, they just nodded him on and followed his upward progress with puzzled frowns.

On either side of the white stairs were small buildings surmounted by cupolas. Each had a separate door and their only windows were arrayed in a ring around the very peak of their domes.

He kept running until he got to the tier of buildings that was third from the top. He swerved to the left, pushed through the door with the familiarity of frequent use.

Druadaen ran out of the daylight, into the brief darkness of a tiny antechamber, and then emerged into the brightness that shone down from the skylights to illuminate his father's patientium.

It was empty.

There was, however, a faint scent of sea and sandalwood, and, on the platform where his father had lain for five years, there was a very small silver leaf.

As Druadaen approached, it crumbled to dust.

Journal Entry 64
2nd of Green Passing, 1792 S.C.
Tlulanxu

Within the week, I will finally be inducted into the Legions.

Reading that over, I am tempted to cross it out and start again. I have seen how often Fate snubs those who attempt to impose their own certainties upon it. But all my friends, all my docents, even the cadre of the Training Legion, assure me that this outcome is certain. I was not aware until the Training Legion's Pretor informed me, just three days ago, that my assessments, both physical and aptitude, are among the highest on record. And he intimated that various letters written on my behalf (by whom, I wonder?) attest similar levels of promise.

But I cannot resist the sardonic observation that Fate has blessed me with the most promising attribute of all: I am an orphan.

I first became aware of the strange correlation between heroes and parentless origins when helping an aged Saqqari scholar locate obscure tomes pertaining to what is effectively the prehistory of Arrdanc. I refer to that time when humankind was rising up into the vacuum of power left after the great kinslaying wars among the Uulamantre. (The events recounted in the *Costéglan Iavarain*, although that seems to be comprised of at least as much legend as history.) In fetching and replacing the various scrolls and codices the scholar required for his sprawling researches, I also had the opportunity to peruse a good number of them.

What I discovered was that at least half of the heroes of note (and almost all the greatest of them) were orphaned early, raised by adoptive parents, or had otherwise enigmatic, mysterious or untraceable origins.

This cannot be coincidence. Persons with such meager backgrounds are rarely alluded to, let alone individually mentioned, in either historical or apocryphal annals. Quite the contrary, regardless of the country or culture, most powerful figures arise from lineages wealthy in silver, repute, or both. Hardly a surprise. Some consecrants suggest that this is how gods—or Fate—reveal which families they favor the most. I propose a much simpler, mundane conclusion: that having wealth and prestige makes it easier to accrue more.

But when it comes to the great heroes, this correlation between plentiful assets and profound accomplishments inverts. Humble beginnings almost seem to be a prerequisite for attaining mythic stature. Indeed, if you examine the origins of heroes whose names endure because of their *deeds*, you shall discover that the overwhelming majority of them began as farm boys or milkmaids or (particularly) hand-to-mouth orphans subsisting on what they found in alleys.

This not only defies all logic; it aligns with the axiom that fact is often stranger than fiction. Because the only thing that would be *more* impossible than this seemingly preposterous correlation is the notion that storytellers would dare choose to spin tales of such unlikely heroes. Surely, such improbable scribblings would be profitless objects of general ridicule and critical contempt!

The only reasonable explanation for orphanhood as a near-prerequisite for becoming a great hero is that there may be people who are strengthened rather than weakened by such early adversities. And because those who survive their dire childhood trials continue to accrue greater skill and force of will, their repute arises not just from their deeds, but from the stark contrast between their achievements and their beginnings. But even as I write those words, I find myself doubting whether that alone could explain the immense implausibility of the phenomenon.

Whether or not these absurd correlations have any merits beyond amusement, I may be sure of at least one thing: they do not apply to me. The fiber of my being is certainly not the extraordinary kind from which legends are woven. But in the unlikely event that much lesser persons might yet enjoy some small benefit from humble beginnings, then perhaps it shall add to my chances of being inducted into the Legions.

Either way, the Archive Recondite has been a good haven and

the only unchanging factor in my life since my parents passed. Still, I have no regrets leaving, no more than a bird taking flight from a safe and necessary nest.

Well, I do have *one* regret, I suppose: never being allowed to enter the Reserved Collection at the very lowest level of the Archive. Shaananca refused to let me run even a single errand down there. But I cannot in good conscience blame her. The rules for entry are very clear and very strict, and all researchers who wish access must be approved by a special council of the Consentium.

But ultimately, that regret is but a nostalgic distraction. My eyes and thoughts must be focused on my future. Which is to say, upon the Legions.

CHAPTER SIX

Druadaen emerged from the Archive telling himself that there was value in the further delay of the Legions' notification of his acceptance and assignment. It gave him an opportunity to exercise and strengthen what was arguably one of his weakest attributes: patience. Still, the disappointment of having to wait another week pulled at that resolve like the strong, steady undertow that had taken more than a few swimmers near the rocks west of Tlulanxu's wide bay.

Consequently, Druadaen was so distracted when the first alarm gong rang that he didn't even register its significance. But when a second, higher-pitched one followed, the war between discipline and disappointment evaporated because that sound signified the start of an *actual* war. Whether a full-scale assault or a small raid, any attack on the capital of Dunarra was deemed a formal commencement of hostilities.

Druadaen scanned the skyline, found what he was looking for: brightly burning white-pink signal fires atop two of the towers that overlooked the main docks. *An attack from the sea, no less?* he wondered as he began sprinting in that direction. It was hard to imagine how an enemy's ships could have slipped undetected past the outposts and patrols until they were upon the city itself.

As he rounded the corner of the street that sloped down to

the waterfront, his path was blocked by an apparent confrontation between citizens and the city watch: something he had never seen during all his years in Tlulanxu. More peculiar still, several bodies were visible further down the hill.

Had the watchmen confronted those citizens with deadly force? If so, nothing like that had occurred in living memory, and there was no tension in the city, let alone unrest.

A moment later, the actual cause of the casualties became clear; the air in front of and around him came alive with the rushing whispers of rapidly descending arrows. Black from point to fletching, they were longer and heavier than those used by archers. Most clattered down upon the cobbles, but several found softer objects: awnings, crates...and people. Three fell, two screaming as they did. The third dropped limp and silent.

One of the watchmen glanced at Druadaen, who, unthinking, had started running forward to help. "Boy!" the man yelled, even though he was almost three inches shorter, "get back! Don't you see that—?"

Another humming deluge of heavy black arrows. More people went down, and the watchman's warning ended abruptly, one of the shafts protruding from his left temple as he hit the cobbles.

Druadaen ran to the body, scanning the darkening sky. He had yet to train at sea, but he was certain that these arrows were the kind flung by scorpions: mass launchers that were often found on the walls of fortifications—or on the decks of ships. Sure enough, another flight was rising up the docks, the swarm of dark shafts slowing as they neared the apex of their arc. Druadaen grabbed hold of a confused child and darted for a doorway. They reached it just as the lethal spray hit the street.

"Who is—?" the child began.

"Stay here until guards tell you it's safe to move," Druadaen said sharply, then ran back to the body of the watchman. If there was to be a battle, then he would be damned if he was going to remain unarmed.

The equipment was typical: a refurbished Legion sword, leather armor, a now-broken lantern. Not much with which to meet invaders. But just as Druadaen began to rise to run in search of other defenders, he noticed a loose, braided cord around the dead man's neck: a watchman's whistle.

Druadaen snatched it off and dodged back around the corner

just as more arrows came down, sounding like a torrent of wood and steel.

The small badge that marked Druadaen as being a final-year member of the Training Legion had never been useful. But this night, that small sigil—or maybe the larger and rarer badge of authorization from the Archive—satisfied every guard he encountered as he made his way to the top of the city walls. There, he gave a wide berth to the troops that were manning the battlements and the officers that were receiving reports and sending instructions. If he got in anyone's way, it was a surety that he would be sent—or brusquely escorted—off the broad wallwalk.

Once overlooking the roofs that marched down toward the waterfront, Druadaen saw almost everything he expected. The shining armor of Legion cohorts marked the positions they had taken around the point of engagement, ready to deflect and contain attackers attempting to make deeper inroads into the city. The signal fires in the bay-ringing watchtowers fluttered on and off as iron shutters opened and closed to send coded messages. Fast, yawl-rigged cutters kept their beams toward the landward breeze, angling in rapidly toward the docks. Every step, every procedure was being executed exactly as he'd been taught.

But the one factor that did *not* fit any of the military histories or training scenarios Druadaen had studied was the attack itself—or rather, the seeming lack of one. Although dusk was becoming night and the streets near the waterfront were dark, two things seemed certain, regardless of the deployment of the attackers.

Firstly, although they had apparently come from the sea, they hadn't been detected crossing the bay. That suggested either some strange kind of ship or mancery. Or perhaps the attackers had come in on one or more merchantmen, concealed in their holds while awaiting the word that would loose them upon the city. That might also explain the volleys from scorpions; they were the most compact and swiftly reassembled naval weapons. They could have been brought above-deck piece by piece and readied under tarps.

Secondly, whereas outnumbered attackers typically move as quickly as possible to their objective, this group had apparently established a perimeter just beyond the docks, barely pushing into the constricted streets and alleys there. That kind of deployment was not for mounting an attack but securing safe egress for evacuation. It was, essentially, a protective position which could easily be collapsed inward after any withdrawing forces had embarked.

But neither of those enemy activities had *delivered* any forces so significant that they would need such provisions for withdrawal and then maritime transport.

Druadaen frowned. Was there any reason for an enemy to mount an attack that was restricted to the projection of a small defensive ring around a few ships firing blind volleys from hastily assembled scorpions, but without a landing force of any size? No: that made no sense.

Unless...

Could the landing force already *be here, but in disguise?* Druadaen wondered. *Or hidden?* But no: that did not make any sense, either. Tlulanxu, like the rest of Dunarra's cities, had been constructed to preempt the plots of saboteurs and infiltrators. The final decades of the First, or "Silver," Consentium had taught the propretors the cost of keeping their cities truly open. On several disastrous occasions, enemy forces had trickled in, dispersed into separate hiding places, and then arose when given a subtle signal to wreak havoc.

But if there were such forces somehow lurking somewhere in Tlulanxu, what could they possibly achieve given their unavoidably small numbers? And why had the attackers on the wharves established their foothold before the landside operation had launched?

Furthermore, why spoil their surprise by launching scorpion volleys that caused more reaction than casualties—most of whom weren't even soldiers? These attacks weren't meant to wound the bear in its den; they were just poking at it. Which made less than no sense.

Unless that was exactly *what they intended to do.*

Druadaen's thoughts swerved down a new and serpentine path: *Just because there's no sign of trouble in the city, it does not mean that there still isn't trouble arising in it—just very quietly.*

Druadaen's head turned a slow half circle as he inspected the twilight skyline of Tlulanxu. Somewhere, among all those silhouetted buildings, there might be a much smaller enemy force preparing to attack...what? The Propretorium? The Temple District? The Arsenal? The Collegia?

He closed his eyes. *The attack on the docks is a distraction, so the main attack is to be aimed elsewhere. And it cannot require a very large force. And given the restrictions on entry, there is no covert way to slip many people past the gate guards. So the enemy's biggest tactical problem is to find a means of ingress for a force that is large enough to prevail and yet small enough to move within the city without being immediately detected.*

Furthermore, if any of that force meant to escape, they would have to be able to reach the docks. In all likelihood, then, the target would be on the bay side of the city. Or, to put it another way, someplace close to where Druadaen was standing at that very moment.

He turned slowly back to the right, looked anew at that familiar stretch of wall and what lay on the other side of it: the trade quarter. Merchants from all over the globe. There was no way to know how many persons might remain on the ships that docked there. And with the city's military attention now focused on the Dunarran part of the waterfront, there would be less vigilance near the foot of the walls in that area, where the most common problem was drunken brawling or spiteful urination against the immense foundation stones.

Druadaen began walking in that direction, letting his gaze run ahead. Almost all the troops on the wallwalk were moving in the opposite direction: eastward toward the point of attack. Their eyes were hard, determined, intent, and showed what was in their minds: absolute focus on their current orders to repel the attackers. If he meant to accost them and compel them to believe an inexperienced cadet's assertion that the attack on the docks was actually a diversion, Druadaen would need clear and irrefutable evidence.

He reached the overlook where, five years earlier, he'd sprinted along rooftops in order to sit by his father's body before running on to the epiphanium. He glanced down into the trade quarter. Linens, still pinned up in most of the stalls, moved like angry nighttime clouds. Buffeted by the wind, they made the bazaar a broad expanse of shifting shadows and random movement. Which was completely at odds with the merchants' prudent habit of carefully folding and storing all their wares at the approach of dark.

He stopped and stared down at the still-bedecked stalls. However, they were perfect for obscuring the approach of stealthy attackers and tricking the eye of those whose job was to watch for them. Still, it was not evidence of an infiltration; it was merely atypical.

Druadaen pushed on, reaching the small towers that flanked the gate and marked the beginning of the street that led to Commerce Way: the only artery that connected the trade quarter with the heart of Tlulanxu. Two guards were there, attention riveted on the unfolding drama half a mile to the east. One noticed his attention. "Ai, lad! Not a night to be on the walls."

Druadaen recognized the voice as belonging to the same guard he'd routinely encountered five years ago. That this fellow was still here, at the same post, was no surprise; he was congenial but almost too tolerant, as well as profoundly conventional.

Druadaen nodded. "Where's the rest of the gate watch?"

The fellow gestured east toward the docks. "Called to the excitement. And half who should've been standing duty tonight are sick. Bad food, I'm told."

Druadaen wondered if the food had been bad or poisoned. But without any way to confirm the latter, it once again failed to rise to the level of "proof." He nodded at the guards and turned to gauge his leap to the nearest roof within the city proper.

"You still playing at mountain goat, lad?"

"Just for old times' sake," Druadaen called back, and jumped.

His legs were longer and stronger . . . but that was what nearly undid him. Having used a bit too much force, and with his heavier chest and broader shoulders having raised his center of gravity, he landed awkwardly, a twitch away from falling three stories to the cobblestones.

Druadaen sidestepped gingerly down the slate shingles, peered back at the gate. It didn't appear to be open, but he also did not see any guards. Again, hardly worthy of sounding an alarm, not unless he scrambled down to the ground to confirm his suspicions of foul play. But if infiltrators *had* slipped in, there wasn't a moment to spare. It meant that after eliminating the guards silently, they had reclosed the gate to create the appearance of normalcy and were now well ahead of him. So it was time to dust off his old roof-running skills.

That proved easier to resolve than accomplish. Although well over six feet tall and well muscled for his age, that now worked against Druadaen, who barely completed leaps and maintained balance that would not have required any special effort or attention just five years ago. He still made reasonable progress along the roofs but dislodged no small number of terra-cotta and slate shingles doing so.

As he approached the ridge of the fifth roof, he realized that the next street was too wide to jump across and, in the process of surveying his other options, he finally saw what he'd been looking—and fearing—to find:

Six still forms on the cobbles beneath him. Twenty yards further on, there were another two. And just before the road ran around a blind corner, one more. A trail of bodies that marked a path to the Temple, or possibly Consular, district. Either way, they first had to go through the oldest part of the city, dominated by twisting roads and stores and workshops instead of dwellings. A perfect route of approach for infiltrators on their way to—well, wherever they were going. But unless they knew the streets and roofs better than he did, Druadaen was sure he could get ahead of them.

Assuming I don't break my neck first.

As Druadaen approached the harborside end of Commerce Way, he realized that the plan he'd concocted while running across uneven roofs was not as original as he'd thought. It was merely a vastly simplified reprise of the tactics employed by the first Ballashan emperor, Hafshanis, at the pivotal Battle of Thēda-Shri, back in the early years of the First Age.

But Hafshanis had enticed and misled his enemies with an entire—and ultimately, much battered—cohort. Unfortunately, tonight's version of the ancient ploy would fail if the enemy inflicted even one casualty. Namely, Druadaen himself.

Having managed to follow a mostly straight line over the roofs, he finished by clinging to the underside of a long, arching walkway built across what locals referred to as "The Throat" of Commerce Way. Twelve yards beneath Druadaen's dangling boots, four thoroughfares joined to become the wide, brick-and-cement commercial artery whereby trade moved into and out of Tlulanxu's trade quarter. From there, the broad avenue ran into the heart of the city, as straight as a quarrel-shot. Its four separated lanes had few intersecting streets or alleys, ensuring a minimum of traffic from its sides. As a result, there were few impediments to the steady stream of ox-wains that made it possible to move so much material into and out of Dunarra's capital on any given day.

Druadaen swung from the bottom of the elevated walkway down to a balcony, dropped to the peak of a gable, and finally slid to the ground along one of the decorative half columns that framed it. Remaining in a crouch, he glanced back toward the conjunction of streets at The Throat: still no sign of the infiltrators. But that was sure to change soon enough.

Druadaen shifted the sword into his right hand, then fished the watchman's whistle out of his pocket. He blew into it as hard as he could for a full minute. Then he turned and ran north, blowing it again but keeping close to the center of Commerce Way so that the sound might spread equally in all directions.

Druadaen's stamina and strength were deemed very high, even by the standards of the Legions, but after sprinting and blowing the whistle for three hundred yards, he experienced a sensation he hadn't felt for a decade: light-headedness. He glanced behind as he caught his breath.

There was movement in the darkness beneath the walkway from which he'd dropped down. However, there were no glints of weapons or armor, and the infiltrators courted the shadows so well that Druadaen could not estimate their numbers.

He darted away from the median of Commerce Way, making for the side drowned in the hard-edged shadows cast by the rising of the night's first moon: Latharos. As he did, he heard a single air-shivering whisper well behind him: the release of a small arrow, probably from a shortbow.

As the shaft sighed through the space he'd occupied only a moment earlier, Druadaen reached the outer edge of the shadows and continued sprinting until he came up against the buildings on the southern side of the avenue. Soft but fast footfalls were approaching, although still well behind him. Staying in the ink-black shadows cast by Latharos, he literally ran for his life.

Druadaen maintained that pace for the three hundred yards it took to reach the spot he'd had in mind since leaping down from the city wall to the first roof: a wide opening to the right. To casual observers, it would appear to be the mouth of a cross street. In actuality, it was a wagon-access apron for a large warehouse located just a few yards shy of the second elevated walkway that arched across Commerce Way, a near match for the one that spanned The Throat.

Druadaen rounded the corner, kneeled, and caught his breath.

Still in deep shadow, he checked his gear to ensure that nothing reflective was exposed. Then he leaned his head forward just far enough to have one eye peeking around the corner.

A mass of dispersed, crouching figures was flowing in his direction, unusually silent.

Druadaen inhaled as quietly as he could. *Well, this* was *the plan.* He meant to move...but didn't. *So, have you lost your nerve?* Still balking, he added, *You don't* deserve *to be in the Legions.*

That was a rebuke he could not tolerate, not even from himself. He sucked in a deep breath, tensed the muscles of his throat, and bellowed in his best parade-ground voice: "Dress ranks! Stand ready! Subaltern, report!"

He stood, leaned around the corner...far enough to ensure that his silhouette and light-colored tunic would be visible.

An arrow whiffled past. Most of the cloaked figures continued approaching, concealed by the same black shadows that had kept Druadaen alive as he'd sprinted away from them. He jerked back behind the corner and tried to make his voice even deeper, more from his chest: "Front rank: shields low! Second rank: shields high! Marching wall, on my command!"

Out in the street, he heard short, hissed snippets of what sounded like low-caste S'Dyxan: the sharp, hasty whispers of an urgent debate. Before it could die down, Druadaen blew the whistle again, as long and hard as he could. When he was finally too winded to go on, he tried to listen in between gasping attempts to fill his lungs.

There was no sound coming from the street, now. Which meant they were advancing, but slowly, cautiously. Druadaen flattened himself against the wall and thought, *Well, if what worked for Hafshanis is going to work for me, it had better do so soon.* He slipped the sword's pommel-fixed lanyard around his wrist, wishing he had a shield and helmet, too. He listened again for movement—either out on Commerce Way or overhead on the nearby walkway—and tried to put everything out of his mind other than the corner just two feet away: the place where the first enemy scout was sure to appear.

If he'd been wearing a helmet, he would not have heard the approach of soft leather boots: the kind that S'Dyxan assassins were said to favor. He drew back the watchman's sword, saw a slight change in the shadows just beyond the corner. Then: movement—

He swung the sword.

And missed. The S'Dyxan—a wiry, middle-aged veteran—cleared the corner in a low crouch and came up just after Druadaen's blade completed slicing the air over his head. His teeth flashed as he saw his boyish adversary and stepped forward with two readied shortswords.

But he fell sideways, two black-fletched arrows thudding into his leather armor, another transfixing his neck. And the high angle of those impacts told Druadaen that the whistle had been heard and that his ruse had worked. All along the near span of the second walkover, Legion archers were rising to fire, having responded to the whistles and taken their positions silently.

Stepping over the slain S'Dyxan, Druadaen waved up at the bowmen, saw a steady stream of more Legion helmets moving behind them and then further out along the walkway. If any of the Legiors saw him, they did not acknowledge; they were too busy firing their composite bows down the length of Commerce Way.

A command—an order to charge—was shouted in S'Dyxan and a brief roar answered it—just before it spun apart into cries of dismay and pain. Druadaen risked peeking out around the corner again.

Back upon the walkway that arched over The Throat, moon-reflecting gleams marked the steel helmets of even more Dunarran bowmen: the ones that had converged upon the point where Druadaen had first blown the watchman's whistle. Their arrows hit the rear of the charging S'Dyxoi who, scrambling for cover, learned too late that Commerce Way's lack of side streets had a tactical purpose as well. Like snakes that had crawled into a tube, the S'Dyxoi now found it stoppered by withering bowfire at both ends, and without any exits or cover along its length.

Druadaen sighed, realized he had been sweating so heavily that his clothes were almost as wet as if he had jumped into the bay. He retreated to the back of the warehouse's loading apron, found where the shadows were darkest, and remained there, ready and watchful. As much as he hated it, he had to admit that doing anything else would only put him in the way of real soldiers, lethal arrows, or quite probably both.

CHAPTER SEVEN

The next day, after lugging supplies and new holdings into the outer chambers of the Archive Recondite since lunchtime, Druadaen finally slipped back into the reading room. Only one researcher was still in the Archive: the aging court scholar who had been sent, or at least funded, by the Orchid Throne of Saqqaru. Scribes in the various wings and collections of the Archive had been speculating on the purpose of his visit for months, some whispering that he had traveled here at the behest of the Most Serene Empress Reconcilera herself. The fellow was even now moving another armful of codices and scrolls to his study chamber. Since the small rooms had been purposely built to block sound and were considerably taller than they were wide, they were more commonly called by a sardonic nickname: oubliettes.

Druadaen started across the wide reading room toward the burdened fellow, called in a low voice, "Honored sir, may I help you with—?"

"Hsst! *Hssssssssst!*" the Head Facilitator nearly spat at him. "They are meeting! Have care or I shall report you!"

For what? Druadaen wanted to ask. *Doing my job?* But he only whispered, "Apologies. I have been elsewhere most of the day." That elicited what might have been a conciliated grunt from the Head Facilitator. "Who is meeting?"

The Facilitator sighed and looked up from the codex open

before him. "The honored Master Archivist has been closeted with the Pretor that the Legion has detailed to oversee our security: Alcuin IV."

"The grandson of the Propretor Princeps? Here?"

The Facilitator looked up testily at Druadaen's amazed tone. "It is not so unusual," he objected haughtily. He firmly closed the tome before him: a compendium of all known records and references pertaining to an obscure folk dance practiced by a long-vanished people. "We do important work here," he sniffed.

From the other side of the reading room, someone cleared their throat. He looked; the aged Saqqari scholar was nodding and waving him over. Druadaen headed in that direction, bowed as he came close, but the wizened fellow gestured for him to follow into his oubliette—the largest that communicated directly with the reading chamber.

As he entered, the Saqqari rounded on him. "You have done an admirable job finding all the tomes I requested. All but one, that is."

"Yes, sir. Apologies, sir. I discovered that it is not in the main holdings of the Archive Recondite but is part of the Reserved Collection."

The fellow smiled. "You are diligent. And you are correct. The tome is indeed in the Reserved Collection."

Druadaen frowned. "Then why did you send me to find it, sir?"

The Saqqari's smile became shrewd. "Tell me: Have you ever been down into the Reserved Collection?"

"No, sir. But I have wanted to see it for many years."

"Well, 'many years' is a matter of personal context, my young friend. Now, do you remember the subject of the tome I requested?"

"Yes, sir." A strange question, since he had just been asked to find it this morning. "It is a very old tome about the Great Beasts," Druadaen answered. "Although the author used the word *direkynde* instead." Which was an improbably archaic term for various large, rare, and usually ravenous creatures, the most legendary of which were dragons.

The Saqqari bobbed. "You are correct. One day, you should read it. So, since you could not be sent for it, what became of my request for the volume?"

"It had to be retrieved by Master Archivist Shaananca herself, since the Head Facilitator was out of the Archive when you submitted your request. But she is still conferring with Pretor Alcuin, so I cannot bring it to you immediately."

He smiled. "I quite understand. You need not rush." His smile became a grin and grew shrewd again. "Besides, I am in no great haste to see it."

Druadaen hoped his smile hid his profound puzzlement as he bowed out of the room. "Still, sir, I shall see if the meeting is over."

He entered the corridor leading to Shaananca's outer receiving room and beyond it, the vault that was purportedly the entrance to the Reserved Collection. The two doglegs he had to navigate were supposedly there as a sound barrier, but to Druadaen's eye, they also looked to be defense points that would prove easy for a small number of defenders to hold against a much greater number of attackers.

He inspected the walls as he emerged from the second one, searching for other features that would confirm or disprove his conjecture, vaguely aware that he could hear voices through the open door that led into Shaananca's rooms. He was still mulling over the construction of the second dogleg when he heard a male voice finishing a statement: "—no indication that the other night's attack was related to the one which orphaned him almost nine years ago."

"I am relieved to hear it," answered Shaananca through a sigh.

Druadaen froze, both his body and mind. *They are talking about* me. *Why? Should I back away? No! If I'm heard, who knows what trouble* that *might make?*

But by that time, the conversation had moved well past the point that had stunned him into immobility.

"—that attacked the docks two nights ago were unquestionably from Tsost-Dyxos." That term for the attackers—which, elided, produced "S'Dyxos"—had fallen out of routine use centuries ago. It had been that long since there had been anything other than colonial skirmishes between the two nations.

"And their sudden disappearance?" Shaananca asked.

"It wasn't mancery," Alcuin's voice replied after a pause.

"I didn't suppose it was," her voice answered calmly.

"Well, most did. After all that smoke shot up and they were suddenly gone, you can imagine the talk. Before we could announce that we'd found their armor floating in the water—unclasped and without any sign of blood—the rumors had started. And once kindled, they spread like a grassfire."

Shaananca's voice was mild...which Druadaen knew was often her precursor to springing a rhetorical trap. "And once the Tsost-Dyxoi were submerged, how did they get out of the bay without being seen? There were certainly enough of our boats crisscrossing those waters."

Alcuin sighed. "That part of their escape—ironically, the part that hasn't set the wheels of the rumor mills spinning—is the part that *did* involve mancery. Or at least alchemy. I'm told either could have allowed them to breathe underwater, or not need to do so for some time."

"More likely the latter," Shaananca answered, "but not so long that they could have strolled along the bottom of the bay and so, to the sea."

When Alcuin spoke again, he was clearly restraining profound frustration. Anger, too. "Well, I shall not solve this mystery before I depart, that much is clear. At least their infiltration from the trade quarter was straightforward; no mysteries there."

"And I shall discover the means whereby those on the dock escaped. Certainly before you return," Shaananca answered.

"You sound very confident, Master Archivist."

Druadaen heard the small smile in Shaananca's voice. "Young Alcuin, Tsost-Dyxoi may be meticulously stealthy when approaching a target, but their tidiness upon departure is typically quite minimal." A pause. Then: "When do you depart for Saqqaru?"

Dark laughter. "You weren't informed?"

"Why would I be?"

"Well, you and Grandfather seem to coordinate on all such matters directly. And privately. Take the recent appeal you made to him concerning this boy-hero's upcoming assignment. By the time I heard about it today, it was already on the desk of the Archpretor of Legions."

Druadaen blinked. *They're talking about me* again?

"I would not have sent word at all, had it not been for the events of two nights ago. Now, additional considerations are warranted."

Alcuin nodded. "Very well; they shall enter our deliberations, I assure you." As he finished speaking, he also began walking.

Druadaen braced himself in anticipation of being discovered, but then realized that Alcuin was not yet exiting but moving to pick up objects: probably helmet, shield, and weapon. Starting with one very long backward step, Druadaen reversed down the hall as quickly and quietly as he could.

He was hard at work, gathering scrolls left in the various oubliettes when Shaananca and Alcuin finally passed through the reading room on their way to the funicular platform. Shaananca reentered a moment after the pulleys began groaning, closed the doors, and then smiled brightly at the Head Facilitator. "Lanaral," she said, "I wonder if you would be so kind as to locate the restricted papers on the slaying of Alcuin III? You will find them under the title 'The Steppney Inquest.'"

The Head Facilitator murmured compliance and disappeared through the door that led to the Reserved Collection. Druadaen looked after him wistfully...

"Druadaen!"

He started, dropped the refuse he'd collected from the oubliettes.

Before he could reply, Shaananca speared him with her eyes. "You heard nothing. Do you understand?" She hadn't used that tone with him in years.

"I understand." He didn't even consider denying he'd been outside her office, listening.

Shaananca's stare was unwavering. "You heard *nothing*," she repeated.

Ah. "Apologies, Master Archivist, but I do not know what you are referring to."

She nodded. "I think I can smell your dinner being prepared." His dormitory was over a mile away. "And just beyond, unless I'm much mistaken, I can hear your bed calling to you."

He barely heard her last words; the door to the funicular platform was already closing behind him.

Two weeks after the S'Dyxan attack had been thwarted, Druadaen found himself slowly mounting the stairs to the Archive's cupola, frowning as he did. If word of his deeds had been made known to the high and the mighty, they had evidently kept it among themselves. The detection of the infiltrators and the tactics leading to their summary defeat remained unattributed.

But the lack of recognition was merely an annoyance. Yes, it would have been nice to have been publicly praised for his actions that night, but Druadaen's focus—indeed, his world—had narrowed to a single concentrated point: assignment to the Legions.

He reached the top of the stairs, looked over dawn-lit Tlulanxu. It had become his home. But it was long past time for him to leave it and start the next chapter in his life. Maybe today.

But when the day came to a close, he was no closer to that departure. Instead, since becoming the most senior assistant, he was the one entrusted to perform the last tasks of the day, which included a final check and cleaning of the oubliettes. Somehow, despite being at the bottom of the funicular's long, tubelike shaft, there was still an astounding amount of dirt and rubbish that daily found its way down into the Archive Recondite. Druadaen suspected mancery: an old curse left behind by some nasty-spirited old trickster who had been slighted or thwarted by an assistant. Unfortunately, whatever the spell might be, it had shown no sign of relenting in the nine years that he had worked there.

Druadaen's final task was to secure the Archive itself, which involved waiting for the two guards posted there during the night. They officially witnessed him secure the many vaults and concealed repositories that held artifacts and codices so ancient and (to him) mysterious that they were tempting targets for thieves and mantics alike. Typically, this job fell to Shaananca, but she had been called away a week ago—in the field with a legion, from the sound of it. Lanaral had left a few days later to fulfill his annual work-tithe on a fishing smack that plied the shallows where Dunarra's east coast touched the Nyrthule Sea. So on this day, when he heard the cables of the funicular creak into taut readiness and then squeal and grumble, he hastened to complete his tasks: apparently the guards were a quarter hour early.

After checking that everything was in order, he went out to the platform—and discovered Shaananca smiling at him as she descended from the car. "No greeting?" she teased.

"I'll have to come up with a new one. The one I exchange with the guards is...unsuitable for present company."

She chuckled as they walked into the reading room. "Things seem in fine order."

"Yes, and I am ready to depart."

She nodded, looking around appreciatively. "You are indeed done for the day."

"Well, yes, I am, but I was referring to my time in Tlulanxu. But I'm still waiting for assignment."

"Yes," she said, "I know."

"You do?"

She nodded and handed him a scroll. He had a faint peripheral impression that her face was set in one of its inscrutable masks, but he didn't stop to make sure; he was too busy carefully breaking the wax seal and then unfurling it so that he might save it unblemished for posterity.

He read the document. He frowned and read it again.

He looked up. "This must be a mistake?"

Shaananca's eyes were distant, but he could see pain in them. Pain and knowing and other things for which he had no name. "No," she answered eventually. "It is not a mistake."

"I . . . my assignment . . . I have been made an *archivist*?" he roared.

She nodded.

He discovered he was panting, harder than he had while leading the S'Dyxoi into the ambush along Commerce Way. It made no sense. He had been given the highest ranking in the Training Legion, had excelled in his classes, and his weapon proficiencies were among the highest in his age cohort. "What did I do wrong?" he wondered, his voice breaking for the first time in years.

"You did *nothing* wrong," Shaananca insisted.

Druadaen detected a strange, tortured twist in her voice. He looked at her. "Did *you* do this?"

She closed her eyes. "I did not stop it."

"Did you *suggest* it?"

"I did point out that you had gifts uniquely suited for this role. Which, by the way, is *not* that of an archivist. You are a Courier working on behalf of the Archive Recondite. You will travel the world. You will see great cities. You will—"

"I will not do this willingly."

She sighed. "I assumed as much."

"And I will never relent in my appeals to be given the assignment I have worked toward, the one I deserve, the one for which I am perfectly suited." He'd never claimed such things before, but now that he had, he would not foreswear them.

"I assumed that, too." Shaananca nodded. "And in the fullness of time, I will add my voice to yours in pressing that you be given an assignment along the lines you wish."

He recoiled. "'*Along the lines* I wish'? But you know *exactly* what I wish, and you could have spoken for it now!"

She nodded. "Perhaps. But not successfully."

Druadaen let himself half fall into a chair. "So I am to be made a Courier." He felt as if all his organs had been removed. "I will not accept that life."

Shaananca rounded on him. "Pay closer attention. I did not say this is your life. I have made it very clear to others it must *not* be. But it is decided that before an assignment to the military may be considered, you should travel, learn the ways of ships and the sea, hear many languages, see many peoples and places."

"And how long must I serve as a Courier?"

"I am uncertain. But rules stipulate that one cannot serve as an Archive Courier for *more* than three years."

Druadaen found that curious. "Why?"

Shaananca settled back. "Because the paths you travel, places you go, and contacts you develop will become known by then."

"And so?"

"And so, you could be intercepted and your portfolio lost. And your life along with it."

Druadaen sat straighter. "My life? I could be killed for a packet of old papers?"

Shaananca raised an eyebrow. "It beggars belief to think that you might have failed to notice the precautions, and the defenses, an intruder would have to pass in order to reach the Reserved Collection."

"I have noted them. Although now I suspect I have not noted *all* of them."

"You have not. If you have, then we have done a very poor job of concealing them."

Druadaen reconsidered the Archive, then also reconsidered the many possible destinations along the path the S'Dyxan infiltrators had been following. "Might the Archive have been the object of the recent attack?"

Shaananca's eyes seemed to grow almost opaque. "It is not beyond the realm of possibility."

He sighed. "Well, it's hardly the Legion or even the Ord Ridire, but being a Courier certainly doesn't sound dull." A year or two would be a small price to pay for a life in the Legion. "I suppose if I must wait, there are worse ways to serve. So long as I am assigned to the Legion, at the end."

She nodded. "You will certainly be made a soldier, that much I can assure you. But once again, the precise assignment is not within my power."

He nodded. "I understand." *But once I am made a soldier, where else would I be assigned* but *the Legions?* Druadaen let that relaxing reassurance wash over him, thinking: *So really, what could go wrong?*

PART THREE

CONUNDRUM:
THE BENT

Journal Entry 126
6th of Scythe, 1797 S.C.
Tlulanxu

Just before embarking upon my first assignment as an Archive Courier, I remember consoling myself with the surety of joining the Legion when I finished. I thought, "What could go wrong?"

The answer turned out to be, "Quite a lot, actually."

Since that day, I have traveled the seas for almost three years as a Courier and had many so-called "adventures." I sailed on many ships, almost always Dunarran, to many lands. We were nearly shipwrecked off the coast of Uanseach, beset and almost boarded by Sikassian privateers within sight of the docks of Hadezh on Mihal'j, and attacked by some great tentacled beast while at overnight anchorage near Crovae, the Irrylaish gutta-percha colony on the west coast of Solori. I stood ready in cuir-boulli and with sword drawn each time. And each time, I was told to guard the portfolios bound for the Archive Recondite, at the cost of my life if necessary. It seemed a genuine command to address a genuine concern, but I cannot help but suspect that it also reflected a desire to keep a young, untested warrior out of the way of the seasoned soldiers already lining the gunwales or standing to the weapons mounted on the centerline pivots.

I have tallied all the places I made landfall and it turns out that I have seen and walked the streets of just about three dozen port cities beyond those of Dunarra and her three ancestral and closest allies (Teurodn, Connæar, Irrylain). In the course of doing so, I learned an average of three hundred words in a dozen different languages, was trailed by various thieves through various bazaars, and visited scores of scholars—all of whom demonstrated one constant despite personal or cultural differences: a stultifying obsession with their subject of expertise. In many cases, this focus became so myopic that any aptitudes they'd had for interacting with other humans had long since grown stiff and unserviceable with disuse. But they had not lost their appreciation for silver, and Dunarra is renowned for its generosity when paying for noteworthy tomes, artifacts, insights, or information.

In the course of securing and transporting those objects, I drew my weapon half a dozen times and used it only once. That occurred when an arranged meeting with a reclusive scholar in the Sqa'ene highlands of Solori turned out to be a ruse. It was arranged by a bandit-lord who dwelt just beyond the borders of Qu'unatliqlan and who possessed an ear in its court. The one prisoner who survived revealed to whom that ear was attached. It did not remain so after we made our report. In countries such as Qu'unatliqlan, where an autocrat's words—and whims—are law, justice is often remarkably swift, and punishments are often fashioned to fit the crime.

I was two moonphases shy of twenty-one when my assignment as an Archive Courier came to an end and I eagerly tore off the wax seal on the back of my new orders. At last! A posting to the Legion!

Except that was not the order conveyed by the document. As Shaananca had assured me, my case had come to the special and particular attention of all manner of highly placed Consentium commanders and intelligencers. And, as she had also been certain, I was indeed made a soldier. But not with the Legions; I was assigned to the Ord Ridire.

I will admit that it is the most desirable military posting after the Legions. If they are the Consentium's sword and shield, the Ord Ridire is its swiftest lance, both on and off the battle-field. It is they who patrol the areas along—and sometimes well beyond—Dunarra's borders.

But there is a branch of the Ord Ridire that serves the Consentium in a very different role: as its ears, eyes, and sometimes, daggers. Operating in small groups, these are the Outriders, who rarely travel in teams greater than three or four. Certainly, I reasoned, shining service as either a cavalryman or scout would earn me an eventual transfer to the Legions.

But my first assignment in the Ord Ridire was in neither of those customary roles. Rather, no sooner had I unloaded my kit from one ship than I was sent to another. I was to be a subaltern aboard an Ord Ridire barquentine. Which must sound very confusing: Why would a horseman serve as ship's crew?

The answer lies in the Ord Ridire's ancient origins as a band of borderers who patrolled and defended the frontier for those peoples who dwelt in the lands between Aedmurun and Tlulanxu, which ultimately amalgamated into the nation of Dunarra. However, once that state evolved into a continent- (and then globe-) spanning Consentium, the Ord Ridire was tasked to detect potential threats well beyond the borders—including overseas. So although their mobility expanded to include hulls as well as horses, the name did not change.

However, the definition of "threat" changed considerably, expanding beyond strictly military matters. Disruptions in distant dynasties, shifts in power among continent-spanning guilds, regional impacts of new alliances or old grudges: monitoring these events fell to the Outriders, whose emphasis upon small numbers and the ability to blend into different cultures made them a natural fit for the Consentium's evolving needs. Consequently, even as their numbers grew, they evolved too, becoming intelligencers as well as scouts—but still carried on Ord Ridire ships.

I suppose it was inevitable that I was tapped to serve aboard such vessels. I had more time at sea than any recruit except for those who had come from harbor towns, but also had grown up handling animals and riding. So whether at sea or on land, I knew how to get around quickly. Also, my time both as an assistant in, and Courier for, the Archive Recondite had acquainted me with where and how one goes about getting needed information.

The ships I served on mostly sailed the Sea of Kudak, a great inland pocket of the ocean. For almost two years, we crisscrossed those relatively calm waters between Silvallash, Sanâllea, Leannedor, the free city of Menara, and our own ports. We carried news, delivered sealed orders, and transported factotums and agents of the Propretoriate—sometimes out of harm's way at the very last second. Or a little bit later than that.

Six months ago, upon porting in Tlulanxu, I found new orders awaiting me. Surely, I had finally been posted to the Legions! But no, I was still in the Ord Ridire. I was simply being transferred to the Outriders. I had never sought solace at the bottom of an ale mug before, but I did that night.

Understand: To be made an Outrider is a great honor and

a noteworthy compliment to one's abilities. Their missions are at such remove and the consequent need for independent action is so high, that the military Pretors consider it one of the most demanding of assignments a soldier may be given. But inasmuch as my desire to serve in the Legion continues undiminished and unwavering, I consider it just another detour.

Since then, my duties have been light and largely uneventful. I am the youngest of our three-man team and we have ranged up and down the western border of both Dunarra and Connæar, watchful for incursions that never come. We venture further over the border, from the open town of Steppney all the way down to Menara on the coast, when we have information or informers to pick up.

The most important are those who come bearing report of the antagonistic rulers of Khassant, just to the west. On several occasions, we were compelled to stand off Khassa riders that meant to either retrieve or silence a fleeing informer. On one occasion, they loosed a few arrows at us, probably more out of annoyance than intent to start a skirmish. Most of their shafts missed, one hit my shield, another caught the horse of one of the other Outriders in the meat of its haunches. While he controlled and drew his shaken mount out of range, we let fly arrows in return.

Our bows are not as handy as the Khassa pony shortbows, but ours have greater range and power, being slightly longer and of composite construction. One of the pursuers slipped more than fell from his horse: the Khassas use no saddles and only primitive stirrups. Recovering their motionless comrade, they withdrew, shouting as they did. No doubt it was some of the extraordinarily colorful Khassa taunts about the lascivious nature of all our female ancestors, but I was too far to hear much of it clearly.

That was three weeks ago. With winter nearing, we were withdrawn from our patrol circuit, replaced by a larger but less wide-ranging Ord Ridire unit. The other two Outriders in my group immediately returned to their families. I was at loose ends and put in a request for any missions that might want filling; I had no desire to sit idle, although I have accrued an immense amount of leave time.

It turned out there was a job that needed doing up north, in what is called the Plain of Grehar, or to adopt the corrupted version, the "Graveyard." It is a stretch of open land beyond the western frontier that starts in Connæar and continues along the contiguous border of its northern neighbor, Teurodn. Its ominous nickname comes from being one of the places where the Bent most frequently raid, even in the winter months.

Once I heard the destination, I also guessed the nature of the job: to help a lone, but more experienced, Outrider to observe and report on Bent activity in the region. The Graveyard attracts particular attention in this regard, since an increase in raiding there is one of the most reliable barometers of when their numbers are approaching what is called either a horde-mass or a "Hordeing."

Having asked for an assignment, I could not then reject this one. So, I will be spending the next two days in the Archive, learning more about the Bent and then departing on what is roundly held to be one of the most miserable missions that any Outrider can be given. My destination is a small camp, or possibly blockhouse, of bountiers: men whose gruesome profession involves tracking and killing Bent to trade their thumbs for coin. To say that I am traveling to a place that might well be as squalid and unsavory as it is unsafe would be an understatement.

So this time, as I prepare to face another new challenge, I am *not* thinking, "What can go wrong?"

Creeds and cruppers, I'll be happy just to get back alive.

CHAPTER EIGHT

Druadaen slowly brought his mount to a halt, turned in the saddle and took a last look behind. The sheer sides of Dunarra's wallway and its uniform towers were just barely visible over the highlands to the south. It was, in fact, the view he'd grown up with. Those distance-dimmed, angular shapes were his earliest memories of looking—and longing—toward where his parents traveled to do their mysterious work, where almost all their books came from, where traders from as far as Teurodn converged, and where all his boundless hopes and dreams had resided.

He turned his back on the dim shapes on the southern horizon and urged the horse into a slow forward walk. To the right was the stream that ran just east of their house, which was now just a half-overgrown hump of blackened beams and sprawled foundation stones.

It was his first return to the place where his life had gone awry. He had not exactly avoided it, but he'd had no reason to pass it, either. His bordering work along Connæar's frontier had never brought him closer than twenty leagues. But heading north from the wallway out of Aedmurun had been the fastest route further north, so here he was.

He glanced at what was left of the house in which he had grown up . . . and felt nothing. No surprise: he had expected it to be an anticlimactic return, and it was.

He urged his horse into a faster walk, past fields where harvest preparations were under way.

The missions that had taken him into the countryside of other nations had usually been hurried—not to say perilous—episodes requiring constant watchfulness. But that wasn't the case as his northwesterly journey would only gradually angle closer to the border. Consequently, he began passing through communities of a type he had never had the time to visit.

Although Connæar became a protectorate of Dunarra when its royal family was systematically exterminated late in the Second Age of the First Consentium, the Propretoriate had been careful not to impinge upon the political or cultural life of their neighbor. The close association had certainly benefited the military and bureaucracy of the much smaller nation, but it had neither the resources nor the resolve to maintain the standards that prevailed over its southern border. Here, every town was a unique entity with wild variations in the quality, cost, and availability of lodging and meals.

Druadaen noticed a similar degree of variation in Connæar's defenses, particularly in the design—and condition—of its fortifications. Not only was the emphasis on castles rather than forts, but the construction was more crude. The architecture was only indifferently informed by the main strategic objective: to arrest incursions by either human or Bent invaders. And although the garrisons and their commanders were always amicable when he sought advice on local lodgings, they also seemed relieved to see him go, as if his mere presence was simultaneously an intrusion and an indictment.

However, these modest measures of similarity between Connæar and Dunarra abruptly ended when Druadaen crossed the border into Teurodn.

He had certainly expected differences. Although Teurodn was another centuries-old ally of Dunarra, the roots of its peoples, its culture, and its language were all quite different. As a strong central monarchy that forbade serfdom and indentured servitude, it was one of the more enlightened nations on the continent of Ar Navir. On the other hand, disputes ranging from affairs of honor to irresolvable legal disputes were frequently settled by melees between not only the direct antagonists but their blood-oathed supporters.

Druadaen's descent from the low mountains straddling the border of Connæar and Teurodn also signified his arrival at the western limit of human habitation. According to his fellow Outriders, the Graveyard's borderers were ready folk who lived rough lives and came from humble origins. Almost every one of them was, or traced their ancestry to, persons expelled from the more tamed countryside to the east or the descendants of refugees who started out as border-dwelling squatters but were absorbed by the slow westward advance that had new squatters always settling a little further out upon the stark grasslands of the Plain of Grehar.

He had thought that living at the fringes most vulnerable to Bent raiders would instill a greater desire for superior protection and the ability to defend themselves during those periodic attacks. But as his horse crested and then shuffled casually down the last hillside into Teurodn, he found himself staring at the local version of a stronghold.

Its ill-fitting gray stones were so undressed that orderly courses of them were only evident along the bottom of the walls and at a few other key junctures. The rest had been pieced in and supported (one could hardly call it "reinforced") with what looked more like wall plaster, not mortar. Druadaen tried to imagine what its ground plan would look like, gave up as quickly as he'd begun.

The physical details of the castle didn't seem to have much impact on the morale of its complement, however. They seemed as alert and ready as any other garrison. Of course, it was probably the most impressive construction they had ever seen, with the possible exception of the village temple. Druadaen scanned for that other edifice and, when he finally detected it, he decided that no, it was definitely *not* more impressive than the "castle."

As he reached the outskirts of the village, he was peripherally aware that its inhabitants were staring openly as he rode slowly toward the temple. In addition to being an extremely humble structure, it was also mystifying; he could not discern what gods or pantheon it was dedicated to. To the best of his knowledge, few Teuronds dreamwalked in the Creedlands of the Helpers. Most of them remained devoted to the pantheon of the Nyrthulean peoples who had settled—or, according to some histories, invaded—the northern extents of Ar Navir. But this temple did not seem to be aligned with those, either.

That indeterminacy proved to be the clue to understanding

the temple's actual role; it was, for want of a better term, a shared space for any number of devotions. It probably did not welcome *all* creeds: some deities would not abide the presence of another's sacrists or symbology. But Druadaen saw the unmistakable side building that no doubt served as a rude epiphanium, just as the architecturally distinctive broad steps and hollow offering stelae indicated that it was a temple of some kind.

As he rode past, he noticed a long stretch of open land behind it. *Well*, he revised quickly, *not* entirely *open*: ironically, here at the approaches to the Graveyard he had finally encountered an *actual* graveyard.

Druadaen had heard about them, of course. There had been some in Connæar. But they had been small; the greater the proximity to Dunarra, the more profound its cultural influences. Within a dozen leagues of the wallway, devotion to the deities of the Helper pantheon prevailed and the rites were close kin to those practiced just over the border, particularly those pertaining to the deceased: cremation and scattering the ashes upon moving water. Graveyards were more common the further north one went, but remained comparatively infrequent until one crossed the border into Teurodn.

Druadaen had seen a few graveyards in the distance as a child, and more recently as an Outrider, but this was the first time he was close enough to make out the individual headstones, stelae, mausoleums, and other grave markers. He had always labored to keep an open mind toward the practice of burial, but now, seen up close, he could neither dismiss nor suppress his innate reaction: that it was morbid, ghoulish, and more than a bit primitive.

His gaze traveled from the weather-bitten monuments to a restive crowd that was gathering where the fields touched the grange on the village's outskirts. As its numbers and general level of agitation grew, he wondered if, perhaps, the difference in death rites was a reflection of the difference in the lives these people lived. The extraordinary number of children, the equally extraordinary number who died before they came of age, the number of hobbling, untoothed ancients who were not even seventy years old: death or its harbingers were everywhere he looked. Even the masses of children were a grim, preemptive adaptation to the numbers that would be taken by disease, injury, infection, hunger, and mishap.

Maybe, then, the tradition of burial, of graveyards, was just another accommodation of the omnipresence of death, a means of resisting the physical parting of all the family, friends, and neighbors who were constantly passing into the creedlands. He imagined that reliance upon the comfort and reassurance of dreamwalks were just that much more critical in such a place.

As if in answer to his speculation, the crowd ahead let out a ragged chorus of angry shouts as two figures broke away, running toward the fields. One was young and swift; the other was gray-haired and limping with the steady regularity of an accustomed infirmity.

Druadaen turned his horse in the direction they were running, gently spurred it into a fast walk. He was curious, but he also reminded himself that this was not his culture, not his community, and so, not his business.

The crowd was rapidly gaining on the two fleeing figures, but not because of the older one's limp. Rather, the younger one—small and short-legged—was losing ground because he lacked the stamina to keep running. The old fellow turned—frayed robes and long beard swirling—and began hobbling backward, facing the mob while remaining between them and his young companion. He raised a gnarled wooden staff in a gesture of either physical defense or mantic warding; Druadaen could not determine which.

"Stand aside!" one of the mob's leaders shouted.

"You mean to harm him," the old fellow yodeled back.

"That's no business of yours, gritch."

Gritch: provincial slang for a "green witch." So he was a nativist, Druadaen concluded as he neared the back of the crowd, which was starting to encircle the pair. But those who started flanking around from the rear saw Druadaen and stopped, uncertainty writ plain on their faces.

Their hush spread to the front of the crowd. Whispering took its place. Heads turned, among them, those of the leaders. "What's your business here?" an older man asked, frowning at Druadaen's armor and gear; as an Outrider, he was not accoutred in Dunarran standard.

Druadaen simply shrugged.

"Well, move along, then," another said. But it was a tentative suggestion, not a command.

Druadaen made no response. He simply remained in his saddle, watching.

As he'd hoped, the mere presence of an unidentified soldier

sitting on a large horse to the rear had forestalled any slide into ungoverned frenzy and now kept it from restarting. Watchful eyes often were most unnerving—and powerful—when the identity and potentials of the watcher were unknown.

The leaders turned wary backs upon him, shaking rag-wrapped clubs at the youngster cowering behind the nativist. "We've got some nice branches for you right here, boy."

"You shall not harm him," the old man said in a surprisingly sharp and firm voice.

"They will if I say!" shrieked a woman.

"And who are you, hag?"

"His mother," she wailed.

The boy ducked his head in shame or dismay or both. The old man straightened, eyes squinting as if his vision was failing. "And you—*you*—would subject him to—?"

"She'd teach him the meaning of his choice before it's too late," a man roared. He waved yet another stick capped by a smeared rag. "A good beating might shock some sense into 'im!"

"Ya," agreed another loudly. "And if not, well, he might as well get used to living covered in beast dung!"

Druadaen understood the stained bags and the rags, now.

The old man's perplexity had transformed into haughty disdain. He seemed to grow half a foot as he stared down the mob. "Free animals do not live in their own filth. Only 'domesticated' boars—swine—do that." Then he peered over their heads at the dingy cottages and tilting sheds at the edge of the town. "Of course, they may learn that habit from some of the breed that see fit to enslave them."

The mutterings of the mob ebbed briefly, but when they rose again, they were low and dark. Outrage at one of their own had now widened to include the nativist. The leaders started edging forward, shaking the rags from their clubs.

Druadaen sighed. The mob's desire to chastise and punish was stupid, but the nativist's contempt and insults hadn't been much better. They all deserved whatever they were about to do to each other . . . but the youngster's desire to go with the old nativist seemed genuine, innocent.

Druadaen touched a spur to his horse's flank. The sound of its slow forward walk froze the tableau just as combat was about to be joined.

The crowd parted before the charger, staring at Druadaen. And at his sword and armor. It was not the calculating assessment of possible attackers: more a somber recognition of the latent threat.

Druadaen let the horse proceed as slowly as it liked. Not because it gave people more time to get out of the way, but because each second that passed meant that the raised clubs lowered a little further, allowed rage to be replaced with cautious reassessment.

He reined the horse in gently when he was ten feet away from the speakers clustered at the front of the mob. "Has this young man broken a law?"

"Who are you to ask?" asked the most flush-faced of the group.

"Why should you care? Do you mean to keep this matter a secret?" Druadaen assessed the size of the crowd. "If so, you are going about it the wrong way."

"He disrespects our traditions, going to live in the wilds, apprenticing to a gritch. He'll probably become a beast himself!"

Druadaen nodded. "So, he has soiled your traditions and you mean to soil him for doing so? For choosing a different path?"

The mother's head went back as she shouted through her sobs. "He is going to his doom, his eternal death, if he goes with that gritch!"

Druadaen frowned, glanced at the resolute, but softening face of the old man. "He does not look like an evil man, nativist or not."

"I do not fear for my boy because of an old *gritch*," the mother shouted impatiently. Heads in the crowd nodded.

Druadaen was not able to keep a frown off his face. "Then who is threatening your son?"

"If he adopts the old man's ways," said a short, wide-shouldered farmer who bore a strong resemblance to the woman, "we will not find him in any god's creedland. He will be in the Great Tract of the gritches—er, druids," the man finished, using the term common among those whose ancestry and idiom was sprinkled with echoes of the Uanseachan migrations of past millennia.

Druadaen shrugged. "The creedlands are not for all persons. Even consecrants say so, when pressed. They say the gods know this, and that it is by their wisdom and will that the Great Tract exists."

"But we will not see him when we die," the mother cried desperately. "He will not pass with us. He shall be gone forever!" She hid her wet face in chapped hands.

Druadaen nodded, made his voice as gentle as he could. "You seem to love him greatly."

"We do," the apparent uncle answered as she sobbed.

Druadaen stared at the dung they were holding "You've chosen strange ways to show love. Besides, you cannot know the final journey the boy begins with these steps. It is said that some who wander the Great Tract in their youth discover that once there, they finally hear the whisper of a god and so come to end their days in a creedland. And others who leave the epiphanium devoted to a god, and nightly dreamwalk in that creedland, ultimately realize that their deepest longing is for the unfettered freedom of the Great Tract. I am told that neither outcome is frequent, but they do occur."

"And what is to become of my sweet boy," the mother sniffled into her sodden sleeves, "wandering alone through trackless wilds, in both his waking and sleeping hours? What kind of life is it, running with wild beasts?" Her voice darkened. "Or what might be worse."

Druadaen nodded somberly. "And still, there are worse fates than those."

"Name one!" she snapped resentfully.

"To close one's eyes and be happy not to dream at all," he answered.

The uncle frowned. "And how could any being find happiness in that?"

Druadaen shrugged. "They might, if dreaming meant being trapped in the Wildscape."

The silence after that statement seemed to grow more profound with every passing second. Maybe because his tone told them he knew—personally—whereof he spoke.

As the crowd's quiet gave rise to restless movement and averted eyes, the nativist put a gentle hand on the boy's shoulder and, nodding his thanks, slipped away into the sun-bleached posts and desiccated tangles of the dying vineyard that abutted the field.

As the two of them disappeared, the crowd began to drift away, back to their homely cottages and sheds. Several turned their backs and, probably believing themselves unobserved, made subtle warding signs. Druadaen waited until the field was empty, then turned his horse to the west and eased it into a walk.

Toward the scraggle-grassed Graveyard.

CHAPTER NINE

The wind running in from the north was not just cool, but cold. The circumpolar sea was one hundred and fifty leagues away, but there was nothing to block the frigid gusts it sent down the length of the Plain of Grehar. *Yet another reason the locals call it the Graveyard*, Druadaen reflected as his mount's flank rippled at the chill. And with the midday skies growing increasingly gray, the augur of rain made the prospect of a second night upon the flatlands not merely unwelcome but potentially dangerous.

Between the isolation, the cold, and the lack of wood for a fire that would have marked his location anyway, the previous night had been one of the most miserable Druadaen could recall. He was well acquainted with all those conditions, but not all at once, and not alone upon the doorstep of the Bent. Their burrows were still distant, dozens of leagues to the west, but they were among the least predictable of humanity's foes, often ranging far away from their havens.

Indeed, Druadaen's most pressing concern regarding distance was not knowing how many more miles he had to travel before reaching the bountiers' blockhouse. The directions and crude map which he'd been given had proven increasingly insufficient for navigating the flat and essentially featureless Plain of Grehar. Had Druadaen not spent years as a Courier, learning to navigate by the stars alone, he would have had no idea where he was. This way, he did have *some* idea of his location—but it was certainly vague, if not utterly wrong. In which case, the weather was a far greater threat than either the wolves he had been able to detect and avoid, or the Bent, of whom he had seen no sign.

However, as he surveyed the horizon from the back of his horse, he caught sight of black specks in the sky to the north. Birds. Circling lazily. Almost certainly vultures. Since they were still aloft, they were either waiting for their intended meal to become helpless or for an ongoing struggle to conclude. Either way, it was the sort of situation that most riders would wisely avoid.

However, part of an Outrider's training was to recognize when certain risks made survival more likely rather than less. And in this case, the risk of meeting potential foes beneath the circling birds was worth the possibility of an encounter that might either help him locate the bountiers quickly or lead to some other opportunity for shelter. Because the alternative was wandering uncertainly northward on a trackless steppe with lethal cold threatening.

He drew his sabre and tugged his mount's reins in that direction.

Slight rises and dips passed for notable terrain features on the windy Plain of Grehar, one of which obstructed Druadaen's view of the vulture-marked area. Until, that is, he came over a long, low hump of grassland—and discovered a savage melee in progress. He spurred his horse into a gallop.

Six humans had gained the upper hand over what he could only assume was a small party of Bent. Three of the heavily-built beings were already sprawled in the low grass. The last one standing was doing an impressive job of parrying the swords of two attackers with an axe, a feat that Druadaen would have considered impossible.

However, one of the two bow-armed bountiers had maneuvered to the flank of the fight. He drew a bead, waited a moment, and then loosed.

The long arrow hit just under the Bent's right armpit as it raised that elbow to control the completion of its axe's swing to the right. The big hunting point made a hard *thock!* as it penetrated the armor there: cured hide of some kind. The Bent warrior staggered but did not fall, despite having almost half a foot of shaft embedded in its right lung.

But that momentary break in its action and awareness was the opening the two humans had been looking for. They cut, slashed, and stabbed with their swords. Several hits and the axe flew away. The next blow, a heavy cut to the left leg, dropped the humanoid. The small battleground was motionless, except for the charge of Druadaen's sod-pounding horse...

...and one of the fallen Bent who rose swiftly to one knee, right arm cocking back to throw a hatchet at the bountiers.

The humans turned, saw both. One pointed at Druadaen, another at the Bent, a third hastily tried to nock another arrow.

But before any of them could react, the sound of Druadaen's charging horse brought the Bent's head around in surprise. He turned, tried to shift his aim—but not before Druadaen rode past, just to his right, sword sweeping high through an uppercut.

In the same instant that Druadaen realized how badly his arm had been jarred, the reason for that impact tumbled through his field of vision: a severed hand. He pulled the horse into a tight caracole for another pass.

The shrieking humanoid recovered from the blow, tried rising and running despite a freely streaming chest wound, deeply gashed thigh, and missing hand—but went down before he'd taken a step, an arrow sticking up from between his shoulder blades.

Two of the bountiers trotted over a moment later, one stopping to smile up at Druadaen as the other leaned over to check the much-mauled Bent, dagger at the ready.

"Didn't expect to see another hunter out here," said the one who'd approached Druadaen, "but we're glad you happened by when you did."

"Not if he wants a share," muttered the other, who had pulled up the lolling head of the humanoid. "This one's done," he shouted over his shoulder at the other four bountiers.

Druadaen had been in enough engagements so that they did not exactly terrify him, but just put him on edge, mind focused and blood pumping. But he was not prepared for what he saw when he looked back at the other bountiers. The big humanoid that had taken the arrow in the lung was still not dead, so the youngest of them casually hacked at the side of its head. Druadaen started as bright red blood jetted out: until that moment and the color contrast, he had not realized that the Bent's skin was not just green but *bright* green. Like sweetgrass in summer.

The second, and even greater surprise, was the reaction of the oldest of the humans: "Piss and porridge, lookit yeh done, ye gob! Ruined the ear, and they only take pairs. Now we'll need the thumbs, instead." Swearing in a language Druadaen did not recognize, he set about the necessary butchery with a dagger. When the Bent stirred, he muttered, "Ah, be done, you!" and paused long enough to push his dagger through the fallen creature's eye.

Swallowing, Druadaen realized that, regardless of what the books said about the Bent—the savagery, the atrocities, the millennia of mutual loathing—the body lying dead on the sourgrass had too many features in common with his own to think of it as a creature ever again. It *was* a being, ugliness and brutality notwithstanding.

The grizzled veteran looked up from his work. "'Ere, now, rider; what're ye staring at?"

Druadaen started. "The color—the skin. It's so... bright."

The hunters looked at him. Their leader screwed up his face. "Bright?"

"The skin. The green, I mean. Much brighter than I expected."

The hunters didn't change their positions or even their expressions, but something in their eyes changed, all in the same moment. "So," mused the leader, rising, and passing two dripping thumbs to one of the other hunters, "first time you've killed *pekt*?"

Druadaen frowned. "Killed what?"

A few smirks, a few eyerolls. The leader tried a different term. "*Urzhen*?"

"Oh! Yes... but no; this is the first time I have fought them."

"More like the first time he's *seen* them," added the one who'd been the clear target of the Bent whose hand Druadaen had lopped off. "Urzhen: isn't that what the scribes call them?"

Druadaen nodded. "Yes." He considered. "Most of them."

"Well, we're not scribes and no one else actually calls them that"—he paused, studying Druadaen more closely—"Dunarran." He didn't *quite* say it as he would an epithet. More disconcerting was the ease and speed with which the man had identified his origins.

The leader was frowning at the fellow. "'Ere now, you greedy southern bastard, mind yer tongue." He shook his head, came toward Druadaen. "Don't mind 'im; they've no manners in Sanâllea, apparently."

Druadaen shrugged. "My experiences led me to conclude otherwise."

The voice of the Sanâllean was more interested, but also more wary. "You know Sanâllea?"

Druadaen nodded. "Not well, but enough to appreciate that its people are very gracious and polite, unless they've decided you're a person who cannot be trusted."

"Like you?"

The leader bristled, but Druadaen drifted a stilling hand in his direction. "I was speaking of the Silvallashan agent we helped bring to justice." He shifted into Sanâllean. "It was our pleasure to be of service to King Truciero on that day."

The Sanâllean bountier's eyes widened but he said nothing.

The leader laughed, glanced at him as he hooked a thumb toward Druadaen. "This feller sounds almost like you when you start spouting that southern gabble."

The Sanâllean muttered something inaudible but clearly resentful.

Druadaen sheathed his sword, dismounted, drew his composite bow from its scabbard. Seeing their puzzled looks, he explained. "There were wolves following me. For several hours. They'll be here soon."

The archer who'd taken down the big urzh shrugged. "No, they'll wait until we leave."

Druadaen looked at the corpses of the urzhen. Of course: there was no way to burn them, no time to bury them . . . and he had the distinct impression that the bountiers would have laughed at the idea. "So, the wolves, eh, dispose of the bodies you leave behind?"

"Down to the last bit of gristle," the leader assured him. "Of course, if we ever wind up like them, I'm sure we'd get the same treatment. Now, since you're obviously not out here to hunt urzhen, why are you riding in the Graveyard?"

"I am here on a mission."

The Sanâllean scoffed. "Like I said: he's a Dunarran. They're *all* on missions."

"Gradda!" the archer barked at him. "You mind your slimy tongue."

The leader smiled as though no harsh words had been uttered. "And what mission would that be?"

"To seek word of another Dunarran: the Outrider Garasan. Possibly to help him finish assessing the Bent population."

Looks were exchanged among the humans. It was the archer who looked away first. "Well, I suspect he certainly achieved that."

Druadaen was glad they seemed familiar with the Outrider's name, but the archer's tone seemed bleak. "What do you mean?"

The leader stepped forward, put a hand on Druadaen's shoulder. "Come along and have a cuppa at our base. Better to talk there."

"Safer, too," the slim Sanâllean muttered. He jerked his head at the earless corpses of the Bent. "Let's make away before we find out if these *pekt* had friends in hollering distance."

CHAPTER TEN

After almost two weeks on horseback, Druadaen was glad for the chance to walk the two miles to the bountiers' base. He had expected them to maintain greater distance between their refuge and their very vengeful prey, but they explained that outrunning the Bent over any significant distance required horses—and out on the Graveyard, horses were more of a risk than a benefit. Even if there was enough wood to build a barn, the Bent would smell the horseflesh and swarm until they had devoured every last morsel of it.

Over the centuries, ambitious bountiers had occasionally attempted to create bases large enough to accommodate stables and scores of men. But whenever a human base became that large, it drew the pekt like flies to honey...or other substances. Between what they perceived as a territorial challenge and the richness of such a target proved irresistible to them, who would make common cause with other Bent species to remove both the meat and the human interlopers. It was apparently much the same wherever bountiers worked, whether out upon the Graveyard or in the foothills of the Cleethpale Mountains that ran down the center of northern Ar Navir like a spine.

Indeed, there was apparently more variation among the bountiers themselves. Those who worked the Cleethpales were an amalgam of Clearwall borderers, hunters, and outpost garrisons.

They all had families, and often property, nearby so they were motivated at least as much by protecting those they loved as they were by love of coin. Conversely, those who worked the Graveyard had only one reason for being where they were: to collect the bounty on the Bent.

As such, they were a rougher lot than the others. Only a few were from nearby Teurodn, and none of them hailed from its western borders. Indeed, not a one of them had families back in the human realms, which they called the Lands or the Streets. Their pursuit of the Bent was year-round, save the latter half of winter, when their prey remained in their warrens. The reasoning of the pekt reprised some of Druadaen's own recent concerns; if a raid necessitated traveling beyond the ready reach of shelter, then the weather was likely to be even more deadly than humans.

Druadaen did not ask questions as they walked, but he heard occasional phrases in Connæaran, Midlander, even Khassan and Bleklish, and usually in native accents. However, most of their exchanges were in the polyglot merchant's tongue known as Commerce, and their dress, weapons, armor, and opinions were as diverse as any group that Druadaen had ever encountered. The only thing they had in common was a dogged pride in being professional, which was to say full-time, Bent bountiers: self-styled mongrels who paid court to no king, and made a living with their own bloodstained hands. In this case, at a rate of fifteen marks of silver-copper billon for every matching pair of ears or thumbs they brought to the paymasters of border garrisons.

Under other circumstances, Druadaen would have had some concern for his safety among such a group. Whereas he'd met many soldiers who'd become hardened to killing, these men had become indifferent to it. However, out here, even he felt the quick, reflexive embrace of a kinship and bond stronger than any personal differences or material disputes. And not because he had put his sword alongside theirs, but because they were just a small group of humans bivouacking at the very edge of the Bent lands, and so, were never more than a few heartbeats away from the possibility that they might be overrun and massacred.

Druadaen, who had been scanning the horizon for their camp, finally asked, "Where's your blockhouse?" The odd looks he received was the first indication that the information conveyed by his commander had been flawed in yet another particular. "So," he concluded, "you *don't* have a blockhouse."

The archer, a taciturn Bleklauner by the name of Omur, shrugged. "Can't really say that we have a house at all."

"Then where do you live?"

They topped another of the Graveyard's low rises and the leader—Fronbec—pointed down the slope. "There."

Druadaen looked for some kind of construction at the base of the next rise, then noticed a narrow path cut into the backside of the slope they were on, just a few feet below them. "Tunnels?" he exclaimed. "You live in tunnels? Near the *Bent*?"

Gradda shouldered past him. "They don't dig out here. The soil is too sandy. It caves in."

Druadaen kept staring. "So, does that mean you are better at tunneling than they are?" Even to his own ears, his voice sounded not merely incredulous but doubtful.

"No," Fronbec answered, waving for Druadaen to follow them. "It started as a sod house. Oh, about fifty years ago."

"Sixty," corrected Omur flatly.

"Or sixty," Fronbec conceded with a good-natured smile. "Over time, groups of bountiers expanded it. Rains smoothed the sod into the slope, and ice hardened it. Now, be sure to step where we do."

Druadaen nodded, took care to watch where his horse placed its hooves.

Omur nodded approvingly. "If he steps wrong, he's done for. When the Bent stumble into one of our traps, it's just a stake through their foot. With a horse, it could be split hoof, a broken fetlock, or both."

His mount just barely fit through the sod house's relatively narrow entry and took up almost a third of the antechamber. But as Druadaen hitched the horse and removed the tack, he became aware that this spacious, circular room had a purpose beyond the shedding of mud- and blood-smeared gear. Almost a dozen inward-facing murder slits lined the walls between the entry and the much sturdier inner door.

The last to enter, Omur shut and barred it, then headed toward a narrow tunnel at the other end of the barracks-like interior.

"Mind we weren't followed," Fronbec called after him.

"That's my job, isn't it?" Omur disappeared into the narrow slot in the far wall.

"Where's he going?" Druadaen asked.

"Watch post," Gradda muttered.

Druadaen frowned, recalled the shallow, featureless dip in which the sod house was located. "I saw no watch post."

"Kind of the point," the Sanâllean grunted.

Fronbec chuckled at Druadaen's annoyed frown. "Come have a seat with us." He gestured to stools arrayed around a small, homely firepit with a hood and wooden tubes venting the smoke up through the ceiling. Noticing Druadaen's silent study of the arrangement, he explained: "Plenty of peat, out where the sweetgrass meets the sourgrass." He tapped one of the tubes. "Doesn't make much smoke, and what there is goes through wet sandstone before it reaches air."

"And the Bent haven't found you by the smell?"

Fronbec shrugged. "A few have, but they're most oft loners, scouts—and only one or two have ever lived to carry word to others. Assuming they didn't meet some other fate on the plains first." He sat, poured already-steeping birch tea into cups, handed one to Druadaen. "Mind'ee; the reason we can camp here at all is because it's a skip beyond where the Bent are wont to rove, even if they mean to raid over the border. And if that's their purpose, they'd fain dodge us. Needs must that it's quick in and quick out for them. If they haven't put at least three leagues between themselves and the frontier before the Teurond cavalry arrives, it's like as not they won't see their warrens—or anything else—again."

He took a long draught of the tea, raised an index finger to point at Druadaen as he drank. "Now, about this mission of yours..." His voice trailed into a silence he clearly meant Druadaen to fill.

Druadaen obliged. "Garasan journeyed to the Plain of Grehar to gather word of the Bent: how many are seen, where, and how frequently. I am told it was his intent to learn more about their...er, habits."

One of the bountiers who hadn't been in the fight against the urzhen raised an eyebrow. "Funny he didn't ask, then."

"Hi-yeh, but he was cagey," Gradda murmured. His eyes shifted sideways to assess Druadaen. "Cagier than yerself, at least."

"Aye," Fronbec allowed, "but our new friend is a good bit younger, now, ain' he?"

Druadaen had to raise his hands to break in. "Wait: Garasan was here?" Silent nods. "And you said, 'he *didn't* ask.' So, has he gone to investigate the warrens of the Bent? Have I missed him?"

"Well, no and yes. He hasn't gone into the brutes' warrens, but you have most certainly missed him."

Druadaen pushed down a surge of impatience at the opaque answer. "Well, do you at least know where he was headed? Or if he means to return here?"

Silent looks were exchanged before Fronbec cleared his throat and said, "He...eh, was finished with his travels."

"Very well, but where did he *go*?"

They all nodded westward.

"How long ago?"

"Two weeks, maybe three."

Bedamned, easier to get a bone from a bulldog! "And where might I find him? Are there further camps to the west?

"No," Gradda muttered, "but plenty of pyres."

Druadaen stared, frowned. "Pyres?"

Fronbec was watching him steadily, even sadly. "Yes: pyres."

"Oh," said Druadaen. "I see." But he didn't, not right away. The news that the veteran Outrider was dead had always been a possibility, but he'd never taken that thought to its logical conclusion: that he might have to carry on his work alone. The new weight of his mission hit him like a physical blow. It was a moment before he'd recovered enough to ask, "Why a pyre? Why not bring his body back?"

"It's tradition, you might say." Fronbec shrugged. "It's become an expression of ours, that a dead bountier has 'gone to the pyres.' No way to bring a body back over all those leagues, not if his mates mean to outpace the Bent. So there are pits, near the peat fields, where we burn 'em."

Druadaen put down his cup, tried not to feel sick. "How did he die?"

"Well." Gradda punctuated his succinct answer by draining his tea and expelling an exasperated sigh. "He died well. Can't say more than that."

Druadaen shook his head. "But if you saw him di—"

"What we *saw*," emphasized Gradda, "was your friend getting feathered with arrows. He was already behind us, and he couldn't keep up. Then he couldn't stand up. And then they were around him, hacking, their axes red. We didn't watch any more."

"We *couldn't* watch any more," Fronbec amended. "Not if we wanted to get away alive. There were still too many of the brutes."

The long, low room was still until Druadaen cleared his throat. "So Garasan 'went to the pyres.' But his body . . . he's still back there?"

Fronbec started as if someone had stuck him with a pin. "Gods, no!" He studied Druadaen. "We go back to take care of our mates. When we can. In the case of your friend, we were able to get far enough ahead of the chasers to lay an ambush for the Bent who were tracking us. Then we doubled back and saw to your friend." He nodded somberly. "Burned 'im, or at least tried to. Just like with our own dead." He scratched at his half-full beard. "See, lad, Bent ain't picky about their meat, if you take my meaning." He met Druadaen's eyes. "But then, burning's a fit end for you Dunarran folk. That's your rite, i'n't it?"

Druadaen nodded, felt the answering silence grow heavy enough to smother them all.

"Well," Fronbec muttered, "I'm sorry you've come a long way for nothing, young sir."

Druadaen sighed, then squared his shoulders. "I haven't. I am charged to continue Garasan's mission if he failed to complete it."

"You mean counting the Bent? Well, we can tell you what we've seen these last weeks. And I remember him writing in a small journal before that, I think."

"That will be a start, at least. It is also my responsibility to collect any remaining personal effects for his family."

"He had family?" asked one of the other bountiers, as if the concept was not merely novel but alien.

Gradda's voice was flinty. " 'Gather his effects'? Does that include bounties?"

Fronbec held up a hand, shot a warning glance at the Sanâllean. "Er . . . we didn't have cause nor right to know aught about a man's purse . . . at least not while he was alive," the grizzled bountier muttered. "So it was hard to know what might have been his," he concluded lamely.

Ah, but since Garasan was dead and you never expected any- one like me to show up looking for him . . . Well, any money the

Outrider had brought with him, or bounty he was owed, hardly mattered anymore. "By effects, I mean letters, keepsakes, any of his gear that would be welcome to the Legions or as a legacy for his family."

Gradda seemed to relax, more than he had since the melee with the urzhen.

"Well," Fronbec mused, chin in hand, "we set aside almost everything he left behind that day. But if the fire did its work, then everything he carried was lost. Had to douse him with oil and make away with our own lives. Fires draw the Bent like a candle draws summer moths."

The rest nodded, adding their own details of Garasan's pyre. A few had made warding signs to protect Garasan's body until it was ash. Others offered short prayers to their gods. Then they left the Outrider's corpse to whichever agency of fate was destined to devour it first: the growing flames or the greedy jaws of the Bent. And none had been back since, so it was unknown how completely the body and gear had been reduced.

Druadaen had heard their accounts as if they were speaking through a tube filled with cotton. He nodded his thanks, asked, "Do you plan to hunt out there again?"

Fronbec shook his head. "Too late in the season, now. Remember the rain that was threatening as we came in? One cold, hard blow from the Boreal Sea would freeze it, and then we'd be catching our death of lung fever. Hunting the Bent near their lairs is warm-weather work. Now, we're just picking off small raiding parties: the brutes who haven't gathered a larder to see them through the winter and who don't think much of their chances of stealing from—or eating—their neighbors."

Druadaen nodded, considering. "In your opinion, are the Bent nearing horde-mass?"

All but two of them stared, grumbled at the unfamiliar word. Fronbec looked like he'd eaten an old lemon. "What the witch-quim is a 'horde-mass'?"

"A horde-mass is what creates the emergence of a Horde. It is when the Bent population has become so great that they can't continue to support their numbers unless they start raiding the surface for food."

"Oh," Fronbec said with a blink. "That? We just say they're a-hordeing. Some call it a PekTide. And hi-yeh, it's nearing. The

last two springs, there have been a few more Bent raiders abroad."
The older bountiers nodded along with him. "So they'll all come
a-ravening out of their burrows sometime late this spring, I wager."

Druadaen hoped he suppressed his surprise at the answer,
looked around at the cramped, homely burrow in which the
bountiers themselves lived. "And how will you survive that...
er, PekTide?"

All of them laughed. "By not being here, lad!" Fronbec chuckled. "Only a fool stands his ground when the flood is higher
than his head!"

An eminently logical answer, but Druadaen's interest now
fixed upon the one just before, which, as he reflected upon it,
made little sense. "You believe the PekTide is coming because of
a *slight* increase in warm-weather raiders?"

"Hi-yeh," Fronbec nodded. "And because it's about time for a
Horde. Some thought it would be this year, but that didn't feel
right to me. The raiders were all pekt. No other kinds of Bent.
Not even any Reds among the Rotters."

Druadaen hoped to eventually learn what all those terms
meant but, more immediately, he needed to reconcile the points
at which Fronbec's assertions failed to align with either common
sense or the laws of nature. "But if there are already so many
Bent living underground, wouldn't that require an equally large
increase in the number who would have to come to the surface
to get food? Both before and during the winter?"

Fronbec shook his head so vigorously that his long gray locks
swayed back and forth. "Ye're not talking animals, now, lad. Ye're
talkin' the Bent, and when they come in numbers, they boil up
all at once. It's their way."

"Yes, but how can their numbers grow into a, uh, PekTide if
they don't get a *lot* more food?"

Most of the bountiers shrugged. Their leader seemed a trifle
annoyed. "Listen, young, er, 'sir,' no one goes deep enough to
learn such things. Or if they have, they don't come back to say.
So we don't know. And we don't need to. Could be magic in 'em,
I suppose. But my guess? They feed on each other."

"Well, we know the Reds do, right enough," said Gradda. The
others agreed with solemn nods.

Druadaen controlled the impulse to shake his head at the
bountiers' circular reasoning: if the Bent preyed upon each other,

that would *diminish* their numbers, not increase them. It recalled the folly of the old fable in which a castaway on a barren island tried to remain alive by devouring his own body, bit by bit.

Unaware—or at least unbothered—by the contradictions implicit in his explanation of how the Bent repopulated into Hordes, Fronbec adopted a posture not unlike some of the more self-important docents under which Druadaen had studied. "The Bent don't make plans, y'see. Their actions are naught but what's in their nature. Ruled by their lusts, they are. When they want something, they want it right away and go straight after it. It's an old borderer's adage that 'to get to water, a burning pekt will run through oil.'"

The snickers of his comrades encouraged him to greater heights of oratory. "And of all the things a pekt wants, victory stands first. And the more blood, the better. What little mind they have is always on that, even more'n rutting or eating. Although truth be told they go about all three in much the same way!"

He smiled at the bountiers' laughter before continuing. "So not only do pekt welcome battles, they *need* 'em. Stands to reason, then, that bloodlust is in their marrow, that if they don't get their fill of fighting and killing, their lust for it will drive 'em mad. Well, *more* mad.

"And that's why there's no sense in 'em, and why they have no interest in parley. As borderers say, 'Bent will talk peace when cows eat meat.'" He shrugged. "So when there are too many o' 'em in those burrows, they go after each other, natural enough." He leaned back and finished his tea at a gulp. "And there's all the answers you need, young feller." They all looked at Druadaen expectantly.

Sorry to disappoint, but . . . "I thank you for sharing all this knowledge. As you will no doubt appreciate, though, my commander will expect that I find Garasan's body or what is left of his pyre, to both confirm his death and gather observations of the site." *And while I'm at it, try to find a way of learning more about the Bent. Risky, but maybe that will help me get my posting to the Legions.* "To that end, I would be most grateful if you would tell me how to reach it." Even Gradda shook his head sadly, as if Druadaen had announced his own funeral.

"I'd talk you out of it, if I could, lad," Fronbec muttered. "As I say, we shall not be back that way until spring. If then. And you'd do better risking your life at dice than going out there alone and unfamiliar with the land."

His eyebrows rose in response to a sudden inspiration. "Now, what if I could give ye the name of one or two fellows just a shade older than you who've actually been in those burrows? They're down southways now, what with the cold coming, but they might be willing to bring you back with them in spring. Would that suit you? Enough to set aside this mad-risky scheme of yours?"

"Why, yes!" *Actually, no, but when I'm done, I'll be sure to seek them out.* "Who are these bountiers?"

"Well, they're not bountiers, exactly. More travelers in the service of fortune, as t'were. Come, I'll tell you how to find them as we eat."

As Druadaen consumed a very fine and filling dish of Sanâl-lean *olla podrida*, he listened to Fronbec's fragmentary description of two persons who sounded far more like highwaymen than canny scouts or astute observers of a different species. But the old bountier insisted that they had been in the tunnels of the Bent for some time and, having lived to tell the tale, were likely to know more of that conglomeration of related races than any-one else. At least anyone that a fine, upstanding Dunarran was likely to meet anywhere—except, perhaps, over crossed swords.

As Druadaen tended to his gear, he turned their names, descriptions, and details over and over in his mind, resolved to commit them to memory. He continued the repetitions as he stretched his length upon a straw paillasse, and resolved to keep doing so until the sheer dullness of it carried him over the murky border into blissfully dreamless sleep. He hoped.

Druadaen checked to make sure the girth was not too far forward on his mount as Fronbec and Omur approached.

"Last time I'll say it," the older man said. "If you take that horse, you'll regret it."

"I must."

"They'll see you—or smell you—and that will be the end of your mission, lad."

Druadaen couldn't suppress a grateful smile; there was abso-lutely no practical reason for Fronbec to be solicitous. Frankly, it was probably better for the bountiers if he never returned to make a report. He nodded. "You've made the risks very clear. But you've also said that there shouldn't be many Bent out raiding anymore."

Omur shrugged, face impassive. "There aren't. But there are always some. And those that are will see you profiled against the horizon or smell the horseflesh. So if they're out there, you'll find 'em. Which is to say, they'll find you."

Druadaen checked that his gear was secure and swung up into the saddle. "I will be back to collect Garasan's journal and other belongings. Thank you for holding them until I return."

Fronbec shrugged. "Least we could do. Just . . . don't travel at night, don't dally anywhere too long, and grow a pair of eyes in the back of your head. And I know it's a bother while you ride, but keep that bow strung. You may want it in a hurry."

Druadaen raised his hand in farewell, turned the horse slowly, and urged it into a trot toward the west.

CHAPTER ELEVEN

Druadaen's best guess at the remaining distance back to the sod house was only six or seven miles. But it might as well have been a hundred. And for the hundredth time since the pekt had started hunting him, he repented the choice he'd made four days ago: *I should* never *have gone to Garasan's pyre on my own.*

For the last two hours, the pekt horns had been silent, but that was not a good sign. The one reasonable explanation was that they had found his trail again and were now more concerned with giving away their own position than trying to summon the more far-flung chasers to join the end of the hunt.

Although they were too numerous to fight, he'd had to resist the temptation to turn and make a final stand. That impulse had grown as his pace slowed and his breath became more ragged. *Take some with you before you are quaking too hard to have a still hand on your bow,* he'd thought. *Or wield a sword before you lose all the skill and speed you trained so hard to acquire.*

But, for the first time in his life, Druadaen realized that giving in to that final resolve was, in some way, also surrendering his best hope of survival: to keep going, as fast and as far as he could. Only by buying every possible minute could he maximize the chance of being saved by the only force that could still change the outcome: luck. Maybe one or more of the bountiers was out upon the Graveyard, or maybe the pekt would be attacked by hungry wolves. He could elect to go out in a final flash of dubious glory, but what had Fronbec said? "Only a fool stands his ground against a flood that's over his head." Words to live by. Or today, maybe to die by.

Druadaen kept running.

The fourth time that Druadaen stumbled and fell, he was only twenty yards south of a rise that was actually higher than he was tall. He lurched to his feet, forced himself to start jogging up the slope.

A ringing rose deep inside his ears. The sky spun and suddenly blackened.

He woke up staring at the undersides of gray clouds: the Graveyard's perpetual shroud. Each breath a sharp, wheezing struggle, he rolled to a shoulder, pushed upright, and finally heard what he'd been listening for: the cries of the pekt.

It took a moment for his eyes to focus, to make out the stooped, loping figures closing from the south. He rose shakily to one knee, put a hand to his sword's hilt, drew it an inch so that the blade wouldn't hitch on its way out of the scabbard.

He reached for his bow and, not for the first time, was glad for its compact design. Larger than a shortbow or typical horsebow, but smaller than a full composite bow, he could use it from a kneeling position. His heart was hammering hard enough without trying to stand, which would also have given any pekt archers an easier target. And if he kept trying to outrun them, he'd be dead in a minute, maybe two. But with a bow, he might drive them to ground, force them to flank him, and so buy even more time.

He reached behind to the quiver, fingertips on the fletching of the first arrow, and felt it flop oddly against his back. He finished pulling it over his shoulder.

The shaft was half-snapped, just an inch forward of where the fletching began. Odd. Druadaen frowned, drew another.

And discovered himself holding another ruined arrow, broken at more or less the same place.

He unslung the quiver and saw the cause. When he'd blacked out, he'd fallen against a hard lump of prairie: probably a rock with a thin cover of soil and grass. The quiver had broken his impact, but at the expense of far too many arrows. Only six remained.

Well, Druadaen thought, *I won't be buying quite as much time as I had hoped.* He labored to pace his breathing, surveyed the oncoming pekt.

Three were much closer than the others: barely one hundred and fifty yards away. Probably the first ones to rediscover his trail, or sent ahead as harriers because they were faster. They were slender—well, skinny—for pekt and one had a horn around his neck. No sign of bows.

The next group—probably twice as large—was still almost five hundred yards off. Some in that group were larger, but they were charging to close the range. It was too far to be sure if any had bows, but several had two handed axes or polearms. On the rest, he spied the curve of shields carried on their backs. So, few archers, if any. Druadaen nocked his first shaft and strove to still the pounding in his temples. If he could bring down the first three, that might—*might*—cause the rest to approach more cautiously.

As the first group reached one hundred yards, they began a headlong charge; if they had any thought to make themselves difficult targets, they gave no sign of it. Druadaen drew to his ear, chose the horn-bearer in the middle, breathed deep, and was hardly aware of loosing the arrow.

Despite the flatter trajectory of the composite bow, he still overestimated the rate of drop; the shaft missed the top of the pek's head by a hand's width.

By that time, Druadaen had drawn the next arrow from over his shoulder and was sighting along it. As the targets grew in size, he felt the forces affecting the shot—their charge, the arrow's trajectory, the breath of the wind—all align. As he relaxed his fingers to release the arrow, he realized that the throbbing in his temples was finally subsiding.

The arrow—a broad-headed hunting point—drove into the pek's chest, just to the right of the sternum. He staggered, stumbled, fell.

Druadaen was barely aware of nocking the second arrow and loosing it in one fluid motion. And, as was often the case with the shots he thought about the least, it hummed to a quivering stop just below the base of another pek's neck, driven into the collarbone.

But the third of the three—the smallest—was also the fastest.

Druadaen had just enough time to pull another shaft over his shoulder and draw the bow before realizing that this pek had learned from the error of his fellows: he dodged as he came within twenty yards.

Druadaen checked his release, rode along with his target's motion, knowing that the pek would have to break stride to resume his charge—

There! A final, feinted sideways step became a forward stride, and Druadaen loosed the arrow.

It hit, but not where he'd intended. The pek howled as it transfixed his left thigh. He stumbled, righted himself, started limp-sprinting forward. In that moment, Druadaen drew another arrow and waited for when his enemy's gait broke and slowed: the point where he had to drag his wounded leg forward.

Druadaen loosed his fifth arrow when the pek was only ten yards away. It hit and cut through the uncured chest armor with a sibilant *sss-thk!*

The pek toppled forward. If it hadn't already been dead, its forward fall finished the job, driving the arrow the rest of the way through its torso before it broke.

Druadaen drew his last arrow and surveyed the field. It was possible that some of the other arrows were salvageable, but it would take too long to cut free those that had hit. The one that had missed was over a hundred yards away: still too far, even though the half dozen pekt that had been racing toward him were now in a slow, crouching approach. As he watched, two of them angled off to either side: flankers.

So he'd bought himself some time, after all, but probably not more than a minute, maybe two. Before drawing his last arrow, he took the shield from his back and laid it where he could snatch it up quickly, then paused, considering the comparative merits of using his left hand to wield the shortsword, instead. Its quillons were fashioned to catch an attacker's weapon and it preserved his agility.

But there were six pekt, and not only were most of them quite large but several were armed with two-handed weapons; the force of those blows was likely to be more than he could parry, let alone catch, with a shortsword. So he would rely upon the sword and shield, just like the Legions, and hope for the best.

However, that hope was becoming increasingly forlorn. The

pekt had paused to sound their horns again, probably calling even more of their fellows to the final slaughter. But the second sonorous summons stopped abruptly. In the next instant, the pekt unaccountably begun to move away, breaking into a trot a moment later.

Druadaen stood wondering after them. Was it some kind of trick? Apparently not, because they had begun to run. Was it possible? Had his archery broken the nerve of six pekt warriors when he was down to his last arrow? Could he possibly be so lucky? Had he, in fact, prevailed?

Druadaen's heart was thumping out such a wild tattoo of victory and relief that he almost missed the similar pounding that, like dull thunder struck from the loam of the plain, rose swiftly behind him.

He turned—and was almost killed where he stood. Horses—percherons in leather barding—came galloping over the rise, so close on either side that his hair was ruffled in the wake of their passing. The riders wore metal cuirasses and were otherwise cased in mail and streamed toward the routing pekt. Their narrow lances lowered, steel points winking faintly.

Druadaen laid aside his bow, drew his shortsword, then his longsword and, ignoring his shield, walked unsteadily forward to help his rescuers however he might.

CHAPTER TWELVE

Druadaen watched as several of the King's Own Border Cavalry of Teurodn secured their only casualty to the saddle of a horse. Ironically, the rider hadn't been killed by a pek. At least not directly.

The fleeing raider had rounded on his pursuers and struck a desperate blow with his saw-toothed polearm. The rider had flinched out of its way, but the sweep of the weapon caught his mount squarely in the side of the head. The horse went down, the rider was thrown, and he died the very next instant; his brow hit the loam and snapped his neck backward.

The pek that had struck the blow met the same fate as the others: run down and speared from behind. What followed was both understandable, if arresting. The cavalrymen casually dismounted and butchered any survivors with the same detached boredom that the bountiers had. They didn't bother to take the ears or thumbs, however.

Their commander, who was almost as tall as Druadaen, stood observing his troops. He was surrounded by a handful of the oldest in his command, two of whom were not wearing the colors of the King's Own Border Cavalry. Their tunics and equipment bore devices of a heraldic nature, but Druadaen had no idea what their significance might be.

He'd been grimly resolved to help them dispatch any of the pekt who'd survived, but between his exhaustion and the cavalrymen's prompt action, his assistance had not been needed. Relieved, he lowered himself to the grass to rest, observing that he'd better do so while he could.

As the balance of the troopers checked the pekt lying within sight, three had fanned out to the south, scouting for more of Druadaen's pursuers. Upon returning, only one had anything to report: a group of about a dozen that was running back out onto the plains. The final horn blasts of their dead fellows had probably been a warning that humans were upon them, and of all the foes that pekt feared, armored cavalry topped the list.

When no one was looking, Druadaen slipped one boot lower until he could see his heel; it was wet with blood. The heel itself wasn't bleeding—the skin there was too tough—but somewhere on the soles or sides of his feet, the endless running had finally rubbed him raw. He smiled; blood and pain were hardly a concern after the two desperate days now behind him. Maybe, when he could find a minute away from his rescuers—

The commander sat next to Druadaen. Trying to hide his heel was now pointless, particularly since the blood was apparently what had drawn the officer over to him. "One of my men is moderately skilled in chirurgy," he offered.

"My thanks, sir, but it is not a wound. It's from running."

The man frowned even as he smiled. "It appears you've done a great deal of running, then."

Druadaen glanced at the flanks of the nearby horses: still lathered and slick. "I am apparently not alone in that."

The officer raised one eyebrow, but his frown had disappeared. The new expression on his face was difficult to read fully, but it had elements of both surprise and approval. "Well, at least we can get you some bindings."

"I would be most grateful for that. Wherever we are bound, it won't be a short walk."

The other's frown was back. "You intend to walk? I recommend otherwise, unless you derive strength from pain. We mean to leave as we came: riding."

Druadaen counted the remaining horses. "I do not see how we may all ride. Including myself and the body of your man, you have need of twenty-one mounts, but only have nineteen."

"We have that well in hand." The rest of his command staff— or bodyguard?—sat in a rough arc centered on him. "You and another will travel in tandem with the riders of the two largest horses. Their gear will be shared out to the rest of the troop so that we may all be mounted and travel at reasonable speed."

"How far do we have to go?"

"Well, that depends upon your destination. Although," he mused, his eyes flicking quickly between Druadaen's sword, bow, and helmet, "you are a long way from where those were made."

Interesting. "As you imply, we are indeed a long way from Dunarra."

The man nodded but his eyes remained noncommittal. "So, share your tale; what has you playing the fox to the pekt's hounds out here upon the Plain of Grehar?"

Druadaen looked up; more than half the troop had collected around them, seated in a circle. "Fair warning: the tale is not short, and it seems our enemy could be gathering greater numbers."

The Teurond officer waved a lazy hand toward the west. "The chance that they would return is extremely small, and the men on watch are extremely keen of eye. We need not worry about being surprised. So, please: tell your tale."

Druadaen did. When he reached the part where, upon leaving Garasan's pyre-pit, he began suspecting that his horse's barrel was swollen with lethal colic, one of the younger cavalrymen guffawed. "Just what you'd expect of a Dunarran. Can't tell sourgrass from sweet."

The officer's only reaction was a forced, wan smile. "So, you followed the pekt tracks you found near the pyre-pit?"

Druadaen nodded and finished his account: his shadowing of the pekt, his horse's sudden immobility, its shrill whinnies of agony, his remorseful silencing of them, the pekt's sudden turn in his direction, and, finally, the two-day pursuit that followed. His listeners were, by turns, startled by his intents, amazed at his stupidity, and baffled at his unwonted boldness.

When he was done, the officer nodded slowly at Druadaen's bow, his blonde locks bobbing. "You speak as though you come from the city, but you do not shoot that way."

"You are correct. On both counts. But no amount of archery would have saved me. For that, I am in your debt. Particularly his." He glanced sadly at the body over the back of the most distant horse. "So I must ask: By what stroke of luck"—*if that's what it was*—"did you happen to be in this desolate spot to rescue me?"

"We were riding to the south and saw the buzzards."

Druadaen frowned. "I haven't seen any buzzards since I arrived."

The oldest of the officer's veterans explained. "Simple reason fer that, young si—er, fellow. A regular buzzard would starve on these plains. Not much prey and even less carrion. So Grehar vultures fly high until they're ready to feed, so high you won't see 'em unless you know when and where to look."

"And you did?"

"Well, we did hear urzhen horns," added another. Druadaen had begun noticing that they did not use the world "pekt" when referring to the Bent. "Stands to reason they might have already brought down some quarry. Or made a meal of one of their own."

"Even when they are above ground, raiding?" Druadaen shook his head. "But when I read about them—"

"Oh," exclaimed one of the youngest riders, "he *read* about them! Bollocks! He's been learning about urzhen from a *book*! Y'see how it is?"

"Is he mad?" asked another.

"Well," the younger one observed facetiously, "that *is* a Dunarran accent—"

The officer spoke to Druadaen as he cut a sharp glance at the pair. "You'll forgive the terrible breeding of some of my men, I trust."

Druadaen shook his head. "I took no offense."

The officer was staring at Druadaen. "You took no offense? Truly?"

Druadaen shrugged. "Since coming north of Connæar, I have learned at least this much: that when it comes to your lands and your ways, what little knowledge I have is far outweighed by my ignorance."

He sat in a ring of faces suddenly trying to conceal various degrees of surprise and even confusion. The officer was the first to speak. "You are very tolerant, Sir . . . ?"

"I am Druadaen. Just Druadaen."

The officer nodded decisively, and his eyes were, in that moment, no longer guarded. "He is a Dunarran, just as he claims," he assured his men.

Druadaen, surprised to discover that his origins had not already been a foregone conclusion, was further bewildered by the sudden torrent of strange statements and presumptions that peppered a rapid exchange with their leader:

"But, aren't all the Dunarrans nobles, Si... er, captain?"

The Teurond captain shook his head. "You have the matter backwards, Khrefdt. There are no Dunarran nobles at all, nor do any have hereditary titles."

"No nobles? That's anarchy!" one blurted out.

"And still, they're all filthy rich?" another exclaimed.

Which made Druadaen laugh. The Teuronds stared at him, one or two frowns suggesting incipient resentment. "I assure you," Druadaen added, "we are *not* all rich."

"I hear tell that none of you starve," another put in.

"Well, I suppose that's true, but—"

"Then you're all rich, nobles or not."

Druadaen thought to dispute that, but his mind was suddenly filled with images of the thin, bedraggled borderers who lived beside the Graveyard and their ramshackle villages. Perhaps this fellow had a point after all.

The officer held up a hand to still any further exchanges. "I wish to confirm what you shared regarding your orders. You were instructed to complete the mission on your own?"

Druadaen shrugged. "If need be."

The other grunted. "It would seem success enough to return home with the Outrider's notes and personal effects. Especially for a lone, junior Outrider."

"I certainly see the wisdom of that now, Lord...?"

The captain waved away the attempt at discovering his title, if he had one—which Druadaen was beginning to suspect. "I am just Darauf."

His men exchanged glances.

Darauf had not paused. "Druadaen, either you are the most dunderheaded man I've met, the most courageous, or perhaps the most desperate." His tone turned sly at the end.

"Desperate for what?" asked the youngest of the riders.

Darauf smiled at Druadaen. It was not unkind, but it was decidedly inquisitive. "Why don't we let our guest tell us?"

Druadaen sat very straight. "It has been my goal since childhood to be inducted into the Legions. That still has not happened." He shrugged. "I reasoned that brave deeds might change that. I will never know, now." Without looking, he was very aware of the exact location of the dead horseman strapped across a saddle. "And others have paid a terrible price for that ambition."

Darauf's voice was surprisingly mild. "Druadaen, we patrol these wastes to do exactly what we did today: kill the Bent and save fellow humans who are about to run afoul of them. Your intent—to learn more about your enemy—is commendable. Indeed, as I reflect upon it, it might well be a wise—if unintended—indictment of a dangerous complacency in us." His men snapped straight, frowning, perplexed. "We have fought this enemy for so long that we presume to know him so well that there is no point in further study of his ways. Yet history and aphorisms alike tell us that such arrogance is a frequent path to ruin." The Teurond commander, who was apparently not much older than Druadaen, glanced around the circle of faces. Their deference and respect was immediate and absolute.

"Sir—" Druadaen began.

"Darauf," the other corrected with a mild smile.

"Darauf," Druadaen repeated, "I realize that Dunarrans may have a, well, a mixed reputation in these lands, but I was not aware that others would try to imitate us."

"It is not frequent," Darauf affirmed with a nod, "but it does happen." His face darkened. "Some unscrupulous blaggards go to great and murderous lengths to secure the trappings of your Outriders and so invite individuals to assume that they are Dunarrans. A handy disguise for those with basest treachery in their hearts."

Druadaen nodded. "You have been to Dunarra, then?" Darauf shook his head. Sadly, Druadaen thought. "Then you have met many Outriders?"

"You are only the second," he answered.

"Then you are to be congratulated on your rapid identification of my gear," Druadaen said with a long, deferential nod.

"We were on the lookout for 'em, anyway," chirped the dimmer companion of the youngest rider.

The veterans stared at him; his rank-and-file comrades stared away. Pointedly.

"I do not understand," Druadaen said. And waited.

Darauf sent one cross glance at the hapless and loose-lipped cavalryman and then turned toward Druadaen. "In point of fact, we were informed of Garasan's presence shortly before he arrived. Then recently, we received word that he had gone missing and might be dead. We were given special orders to venture further out into the plains to see if we could find any trace of him and be ready to render assistance to any other Outriders who might mean to join—or search for—him."

Druadaen nodded. Superficially, it sounded plausible... except that it took weeks for conventional communiqués to make their way from Dunarra to Teurodn. So the arrival of the messages Darauf was referring to had either been incredibly fortuitous in terms of both speed and timing, or the message had been conveyed through more unusual means. Means involving miracles or mancery. Which would in turn suggest that Garasan's mission possessed a level of urgency of which Druadaen had not been apprised.

"So," he asked casually, "if you had not run across me in such a timely fashion, where were you headed next?"

"The sod house you have mentioned. It was, after all, the last known location of your predecessor."

Which was a true enough answer. But it was also an extremely unrevealing answer. It would have been Darauf's next logical destination whether he was searching for Garasan *or* Druadaen. But there was one other inquiry that might shed light on which of the two Outriders had been the main focus of his mission: "I see that I was doubly fortunate, then."

"How so?"

Druadaen effected a casual shrug. "Well, firstly, you just happened to be at the southernmost extent of your patrol circuit. Otherwise you would not have been here to save me today."

Darauf nodded, a small grin starting on his lips. "And secondly?"

"Why, that you were traveling so *far* out upon the plains that you were able to see the high-flying buzzards at all... and so, find me."

Several of the cavalrymen, including two of the veterans, exchanged what they obviously meant to be surreptitious glances, but Druadaen had been watching for them.

Darauf replied with a shrug. "You are right. It is not customary for us to range so far from the border itself."

"So your own borderers tell me. And speaking of the borderers down at this end of your patrol circuit, did you by any chance come across an old nativist while you were there?" The new flurry of glances among the riders were not only less subtle but frankly surprised.

A slow smile spread across Darauf's face. "Why, no, we did not chance upon such an individual. Why do you ask?" His smile continued to grow.

"No particular reason," Druadaen answered with a matching smile. *And you even managed not to lie about meeting the nativist, because if you specifically went* looking *for him, then you didn't "chance upon him."* "So it seems that your timely appearance was merely fantastic luck."

"The world is *full* of fantastic twists of fate and fortune, good and bad. And who can say why they happen as they do?" Somehow, Darauf's wide smile had grown still wider. "Now, as I have some small experience fighting urzhen, I would be pleased to answer any questions about them you might have."

Druadaen thought, then gestured toward the bodies scattered beyond them. "Is this typical of their raiding parties?"

Darauf nodded. "Unless they are nearing horde-mass"— Druadaen noted his use of the same term scholars typically used—"the Bent rarely send out bands larger than a dozen males."

"Why no more?"

One of the veterans leaned in. "Because they don't like to share, young sir. Until they come out in force, that dozen or so is providing for as many as six to ten females and a dozen young. Varies by season, though. Might be as many as thirty if it's summer. Elsetimes, they're busy dying from hunger, disease, or fighting."

"You mean, against bountiers?"

Darauf shook his head. "No. Rival tribes. Or sometimes among their own, if food is scarce and there are a good number of young or weak ones."

Druadaen's revulsion was overtaken by wonderment: *How the hells do they survive?* Then he realized he'd muttered his amazement aloud.

One of Darauf's eyebrows rose slightly. "I believe I just answered that."

Druadaen waved a negating hand. "No, no: I understand what you have explained. But there is a larger question, one for which the bountiers had no real answer. If the Bent do not grow their own crops, and if the food available in the Under cannot even sustain minimal numbers of them, then how do they ever attain horde-mass? Where do they get all the food that is required to amass that population?"

Many of the cavalrymen gave him the same kind of stares that the bountiers had. But Darauf and one of his veterans regarded him quietly, carefully. "You ask interesting questions," Darauf murmured. "Should you once again find yourself on these borders, or in Teurodn itself, ask for me."

Druadaen smiled. "Teurodn is a large realm, so where should I seek you? And, assuming your name is not unique, by what title should I ask after you?"

Suddenly wide-eyed, two of Darauf's men stifled guffaws at the question, as if it was a jest. Their captain merely smiled as he shifted his body to face in the direction of that pair. Their flawed efforts at self-control became instantly and fully effective. "Just ask for Darauf. The borderers will know where to find me."

He rose. "We should be on our way. We will see you safely to the sod house and provide you with a mount. Not so precisely trained as yours, but spirited and strong. And once we part ways, I know of a fellow who might have the information you seek about the Bent. Or, if he does not, I suspect he might prove to be a very helpful guide, should you return to find definitive answers to your questions.

He stared into the west. "The sun is coming to the end of its daily work. No reason to be abroad in the dark. The Bent might be tempted to once again try cases with us on terms more favorable to them. We ride."

Journal Entry 141
13th of Snowbird, 1798 S.C.
Tlulanxu

It has been three weeks since I crossed the snow-dusted border back into Dunarra, and about two since arriving back in Tlulanxu. And once here, I learned the deep truth of the axiom often used by the Keepers of the Ar: "You never put your foot in the same river twice. That is because the river is always changing. As are you."

As best as I can tell, nothing has changed in this city or the nation around it. Everything looks and sounds the same. In part, I have always appreciated Tlulanxu because of how safe it felt. Even the S'Dyxan raid didn't change that. But now it feels *too* safe.

I have looked at that last sentence for a full minute, trying to determine why it feels incorrect. It isn't untrue. It isn't even inaccurate. But it is lacking. It is not the degree of safety here that feels excessive; it is the sense that while many Dunarrans are well trained for many emergencies, they rarely *experience* any of them. And so, I am no longer like them in that regard.

It is even true of the Legions. It has been centuries since a true Dunarran army has marched into battle against a foe which has any hope of defeating it. So our foes no longer try. As a result, not even half of all Legiors see combat, even in small border incidents.

So now, when I pass Legiors in the street—their faces serious, competent, alert—I cannot help wondering, *but have you ever been so far beyond the boundaries of human society that you have no idea how best to stay alive just one more day? Or if it is even possible?* Because I have. And in ways I do not yet fully realize, that has changed me.

What has not changed are the habits I picked up during my years at the Archive. Such as: when confronted by a problem, seek the wisdom recorded by others who confronted it before you. And so I have come full circle, back to the Archive and Shaananca.

She was glad (although unusually unsurprised) to see me, and without so much as a frown or a *tsk*, she escorted me down to the very place I had spent a decade trying to enter: the Reserved Collection. Now, she simply smiles, waves a hand at the many strange shelves and glass-protected cases, and leaves me to my researches. Unattended.

As I said, it is the same Tlulanxu, and yet, it is entirely different.

The sources on urzhen were greatly varied in both style and substance. However, what the collection lacked in cohesiveness it amply made up for in diversity, ranging from dry, learned (and often unintentionally amusing) tracts by scholars to utterly accessible (but likely exaggerated) firsthand accounts. A small number of the writers combined both insight and readability in tolerable measure. The best was a campaigner whose career included both service beneath national banners and in the company of free-spirited bountiers. He was also a keen observer of the urzhen traits that seem to predispose them to become the scourges they have been to what he calls "the civilized lands":

> Unfortunately, the patience required for farming is neither native nor congenial to the Bent. Most of them are not even particularly good hunters, just as few of them are good archers. Their impulses lead them into lives of scavenging and marauding, no matter the community in which they are raised. Rather than track difficult prey or snare small game, they invariably prefer the larcenous titillations of stealing kills and raiding other sapient creatures for what they possess.
>
> However, if they are not careful—and as a rule, they are not—many, if not most, of these raids become deadly debacles. Lacking the organization and discipline to pillage with anything like speed or efficiency, the Bent are frequently overtaken by human riders, who harry and delay them until overwhelming force can be brought to bear. It is not uncommon for every last one of the Bent to be slain.

However, every decade or so, one or more great orc leaders can bring together the fragmented tribes by appealing to the one thing they all have in common: seething hatred (and envy!) of the prosperous humans who have dealt them so many defeats. Using this sentiment as a rallying cry, those leaders can whip the ranks of the Bent into a frenzied wave of slavering marauders who are also very hungry. This is due to the periodic surge in numbers that also seems to quicken an instinctual drive to go a-hordeing. Or as countryfolk whisper (while making warding signs), it causes them to burst forth in a massive "Pekt-tide."

This wave of urzhen is the bane of frontier existence. They emerge from their mountain warrens like a raging flood that swallows up everything in its path. Until, that is, that tumultuous flume of bestial humanoids runs into a truly fortified position. The patience required to mount an effective siege, along with the ever-mounting threat of retaliation by organized human troops (whose cavalry strikes terror into them) typically undermines whatever modest coherence the host possessed.

And so the Horde is eventually reduced to ever-smaller bands that eventually drift back up into the hills from whence they came. Indeed, their cowardice is so complete that the fast-moving warriors often abandon the dependents who traveled with them (since any who remain behind in their warrens may starve before the raiders return). Consequently, the females and young who were the Horde's scouts, throat slitters, porters, etc., are found by the pursuing humans, who are obliged to stop long enough to dispatch these troublesome vermin and burn them en masse. A most annoying interruption of their avenging pursuit of the remains of the Horde!!!

As were many of his contemporaries, this chronicler saw the Bent as little more than animals and evinced excessive excitability in both his diction and punctuation (!!!).

However, out of all the treatises and accounts I have read, only a handful have ever mentioned the perplexing speed with which the Bent reproduce. Considerations of how that phenomenon occurs are rarely touched upon. Most dismiss the quandary the same way the bountiers did: they presume it is effected by whatever deities the Bent might worship. A few do admit it is a puzzlement, but only one went so far as to attempt to discover its cause. Indeed, his last entry declared his determination to solve the mystery or die trying. As that was the very last page in the very last of his journals, it seems that—sadly—he was as good as his word.

Which means that after more than a millennium of accumulated accounts, two critical questions remain unanswered: By what miracle of reproduction do the Bent recover from near decimation every ten years to flood forth in yet another Horde? And, if it is not the work of the gods, then from whence comes all the food that fuels and sustains such growth?

I had hoped that the Reserved Collection would hold some useful clues or insights. Of clues there were none, and of insights, only one that was useful: that we do not know enough about the lives of the Bent to even hazard a reasonable guess. Leaving me with but one option: to seek the answer myself.

I once again hear Darauf's voice wondering if I am brave, mad, or desperate. I know I am not brave, for I am no stranger to terror. And my desperation to join the ranks of the Legions, while no less powerful, has become less urgent; if it takes longer than I hoped, so be it. Lastly, insofar as madness is concerned, more than a few have wondered that, and I sometimes wonder if they are right. But when all those explanations for my commitment to this investigation are put aside, the real reason I want to answer the mystery of the Bent becomes clear:

Insatiable curiosity. If the sudden surge that leads to a hordeing is the act of gods, I wish to know, because then we are indeed little more than their playthings. And if it is not, then what strange and undiscovered truth has shaped their existence for these many centuries, hidden in their dark and distant warrens?

It seems as if fate is trying to smooth my start upon that journey of discovery. I have now accumulated a full year of leave from my duties. Also, upon my return, I was specially commended for my attempts to recover all of Garasan's effects and reports and, as a reward, have been given permission to travel as I wish during my leave. Lastly, while I am hardly wealthy, my accrued stipend will allow me to fulfill any needs that my Legion-assigned equipage does not address.

Now, if only I can locate the fellow who both Darauf and Fronbec mentioned. His last known whereabouts are in the free city of Menara, not far over the border from Aedmurun. I do not know if I possess enough coin to pique his interest, but no other course of action presents itself.

However, finding him may prove easier said than done. He is just one more itinerant sell-sword of questionable reputation in a free city notorious for its black market, double-dealing underworld, and constant churn of persons from the furthest corners of Arrdanc. And my only lead is a name, which I must hope is uncommon enough to be distinctive on those unpredictable streets:

Ahearn.

CHAPTER THIRTEEN

As Druadaen approached the time-gnawed sign over the tavern entrance, it swayed in the wintry breeze running in from the sea. The wooden placard's legend appeared to have been modified, either genuinely or as part of a conceit suggesting it had been "forcibly altered." The gaily-painted "original" name of the tavern—Truth or Consequences—had lost almost half of the first word to a deep, ragged gouge in the wood. Two replacement letters had been scrawled beneath it, rendering the dire "new" name: Truce or Consequences.

Druadaen was still not entirely accustomed to the quirky, even perverse, names of taverns beyond the borders of Dunarra. To date, most of his lodgings had been at inns with the predictably staid labels that guests associated with conventional—and therefore, safe—establishments.

But most taverns brought in their pence and marks through drink, food, and a broadly accepting atmosphere—which was to say, lax attitudes about taproom behavior and complete indifference to the professions of their patrons. Predictably, the more boisterous the establishment, the more its name reflected the freewheeling and even iconoclastic nature of its clientele. And judging from a label like Truce or Consequences, Druadaen could only expect that this would be a very "lively" tavern. He made sure to push open the heavy door and enter all in one motion; anything else might look like hesitation and so, trepidation.

It was not what he'd expected. Most of the tables were full, but instead of loud debates and drunken arguments, heads were low, and shoulders hunched into each table's own furtive buzz of conversation. That gave Druadaen a better opportunity to take in the low-ceilinged taproom, which sprawled to the limits of the building's four walls, the far corners dim. The scent of various smoke-herbs was in the very wood of the place, old and musty beneath the more immediate odors of salt-cured fish, cheap bread, and the sour tang of spilled ale.

No one looked up and no eyes followed him as he walked in. Or at least, none that he could detect. A barboy passed, nodding, waving vaguely deeper into the room. Druadaen wandered over to the rickety driftwood bar that wasn't much more than a long, high table with saw-toothed skirts made from sun-bleached strakes. The barkeep nodded what might have been a greeting, flipped a hand at various bottles on the table behind him. The boy's resemblance to him, even in the gesture, was unmistakable.

Druadaen affected a casual inspection of the various libations, using his movement along the bar to give him a viewing angle into the taproom so that he could casually scan for—

Ahearn—it had to be him—was sitting at a table near the farthest corner from the door. He was as large as described: almost Druadaen's height, but somewhat more thickly muscled. However, since a man of that description was hardly unique in Menara, it was his two companions that made him easy to spot.

Sitting to one side of Ahearn was a lithe, slightly older man with a dark-rust complexion, the type usually associated with the nations of southern Mihal'j. On the other side was a wolfhound of such immense proportions that the chair beside his master had been removed to give the dog enough room to sit. Even with its haunches on the floor planks, its head was higher than Ahearn's and that of the others sitting at the table.

Which was not only more full than Druadaen had anticipated but populated by persons he would not have expected encountering in Menara. Or any other human city.

One appeared to be aeostun and, like many of that race, her/his sex was difficult to determine. Not that it mattered to the aeostu much or that it was any of his business, but that ambiguity frequently made them unwelcome in human lands other than those that had frequent contact with them, such as Dunarra, Alriadex, and Irrylain.

Even more surprising was what appeared to be an urzh woman who was almost as heavily built as Ahearn. But there was one aspect of her appearance that made Druadaen wonder if she wasn't HalfBent instead; there was no green tint to her flesh. Indeed, her skin tone was no different than those of peoples who lived near Arrdanc's middle latitudes.

The third and most impossible being at the table was not merely an urzh, but a *very* green-skinned one. The heavy jaw and blocky build were consistent with the ones the bountiers had more frequently called Rot or Rotters, although he'd never determined if that epithet was inspired by specific traits or just general disdain. And most amazing of all was the reaction his presence elicited from the other patrons:

None at all.

As Druadaen gestured toward a tap and waited for a half-beer (probably simply watered down, here), he also noted that the various individuals at the table did not evince the easy postures or proximity of a close-knit group. The two humans were companions, the two pekt were something similar, and the aeosti was too aloof to determine which, if any, of the others she/he was affiliated with.

He pushed two copper pence across the bar in exchange for the mug being carried by the barkeep, who eyed the two small coins and then stared in exasperation at Druadaen. Who pushed another pence into contact with the first two, received his drink in exchange for them, and wandered toward a table along the far wall, midway to Ahearn's table.

Reaching it and planting himself on a rough stool felt like coming to the end of one journey and the beginning of a new one. Druadaen had visited many foreign and perplexing places as a Courier and an Outrider, but always in the company of other Dunarrans. No longer. Druadaen was no stranger to the free city; Outriders often had reason to visit its streets or surrounding areas. But this was not the Menara he knew. His forays into its questionable precincts—such as this one—had been rare and very brief. So he had remained cautious while seeking leads on Ahearn's whereabouts and divested himself of any gear that was distinctly Dunarran. Avoiding notice meant remaining innocuous; he knew full well he'd never manage to blend into Menara's ever-shifting and ever-bustling shoreside quarter. Transients accounted for over half the population and had only one thing in common: they had come seeking their fortune.

Once his inquiries led him to Truce or Consequences, his trained reflex had been to gather information on its interior. But experience and common sense told him that any attempt at scouting its layout would have only one certain result: he would be detected doing so. So the only way to avoid the possibility of walking into a scenario of someone else's making was to enter the tavern as a complete unknown.

So far, so good, he thought as he sipped the horrid half-beer. He leaned back, trying to appear more relaxed than he felt, and purposely missed placing his mug squarely on the tabletop. Half on the edge, it tilted, slid, hit the floor.

Druadaen jumped to his feet, stifled a curse, and shrugged apologetically as the barboy tromped wearily over. He laid three more pence on the table. The boy nodded and returned to the bar, calling for a bucket and some rags.

As Druadaen started to sit back down, he straightened with yet another suppressed curse; there was a puddle on his chair . . . just as he'd planned. That gave him a reason to glance around for another empty table. The only one was adjacent to Ahearn's, and none of its occupants seemed to notice the commotion, let alone attach any significance to it. Wiping half-beer off his britches, Druadaen made his way there and slid into the chair closest to the wall . . . which providentially positioned his left ear at an oblique angle to the center of Ahearn's table.

Well, he thought, *that worked well*. Had he gone directly to his present seat, even a half-wit would have been suspicious. Instead, he wound up there through an embarrassing sequence of mishaps. Now, if he overheard a likely point at which to enter the conversation at the next table . . .

But understanding their rapid, irritated exchanges was challenging. The two humans had a good command of Commerce, but the pekt woman's was stiff and halting. The other pek mostly grunted, and when the aeosti spoke at all, it was usually a mutter to herself—and in her own language.

"This is rich," Ahearn was saying. "You approach me, a *human*, to guide *you* in the Under . . . and then you have the nerve to quibble over the price?" He snorted and drank a great gulp of whatever was in the tankard in front of him. "I'm surprised you're willing to take on the shame of having a thinhide like me show you around your own home."

The female pek's voice was hard, her words clipped. "Do I look like the Under is my home? Besides, shame is put aside where an oath must be kept."

"And what oath is that?"

"I swore to my companion, Kaakhag, that if he agreed to wear my tribe's colors, I would help him find and free his get-brother."

"Well, doesn't he know the way back to his own home? Why do you need us?"

"His tribe lived in the Gloom, but it was defeated in battle. The chief was wounded, and the survivors went deeper. Down toward the Black, where the Rot gives way to the Red. I am told you are familiar with such places."

Ahearn's response was apparently stilled by his companion. "We *may* know such places," the other human said. "But if his tribe is no longer in its old haunts, then how do we find them?"

The pekt woman shrugged. "Tribal hashes. We will go to the last place where his tribe had its great hearth. From there, you will guide us deeper into the tunnels and he will watch for their hashes."

Ahearn shrugged. "Just one thing puzzles me: Why does Kaakhag not tell the tale himself?"

"He cannot. His tongue was taken from him."

"A punishment?"

"A precaution. He was young when the tribe captured him. But he was never accepted by them, and, as he grew older, they did not want him to be able to speak of things he saw while serving their colors. Such as secret places and passages."

"And these, er, secret places and passages: Is that how you mean for us to enter the deep without being filleted?"

"It is."

"Well, I think we should get another opinion. You!" Ahearn's voice was slightly louder, and more direct. Almost as if he'd turned in Druadaen's direction.

"Yes, I mean you! Don't keep pretending. You *know* I'm talking to you."

Druadaen ground his teeth together. *By the hells, how did they know I was—?* But it was pointless to wonder.

Without any idea of what might happen next, Druadaen turned and answered, "Yes?"

CHAPTER FOURTEEN

Ahearn was grinning at Druadaen. The aeosti was smirking. The dark man was expressionless but shrugged. "Well," he said reasonably, "if you're going to keep listening to us, you might as well sit at the table."

"That's very kind of you, but—"

Ahearn held up his hand. "No buts. And no kindness involved. This is business."

Druadaen felt his wariness increasing. "Business?" he repeated uncertainly, stalling. Typically, eavesdroppers were sharply rebuked and sent packing, not invited to join the offended. *No: something's wrong here, but I'm where I need to be, so...* "What kind of business?"

Ahearn indicated his nearly full table. "You want to listen and find out? Fine. But that's not free. So you're standing for the drinks as long as you sit here." The aeosti edged away from the only empty chair. "Just stay quiet."

Druadaen nodded, occupied the chair, and felt a strange calm. He couldn't even afford the mental distraction of trying to puzzle out what Ahearn might be up to. That was a distraction from the only thing that mattered: remaining alert for signs of a sudden threat.

Ahearn turned back to the pekt woman. "So let's suppose we have a passing knowledge of the Underblack and the Red." He pointed at Kaakhag. "He still has almost all the knowledge you need. The moment he tweaks to any signs left by his tribe, he'll be able to follow them. Our knowledge of the deeper tunnels might not even be needed. So what you're *really* doing is hiring us as sell-swords. And since what you propose sounds very much like suicide, you'd better be able to pay appropriately." He leaned back, crossed his large arms. "So, what are you offering?"

The woman sat very straight, seemed to be steeling herself to speak when Kaakhag put his green hand on her arm and shook his head slowly, but emphatically. She snatched her arm away, squared her shoulders, and said, "My axe in your service. For one year. Where you lead, I shall follow."

Ahearn stared, stopped in mid-sip. He blinked and then stared again; the reaction might have been either theatrical or genuine surprise. "You're serious?" He sipped again.

"I am. But heed this: you are my war chief. And that...is...*all*."

Ahearn sputtered out his most recent sip of beer. "Oh, have no fears on that count," he mumbled. He seemed both surprised and amused and was doing a poor job at concealing either. "I mean no offense to your axe or...or to the rest of you, but I'm interested in coin. I have no need of your service."

"Haven't you?" Her eyes were as sharp as her voice. "The tasks you are said to have undertaken within the past few moonphases could not be carried out by three. And she"—Umkhira tilted her head at the aeosti—"is new to your colors." Ahearn almost managed to hide his surprise at her insight.

But she wasn't done. "I am also not blind to your gear: sturdy but old. In want of improvement. Hardly what one would expect from a successful fortune-seeker."

Ahearn's gaze had settled on her and become shrewd. But he aimed his voice at Druadaen. "So, what do you think? Surety of service for the surety of suicide? Can *you* see any gain in those terms, lordling?"

Druadaen ignored the jibe that was also an exploratory jab. "If those were her terms, they would be pointless. But I do not see that as an accurate statement of what she is offering."

Every pair of eyes at the table turned toward him—except those of the dog, which was licking noisily at some spot well beneath its belly. Druadaen took the time to look into each face and also to collect his thoughts and formulate a quick strategy.

"Firstly," he began, "from the look on Kaakhag's face, I think he fears that he alone will not be able to be your guide. After all, any hidden entrances he knows of are also known to those who held him and might be firmly held."

The pek nodded vigorously, made tangled motions with his hands.

"So I suspect that there is value in having more than one person familiar with the tunnels, the habits, and the language of the pekt."

They all started at the word "pekt." Before Kaakhag's **and** the woman's immediate frowns could become snarls, Ahearn interceded. "Here, now! No reason for slurs! I thought Dunarrans were taught better manners than that."

Druadaen pushed past the deflation of being so readily identified as a Dunarran. "I ask your pardons," he said quickly to the two glowering beings to his right. "By what name would you be called? Urzhen?"

That term melted the frowns, brought relief to the human faces.

The woman's chin came up sharply. "A proper, if imprecise, term, but it will serve. Now, back to my proposition. You reason correctly, newcomer. I need both a guide into the Under and swords that know what it means to fight—and hide—there."

Druadaen resumed by nodding meaningfully at the pair of humans and then at the pair of urzhen. "So then, my second point: If the mission has four individuals familiar with the Under, and possibly a fifth"—he glanced at the aeosti—"it hardly seems like suicide. Particularly since you will only accomplish your end by focusing on stealth rather than combat. I suspect that if your numbers were much greater, it would lead to more frequent discoveries by your adversaries. Which would be your undoing."

Even the aeosti nodded at that.

Ahearn leaned back and smiled at his dark companion. "Pay up."

The man sighed and tossed a mark onto the table.

Druadaen frowned. "There was some wager?"

The companion nodded glumly. "Specifically," the dark man muttered, "whether you really *are* a Dunarran."

Ahearn chuckled. "Anyone could pick up the little odds and ends you're still carrying from your homeland, and you wouldn't be the first fellow who'd wandered into this kind of tavern looking like he was fresh out of a scriptorium. But when you opened your mouth just now—!" He hooted out a sharp laugh. "No one does that quite the way a city-schooled Dunarran does! 'I conjecture!' Every one of you comes out of the womb equipped with a scholar's palaver!" Ahearn's mouth remained smiling, but his eyes suddenly weren't. "But what I *still* can't figure out is why you were looking for me."

Druadaen saw several things in the same instant. The two urzhen were even more surprised than he was at Ahearn's revelation. The aeosti was as well; she/he was just better at hiding it. Ahearn and the dark man were both watching him like stooping hawks, but without any bodily shift which presaged anticipation of combat. Not immediately, at least.

Druadaen sighed; this was the crossroads, then. The tavern's purportedly original name rose up like a suggestion: truth or consequences.

He inhaled slowly. "I will answer that by way of my third and final comment on this warrior-woman's proposition: that there is yet another person willing to accompany you into the Under."

Ahearn's eyes widened, then narrowed. "You? Really?" He shook his head. "What's this about, Dunarran? Why in the hells would you be eager to rub elbows with underkin? A death wish?"

"No. Curiosity."

The smiles elicited by his reply were neither amiable nor kind. The dark man leaned sideways toward Ahearn. "That's so perfectly Dunarran, I almost feel I owe you another mark."

Ahearn nodded, his eyes still on Druadaen. "Make it a pence and we'll call it even." He shook his head again. "Still, why would you be curious about such things?"

"Because when I was with the bountiers out upon the Graveyard, they only understood how to hunt the urzhen. They knew nothing about them as a people. In particular, they had no way to explain how the urzhen could achieve a Horde every eight or nine years, no matter how terrible their casualties had been during the previous Horde."

The response was stunned silence. "You went 'exploring' out on the Graveyard?" the aeosti asked eventually, her tone both doubtful and sardonic. "Alone?"

Druadaen simply nodded.

Ahearn's companion glanced at him. "That's how he knew to look for us. He must have met Fronbec."

"I did, but you were also recommended by the leader of a troop of Teurond cavalry."

Ahearn frowned. "And what was *that* worthy's name?"

"Darauf, captain of the King's Own Border Cavalry."

Ahearn sputtered out more beer. The urzhen woman frowned. The big green male growled. The dark man became very still, and his eyes widened.

The aeosti was the only one smiling. "You have no idea who you actually met, do you?"

Before Druadaen could formulate an answer, Ahearn muttered, "That 'captain of horse' is a crown-lord! He's the grandson of King Tandric V and eldest son of Prince Alaxöman of the line of Teurodn. Eight or nine years ago, he made a name for himself as the scourge of the last Horde." He put both fists upon the table. "But it's strange as spider teats that any Teurond crown-lord knows *my* name."

Druadaen shrugged. "And yet he does. Maybe when we go back that way, you can ask how he came to be acquainted with it."

The mute urzh slammed a large-knuckled fist on the table. He made a tortured sound deep in his throat.

The urzh woman nodded. "I believe Kaakhag means to say that he would rather kill the crown-lord than ask him questions."

Druadaen shrugged; no surprise there. "And you?" he said, turning to face her directly. "Your opinion of the captain seems similar, if not so intense."

She shrugged. "To most of you, we are all alike and, so, are all marked for death. In this regard, the spawn of the House of Teurodn are no better or worse than their subjects. But Darauf's name is known above others because he killed so many of our people."

Druadaen frowned, puzzled. "*Your* people?"

She frowned back, equally puzzled at his reaction. "Of course, my people. Despite the differences among those you call the urzhen, ours is one blood and one destiny."

Druadaen shook his head. "But, you...are you not HalfBent?"

She started. "What? Why do you think such a thing?"

"Well...because you're not green."

She rolled her eyes. Kaakhag's laugh was like broken wagon wheels bouncing over loose stone. The others leaned back, a modestly amused audience.

The woman's stare was baleful. "We are not *born* green," she said. Her tone added, *you idiot.*

Druadaen might have blinked. "But, all of you—"

"What you see is a dye, human. It has useful properties and identifies any underkin so colored as a warrior, a raider."

"But you...aren't you a warrior?" It took Druadaen a moment to realize that the male urzhen's immediate reaction—a rumble of grunting snorts—was a long snicker.

The woman was rolling her eyes again. "Yes, I'm a warrior," she explained through a long, exasperated sigh. "But...well, do I *look* like underkin?"

Feeling trapped, Druadaen tentatively replied, "Erm...no?"

She closed her eyes and shook her head.

"Umkhira is a Lightstrider," the dark man explained. "Her kind of urzhen live on the surface—and *only* there. That's why she knows so little of the Under. Much less than Ahearn and I do, in fact."

Druadaen nodded. "And this is why I must go to the Under: to discover just such distinctions and details concerning the urzhen."

A dangerous growl welled up from Kaakhag's barrel chest. He made a slashing gesture with one hand.

"'So you can come after us in our lairs?'" Umkhira translated.

Druadaen had been able to intimate that much; he was already shaking his head. "Although the knowledge I hope to gain might be used that way, it is not why I seek it. As I said, your existence holds mysteries that defy the laws of nature. Specifically, the numbers and growth of any species is limited by the resources it may access. But if that is true, then—according to all the facts I have been able to gather—it should be impossible for the urzhen of the Gur Grehar to ever grow into a new Horde."

Kaakhag shrugged, waved dismissively and gestured downward.

Druadaen turned to Umkhira. "He attributes it to gods in the earth?"

Her gaze quickly went from imperious to curious. She nodded, then frowned. "You are very odd." Her tone was not insulting, just frank.

Ahearn laughed. "Well, we *have* established that he's a Dunarran, so no surprise there. It's said that most of the young ones are half philosopher and half fool. For instance, did you really think it likely that any of the locals you asked about me—however indirectly—were going to keep it a secret? That once a stranger they'd never see again had crossed their palm with a little copper, or even billon, that they wouldn't make another pence or two by coming to tell me?" He leaned back slightly. "You walked straight into this, lordling."

Druadaen shrugged, hoping the motion would disguise how he shifted in his seat so that he could stand more quickly... and how his left hand cheated backward, closer to the hilt of his sword.

Ahearn shook his head, raised his empty hands. "Now, now. No reason to get nervous. If we meant to roll you, we'd have put you at your ease, and then—"

"And then attacked me in a nearby alley?"

"Attacked? Such an unpleasant word. Let's just say that, at the end of our business together, we'd have had what's in your purse and you'd have still had what's in your veins."

Druadaen shook his head slightly. "And that reassurance is exactly what you'd say if you wished me to lower my guard to make the same thievery that much easier when we leave." He watched for the response: this moment, too, was a crossroads.

The dark fellow glanced at Ahearn. "He's not gullible. Just inexperienced. We can work with that."

Ahearn nodded. "Very well, then, consider yourself part of the company."

Umkhira sat erect at the word "company." "So, you accept my offer?"

Ahearn rubbed his chin. "I do. The damnedest group I've ever worked with, but there's often opportunity in that." Now it was the aeosti who rolled her eyes. "And what are you fussing over?"

She tilted her head toward Druadaen without deigning to look at him. "Really? This one? Who will be responsible for changing his"—she struggled to find a word, gave up—"*jesa*?"

Before anyone else could puzzle out the Iavan word, Druadaen calmly said, "The word you were looking for is 'diapers,' *Sahn*."

The aeosti started at the last word.

The dark man frowned. "I don't know that term."

"It is a pronoun," she explained, abashed. "For when one of my people are newly met and we are not yet fully... known." She turned to face Druadaen directly. "*Veth*," she apologized contritely. "I am called S'ythreni."

He nodded, glanced at Ahearn. "So at what point did you decide *not* to rob me?"

Ahearn laughed. "Oh, pretty much the moment you came in the door. We wouldn't have done so, anyway. Not unless you turned out to be a right bastard. Might've given you a sharp scare for your own good, though."

"And why did you not do that?"

"Heh: the day's not over, lordling," Ahearn said with a wink. "Truth, though: You might be a bit of a swell, but you know to wear your weapons lower, a little further back, and on a lanyard with loose loops tucked where they won't snag. Also, with your sword on your left hip and a long-quilloned dagger on your right, you're rigged for a cross-draw or I'm a fish's father. And that's no costume you're wearing, but your own gear: fits too easily and it's weathered where your body's creased it." He stretched. "And besides, your timing could not be better."

"You mean regarding Umkhira's proposal?"

"Well, that too, but I'm speaking about more pressing matters."

"Such as?"

The dark man's eyes flicked at something over Druadaen's left shoulder. "That," he muttered.

A man of middle years was approaching the table. His profession was not evident from his attire, but there was no mistaking the way the three men with him made their coin. All were in leather armor, had their hands on the hilts of their weapons, and had the empty eyes of trained killers ready to ply their trade if necessary.

The man stopped a few yards away; his retainers continued a few feet further, arrayed themselves as a living wall between him and the table. From behind that screen, the man inclined his head slightly. "Elweyr."

"Bannef," Ahearn's dark companion answered with a similar nod.

"You wanted to meet about a book."

"Indeed I did. And still do."

The man glanced disapprovingly at the other figures around the table. "You said you'd be coming alone."

Elweyr shrugged. "So did you."

"And who are these others?"

"Potential partners of his," Ahearn explained with a table-sweeping gesture.

"Convenient how you managed to double your numbers by

having this little meeting just before we do business. Did you mention anything about that to the three of them, I wonder?"

"And I wonder how it is that you knew Elweyr was part of a group, and how you had such detailed information on its numbers." Ahearn had leaned forward and shifted sideways as he spoke.

Ready to stand and draw steel, thought Druadaen.

"Now," finished Ahearn, "are you two gentlemen going to do business, or what?"

Bannef's smile was cool. "I think the answer is 'or what.'"

Ahearn raised a palm. "Ah, a shame, that."

Druadaen mentally rehearsed the angle at which he'd need to make a grab for the hilts of his two weapons while sitting.

Elweyr put both hands flat on the table. "So you have no interest in selling that treatise you were dropping hints about?"

Bannef's smile widened. "I can't sell an object I don't possess."

Ahearn sighed. "And never did, I wager."

"You'd win that bet."

"And if we were to wager that the only reason you're here is to take Elweyr's own book from him—?"

"You'd win the bet and lose the book. Which is exactly what will happen now." Bannef turned toward Elweyr. "Turn it over." He waved two fingers in the air.

Six other men in the room stood. Everyone else started to leave. Quickly.

"Well," murmured Ahearn, "*this* is interesting."

CHAPTER FIFTEEN

Ahearn calmed his restless dog and craned his neck until he caught the tavern owner's eye. He gestured to the ten men arrayed against them. "Thanks for the warning, barkeep."

"Yeh, just my way of thanking ye for bringing *that* in here." He glanced at Kaakhag and spat; the gob hit the planks as loudly as a wet palm.

Umkhira put a restraining hand on Kaakhag's arm and stood. "Human, you will repent that stain on your honor."

The barkeep laughed. "Eh? On *my* honor?"

S'ythreni looked sideways at him with narrowed eyes. "She means you took money for the urzh's drink even as you were laying a trap for him. You betrayed a guest."

"And who asked you to explain, you sodomizing slut?"

Druadaen started at both the bigotry and ignorance of the slur.

Umkhira's hand was on the handle of her hatchet. "I await your apology, human," she repeated slowly as the standing men wrapped fingers around the hilts of their own weapons.

"And I'm waiting for these men to be done with you so's I can wipe your filthy *darger* blood off the floor." He turned his back, grumbling as his last patron hurried out the door. "Mebbe then I'll have a respectable estab'shment again. The room is yours, Bannef."

Bannef managed to appear both bored and impatient. "Well,

140

now that there's no further chance of interruptions, tell me exactly where your book is, and we can avoid any unpleasantness."

Ahearn pouted. "Well now, the shame of it is that we don't have his much-vaunted book with us."

"A shame for you," Bannef amended. "We know where you're wont to flop, to hide, to run. So when we're done with you here, we'll just find your current lodgings and take it."

"Strange, but I don't think you will."

"And I don't think you're leaving here alive if you give me any more lip, you hound-buggering bastard." The dog stood slowly, growling at Bannef, who pointed at it. "And if your mange-ridden he-bitch comes at us, I'll gut it myself."

Ahearn sighed through a genial smile. "Now, I can see how you might be frustrated right now, might even feel the need to fling a few insults at me. But insulting my dog, too? That's just not right."

Bannef was confused. "Your dog?"

"Why, yes: my dog. See now, I'm a forgiving type. Sticks and stones and all that. But my dog is a sensitive soul. An insult like yours can make him sad for a week." Ahearn's smile became sharklike. "So you're going to *apologize* to him. Right now." And he waited.

It took almost a full second for Bannef to react, by which time, everyone at the table had risen. He raised his hands—a clear prelude to a mantic pass—and his three main bodyguards drew their weapons.

But before those blades cleared their sheaths, Umkhira had leaped toward their wielders, her hatchet whirring round their ducking heads as the lead two backed up, parrying. But the third was stepping past her, moving to get on her flank, sword cocked back.

Druadaen cross-drew his blades and jumped forward.

The bodyguard heard the sounds, spun on a foot toward the new threat, and swung at Druadaen.

Who caught the approaching blade between the quillon and tang of his dagger, snaring it with a quick turn of the wrist. The guard's eyes were wide upon Druadaen's ready longsword—

—which was almost knocked out of his grasp as S'ythreni's passing shoulder struck his elbow. "Oaf," she muttered as she sprang after the guard.

Who used the moment to pull his own sword out of Druadaen's loosened control—and just in time to block the gleaming blur of the aeosti's slashing blades.

Druadaen was about to close in to help when a blow from the *other* side nearly tumbled him. Kaakhag had leaped over the table to join Umkhira, swinging his chair as he landed an inch too close to Druadaen. The urzh's mass forced the two guards there to take yet another backward step, giving Umkhira a moment to sweep her left hand down toward her boot and bring it up again, holding a narrow dagger.

Still unengaged, Bannef had raised a hand toward Ahearn, seemed surprised when nothing happened, glanced toward Elweyr. Druadaen, recovering from his near fall, spared a glance in the same direction: the dark man's hands were held in the shape of a bowl, his eyes focused on some place beyond the limits of the room—or maybe the world.

Ahearn finished rushing around the table and, slipping through the gap left by the urzh's leap, joined Umkhira and Kaakhag as the center of a rough skirmish line. Together, they forced the two guards back upon Bannef, who ran toward the safety of the other men he had secreted throughout the taproom.

Druadaen reentered the fight against the man whose sword he'd trapped and who was continuing to parry S'ythreni's relentless flurry of strikes, one of which had opened up a bright red seam on his thigh. Seeing Druadaen approaching again, the guard raised his sword to block the new threat—and as he lifted that arm higher, the aeosti leaped in. The tapering point of her left-hand shortsword took him in the underarm gusset; he fell with a sigh, bleeding heavily.

An instant later, the other two guards were overwhelmed by the stronger, relentless attacks of the two urzhen and Ahearn, whose double feint caught the largest of their opponents off-guard. The soldier of fortune's blade plunged into the man's shoulder joint. A howl, a stumble, and then Kaakhag brought what was left of the chair down on the thug's head, sprawling him. Ahearn's dog, finally clearing the table, dove for the man's throat.

The last bodyguard spent a fatal moment trying to decide what to do next—and never got a chance to do anything; as he sidestepped the arc of Umkhira's hatchet, he walked himself into the sweeping tip of her razor-sharp knife. His windpipe half-severed, he fell backward, gargle-yelling through the rush of blood.

But Bannef was beyond reach, having abandoned whatever mancery he was attempting as he fled behind the advancing gang he'd gathered to the tavern in secret. Druadaen and S'ythreni were already parrying that poorly armed group's tentative cuts and lunges. Elweyr cursed, unable to track his mantic adversary through the frenetic melee, just as Ahearn and the urzhen swung round to form a line against Bannef's remaining forces...

—and just as the mancer smiled and made an invocational gesture toward the door.

It crashed open and more men—better armed than the others—began swarming in. The half dozen defenders around Bannef backed up, falling back a few steps toward this new, growing force.

Druadaen assessed the rapidly changing odds. He and his companions were now facing a total of eleven adversaries and more were still coming through the door. Not promising.

Ahearn had apparently made the same estimate. "Elweyr, we need—"

S'ythreni interrupted sharply. "He can protect or attack; can't do both."

That made the course of the melee—both leading up to and after this point—much clearer to Druadaen. Elweyr's and Bannef's mancery had effectively cancelled each other out. A strategy that had, until now, favored the Dunarran and his companions, who were more capable fighters. But with the influx of Bannef's new foot soldiers...

Druadaen let his dagger dangle on its lanyard long enough to snatch one of the guards' swords off the floor. With a *hssssttt!* he tossed it to Kaakhag.

The urzh, who reached in front of Ahearn to snare it, regarded it as he might an unsavory meal, but resigned, tossed away one of the two chair legs he was now wielding.

Ahearn, at the center of their rough line and with his dog poised to leap at enemies, nodded as the first rank of Bannef's fresh warriors approached cautiously. "Ready?"

Druadaen shrugged. "One is or one dies."

Ahearn grinned. "*Typical* Dunarran. Here they come."

Several of the enemies in front rank had bucklers: not as good as a full shield but a reasonable defense, and not too awkward for indoor swordplay. Blades raised, they advanced at a measured step, holding a rough line that would be much harder to break. Or survive.

Druadaen let his sword rest back upon his upper arm, fell into that trancelike state where he could see the entire tableau while maintaining focus on his first intended target...

The first rank of attackers took another step forward—and, as one, fell flat on their faces.

Bannef glanced toward Elweyr in panic, then, confused, made gestures toward the men on the ground—without effect.

Behind, Elweyr was muttering curses. Ahearn started forward, shouting, "Now, let's gut them while—!"

But S'ythreni shouted, "Wait!"

As the word left her lips, the rest of Bannef's men either staggered to chairs or fell into awkward sitting positions on the floor.

The color drained out of the duplicitous mantic's face. He sprinted for the still-open door—and drew up short before a figure standing in it:

Shaananca.

Who smiled at the speechless Bannef and nodded slowly at him.

The mancer's mouth worked silently. His eyes drifted slowly toward the ceiling and he swayed where he stood, but otherwise did not move.

Shaananca stepped around him, avoiding the fighters sprawled in chairs and dazed upon the ground. Three men and a woman, all armed, alert, and chillingly calm, moved into the room and formed up on her, two trailing to either flank.

Ahearn's voice was barely more than a whisper. "What's this? Are you—?"

Druadaen cleared his throat. "The four who just came in are Outriders."

"Dunarrans?" breathed Ahearn.

"They do not look it," asserted Umkhira.

"That's the idea," Druadaen explained.

"And the woman?" Elweyr muttered warily from behind.

"She's—uh, she's a librarian."

"A librarian?"

"Well...she's an archivist, to be exact." Even in Druadaen's ears, the clarification sounded ridiculous. He stepped forward to meet her, sensed the others trailing in his wake. Cautiously. "Shaananca," he said.

Her eyes opened wide, but her smile was mischievous. "Just my name? Not a 'thank you' or a 'hello'?"

He gestured at the stunned, wounded, and dead around them. "Respects, but... it's hard to even believe you are here. If it really *is* you..."

"You require proof?" Her eyes narrowed, but not disapprovingly. "Shall I share the name of the first girl to which you took a fancy when you began school in Tlulanxu? And her reaction when you told her?"

Druadaen felt himself flush as his companions edged closer, eagerly. "That will not be necessary, Shaananca."

"I thought not," she replied primly. Disappointed murmurs arose not only from his companions but two of the Outriders.

"Shaananca, I have only one question for you: Why are you here at all? And of all times"—he gestured at the shambles around them—"why now?"

"I'm here because you and your associates had particular want of my presence."

Druadaen waved away her maddeningly ingenuous answer. "Shaananca, please: enough games. You understand what I am asking. When I left Tlulanxu, I did so by ship that ported here. I immediately boarded another ship to Sanâllea but slipped over the side before she sailed. I even arranged for a friend from my Courier days to pick up the chest I'd brought aboard when the ship reached Caratta."

Shaananca nodded. "Yes, and you created a second false trail by riding back over the Connæaran border and dropping clues suggesting your ultimate destination was the coast of Teurodn." She nodded again. "Quite professional, actually. Just enough variation not to be entirely predictable."

Druadaen could feel, as well as peripherally see, the stares of Ahearn's band. "And yet, it was all for naught."

Shaananca stepped closer. "My dear boy," she murmured, "do you really believe that if powerful people wish to remain apprised of your whereabouts, that they would fail to do so?"

"No, but I am surprised to learn that my 'whereabouts' are of such keen interest to people who oversee far more important matters." The sudden stillness of his companions suggested that they might be considering the worrisome conclusions that could be drawn from his statement, if true.

Shaananca folded her hands. "It often happens that a person whose life is touched by the actions of great powers assumes that it is the result of those powers' careful deliberation and settled intent." She smiled. "That is natural enough, since it may change their life quite profoundly. But the fact of the matter is that such a touch is usually a matter of chance, coincidence, or incompetence."

Druadaen almost smiled. "And you are trying to convince me that is how you came to be here? By chance?"

Her smile dimmed, but only slightly. "I am trying to convince you that I have sworn the same oath of service that you have, and so I may not reveal what I do and do not know. Just as I am prohibited from publicly sharing any of my guesses"—she looked at Ahearn—"or 'conjectures.' Which is apparently held to be a favorite word among us Dunarrans."

Ahearn's scalp seemed to jump backward on his head.

"Besides, when it comes to following your progress," she finished, "I hardly need reasons other than my own."

Even as his heart was warmed by those words, his head became wary. "And what are your reasons?"

Shaananca smiled again. "Druadaen, you are often wiser in the ways of the world than your limited experience of it would lead one to expect. But when you entered this city on your own, you were sure to enter places like this."

"And what sort of 'place' is this?"

"A place where the rough texture of reality was likely to take your idealistic self by surprise, and fray—or even shred—the smooth morality which you have yet to shed." She frowned. "And perhaps, never will. I cannot tell, anymore. But regardless, here we are."

He smiled. "Yes, here we are."

Shaananca looked over his shoulder; her smile returned, but with a wry cast. "And in such proud and estimable company."

Druadaen shook his head. "They are good folk."

Shaananca cocked an eyebrow.

He almost grinned. "More or less."

"Less I suspect," murmured Shaananca, studying Kaakhag's heavy, brooding brows before glancing quickly at Ahearn's ill-shaven and wary face. "Much less, perhaps."

Druadaen felt torn between trust of her and a quick, natural loyalty toward those along whose sides he had fought. "What do you mean?"

"I mean they had other plans for you."

"You mean that they meant to give me a scare?"

Shaananca's smile became brittle and her eyes moved between Ahearn, Elweyr, and S'ythreni. "Oh, they meant far more than that, had things not worked out to their liking. Besides, it was they who spread the word that they would be at this fine establishment today. And timed it so that you would be here when the rival thaumantic arrived at the door, thereby making you a de facto recruit to their side. They had no great concern for your safety, Druadaen. Quite the contrary."

Ahearn swallowed, and when he spoke, it was in a voice all at once determined and yet as reluctant as a serf contradicting a king. "If you know so much as that, lady magistra, then you must also know we would have drawn no blood unless he sought us to harm us. And we freely admitted as much before this room became so—lively." He looked away. "As far as the timing of our meeting, I can only say this: we would have seen to his wounds as if he was one of us."

"If he had lived, that is," Shaananca added flatly. "Which seemed very much in doubt, from what I could tell." She studied Ahearn, looked at his two followers. Her expression softened. "So, no less a rogue than your actions suggest—but one equipped with a conscience, it seems." Then her gaze shifted back to Druadaen. "You realize, of course, that the Propretors might wish to put you in irons for this, my boy."

Druadaen swallowed, nodded. "My deeds are my deeds. There is no gainsaying them or the Propretors."

"You could flee." She looked at the others. "With them." Ahearn nodded. Eagerly, almost.

Druadaen shook his head. "If the Council determines that my actions today jeopardized the Consentium's relations with Menara, then I must stand to answer for them. I shall not run."

"And you shall not need to," said Shaananca with a rueful smile. "That much can be arranged. But be warned: I will not be able to intercede should there be a repeat of this event. It is not just the Consentium that must be placated when they learn of this." She looked around the taproom. "The mayor of Menara will have words for our emissary here in the free city, and you may rest assured that his placation will carry a cost."

"And the militia will be looking to have our guts for garters," Ahearn said with a long sigh.

Shaananca looked at him. "You, too, are free to go. All of you. But in the case of the officers of the city militia, I can only delay, not prevent, their inquiries. So if you wish to go, you must go immediately."

Elweyr sighed. "With respect, magistra, we cannot. Since we anticipated Bannef might prove faithless, all my thaumantic references are secreted inside the city."

Ahearn nodded. "Along with our modest wealth."

S'ythreni snorted at the word "wealth."

Shaananca shrugged. "If you return to that place, you could encounter further associates of these brigands"—she gestured at the slowly rousing foes around them—"or the watch, who will certainly have been told of the events here."

"That's a risk I will have to take," Ahearn asserted, before shooting a hard stare at Elweyr and S'ythreni. "By which I mean *me*. And *only* me. This was my doing."

"But I was the one who—" started Elweyr.

"There will be no argument. It was my decision to make, and I agreed. Eagerly."

Shaananca cocked her stately head. "Why do you feel compelled to do this?"

"Well, it's just the way of it, yeh? Comes with being the leader, if it's a true leader that you'd be. Besides, I have..." Ahearn could not help looking away. "I have debts that need paying. Just outside of town. And they are not the kind one may pay with labor or service."

Shaananca appeared to grow thoughtful.

Druadaen looked at her and shook his head. "Ahearn will leave the city with the others—"

"I will not! I have to—"

"To undertake take a task that would be the end of you? No, *none* of you can go. But I can because I am not known to travel with you. No one has any reason to follow me, to suspect that I might lead them to your secret cache. Once I have your goods in hand, I shall ride from the city and meet you at a safe place."

The others stared at him. Ahearn's face wore an expression that might have been—guilt? "You—you would do this? Think well, lordli—er, young fellow. If you are wrong, you could wind up...well, in a very bad way."

"Unlikely, and—"

"And unnecessary," Shaananca interrupted, turning to Druadaen. "Also, the swordsman has no debts."

"What?" Druadaen and Ahearn asked in unison.

She looked at the soldier of fortune. "You have no debts."

"With respect, ma'am, I have..."

"You have no debts." Shaananca emphasized, and smiled. "Not anymore. Those that exist presently shall be seen to. After that, your responsibility is yours to fulfill."

"But you don't even know in whose debt I—"

"In fact, I do, now, and I commend your resolve. A visit will still be expected, though." She turned toward Druadaen. "Better and better I deem your choice of companions. Better and better. And they seem as willing to stand with you as you were to stand with them. That, at the very least, deserves coin." Which Shaananca extended toward Ahearn on a clean, aristocratic palm.

He slapped it away, his cheeks reddening as the silver clattered across the floor. "Keep your filthy money. We fought as mates." Only after the words left his mouth did he remember who he was speaking to. The flush fled his face, but the defiance remained.

Shaananca was neither surprised nor angry. Instead, a small smile creased her lips. "Excellent."

"Excellent?"

"You value your pride above coin." Shaananca scanned the group's gear. "And considering your means, that is a luxury you can ill afford. Excellent, indeed." She turned back to Druadaen. "You may have chosen your companions well enough after all, Druadaen. Perhaps there is hope for you yet."

"Perhaps," he agreed. "But only if we leave quickly."

CHAPTER SIXTEEN

Ahearn spurred his horse to catch up with Druadaen's. "She decided me, Dru," he muttered.

Dru? "I am not 'Dru.' You may call me 'Daen. If you must."

"Ah. Have it as you will. As I was saying, Dru, your aunt the wizard is what decided me about you."

"Did she? Besides, Shaananca is not my aunt and not a wizard."

"You think not? How did she drop those guards in their tracks? And from outside the building, no less?"

Druadaen considered. "So that wasn't Elweyr?"

Ahearn shook his head. "No. And he wasn't happy to admit it. He's got quite a varied bag of tricks, he has. But his mancery wasn't working any better than Bannef's. Still think that your aunt isn't a wizard, Dru?"

"*'Daen.* And no, why should I?"

"Well, who do you think knotted the nuts of *both* of the mantics in the taproom? Some wayward god?" He snorted. "That was your magic auntie, right enough. Who, it seems, can send spells clean through walls. An' good it is she can, or we'd have been fresh mince by the time Bannef's lot was done with us."

Druadaen frowned. Yes, Shaananca had touched his mind once, and even called forth forgotten memories—but a magistra? Or, to use the old, superstitious term, a wizard? "The magists of Dunarra are not secretive about their calling or their craft. Why would she be?"

"Can't guess because I don't know her or Dunarra. But here's what I *do* know: she had heard what we were saying—word for word—at the table before she walked in. You're saying that wasn't mancery, right there?"

Druadaen shrugged. "Well, perhaps a *little* mancery."

Ahearn's responding scoff was a bluff, rather than derisive, sound. "No one is a 'little bit' of a wizard, Dru, same as no one is a 'little bit' dead. I've seen more than a few mantics in my time, tried cases with some. But none like her. Hells, Elweyr's among the most skilled I've seen, but even he couldn't protect us or harm them, no matter what he tried. And he's a mantic with many options."

"So he's a thaumancer, then?"

Ahearn stared at Druadaen. "So you know a bit about magic, then?"

Druadaen shrugged. "I know what I read."

"They teach that kind of thing in Dunarra, do they?"

"Well, not as such. But I was...I guess you'd say I was apprenticed to Shaananca at the Archive Recondite. And I read, um, widely."

Ahearn eyed him. "I'll bet you did. Same as I'm sure she's *just* a librarian." He stood in his stirrups as they topped a low rise. "So. We've arrived." He nodded at a thatch-roofed cottage in a small glen beneath them. "Wait here." Without another word, he prodded his horse into a canter, clods coming up behind its hooves.

The rest of the group drew up alongside Druadaen. S'ythreni was the only other one riding, sitting a fine-boned horse that seemed almost as aloof as she was. Elweyr was hanging on to the saddle and panting. He fell heavily upon the grass. Druadaen dismounted as Umkhira sat with slow, deliberate stateliness. Kaakhag dropped unceremoniously beside her, scratching flakes of old skin from his neck. S'ythreni surveyed the group, seemed quite happy to remain mounted.

Druadaen stared down the hill at the cottage. "Who lives there?"

"Private matter," Elweyr wheezed. "Even I. Don't know."

S'ythreni's voice was slow and certain. "But. You. Suspect."

Elweyr stared up at her. "I also. Know to. Mind my own. Business."

Druadaen nodded once down the hill. "But this is where Ahearn owes—well, owed—his debt, yes?"

Elweyr nodded, breathing more easily.

"I was not informed," Umkhira stated flatly, turning toward Druadaen.

Druadaen was so surprised by the sudden pronouncement that he blinked. "You were not informed of...what? Ahearn's debt?"

"No! His affairs do not concern me. However, what happened at the tavern does. Neither Ahearn nor his companions may hope I will hide their dishonor with my silence. It is unjust." She pointedly kept her eyes on Druadaen. "I was not informed that they intended to meet the human book-mantic while we were in the tavern. Nor that they suspected treachery."

"We didn't expect it," Elweyr protested. "We just knew it was a possibility."

Her eyes flicked hard in his direction. "You put us in a position where we were obliged to fight your foes, having never agreed to do so." She glanced up at S'ythreni. "And you, an aeosti, were a willing party to such duplicity?"

"It was a tactic," she temporized.

"It was the littermate of a lie," Umkhira spat.

Elweyr sighed. "If we hadn't worked the timing that way, we could very well have wound up dead. We thought that if Bannef had anything dishonest in mind, he would see the numbers at our table and reconsider." He shrugged. "Clearly, he misled us from the start. But not only are we all still alive, but now a company setting forth upon a profitable journey."

Umkhira's large chin raised indignantly. "We are here only because of the Dunarran's, eh, mentor. And as for a profitable journey, that has yet to be seen." She turned back to Druadaen. "All urzhen are accustomed to dealing at arm's length with humans. They think nothing of lying to us." Her voice didn't soften, but it lost its strident edge. "But it seems that your code of honor might extend even to urzhen. So I warn you: think well on traveling too long with such treacherous companions as these."

"As though urzhen are any different," S'ythreni sneered.

"*My* people are," Umkhira said in a slow, deliberate, and dangerous tone.

Druadaen leaned toward her. "'Your people'? Do you mean Lightstriders?"

She nodded. "Among us, if we are negotiating, it takes one of two forms. It is either on our feet in parley with an enemy—so trust cannot be expected—or seated over shared food and drink. That signifies that trust may be assumed."

Elweyr made a pensive sound. "And none of you ever stab another in the back after sharing a meal?

"Not if we agreed to part ways as *h'adzok*."

"*H'adzok*?" Druadaen repeated. "What is that?

S'ythreni explained. "It means that although you are not friends, you are definitely *not* enemies. There is a truce between you, and to change that honorably, you must inform the other before taking action against them." She sighed. "Would that humans were so scrupulous."

"Hey," Elweyr complained, "whose side are you on?"

"Mine. As I have been from the start."

Elweyr shot her a look that was not angry but very disappointed.

Druadaen turned back toward Umkhira. "I have another question, but I am concerned that the mere asking of it may offend."

The Lightstrider studied him with a small measure of surprise before replying. "When one takes such care in asking a question, it is surely not meant as an insult. Ask, human."

Druadaen glanced briefly at Kaakhag. "I have seen differences among the features of your kind. I have seen urzhen with . . . well, your kind of features."

"You mean, features more like unto humans."

"Yes. But the ones I have seen before now were green. *Very* green."

She frowned. "Bright green, as though they were painted?"

"Most, yes. But one was more dull in color."

She nodded. "The bright ones were dyed for battle. It signals that they are raiding along with their urzhen kin from the Under." She shrugged. "The other one: Was he or she about the color of Kaakhag?"

Druadaen glanced at the big urzh again, nodded. "He was."

"Then he was of mixed blood. Part urzh, part ur zhog."

"Ur zhog?"

"That is the proper name for Lightstriders."

Elweyr pushed himself up to his feet. "First lesson you learn in the Under: you can't know an urzh's background just by their features and physique." He gestured to Kaakhag, who was now brushing skin flakes off his rough jute tunic. "That dull green one was probably dipped, like him. The mix enters their skin and both protects them and marks them as tribe members for life. So it's a near certainty he was raised among the Rot."

"'The Rot'?"

Kaakhag thumped his chest.

Umkhira sighed, uttered a string of syllables that sounded like an irritated hog with a gullet full of pebbles. Kaakhag shrugged, made a brief reply with his hands. The Lightstrider huffed, stood, and walked impatiently down the slope. Druadaen stared after her.

"Shall I translate?" the aeosti asked through a sigh.

"Yes. Please."

"She told him she cannot understand why the urzhen welcome the label 'Rot,' because the green color encourages humans to associate them with decaying meat and fungus."

"And he answered—?"

"That if humans get scared at the mere color and smell of rotting flesh, then all the better. Then he added that although she's a friend, she should mind her own business." The aeosti smiled impishly. "Or words to that effect. I claim no great command of urzhen hand speech."

Umkhira called from down the slope. "Ahearn approaches." The rest stood.

As the swordsman ascended the gentle rise, leading his horse, Druadaen was struck by the way he moved. Light on the balls of his feet and yet inexorable. The image of a cast-iron tiger sprang to mind.

He swung up onto his horse while still a few yards away from the others. Hardly necessary, but an effective and silent way to signal that he was intent on moving on. And avoiding conversation. But he did grin at Elweyr as he lifted the flap of a saddlebag. The binding of several hidebound books peeked over its rim.

The dark man smiled broadly. "My codices!"

"Every one of them," Ahearn affirmed. "Thanks to Dru's magic auntie."

Druadaen decided on a different approach to discourage use of that nickname. "Just as I told you she would, 'Hearn."

He started. "'Hearn?" He looked at the others. "Who put the

Dunarran up to this?" Surprised stares and shrugs were his only answers. His eyes drifted back to Druadaen. "Can't say I like that name—or the familiarity."

"Can't say I enjoy them, either. But it's up to you. It's either 'Hearn and Dru and irritation. Or not."

The others' eyes moved between them, expectantly.

Ahearn frowned, but it suggested more calculation than displeasure. "You've got some salt in you," he said. "I'll give you that."

"He handles his blades well," Umkhira added. "Sure and strong."

"Stiff, though," S'ythreni muttered. "But *real* experience will file down those training-field edges soon enough."

Ahearn's eyes were still fixed on Druadaen's but gradually changed from stubborn to frustrated, and finally, to resigned. "Well, I suppose we should get under way, *Druadaen*."

"I agree, *Ahearn*."

The soldier of fortune rolled his eyes, smiled crookedly, brought his horse around to face north, and urged it into a walk.

Upon reaching the next crossroads, Ahearn tugged his horse's head left. Westward.

Druadaen reined in his mount. "We are heading north to the Graveyard, are we not?"

Ahearn shrugged. "Close to, but we'll track west first."

"And then go due north, straight to Gur Grehar?" Elweyr, perched awkwardly on the back of S'ythreni's saddle, sounded less than enthusiastic.

"It is wiser," Umkhira added, breathing heavily. The initial walk from Menara had been five leagues. Since resuming, they had covered almost five more, and always at the fast-walk pace of the horses.

"Why?" asked Druadaen, still looking north. "This way, we will make Stammadous in two days, at most. Beyond that, we cross into Connæar and so, travel on First Consentium roads in safe country with ready provisioning almost all to the southern tip of the Graveyard."

Ahearn stared at him, seemed to be trying to find words.

Probably more tactful ones than those S'ythreni blurted out. "And I'm sure the Connæarans would be delighted to allow *them* over the border." She jerked her head at the urzhen. "And I'm not so sure how they'd feel about me."

Druadaen shook his head sharply. "Connæar may be a protectorate, but it is still *Tar*-Connæar; one of the three Shield Realms. It has not forgotten its friendship with all Uulamanthi, whether Iavan or L'fahn."

S'ythreni looked somewhat mollified, but her eyes remained on the urzhen and her lifted brow and steady gaze was the equivalent of a steadily tapping foot as she waited for him to address that thornier issue.

Druadaen shrugged. "As to urzhen, I cannot say."

"Yes, you can. I hear a hint of a Connæaran accent, human: probably acquired when you were a child. And so tell me, how many urzhen did you see in Connæar while you were growing up?"

Druadaen shook his head. "None."

"That's one problem," Ahearn said, now that the ticklish subject of species had been aired. "But there are others. Not the least of which is that if the Lord Mayor of Menara wishes, he might send inquiries far and wide for news of us. And you can be sure Bannef will, because I'm equally sure that your nice magic auntie did not stoop to putting him out of our misery while tidying up the mess we made. So the only way we can disappear is stay away from the big roads, to travel overland."

"You mean, in the wilds."

"In the wilds," he agreed with a nod. "At least the ground to the west is level and Elweyr and I have journeyed there before. We know where to hunt, forage, find shelter."

Umkhira raised her chin. "Not as well as I do. Those lands are my home."

Druadaen shook his head. "Then you have my condolences regarding your neighbors."

Umkhira stared, shook her head. "I have no wish to speak of the Khassas. But I would rather pass close to them than to your lands, Dunarran."

Ahearn held up a hand. "The point is that half of us are well accustomed with the route that avoids the Plains of Grehar by going west and then directly to the mountains of Grehar themselves. Besides, there are several different options that will help us quicken our progress as we pass near Khassa lands, and after."

"You refer to shortcuts?"

"Well, those, too," Ahearn admitted with a smile. "But if we're to camp in a safe place near Khassant, we need to press on."

Druadaen shrugged. He had been over these roads before, but not so often that he had a local's familiarity with them. And he knew little about the more northerly borders of Khassant. Conversely, the others were almost certainly correct about the border with Connæar: guards there would be far more likely to seize the urzh as prisoners than allow them entry. He turned his horse in the same direction as Ahearn's: westward on what the locals called the Steppney Road.

"Ho, the camp!" cried Ahearn's voice just before he rode out of the dark and into the fluttering circle of light cast by the fire. "See?" he cried gleefully. "That hasn't been so bad a detour, has it?"

S'ythreni and Umkhira appeared on either side of him, and this time, the urzh was on a horse. And each of them was leading yet another.

Kaakhag stood and hooted in mirth as Druadaen gaped from his place near the fire. "*This* was the reason you wished to travel west? To steal horses?"

"Now, Druadaen: 'steal' is a very debatable term in this instance. I'm thinking it's more a matter of recompense."

"For what?"

Umkhira nodded. "I agree with Ahearn. We have both been wronged by both the local hetman, Paftrelt, and the liege-sworn patrols of *Khassant taku Kalazhmaf.*"

Druadaen was too surprised by the purloined mounts to reflect on the Lightstrider's use of the formal name of the Khassan realm. And before he could recover, yet another four-legged silhouette appeared at the edge of the firelight. "And an ox? Really?"

S'ythreni stared at Druadaen as if he was a half-witted rabbit, then glanced at mirthful Kaakhag. "Does *he* look like he can ride a horse?"

Druadaen shook his head, half to agree with S'ythreni that no, the big urzh was far more likely to consider a horse food than transportation, and half to clear it of the day's accretion of surreal developments. "And how does this help us avoid detection, which was one of the reasons you gave for traveling on this route?"

"Well," said Ahearn, folding his hands on his saddle horn and looking slightly hurt, "firstly, neither the Lord Mayor of Menara or Bannef are going to make inquiries in Khassant, and certainly not out here. Secondly, with all of us riding, we can double the pace we had yesterday. In two days we will be far beyond the reach of the swinish goatherd who so generously provided the new mounts."

"Why do I think that this hetman—Palfrekz—is not merely a 'goatherd'?"

"Well, now that's a fair point, but then there's the matter of settling accounts with him."

"Took one of our horses a year ago," Elweyr muttered. "As the 'toll' for crossing his lands." He spat.

"And you agreed?"

Ahearn smiled indulgently. "You don't argue with a dozen riders on fresh mounts and more'n a score of liege-troopers just a long whistle away."

Druadaen shook his head, looked at Umkhira. "And you agreed to this? What did this Paftrelt ever do to *you*?"

"He owes a blood debt," she said slowly and quietly. "He killed two of my tribe. We had been forced to cooperate with the Khassas, believed we were still welcome at their hearths. Either Paftrelt did not know or did not care."

"Probably both," Ahearn mused.

Druadaen simply shook his head, realized that he had been the only person in the group who had been unaware of this further reason of "detouring" to the west.

Umkhira looked uncomfortable. "It was wrong not to inform you of what we intended. But that is why we did not allow you to follow us. It is also why we left Kaakhag behind: to protect you and see you back to your border, should we have died."

Druadaen wasn't sure whether he felt more mollified or mortified that the rest had conferred on how best to "protect him."

Ahearn dismounted, led his horse to one of the two hitching stakes. "We'll leave in three hours. Paftrelt won't miss his livestock until then, but he'll come looking, right enough. And there's no covering our tracks. And we need to follow the big stretch of sweetgrass before riding through the Hasgar Woodlands." He frowned. "It's mostly sourgrass as we get closer to Gur Grehar."

Umkhira nodded. "Yes, but at least it is good hunting country. And if any of my people are there, we shall have safe passage... and the Khassas shall not."

"Still, I won't feel safe until we've made it into the wilds, not with the buggering goatherds hard upon us. 'Never turn your back on a Khassan,' eh? That's the saying at least." He looked at Druadaen who was staring into the darkness. "That's a Dunarran axiom, isn't it?"

"It might be. I would not know. I did not grow up in Dunarra and have no family there. So, many of the things that are common knowledge among its children remain unknown to me." He finished, noticed the silence, turned and looked.

They were all staring at him, surprised, even abashed. Even Kaakhag. And then, as if suddenly and intensely uncomfortable, they all looked away.

"We've a long journey ahead," Ahearn mumbled. "We'll ride at first light."

He kicked dirt into the fire, smothering it.

Journal Entry 149
6th of Lion, 1798 S.C.
Plain of Hasgar, two days south of the
headwaters of the Sendra River

The sun is setting and there is little light by which to write. Besides, my fingers are too cold to hold a stylus much longer.

We have traveled just over one hundred thirty leagues in seventeen days. That may not sound like much to those who travel upon Dunarra's wallways—or any First Consentium road, for that matter—but over open country and at the onset of winter, it is respectable.

The horses have benefitted from the modest pace. Their hooves show little wear and because they have had ample time to graze, none have suffered from colic. And, thanks to S'ythreni's and Elweyr's expertise at finding sweetgrass, our fine-gutted mounts have remained healthy and strong.

The only mount which shows any sign of weariness is the ox. Our progress has been at the limit of the fastest movement it can sustain, and that pace has exhausted it. Fortunately, although incapable of a horse's bursts of speed, it has greater endurance. On any given day, I doubt we lost more than two leagues because of it.

The creature which has cost us the most time is, ironically, also the fastest over short distances: Ahearn's wolfhound Raun. Although he, too, has admirable endurance, our steady movement has been terribly hard on his paws. As a result, we are compelled to stop far more frequently than we might have otherwise. On the other hand, Raun's senses—on the trail and at night—detected both enemies and game that we would have otherwise missed.

Thanks to him, we had a reliable supply of meat without needing to spend additional time searching for it.

Some of the creatures we have encountered were unfamiliar to me. The most memorable was an undomesticated example of one of the many species now used as titandrays: a bedoq. It was at least fourteen feet at the shoulder, and, like most titandray, is broad-gutted, grazing without concern upon sweet- and sourgrass alike.

We lost the better part of one day when Umkhira detected ur zhog tribal hashes that the rest of us missed until she pointed them out on rocks. She rode ahead and cleared our passage, returning with two days' worth of food for us and a young male Lightstrider who shall trail us and then tend to our mounts once we enter the Under. When I expressed my appreciation, she explained that neither form of assistance was motivated by generosity. Her people were simply giving us the means to travel through their lands without needing to stop, and to ensure that our mounts would be safely waiting for us so that we could return to our own lands. As quickly as possible.

As cold as it is becoming, I am daily grateful that we are not out on the Graveyard. This route keeps us in the lee of the highest part of the Gur Grehar range, which blocks the rush of cold gusts rolling down from the Boreal Sea. But since we are now verging into a region dominated by various species of Bent, we cannot risk a fire at night. Not only has that been uncomfortable, but it has emboldened various strange creatures to come snuffling around our camp. We had to kill one Umkhira calls a giireyza, and it is like nothing I have ever read or heard about, much less seen with my own eyes. Scaled with chitinous plates, it reminded me of a furred lizard with rows of dark spots where normal animals have eyes. Umkhira explained that it has only rudimentary vision as we think of it but can see the heat of its surroundings with extraordinary sensitivity, making it a particularly dangerous nocturnal hunter. However, after feeling a few arrows lodge in its scales, and one which slipped between them to draw its (purple) blood, the giireyza fled back into the night.

Tonight we are sheltering in a cave with a relatively narrow mouth which opens into a wide chamber. After gathering enough fodder, we shall leave our mounts here, in the care of the young Lightstrider groom who has been following us at a distance as we travel. Hopefully, we will discover our mounts—and him—in good condition when we return.

If we return, that is. We could be detected and overwhelmed while in the upper tunnels, those known collectively as the Undergloom. It is also possible that, like Ahearn and Elweyr, we may be forced down into the deeper, more daunting tunnels called the Underblack. Of course, that is also where the hidden truths of urzhen population recovery are likely to be found, so I cannot help but hope that we may have reason to journey there, albeit briefly.

I cannot write more; darkness is fully upon us.

CHAPTER SEVENTEEN

Hidden in shadows cast by the foothills of the Gur Grehar, and the sound of their movement masked by the rushing rapids they had followed upstream, the group crouched silently, observing the entrance to the Under. As they did, Ahearn put a calming hand on his soundless wolfhound; the fur along the length of Raun's spine was standing stiff and upright.

Kaakhag peered through the underbrush, then nodded and signed to Umkhira, who translated in a rough whisper. "The dog has spotted the guard beasts where Kaakhag suspected they would be. Also, as with many that lair near small tunnel openings, they are feral."

Again, Druadaen was the only one who needed clarification. "Please explain why that is important."

Umkhira looked at him as if he had asked why one drank water through one's mouth. "Small openings, such as the one in this rock shelf, are not much used by underkin. So any animals maintained near its entrance are merely wild creatures that lair nearby because the urzhen put out scraps of food."

Druadaen frowned. "So, the creatures cannot be ordered to attack. Their value lies in the probability that they will become agitated and so alert the guards when intruders approach."

Umkhira nodded. "Correct, which is why naturally combative breeds are preferred. As is the case here."

Ahearn groaned. "Let me guess: badgers."

Umkhira nodded again. "Kaakhag sees only one burrow and two creatures. Both have darker pelts, so they are younger. It is unlikely that they have offspring old enough to be lairing nearby."

The wolfhound's eyes were riveted on the animals; he snorted hoarsely. Druadaen glanced from Raun to his master. "I have never seen a dog so well trained to silence."

"And you're not seeing one now," Ahearn said, shrugging one shoulder. Seeing Druadaen's puzzlement, he expanded: "'Raun' is an Old Teurond word, meaning 'mute.'"

"So, he was whelped this way."

Ahearn's brow furrowed. "No, some bounty hunter is responsible for that. No scar though, so they probably did it while the litter was new."

Elweyr cocked his head. "Or it was faunamancery. It's said to be tricky knife-work, cutting voice cords."

Druadaen shook his head. "But why do it?"

Ahearn pointed at the tunnel entrance, not fifty yards away. "So that he can be brought this close to quarry. There's some bounty hunters as pay good coin for that." He ground his teeth. "Meaning there's always someone willing to mangle pups for profit...the bastards."

Druadaen nodded at the bitterness in Ahearn's voice. "You sound ready to mangle *them*."

The swordsman nodded back, then expelled a great breath. "Sitting in the bushes won't get this done. S'ythreni, how quickly can you get off a second shot?"

Druadaen turned, expecting to see the aeosti with a bow in hand, but was surprised to discover her readying a complicated crossbow. Its mechanism was not as heavy as the counter-geared steel-sprung arbalests he knew from Dunarra, but the already-taut lathes were made of glossy, jet-black wood: almost certainly Solorin ironpith.

"I will need a five-count," she replied, apparently determined *not* to notice Druadaen's interest in the weapon.

"What?" hissed Ahearn. "No faster than that?"

Her brows knitted. "No."

"Druadaen?"

"Yes?"

"Are you any good with that bow of yours?"

Druadaen decided to consider Ahearn's phrasing as brusque banter rather than actual doubt. "I am competent."

Umkhira looked away. Elweyr sighed. S'ythreni smirked. Kaakhag made the gravel-gargling sound that was his equivalent of a smothered chortle.

Ahearn closed his eyes with a long-suffering look on his face. "The targets: can you hit one from here?"

Druadaen was beginning to think that Ahearn did, in fact, doubt his abilities. "I am confident that I can."

"We need certainty: Yes or no?"

He turned toward Ahearn. "Are you asking about my skill as an archer, or as a soothsayer who can anticipate every twitch of the wind?"

S'ythreni may have snickered appreciatively.

Ahearn was not amused. "You don't inspire confidence, Dunarran."

"And you ask for that which no mortal can promise." He waited, shaft nocked. "I see that Umkhira has a self-bow. I have seen a wrapped longbow among your own gear. I am not the only archer. Choose one or several. It is of no matter to me."

The eyes of the group moved between him and Ahearn in the following silence.

Ahearn waved away their staring match. "Just hit a damn badger."

Druadaen nodded, stood next to S'ythreni, moved until the foliage did not block his aim nor the draw of his bow.

"You're stiff," she muttered. "Just like a human."

He ignored her. "The one on the right or the left?"

"The one on the right is bigger. That's mine."

"I concur. My bow hasn't the power of an ironpith crossbow. I will fire on your count of three."

S'ythreni murmured "One..."

Druadaen focused the way his father had taught him: aware of his body, the bow, the target, the space between, but not calculating so much as absorbing the relationship between them all. Alert to subtle changes, ready to shift in accordance with them.

The instant S'ythreni fired the crossbow on her count of "three," the smaller badger's head halted in mid-turn, perhaps hearing the weapon's string slapping against its lathes. Druadaen checked fire to follow the target's motion and loosed the shaft—at the same moment S'ythreni shouted, "Shoot!"

Even as her quarrel hit and rolled the larger animal, the

smaller one was already beginning to reverse direction—just as Druadaen's arrow drove into its belly. It kicked and flipped, a surprised hiss starting to rise into a squeal—

Which Druadaen's second arrow killed in its throat.

S'ythreni was staring at him as he recovered to the ready stance; loosing two shafts so rapidly had uncentered him.

"That was pretty 'competent,'" Elweyr muttered behind him.

Druadaen shrugged. "I hit a still, unsuspecting target. That is hardly proof of great skill."

"It's good enough for me!" Ahearn said emphatically before remembering to whisper. "Now, we'll angle west until we come up against the skirts of the outcropping. Then we'll work along it until we reach the tunnel mouth. With the noise of the falls behind us, even bat ears like his"—he jerked his head toward Kaakhag—"won't hear us coming."

Ahearn's prediction was correct; the two Bent just within the opening to the tunnel did not hear the group coming. They probably wouldn't have even if the waterfall had somehow been silenced; they were engaged in a heated exchange that was completely audible to Druadaen and the others as they crouched close around the entrance.

One voice was high-pitched, arguing—or complaining—so constantly that it was hard to imagine how the speaker breathed. The other voice was more typically urzhen and was bored and dismissive whenever it deigned to respond. Which wasn't often.

Kaakhag made quick hand signs. Umkhira turned, explained. "They are arguing about who shall return to the closest darkstream— erm, underground river, which is apparently shared by their two tribes. The bigger one is an urzh and is telling the other to fetch more water before they run out. He refuses."

"Why?" asked Ahearn.

"Because he is a g'ban and has gone the last three times."

Druadaen shook his head. "G'ban?"

Elweyr muttered over his shoulder. "Ur gaban. Smaller, wiry, never seem to sit still."

"Or to shut up," Ahearn sighed. He drew his sword. Kaakhag saw, made rapid movements of negation. "Oh, be still, you great green lump. I'm not such a fool to just stroll in and lay about. If they get the chance to sound an alarm, we're done before we've begun."

Kaakhag was gesturing frantically, Umkhira falling behind

in the translation. "He suggests that we wait. The urzh shows no willingness to go and they are both hungry and thirsty. Eventually, the g'ban will relent and go. When he does, we can rush the urzh. With our numbers we will kill him so quickly that he won't have a chance to sound an alarm. Then we can follow behind the g'ban at a distance."

"Why?" S'ythreni asked sharply. "So we can find both their tribes and be drawn into an even larger combat?"

"No," Umkhira said carefully, studying Kaakhag's rapidly moving hands. "He says that it would be unusual for any surface entrance to lead straight to a darkstream. Most water in the Under is gathered from, eh, drippings. It is not pleasant in one's mouth or in one's gut. Access to a river is often like a crossroads on the surface: a place where many gather and trade. They are often *h'adzok-gar*—truce-places. We would come upon more guards before getting there."

Elweyr sighed. "So we're cut off from going deeper."

"No. That is what he is explaining now. There are almost always tunnels that go around a *h'adzok-gar*, particularly one with running water. That way, tribes may move, hunt, attack each other without bringing their business into or through a truce-place." She stared at Elweyr and Ahearn. "How do you not know this, if you dwelt in the Under?"

Ahearn's smile looked more like a feral display of teeth. "Because as I said, we had to go—and stay—deep, where such niceties as this don't exist. So, if I follow Kaakhag's reasoning, he's suggesting that when we're done with the g'ban's lazy chum here at the entrance, we follow along behind the little grubber until we find a side tunnel, and use that to go further in."

Umkhira nodded. "Yes. He says that side tunnels to the surface tend to be narrower and are only used if a group wishes to exit or enter the Under without encountering others."

"Well, that describes us well enough." Ahearn looked thoughtful, then shifted his glance to Druadaen. "You like Kaakhag's plan, Dunarran?"

Druadaen spoke slowly. "It has merits."

"But . . . ?"

Druadaen shrugged. "Our objective is to enter undetected. There are two threats to that." He pointed into the cave mouth. "We should eliminate both, if possible." He held a hand up toward the now-frowning Kaakhag. "I mean no disrespect, but have you actually been in this tunnel before?"

The urzh crossed his beefy arms, looked away, but shook his head.

As I thought. "Then we cannot know how sound carries. Or if there is a bolt-hole with an escape passage that is large enough for the ur gaban but not for us. There are other possibilities, but they all point to the same conclusion: the only way to be certain that our entry remains unreported is to quickly eliminate *both* of the beings that could report it."

Ahearn looked at Kaakhag. So did Umkhira. The urzh's frowned deepened and he grumbled before looking away again.

Ahearn studied Druadaen from the corner of his eye. "So, what's your plan for getting the little grubber before he can slip away?"

Druadaen had to force aside a wave of reluctance. His day-dreams of Legion service had always conjured images of faceless ranks of human enemies. But this? This was as intimate and yet as impersonal as killing rats: worse, because these were thinking beings, regardless of their proclivities. Speaking about killing them as if they were vermin—well, his boyhood visions of life as a Legior hadn't prepared him for that.

No matter. You sought this. See it through. Druadaen glanced at Raun. "Shortly after leaving Menara, you mentioned that you had just recently bought, er, barding for the dog?"

Ahearn nodded. "It's in the pack with the rations and pots. Figured we'd need it once we were in the tunnels."

"We need it now. Ready him while I explain."

Umkhira slipped into the dark cleft in the rockface with no more sound than a gust of wind. Kaakhag followed, considerably louder.

Druadaen snapped "Now!" at those behind him and leaped into the cave mouth.

As he plunged into the darkness, he shifted the patch over his right eye to his left, then drew his dagger.

He bumped around a corner and heard, rather than saw, a loud melee breaking out just a few yards ahead of him. Covering his right eye for a few minutes had made it slightly more sensitive to the limited light but not much. He kept his weapons in a guard position, muttered, "Ready."

Beside him, S'ythreni muttered back. "Here." More loudly: "Elweyr...now!"

The sound of the melee up ahead stopped...just as a shaft of yellow lantern light streamed in over S'ythreni's head and Druadaen's right shoulder.

Umkhira and Kaakhag had leapt away from the urzh in different directions, leaving an open path to the desperate Rot guard. And the aeosti was at the other end of that path, head down over her crossbow.

The bolt snapped away from the lathes as Umkhira shouted, "The g'ban!"

The Rot, blinking in the brightness, came forward—straight into the quarrel. He grunted, fell back heavily, would have sprawled if he hadn't been so close to the wall.

"Ahearn!" shouted Druadaen.

The broad swordsman rushed in, shortsword out and the dog at his heels. He pointed into the darkness. "Chase!" he shouted. "Hold that light higher," he added as he headed after the bounding wolfhound. Elweyr complied, and Druadaen took a moment to assess.

The chamber was an uneven, rough-walled oval. Umkhira and Kaakhag had already jumped back into engagement with the staggered and bleeding urzh. S'ythreni was reloading. Ahearn had disappeared into the gloom, cursing. Maintaining his defensive guard in front of Elweyr, Druadaen asked, "Alarm?"

"Not that I can se—yes! Just behind S'ythreni. Pot hung as a gong."

At which point multiple attacks connected with the urzh, who fell his length with a strangled cry. S'ythreni raised her crossbow, aimed it down the black passage Ahearn had plunged into—and out of which came a high-pitched shriek. Then two howls. Then silence.

"Ahearn?" called Druadaen.

"Keep it down, Dunarran. Are yeh trying to call them on us?" The swordsman emerged from the tunnel. "Don't shoot me, lass!"

"I've been watching you the whole time," S'ythreni muttered. "Urzhen aren't the only ones with good night-eyes, you know."

Druadaen made a mental note of that as he asked, "The ur gaban?"

Raun emerged from the darkness, his maw dark red.

"Never mind," Druadaen amended. He made to join the others. Ahearn waved him back. "You just keep Elweyr safe."

"I can fight as well as the rest of you," the dark man said. Judging from his equipment and armor, Druadaen had no reason to doubt that claim.

"Aye, but you're my only friend, you damn fool."

"I'm also the only mancer you have."

"Well, that's true as well. Now keep watch and protect us while we take a look at these bodies."

Druadaen realized soon enough that "taking a look at the bodies" was simply a euphemism for searching, stripping, and then dragging them outside. When Druadaen raised an eyebrow, Umkhira explained, "In hours, scavengers will arrive. They will leave nothing behind. So there will be no hint of the fate they came to, or that there was even a battle here." Which was certainly prudent.

Equally prudent, but also unanticipated, was the businesslike review of the dead's possessions. It was not the speed and thoroughness of the process which Druadaen found arresting, but the ghoulish detachment. Druadaen volunteered to stand watch as the others inspected the weapons, tools, portage, cookware, coins, and assorted baubles. He wondered aloud, "How will we carry all of that?"

"Well," Ahearn answered, "Kaakhag is traveling light; escaped with his hide and not much else, we were told. So whatever he can't carry, we split amongst us. I just wish the g'ban hadn't been ready to take a second cut at Raun. Might have taken the little grubber alive if I hadn't had to take his hand off. But he could've gutted that damned fool of a dog."

"Raun was a 'fool'?"

"Yeh: tried to hold the bugger rather than take chunks out of 'im and so got quite a swat from the grubber's hatchet. A second one might have broken bones through the leather—or worse, sliced through."

Umkhira looked up as she dragged the body of the ur gaban closer to the lantern. "And then you let the dog finish him?"

"Aye. Shame, though. Could have used the gobbler as a porter. Maybe ask 'im some questions about these parts of the tunnels."

Druadaen goggled at the idea. "But he would have fled. Given us away."

"Always a risk in the Under, Dunarran, but it's the way of

life down here. The weak serve the strong if they want to live. And all he would have known is that we're a strange but dangerous bunch—and that if he didn't make a clean escape, he'd be as good as dead. He'd have been useful, for the short time we'd 'ave needed 'im."

Umkhira was frowning. "I understand that this is how you and Elweyr survived in the Under, but I share Druadaen's misgivings over increasing our numbers. A task such as ours must depend upon speed and stealth."

Ahearn glanced at her, then turned to look at Elweyr.

Who shrugged and nodded. "They're right. Old habits die hard, but they'll get us killed, this time."

"Ah, I suppose you've the right of it." He studied the rusty knife blade he'd extracted from the rubbish of the urzhen's rude camp. He smiled. "This was like coin to us, down here. Remember, mate?"

Elweyr nodded. "But this isn't our world anymore, Ahearn. So unless we mean to stay, that's not worth the weight of carrying. We've found and packed everything we can use. So leave off, you lazy bastard, and help me get the second body outside."

CHAPTER EIGHTEEN

Kaakhag had been correct about the smaller side tunnel that plunged downward. With the exception of tribal hashes on the wall—often foully defiled—they encountered no Bent or signs of their presence before reaching it.

The movement downward brought increased dampness for a time, but that passed quickly. It did not come from the rocks, Kaakhag explained. It began as the humidity drifting in from the entrance, which cooled as it descended. Eventually, its effect upon the lower rock and air became so diffuse that it was unnoticeable.

The side tunnel led to a surprisingly dry chamber. Or at least that's what the two urzhen told the others. Druadaen expected S'ythreni to offer some sardonic counterpoint—she rarely missed such opportunities—but the aeosti was silent. He couldn't make out her features in the almost undetectable light coming from Elweyr's hooded lantern, but even her gait seemed pensive.

He leaned toward her. "Do you have misgivings about this chamber?"

She muttered something that sounded simultaneously annoyed and noncommittal.

Elweyr leaned over Druadaen's shoulder. "She can't see very well down here. No wet rocks nearby."

Druadaen did not see any logical connection between the two statements. "What?"

Ahearn hissed the answer back over his shoulder. "Bent see ... well, they see heat, is the only way to describe it. Aeosti see better than we do in the dark because their eyes see more light. So without the lantern reflecting off anything nearby—"

"I'm nearly blind," S'ythreni finished bitterly. "I certainly can't see well enough to shoot. Any other pressing questions, Dunarran?"

"Just one. About your shooting."

She sighed. He could imagine her eyes rolling. "Yes?"

He glanced at the vague shape of the crossbow still in her hands. "Iavarain visit Dunarra, so we do hear their stories and how their customs are different than ours."

"And this concerns my shooting—how?"

"Well, I have seen evidence that some of the human truisms about your race are not without some basis in fact. For instance, it is held that almost all Uulamanthi—both Iavan and L'fahn—are renowned for their natural talent for the longbow." He glanced at the crossbow again. "So I cannot but wonder why your weapon of choice is—"

"Shut up."

Druadaen pushed down annoyance. "I did not know that question would offend you. I retract it and offer my apologies in its place."

"Yes, well ... it is a personal matter." She muttered more loudly at Ahearn's back, "So are we going into the chamber or just going to stand here?"

"I'll tell you when the urzhen return; they're scouting ahead."

Umkhira's voice reached out of the darkness toward them. "We have finished." Druadaen heard the larger Rot's heavy tread halt just beyond the faint circle of light. "Kaakhag believes he has been in this chamber before."

"He *believes*?" repeated Ahearn in exasperation.

"It was only once, and years ago. He and others were returning from a raid upon another tribe. Because this route is rarely used, few know about this chamber. Therefore, he suggests we rest here and then press on."

Elweyr's voice suggested a frown. "This day isn't even half over."

"True, but since we do not know what lies ahead, we may not find another place to sleep for more than a full day from *now*. If Kaakhag is right about our location, we are barely a mile from where the tunnels become more frequent, wider, and patrolled.

We may have to move quickly and without much warning to avoid becoming known to the tribes that clash and hunt in those areas as we search for a passage down toward the Underblack." A pause. Druadaen heard arms moving, hands smacking. "He wants to know if either of you, Ahearn and Elweyr, recognize this place."

"No," they chorused. Ahearn's voice continued: "The only time we dared to come this far up from the Black was when we finally had strength enough to fight all the way out to the surface. So we won't be of any help until we've gone a good bit deeper. Can we risk a light?"

"It is not prudent."

"But..." started Druadaen.

"Yes?"

"How do we find a seemly place to... That is, is there a best spot for us to...eh...?"

"Godsblocks," hissed Ahearn. "Come; I'll show yeh."

S'ythreni snickered. "I *told* you someone would have to change his diapers."

As it turned out, Kaakhag's memory was accurate; he had slept in that chamber once before, which, aside from the scurrying of rat's feet following along a far wall to avoid them, was without noise or visitors.

The tunnels that started a mile beyond it were smoother underfoot and showed other signs of frequent use: rock blackened with the soot of old torches; scraps of leather and sheared bronze rivets; faint pongs of waste and sodden cloth; and, of course, the occasional rat skeleton or larger bones that had been cracked open for the marrow.

Twice they paused as Kaakhag and Umkhira went forward alone and later returned with a report on the Bent ahead and how to avoid them. But the third time they were gone longer and came back more carefully.

"We have come to a place where several tribes have been warring," Umkhira explained, pausing as Kaakhag signed a long explanation. "It is a crossroads—no: an intersection—with five branches. Well, six, counting the one that connects to it from here. Three are tunnels into the more populous warrens in this part of the Under. Another leads to a lake with a high ceiling. He knows that place by reputation. It is Bebga Oog: the Puddle of Drowning."

"We heard of it," Elweyr commented. "A lot of tunnels lead

there. A mile or more across, but when you approach it, you don't hear any water sounds, don't see a drop or a waterside shelf or scree shore. The edge comes right into the tunnels, the surface smooth and almost level with the ground. Like a puddle."

"And the fifth passage?"

"That one will lead us down to the very edge of the Black."

"And that's the one being guarded?"

"It is."

"Well, let's see about relieving the guards..."

Keeping his head turned toward the intersection that was somewhere ahead in the darkness, Druadaen took the lantern from Elweyr. The thaumantic inhaled deeply and focused himself in the same direction, ready to react when the corner of the right-hand tunnel became briefly visible. He started murmuring repetitive syllables to himself. Or maybe to the universe.

Druadaen spoke to the pitch-black space just ahead of him. "Umkhira, as soon as you—"

"Hsst. Quiet. Soon now. Wait, wait...now!"

Druadaen lifted the lantern hood slightly. The light washed forward, picked out the corners of the intersection.

Elweyr's muttering concluded on a single syllable and a faint gesture at the back of an urzh, just barely visible at the mouth of the tunnel to the right. Its spine stiffened slightly. But otherwise, it did not move. At all.

Another one emerged from that same tunnel, started poking its friend in the same instant it noticed the light.

S'ythreni fired her crossbow.

The quarrel leaped across the twenty feet in a blink. The urzh—almost as big as his friend—staggered back, the fins of the bolt protruding from the center of his chest, a dark stain spreading rapidly outward from it.

"Light out!" Ahearn hissed. "Everyone: hand on the shoulder in front of you. Kaakhag, you lead us. Elweyr, you keep holding the first urzh. He's an easy target, Umkhira. Make sure you—"

"I know my job," she muttered bitterly. "Executioner." She moved forward, axe already in motion.

After getting through the intersection, they kept moving for hours. How many, Druadaen could not guess. At one point, he thought he heard shouting behind them. Later on, a faint winding of horns. But they did not stop until the twisting, narrow passage leveled off and opened into a long, wide chamber. There were so many opposed stalactites and stalagmites that peering through the entry was like staring down the length of some immense creature's tooth-lined gullet. "Hold," panted Umkhira, "Kaakhag says we are safe here."

"Are they still behind us?" Druadaen asked. That earned him several puzzled expressions. "I heard shouting, horns," he explained.

"Oh, that?" Ahearn chuckled. "That wasn't them coming after us. That was them going at each other."

Umkhira nodded. "When we slew those guards, the rival tribes must have heard it and gathered for an attack. It is likely that they have been engaged with each other since. Even if they found our trail, I doubt they had the time or warriors, let alone need, to follow and discover who killed the guards."

"And quite the job you made of that," Elweyr commented with a rueful look at Umkhira's blood-spattered leather armor.

Kaakhag signaled abruptly, looked at the mantic with contempt. "Killing should be quick, not pretty," Umkhira translated with a nod.

"Not what Elweyr was getting at," Ahearn said testily. "He's worried about all that blood on you and the trail it leaves."

Kaakhag's shrug was dismissive.

Umkhira's wasn't. "It could not be avoided. It was the price to be paid to achieve what Druadaen rightly defined as our most important objective: to get into the lowest levels of the Undergloom undetected. It was to achieve that end that we also took so much of their gear. Including things we do not need."

Elweyr frowned. "Such as?"

She held up a necklace of large fangs and even larger claws. "Trophies. Another sign that will make other urzhen think it was Bent who killed the guards. Among many of our tribes, when you slay a foe, it is believed that by taking their trophies, the fame and deathpower of those triumphs transfer to you. None but urzhen—and none but those of Under—would care for such things.

"Although the two guards did not have much food or water, we took what little they had. Also, their weapons are still serviceable, and they had some useful ointments and dyes. So we took all those as well." She translated an addition from Kaakhag. "Underkin will see the missing gear and believe the guards were ambushed by a few tribeless marauders." She shook her head, ending the conversation. "We have had our rest. We should continue. Now."

"So you think they might be following us, after all?" S'ythreni asked.

"I think that the urzhen of the Under are always restless. If the clashes over the intersection do not distract or damage all sides sufficiently, some of them may eventually wonder at the killing that preceded their battle. If they are bored or restless enough, they might decide to follow us. So we must reach the darkstream quickly, that we may cleanse ourselves and stop leaving a trail."

Shortly after reaching the stream, Kaakhag led them into a long untraveled stretch of tunnel, honeycombed with side passages of all sizes. Before they'd gone more than a hundred feet into the tangle, he gestured toward the lantern and made a few hasty hand signs.

S'ythreni frowned, glanced an Umkhira. "What does he want?"

"He says that this is a good place to use the light. Unhooded."

"Why?"

Ahearn nodded. "Because this is not where the Bent live. No matter the breed, all of them need big caverns to house their numbers. But those caverns must also have only a small number of tunnels that lead to them: that way, a tribe has fewer points of entry to watch and defend. For these reasons, the Bent do not live in areas like this, cut through with more passages than an ant-hill. So there are none close enough to see our light, which will enable us to move more quickly."

Druadaen frowned. "But won't it attract the creatures that live here?"

Kaakhag grumbled and made more signs.

Umkhira nodded. "Yes, but it should also keep them from approaching too close, once they see how large our party is."

"*Should* keep them from approaching?" S'ythreni repeated.

Umkhira did not even need to translate. She shrugged. "If a creature is large, or desperate enough, nothing will deter it. That is no different than it is on the surface."

The group pushed onward, the lantern revealing a twisting grotto that seemed like stony latticework. Fungi was more plentiful, several kinds of which glowed dull green or dull yellow. Spiders the size of pot lids popped out, rows of black-bead eyes aimed at the passing light before they disappeared as suddenly as they had appeared. Rats scurried at its dim edges, never in great numbers but almost always present. And there were other, slightly larger creatures that were barely seen—furtive serpentine flashes of movement—but of which they found remains: a long, flexible skeleton that seemed a perverse cross between a weasel and a salamander, topped by a toothy skull with four eye sockets.

S'ythreni shivered. "What are those?"

Umkhira had to study Kaakhag's hand gestures carefully. "Individually, they are not deadly to us. In greater numbers, they can be, but they do not seek us out. We are not food for them."

"What is? The rats?"

"No, they cannot eat the rats either, and the rats cannot eat them. Nor do they and the rats eat the same things. And yet they fight each other. Fiercely. Eagerly. To the death."

"So nothing to worry about?"

"Not much. But Kaakhag says that we should continue to move. Quickly."

They did.

After emerging from what Druadaen thought of as the filigree tunnels, they found another safe place to sleep. On its walls, Kaakhag discovered the first hash of the tribe from which he had been providentially separated, and so, escaped. But the sign had been subtly altered, and he was not sure what that portended.

The next day's travel, while swift, was frequently interrupted. Three times, they came to corners or tunnel branches where there was no way to avoid the Bent that were guarding or watching them. All three combats were short, brutal, and had many of the same features as their attack to enter the tunnels, the ambush at the intersection, or a liberal mix of the two.

As they went deeper, Ahearn and Elweyr demonstrated increasing knowledge and familiarity with their surroundings. They knew which tunnels to avoid and which to travel, simply by glancing at them. Narrow, rough, and twisting? Likely to be safe. Broad, smooth, and straight? Too likely to run into large numbers of Bent. Kaakhag had many of the same insights, but he lacked their skill for reading changes in the rock itself as predictors of how the tunnels might change ahead, or for locating and harvesting the glowing lichens. If kept moist, the matlike growths continued to give off a very faint green glow. And while it was barely enough for humans to work by, it improved S'ythreni's vision to a level that she likened to human sight at dusk.

The lichens had become a major factor in all the day's ambushes but were now the linchpin for what they hoped would be the last attack before finally reaching the subterranean no-man's-land between the Gloom and the Black. As they finished positioning themselves for what Elweyr had aptly called "yet another roll of the dice," Druadaen could smell as well as hear exhaustion. A single fight made even the most stalwart warrior tense. Four in one day left their nerves as raw as their muscles were weary.

Hearing Kaakhag approach, Druadaen held the covered lamp higher so he would not hit it while moving to his position up front with Umkhira. In the dim light, he saw the Rot make an unfamiliar hand sign. Before Druadaen could ask, Elweyr muttered, "Means the guards will be changing soon. Thirty minutes or so."

"So is he telling us that we should hurry up or wait?"

"Neither. Urzh are even worse guards than we are. They lose focus easily, become impatient, then bored, then drowsy."

"So he is saying they are probably less attentive now?"

He smiled. "Some urzhen can go to sleep standing, like horses. Don't know how they do it. And those who could explain aren't about to admit they sleep while on watch." He shrugged at Druadaen's stare. "Just another of the things you learn if you live down here long enough." Elweyr exhaled and turned his eyes into the leading darkness, allowed them to become heavy-lidded. The group hadn't required any mancery during the last two engagements, but he remained ready to intervene.

"They're ready at the corner," S'ythreni said from her kneeling position. Ahead of them, Umkhira was flat against the left-hand wall, a battered pewter cup in her hand, luminous lichen wrapped around it and tied off through its handle. S'ythreni had a small clump attached to the rear of her belt.

Ahearn muttered something to the two urzhen at the corner; they readied their axes. Maintaining a crouch, S'ythreni moved forward, Druadaen and Elweyr following close behind.

Ahearn's fist raised, silhouetted against the dim glow of Umkhira's lichen. Two fingers extended, then folded away. Then one finger extended, very straight. It disappeared, then reappeared waving slowly from side to side.

So: two Bent. One was alert. The other was drowsy. "Stand ready," Ahearn hissed back. Beside him, Raun rumbled impatiently. "Now!"

The rush of action was tense yet familiar. The lichen marker on Umkhira's back disappeared around the left-hand corner, accompanied by the sound of heavy footfalls: she and Kaakhag were charging the guards. In close file behind S'ythreni, Druadaen and Elweyr moved rapidly past Ahearn and Raun.

The aeosti slipped to a knee at the corner and leaned around. Druadaen emerged behind her, ready to uncover the light, spotted the lichen-wrapped cup that Umkhira had hurled ahead for S'ythreni's benefit. The sharp slap of her crossbow was answered by a startled howl and then the clash of weapons, some of which clattered against shields. The green glow didn't outline the figures in the desperate struggle but flickered as rapidly moving legs passed in front of it.

Something heavy hit the ground; "One," called Umkhira, announcing the first enemy casualty as weapons kept cracking into each other. Ahearn muttered and in the next instant, a breath of air and rapid patter of canine pads went past Druadaen: the wolfhound was racing for the one that was down. He nudged Elweyr, who took the lantern from him and half-raised the hood.

Druadaen ran toward the melee, drawing his dagger and muttering his name as he closed. Umkhira and Kaakhag shifted to either side of the remaining guard.

Druadaen charged into that space, launching into a lunge... that he arrested abruptly.

But the Rot guard, having to shift to defend against a third adversary, couldn't take the chance or time to watch for a feint. He turned toward the new attacker to parry...

The moment he did, Umkhira launched a genuine attack. The guard responded in the only way he could: re-angling to face the two of them.

Which was what Kaakhag had been waiting for: a rear-flank opening. His axe, waiting poised on his shoulder, now swung sharply forward, cutting the air with a faint moan.

The sound of the impact was ghastly: a shearing of leather and muscle; a splintering of bones. Druadaen felt a shower of hot liquid along his arm, saw it spattered by what looked like a spray of ink: lantern-lit blood. The final Bent guard fell with a cry, sucked in more air as he gasped, seemed about to scream—

But Raun was there, jaws snapping fast on the guard's throat, crushing the Bent's voice box as Elweyr covered the light again. The only sound that escaped into the dark tunnels was a pathetic gurgling wheeze.

Umkhira had apparently forgotten the two guards they had just slain: she was scrutinizing something on the wall behind them.

"Can you tell what they were guarding?" S'ythreni asked when the final grisly sounds of the dying guard subsided.

If Umkhira heard her, she gave no sign of it.

The silhouette of Ahearn's lower legs stepped into the dim circle of light being shed by the lichen-covered cup just a few feet beyond the bodies. After a moment's pause, he said, "They were set to guard the tunnel we've been looking for." He gestured into the farther darkness. "Which is five steps in that direction. Follow me; I know the way by touch, from here."

CHAPTER NINETEEN

Druadaen reflected that if someone had told him six months ago that he would have considered any part of any cave a comfortable and welcome place to relax, he would have doubted their sanity. That was no longer the case.

The soaring cavern into which Ahearn led them looked extremely unpromising. The masses of stalagmites made it almost impossible to move through, and paradoxically, Ahearn seemed determined to move to the almost inaccessible rear wall. He followed a winding path, barely wide enough for one, which ended at the foot of a sizable "pillar": the joining of a stalactite and stalagmite into a column. Not breaking his stride, he was about to collide with it when he sidestepped sharply to the right, then just as quickly to the left...

And disappeared.

"Come on," his voice called. "Don't lollygag out there where you might be seen!"

Druadaen followed Ahearn's steps and discovered that although the top and the bottom of the pillar were flush against the back wall, the column itself stood out from it by about two feet. And in that concealed space was an opening in the wall, a little over two feet wide and five feet high. Druadaen slipped through.

He emerged into a roughly oval chamber with a small pool of water at the rear. This ceiling had only a few stalactites; it was dominated by cracks and rents that led up into darkness.

Ahearn noticed Druadaen inspecting the lightless scars in the rock, then the ground immediately underneath it. "Yes, that's the black of a cook fire," he said, nodding at the circular charring just beyond the toes of Druadaen's boots. "The gaps above it carry off most of the smoke. Doesn't look like it's been used since we were here."

Elweyr, one of the last to file in, added, "Doesn't look like anything at all has been here but rats, and not a lot of those, either."

Umkhira, who until now had been distracted since the aftermath of the fight, seemed to awaken to her surroundings. "How did you find this place?"

"Partly luck, partly method," Ahearn explained, hands on hips as he inspected the walls in the full light of the lantern. Holes had been bored into them in various places. Elweyr began cutting through the hafts of two spears they had salvaged earlier and inserting the lengths into the holes. A pattern of hooks for hanging gear began taking shape.

"There's a method to finding a cave like this one?" asked S'ythreni dubiously.

Ahearn nodded. "Yes. It's called persistence. In the Under, you don't waste anything, including the opportunity to take a careful look at every new place you visit. You never know when you're going to find something useful." He looked around the chamber fondly. "But we never expected anything quite like this."

Druadaen heard the pride in his voice. "It was you who found it, wasn't it?"

The swordsman smiled. "Guilty as charged. I wasn't the first, though. We found old—nay, ancient—gear here that day. Broken bronze swords and other cast-offs."

"Ballashan empire," Elweyr added confidently. "Although it could have been left here by Bent who'd found it someplace else. It might have gone from tribe to tribe for centuries. Or longer."

"Either way," Ahearn summarized, "we spent almost a year in this place, growing the force we eventually used to get back to the surface."

Umkhira, still distracted, was aware enough to frown and observe, "It has not been so difficult getting down. Why was it more difficult to go up?"

"Well, we didn't know about the entry we came in—or any

other—when we started out here in the Under. Not even the one I came in through. I'd remember it if I saw it, but...once I was captured, I lost all track of where I was. Prisoners and slaves don't get regular briefings, y'see."

Kaakhag rumble-chortled ruefully, signaled, had to prod Umkhira to get her to translate. "How did you wind up in this place? He has never heard of humans seeking to enter the Under. Even bounty hunters are not so greedy or foolish."

"Well," Ahearn muttered, "if it hadn't been for this one"—he poked Elweyr—"I'd never have been here at all. But *someone* had to bring him back!"

Elweyr felt the stares of the others and rolled his eyes. "I was returning from study. Up in Eld Shire."

"A true crossroads of sophisticated mancery!" S'ythreni's tone was facetious, but Druadaen noticed that, as was often the case, her tone was a little less sharp when addressing Elweyr.

He shot a rueful smile at her. "You go where you find the teachers you need. The short of the tale is that the caravan with which I was returning was about a day away from the river Rye-pare when it was overrun by Bent."

"Urzhen?"

"Mostly, but there were some kaghabs mixed in with 'em, and they're big enough to kill horses with one or two blows. Which they did. Half of the caravan was lucky enough to get away." He sighed. "I've never been particularly lucky."

Umkhira seemed to awaken into the conversation. "I must differ. You are alive. That is surprising and unusual enough."

He nodded. "It is, but it was not a matter of luck. The tribe's shaman—who might have been HalfBent—apparently went through the loot from the caravan, found my books, and figured out that they were mine."

Umkhira frowned. "An urzh shaman spared you because you could *read*?"

"Not because I could read, but because I was studying mantic scripts and glyphs. And I was still young enough that I wasn't a danger to him or the tribe he was with."

"Wouldn't seem to make you very useful then, either," S'ythreni observed.

Elweyr shrugged. "He thought I could show him how to read thaumantic codices: what he called 'human mancery.' He got it in his head that maybe he could learn to master those and still channel his god's bestowals."

S'ythreni stared. "Even for an urzh, that's..." She shook her head. "Was he really that stupid?"

Umkhira looked angry but said nothing.

Elweyr shrugged. "Well, he couldn't know if he didn't try. Besides, do you actually *know* it's not possible?"

S'ythreni frowned. "Well, they've never done it."

"Not unless they are heretics," Umkhira snapped. She continued without looking at S'ythreni. "What is truly stupid is to speculate on a matter of which one has no knowledge...particularly when in the presence of one who might."

S'ythreni's face became calm, almost blank. With sudden, chilling certitude, Druadaen recognized what that expression signified: a completely dispassionate readiness to kill. "And you have such knowledge?" she asked quietly.

"In fact, I do," Umkhira replied, almost haughtily. "What Elweyr recounts is not often done among urzhen because it is heresy to do so. As it is among human gods. And Iavan as well, if my dams and sires told me true."

"They did," S'ythreni said with lethal mildness before she turned back to Elweyr. "And did this shaman master both?"

Elweyr shook his head. "Not while I was there. He didn't speak much Commerce and I didn't speak a word of urzhen, so communication was slow. After he was done cuffing and threatening me over our lack of progress, he began to realize that part of the problem was the limitation of his own language; it doesn't have the vocabulary needed for that kind of discussion. So he decided to get, well, language tutors."

Druadaen glanced at Ahearn. "And is that where you enter the tale?"

"Well, yes and no. It is where I enter the tale, but not as a tutor." Clasping a knee, his posture and tone became positively bardic—to the point of caricature. "As it so happens, I was one of the lucky ones in that caravan where Elweyr's tale of woe began. Made it back down to the Sea of Kudak and then over to Menara, where I was at loose ends for some weeks.

"Then, one night, I discovered a very discreet but worldly couple waiting at my lodging before I could get in my cups. Somehow, they had heard that I was recently arrived from adventures in Eld

Shire, where I had almost ended my days as an urzhen delicacy after a savage caravan attack. They wondered what more I knew of the region and the urzhen who lived in it.

"Of course, they were this fellow's parents, and they already knew more than they let on."

"Such as?" S'ythreni drawled.

"Well, they knew I had been bountying up near the western arm of the Gur Grehar, so I was sure to know about the Bent in that region. They also knew I'd spent my way through the meager earnings I'd brought back. So between their generous offer and my imminent penury, I took passage back to find and retrieve him...and promptly got snared myself."

He laughed. "But some little bit of luck was attached to my sorry carcass, even so. The raiders what laid their scrabbly claws on me were from the same tribe that nicked Elweyr. And they proceeded to bring me before the very same shaman. But most important of all, not a one of them had any inkling of how much I knew of their ways and language." He grinned. "We plotted our escape in the very middle of 'language lessons.'" He glanced toward the outer cavern. "When we finally ran, we passed within five feet of this place."

Kaakhag poked Umkhira to convey his question. "And that is how you came to learn the ways of the Underblack?"

"It is," Elweyr answered. "We knew they would not want to follow us further down; the Rot often lose hunting parties there."

Kaakhag made startled signs. "So you knew it was suicide, then?"

"*Near* suicide," corrected Ahearn with a smile and a finger raised in didactic exception. "We also knew that the bodies of hunters who'd run afoul of beasts, rather than the Red, would still have gear on them."

"That was a mad wager with your lives," S'ythreni breathed.

"Not so mad when it's your only chance," Ahearn said with a philosophical smile. "Besides, in his time among the Rot, Elweyr had learned the way to the Grotto of Stone Bones."

"The what?" asked Druadaen.

"The way we're going to get out of here, once we've found Kaakhag's get-brother. But we'll have to be smart and fast, we will. Last time, we had twoscore Bent warriors and porters helping us."

Druadaen tried to keep the disbelief out of his voice. "So you two became the leaders of a whole tribe?"

Ahearn looked like he was about to say "yes" when some iota of humility intervened. "Well, not really a tribe, but a *hrug*, a gang. We're not Bent, so we *couldn't* be the head of a tribe. But that's a story for another time. Kaakhag there looks like he has an urgent point to make, water to release, or both."

Umkhira was so distracted she did not immediately realize that the group was waiting for her translation. "He says that in the places we were today, he has seen the hash of the tribe that held him, but it has been changed. A new sigil has been blended into it."

"You don't see that, often," Ahearn muttered.

Druadaen leaned forward. "What does it mean?"

Elweyr shrugged. "It means the chief Kaakhag knew has been replaced, but the tribe itself was not defeated or absorbed by another tribe."

Umkhira was frowning. "It may have been the only hash Kaakhag saw today, but I saw something else on the wall near the site of our last skirmish." She glanced at Kaakhag's agitated gestures and explained to him, "You did not see it because it is not meant to be seen. It is a pattern of nicks and cuts in the wall, widely separated."

Ahearn nodded slowly. "And what do those marks signify?"

She squared her shoulders, the way Druadaen had watched her do in Truce or Consequences just before uttering words she was loath, but honor bound, to speak. "It is a Lightstrider sign."

S'ythreni goggled. "Down here?"

"It is a sign of danger and distress," Umkhira continued without stopping. "The Lightstrider who made it is a young huntress, part of a tribe with which mine occasionally intermarries." She sighed, closed her eyes. "I may not ignore it."

Ahearn shrugged. "So?"

Her eyes opened into a wary squint. "I gave my word; you command my axe for a year."

Ahearn squinted back, as if he was insulted. "So you did. But if you think I am going to demand that you forsake a stripling of your own kind..." His voice was firm, but his eyes became pained and hard. "If you believe I would ask such a thing, I free you of your oath. I have no need of followers who think so ill of me. But first things first: Does the mark show where this young huntress is?"

Umkhira's voice suggested she had a hard time believing what she was hearing. "By leaving the marks beneath the new hash, she is indicating that it is the tribe that holds her."

"Well, then," Ahearn resolved with a slap of his knee. "Our paths continue together at least a little way further. I don't suppose she passed any information on this tribe or its chief?"

Umkhira shook her head.

But Elweyr was frowning. "I would appreciate it if you or Kaakhag would draw the tribe's new hash for me," he murmured. "It's been too dark for us humans to see it."

"Very well," Umkhira replied as her finger started tracing a sigil in the dust.

When it was done, Elweyr looked at it for several long, silent seconds. Then: "It's his."

"'His'?" repeated S'ythreni.

But Ahearn was rising slowly to his feet, face suddenly pale with rage and shock. "It can't be."

Elweyr just nodded. "But it is."

Druadaen looked back and forth between them. "You mean... the shaman who held the two of you as slaves?"

They nodded, then Ahearn turned to his friend. "How'd you even know to ask?"

"I didn't... not until Umkhira mentioned the young huntress. Then, I started seeing the pattern."

Ahearn raised an eyebrow. "Make sense, man. A young ur zhog hostage was part of a pattern that includes *us*?"

Elweyr nodded. "First, he's trying to learn how to read—or just speak—human language from me. Then from you. And now he keeps this young Lightstrider a prisoner rather than just killing her. That's why I suspected, Ahearn; it's part of a pattern. And the pattern points at what he's really after."

"This shaman is keeping captives to learn from peoples that know more about the surface world than he does." Druadaen frowned. "I think that's why he's situated himself here: he's trying to get control of a major passage that links the Underblack and the Undergloom. Which will increase in importance as the hordeing gets closer."

Umkhira frowned. "So he would collect tolls? But even if he could, the Red and the rest of the underkin could simply use other passages to the surface. I am told there are many."

Ahearn shook his head. "There are, but the one beyond these chambers is the widest and the most direct. No doubt some under-kin will forge their own paths, but they'll have to go through the Rot and that's a messy and uncertain business, at best."

S'ythreni's slow smile was half ironic, half admiring. "But if they're willing to pay a toll to the shaman, any Bent coming up from the Black will know they can reach the surface quickly and without a fight."

Druadaen nodded. "And that's where the shaman's knowledge of the surface becomes crucial. He not only provides them with the fastest route out of the tunnels; he can tell them the quickest way to get to choice places to raid and pillage. Meanwhile, the other Rot can emerge through other tunnels and become the guides or even leaders of the underkin, since they've spent the last ten years raiding it from time to time."

Umkhira was nodding as Kaakhag signed at her. "He says that this all sounds very well, but that the Red and the underkin will not know, or want, to arrive with coin to pay a toll. They will only have weapons, hunger, and the desire to kill. Anything."

Elweyr nodded. "All true. But if the shaman is clever—and this one is—he won't ask for payment in coin or goods. He'll want recruits. And with too many mouths to feed, the underkin will be happy to part with a few of their underlings. And then he turns around and sells the other end of the deal to the Rot by telling the tribes of the Undergloom that he can ensure that when the Red and other kin-eaters go a-hordeing to the surface, that he can prevent clashes by keeping them on an agreed-upon route. And all he needs from the Rot is their cooperation . . . and modest compensation."

S'ythreni cocked a long eyebrow. "More slaves? More service?"

Druadaen nodded. "He doesn't need the best warriors: just enough followers that he cannot be successfully challenged."

Kaakhag frowned, chin sinking into his hands as if his head were growing heavier by the second.

Elweyr nodded. "And that's when the shaman will start occupying and holding intersections, water sources, and access to better hunting areas."

Ahearn nodded. "And only then does he start charging tolls. Small, and payable in common goods, probably, but it would add up. Before long, he'd not only have more bodies than any three tribes, but more loot than any ten."

Druadaen leaned back. "And to ensure that he does not become a target of envy or assassination, he needs to grow his personal powers—both as a shaman and a mantic. He could become impossible to overthrow."

Umkhira frowned. "If all that is true, he will not join the Horde."

Kaakhag's hand signals were so hurried she could barely keep up. "Yes, you are right. Because even the most successful tribes will lose many warriors, but the shaman's numbers would be even greater when the Horde is finished."

Umkhira nodded. "If these guesses are rough shapes of the truth, then we have many reasons to strike him—the shaman himself—as quickly and as hard as we can." Kaakhag signaled emphatic agreement.

Ahearn nodded back. "Agreed." He glanced at Druadaen, who was frowning; he was less than certain that killing one figure could have such a decisive impact. "First rule of the Under, Dunarran: A group rarely survives the death of its leader. That leader's power and reputation is all that holds tribes and *hrugs* together in the first place. So if we mean to rescue Kaakhag's get-brother and the Lightstrider huntress, we can't just grab 'em and run."

Elweyr nodded. "If we don't get rid of the shaman, he'll keep his forces on our trail. We'll never get out alive. But if we kill him, the tribe will fly to pieces, the weak sticking to the strong like mites clinging to a fleeing dog." He frowned. "Problem is, we don't even know where the bastard is holed up."

Kaakhag gestured back toward the entry. "There are only a few chambers in this part of the Under big enough to hold a single tribe. So if he means to grow larger than that, he will need to claim more than one of them," Umkhira translated. "He will leave hashes on them as warnings to others. So if your guesses are right, he will be easy to find."

Umkhira looked up, added. "Besides, my kinswoman will have left more of her hidden signs. So if you are right about why the shaman has kept her, she will not be far from him."

S'ythreni stared around the group. "My worry is that right before arriving here, we killed at least one pair of his guards. So *he* may be looking for *us*, too."

Ahearn shook his head. "No. So far, we've been like a fly

dancing at the far strands of a spider's web. He's no doubt noticed a tug or two, but that's nothing strange in the Under. And as Umkhira pointed out, we've been careful to pilfer the bodies and leave 'em just as he'd expect passing raiders to do."

She smiled. "I guess I'll have to forgive you for agreeing to take all the 'useless' gear."

Ahearn smiled back. "See? Always a method to my madness."

"Always?"

"Well,... usually. Now, let's get fed and get to sleep. We've much to do, come the morrow."

CHAPTER TWENTY

After two days preparing, planning, and fruitlessly listening for the sounds of urzhen in the tunnel beyond the outer cavern, they crept forth, all unnecessary gear left in the hidden chamber. If they survived, they'd hopefully have the chance to return and reclaim it. But if they had to flee for their lives, every ounce that they left behind made it just that much more likely that they'd be able to outpace their pursuers.

Their plans were not so thorough or detailed as those they'd settled upon before prior attacks, simply because they were relying far more upon conjecture than information. Of the five suitable caverns Kaakhag knew to be in the area, three were both close to their chamber and close to each other—so close that if the shaman was residing in any of them, the tribe would need to maintain control over all three. If they didn't, any unoccupied cavern would be a handy place from which an adversary could mount an attack with a large force. That made Kaakhag's knowledge of Rot territory hashes particularly important; those were the only means whereby they might have some idea of which of the three—or the others—was the shaman's personal seat of power.

After passing the rat-gnawed remains of the two guards they had defeated days before, the group began moving quickly. Presuming they were in enemy territory meant that every passing minute increased the chance of bumping into various urzhen simply going about the tribe's daily business. The only way to reduce the odds of that occurring was to move more quickly, but the only way to achieve that was to somehow improve the visibility for the three humans. So they resorted to an expedient that they had previously used in a more limited fashion and only for conducting attacks: small patches of glowing lichen, now affixed to each of their backs. That enabled the humans to see where Kaakhag and Umkhira were leading them and also allowed Ahearn to remain at the back with Raun, whose ears were their best protection against surprises from behind.

After half an hour, in which they passed through several four- and five-way intersections, Umkhira called for a brief halt to warn them that, according to what Kaakhag had been told, they were now nearing the outer guard points for the first of the three caves that could house the greater part of the shaman's tribe. But when they continued on, they passed those points without encountering any living creatures and so, followed the tunnel all the way to their first destination.

It was a single immense chamber rather than a complex of sizable caverns, and it showed signs of recent use, but only as a lager, or maybe a meeting place. The subtle spoor that would have marked it as jealously held territory—debris, scat, cooking circles—was absent. Since it was also the site closest to the tunnel that led down into the Black, Druadaen wondered aloud if this might be where the shaman met the underkin to parley. Kaakhag and the other two humans simply shrugged; there was no way to know.

Another ten minutes of walking brought them to a fork in the tunnel. Kaakhag studied the stone around that split, looked up both passages, and then led them into the smaller of the two. Better to assess that one first, he explained, since its size made it the less likely candidate.

They moved barely ten minutes in that direction before Kaakhag called a halt to their cautious forward creeping and turned about. They hadn't encountered any outlying guard posts or defense barriers, the tribal hashes were sparse, and Umkhira had seen none of her kinswoman's secret signs.

Upon returning to the fork, they entered the larger passage and, within minutes, encountered clear signs that they were approaching the shaman's seat of power. Kaakhag pointed out the significant increase in tribal hashes and Umkhira reported seeing the huntress's signs. Other passages branched off, but Kaakhag did not even bother to investigate them; he knew them to be minor connectors to other tunnels.

Ten minutes later, he called for a halt and went ahead on his own. He returned within the minute, motioning that the time had come to cover the glowing lichen markers on their backs. Umkhira began translating the gestures that only she could see, now. "He says that there are four Rot up ahead, guarding the entrance to the main tunnel into this cave complex. One of them is very large, probably a kosh."

Druadaen frowned. "I do not know that word."

"It's slang for 'kagh urzh.' Means he's a beefy fellow," Ahearn explained. "Born so large that his chief made sure he had enough food and training to grow into a big, powerful warrior. Better weapons and armor, too." Ahearn make a *tsk* noise. "But what worries me is that there are four watching the entrance."

Umkhira murmured. "Why? We expected a large number patrolling any entry to the shaman's seat of power." She paused, then added Kaakhag's comment. "You claimed Elweyr's mancery can overcome that many."

"Yes," Elweyr muttered, annoyed. "But while doing so, I can't move quickly. I'll have to keep concentrating on the thaumate."

"Why this time and not the others?" Umkhira asked.

Ahearn interceded for his friend. "If he wanted, Elweyr could dazzle this lot until their eyes crossed and they fell over. But here, we can't afford the sound of them hitting the ground or awakening later to discover themselves all passed out in one great heap. The dimmest Bent ever whelped would still know to sound an alarm."

"So," Umkhira said after a pause, "we must use the same methods we did at the first intersection we had to cross, the day we entered."

Elweyr nodded. "Yes. The first guard had to be dazed and *held* that way. If he'd just fallen over unconscious, the second guard wouldn't have stepped over to check on him. He would have sounded an alarm."

Druadaen saw the difficulty. "But here, you have to hold four in that kind of daze at the same time. So that they will have no memory of us passing."

Ahearn nodded. "All of which takes more concentration and more magic—"

"*Manas*," Elweyr corrected with a long-suffering sigh.

"*Manas*, magic, power, hoo-doo. Call it what you will but holding those Bent unaware will cost you dear."

S'ythreni's voice suggested more than mere practical concern. "Elweyr, is it safe to spend so much?"

He answered in a tone that was the equivalent of a shrug. "Thaumancy doesn't personally drain the wielder the way other mantic disciplines do. But the less *manas* I have left, the less likely I am to succeed at constructing additional thaumates."

"'Constructing additional thaumates'?" repeated Umkhira slowly.

"That's wizard-talk for 'cast more spells,'" supplied Ahearn. "Now, let's be about finishing this business. Do either of you see fireglow coming from behind the entry they're guarding?"

"Yes," S'ythreni and Umkhira answered in unintended unison. The latter added, "Kaakhag says it is not bright enough for work, so many will be sleeping."

"Good," Ahearn muttered. "Now, be mindful of your noise. We'll creep along so that Elweyr can befuddle any guards before we get to 'em. But if one of them manages to yell out, then it's all lights and all speed following Kaakhag into what lies beyond. As the only one who's lived in this part of the Undergloom, he's got the best chance of getting us straight to the shaman."

S'ythreni's mutter was dark and tense. "I just hope he's right about there being side passages out of this place."

Ahearn sighed. "He says there will be, and that's good enough for me." But the swordsman's resigned tone seemed to add, *and how could we ever hope to know if he's wrong?* "Now: Any more questions?" Silence. "Well then, ask favor of your gods and let's get on with it."

Getting through the main entry into the complex was almost anticlimactic. They waited as Elweyr, face coated in a heavy layer of char, leaned one eye around the corner and went completely still. He stayed that way so long that Druadaen began to wonder if his dazing mancery could rebound back upon himself.

But eventually, he waved the others on with the hand he'd kept back behind the corner. With Druadaen now bringing up the rear, they approached casually but remained watchful; if Elweyr's control slipped, they would have to attack swiftly.

But they simply walked past the dumbstruck urzhen, whose eyes were blank and unblinking. Umkhira and Kaakhag still led the way since both might be briefly mistaken as belonging in this place. Ahearn was right behind, sword in one hand, Elweyr's upper arm in the other; he seemed to be supporting and steering his friend. Raun padded silently behind, followed by S'ythreni, who was ready to step out and bring her crossbow to bear.

Although there were no fires in the tunnel itself, the collective glow emanating from side caverns seemed reasonably bright to Druadaen's dark-adjusted eyes. Nearing one of the larger light sources, Umkhira signaled for a halt, then touched an eyelid. The others peered ahead.

Two guards flanked the entry, leaning on the wall. Ahearn looked apologetically toward Elweyr, who waved off the concern: their plan presumed that his mancery would be needed frequently at the outset. While slaves of the tribe, the two humans had noted the shaman's unusual prudence, which had made their escape that much more challenging. It was he who had convinced the prior chief to place small, separate watches near each large chamber, not just the main entry.

Ahearn and Elweyr had expected no less here and so, had planned accordingly. Once again, Elweyr reached forth a steady hand, eyes focusing someplace well beyond the dank cave walls. After a moment, he nodded and they moved slowly forward. They peered in cautiously as they drew abreast of the entry; the cavern was high-roofed and immense, at least twoscore prone urzhen scattered about, either sleeping or lounging.

But one very young one was awake and came sneaking toward the now-motionless guards. He or she stared at them for several seconds, bewildered, before even noticing Kaakhag and Umkhira. The little one's eyes grew very wide and round and she/he scampered back into the cave, whispering loudly.

"Quickly!" Umkhira whispered as Kaakhag gestured for them all to follow. No sooner had they swept around the next bend in the tunnel than they heard flat feet come slap-slap-slapping out of the entry they'd just left behind. After a few moments of silence, a higher-pitched mutter was audible, but began fading; apparently, the speaker was heading back into the cavern.

Druadaen made ready to move, but Kaakhag held up his hand, cocked his ear to listen.

They all heard what came next: a hissing remonstration, a meaty smack, and a young howl that was quickly muffled.

Umkhira translated as Kaakhag's hands resumed moving even as he did. "It was unlikely the whelp would be believed, but it was best to be sure."

"I quite agree," muttered Ahearn, wiping sweat off his brow. "Onward, then."

The second cavern dormitory they passed had only one guard. Elweyr breathed a sigh of relief. "Well, this should be a little easier." He turned to Umkhira. "Get as close as you can. Signal when you're ready to move."

"What are you going to—?"

"This one's alone. If he's found unconscious, the assumption—including his own—will be that he fell asleep on his watch. Stand ready to catch him."

She courted the shadows to get within fifteen feet of the Rot, then flashed her palm in readiness.

Elweyr reached out, frowned as if he was trying to perform a balancing act with his eyes closed, concentrated even harder.

The solitary guard yawned, reached back to steady himself against the wall. He slumped, his weapon hanging loosely in his hand. As he half slid down the wall, Umkhira stepped in to catch the guard before easing him down into a sitting position. He was already snoring faintly.

As they crept past the open cavern—almost twice the size of the other—Ahearn leaned toward his friend. "Good work, Elweyr. Always said you were the finest mancer I ever met."

"So it looks to you." Ahearn stared at him. "I'm exhausted already. A truly accomplished thaumantic would carry off what I have as if it was all just a few steps in an easy dance. But today, every step is like pushing through cold treacle."

The third chamber was smaller and unguarded, but one glance inside told them that it was not merely another general sleeping area; this was more like a barracks. Large forms, some of them not urzhen in outline, slouched or slept, slaves nearby. Ahearn waved Kaakhag to move past; they were undetected, and they hadn't much further to go.

But the big, mute urzh either didn't notice, or chose not to. He closed his eyes, lifted his head, nostrils flaring. A pained look came over his face. He signed briefly. Druadaen knew what it signified before Umkhira could translate. "He smells his brother in there. Probably one of the slaves."

Ahearn moved slightly closer to Kaakhag. "Now listen: I'd want to run in there, too. No waiting; just get him and be gone. But if you do that, then this is where our fight begins. And probably ends. And even if we're lucky enough to get away, the shaman would send his hounds after us. And what would become of the young Lightstrider?" The urzh looked back at him, frowning but neither surprised nor angry. "You said it yourself, Kaakhag; the only safe end to this is to send the shaman to whatever creedland will have him and for us to slip out the escape passages he's likely to have back near his own cave."

After a long, silent moment, the urzh nodded and moved back to the head of the group. Ahearn drew a deep breath, released it slowly, and followed the big Rot deeper into the complex.

CHAPTER TWENTY-ONE

The shaman's seat of power was located at the far end of the cave complex. But even if it hadn't been, they'd still have known it for what it was.

The entry had clearly been carved out of the solid rock, with slowly burning torches in crude cressets to either side. The opening itself was higher than it was wide and had a dogleg bend just five feet within. And its solitary guard was an immense creature that resembled a bizarre mix of urzh and perhaps ur gaban, which Ahearn and Elweyr alternatively called grubbers, grabbers or gobblers.

However, this being's faint similarity to that small species did not go beyond its facial characteristics. It was at least eight feet tall, with arms proportionally as long and muscled as an orang's. The group held their breath as Elweyr exerted his now familiar thaumantic power upon it. And they all exhaled in relief as the spell—or thaumate—proved so effective that the towering monster simply lay down, curled up, and promptly went to sleep.

Directly in front of the entrance.

"Well, *that's* not very helpful," S'ythreni sneered as the group approached. She glanced at Ahearn, produced what looked like a pin. "Shall I do the honors?"

He held his sword ready, gestured at the snoring creature with the other. "By all means. I don't fancy fooling with a *kaghab*."

The aeosti checked the being's limbs, found a loose fold of flesh in its upper arm, inserted the needle.

Druadaen started. "Won't that make him wake up?"

She withdrew the pin. "On the contrary. It will make sure that he *doesn't.*"

Kaakhag grunt-laughed, inspected the entrance closely. Ahearn stepped away from the kaghab, looked at the big urzh, who shook his head.

S'ythreni sighed. "Let me guess: he never heard about, let alone entered, this part of the complex."

Ahearn shrugged. "As he told us, when he escaped, the last chief still refused to leave any forces in these caves. So, we go with the simplest plan: run in fast, fight hard, and use everything in our bag of tricks until we get rid of the beady-eyed bugger running the show. As soon as that's done"—Druadaen almost laughed at the certainty in Ahearn's tone—"whoever's closest to the entry stands watch there. Best if it's someone with a bow"—he glanced at Druadaen—"because we need to keep the tunnel clear if we're going to backtrack a bit to fetch Kaakhag's get-brother." The big urzh nodded vigorously. "Anything to add?" Ahearn finished, looking around the group.

They shook their heads as Elweyr passed out a vial to each as they crouched in the shadows. Druadaen stared at it as the others began anointing their weapons with the contents: a faintly yellow fluid.

"What is it?" Druadaen asked, holding it out.

"Poison. Adder venom." Elweyr answered. "The color is from the fixative that will keep it on your weapons. Give it a few seconds to set," Elweyr answered.

Druadaen started at the explanation, then glanced at S'ythreni, then down at the small, flapped pocket to which she'd returned the needle. As grim understanding grew, he stared hard at the other two humans. "No one mentioned poison when we were making our plans."

"Hoped we wouldn't need it," Ahearn muttered as he started dabbing it on several arrows." He glanced at Elweyr. "Is that all we've got?"

The thaumantic shrugged one shoulder. "Couldn't make any more."

Druadaen hissed, "You *made* it?"

"Well, I'm also an alchemist."

Druadaen opened his mouth but the overlapping surprises kept any coherent sound from coming out.

Ahearn saved him the trouble. "We haven't the time for this. Yes, he's an alchemist and a damned fine one. Yes, alchemists make poisons. And yes, we need to use it now. Much as I regret it."

"Well . . . at least you regret it."

The others all stared at him. "He regrets having to *waste* it," S'ythreni murmured with a small smile.

Druadaen stared at her, then at Ahearn, who held out the poisoned arrows. "Here. Don't rub them together."

Without thinking, Druadaen leaned away. "I am no assassin!"

"And down here, ye're no soldier, either, Dunarran." Ahearn jerked his head toward the final chamber. "You think this lot would scruple to do otherwise, if our places were reversed?" He pushed the arrows at Druadaen. "We can argue later. Now, it's time to do our job."

Druadaen did not reach for the arrows. "If I take them, it does not mean I will use them. Not unless we are in dire need."

Ahearn rolled his eyes. "Now you *do* sound the fool—and without even a hint of the philosopher. We *are* in dire need, every second we tarry in this place. I'd have used poison before if we'd had enough. But now's no time to be saving it for later, nor for you to get dainty on us. When we pass through that opening, we can be certain of only one advantage: surprise. So if we use these quickly enough"—he shook the arrows in his fist—"it just might make the difference between us living and dying. So you'll use 'em, or you'll answer to me if any one of this group dies because you didn't." He pushed the arrows at Druadaen again.

Who accepted them as if they were vipers. Which, given the source of the poison, was not entirely inaccurate.

Ahearn emitted a satisfied grunt. "You ready?" he asked Elweyr.

The mantic nodded and produced a small metal ball from a flapped pouch. He touched it; the top sprang open, like a round six-fanged mouth. Inside was an even smaller ball, made of crystal and clutched by a small clasp.

Elweyr removed the crystal sphere. As he did, Ahearn shifted to stand behind him, lifted his traveling cloak as if to shield him from something.

Elweyr's eyes closed, he folded his hand into a fist that

concealed the sphere. A moment passed—and then his fingers were suddenly glowing. "Eyes," he muttered. Druadaen did not know what he was referring to... but discovered an instant later; the thaumantic unfolded his fist to reveal a blinding kernel of light resting on his palm.

Druadaen spun his head away from the painfully bright glare. As the green-blue afterimage faded, he peripherally saw Elweyr return the crystal sphere to the clasp and reseal the top of the metal ball.

Darkness rushed back in at them. Ahearn lowered his cloak. Kaakhag uncovered his eyes, glanced behind him, nodded reassuringly.

"Well and quickly done, my friend," Ahearn muttered to Elweyr. "No one saw, so no one's the wiser." He looked at his sword, tested a two-handed hold on the hand-and-a-half grip, then gazed slowly around the group. "Remember: make your first strike to any flesh you can reach. A graze with this poison is as good as a blade to the heart. Let's go."

After the dogleg, the entry ran straight back, with firelight from the far end illuminating it enough for S'ythreni's sight to be more helpful than the urzhen's. While the Bent ability to see heat allowed them to operate in total darkness, it came at the cost of detail. With enough light, the aeosti's eyes were far more likely to detect the thin strands or slight seams that might trigger an alarm—or traps and snares.

As they neared the far end of the tunnel, though, she faded back to the rear again, allowing the two urzh to move back to the front, Ahearn at their backs. "Ready your bows," he muttered over his shoulder. Druadaen felt a pulse of fear as he sheathed his sword. Yes, he'd had a bow in hand during their earlier melees in the deep. But on those occasions, they had known the numbers they'd be facing and in what positions. Here, if they were suddenly confronted by a pack of Bent at arm's length, he'd have nothing more than a thin curve of wood and bone with which to fend them off.

"On three, then," Ahearn murmured. "One, two..."

Druadaen didn't really hear the "three." If fear and hesitation had been put aside, it was just a vague sound that marked an abrupt transition: from routine perception to the keen—yet time-slowed—sensory acuity of combat.

The two urzhen bounded forward into the chamber, Umkhira coming close enough to one of the enemy—either reclining or sleeping—to kill him with a single heavy chop.

Ahearn ran in, veering slightly to the left. Raun followed at his heels until the fighter pointed at the mass of prone figures against that wall, loosing a sharp whistle as he did. The dog shot toward them as if he'd been launched from a catapult.

Elweyr stepped into the room, manipulated the metal ball, sent it rolling swiftly over the unusually smooth floor.

As he did, Druadaen came up on the thaumantic's right, drawing his composite bow. S'ythreni was on Elweyr's other flank, her own weapon ready. They sought, and quickly found, two targets in the wide lane that the three in the front rank had left open by pushing to either side as they entered.

S'ythreni's crossbow slapped sharply and one of the first rising figures—clearly a kosh—was hit in his thigh; his skirt of armored hide pleating, hanging loose for comfort, had failed to intercept the quarrel. He staggered, fell to that knee, started to rise, but then convulsed as the poison began to do its work.

Druadaen had drawn down on another rising figure when he realized that he still had the same unpoisoned shaft nocked. He hesitated: Shoot quickly or with a poisoned arrow? Prejudice against poison fused with urgency; he fired what he had ready...yet as soon as he'd loosed the arrow and saw it drive the second kosh to the ground, he was glad he had inadvertently saved the poisoned one.

Because a new target was rising...and continued to rise until it loomed even taller than the kaghab that had guarded the entry. This creature's face wasn't ur gaban or urzhen but was decidedly asymmetric; the deformed and oddly small head looked down at him from atop a massive body weighing well over five hundred pounds.

The next thing Druadaen was aware of was a second, and poisoned, shaft leaping off his bow as he shouted, "Monster!" because he didn't know what else to call the being. Hardly noticing the impact of the arrow, it started forward, a length of timber swinging up in its grip—

Elweyr's metal ball stopped rolling; with a sharp *clack!*, both the lower and upper halves sprung open. On the bottom, six legs snapped outward, fixing it in place as the six segments on top flipped back, revealing the actinic crystal sphere.

Brilliant light flooded the chamber. The "monster" flung up a massive, stub-fingered hand to cover its eyes. Druadaen saw his chance, brought another poisoned shaft over his shoulder, loosed it. As he watched for any sign that the venom was taking effect, he nocked another arrow and noticed that even more mammoth hulks were rising, bellowing, shielding their eyes. And he thought: *Ahearn was right; we* don't *have enough poison.*

Peripherally, he caught glimpses of the others:

—S'ythreni cursing as she fought to pull the lathes of her crossbow back more rapidly;

—Kaakhag's axe rising and falling, trailing red mist as it cut deep into urzhen who'd been lounging instead of standing at their posts;

—Umkhira and Ahearn sweeping deeper into the room on the left, where the majority of the kosh were still struggling to shrug into their armor while also protecting their eyes;

—and just beyond them, Raun as he leapt from one rising urzhen silhouette to the next, teeth making dull ripping sounds as he went.

Druadaen was about to loose a third poisoned shaft when the first and largest of the "monsters" began to stumble. "Two hits is enough," he snapped at S'ythreni as he shifted his own aim.

Just as her crossbow cracked again. "Now you tell me," she hissed.

Druadaen had the next closest behemoth lined up, but this one had a cured hide covering most of its torso. But the crude kirtle did not reach to the knees. He adjusted low, fired, saw the shaft go between its legs, cursed, was mollified when a kosh shrieked behind it. But it was still lost time and a lost shaft.

Druadaen had drawn on the monster once again when it abruptly cast out its free hand, as if suddenly blind. "Leave him for blades," Elweyr muttered loudly across the gap between them.

Druadaen shifted his aim to the third, and apparently last, of the huge creatures and let fly at its unarmored chest. The shaft hit and went deep, dark blood welling up, but the creature shrugged it off as if it was a nuisance.

As Druadaen readied his last poisoned shaft, he saw an armored kaghab moving rapidly through the nearly equipped mass of urzhen. "S'ythreni—" he started, just as her crossbow clapped sharply and the bolt hummed into the long-armed Bent.

It quickly recovered from the impact but began tilting sideways as it resumed moving. Druadaen released his second arrow at the last of the larger monsters and, a moment later, it too began evincing similar unsteadiness.

He considered: Continue to use his bow or go to his sword? Peripheral vision showed Umkhira and Ahearn hacking and goring the monster's blinded cousin; it had already absorbed enough damage to kill any three humans. Druadaen drew another arrow, aimed over his companions and loosed at its head.

The monster moved erratically; the shaft skimmed past its ear. He reached for another arrow, glimpsed Raun and Kaakhag on opposite flanks embroiled with the urzhen who were just steps ahead of the large, central mass of their fellows. Druadaen drew, fired, saw the arrow hit the monster square in its chin. Although the wound did not seem serious, the monster roared and grabbed the long shaft, tugging to pull it free of the bone. During that brief pause, Ahearn glanced toward Elweyr, who shook his head: still no sign of the shaman.

Druadaen cursed silently, dropped his bow, hoped it would survive underfoot in the general melee soon to be joined, hoped the same for himself, cross-drew his blades...and watched as a great number of the charging urzhen abruptly slowed, as if each one of them was now burdened by a great load of rocks.

"This won't last long," Elweyr muttered. His voice was becoming strained.

Druadaen rushed into the suddenly paralyzed center of the enemy, hoping to intercept enough of the unaffected ones to buy time for the two flanks of his own force to rejoin and form a skirmish line. Otherwise, they risked being swarmed, surrounded individually, and defeated in detail.

The closest Rot was swinging a mace wildly, a buckler almost forgotten in its off hand. Druadaen lunged, which caused the urzh to check its headlong charge and swing before he was ready. Druadaen leaned away from the arc described by the mace, then rolled his wrist as he swayed back in, cutting low for the inside of his enemy's off-side calf. The urzh howled, tried stepping back, but fell, the muscle severed.

A moment later, the monster Elweyr had blinded finally toppled, his backward fall crushing two of the Rot beneath him. Umkhira and Ahearn glanced over, saw Druadaen's position, swung toward him. Seeing that, he cheated a step to the right to close the distance to Kaakhag, who was likely to prove the weakest part of whatever line they could form. Like many urzhen, his training and choice of weapon were suited to his temperament: to attack ferociously and so overwhelm his opponent that he had little need for defense. At least Kaakhag was not one of the Bent who insisted on rejecting a shield in favor of wielding a two-handed weapon.

Ironically, Druadaen spent the next half minute being very glad for the Outrider emphasis upon fighting with two weapons rather than a shield. Light-footed evasion, dodges, and fast flurries of parries were all that was keeping him alive. Occasionally, he managed to catch a slow or overextended arm or leg during one of the rare moments when he was not repelling attacks. But step by step, he was being forced back, unable to hold his ground against so many. Before long, he would tire and without having inflicted many casualties.

What he saw from the corners of his eyes was not reassuring; his companions were even more beset than he was. Ahearn was not only skilled with a bastard sword but was surprisingly quick and agile for so large a man. However, he too was having to fall back slowly to keep Umkhira on his flank.

She was swift enough with her shield but had never been taught to use it to deflect, rather than directly block, the axes and maces that were hammering at her now. Her face showed pain and weariness as she tried to reach out effectively with her one-handed axe. Kaakhag was only engaged with two enemies presently, but his skills were markedly inferior to Umkhira's: he, too, was being driven back.

And the shaman had yet to bring his own powers to bear upon them: a very bad sign, given that they were becoming increasingly vulnerable with every passing second.

As if conjured by Druadaen's misgivings, their true foe finally made his presence felt: the sluggish urzhen lagging behind the center of their line were suddenly freed of Elweyr's burdening mancery. They charged forward to join the others already forcing back the intruders' uneven and shaky line.

A moment later, a small opening in the far wall of the cavern—little more than a crevice—began vomiting a slow stream of kosh: fully armored, weapons at the ready. The only reason they were not emerging twice as fast was that many had shields, which forced them to twist sideways as they exited whatever chamber was behind them.

As his attackers turned to confirm the arrival of this reserve force, Druadaen leaped forward, cross-cutting one, rolling his wrist and elbow to quickly redirect his sword point into another—and then gave ground, using the break in tempo to peer closely at the wall near where the kosh were emerging.

S'ythreni confirmed what he thought he saw: "Back wall has slits."

Elweyr cursed, and Druadaen knew enough about mancery to understand why. With the shaman positioned to see and send his powers through a murder hole, Elweyr had no way to be certain of hitting him and would be unable to ascertain the effects if he did. So, if they couldn't figure out some way to attack him without fighting through his still-deploying forces...

Elweyr shouted, "Stand close! Now!"

Druadaen and his companions all backpedaled toward the mantic; even Raun broke off and ran for the outward-facing cluster.

As he arrived, Elweyr brought both hands together in a ring, creases stark in his face. His eyes went blank for a moment—

Then, as they flicked open in profound confusion, a screeching cackle echoed out through the murder slits in the back wall. "Godsblocks!" swore Elweyr, whose rapid blink looked more perplexed than aggravated.

"Again!" demanded Ahearn.

"Trying," the mantic murmured as the urzhen crashed into the four on the line. S'ythreni stood behind them, crossbow aimed at the rear wall. Elweyr repeated his gesture, but the same result: nothing—except this time, he shot a rapid glance at Druadaen. In the course of an instant, his expression transformed from confusion, to fury, to dread, and finally, resignation.

"Elweyr?" Ahearn howled.

Another cackle came from the murder slits, followed by threats in mangled Commerce, promising that they would now feel burning ants beneath their skin, be unable to fight or even stand...

But nothing happened.

The same voice unleashed an infuriated screech, yelling profanities at urzhen deities.

In the dark behind one of the slits, Druadaen saw a shift in the shadows. While parrying, he shouted, "S'ythreni!"

She was already head down over her weapon, smiling. "Behold the price of blasphemy," she whispered as her ironpith crossbow discharged with a sharp slap. The quarrel flashed straight through the slit.

The resulting scream stopped the Bent in mid-attack. When the scream became desperate shrieking, some of them wavered. Several of the kosh, the last that had emerged from the secret chamber, ran back through the crevice, shouting for their leader.

"On me!" Ahearn hissed as he shifted to the left rear, getting the group clear of the entry. "Stay out of their way and make a half circle, backs to the wall."

They did, Kaakhag trailing a generous amount of blood from a deep cut in his left thigh. But as he limped to comply, he also nodded his approval at Ahearn's orders.

The shaman's shrieking became convulsive, then spastic, and finally transitioned into a keening gargle.

The urzhen in the chamber—well over two score of them—had already begun to glance at each other fearfully when the kosh that had entered the rear chamber reemerged at a run, shouting and swinging wide of the intruders as they made for the exit.

Druadaen could only make out two of the words they yelled "—is dying!—" before all the Bent in the chamber broke ranks in an urgent rush to flee the cavern.

CHAPTER TWENTY-TWO

"Well," said S'ythreni in a fey tone, "I never thought I'd wind up being an urzhen god's hand of vengeance."

Ahearn wiped sweat from his brow when the last of the retreating footfalls gave way to silence. He positioned himself to one side of the entry, motioned Druadaen toward the other, then nodded at Elweyr. "Good on you, stopping that bastard's god! He was ready to plow us under, he was."

Elweyr was frowning, looking among the bodies. "I didn't stop him or his god," he muttered.

"Well, then it's our great good luck the old swine was muffing his miracles."

"He wasn't muffing anything."

Ahearn glared at his friend. "Well, then what the blazes stopped him?"

Elweyr looked at Druadaen. "It was him."

"What?" Druadaen asked in unison with Ahearn.

"How could that be?" the swordsman continued. "You said the Dunarran hasn't the smallest bit of mancery about him."

The thaumantic shook his head. "I know what I said. And I stand by it." He glanced toward Druadaen again. Sheepishly, this time. "I checked, shortly after we met you at the tavern. Just a precaution early on, you understand."

Druadaen *didn't* understand and didn't like it, but nodded;

at the moment, he wanted to hear what else the thaumantic had to say.

"I am certain it wasn't that shaman; I've tried cases with enough of them to know . . . as you're well aware. Their power doesn't come from either elemental or protean *manas*. You can feel it comes from somewhere—or some*thing*—else and is arriving for a specific purpose."

Elweyr shook his head. "But here, there was no opposing power of any kind. Nothing that worked *against* my thaumate. The moment its outer edge reached him"—he pointed at Druadaen—"it was gone. It didn't even fold in on itself, the way a failed or broken construct does. It just winked away. Instantly."

Ahearn was irate. "Well, what the hells would cause that?"

"The hells might be where you'd have to make your inquiries," Elweyr said.

"Do we have the time for this?" S'ythreni sighed. Umkhira grunted and nodded profound approval of the aeosti's point.

"In fact," Ahearn snapped, "we don't dare *not* to take time for this. If Elweyr is right, then we need to know when his mancery will work and when it won't. Or are you two happy to live in ignorance and roll the dice every time?"

The aeosti and the urzh did something either rarely did: closed their mouths tightly and looked away . . . and in Umkhira's case, to start in surprise. "He's gone," she muttered.

"What? Who?" Ahearn asked irritably.

"Kaakhag."

Ahearn started to scan the cavern, but Umkhira shook her head. "He left a trail." She pointed: an unbroken spatter of blood led from where they'd clustered against the wall and promptly mixed into the drops shed by the wounded Rot they had routed.

"Well, that ties it," Ahearn fumed. "We'd best go get him right—"

"No," interrupted Umkhira. "*I* will get him. Any Rot who did not already see me in here may stop for at least a few moments, wondering what a Lightstrider is doing in the Undergloom. But if they see a human, they will simply attack."

Ahearn stared at her for a moment. When she did not move to go after Kaakhag, he shrugged, "Well?"

Umkhira shook her head. "It would be unwise for me to go after him so soon. Right now, the tribe is either still learning of what has happened or is in blind terror of us: we reached and killed their leader in a single battle.

"But if I go to their tunnels and they identify me as one of the intruders, I had better be able to smite them by the dozen, or I will seem vulnerable. That will turn their terror to rage, and they will come back at us. Quickly."

"They will anyway," S'ythreni observed.

"Yes, but it could be a quarter of an hour before they are calm enough to reflect upon what they know about us, what they don't know, and how to respond."

Druadaen frowned. "And what of your kinswoman?"

Umkhira nodded. "She is already here." She pointed at the crevice leading to the almost-secret chamber. "I heard her during the combat, and I have tarried here too long." She began to stride to the back wall.

S'ythreni finished recocking her crossbow and held it in one hand as she drew a shortsword with her other. "I'm coming with you."

"I am safe on my own."

S'ythreni shrugged, then smiled. "Yes, but are the valuables?"

Umkhira blinked. "You are bold indeed if by that you mean to question my honor, aeosti."

S'ythreni rolled her eyes. "And you are being foolish indeed if you think I'm being serious, Lightstrider." She slipped around Umkhira. "We need to make a quick search, and only you and I have the eyes for that job. Let the humans pick through the bodies and guard the entry until Kaakhag returns."

Umkhira, frowning uncertainly, followed S'ythreni, muttering to herself.

Ahearn spat. "Well, this is a fine fix. I swear, Dunarran, if you knew of this and didn't tell—"

"There seems to be much questioning of honesty, at present," Druadaen interrupted. "Let us not leave this chamber with a debt of honor to be settled between us, Ahearn."

Who started, then studied him with narrowed eyes. "You'd lose. Badly."

Druadaen shrugged. "Even if my courage was wanting, I would not tolerate the suggestion that I might have withheld such information. Bring it up again, and I shall ask for satisfaction. In the meantime, I have pertinent questions for Elweyr." He turned to the thaumantic. "Clearly I do not disrupt all your thaumates. You have invoked many since we came into the Under."

Ahearn visibly shook off his anger and raised an eyebrow. "Now there's a point I should have seen right away."

Druadaen elected not to express his profound agreement, keeping his focus on Elweyr, instead. "There must be a reason for both outcomes. You are the only among us who have the knowledge and senses that might discern some pattern under which both might occur. Do you have any speculations on that?"

Elweyr's eyes narrowed and he started nodding. "There *is* a pattern, Druadaen, but the key to it isn't what happened here in the Under." He rightly perceived the complete lack of understanding in both men's eyes. "What happened in Menara is *also* consistent with this. Remember when I couldn't create the protective effect in the tavern? And then Bannef couldn't bring off whatever mancery he'd intended? I thought I'd failed, and we thought that Shaananca had projected something to stop Bannef from outside the tavern."

Ahearn nodded. "But maybe it was this fellow, all along. Bollocksing the spells."

Elweyr winced at the term "spells" but nodded. "He was within the boundaries of all those thaumates. But all the others since then—the dazes I imposed upon all he guards we've encountered so far—did not have him within the field of their expression. Or on the path between the mantic and their attempted construct."

Ahearn shrugged. "So that's good news, yeh?"

Elweyr was rubbing his chin. "It is. In fact, it could be very good news. But I have to think on that. Now, who's going to look through these bodies?"

"You and Druadaen."

"Me?" Druadaen raised an eyebrow.

Ahearn grinned. "You'll be close enough to help if I hear the buggers coming back. And searching through a slew of bodies is different than going over one or two dead. Separate skill. Learn from Elweyr. He's the best. Aren't you, chum?"

Elweyr only shrugged. That was probably as close as he would come to agreeing with his friend's hyperbole.

As they sped through their grisly task, Druadaen watched the thaumantic, who had a clear routine: first assess weapons, then anything on the fingers and neck, and lastly the contents of pockets and pouches. But what Elweyr's trained eyes could read almost instantly Druadaen found himself puzzling over for much longer. Partly because he was frequently distracted by the bodies themselves.

Although the great majority of the urzh were Rots like Kaakhag, there were others that were clearly of the Red. And the difference was not restricted to the color of their sclerae. Many of their eyes were not only larger, but almost as round as a tarsier's. Their jaws were either furnished with tusklike incisors and more dramatically prognathous or had smaller jaws with a wider mouth jammed with a crooked mix of sharklike teeth interspersed with fangs as thin and pointed as those on an anglerfish. Almost all of them had twisted, tapering ears akin to the ur gaban, but in many cases, were almost perpendicular to the side of their head.

He encountered two other creatures which, despite their bipedal physiology, looked as though they had interbred with animals. "Are these Beastkynde?" Druadaen asked, using the term that he'd most frequently encountered during long hours reading in the Archive Recondite.

"Shifters, you mean?" Elweyr answered. "No. Shifters won't associate with the Bent. And vice versa."

Druadaen kept looking at the strange faces, which from some angles looked almost like a short-muzzled canine, and from others like a weasel or hyena. "And these are—Bent?"

"Yes... although not one of the ur species. They're called hyek. Not usually found in the Under, but during winter, anything is possible." He saw that Druadaen was edging toward the largest of the small-headed, immense-bodied monstrosities that had barely succumbed to two poisoned arrows. "Don't bother with the blugners; they won't have anything you want."

"Is blugner another term for... er, a giant?"

Elweyr stifled a laugh. "A giant? Gods, no. According to what I've been told, they aren't big enough. And no, they aren't Bent."

"Why?"

Elweyr shrugged. "Well, they don't consider themselves Bent, and the Bent feel similarly. You can call them underkin; that refers to any race that lives down here and walks on two legs."

He pulled a ring off another blugner's bloody finger, which was shaped more like a stump than a digit, yet furnished with a nail the length and shape of a talon. He glanced back at the body. "But blugner are more often referred to as Deepkin." He smiled at Druadaen's quizzical look. "They're the most dangerous and mysterious of the underkin. No one knows much about them. They're not even related to the Bent, so far as anyone can tell. Take a closer look at your blugner, there where the kirtle has separated, and you'll see what I mean."

Druadaen did, and was confused for a moment, distracted by the exposed chest. He wondered why any creature with just two arms would have multiple sets of pectorals—until he realized they were teats. Bile rushed up; he swallowed it back down.

Elweyr nodded at the barrellike torso. "Those dugs mark it as a sow. Which is an apt term for how they whelp and raise their young. No, keep your questions for later; we have to get back to work. I doubt we have much time left."

Druadaen worked for another five minutes, turning over bodies, rifling through pockets and pouches, trying not to feel like a bandit...but quite aware that, from the perspective of the Bent, that was exactly what he was. Of course, it was no different than what the urzh did to each other—as Kaakhag pointed out every time they had bodies to search—but that hardly mattered: each being's context was their own. And Druadaen's kept telling him that since entering the Under, he had not just traveled far down into the earth but might have sunk even further than that as a person.

He returned to the door with his meager findings: mostly pie-sliced pieces of copper coins and inferior billon: too much copper, too little silver. Elweyr had done a little better, but not much.

Ahearn smirked at both their palmfuls of coin fragments, glanced at the room behind them. "I remember when all those weapons, all that gear, was pure treasure. Now, we just turn our noses up at it."

"Well," S'ythreni said as she emerged from the crevice in the back wall, "you won't turn your nose up at this." She was cradling a shield filled with a wild variety of objects and coins.

"Or this," added Umkhira, who followed her, one hand grasping several weapons, the other steadying her fellow Lightstrider, who appeared to be a young teenager with unusually sleek, muscular limbs. She was rubbing her wrists, which were badly abraded; whoever had tied them had used very tight knots.

Ahearn spared a glance away from the entry. "She can travel, then?"

"Yes, and warns us that we should leave quickly."

"Aye, we know that the rest will—"

"No: we are in a battleground."

Ahearn gawked at the bodies they were standing among. "This is news?"

"Do not be dense, human. She means that we have walked into the middle of a war."

Elweyr pinched the bridge of his nose between two fingers and rubbed intensely. "A war? Between whom?"

"She—Zhuklu'a—does not know. She only heard parts of conversations and does not understand Undercant any better than she does Commerce. But on both sides, prisoners have been taken and many executed. Trophies and treasure have clearly been seized—or offered as tribute—from other parts of the Under. And there is much movement."

"Then why didn't we detect any?"

"I have not had the time to question her in detail, but it sounds as if the war paused when the ur gurur—those you call blugners—arrived about a month ago. Since then, no other tribes dare approach the tunnels to the Underblack."

Druadaen glanced at Umkhira. "Didn't Kaakhag say that when the killing among the Bent becomes routine, they are at the cusp of hordeing?"

"I think you can ask him yourself in a moment," whispered Ahearn, listening at the entry.

S'ythreni rolled her eyes, drifted to his side, listened, then said, "We know it's you, Kaakhag. Hurry in."

"Can you teach me how to do that?" Ahearn asked with a smile.

She touched her narrow but high ears. "Come back when you have a pair of these."

Kaakhag limped in, helped by another Rot, whose stare was simultaneously desperate, fearful, and hostile. Kaakhag signed at him. The fellow signed back and seemed to relax. Slightly.

Ahearn stood directly in front of Kaakhag. "This stripling of a Lightstrider says we're in the middle of a war. Is that—?" He didn't bother to finish: Kaakhag's hand signs were emphatically affirmative and kept adding details.

Umkhira may have gone slightly pale. "According to his get-brother, the shaman has already started negotiating with powers in the Underblack. The blugners were, ah, resettled here to ensure he remains in power while final terms were agreed upon."

S'ythreni nodded, cocked her head in the direction of the crevice. "I am no expert at such things, but I'd say this shaman was preparing to build an army, too."

Umkhira sighed. "The aeosti speaks truth. Behind the back wall, there is a second, smaller chamber that you might call a storehouse or maybe an armory. Weapons have been stacked there, along with shields and armor. About half still bear the marks of the tribes that made them."

Elweyr frowned. "So: taken in battle, not given as tribute."

Kaakhag nodded as Umkhira continued. "Other weapons have been broken apart. Much of the iron and bronze has been reduced to raw stock, possibly for reworking into new weapons."

"So," Ahearn sighed, "we were in time to rescue these two lovelies but too late to finish the job safely."

"What do you mean?" Druadaen asked.

Ahearn jerked a thumb at the passage through which they had entered. "Well, there's no going back that way, is there?" He glanced at the two Rot brothers, who shook their heads so hard that drops of sweat flew. "So that leaves us the back door. Which I'm guessing you lasses found straight away?"

"We didn't have to," Umkhira explained, with a gesture toward Zhuklu'a. "She showed us. He kept her close, so she saw things that only a few in his own tribe know about."

"Does she happen to know if that passage leads back into the Undergloom, or down to the Black?"

"Black," Zhuklu'a said without hesitation, but with a thick accent.

"Of course it does," Ahearn nodded sardonically. "Wouldn't be much good as an escape route, otherwise. Meaning we're pretty much caught between a tribe whose shaman-chief we've just decapitated, and his new underkin allies. And that," he finished, turning back to Druadaen, "is what I meant by saying it's too late to finish this job safely. Because as it turns out, getting *into* the Under wasn't the problem; it will be getting *out* that may undo us."

But Kaakhag was gesturing again, as wildly as if he had been having a fit.

Zhuklu'a surprised everyone by translating even more easily

than Umkhira. "He says we will have *no* chance getting out if we stand here talking. We must flee. Now."

"And we will, although I think the Bent we fought in here are still running in the other direction."

But Kaakhag was not mollified. Instead, he became more agitated, limping over to the second largest of the blugners, gesticulating.

Druadaen followed him, studying the huge body.

"What's he on about with that blugner sow?" Ahearn muttered, holding a pair of crude urzhen rucksacks steady as S'ythreni and Umkhira loaded them with the valuables they had found.

Zhuklu'a frowned. "He says the blugner sows travel with at least one other female. Always."

"And so? Maybe the other was killed earlier, not in this chamber."

This time it was the brother who made desperate motions. "No, because then this one would not still be here. He says the sows ensure their safety through alliance with each other. And when one of an allied pair dies, the other goes in search of a new Sister Sow."

Elweyr spoke from where he was applying a salve to Kaakhag's leg. "Well, then maybe the other sow will get the word and look for her new Sister."

"He says no, that is not what the other sow will do."

Druadaen stepped closer. "Explain."

Zhuklu'a looked back and forth as she conveyed the brother's rapid gestures. "The Sister who still lives was here to help keep the shaman alive. She has failed. And she lost her Sister. She needs to find us before she returns to the Underblack. If she does not, um, pay that, um—'debt of duty'?—then she will lose her position here and become an outcast in the Black. But if she succeeds in making good her failures, she will be allowed to search for a new Sister Sow and to return here as matriarch."

"Well," muttered Ahearn, starting to tighten his gear for fast travel, "I see why the two green brothers are so eager to leave. We'd best steal a march on the other sow and frustrate her plans."

Zhuklu'a shook her head. "Leaving now, even moving as quickly as we may, will not be enough. This I know as well as they do. The blugners have a sense of smell unlike any other creature. Imagine that scents are like voices in a crowded room.

Now imagine what it would be like if you could hear all of them clearly, no matter how many there were. Hear each word, understand each speaking."

She looked around the group. "That is how the noses of blugners work. Particularly the sows. So the sow will be able to follow wherever we go. Unless we can somehow run far enough and fast enough that our scent will fade faster than she—and the tribe—can follow."

Ahearn and Elweyr exchanged glances. That latter looked away and shook his head: not in negation, but resignation.

Ahearn just sighed. "So we'll have to go down into the tangliest part of the Black," he muttered, suppressing what might have been a shiver. "Just like we did the last time we had to run for our lives in this gods-forsaken place. So let's step lively."

CHAPTER TWENTY-THREE

They ran without caution, wads of glowing lichen held aloft to light their way. Long weapons were too cumbersome for running in the tight passage, so they held only shortswords or daggers in their other hands. Besides, if they did encounter anything, it would be so sudden and at such short range, that only a short stabbing weapon was sure to be useful.

The passage led into what Druadaen first perceived as a dark tunnel with a very distant opposite wall, but the eyes of the urzh and the aeosti quickly discerned that they were, in fact, on the ledge of a precipice. Safety and speed required proceeding in single file, staying close against the wall, two urzh at the front and two at the rear. Ahearn asked how far the drop was. Umkhira answered that she did not know. Well, Ahearn wondered, maybe she should take a look and find out. She shook her head and explained that she *had* looked; she just couldn't see the bottom.

Silenced by that dire report, they hurried as best they could along the ledge. Even the dog seemed to stay unnaturally close to the wall.

After almost two miles, the ledge bored back into solid rock. In this tunnel, the stone underfoot was much rougher: not often used, the Rot explained. At the first intersection, though, all the urzhen started sniffing. A moment later, Druadaen detected the odor: the sour, rotting-eggs smell of sulfur.

Ahearn and Elweyr exchanged glances. "You think we're close?" asked the swordsman.

The thaumantic shrugged. "Could be. But we need better light if we hope to recognize a familiar tunnel."

"A light may be our death," Umkhira muttered.

"Could be," Ahearn agreed, signaling for a halt while he rummaged in his pack and produced a very small bull's-eye lantern. "But it could also be what saves us. By following that smell, there's a good chance—if we come across tunnels we recognize—we'll find the way to a safe place we know. One that will throw the blugner sow off our scent."

"How?" Druadaen asked.

Ahearn kindled a small flame in the lamp. "You'll see."

"If underkin don't see us first," Umkhira added.

Ahearn grinned and shrugged. "No perfect answers in the Under, Lightstrider." Playing the lantern's beam from one wall to the other, he started forward at a quick jog. Muttering darkly, Umkhira followed, gesturing for the others to stay close.

It was impossible to even guess at the passing of time after that. Druadaen couldn't measure it by the limits of his own endurance because they weren't always running. The two other humans made frequent stops to examine their surroundings, particularly when the smell of sulfur either grew fainter or stronger.

And then there were the moments when someone—often the urzhen, but usually S'ythreni—reported distant sounds. That meant covering the lamp and lichens as they crouched flat against the roughest part of the nearest wall. The time spent in the black silence could have been ten hours as easily as ten minutes, but whatever they heard ultimately did not come their way.

On one occasion, Druadaen asked if it was the sound of their pursuers.

Umkhira met his eyes with a baleful stare. "No. Worse."

"By which you mean...?"

"The sound was from in front and below. So, underkin."

"Or Deepkin," Zhuklu'a added, her voice hushed not against fear of detection, but in dread.

Eventually, Druadaen stopped trying to keep track of time. The dark, the sweat, the constant need to pay attention to the rough footing, and the constant threat of sudden attack made it far easier to suspend consciousness in a state of what one of his docents had called an "eternal present": no past or future, just immediate experience.

Until the tone in Elweyr's sudden "Wait!" snapped him back into the present.

Ahearn had seen whatever the mantic had. "Yes! No doubt about it. This is where we fought that band of Red kosh. Nasty business."

"So, we are close to this hiding place you spoke of?" Umkhira asked in a low tone.

"Well, I wouldn't say it's close, exactly," Ahearn temporized. "But we know the way from here."

Whether it was, in fact, fairly close, or because they had no more pathfinding interruptions, or simply because there was a promised end to their desperate journey, Druadaen did not feel much time passed before Ahearn called for a halt and went forward with Kaakhag and Umkhira to scout the chamber that was their destination.

They came back quickly. "All clear," Ahearn announced almost cheerily. "Quick now; boots off and follow me."

"Won't that leave a stronger trail for the sow?" Druadaen asked.

"That's the idea. You'll see. Now, come on!"

They followed Ahearn past a craggy opening from which the distant sound of running—or was it falling?—water emerged, along with a pungent surge of the sulfur scent. Two hundred yards past that, they came to a six-way intersection where a swarm of rats approached, then scurried away when Ahearn and Kaakhag ran toward them. Without breaking stride, Ahearn led them down each of the other five passages for about thirty yards.

At the end of the last, he stopped to pull his boots back on, gestured for them to do the same. "Back we go," he explained. "And long steps, now. Less of a trail, that way."

Reaching the opening again, he made hand gestures indicating that they should relieve themselves near the entry before following him single file.

Umkhira stared. "That is not so easily done for my sex!"

"Aye, just be as quick as you can," he muttered, taking almost comically long steps inside, Elweyr and Raun following just behind.

After finishing Ahearn's physically and socially awkward instructions, they followed his steps to the far end of the cavern. A wide sheet of sulfur-reeking water fell ten feet from a cleft along the back wall. It sent up a vaporous spray as it splashed into a shallow pool. That, in turn, ran off into a crevice that spilled into an apparently bottomless fissure.

With one hand firmly holding Raun's collar, Ahearn stuck a glowing patch of lichen on the tip of his shortsword and walked straight into the solid sheet of water—and disappeared through it. Elweyr followed immediately.

"Well," Ahearn called through the rush and splash of the dully glimmering curtain, "what are you waiting for?"

The chamber beyond the waterfall was a breeding ground for snails, which supported a small population of rats with freakishly large and luminous eyes. By the time Druadaen entered, the last of them were hurrying to the rear of the small cave, doing their best to become invisible.

Ahearn shrugged out of his gear, arranged it in the careful fashion he did when bedding down in the dark; all his weapons and other needful objects were in precise locations, and all in arm's reach. Druadaen had adopted a version of that for himself; if he had no way to react until there was light, it was unlikely he'd last long enough to react at all.

S'ythreni seemed to pout. "So now we have to sit in the dark."

Ahearn nodded. "Unless you want to become somebody's— well, some*thing's*—dinner."

"But we can talk?"

"That should be safe, but there's no way to be sure. I'm not so worried about the sow or warriors from the tribe; Raun will hear them long before they could hear us through that waterfall and all the echoes of the overflow plunging into the crevice. But some creatures of the Underblack can be very, very silent. So if one of them happens to come up this high, they could get close enough to hear us before Raun hears them."

S'ythreni sighed, looked around. "How did you endure the boredom of this existence?"

"Oh," Ahearn smiled broadly as he gathered strips and bits of hide from the urzhen gear they'd all accumulated in recent days, "our time down here wasn't the least bit boring. It's rather invigorating, living in constant fear of one's life."

Her answering smile was small and perhaps abashed. But only slightly.

As the rest of the group arranged their packs and sleeping rolls out of the line of sight of the narrow entry and as far away from it as possible, Elweyr was using Raun to flush out the rats at the back of the cavern. One by one, he extended a hand in the direction of the large-eyed rodents and, in a moment, their movement stilled and they sat. Raun was apparently familiar with this routine. The instant a rat became quiescent, he turned his aggressive attention to another.

When four had been gathered, Elweyr called for each person's sanitary rags. All but Zhuklu'a was moderately revolted; she seemed intrigued. "I have none to share, but what do you intend to do with them?"

Elweyr answered by way of demonstration. He wiped the first rat with each rag, and then proceeded to do the same with the others, leaving only one unwiped. He ignored the group's mutters of complaint and disgust and gently scooped the other rats into a satchel and nodded to Ahearn who whispered, "Wait here," and followed the thaumantic through the sheet of water.

"Well, that's revolting," S'ythreni hissed.

"I do not like it, but I think I see their intent," Umkhira replied.

"So do I—creating a false scent trail—but I'll be unboled before I'll ever use that rag again."

"'Unboled'?" Zhuklu'a asked before Druadaen could. But Umkhira made a gesture for the young Lightstrider to desist when S'ythreni affected not to have heard her curious echo of the unfamiliar expression.

Druadaen used what little aeosti he had. "I know that word not."

"You're not supposed to, Dunarran," she snapped in Commerce.

"*Veth*... your pardon, please," he murmured, not sure which language she would prefer.

She nodded tightly but did not look at him.

Shortly afterward, Ahearn and Elweyr returned, the latter looking drawn. In response to the questioning glances, Ahearn just shook his head. "Long day for him. More concentrating than even a wizard should try, I suppose."

He hung the satchel up and pulled out the sanitary rags. They had been washed, wrung dry, and smelled of sulfur. Which was, frankly, a considerable improvement. "Sorry to impose that way," Ahearn murmured, "but if you want to leave a trail, well..."

The urzhen shrugged. Druadaen waved off the apology as

unneeded. S'ythreni just took the rag and stretched it out to dry further.

"So," whispered Druadaen, "I assume you took them to the intersection."

Ahearn nodded.

"And does Elweyr have to remain awake in order to, er, keep influencing them?"

Elweyr's voice was ragged. "Not how I did it. I let the thaumate— an affinity construct—lapse. Too hard to keep up that many, impossible at a distance."

Umkhira's head tilted quizzically. "Then how can you be assured they shall go where you wish?"

"Because the moment I let the affinity lapse, I created a sense memory in all of them. They now believe they must continue to flee downward, because something from the higher tunnels is chasing them."

"So," asked Umkhira, "will this mislead the sow?"

"I don't know. It's possible," Elweyr sighed. "But I wouldn't bet my life on it."

"It seems to me that you just bet *all* our lives on it." Although it was Zhuklu'a's voice conveying the statement, Kaakhag's irritated gestures largely spoke for themselves.

Druadaen looked away from the exhausted mantic and before he realized it was glaring at the urzh. "And what would *you* have done instead?"

Kaakhag's face cycled through surprise, suppressed rage, then surly disdain.

Druadaen stood. "Elweyr has done the best he could, and I have yet to hear your plan. I suspect that is because there is not one to be found. It is as Ahearn said when we finally located the tunnel that brought us to this refuge: there are no perfect answers in the Under."

Kaakhag started to rise, but his brother tugged him back down. Their brief exchange of signs made Zhuklu'a lift a hand to rub her nose. And so, stifle a laugh.

"What did he say?" S'ythreni asked.

"That sometimes, thinskins are right and urzhen are wrong... and this was one of those times."

Druadaen was careful not to react or even look in their direction. Instead, rather than sitting, he picked up his rucksack and rummaged through it as he walked toward Kaakhag. The urzhen and his brother looked up, uncertain but still defiant.

Druadaen removed his hand and pushed it toward Kaakhag, unfolding it to reveal what he'd fished out of his rucksack.

Kaakhag looked, then sniffed, at the dried meat, his brow rising in surprise.

Druadaen pushed it closer. "Here," he said. Then, struggling to pronounce the urzhen word correctly, he said, "*H'adzok?*"

Umkhira smiled. "You remember."

Druadaen smiled back. "'Truce' is an important word to learn in any language."

Kaakhag just gaped at him. Then, reminded to act by the elbow his brother jammed into his ribs, he stood and nodded. "*H'adzok,*" he agreed, and waved away the proffered food.

Druadaen shook his head, held the jerky out again. "*K'teff.*"

Umkhira blinked. "Where did you learn the word for 'honor'?"

Druadaen grinned back at her. "Books *are* useful, you know."

Kaakhag was frowning at the dried meat. The token was not merely a means of putting aside any hard feelings but was the formal exchange—the act of honor—upon which *h'adzok* was contingent. The Rot nodded again, very seriously, and accepted the meat. "*K'teff, sut.*"

Honor, yes/accepted. Druadaen returned the nod, returned to his seat, and noticed Ahearn watching. And, then ever so quickly, flash a pleased wink at him.

In the near-dark and the silence that followed, time once again became fluid, defied attempt at measurement. Minutes rolled together into an hour, maybe another, or maybe many; Druadaen could no longer tell.

He might have dozed or become caught up wholly in his drifting thoughts and memories. But regardless, he jerked upright when Raun rose, legs stiff, moving toward the narrow opening. Ahearn reached out, drew him back. He covered the one exposed patch of lichen and began rebuckling the straps on his armor. The others began to do the same. Druadaen resisted the urge to catch up; silence was more important than any protection or weapon, at this point.

In the utter dark, S'ythreni's eyes could not see through to the outer chamber, and the temperature of the sulfur-laced water had a similar effect on the urzhen's heat-seeing eyes: "a thick veil" was how Umkhira had described it shortly after arriving. And only Raun's ears might have been able to discriminate the sounds of an approach through the constant spill and churn of water.

Until something audibly thumped on the stone floor of the outer cavern. Voices arose, were hushed by others, some far deeper than the first ones: almost certainly the kosh cadre that had survived the attack on the shaman's chambers.

A minute passed, then—probably—another. Voices began murmuring again. They passed the waterfall, paused for a moment, then reversed and grew more distant, receding back toward the tunnel. A jabber of hushed voices followed them, diminished, and were gone.

CHAPTER TWENTY-FOUR

Druadaen looked up when Umkhira came back through the waterfall. "We were becoming concerned."

She shrugged. "It is wise we waited so long before sending out a scout. They remained near the intersection for quite some time."

Ahearn nodded. "Aye, once they realized we'd tricked them with the scent, they waited there in case we backtracked, tried to make good our escape by getting behind them. Now come over here and help us puzzle out some of these tribal trinkets we found among the coins."

Druadaen turned away from where the others were sorting the spoils of the battle into shares . . . and discovered Zhuklu'a staring at him. She did not avert her eyes. "Yes?" he asked.

"I understand why the others are here. But not you. You show no interest in the profits of your victory. You have no loved one to rescue. You have no honor to restore, nor vengeance to satisfy. Why are you here?"

Druadaen told her in as few words as he could.

She frowned throughout, but at the end, she nodded. "So you are like a hunter, learning as much as they may about their prey."

Druadaen shook his head. "Others might use what I learn that way, but it is not why *I* am doing it. I am trying to understand how urzhen—er, the Rot and the Red—repopulate so quickly that they go a-hordeing every nine or ten years."

Her frown returned as she looked at him from the corner of her eyes. "The urzhen of the under all have many young. All the time."

He smiled. "Yes, I understand that part. What I do not understand is how they get enough food to feed so many mouths."

She thought, then nodded. "That is a wise question. I had not thought to ask it, but as I hear your words, I come to wonder the same thing."

Druadaen felt his spine straighten slightly. *The only reason she would now wonder the same thing is if she has noticed the imbalances that almost certainly hold the clues for solving this mystery.* "Were there any groups or tribes that seemed to be consuming more food than they were gathering?"

She shrugged. "That is hard to answer. I did not live so long among the shaman's tribe. And even as I arrived, he was getting much food as tribute and in trade."

"I understand the tribute. But what of the food which he got through trade? Who had it and what did he trade for it?"

She frowned again. "He traded mostly with other Rot. Sometimes Red. It was often spoils from battles. But then there were other times…" Frustrated, she shook her head. "I do not know how to say these things."

Umkhira leaned toward them. "What is it you do not know how to say, *eshzha*?" It was an affectionate ur zhog term for a girl on the cusp of womanhood. Zhuklu'a's voluble reply caused the older Lightstrider to frown also, but in the end, she nodded and said to Druadaen, "She believes that the shaman traded his skills—in language, in knowledge of the upper tunnels and surface—for food."

"And with whom did he do this trading?"

Zhuklu'a nodded her understanding of the question. "Red, usually. Tribes from the Black."

Druadaen frowned. "But how is that possible? Doesn't the Underblack have less access to food than the Undergloom? And so the Rot usually have more than the Red?"

"That is correct," she replied, Umkhira nodding over her shoulder.

"Then how can the Red trade away that which they need even more than the Rot?"

They shrugged in unison. "You should ask Kaakhag," added Zhuklu'a.

Druadaen smiled. "I did that the first night of our journey north."

"And what did he say?"

"He shrugged. Just the way you two did."

Zhuklu'a frowned. "Maybe the food comes from the Root."

Druadaen frowned at the unfamiliar term. "What is the Root?"

"It is . . . eh . . . eh . . ." Frustrated, she released another stream of the far more complex Lightstrider dialect at Umkhira.

Who explained: "She says that whenever the Rot or the Red cannot explain something, they believe it is the doing of the Root. It is all just legend."

Druadaen nodded. "Still, I would hear about this 'Root.'"

Zhuklu'a sighed, shrugged. "It is the Root of the World. It is where the Bent were born into existence, along with the rest of the underkin. And it is the rock-womb which continues to spawn Deepkin unto this very day."

Druadaen tried not to sound too incredulous. "And it is right here, in the Gur Grehar?"

Umkhira smiled. "Wherever there is an Under, there are many underkin who are certain that the Root of the World lies directly beneath them."

"I told you. It is all just legend." Zhuklu'a's tone was slightly abashed but also slightly petulant.

Druadaen reflected that one of the many constants he had noticed among all races was that, during their adolescent phase, most of them became prickly. "Yes. It is easy to see how such a legend would arise, since every eight or nine years so many Red and underkin pour out of the Underblack to give rise to yet another Horde."

"That is what the Unnamed believed," she agreed.

"The Unnamed?"

Zhuklu'a flapped an annoyed hand at herself. "The shaman. He refused to share his name. He believed that if spirits learned it, they would have power over him. So he called himself the Unnamed."

"And he believed that when the underkin of the Black go a-hordeing, many come into being at the Root of the World?"

She nodded. "Soon after I became a slave from whom the Unnamed hoped to learn languages, I heard him talking to a kosh war chief. They did not agree on much, except that, starting three or four years after each Hordeing, urzhen and other under-kin begin wandering up from the deepest tunnels. These are the places where even the Red dare not go: the lairs of the greatest Deepkin and the monsters that live among them."

"When you say 'wandering up,' do you mean that they are alone, or that they do not know where they are?"

She shrugged. "Both. The kosh chief said that many who come from the deepest Black only know a few, simple words of urzhen. That they were like children, but fully grown. And they are almost all males."

Druadaen felt a chill run slowly down his spine. "And the Unnamed believed they came from the Root of the World, that they had been sent by...by the gods?"

Zhuklu'a shook her head. "I do not know. The Unnamed always said that the gods had made the Root of the World holy by anointing it with their own blood, but he never said that they created it." Seeing Druadaen's questioning look, she clarified. "He said it many times in his rituals. I did not misunderstand it, and he was not misspeaking."

"I did not think either of those things. Tell me, how did the tribes of the Underblack feed these new arrivals?"

"I do not know."

"Did they trade with the Undergloom for food from the surface?"

"I was not present in those days, but I do not think so."

"Then how did the Underblack feed those new warriors?

"I cannot say, because I had no reason to ask. And he had no reason to tell me, a mere captive and slave."

Druadaen nodded. "Zhuklu'a, what you shared has been very useful. I wonder if you would continue to help me with your knowledge."

She started, checked with Umkhira to make sure she had understood the Commerce correctly. "My knowledge?"

Druadaen nodded and waited.

She shrugged. "You were one of those who saved me from an end worse than death. If I know a thing, I shall share it."

Druadaen pushed aside a sudden sense of irony. Chance, rather than strategy, had given him exactly the witness he needed to answer so many of his questions. "That is a great help to me. So, in addition to telling me everything you remember about the shaman and his dealings with the Underblack, I would also like you to tell me everything you remember about the food."

"Food? You mean when I was a prisoner?"

"Yes. But not just what they gave you to eat. Tell me what other foods you saw, how often, how much was eaten, and by whom. Both those in that tribe and any others you saw or heard of."

Zhuklu'a frowned. "That is a long, long saying. Are you sure you want me to tell everything?"

Druadaen smiled. "Yes. Everything."

Shortly after they woke into the dark of what Kaakhag assured them was a new "day," Ahearn stood and uncovered the noticeably dimmer lichen. "Time to go."

"Go where?" S'ythreni asked suspiciously.

"First we make our way to the Grotto of Stone Bones. That's our shortcut to the back door."

"The back door?"

"The way out of this gods-forsaken place. So let's be on our way...unless some of you want to remain?"

Within two minutes, they were in the tunnels, heading toward the Grotto of Stone Bones.

CHAPTER TWENTY-FIVE

The journey took the better part of that morning, mostly because they learned they were not alone in that area of the tunnels. They found the remains of two of the shaman's tribe, as well as an absurdly large rat that had been squashed by a single blow to the body: almost certainly the work of the blugner sow.

But the blood was barely sticky anymore. It had been in the air long enough to darken into a maroon-brown color and harden around the paw prints of some predator that had discovered the corpses while they were still fresh. The larger muscles had all been consumed and the urzhen bodies had been gutted for the choice organs.

Umkhira surveyed the walls as if a monster might jump out at them. "We are in some creature's hunting ground."

Ahearn nodded as he stepped over and around the bodies. "No doubt. Whatever found the kills wasn't shy. Stayed around to gorge itself quite thoroughly. So either this creature is on its own ground or is so big that it doesn't care. Let's go; we've another hour ahead of us before it's safe to stop." He reflected on that statement. "Well, saf-*er*." He gave the sign for Kaakhag and Umkhira to resume the march.

The Grotto of Stone Bones was aptly named. The cavern's ceiling arched as high as those in the slate-roofed temples Druadaen had seen in the coastal cities of Nyrthule and was plainly visible due to the complete lack of stalactites. In their place, however, were what appeared to be partial skeletons of great creatures, forever flying or hovering over a veritable army of their cousins that protruded in still denser profusion from the floor and walls.

Zhuklu'a sucked in a sharp breath when she stared around at the remains of the ancient behemoths that had somehow been trapped in the stone. "*Aa-hai!*" she gasped. "Is this a...a tomb? Or a burial ground?"

"Might be," Ahearn answered with a shrug. "But judging from their skeletons, these beasts were just that: animals. No sign of tools. Just ribs and teeth, some bigger than those of the largest titandrays."

"I wonder what became of them, elsewhere in the world?" Umkhira murmured, gazing at the brown and black bones that were every bit as hard as the rock in which they were trapped.

"Maybe they only lived in this one place," S'ythreni offered as they finished making sure there were no live creatures lairing or lurking in the cavern.

Druadaen shook his head. "No. At one time, they lived all over the world."

"How do you know?" asked Zhuklu'a, wondering eyes on him.

"Books!" laughed Ahearn as he lit the small lantern. "Am I right, Dunarran?"

"You are. Written by a few scholars from many different lands over many centuries. These stone bones are called 'fossils.'"

Ahearn smirked. "And so what happened to all these great, stone-boned creatures? They all die trying to swim? Heyah! Maybe this was their natta—not-ah—er..."

"Natatorium," Elweyr supplied. "But no, Druadaen is right. There's mention of them being found in deep caves of almost every continent. Probably weren't made of stone originally. Couldn't have walked, let alone float."

Ahearn rubbed his chin as he sat and pulled a strip of dried meat from a pouch on his belt. After tearing off a piece with his teeth, he used what was left to point at Elweyr. "I think I remember you saying as much the last time we were in here." He leaned back, stared up into the frozen shadow-forms of dead or dying gargantua. "Ah, that was quite a battle."

Kaakhag asked a question through Zhuklu'a. "Why would you fight to possess such a place?"

Elweyr grunted. "Didn't fight to possess it. Fought to pass through it."

Ahearn nodded. "Beyond there"—he used his dried-meat pointer to indicate the other end of the Grotto—"the path is narrow, steep, and comes out near a very small entry to the surface, far away from the main tunnels. For all those reasons, that entry—the one I called the back door—is rarely used.

"Neither Elweyr nor I had ever been to it, but we had... well, let's call them recruits... who had seen it and knew of the path that led to it, the one right there at the other end of this cavern. One small problem: none of our lot had ever been to the Grotto themselves and had no idea how to reach it from our lager in the Underblack. So to get back to the surface, Elweyr and I had to find this place first, and then head up. But there were so many of us that we attracted more attention. And that meant more battles.

"So," Ahearn finished, "because we've smaller numbers now, we traveled faster." He frowned. "But when we come to the back door itself, I *could* wish there were a few more of us. But we'll just have to make do—and make better plans—when that time comes."

Druadaen nodded. "So let us not tempt fate, but eat quickly, drink sparingly, and be on our way."

Ahearn smiled. "A fine-sounding plan, but you haven't been up the bloody passage from here to the Pool of the Warrior."

Druadaen frowned. "What is the Pool of the Warrior?"

"You'll see. All of you: drink *deep* from your waterskins. We've a long, steep way ahead of us."

Ahearn had not exaggerated. The passage upward was more of a climb than a walk, and in order to save what lamp oil they had left, they had to rely on the fading glow of the few remaining lichens.

When they finally emerged back into a more typical tunnel, it required another half hour to reach the Pool of the Warrior.

Druadaen had expected a large chamber to go along with the grandiose title. Instead, it was relatively small, no more than twenty feet across, with a roof that reminded him of the underside of a small dome. The Pool itself was barely ten feet across and even in the dim light, the edge of it was clearly covered in slime, the kind that results when pond sedge begins to die off. However, although this was the place where the Rot were supposedly confirmed and created, there was no smell of decay. The prevailing odor was more akin to the sharp, acidic smell of a freshly squashed ant mixed with the reek of sweat-soaked clothes.

Zhuklu'a entered with the surety of prior experience, reached up into a crevice hidden behind a fold of rock in the rough wall, and produced two torches and two jars.

Ahearn came forward eagerly as she made to hand off the container. "I didn't dare hope we'd find any, but this is better than gold, it is."

Curious, S'ythreni leaned close. She leaned away abruptly. "Well, it's certainly not valuable as a perfume."

Elweyr smiled, shook his head. "No. It's the dye for the Pool. But on us thinhides, it almost makes us invisible down here. Seems to muddy or block the urzhen ability to see heat."

Zhuklu'a translated the brother's rapid hand motions. "To use it that way is to...uh, show disrespect for a god-gift meant for the Bent alone."

Ahearn shrugged. "Well, apologies to your gods, but also our thanks. This dye saved my life, and Elweyr's, more than once. We never did have enough of it."

The brother muttered something dark as Kaakhag nodded, but also shrugged, palms upward. *What's done is done and you can't expect any better of thinskins*, was Druadaen's translation of the gestures.

Around a mouthful of dried meat, Umkhira nodded toward Kaakhag. "It is time we go on ahead, if you know the way."

He nodded, but hesitantly.

"Well," Druadaen asked, "does he, or doesn't he?"

Ahearn put out a temporizing hand. "He does, but the memory is not fresh. I suspect we shall have one or two wrong turns before getting there."

"And why are they going alone?" S'ythreni asked. "Why should any of us stay here?"

Elweyr stared at her. "Because two people are a lot less likely to be seen than eight, and because urzhen don't move blind down here."

Umkhira accepted one of the jars from Ahearn and walked toward the brother who, like the shaman, had apparently decided it was not safe to share his name. "Get-brother of Kaakhag," she began solemnly, "I did not know it would be an offense to your gods to use this dye directly upon my body, for I am not familiar with all the ways of the Rot. I ask your forgiveness that I must anoint myself with this dye, so that I shall be less visible to any underkin whose paths we may cross."

"Brother" frowned but, after glancing at Kaakhag, nodded.

Umkhira offered a slight bow and stripped without any delay or modesty. S'ythreni rolled her eyes as the powerfully built Lightstrider covered her skin with a thin layer of the dye. When Umkhira had slipped back into her hide armor, she glanced at the humans and S'ythreni. "Did you see or smell the spoor as we neared this chamber?"

Druadaen was once again prepared to feel like the only person in the group who had no idea of what was going on, but on this occasion, the others shook their heads as well.

Umkhira nodded. "Whatever fed on the bodies we found earlier today seems to have picked up our scent from the site of that kill."

"And it followed us all the way here?" S'ythreni asked, disbelieving. "It would have had to track us to the Grotto and follow us from there. Except that means it could only get here behind, not ahead, of us."

Ahearn tilted his head. "Now that's not always how it works down here. If that beastie tracked us to the Grotto, found us gone, but caught our scent in the upward passage, it might know where the other end comes out. So, as it's likely too big to fit through that passage, it probably just took another route here."

"So if there's another route, why did we just struggle up that underground goat trail?"

"To avoid everything else in these tunnels," Elweyr sighed. "And if we hadn't, it's likely that the creature on our trail would have overtaken us. Because if it's big enough and quiet enough, it wouldn't need to be cautious."

With nods, Umkhira and Kaakhag crept back to the entrance, listened, then slipped out into the tunnels. If they made any sound as they moved, Druadaen could not hear them.

When they were gone, he asked Zhuklu'a, "How did you know where to find the jars and torches?"

"Because they are a female responsibility," she said through what sounded very much like an animal growl. "We attend the one being Dipped. We are the ones who make any patterns in the dyeing if they are required."

Ahearn shook his head. "A daylong bath to become green. I've never been able to figure out all the fuss over it."

Zhuklu'a stared at him. "You led many urzhen in these tunnels. How is it you do not know more about their ways?"

He smiled. "Well, little huntress, down here, leading urzhen means losing them right and left. So you don't learn a great deal about 'em, y'see."

"Then I doubt you know that any who come here to be marked as warriors may not eat or drink for three days before."

Ahearn's smile was mischievous. "Is that a ritual cleansing, or a way to make sure the would-be warrior doesn't add to the holy broth with a bit of his own water?" His grin widened. "Or what might be worse."

Zhuklu'a was not amused. "It is both. If the Dip is soiled, it must be replaced. To the Rot, this rite is not just important; it is useful."

Brother signaled at her. She translated: "Becoming Rot is a test. The Dip burns every second you are in it. For months after, it chafes and itches until finally, you shed that layer of skin."

"All to make yourself green?" wondered S'ythreni.

Zhuklu'a shook her head. "You do not perceive. Becoming the Rot means you have sworn an oath that everyone can see. That you will live the life of a warrior. That you are a killer and that your very skin declares that."

Brother signed. Zhuklu'a had to ask him to repeat it before she explained, "He says that the patterns—made by covering that part of the skin with wax—promise and declare other things. He says that no race wears their oaths as openly and permanently as do urzhen. There are other temporary markings, but they only have meaning among—"

S'ythreni held up a hand, tilting her head. Then she was unsheathing her weapons. "The creature tracking us: it's approaching."

But Zhuklu'a grabbed her arm, stared urgently at the others, and hissed, "You must trust me."

"Why?" asked Elweyr.

"Because we do not wish to fight what is coming."

"And so—?"

"And so, we do this!"

Without further explanation, she held her nose, closed her eyes and mouth tightly, and jumped into the Pool of the Warrior.

Druadaen was hitting the slimy, fetid Dip before he was even aware he'd decided to follow her.

CHAPTER TWENTY-SIX

It was only when he hit the Dip that Druadaen realized his eyes were still open. The oily fluid did not merely sting them; it felt like deep-plunging daggers.

He almost opened his mouth into a gasp before remembering that he would not only alert whatever creature was stalking them but swallow a mouthful of the noxious liquid. He tightened his lips even more and clenched his jaw for good measure.

Even if he'd been able to open his eyes, he doubted the glow of the dying lichen could have penetrated the murk of the Dip. But after half a minute under the surface, he felt vibrations through the rock at his back; some heavy creature was circling the Pool. Then, something stuck down into it—a claw?—but was hastily pulled out.

Despite years spent swimming in Tlulanxu's bay, Druadaen was beginning to wonder if he could hold his breath long enough when he distinctly heard, and felt, rapid movement through the rock. It became steadily fainter, then faded away entirely. He decided to count until twenty to be sure...

But he only reached "twelve." Zhuklu'a's hand shook his shoulder. Druadaen stood, extending his toes to the bottom of the Pool to keep his chin above the Dip. He moved slowly, carefully, to keep it out of his eyes. He glanced at their rucksacks, still in an unmolested line against the wall. "Why did it not detect us? Or rip through our bags?"

Brother shrugged, signed as Zhuklu'a translated. "He says if it is the kind of creature he suspects, it would avoid the smell of your dried meat. The smoking and spices would sicken it. As for us, it would be unable to detect our scent through the reek of the Dip, particularly while we were under the surface of the Pool."

"Fine for urzhen, perhaps, but I am glad to get out," said Ahearn, as he clambered out of the Pool. He glanced over his shoulder at Druadaen. "You stay in there much longer, and you will become famous."

"As what?"

"As the first green Dunarran."

"Then that is what I shall become."

Half out of the Dip, Elweyr cocked his head. "Why?"

"I'll answer your question with one of my own. If the creature should return, and we fail to hear it in time, how quickly can you get back into the Pool without making a splash? One loud enough to reveal exactly where we are hiding?"

The group started exchanging glances.

"And so," Druadaen finished, "if it knows to go fishing for us in the Pool, it is just a matter of time before it scoops us all out."

The others settled further down in the Pool. Ahearn, grumbling, slipped back over the side. "I'll be scratching at my privates for months," he groused.

"Better than having them devoured by whatever monstrosity is hunting us," S'ythreni muttered. "What I want to know is why this pool is in such a dangerous place?"

Zhuklu'a regarded her blankly. "Where else would you put a pool for those who are dedicating their lives to the warrior's path?"

"Fair point," the aeosti conceded. "But still, it seems like the tunnels here are on a thoroughfare to whatever dark hells are beneath us."

The young Lightstrider nodded. "They are. The Pool is very close to one of the widest, if winding, ways down to the Black and the Root itself. So while dangerous, this place also connects the Rot to their beginnings. Or so they believe."

Druadaen murmured, "I am curious—"

"When are you not?" Zhuklu'a interrupted, but her expression was amused rather than annoyed.

He smiled. "When the Red wander up from the Root of the World, are they already Dipped?"

She raised an eyebrow, turned to Brother, who was already signing his answer. "Some of the shaman's new allies mentioned that those who came up from the Root of the World were neither Dipped nor Scorched."

"Scorched?"

"That is how they are given their red eyes. Their lids are pinned back. The eyes are covered with a paste. It burns terribly."

Druadaen frowned. "Why do they do it?"

It was Ahearn who answered. "Not that I ever knew how they got that way, but I can tell you why they do it: an urzh with red eyes not only sees heat better, but light as well. So much so, that nighttime on the surface is like daylight for them. But actual daylight almost blinds them. Even beams from a bulls-eye lantern can—"

S'ythreni held up a hand, head cocked, listening intently. The others settled lower in the water, ready to submerge again. "No," she said finally, "not the monster. Footsteps. Only two people."

Ahearn seemed to vault straight out of the Pool of the Warrior. "Then crouching in muck is the worst place to be. See to your weapons!" He was already moving toward the door, bastard sword in one hand, a dagger in the other.

But S'ythreni was cleaning, not brandishing, her Dip-soaked weapons. "No need."

From out in the tunnel, there was the rapping of metal on stone.

"Well, come on in, then!" Ahearn muttered sharply.

Umkhira and Kaakhag slipped around the corner into the chamber. They nodded to see that the others were almost ready to move, but frowned at the fetid muck dripping from them.

"What news, then?" Ahearn asked.

"Good and bad," Umkhira began, her nose wrinkling. "The good news is that we found the way to the back door without any wrong turns. It is not far."

Elweyr's unblinking gaze was baleful. "And the bad news?"

"That the creature that caught our scent has followed us. It is close."

"We know," Druadaen replied. "It was here. We escaped it by ducking under the Dip."

"Clever," Umkhira nodded, "but also unfortunate. The moment we leave this chamber, you will all be trailing that scent."

S'ythreni huffed in aggravation. "Superb. So what is our strategy, now?"

Ahearn managed to smile and grimace at the same time. "To run like all the hells are right behind us, High-Ears. Grab your packs. Anyone who can't run the rest of the way out of here is staying behind as dinner."

As they approached the small exit to the surface, Druadaen saw why, in addition to being on the other side of the river they'd followed north, this passage was called the "back door."

Only wide enough for one person to pass at a time, it was sealed against intruders. Just a few feet within, a massive boulder was set in the earth, sealing off access to the outside except for a narrow gap between it and the cave wall. A stone disk—probably a millstone, originally—had been rolled into that gap, blocking the opening. From the look of it, persons on the outside would have no purchase on the mill stone, and so, be unable to move it. From the inside, however...

"Druadaen," Ahearn muttered as he strode toward a dark crevice near the entry, "you look like just the kind of strapping and well-educated lad who'd know how to put a lever to good use."

"I am," said Druadaen, following him.

"Then make use of this." The swordsman produced two steel-wood staffs from the notch in the stone.

Druadaen took one of the pry bars, studied the disk blocking the entry. There was no way to get behind it; the gap between the boulder and the cavern wall was too tight. "How do you plan to move it?"

"Why, by getting it to rock back and forth a bit." Ahearn jabbed the end of his rod down into the point where the disk met the cavern floor.

"That could take a very long time," Druadaen commented.

"Well, if it does, then it does. Or do you have a better idea, Dunarran?"

"Actually, I just might."

Druadaen's plan was progressing as he'd hoped. It meant fewer people on guard duty, but so far, that trade had proven quite valuable.

At the other end of the long chamber, the three full-grown

urzhen watched the tunnel mouth. They were the fighters best suited for detecting and fighting adversaries in near-darkness, and while one stood guard, the other two worked to build a deadfall trap. It was poised immediately to the right side of the opening and was designed to be released by one tug on a rope. It was delicate work, and Umkhira proved to be the only one with enough manual dexterity to initially build, and then inter-mittently adjust, the most difficult part: the balanced rock lever that would unleash the stones above it. If the lever was too stable, the stones wouldn't fall, but if it was too sensitive, it wouldn't hold them in place. Elweyr stayed well back from the opening, ready to intervene when and if an enemy arrived.

At the back door, Ahearn and Druadaen pushed at the steel-wood levers, sweating side by side. But instead of just trying to rock it so that it would build enough momentum to then roll it out of the narrow slot between the wall and the boulder, Drua-daen had positioned Zhuklu'a on top of that boulder. Every time the old millstone rolled back toward the two straining humans, she dumped a rucksack full of dirt, grit and small rocks into the narrow space behind it. As a result, that space was filling up, and every time the millstone rolled back upon it, it crushed that ballast into a finer and denser pile: a pile that was starting to become a ramp. Each time the mill stone rolled back, it started its return roll earlier and with more force. They couldn't push it as far anymore, but that didn't matter; as the ramp grew, more momentum from each push was being retained.

S'ythreni, who was filling the rucksacks used by Zhuklu'a, handed the next load up to her and called around the boulder. "Is it starting to roll out of the doorway, yet?"

"Soon," called Druadaen. "Four more loads, maybe five."

"Damn if it isn't working," swore Ahearn cheerily. "I'll never live this down, being tutored by a Dunarran who's just barely left home."

Druadaen cocked an eye at him and was in the middle of formulating a response when Umkhira spat out an explosive oath. He turned, and for a moment, couldn't make full sense of what he saw.

Umkhira had backed swiftly into the chamber from her guard position at the mouth of the tunnel, swinging her axe high, as if she were trying to hit a bird. The other two urzhen—Kaakhag and Brother—tossed aside the last of the rocks they were adding to the deadfall trap, grabbing for their own weapons. Elweyr was simultaneously craning his neck for a better view and lifting the lantern's hood.

Umkhira swung again, then suddenly she leaped backwards—so hard and far that she fell—narrowly avoiding a claw that seemed to grow out of the ceiling.

Druadaen yanked his sword out of its scabbard, ran toward the tunnel mouth, and heard Ahearn and the others following— just as the sudden flare of Elweyr's lantern revealed what was actually transpiring.

Umkhira was scrambling to her feet, shouting a warning in her own dialect of urzhen, but Brother didn't understand it in time to realize that the threat was not just already in the tunnel mouth: it was overhead.

Druadaen had a brief glimpse of four baleful eyes reflecting the lantern just before a sinuous creature leaped down upon Brother, twisting around as it descended from the ceiling. Its jaws made a sound that was part shearing, part crunching as the Rot howled in pain and terror. Kaakhag emitted the only sound Druadaen had ever heard him make—a shrill, despairing wheeze—and charged the monster, axe swinging.

But the blow never landed. One of the creature's six limbs flashed out and hit Kaakhag's calf, cutting a wide gash in it. The force of the blow sprawled the big urzh backwards.

Umkhira, once again on her feet and axe in hand, slashed at the beast even as its hide began to change color. No longer the black of the tunnels, it swiftly matched the gray of the lamplit rocks, the transition revealing its sinuous body: a mass of rhino- hide plates studded with color-shifting spines and spiky fur.

Despite its armor, the creature recoiled from Umkhira's heavy blow and, still dragging the screaming Brother, pushed through the entry toward her...

...just as its fluid motion became a ragged series of hes- itant jerks, as if each movement now required a great deal of deliberation and focus. As Druadaen raced past Elweyr, he saw the cause: the mantic's hands were rigidly extended toward the creature. Druadaen charged to close with it—

And skidded to a halt. If Elweyr was right, if the mere inter- position of his body disrupted the mantic's thaumates...

Druadaen dropped his sword and stepped further away from Elweyr. He swung his bow off his back as Ahearn and S'ythreni ran past. He shook his head at their shouts of anger, surprise, bafflement. There wasn't time to explain and he had to keep his concentration on one thing: stringing his bow faster than he ever had before.

Where the creature's jaws held Brother, dark blood was welling up rapidly—a mortal wound. Umkhira brought her axe down again, clipped off the leg that was holding him. The creature yowl-trilled and pushed toward her as Kaakhag limped back on his now twice-wounded leg and hacked at the center of its long body.

Blue-green ichor fountained briefly. As it stopped, the middle and rear legs on that side scissored, catching Kaakhag between them before he could complete his second swing. Moving unevenly, it dragged him forward as it kept after Umkhira.

As Druadaen got the bowstring's loop into the nock of the bow's lower limb, Kaakhag reached back to grab something, anything, to resist the pull of the monster—and his hand closed around the deadfall trap's trigger-line.

The rocks slid down with a roar, crushing him and that entire side of the creature. Its four eyes bulged in either pain or rage. It lashed out toward Umkhira but missed: she was swift and it was still moving erratically. An instant later, as Ahearn and S'ythreni charged in and started slashing at it from the other side, Druadaen finished the step-through stringing of his bow, brought it up to meet the arrow he had pulled from over his shoulder, drew, and yelled, "Arrow!"

The swordsman and the aeosti jumped out of the way just as the fletching reached Druadaen's ear—and he heard and felt a sharp *snick*! in the grip. The bow shattered loudly.

Whether or not Ahearn and S'ythreni realized what had happened, they leaped back in to press their attack. Having seen the hornlike plates turn the blow of axes, they aimed at the junctures with the points of their weapons.

It might have been an impossibly hazardous strategy, getting in and staying so close, had Elweyr not continued to exert his restrictions upon the creature's movement and the rear half of its left side not been crushed and still partially pinned by the rockslide. After a few tries, S'ythreni's weapons found a gap. More of the ichor leaked out. Ahearn watched for the source, and reversing his grip for a thrust, drove his bastard sword in with both hands. Sickly teal-green blood jetted out and the creature collapsed. The wound continued to gush for several more seconds before the flow began to abate.

S'ythreni stared at the litter of bodies and shouted at Kaakhag's corpse. "I thought you said these things were *small*! Like the rats they kill!"

Zhuklu'a had scampered down off the boulder. "Most all of them are," she said quietly.

"Well... this one wasn't!" S'ythreni sounded like she was about to sob.

"It is from the Black, maybe deeper," Zhuklu'a explained. "Like fish, few of those spawned survive, but the ones that do keep growing as long as they live... and they live a very long time. The oldest go to the deep Black to find large enough prey. They change there: harder armor, bigger claws, sharper teeth."

"Does it matter?" Ahearn sighed grimly, looking back at the stone disk with which they had been struggling. "And we were almost out, too." He spat at the collapsed creature. "Another bit of buggering from the universe, to remind us just how easily we can be bumped out of it."

Elweyr checked to see if Umkhira had been injured, approached the bloody heap of bodies and stones. "The two of us will salvage what we can. The rest of you should finish rolling the stone out of the way. Let's get out of this miserable place."

PART FOUR

Conundrum:
The Giants

Journal Entry 161
8th of Blossom, 1798 S.C.
Tlulanxu

It has taken me some time to adapt to the strangest sensations I have experienced in many, many weeks:

Solitude and calm.

I didn't have a single second alone while in the Under of Gur Grehar. And while silence was not hard to come by in those tunnels, it was in no way calming. It varied between the stillness of the tomb and the protective stifling of all noise, during which imagination filled the surrounding dark with soundless pursuers.

Here, writing in the service hostel maintained for Legiors and Outriders between postings, there is peace in the silence of night. And if I listen very closely, I can hear the tread of the watch, the laughter of distant revelers, the sleepy bellow of a titandray in its paddock. Sounds of a city with no worries beyond those of the next day's round of labor and living. Dunarra may be located upon the same globe as the Under, but they are truly different worlds. And although I welcome and revel in the comforts of Tlulanxu, I no longer feel fully at home in it. If I ever did.

My recent fellow travelers are, to the best of my knowledge, in Menara again. Our journey back was longer than the one north to Gur Grehar. First, we returned Zhuklu'a to her tribe (which would have naught to do with any of the rest of us). A week later, we bivouacked a few days while Umkhira rode to her own kin (who were no more forthcoming with an invitation). After that, we crossed the open lands that separate those wilder western reaches from the border of Connæar, which we paralleled. Our prudent intent—to lessen our chance of encountering troublesome creatures while also remaining as distant as possible from Khassant—was rewarded when we finally drew within sight of the Sea of Kudak and so, parted company.

I did not expect to be missing them, and yet, I do. And not merely in the way of those who have served together under largely benign conditions. It is because we shared living in constant peril, in the midst of enemies, with no hope of help except that which resided in each other.

Before parting, they promised to seek me here, particularly since I had the authority (barely) to give them a writ requesting passage aboard one of the Consentium's routine advice packets that cycles between Tlulanxu and Menara. However, they have much to distract them in the free city, most especially the search for Elweyr's parents. That search is apparently what brought S'ythreni into contact with him and Ahearn, but they did not share any further details with me. Frankly, I suspect that even Ahearn is not in full possession of them. But as he philosophically put it, "One never deals with aeostu without also dealing with their mysteries."

I have my doubts they will avail themselves of the two-day sail from Menara to Tlulanxu, particularly since I felt obligated to emphasize how unlikely it was that we would share further travels. I am still an Outrider, and I am due for new orders, although those are late in arriving, actually. It is a welcome irregularity, but also perplexing.

However, it has afforded me the opportunity to spend time at the Archive and with Shaananca once again as I finish writing my observations of the Under in general and the urzhen in particular. Naturally, for those notes to be useful to subsequent researchers, I took pains to ensure that they built upon the older sources that I had studied (well, skimmed) before my travels.

Alas, that noble intent was stymied. But not by prior differences of opinion or theory or observation: I expected those discrepancies. Rather, the source of my frustration was—and remains—the disregard that researchers and archivists and scholars in general evince for each other's work.

Specifically, I spent my first days back in the Archive Recondite attempting to puzzle out the proper naming scheme for the many beings that earlier texts refer to under the broad label "the Bent." At the end, I realized I could not discover the authoritative and orderly taxonomy of them...because it doesn't exist. They did not merely ignore each other's researches but seemed to subtly relish invalidating it, however they could.

In the end, never have I been so grateful, and secretly proud, to have had the instinct (if not the foresight) to deflect all suggestions to consider a career as an archivist or docent. It seems entirely possible that even I could have become pedantic and hopelessly abstruse...

However, although my notes do expand what has been recorded regarding the Under, I am no closer to answering how, or from whence, the deepest dwelling Bent get the food with which to support their immense communities. Nor how it could be that Bent who are said to emerge from the Root of the World happen to speak the same language, worship the same gods, and share the same culture as those who were raised in a tribe. A logical surmise is that they are outcasts from still deeper communities, but if so, I am wholly ignorant of how far down the Underblack goes or how many layers it has. In short, are there always *still deeper* communities ready to arise just as the hordeing approaches? And wouldn't each layer find it just that much harder to acquire minimal sustenance?

I cannot rule out the commonplace explanation for all of these quandaries: that it is all at the will of the gods. But would the gods regularly rebuild an entire species by the flagrant use of miracles? That seems to press far beyond the implicit limits they themselves have set upon the projection of their will into the world. Sacrists and nativists agree on few matters, but one such is that both peace among the gods and balance in the world depend upon their universal accord to limit the physical exercise of their power. Orthologues report how the deities promised each other to restrict mundane manifestations to finite and particular acts. Otherwise, even the passing of seasons and the spinning of the globe would be their playthings. Whether altered with serious intent or on a whim, the outcome is identical: natural law would not merely be provisional, it would be moot.

Turning away from my failure to make any definitive determinations regarding the Bent and the urzhen, I have shifted my attention to a new mystery that has increasingly pressed at me since Elweyr asserted that blugners, also known as ur gurur, cannot be one and the same as the race commonly called "giants."

It began as a fairly casual curiosity, but my very first researches indicate that Elweyr is almost certainly right. Blugner are not merely considerably smaller, but are always noted as being mis-shapen, often with pronounced asymmetries of both head and body. They are comparatively slow, lacking agility, and have markedly less manual dexterity than any other biped. Their reproduction is extremely different from urzhen and the preeminence of Sister Sows in their groups suggests that females are at least as socially powerful as males, probably more so.

Giants are entirely different. They always dwell above ground, usually in large caves in the sides of hills or cliffs, and if not, then in deep forests. They purportedly prefer hostile climates and regions and are said to surround themselves with Bent and other servitors who routinely patrol their domains in exchange for the decisive power they bring to battlefields. Both reclusive and capricious, they remain quiescent for years and then suddenly fall upon communities, either in groups or alone, but always insatiably hungry. They stand twice as high as the tallest human, and whereas blugner are slow and cumbersome, giants recall humans in their speed and manual dexterity. However, they cannot simply be large humans, because if I were expanded to twice my height and five or six times my weight, I could not even stand, let alone function: it would be a physical impossibility.

During my years at the Archive, I spent considerable time assisting both physicians and scholars of fauna and flora with their researches. As a result, I learned a reasonable amount regarding certain basic principles of physiology. For instance, even with a heart the size of a bucket, a proportionally larger human would likely collapse due to inadequate circulation of blood. While there are many immense mammals, all evince multiple adaptations to meet the circulatory requirements imposed by both their size and weight.

Conversely, according to the archivists who specialize in great fauna, simply expanding a human form to fifteen feet in height does not provide the room nor proper shape to incorporate such adaptations. Likewise, they see no way that the blood may perfuse and then return quickly enough from the small capillaries that service the digits of distant extremities, particularly toes. Consequently, most scholars advanced one of only two answers: that giants are simply creatures of myth or that they enjoy the intervention of deity.

A further perplexity is that in the older texts, they are referred to as belonging to that group of creatures known by the label direkynde. It is a mysterious nomenclature that I might never have encountered were it not for the august and elderly Saqqaruan scholar who took an interest in me when I was an assistant at the Archive, now six years past. I have since learned that he is none other than Aji Kayo, the First Scholar of the Orchid Throne. Also, by a stroke of singular luck, he returned to Tlulanxu just a few weeks ago so that he might expand the research for his magnus opus, about which he is infamously close-lipped.

In hearing his name again, I recalled his exhortations to explore a tome that touched upon the direkynde, the accounts of which are said to be even more disparate and problematic than those of urzhen and giants. Perhaps I shall dip into them tomorrow.

CHAPTER TWENTY-SEVEN

In an oubliette of his own, Druadaen sat surrounded by tomes, vellum scrolls, and parchments made of skin—the origins of which he was glad not to know. It was the noisiest of the private rooms, inasmuch as the cable spools of the funicular were on the other side of the wall. But since their regular operation precluded any hope of sustained silence, there was no reason to keep the door closed, which had the happy effect of keeping the air slightly more fresh.

Which is why, as he was poring over the ancient texts to ensure that the apprentice scholar had copied them accurately, he was able to hear two voices conversing as they approached the door to the funicular.

"So, as I understand it," said a vaguely familiar male voice, "this newest trip to Saqqaru—and points beyond—was *your* idea, not grandfather's?"

Shaananca replied, "And what of it, Alcuin? One of the most important duties of any Pretor of the Council for External Affairs is to be among the most trusted and involved advisors of the Propretor Princeps. Another role is to see to the handling of matters that are either delicate or must remain detached from normal bureaucratic channels. In the case of your journey, both apply."

"Yes, I have heard the logic, and I have agreed with it. But another such journey is . . . well, it's ridiculous. All to fulfill the expectation that any Pretor who *might* eventually become the Propretor Princeps should routinely see the world and so, be seen by it in return. I feel like one of those innumerable princelings who are sent on one of those equally innumerable grand tours required by parental autocrats. Except in my case, one tour was not enough. This is…what, the fifth?"

"Fourth, as you know very well. And this time, it affords you a perfect opportunity to surreptitiously gather information on a matter of interest to both your grandfather and me."

"Indeed? And what is this 'matter of interest'?"

"It is partly of your making. As I understand it, you and your grandfather have further questions about Druadaen's recent journeys and findings. It so happens that an esteemed Saqqaruan colleague who has been conducting related investigations will be taking ship with you to his homeland."

"And in what way are his searches related to your 'matter of interest'?"

"That is best discussed with him during the free time—and isolation—that a shared sea voyage affords." Her tone became gently mischievous. "And while you are traveling with Aji, you might ask him to share a few stories of your father. He will be glad to do so. Both for your amusement and his own."

"Aji Kayo? I'm surprised to learn that he's still alive, let alone still traveling."

"And yet, he is. If he has not already mentioned it, he was a good friend of your late father. I think you will find that he not only possesses useful practical insights, but personal ones as well."

Alcuin's response was slow, somber. "I appreciate your counsel, Senior Archivist." The heavy door to the funicular platform creaked open. "Now, about this young fellow, Druadaen: some of the Pretors have been inquiring into—" His voice was cut off by the closing of the door to the funicular platform.

Druadaen realized his mouth was open. He shut it so suddenly it made a sound like a bottle being uncorked. *The last time I saw Alcuin here, it was because of what I did when the S'Dyxoi attacked. Now it's about research I'm doing on my own time and at my own expense. How is any of that important to him? Why does he—?*

The funicular started groaning. The door to the platform opened, then closed. He could not hear if Shaananca walked away. Indeed, he didn't hear any footfalls at all. But then again, if Shaananca did not want to be seen or heard, she wouldn't be.

Not wanting to appear so quickly that Shaananca would realize he'd overheard her conversation with Alcuin, he counted to twenty before he emerged.

The Archive's reading room was empty.

Or maybe not. He was about to head toward Shaananca's office when he saw a small, waving hand back near the oubliette in the far corner of the reading room. It was Aji Kayo and now, as last time, his wave was a gesture of invitation. Glad at the promise of a brief reunion, Druadaen changed course toward the fellow, who ushered him into his oubliette with a bow.

Without pausing for pleasantries or even a "hello," the scholar scuttled toward a stack of books. "I have something for you," he explained over his shoulder. He returned with three tomes, all thick and relatively new-looking. He placed them in Druadaen's startled hands and smiled up at him. "Dragons. Direkynde. Deepkin. In your language, all the most infamous creatures begin with 'D'...Druadaen." On that final word, his smile became not just mischievous but rueful.

Druadaen raised an eyebrow but succumbed to the magnetic pull of the books. He frowned as he flipped carefully through the first pages of the one on top of the stack he was cradling in his other arm. "This is the reference you had asked me to find for you, years ago."

The Saqqari's smile became puckish. "Your memory remains adequate, I see."

"I am sorry to confess, though, that I am still unfamiliar with the book. And I have never even heard of these other references," Druadaen murmured.

"Neither fact surprises me," the scholar sniffed. "I suspect the bottom two books exist someplace within this archive. And no," he continued, seeing Druadaen's doubtful look, "not even with the documents in the Reserved Collection beneath us."

Wondering what other repositories he might be referring to, Druadaen asked, "Then where did these come from? And why are they all so new?"

"The answer to both questions is the same: I had my assistant translate and copy the editions that are in my Empress's private references. They are less than six months old and quite valuable."

Druadaen bowed. "I deeply regret that I am just this day ordered to my next assignment: to deliver a secure pouch to the Ord Ridire section officer in Shadowmere. I depart tonight."

"Shadowmere? The far side of the world, or near unto. And yet, said to be its crossroads. But why does that trouble you, my young friend?"

Druadaen could feel how crooked his smile was. "I read quickly, First Scholar, but I will not be able to peruse even a fraction of these monographs before I sail."

The Saqqari's face contracted as if he had bitten a lemon thinking it to be an orange. "*A-sai!* You do not comprehend. These are yours. To take. Why do you look at me that way? Is my accent so thick that you do not understand what I say?"

Druadaen was trying not to stammer in surprise and wonder. "N-no, First Scholar. I just—well, I never . . . Sir, I am left speechless by the magnitude of this gift. And the trust entailed thereby."

Aji waved an impatient hand. "You make fine speeches, but they are not required. Indeed, they put distance between us. We are colleagues. I tell you again: speak freely. For we have little time."

Druadaen prepared to exit the room. "Are you needed elsewhere?"

"No, no" he said, almost irritably. "It is simply not . . . prudent for us to confer too much." Even saying so seemed to annoy him. "At least not yet." Druadaen wondered if their relationship had indeed become so collegial and casual that he could openly tell the old man that he had no idea what he meant by his cryptic remarks.

But he never got the chance. The scholar was handing a satchel to him. "Put the books in here. It is stronger than it looks. And that seam at the top will seal fully when placed against the matching seam on the bag, making it waterproof."

"How does it—?"

"Not enough time. It will only recognize your fingers, mine, Senior Archivist Shaananca's, and a few others over whose identities you need not trouble yourself. You can make use of these references, yes?"

Druadaen raised an eyebrow. "So much so that your question is ingenuous."

Aji smiled broadly. "Now *that* is spoken like a colleague. Now, be attentive: I know something of the notes you have been submitting and the new researches you have been pursuing. And so I suspect you shall soon have need of this book on the direkynde and dragons. The other two works are more detailed but are also inconveniently disparate in their methods of analysis and their conclusions. But they contain most of the details concerning what is known of dragons, as well as even larger creatures that might...or might not...have been their forerunners." A sly smile had returned to his face.

Druadaen studied his expression and thought for a moment. Then: "I see that word has reached you regarding what I saw in the Grotto of Stone Bones."

Aji Kayo simply bowed slightly.

"You think the remains I saw there are those of a related species?"

The diminutive Saqqari shrugged. "Who can say? I suppose one would have to ask a dragon oneself." The smallest grin creased his lips.

Druadaen couldn't help smiling in return. "You know me all too well."

"Odd, since we have spent so little time in each other's company. But perhaps I see familiar traits in you and so extrapolate others."

"And what familiar traits do you see?"

"Curiosity. Determination. And maybe a bit of stubbornness."

"A bit?"

Now, it was Aji's turn to smile broadly. "Well, perhaps somewhat more than a bit. Come; I see you wish to ask a question. You need not make a petition to do so. We may come from different peoples and generations, you and I, but that does not mean we are not kin in ways that transcend those distinctions."

Druadaen bowed. Figurative kinship notwithstanding, the First Scholar of the Orchid Throne had just bestowed a great honor upon him: that of being, in any fashion, a peer. "I was wondering about the process whereby bones become fossils; how long would that take?"

"You refer to a natural process? Longer than the world has existed, judging from excavations of cities or skeletons. Those which the historical record shows have been buried for millennia have yet to demonstrate any measurable progress toward petrification."

"Then how could these fossils have come to be?"

The scholar shrugged. "The work of the gods, what else?" But his concluding "what else?" sounded less like resigned acceptance than it did an invitation to ask an actual question: an investigation into some other possible source of the fossils.

Druadaen frowned. "So these vast collections of bones are—?"

"Are not natural at all. Either they are the remains of creatures with bones of rock—"

"Impossible."

He nodded. "Or they were great beasts turned to ash and rock by the acts of gods. Or through mancery that they vested in us for that one purpose."

"Do such spells even exist?"

Aji smiled. "There are none such in contemporary references, nor are they depicted or described in the most ancient annals known to humans. Or Iavarain, for that matter."

"Then how—?"

The Saqqari's interruption almost seemed precautionary. "The sacrists tell us that, in primitive times, these great beasts threatened the survival of the thinking races. And so the gods endued those races with powerful mantic powers to defeat these behemoths."

"And then withdrew those powers when they were no longer needed?" Druadaen squinted at Aji's almost impish nod. "How very convenient."

"Is it not? Now, I must return to my own researches, but I will ask one favor of you."

"Sir, I am at your service."

He reached out and patted the much larger man's bicep. "Come visit me, should you ever journey to Saqqaru. I have something of interest to show you." As Druadaen opened his mouth to ask "What?" the old fellow waved him toward the door. "If I tell you now, it will spoil the mystery. And that will reduce the chance that you will devote the time and effort necessary to visit me in my homeland. So let your unfulfilled curiosity bring you to my doorstep. Until we speak again, my young friend!" He smiled and gently closed the door in Druadaen's face.

"I hear you have been given orders."

Druadaen almost started, but he was in the same complex as Shaananca, so he knew to expect her unexpected approaches. "Yes," he said turning. "As usual, you are extremely well informed."

She smiled at his smile. "I am a librarian, after all."

He chortled. "And nothing more?"

Her smile became sly. "I don't recall ever saying *that*."

Before she could step back, he stepped forward and put his arms around her. She stiffened, but then, after a long moment, relaxed into his fond hug. "Thank you," he said.

"For what?" she asked, holding him back where she could see his face.

"For being there to help me. In the ways I know about, and the others—the many others—that I cannot even begin to guess at."

"I have no idea what you're talking about," she said through a trembling smile.

He shook his head. "Which is, of course, exactly what you must say."

She only looked at him.

He could not remember a time when she did not have a ready rejoinder, and he suddenly felt anxious—for her. "And whether you had any control over it, I thank you for convincing me to have an open mind. First about being a Courier, then an Outrider."

"It is a very different life from the one you would have led in the Legion." Her tone suggested both acknowledgement and apology.

"It is. And I suspect I would have discovered that life to be rather disappointing, by now." He remembered the desperate desires that had consumed him, day in and day out, in the reading room.

Shaananca's eyes searched his. "As I hear it, you depart tonight. A Courier ship that will only port once, at Araxor, before crossing the western ocean to Shadowmere."

Druadaen smiled. "As I said before, you are extremely well informed...for a 'librarian.'" Which reminded him of a task he had to perform before sailing. "I have prepared a packet of notes in my oubliette. It is marked with your name."

She frowned. "And what is the purpose of it?"

"Why, to enter into the collections here. Even if I should fail to return, then at least what I have learned will survive me. It contains information—*pertinent* information—that is not present in the other sources here." He frowned to see Shaananca frown. "It is well-organized, and I have prepared indexing notes. It will not be troublesome to integrate with the other accounts."

"I do not doubt it," she allowed through a deep sigh, "but I cannot keep that packet here."

Druadaen had not felt so confused in a long time. "But—"

"It is not *wise* for me to keep it here," she amended with emphasis. Her tone was steady and firm, but her eyes were... fearful?

Druadaen frowned. "Would my notes endanger you in some way?"

"No. But for now, it is best to keep your observations private, I think."

Druadaen was only more confused, considered her careful tone and words, and then wondered aloud, "Do my notes endanger *me*? How?"

She shrugged; the gesture looked casual, but Druadaen had learned to spot the telltale signs of when Shaananca feigned ease she did not feel. "I am assuredly being overly cautious. And I would not use the word 'endanger.' Let us say instead that those notes could possibly complicate *both* our futures. If shared at this time."

Druadaen studied her before voicing his realization: "You intended that I should overhear your conversation with Alcuin IV. Your reluctance is connected to him, or the matters he must soon address."

Her answering smile was both sad and proud. "Yes. But you have nothing to fear from Alcuin."

"Then who?"

Shaananca closed her eyes. "Suffice it to say that your work here has been noted and observed. Several senior members of the Propretoriate have become acquainted with your travels and discoveries, albeit only in the most general of terms. They are intrigued but are cautious."

"Of what?"

"That is for them to know and them to share. But I suspect that what you have brought back from your journey into the Under has ramifications that they neither foresaw, nor had contingencies to handle."

"What kind of—?"

"Druadaen."

He smothered his question in mid-asking.

"This is not an auspicious moment for your findings to come to light. Please accept that."

Druadaen frowned, then realized why his assignment had been

delayed. "They're sending me as far away as they can. That's why they're sending me to Shadowmere, to Far Amitryea. Because I'll be too distant and too busy adapting to unfamiliar languages and customs and peoples to make any more trouble."

She looked at him for a long moment and he knew, as clearly as if she'd said so, that he was correct. She sighed and nodded. "I will join you at the ship. I have some matters to attend to before I may leave." She offered a crestfallen smile. "The funicular has returned to the platform. I will have it held for you."

CHAPTER TWENTY-EIGHT

Druadaen stepped around a tall pyramid of crates being offloaded on one of the Tlulanxu's protected docks...and almost dropped his sea chest.

Ahearn, Elweyr, S'ythreni, and Umkhira were lounging on stacks made of their weapons, gear, and packs, just beyond the boarding ramp of the ship that would soon carry him away from Dunarra. They grinned at his surprise. Raun rose up from behind the crates against which they had propped themselves, stretching long, stiff legs.

"Well!" Druadaen said.

"As eloquent as always," Ahearn said in a loud voice as he rolled up to his feet. "Thinking we'd let you down, did you?"

Since Druadaen hadn't been thinking about that—or them—at all, his answer was the simple truth: "The thought never crossed my mind."

"Well, here we are," the bluff swordsman continued, "ready for another journey together."

Druadaen put down his sea chest, glanced up at the tall masts of the outsized brig. "I really am quite...touched that you found your way here. But I was just given new orders today, and—"

"—and you're leaving on this ship," finished S'ythreni, tilting her head at the ship beside them. "Yes, we know." She may have smiled.

For a moment, Druadaen's head felt as though it was trying to split itself down the middle. Having just come from learning that his new mission was actually a way to get rid of him, and now discovering his recent companions decamped on a dock in the restricted part of the harbor... well, it was as if some god of mischief was taking delight in buffeting him with one awkward surprise after another.

So stick to simple questions as you find your feet. "When did you arrive?"

"Last night," Elweyr muttered. "Had to promise not to get off the ship." He jerked his head at the forty-foot packet docked at the end of the wharf.

Druadaen raised an eyebrow. "And why didn't they drop you off at the trade quarter, first?"

"Well," Ahearn temporized, "it's not as if they knew they had to do so."

Druadaen frowned... and then understanding arrived. "You told them you were Dunarrans? And they *believed* you?" He tried very hard not to glance at Umkhira.

Ahearn recoiled from his questions. "We most certainly did *not* tell them we were Dunarrans!" Finding himself the focus of Druadaen's silent gaze, he shrugged one shoulder. "Of course, as we were traveling on your letter of recommendation, they may have come to the conclusion that we were your, eh, armsmen and confidential agents."

Druadaen kept staring at him.

A larger shrug. "And we certainly weren't about to ruffle their feathers by pointing out their mistake. Hardly a nice way to treat your hosts, as it were."

Druadaen put one hand—actually, one fist—to his temple. "And you didn't happen to say anything that would have led them to that conclusion?"

"Well, now, if I recall correctly—"

"I will not be party to this subterfuge," Umkhira said, standing. "None of the words spoken were lies, but they were misleading. And I did not disavow them. So I share their guilt."

Everything Druadaen had heard as a child had taught him to fear urzh; now, he had begun to consider Lightstriders to be an absolutely refreshing source of frankness and honor. "Well, now I know how you got here, and why you've remained on the wharf." *Because you wouldn't have made it ten feet beyond the end of the pier before attracting some very keen attention and being asked some very pointed questions.* "But how did you find me?"

"Luck was with us," Umkhira affirmed with a nod. "An officer from this ship had been sent in search of some cargo on the packet. We heard the conversation between them. Apparently, this ship should have sailed two days ago, but was held. For you."

"For *me*?"

"You did not know?"

"I did not."

"Then our fortune is even greater than we supposed."

S'ythreni sighed in bored exasperation. "It's not 'fortune' at all. We were *supposed* to hear that conversation." She shook her head. "Remember what I said about—?"

"Yes, yes: 'It's too coincidental.'" Ahearn offered a very poor imitation of her insouciant tone. "'And they're *such* bad actors.'" He straightened. "Well, however it's come about that we are together again, I call it fine fortune. Now, where are we off to?"

Somehow Druadaen resisted the strong urge to shake his head, as if that might clear it of the surreal turn of events. "I am traveling to Far Amitryea."

S'ythreni rolled her eyes. "Well, we know *that*."

Druadaen considered how freely mariners' tongues wag, particularly in the shadow of their own ship, and allowed that her comment, while snide, was valid. "Shadowmere."

She looked triumphantly at the group. "As I predicted."

"Well, now, that hardly required the gift of prophesy, did it?" Ahearn countered. "'All great quests pass through Shadowmere.' Or so goes the saying."

Umkhira frowned, glanced at Druadaen. "But he is not on a quest. He is following orders."

Elweyr shook his head. "Those orders are to keep him away from here. From making trouble."

Druadaen straightened. "Master Elweyr, it sounds as though you may know more about my assignment than I do."

The mantic shook his head again. "No, but I know how empires work. They get rid of their problems. The only difference between the bad empires and the worse ones is that the bad ones just send you off on errands or to isolated posts. The worse ones arrange for more, er, permanent absences."

Druadaen kept his smile small. "I was also referring to your own experience with quests. About which: How goes the search for your parents?"

Elweyr's gaze fell toward the space between his knees and the wharf planks beneath him. He shook his head.

S'ythreni looked sadly at him. "There are some hopeful clues." Despite trying to sound encouraging, her remark only underscored how unpromising Elweyr's search must have been.

But Druadaen wasn't about to discourage her from displays of compassion. "If they can be followed successfully," he said gently, "I am sure you shall do just that, Master Elweyr." He glanced at S'ythreni. "And you as well, *Alva* S'ythreni." She started and stared at him, surprised and possibly grateful. "I apologize for having forgotten the term, earlier. I confess that I had to look it up when I returned to the Archive."

She murmured something inaudible, waved a hand that dismissed any notion that she might have taken offense.

Ahearn leaned in. "'Alva'? That's Old Iavan, right?" He grinned at her. "So, is that a title of nobility? Are you some high-born high-ear, and been holding out on us?"

Druadaen spoke slowly and calmly even as S'ythreni's back stiffened. "No, it is a pronoun by which one should address all aeostu."

"But when you met her at the tavern you used a different word...eh, *sahn*, wasn't it?"

"Yes, but that term is only to be used when first meeting an aeosti. Or if you are meeting them again after a rebirthing."

"A what?"

"A rebirthing," explained Elweyr with a curious look at S'ythreni, "occurs after Iavarain emerge from their womb-trees."

"Their what?" Ahearn almost shouted in surprise. "I know the high-ears are fond of forests, but...by damn, are you saying she was whelped by a *tree*?"

Druadaen took care to keep his voice level. "Of course not. But there are certain trees that, eh, bond with individual Iavarain." He glanced at her to check for any sign that his simplistic explanation might be giving offense.

Ahearn nodded at S'ythreni's rigid spine. "I see."

"I doubt it," she muttered through gritted teeth.

"Well," he answered testily, "I suppose that explains the

legends of your long lifetimes. And your—well, your perverse coital habits."

Elweyr looked up at his friend. "That's enough," he said.

"What?" Ahearn exclaimed indignantly. "It's not as though the high-ears ever deign to share anything about themselves with us mere mortals. Maybe they all have trees for paramours!"

S'ythreni snorted. "If you ever stopped to listen to yourself, you'd realize why we avoid humans."

"And what is that supposed to mean?"

"It means that we do not like being judged by ignoramuses who think that our mothers and lovers are trees and talk about our 'perverse coital habits.'"

Ahearn crossed his arms. "Well, that's the nicest term I could come up with. Would you prefer 'proven appetite for buggery'?"

The others flinched, but S'ythreni just laughed. "And clearly you are *such* an expert in discerning such things."

"Eh? What do you mean?"

"I mean, your extraordinary skill at detecting 'buggery.' Apparently, it didn't help you realize that Kaakhag and his 'brother' weren't actually siblings."

"What do you—?" Ahearn halted with his mouth open. "Oh," he said.

"Yes, 'oh.'"

He shrugged, glanced at Umkhira. "Did you know?"

She waved a hand. "I suspected. But it was not my place to ask. Nor is it polite to study the actions of others to gain insight into what is an entirely private matter. But they were, eh... very careful. Which is not unusual, when like-sex pairings occur among us. Most urzh frown upon such unions."

"Well, in that way, our races are much alike, then," Ahearn affirmed with a sharp nod before turning back toward S'ythreni. "It doesn't seem to be the way among *your* people, though, High-Ears."

She laughed. "You mean the guilt, the furtiveness, the secrecy? No, human: I first saw that while traveling among *your* kind."

"Well, then how is it—the way of courtship and chapping—among you high-ears?"

"That might be something you'll learn if you ever walk among us."

"Well, maybe I'll decide to do just that some day!"

She smiled unpleasantly. "You don't *decide* to visit. That is by invitation, or not at all. And in your case, I wouldn't hold my breath." Her grin widened. "Or, on second thought, *do* hold your breath. Please."

"I suspect I couldn't breathe even if I was invited, given how rarified the air must be in Iavan society—despite being known amongst us lowly humans for its shameless depravity."

"Because of what you perceive as our 'buggery'?" she asked through a facetious grin.

"Well, it goes beyond what happens in your beds—or trees—doesn't it? We can hardly tell what sex you are, most of the time... and maybe you have the same problem, since your women do every- and anything that your men do, blast them. It's positively indecent. Seems Dunarra, too, is almost as perverted as your lot."

"I believe you mean perverse," Elweyr offered.

"Well, now, give me a moment to decide which I meant more."

Umkhira frowned. "You consider the freedom of Dunarran women to be perverted?"

Ahearn shook his head. "That's not the perversion I'm referring to." When he was met by baffled stares, he added, "Well, what would you call it when so many Dunarrans take multiple wives?"

S'ythreni rolled her eyes. "Dunarrans have multiple *spouses*. It's not just men, but women too."

"And that makes it better?"

S'ythreni shrugged. "Of course."

He turned toward Druadaen. "Maybe a Dunarran can explain it to me, then."

Druadaen sighed. "Dunarrans have longer lives and nature apparently adapted to that; their women conceive much less frequently and do not bear multiple infants..."

"Oh, save me!" Ahearn interrupted with a histrionic clutch at his heart. "A nation of only children! Legions of well-bred, well-educated, and well-spoiled brats! So that's why you take multiple wives—er, spouses? To increase how many children you have?"

"You misperceive. Dunarrans do take multiple spouses, but singly."

"Er... what?"

S'ythreni grimaced. "Really? You don't see it? In the course of a lifetime, they may have multiple unions, but only one at a time."

"Ah, so serial adultery, then. So much more virtuous!"

"Or maybe it is so much *better* than the marital misery of *your* nations." S'ythreni leaned toward Ahearn. "How many human couples still wish to be together after twenty years? Gods, how many can even stand the sight of each other after a second child?"

Ahearn's frown was skeptical. "I still say the Dunarran arrangement is unnatural. I, for one, believe that love—*true* love—can endure. Can rise above all concerns of time and separation." He almost blushed, then seemed desperate to leave the topic.

Elweyr coughed hard, once. When he had their attention, he said, "All this talk proves that all these groups have at least one thing in common."

Ahearn smirked. "And that is?"

"They're all convinced that their own dung doesn't stink."

"Now that," said a familiar female voice, "is well and truly said."

Druadaen smiled as he recognized it and the others craned their necks to discover who had spoken from behind him. As they saw, they began to look away as if they very much wished they were somewhere else.

Shaananca stepped forward to stand beside Druadaen. "Please continue your discussion," she said with a broad smile. "It was just becoming interesting."

CHAPTER TWENTY-NINE

Druadaen smiled at Shaananca. "Your timing is, as ever, singular."

"So you mention almost every time you see me." She surveyed the group, fixed her eyes on the mantic. "Master Elweyr, I have news."

"For me?"

"Yes, regarding your parents. I took the liberty of looking into their disappearance."

Elweyr darted a look at Druadaen; it was simultaneously resentful and grateful.

"Druadaen neither requested I make inquiries, nor knew I was doing so," Shaananca added.

Elweyr frowned. "Then how did you know I'm looking for them?"

"I was able to ascertain," she continued as if the thaumantic had not asked her a question, "that they are alive, safe, and in a secure place but living under different names."

"What? Where? Why haven't they—?"

"Unfortunately, for the time being, it seems that they must remain incognito. So it would probably be safer for them if you did not investigate further. At this time."

Ahearn squinted at Shaananca and then looked toward his friend. "And that's all you're going to hear on the matter, unless I am misreading my Dunarrans."

She seemed not to have heard that comment, either. "I regret that you have not had the opportunity to visit Tlulanxu before undertaking another journey."

"And how is it that you know we don't intend to stay awhile?" Ahearn asked.

Her laugh was musical but brief. "Well, firstly, I am not deaf, and yours was not the conversation of a company that has agreed to part ways. So I presume you leave with Druadaen this eve. Secondly, you have not made arrangements to take a boat to the trade quarter, where you would be able to debark."

"Aye, that's right," Ahearn seemed to recall suddenly, "we're not allowed inside, are we? Keep the riffraff where you can watch 'em, eh?" His tone was merry; his eyes were not.

Her eyes shifted sideways to meet his, unblinking. "It was not always thus, but it became so after the fall of the First Consentium. It was a decision we greatly regretted. But we learned terrible lessons about how even such harmless, oblique jibes as that one can eventually grow into true resentment and hatred."

Umkhira's gaze was untroubled, her voice wondering. "You ruled the world. You did not say so. But you did. Yet you did not anticipate that familiarity and mastery cannot long occupy the same tent? How could you be so wise in other matters and so blind in that one?"

Shaananca's smile became sad as she nodded. "A very fair point and a very good question. And you see how steadfastly we have corrected our imprudent idealism." She shrugged. "We never sought nor declared mastery, so we presumed they would never be imputed to us."

S'ythreni's voice was actually respectful. "Hasn't enough time passed for the Propretoriate to consider adopting a more moderate course?"

She smiled. "Some propose that. Many more advise against it. In fact, until almost a decade ago, we were making progress. And then..." She shrugged and glanced at Druadaen. "I imagine he has mentioned the attack by the S'Dyxoi, just before he began his time as a Courier." When she was met with blank stares, she added. "The one he helped repel?" The blank stares widened into surprise and rotated toward Druadaen. Shaananca's gaze followed theirs, puzzled. "Well, then, I shall tell you—"

Druadaen shook his head. "No time for that. We must board soon."

Ahearn had folded his massive arms, looked terribly amused. "Now, now, we've a few spare minutes. Do tell us, good my Ar mistress."

Druadaen started. *How is it that everyone else can figure out that she's a follower of the Ar?* He turned toward her. "Why have you never told me you are a follower of the Ar?"

Her smile was actually impish. "You never asked." Before Druadaen could fashion a rhetorical riposte, Shaananca turned to Ahearn. "I almost forgot; I have something that might help you. Well, your dog." She glanced down at Raun, who stared up at her. "Most dogs do not enjoy the sea. I suspect he is like most of his breed in this?"

"Aye, an' ye have that right enough. He retches on a short ferry across still waters. Bog only knows how he'll manage a voyage across the great ocean-sea."

"Perhaps this will help," Shaananca murmured, holding out her hand.

There was a shiny steel bracelet just above her wrist. In the space of a single second, the glimmer of the metal seemed to deepen, became like that of a mirror seen through a great depth of pure mountain water. The reflections in it were crisp, lifelike, moved with perfect fluidity...

As did the bracelet itself. It swiftly unfurled itself from around her wrist, the loop flowing into a new shape: a startlingly lifelike image of a dragon. Or, maybe it was...?

Ahearn leaned away from it, almost toppling backward. "Ai! Now what is that? Living jewelry?"

"No," Shaananca explained patiently, "it is a velene."

"A what, now?"

"A Restorer," S'ythreni supplied, almost warily. "Or, at least that is one way to interpret the word." She studied Shaananca from beneath straight, cautious brows. "It's Uulamantrene," she said. Druadaen wasn't sure if she was talking about the word or the velene itself.

"Well," Shaananca said through a chuckle, "there are some abroad in the world who might debate that."

"Oh?" Ahearn asked guilelessly. "And who would those be?"

"The velene," Shaananca explained as if she hadn't heard that question either, "should be able to help your canine companion travel the waves in reasonable comfort. He can drowse through much of the unpleasant motion, if you will permit the assistance."

Ahearn frowned. "What kind of assistance? Or, more to the point, how is it rendered? Will this vermine, er, vermeen, stick my poor pup with a barb? Poison it with a sleeping potion?"

Shaananca shook her head and put her hand down toward the dog.

The velene was a serpentine stream of liquid mirror-steel as it ran from the back of Shaananca's weathered hand onto Raun's nose.

The dog was either too surprised or amazed to react. Until, that is, the velene started to hum. Not in its narrow throat, but through its entire body.

Raun's eyes widened, then returned to normal, then became heavy-lidded. He lay down at Ahearn's feet. In less than ten seconds, he was emitting the wheezing grunts that were the canine equivalent of light snoring.

"By damn," breathed the swordsman.

Shaananca nodded. "Velene are quite helpful." She lowered her hand; the shining dracoform ran back up along its strong cords and age-swollen veins but did not revert into a bracelet.

Ahearn stared at it, then looked uncertainly at Shaananca. "It's a great kindness, ma'am, you giving us this metal beastie as—"

"Understand: a velene is not a gift." It ran up her arm and perched on her shoulder. Its head and neck strained toward Druadaen. "Ah," she said, and edged closer; it leaped up and in one smooth motion, was not merely perched but coiled upon Druadaen's shoulder.

It was surprisingly light and had no discernible smell: just a hint of the odor that lingers in the moment after a lightning strike. He turned his head to meet its gaze, but it only had the shape of eyes, like the face of a statue. It flowed down his arm, swept its tail once around his wrist—and suddenly was a bracelet again.

Ahearn shook his head and scoffed, but there was genuine jocularity in it. "Ah, so *it* chooses...although I wager that choice was never in doubt, eh?"

Shaananca shrugged, smiled at S'ythreni. "I believe there is an ironic aphorism in ancient Uulamantre: 'as predictable as a velene.' But it is much more beautiful in that tongue."

"*Fey-hethre sha velene sotu,*" S'ythreni almost whispered. "I

never thought to witness the source of the saying." She bowed
her head slightly; Druadaen was not certain whether she meant
it for Shaananca or the velene.

Ahearn's calculating gaze bounced between the two of them
and then Druadaen. "Ah. So, magistra, you thought the silvery
serpent might cozy up to high-ears, here."

Shaananca shrugged. "I did not speculate. As the axiom implies,
it is as futile as trying to guess where any given raindrop may
fall. However," she said with a smile and more animated tone,
"we may safely predict at least two things. First, that I must make
my way to my home and my supper. And second, that you must
finish the spirited discussion I interrupted."

Umkhira shook her head. "I am quite glad to be done com-
paring the ways of our peoples."

Shaananca nodded slowly, smiled. "Yes...although that was
not what you were actually discussing."

She firmly embraced a surprised Druadaen and turned quickly,
departing with a quick step behind the crates which had shielded
her approach.

"Now what do you s'pose she meant by that?" wondered
Ahearn, staring after her with an expression of both perplexity
and admiration.

Elweyr looked up. "She means that we were determining if
we could actually work together."

"Ah," Ahearn nodded. "You mean, instead of killing each
other?"

S'ythreni's smile was small but genuine. "Who wants to give
me odds?"

Umkhira's frown could have been because she disapproved
of wagering or didn't understand the reference. "The Dunarran
sorceress spoke both truth and wisdom. If we remain a company,
it shall be in spite of great differences. Both in our traditions and
what we each hope to achieve."

Ahearn's frown was anxious. "Now, now; let's not predict
doom because of a single contentious conversation."

"Single?" S'ythreni repeated, incredulous. "Either your memory
or mine has been scrambled by mancery or malady, because as I
recall it, contention has been the rule, not the exception."

Ahearn waved away what Druadaen considered to be her very
sound point. Instead, he spread wide his hands in appeal. "Besides,

our purposes aren't so askew, are they? We could all do with a little more coin in our pockets, and we've fewer worries to pull us away from that, now." He leaned toward Elweyr. "Thanks to inquiries by Druadaen's magic auntie, at least you're free of the charge of finding your parents."

"For now. And only if I believe her."

Druadaen bristled and didn't care that he did. "Shaananca does not lie."

Elweyr reconsidered. "No, perhaps not. But when she speaks, the words are vague enough to conceal a mountain of unspoken truths."

I would disagree, if I could, Druadaen thought ruefully.

Ahearn jumped into that moment of relative social calm with a sweeping gesture and triumphantly pleased declaration. "And so then here we are: Elweyr, High-Ears and me, with two new partners.

Druadaen raised a bemused eyebrow.

But Umkhira frowned. "I am not your partner. I am oath-bound in your service."

Ahearn rubbed his chin. "And what would you choose to do if I released you of that oath?"

The Lightstrider's frown deepened, but it had changed from dubiousness to pondering an uncertainty.

"Well," Ahearn continued, "take a moment if you must, but don't keep me waiting on that. Druadaen, what say you?"

"I say what I did at the outset: my path is already set. But I appreciate the offer."

"Well, see, and here's where I'm conceiving a fine marriage of our respective interests. You have your further voyages and investigations, yeh? Well, here we are, fresh, rested, and hoping for wider horizons in which to seek our fortune."

"Did you not in fact leave Gur Grehar with a fortune?"

"Well, in a manner of speaking. But when all is said and done, it wasn't *much* of fortune, now was it?"

Druadaen frowned. "I cannot help but notice that you used the past tense: '*wasn't* much of a fortune'?"

S'ythreni rolled her eyes. "The only thing Ahearn does better than finding riches is spending them."

"Now, see here, High-Ears, I resembl—er, *resent* that remark! But truth be told, Ar Navir is expensive wherever you go. And while it is a very fine place indeed, all the ruins and remains of its old empires—and their treasures—are either long since restored as new seats of power or have been picked through many times over.

"But as I hear it, most of the other continents are not so thoroughly reclaimed." His tone picked up a hint of understated—and wholly feigned—praise. "I suspect that's because they lacked the organizing presence of a Dunarran Empire."

"Dunarran Consentium," Druadaen corrected and could not believe what he was about to add. "And you needn't sprain your tongue and integrity with rhetorical contortions. Yes, I suppose it might be best that we travel together. I know you are no great champion of Dunarra or its ways. Still, that does not make you any less of a fine companion when it comes to facing dangers and uncertainties."

Ahearn blinked. "Well, I can't remember a speech that started so hard, and then finished so fine and fair. Well. Well. So it shall be, then."

Umkhira looked between them. "So, who is the leader now? Whose orders have precedence?"

Druadaen sighed. It was the question they had avoided addressing since the first combat against Bannef in Truce or Consequences. And it was probably the further point of discussion to which Shaananca had been alluding. But now it was out in the open and would have to be answered. He folded his arms and glanced at Ahearn. "Well?"

"Now, this is a tricky question, isn't it?" the swordsman mused uncomfortably. "We have agreed to travel with you, but all the others are here because of me. How would one make that work?"

Druadaen shrugged. "As on a ship. On a merchantman, the owner, or Master, is rarely the captain."

Elweyr nodded. "Yes. That makes sense."

Druadaen nodded back but thought: *And of course you'll make encouraging noises . . . because this is the only way you and Ahearn will ever reach more promising places for fortune-hunting.*

"So," Ahearn mused, rubbing his chin, "you tell us where the ship goes—"

"—and what agreements and alliances and enemies it makes along the way—"

"—and I run the ship. Choose the best course, fight off

boarders, decide when and where we must provision, or even—
gods forbid—dive overboard."

"We will need to work out the details," Druadaen answered,
"and hopefully without further strained nautical analogies, but
yes: that is the gist of it."

"And that is something I can live with." Ahearn looked past
Elweyr who was exchanging small nods with S'ythreni. "And
what of you, High-Ears? Fancy seeing the world?"

"The world," she sighed, "is overrated." Worried frowns sprang
up. "But that also means that one place is pretty much as good as
the next. Besides, *someone* has to keep a level head in this band."

"Hey-ah, because I'm *certainly* the tempestuous type," Elweyr
observed drily.

She actually smiled at that, as if the curve leaped to her lips
before she could control them. "Especially you," she retorted
broadly.

Elweyr smiled back.

Umkhira was looking hard at Ahearn. "If you dissolve my
oath, I will not follow you. You have the bounty-blood of my
people on your hands. I do not claim vengeance against you, but
I would dishonor any Lightstriders you slew were I to follow you
willingly. But I will promise you this, Ahearn: if you free me
of my oath"—she turned toward Druadaen—"I will follow *him*."

Druadaen nodded deeply toward her, surprised and silent—
because he didn't trust he'd find the right words and because
they would only sully the moment, anyhow.

But Ahearn was as voluble as ever, smiling broadly. "Well,
then, my fine not-green lass, your bond is no more, and we are
quit of tangly oaths and debts! We are now a company bound only
by the free choice of free beings! Now, where's a suitable libation
with which to toast the beginning of a beautiful fellowship?"

With the lights of Tlulanxu about to dip beneath the dusk-
darkened horizon, Druadaen mounted the quarterdeck to watch
them disappear. He discovered he would not be the only audience
for that silent leave-taking; Ahearn was already at the center of
the taffrail. The swordsman shifted slightly to make room.

Druadaen nodded his thanks, noticed that Ahearn's gaze
was not directly aft, but toward the starboard quarter. There
was nothing but mostly unlit coastline in that direction. Well,

Druadaen amended silently, nothing *visible*. Even though it was almost two hundred leagues to the northwest, he asked, "Looking toward Menara?"

Ahearn nodded. "It's strange to think of being so far away from it." His tone matched the faraway look in his dark eyes.

Druadaen leaned his elbows on the rail. "But it's not your home, is it?"

Ahearn shook his head without taking his eyes off the compass point to which he'd affixed them. "No, not my home." His brief smile had a hint of melancholy. "Not sure where that would be."

Druadaen nodded. Despite the vast differences in the lives they had lived, he had the same feeling. Dunarra might be where he had grown up, but every time he returned, it felt less like home. Instead, he had the sensation that it was drifting further and further behind him, just like the lights of Tlulanxu.

Ahearn's louder, more conversational tone startled him. "I've no desire to live on the sea, but I do like living close to it. Funny thing, that."

Druadaen heard an oblique invitation in his seemingly random observation. "Is that where you met her? Near the sea, in Menara?"

Ahearn's smile was almost gentle. "It's that obvious, is it?"

Druadaen smiled back. "That comment about your living by the sea: it certainly sounded to me like you were, well, fishing."

Ahearn's smile became sly. "Ah, so all that library learning didn't make you dull." He nodded. "That's good. You never know how it's going to be with bookish folk." He sighed.

Druadaen glanced at the dark spot on the coast that still held his gaze. "So: the sea."

Ahearn shrugged. "It reminds me of her. She could be just as changeable, and just as deep. And though you could never be sure what the next moment might bring, you knew she was always there and always would be." He paused. "Until she wasn't."

Druadaen had the strange sensation that, despite having spent months with Ahearn, he hadn't really met him until now.

"She was wonderful," he whispered. "At everything. She sang like an angel but had a tongue as bright and sharp as a silver whip. And handy! She made her living on the water, y'see. No task she wasn't up to."

Druadaen managed not to blink. *And this from the same fellow who railed against women doing men's work?*

"And so cunning with numbers!" Ahearn continued, his eyes drifting up to the first bright pinpricks that shone through the gloaming as Tlulanxu's lights sank beneath the black horizon. "Knew all the stars, she did: both the parts played by their namesakes in the Sagas of Serdarong, and their place on the charts by which captains navigate. By the gods, she was a natural when it came to using that fiddly bit of nautical equipment navigators call an astral—er, austral, em—"

"Astrolabe?"

"Aye, that's it!" He shot a mock-suspicious glance at Druadaen. "And from that careful look on your puss, I'm guessing you know how to use one, too."

"Well, I did spend three years on Courier ships like this one." Druadaen let a few moments pass. "She sounds like an extraordinary woman."

"Aye, that she was." Ahearn's eyes were bright with more than reflected stars. "And hey-ah, you can ask what you will. We're mates, now."

Druadaen nodded, waited a few more seconds. "What happened?"

"Life. Death. Just the natural cycle of things, I s'pose." Ahearn shrugged, his smile crooked and painful to see. "If we'd had all the time ever unspooled by the great clockwork of the heavens, it still wouldn't have been enough. So by any definition, ours was brief." He looked back down to the lightless coast. "Maybe that's the way of things, too. That the more beautiful a thing is, the shorter it seems to last. People no less than flowers."

"And that cottage outside Menara?"

He nodded. "Where she lived. With her family. I . . . I look in on 'em. From time to time."

Druadaen returned his nod, and wondered: Did he go there because it also reminded him of her? Because he somehow felt responsible for their loss? Or perhaps because they, too, had come to care for the rootless sell-sword who had fallen in love with their daughter? Which made them the closest thing he had to family.

Together they watched the night deepen and the stars emerge from it, as sharp and bright as polished sword tips.

CHAPTER THIRTY

The first half of their journey aboard the Courier brig *Swiftsure* was largely uneventful. The seaways were fairly quiet, and the ship was large enough to deter any but the most determined pirates. Even as they skirted the northern limit of the Eshfet Deep that ran like a trench between Ar Navir and the equator-straddling continent of Mihal'j, they saw no sign of the marine cryptigants that sometimes troubled passing vessels, and occasionally took one whole.

The weather was mostly fair and Raun proved to be more reliable than the ship's barometer at predicting when a storm was on the way. At first, Druadaen had to make frequent use of the velene, which invariably unwound itself into a small dragon as soon as he lowered his wrist toward Raun's dry, anxious nose. Within minutes, the huge dog was curled up and sound asleep. Perhaps he came to associate the approach of storms with comfortable sleep because, as time went on, he required the velene's intercession less. Shortly before they began tacking northwest to complete their travel to the far western shore of Ar Navir, Raun ceased to need it at all; at the approach of high weather, he simply trotted down to their cabin, paced through a few turns, and set himself down to sleep.

However, it was only as the last landmark of their home continent dropped behind—Corrovane's fortress-port of Araxor—that the group's talk turned to what Druadaen meant to do on

Far Amitryea after he had discharged his duty in Shadowmere. Which would surely be, as Ahearn confidently asserted, "but the work of an hour. If that."

Druadaen shrugged. "After returning from Gur Grehar, I encountered other impossible accounts of beings that have been worrisome to human communities."

"You mean, you have even more questions about urzhen?" Umkhira asked.

"No: about giants. After the battle with the shaman, Elweyr remarked that blugner are not lesser kin of giants and are not numbered among the Bent races at all."

Ahearn frowned. "Blugner aren't related to the Bent?" He glanced at Elweyr. "And you never bothered to tell me?"

"You never bothered to show interest."

Ahearn shrugged. "Well, I can't think of everything now, can I? So, Philosopher, what have you learned about the giants? Even if they're not Bent, are they really so different?"

"They are. And the differences are stark."

"Such as?"

Druadaen explained in detail. He was concerned that they might become bored, but instead they were not only attentive, but became more so as his description progressed.

When he was done, they exchanged wide-eyed stares. Elweyr finally rubbed his hands together. "And you mean to . . . eh, find these creatures?"

"I do."

"To do what?" S'ythreni blurted out in something that sounded very much like panic.

Umkhira shook her head in resignation. "Unless I am much mistaken—and I hope I am—he means to have speech with them."

S'ythreni cocked an ear toward the Lightstrider. "Excuse me," she said sardonically, "did you say he means to be *eaten* by them?" She straightened, face souring. "Because at least *that* makes some kind of sense. Assuming his final objective is suicide."

"Now, now," Ahearn soothed. "I doubt he means to do himself in"—his eyes shifted to Druadaen—"do you?"

"I mean to learn about them. That would have little value if I did not survive meeting them."

"Aye, aye . . . but what makes you think you *will* survive meeting them?"

Druadaen noticed that Ahearn had used the word *you* rather than *we*. "Well, firstly, I intend to approach them with extreme caution—"

"Oh, well," exclaimed S'ythreni, "I feel *so* much safer now."

"—and to observe them and their routines in detail before announcing my presence. It is essential to keep the initial contact to a single member of their community, obviously."

"Oh, obviously," the aeosti echoed.

Druadaen turned to her. "Note I use the word 'I.' This is because I only speak for myself, for my actions. If you—if all of you—decide against joining me, I neither begrudge nor blame you for making that choice. I freely acknowledge that the risk is considerable."

"Well, and who's averse to a little risk, eh?" Ahearn almost wheedled. "Better than the tunnels of Gur Grehar, surely. He's just assured us that giants live in wide-open caves or forests: easy to run from, in either case. And think of the treasures they must collect! Gigantic, just like them!"

Druadaen was about to object—no account had ever connected giants with hoarded wealth—but Elweyr caught his eyes and waggled a deck-pointing finger slightly. The look on his face was almost as easy to read: *Hold your peace, for now.*

So Druadaen remained silent as Ahearn waxed poetic and inspired about the surety of giants being in possession of long-accumulated riches—because, after all, who would have the nerve to try to take them, either by force of arms or stealth? He ignored S'ythreni's dry counter that it wasn't a lack of nerve, but a lack of idiocy, that kept fortune-seekers from hunting giants.

But Ahearn was undeterred and spun a gossamer and gold-limned tale of the ancestral treasure troves that such insuperable creatures must necessarily pass down from generation to generation, just waiting to be plucked by adventurers as bold and cunning as they! It was delightful to listen to.

It was also sheer fabulation. Or, as Umkhira pronounced in her one-sentence coda, "Those are hopes made to sound like truth. So, they are cousins to lies." And yet, she did not refuse to take part in the venture.

It was late by the time the discussion broke up, having carried straight on through dinner. Although never a sound and ready sleeper, Druadaen had learned during his years as a Courier that nighttime aboard a ship in calm seas was often soothing, which meant longer and more restful periods of slumber, some of which were blissfully dreamless. And if he did find himself wandering through the Wildscape, whatever determined the severity of its typical cavalcade of savage misadventures, chaos, and disorientation also seemed to respond to the quieting effects of the gentle risers.

So it was with relief rather than trepidation that he anticipated the dubious comfort of his cramped bunk and left the others to conclude their meal and deliberations without him.

Druadaen woke in a room which seemed very familiar, but which he did not immediately recognize. Not until he realized that he was still asleep and dreaming of Dunarra.

Except this was not like any dream he had ever had before. It had the crisp sensory edges and detail of reality, rather than the mere impression of being real. The point of view was unusual as well; he was looking over the sloping shoulder of a woman somewhere between aged and elderly.

It was Shaananca's shoulder, he realized when she spoke. "We have had word from the Urn Wardens of Corrovane. The ship has departed Araxor and is underway to Far Amitryea."

Beyond the weary curve of her shoulder and long gray mane of hair, he saw a man of similarly indeterminate but advanced years. Among the neighboring nations, he would likely be deemed halfway through his sixth decade and well preserved, at that.

"These activities of his: Do they pose a risk?"

"I would need to know what you mean by that, old friend."

The man sighed, a frown of regret growing on his brow. "For now, Shaananca, I must ask these questions not as your friend, but as the Propretor Princeps."

Propretor Princeps! So this was Alcuin IV's grandfather, Alcuin II. Druadaen saw both similarities and distinctions between their faces and allowed that his mind had conjured up a very convincing blend of features.

"Very well, Propretor Princeps," Shaananca answered, even more wearily than the other, "but I remain unsure what kind of risks you mean. That he will inadvertently reveal state secrets? No, he hasn't enough pieces of knowledge from which to assemble any such deeper truth. Or perhaps, that he will cause an incident with some foreign ruler? No, because we have seen that is not in his nature."

"Came damned close to doing so in Menara last year," the man interrupted.

"That was a more complicated situation than it first seems, Propretor."

"How so?"

"Alas, to address that adequately requires a great deal of additional background. Do you wish me to—?"

"No, no," he waved irritably. "Let us stay on present issues. So, firstly: You do not believe the lad presents any risk in the conventional sense of the word?"

"Correct, Propretor. But again, I must ask: What kind of unconventional risk do you fear he might pose?"

"It is not he who poses the risk, Senior Archivist. It is his questions, no less than the answers he's discovered. All of which become far more problematic, now that you have been compelled to store his notes in the Reserved Collection."

Shaananca leaned forward. "Is it his findings that worry you, or that they may now be accessed by—?"

"Senior Archivist." She grew silent at his severe look and equally severe tone. "Druadaen is asking not just one, but many questions. And for every question, there are many possible consequences. Any of them could cause one or more of the pillars of our strategic edifice to wobble, maybe fall. And although there is no way to predict which might start tumbling first, it is a surety that one or more will eventually impact the most rigid and fragile of the Consentium's buttresses."

Shaananca nodded. "The temples."

"The temples," confirmed the dream-image of Alcuin II. "And I can only imagine that their response would be—"

Abruptly, the dream was over and replaced with another that was equally vivid. But the change was so rapid that it lacked the lurching nausea of the Wildscape hurling him from one surreal scenario to another as it churned through its constant and chaotic transmutations. This was a sharp, jarring shock, as if he'd fallen through the floor of one reality into another in the blink of an eye.

Ahearn, Elweyr, and S'ythreni were sitting in a tight cluster, just abaft the *Swiftsure*'s midship companionways into the hold. The night was calm, but clouds were scudding across Duryonax, the one risen moon.

"—never would have believed that a Lightstrider would agree to march alongside the Dunarran into certain death. And all for the sake of *knowledge*," S'ythreni was saying. "Knowledge he is never going to get, by the way." She looked from one human to the other. "And you're both going along with this insanity as well? Truly?"

Elweyr shrugged. "It might be insanity for him, but not for us."

"Explain that." Her tone was somewhere between a request and a command.

The mantic shrugged. "Traveling with him means we can listen for word of new places that are likely to be profitable for us to visit."

Ahearn leaned in. "Ar Navir's naught but occasional wars between nations and races, now. The only old sites of wealth are on—or within—the lands roved by the Bent. But Far Amitryea? Now, there's a seat of once great power that, to hear Druadaen tell it, hasn't been able to form up into great nations for over a millennium. Lots of outback that's never been stripped by armies careening this way and that."

S'ythreni nodded. "So if he's determined to parry a giant's paw with his skull, we leave him to it and seek more promising opportunities. Very well. I can accept that."

But Ahearn was shaking his head. "That's not what I was suggesting, High-Ears. I'm for trying to talk sense into him if his quest turns out to be as hopeless as the rest of us suspect."

"Why? So he can conceive of some new but equally insipid quest?"

Elweyr looked up at her. "Do you like the odds of just the three of us trying to locate, then find our way around, and finally drag loot out of old ruins? Because if Druadaen doesn't come, then Umkhira doesn't either. And we are back down to where we were in Menara: just the three of us. I'm not fond of those odds."

"Besides," Ahearn said with a mischievous twinkle, "there's something to be said for traveling along with a feller as well-placed as he is. A magistra, and probably Guide of the Ar, as his auntie? Who must have been the one with the authority to hold this ship in port long enough for him to meet up with us? And who gave him a magical metal monster as a going-away present? I wish I had someone who'd drop in to say, 'Farewell and here's a vermin for you!'"

"Velene," S'ythreni corrected, "and Shaananca was correct; you don't give a velene to a person. They make their own choices."

"You talk of it as if it was alive," Elweyr observed.

"It might be," she retorted. "There's a lot more legend about them than reliable fact. But I agree with at least one thing you've said, Ahearn: having friends who walk around with a velene on their arm means having friends with real power."

Ahearn nodded. "And where would the likes of us find access to that on our own, hey? We could roam across this tired old globe for a century and never even meet such folk, much less find ourselves on speaking terms with them. Mark my words: we stick with that feller, peculiarities and all, and we'll find patrons with bigger plans and deeper pockets than we ever dreamed."

She looked from one to the other again. "So, you're serious? About this idea that we're all one big, happy fellowship of fortune-seekers?"

"In fact, I am," Ahearn announced, a bit defensively. "Naive or not, I have to admit Druadaen may be on to something with these questions of his. Mad as they seem."

S'ythreni shrugged. "It's not the questions I mind. It's the kind of attention they may attract. As Elweyr said the day we left, the Consentium got rid of him for a reason. And whatever that reason is, it will stick to us as long as we stick with him."

Ahearn nodded. "Aye, but that's simply what comes of traveling with well-placed folk, now, isn't it? With greater influence comes greater opportunities, but also greater trouble. So I'm of a philosophical mind on that point. Besides, I have to admire a man who's got the courage to ask unpopular questions and stand by costly convictions—mad as they may be."

S'ythreni shook her head, glanced at Elweyr, who was shaking his own. At her. "Leave his crazy quests aside for a moment. He's pretty good to work with. Learns quickly. Good in a fight. Doesn't lose his head. Almost as strong as Ahearn and definitely more agile."

The swordsman reared back, affronted, but did not interrupt.

"He's got a lot of useful information between his ears and he's able to put it to practical use. And best of all, he doesn't belong to either category of fortune-seeker we've had to deal with over the years."

"And they are?"

Ahearn folded his arms. "Aristocratic second-son adventurers who are ready to grab fame and fortune by climbing to it upon the bodies of their 'lessers.' Or, gods help us, temple-sent, crusading zealots." He shook his head. "Right away, you could tell he wasn't either of those."

S'ythreni frowned. "How?"

Elweyr shrugged. "The way he pitched in beside us in the tavern. And later, how he shared everything that was in his pack. He never held anything back, and he never argued about his share of any gains made along the way."

"So, you're saying he is stupid. Or spoiled. Or both."

Ahearn tapped an impatient toe on the deck. "Or he's simply honest, as strange a concept as that may seem. Gods above and below, if that's stupidity, then we could all afford a bit more of it. You do what you want or what you must, High-Ears, but my mind is made up."

He made to leave but S'ythreni spoke quickly. "It's not that I don't think he's—an acceptable companion. But he's dangerous."

Ahearn and Elweyr frowned. The latter asked, "Dangerous in what way?"

She held a palm aloft. "Yes, he has powerful friends and mentors. Yes, he has surprising amounts of knowledge, even for a Dunarran. But he's *already* attracted far too much attention of people far above his station. That's dangerous under any circumstances, but in his case, no one—not even he—knows why. Or they're not saying."

She looked urgently from one to the other. "Those kind of secrets can hide interests and enemies that could do away with us as easily as they'd pop a soap bubble." She held her hands tightly in her lap. "You haven't...lived as long as I have. Seen as much. All of which tells me that he isn't *possibly* dangerous; he already *is*. And the longer anyone is connected to him, the more his fate becomes theirs. Are you ready for that?"

Elweyr glanced at Ahearn, who recrossed his arms. "Not sure that I am. But likewise, I'm not sure that I'm not. Either way, no harm tagging along for now. It's weeks before we reach Far Amitryea, and then we'll see what we see. Now, let's away lest the Lightstrider wakes and decides to come looking for us."

Druaden tried to speak. Couldn't. Tried shouting—

—and heard the words coming out of his mouth even as he

jerked upright in his bunk and hit his head against the overhead crossbeam. The *crack!* was so sharp that it surprised him even more than the sudden flash of pain.

Rubbing the spot where he could feel a goose-egg lump forming, he saw that Ahearn and Elweyr were not in their bunks. Even asleep, he must have sensed that they still hadn't returned to the cabin, and so the Wildscape had populated a dream with them.

Except, he reflected, he hadn't felt trapped the way he did within the aimless and insane scenes through which the Wildscape incessantly pushed him. In this dream, he'd felt the way he imagined a ghost might, hovering in a room, overhearing others, but unable to act. A very, very strange dream, indeed. And so startlingly realistic. *But still,* he thought with a smile, *it is certainly better than the Wildscape.*

Now, if only he could get back to sleep despite the throbbing in his head.

CHAPTER THIRTY-ONE

Evidently, the crew of the *Swiftsure* sighted the eastern coast of Far Amitryea sometime in the dark hours of the morning, because by the time Druadaen and the others came on deck, she was already several leagues into the Earthrift Channel.

Druadaen peered through the clearing mists at the landmass to starboard: North Omthrye. Its coast rose gently from the faint breakers to broad strands, and occasional farmlands beyond.

"So," said Elweyr's voice behind him, "how many times did your Courier duties bring you here?"

Druadaen moved aside so the mantic had room along the gunwale. "Once, and we never made landfall." He smiled. "We were there to take Outriders off the shore, not deposit our own upon it."

Umkhira had overheard and joined them. "You send Outriders so far from home?"

Druadaen nodded. "Like the mariners among us, those who are based on foreign soil are a special group. They are called 'overseas expeditionaries' and are officially part of the Couriers."

"Officially," echoed Elweyr with a sly smile. "Because it sounds better to say you have Couriers in other countries rather than armed scouts, I take it."

Druadaen returned his smile. "That is the unspoken understanding among us."

"And is that an island to the southwest?" Ahearn shouted, pointing to the opposite horizon.

Druadaen frowned. "No, I think those are the highlands west of Wydshanan, the only realm of consequence on this coast."

A new voice from back near the starboard quarterdeck stairs rose above the hoarse rush of swells rolling past the hull. "You seem passably acquainted with these lands, having never visited them, Outrider Druadaen." The voice was that of Captain Firinne, who had proven to be not only a fine shipmistress, but the very soul of discretion. At least when it came to the unique collection of companions that Druadaen had brought aboard her hull.

Druadaen turned, prepared to raise his hand to his chest in salute, but she waved it off. "You've spent too much time in Tlulanxu," she muttered through a grin.

"My presence here proves that you are not alone in that opinion," he said, hoping his smile wasn't as crooked as it felt.

Firinne's glance suggested she was as astute as she was discreet. "Nor are you alone in being sent on a very small assignment to a very distant land." She winked in response to his surprised stare. "And ships which sail the expanse between Ar Navir and Far Amitryea carry more such hapless servitors than others, I reck."

"The further the better, eh?" Ahearn suggested in a stage whisper.

She looked at him out of the corner of her eye. "I will allow you to draw your own conclusions on that, swordsman. In the meantime, I will ask you all to make ready for action."

Druadaen was the only one who did not spend a long moment staring at her. "Enemies sighted, Captain?"

She jutted her prominent chin westward beyond the bowsprit. "No reason to expect so, and still too far off to see. Just caught sight of topsails ahead."

Ahearn seemed surprised. "Is such precaution customary... Captain?"

She looked at him more carefully this time. "Why do you ask, Master Ahearn?"

"Well, it's just that—well, the short of it is that I had a...a friend who officered ships in the Sea of Kudak. And so, Dunarran pennants were a regular sight, crisscrossing that pond as they do. But sh—my friend never mentioned that your ships take up arms merely upon glimpsing another sail."

She smiled. "Your 'friend' did not mislead you. But the Sea of Kudak is all open water. The Earthrift Channel is less than ten leagues wide here, and ahead, will narrow to three, at parts."

Elweyr crossed his arms. "Good hunting spot for pirates."

Firinne nodded. "And what might be worse. Suffice to say, we take no chances in these tight waters. Too easy for smaller ships to come out of the coves on either side of the channel and box us in. So forewarned is forearmed as they say, and if any mean to stand before us, our course of action shall not be to come about, but crowd sail and cut through." She looked around the group. "Can I count on all of you?"

"You can count on us," Druadaen answered before anyone else could open their mouths. This was a decision for the company's "master aboard" rather than "captain," and he meant to set that precedent quickly and clearly.

Firinne looked at him with a surprised, and pleased, smile. "Very well, then. You'll want your weapons. And if you don't have light armor, speak to the purser; he has some in stores."

The voice from the maintop crow's nest was stentorian but also hoarse from the many reports of the past hour: "A dark gray sword on a white escutcheon, framed by midnight blue. Ship out o' Corrovane, Captain!"

Firinne's return bellow was not only loud but surprisingly deep-toned. "Is she showing a response to our welcome code?"

Druadaen glanced up at the array of colored pennants on the starboard mainstay.

"No, ma'am," came the wind-muffled reply. "Probably hasn't seen ours, yet."

"Or is not really a Greyblade ship," muttered Elweyr.

"Possibly," Druadaen agreed, "but it's more likely their telescopes are more rudimentary." He studied the mantic. "You called it a 'Greyblade' ship. Do you speak Old Amitryean?"

His eyes conspicuously avoided meeting Druadaen's. "Some," he said. "I'm a thaumantic. I spend a lot of time with old scrolls and dead languages."

"Old Amitryean isn't entirely dead," Druadaen pointed out.

"What are you two on about?" Ahearn muttered. "Here we are, possibly ready to cross swords with pirates, and you decide to have a scholarly argument over a few archaic words?"

Firinne had overheard and was smiling shrewdly. "Not just any words, swordsman. And not from a dead language." She nodded at the ship approaching. "Corrovane: *corrov* is Old Amitryean for 'grey'; *vaan* is 'sword.' Your friend translated the name of the nation for us. No mean feat." She nodded to Elweyr who looked simultaneously annoyed and anxious.

"Captain!" shouted the lookout. "She's run up a response. One of the correct codes. And she's run up a counter-challenge."

"Make reply," Firinne thundered up along the mainmast.

Umkhira's gaze roved over the crew, who had reacted with relief. "So, the ship ahead is showing a true flag?"

Firinne raised an eyebrow. "Looks like it. But we'll stay prepared until we're sure. It would be quite a coup for pirates to be able to mimic our safety codes...but when you've been at sea as long as I have, you don't put anything beyond the realm of possibility, Mistress Warrior." She nodded a curt farewell and headed back up to the quarterdeck, shouting orders as she went.

The captain of the Corrovane ship *Atremoënse*—or, *Ready Narwhal*—was like so many of his infamously dour countrymen: taciturn and serious. His first words as he came aboard were, "Greetings. Where are you bound?"

Either Captain Firinne was happy to dispense with formalities and courtesies, or she had ample experience dealing with the Corrovani. "Shadowmere. You?"

"Crynyrcar. Our home port. Your business in Shadowmere: Is it refit or assignment?"

"Some of both." Firinne gestured for Druadaen to stand forward. "This young fellow has sealed orders and summaries for the station officer."

The Corrovani captain kept his focus and speech directed toward Firinne. "You are referring to the commander of your Overseas Expeditionary Consulate, there?" Druadaen could hear the capitals in the way he said it.

The moment after Captain Firinne nodded, the Corrovani turned to Druadaen. "Then your journey will not end at Shadowmere. The station officer, Talshane, departed while we were laying over there. He had urgent business in Crimatha. Do you know it?"

"I know of it, sir. I have never been."

"I've ported at Treve a few times," Firinne interjected. "Is he in the field or the capital?"

"I cannot say. He meant to remain in Treve, I think, but I am uncertain that the circumstances will allow that. He is responding to a sensitive matter that arose on the realm's frontiers. I believe an attempt to poison several of your Outriders was involved."

Firinne frowned. "I appreciate the information, but it is unusually... detailed. Were any of your Urnwards operating in concert with our Outriders?"

The Corrovani may have smiled. "It is always a pleasure dealing with another veteran of such matters. No Urnwards were personally committed to the activities, but several of their servitors were. Your forces at the consulate were overextended, so some of ours were tasked to assist, including she who was to be my ship's sacrist for our return. She is named Padrajisse and was sent by her temple in Shadowmere to assist Talshane in his investigation. She will need the help of our allies to make her return to Ar Navir; we have no other official ship traveling to or from Far Amitryea for the rest of this season. So, if it should be within the scope of your authority and permissions, it would be a great favor and service to the Urn if you would port there before sailing for home."

Firinne smiled thinly. "I would be happy to help our friends of Corrovane, even if we did not need to detour there, now."

The Corrovani cocked his head in curiosity; it made Druadaen think of a quizzical dog.

Firinne explained. "It just so happens that my next orders were not given to me directly. For reasons unknown, they are in the secure pouch carried by this fellow, and which have been sealed and cyphered so that only the station officer—Talshane—can access them. So it seems that I will by necessity be aiming my bow at the very port to which your sacrist has traveled."

He inclined his head slightly. "I shall convey what little we know of the present conditions in Treve, as well as our sacrist's particulars, that you may know how best to seek her when you arrive. Would it be convenient to speak in your cabin, Captain?"

CHAPTER THIRTY-TWO

Treve was by no means a breathtaking city, but there were still a few towering edifices from earlier epochs. It had been the thriving capital of Steelring for eight centuries, dominating affairs on Far Amitryea for at least half of that time.

But that era had ended seven centuries ago, and the many reconstructions since then reflected both the diminished ambitions and dogged pragmatism of its inhabitants. With the exception of fortifications and watchtowers, buildings rarely rose above three stories, but they were overwhelmingly of whole- or part-stone construction and served by long thoroughfares that ran like spokes away from its modest but well-developed harbor.

Debarking just an hour before dusk, Captain Firinne sent a mate to guide them to the small, solid building that was dedicated to the affairs of Dunarra's Overseas Expeditionary Couriers. Its shape and conspicuous patrols made it seem more like a blockhouse in a hostile borderland, but Druadaen and the others received a fair, if terse welcome. They received an equally terse explanation that they should return the next day, when Talshane was sure to be available. And when they inquired after the Corrovani sacrist Padrajisse, only one of them had ever heard the name, and she had no idea where that worthy might be found.

At that point, the choice before Druadaen and his companions was either to return to the *Swiftsure* for another predictable supper and hard bunk, or to part with some billon to spend the night ashore. In the end, they arrived at a unanimous and reasonably economical compromise: to dine on land and then sleep aboard ship.

The mate had no recommendations regarding the city's public kitchens—it was only his second time in Treve—so they returned to Captain Firinne as Ahearn finished securing Raun in their cabin. Firinne nodded and frowned as she considered their options and finally proclaimed "Shan's Shanty," just as Ahearn reemerged.

"That doesn't sound like an inn," Elweyr observed hesitantly.

"That's because it's not," she explained. "It's a tavern. Right near the docks. Only a few minutes' walk. Even if one has been in their cups." She shot a fast, appraising glance at Ahearn.

Who was running a broad hand through his thick black hair. "Now, the thing of it is that ... well, the last time all of us went to a tavern together—"

"Its food is better than any of the nearby inns, its drinks are fairly priced and not watered, and it's under the protection of the mariner's guild."

"Which means—?" S'ythreni wondered.

"Thieves and brigands know not to show their faces in there. If there's a crime committed on or near the docks, the guild knows. And it is the guild that metes out the punishment ... and they have an 'eye for an eye' concept of justice. Literally."

As one, they all began nodding, but Firinne held up a hand that signaled the addition of an important caveat. They waited.

"The only thing you should bear in mind is that we're not the only ship from Ar Navir in port. There's a Kar Krathaun merchantman here, as well. She's leaving on the morrow, so her crew may go ashore for a last night of liberty."

Elweyr rolled his eyes and groaned faintly.

"Is that bad?" Umkhira asked.

"It's not good," he replied sourly.

Firinne grinned ruefully. "Mind your step around them if you can. Now, I have to settle accounts with the purser, a task I find just slightly less enjoyable than a bout of dysentery." With a genial nod, she slipped through the weather deck hatchway into the sterncastle.

Once she was gone, Umkhira turned back to Elweyr. "Why

must we 'mind our step' when in the presence of these, eh, Kar Krathauans?"

He sighed. "Because Kar Krathau has been at war with Corrovane for... well, I guess four centuries now."

Umkhira frowned. "But we are not sworn to the service of Corrovane."

"No, but he"—Ahearn broke in, aiming a finger at Druadaen—"is a Dunarran."

Umkhira nodded cautiously. "So in the case of the Kar Krathauans, it is as the saying has it: 'My enemy's friends are my enemies'?"

Elweyr tilted his head slightly. "Well, yes... but it's more than that. The Kar Krathauans have their own, eh, difficulties with Dunarrans."

Umkhira nodded. "So they feel wronged by the Dunarrans."

"Not so much wronged. More like a... an old grudge between families that once feuded. Same with the Crimathans, for that matter."

She folded her arms. "I do not see why the Kar Krathauans' dislike of the Corrovani would touch the Crimathans. They—we—are on the other side of a wide ocean."

Druadaen nodded encouragingly. "It doesn't make much sense... until you start listening to the local language, and then think back to the speech of the Corrovani captain who came aboard the *Swiftsure*."

She frowned. "Yes, the word-sounds are like unto each other. So, are the Crimathans the descendants of the Corrovani, then?"

Druadaen smiled. "More the other way around, if there is any truth in their legends. At any rate, that's why Corrovane sends ships here to trade, despite the distance; among nations, they are as cousins."

"And yet the Kar Krathauans cross the same great ocean to this place. Why? To be despised?"

Elweyr's grin was crooked. "No: to be provocative."

Ahearn nodded. "I'll tell you the one thing that *I* know about 'em: whereas the soldiers and generals of most warlike nations are more bluster than business, that's not the case with the Kar Krathauans."

"And they despise cowards," S'ythreni murmured. "Their own, most of all."

Umkhira nodded and stood. "Now I understand. I hope we

shall see some of these Kar Krathauns. I wish to observe them. Let us heed the captain's advice and go the tavern with good food and drink."

"Well," drawled S'ythreni, "it appears that the gods of the ur zhog have granted your wish."

"Bloody hell," muttered Ahearn, leading them quickly to a table against the same wall as the door through which they'd just entered Shan's Shanty.

"There are Kar Krathauans in here?" Umkhira asked in a tone that was anything but muted. "Where?"

"Stop craning your neck," S'ythreni muttered. "They're already looking at us."

Umkhira noticed that the entire taproom had grown quiet; indeed, half of the patrons were looking at her. Their faces showed fear, anger, curiosity, sometimes a mix of all three.

"Are my people unknown here?" she murmured as she sat in a chair that had its back to the room.

Druadaen was on the verge of suggesting that was a very vulnerable position, thought the better of it, and answered, "No. But on Far Amitryea, no humans ever make common cause with the Bent."

An unfamiliar voice asked, "A word, if you please?"

They turned, discovered an elderly man several paces away, as if he were cautiously approaching wild animals. Which, given his frank and horrified stare at Umkhira, might have been exactly what was going through his mind. "Of course," answered Druadaen, who made to stand.

The other waved him down. "We're a peaceful place," he muttered. "The odd bar fight over a spouse or a wager, mind ye, but nothing that results in loss of life or limb." Now he was trying very hard not to look at Umkhira.

"So we have been told," Druadaen said calmly, "by Captain Firinne of the *Swiftsure*. Who recommended your tavern above all others." He offered a faint smile.

"Aye? Captain Firinne?" It was unclear if he was surprised or puzzled. "Well, if it's as you say, then you're right welcome here. All of you. So long as you ... well, leave us as you found us, if you take my meaning."

"I shall not disrupt this place," Umkhira said frankly, and again, perhaps a bit too loudly.

He stared at her as if she were preparing to devour him at a single gulp.

Umkhira straightened—rather majestically, Druadaen thought—and assured him, "As I am a guest here, it is my duty to defend your tavern, not despoil it. This is the way of my people."

The owner goggled at her. "Why...why that's well said." He glanced at Druadaen. "She's not from here, I wager? And so well spoke...for a pek."

S'ythreni put her face in her palm; Ahearn rolled his eyes; Umkhira's brow came down.

Druadaen stood. "Sir, it may not be known to you, but pe... that word is very offensive to my friend. She is a Lightstrider, an ur zhog, and is not only well spoken and brave but flawlessly polite and honest. More so than most humans."

The barkeep's responding gulp was so long and loud that Druadaen momentarily feared he had truly swallowed his tongue. But it finally made a voluble reappearance: "Now, I had no intent to give offense. And she's a what? A Lightstrider?"

Umkhira had calmed—slightly—but shook her head as she glanced at Druadaen. "I feared this when you said that there is no contact between Bent and human in these lands. If any ur zhog were ever here, we have long since ceased to be."

Druadaen reached out a hand to the owner's shoulder. "If we are not welcome here, we will leave. But we would prefer to stay. The choice is yours."

The look on the old fellow's face was similar to the one Druadaen had seen on Couriers and Outriders about to plunge into their first combat. The shoulder beneath his palm was trembling: possibly with fear, but more likely, the palsy of age.

The barkeep shook himself and looked up into Druadaen's face, as if seeing it anew. "Why, you and your friends shall stay right where you are. What shall I bring you?"

The evening progressed pleasantly enough. Half of the patrons were locals, as was obvious from their easy and boisterous camaraderie. But there were other strangers like themselves, many from the smaller or greater ships that rode at anchor out in Treve's deep bay or tied to her sturdy wharves.

And then there were the Kar Krathauans. There were four of them, three of whom wore dragon-emblazoned livery of some

kind and were in gambesons: near-proof that they had left much
more substantial armor behind. They were, however, armed with
swords that were broader in the tang but smaller at the tip than
those Druadaen was accustomed to.

The fourth of their number did not have their features nor
their martial presence, and so, Druadaen speculated, might not be
a countryman of theirs. By far the most garrulous, he was also
the most expressive. He was also the only one who frequently
glanced at Druadaen and his companions, wearing an expression
both contemptuous and resentful. But the three Kar Krathauans
with him barely reacted to whatever gibes and detractions he was
muttering. Druadaen, like the others, affected not to notice him.

But they remained peripherally aware of his muted declama-
tions, and so were unsurprised when, on his way back from the
privy, he swerved toward their table.

"Ah, gabar guts," mumbled Ahearn testily, "here we go."

The lean man stopped as if surprised, a full table still between
him and Druadaen. "Well, now, what's this?" He looked around
at the patrons immediately surrounding him. "Why didn't any
of you fine people tell me a circus was come to Treve?"

The few smiles his remark earned were either nervous or
uncomfortable.

"No," he seemed to realize on a second, closer consideration
of Druadaen and his companions. "Not a circus, after all. It's
more of an invasion, isn't it? After all, that is a Dunarran ship in
port, and we all know what they do best: conquer other lands!"

Rather than paying attention to the fellow's insipid insults,
Druadaen had been concentrating on his accent. He was almost
certainly from Caottalura, a frequent—albeit odd-bedfellow—ally
of Kar Krathau.

Disappointed by the lack of response from either Druadaen's
companions or the patrons, he stepped closer. "But it seems the
Imperial Eagle must be molting, if these are the most fearsome
invaders it can deposit on these shores. Human riffraff, an aeosti,
an arse-scratching cave dweller, and just one stripling from the
bosom of Dunarra itself. Here to plant the tattered old imperial
flag, no doubt. Tell me, just what have you come here to accomplish, Outrider? World conquest? Again?"

Umkhira stirred in her chair. As she did, Ahearn shook
his head once, sharply. At the same moment, the oldest—and

largest—of the three Kar Krathauans rose wearily and paced over to their table.

When he'd come to a stop, Druadaen looked away from the slender japester and nodded at the newcomer. "I have never understood the Kar Krathaun toleration of allies such as Caottalurans."

The man's dark brows lowered. "We share common interests."

"Particularly against imperial pretenders," the much leaner man sneered.

Druadaen kept his eyes on the Kar Krathauan. "So that is your point of allegiance with this Caottaluran? Resentment over the Consentium's debatable action, now two millennia past?"

The man's frown didn't disappear but became strained. "We set our own course and mean to have our lands back from the Greyblade usurpers. Those who side with them are our adversaries."

Druadaen nodded. "Fairly spoken."

"You agree with him?" S'ythreni wondered aloud.

"No, but he speaks what he holds to be true, frankly and without insult." Druadaen shook his head. "All too often, it seems, honorable warriors find themselves in association with jackals who have less stomach for drawn swords than baiting words." He shrugged. "But no surprise there: raillery is invariably the preferred weapon of cowards."

The Kar Krathauan's only reply was a single twitch of his lower lip.

But the Caottaluran's response was a swiftly drawn dagger. He aimed the point of the slightly curved blade at Druadaen. "Who are you calling a coward, Dunarran?"

Druadaen shrugged, found it strangely easy to smile. Partly because although the Caottaluran had more mettle and skill than he'd thought, he also saw sloppy execution in the rapid drawing of the dagger. Sloppy enough that he was not a profound threat. Still matching the Krathaun's steady gaze, Druadaen shrugged. "I did not insult any individual, but rather, a *kind* of person. The kind that uses words like needles...but who is always ready to hide behind the blade of a more resolute ally." He glanced sideways at the Caottaluran. "I'm sure you know the type."

In the moment of silence that followed, Druadaen went outside himself as his parents had taught him. He remained ready, but for a single instant, widened his perception to the entirety of his surroundings as a detached observer.

And realized that there were two armed men at a nearby table who had been the only ones in the room who had not turned toward, or otherwise took notice of, the increasingly tense exchange.

So when the Caottaluran tried to combine a sudden slash with a hasty backstep, Druadaen was up in the same moment, pushing his chair back with his calves—and then spinning into a long, leaping stride toward the two suspiciously oblivious men.

Who, just starting to rise and draw, were startled by his sudden charge and the longsword that was clearing its sheath.

Druadaen had a glimpse of Ahearn already on his feet, sword drawn in the direction of the Kar Krathauan, who was doing the same with a resigned look and a smothered sigh.

The Caottaluran had taken a further step back, winding up in a stance not of a knife-fighter, but a mantic. Umkhira was surging up from her chair but had only brought a hatchet. S'ythreni, on the other side of the table, was coming around Druadaen's empty chair, but would not reach the Lightstrider's flank before the two other Kar Krathauans had met her in a headlong rush from their own table.

Druadaen chose the more surprised of the two men with whom he was closing, prepared to feint with a shortcut that he would then wrist-roll into a thrust—

Blinding light filled the taproom. Gasps broke through the terrified silence of the moment before.

"Hold!" boomed a voice that would have suited a king's herald.

Druadaen regretted ceding his advantage over the two men but checked his thrust. The only sound was the Caottaluran's deep gasps for air, punctuated by sputtered curses in his own language.

Druadaen turned toward the source of the light. A tall, almost gaunt woman of middle years stood in the far corner of the tavern, holding aloft a steel-shod stave. Its cap was a pinpoint of intense, almost painful, white light.

"It is unlawful to draw weapons in this public house," she said. Although her slow, solemn tone made it sound like more of a pronouncement than a statement.

"I was insulted! I challenged the Dunar—"

"Your insults were direct, Caottaluran, and they preceded those you impute to him," she corrected loudly. "And you did not challenge before you attacked."

"Such matters are handled otherwise, where I am from."

"If by that you mean Caottaluran society practices ambush and assassination as part of its 'honor code,' why yes, I believe I have heard something like that. But you know the rules of this place. As do your comrades."

The Caottaluran clutched his throat briefly, flashing rage-narrowed eyes at Elweyr's raised fingers before making his reply. "You have no knowledge of what I knew and what I did not, hag!"

"Ah. More insults," the woman croaked. "So, perhaps you are hoping that *I* shall challenge you, now? I shall, if you wish. Here, in front of these many witnesses. And we may settle the matter outside without delay."

The Caottaluran raised his chin. "And how does one duel with the miracles of a consecrant?"

"By using your own mantic powers," Elweyr observed drily. "However modest they seem to be."

Still rubbing at the base of his windpipe, the Caottaluran's intended rejoinder was interrupted when the Kar Krathauan's free hand came down with a clap upon his thin shoulder. "Enough," the broad, dour warrior intoned. He sheathed his sword and glanced at his purported ally. "If you wish to injure your own pride with such mewling, that is your affair. But we will not remain with you if you only mean to exchange barbs, rather than blows. So duel or desist, but otherwise, we depart. The choice is yours. Make it now and state it clearly."

"We shall depart," the mantic muttered, his voice quavering with rage. "But I have a long memory, sacrist." As he sheathed his dagger, it reflected light as if a moving snake had somehow been incised upon it. He stepped back so he was alongside the Kar Krathauan. "And I shall certainly remember you, too, Dunarran."

"Of that I have little doubt." Druadaen shifted his gaze to the man's dour companion. "Your honor is an adornment to your people." The warrior's eyes widened slightly. "But your choice of allies is unfortunate."

The Kar Krathauan shrugged as he moved toward the exit, giving Druadaen's table a wide berth. "Our choices are our own. And your counsel is neither wanted nor needed." He nodded as he opened the door into the night, his men and the Caottaluran hard on his heels.

Druadaen turned to the tall woman as her blindingly bright staff began to dim. "Sacrist Padrajisse, I presume?"

CHAPTER THIRTY-THREE

Druadaen had guessed correctly; their rescuer was indeed Padra-jisse. But his hopes to strike up a conversation with her were dashed within a minute.

She dismissed their profuse thanks, asserting brusquely that, at best, she had saved one of their lives and prevented wounds from being inflicted upon the others. Having kept the Kar Krathauans under observation since returning to the city three days ago, she was convinced the group would have dealt them a swift and decisive defeat. As part of the ship's fighting detachment, they were more imposing in appearance than performance, she asserted. However, she deemed their leader markedly more competent and experienced: he could have proven "difficult," according to Padrajisse.

As far as the Caottaluran was concerned, her inquiries revealed that he had been in Crimatha for some time, and had probably been involved, at least peripherally, with the poisoning of the Outriders. Ahearn had clapped Elweyr on the shoulder, expressing confidence that his thaumantic friend would have made short work of the fellow. Padrajisse agreed, but then warned the swordsman against making further assumptions given his "obvious ignorance regarding mantics and their arts." Ahearn recoiled as if struck, but before resentment overtook his surprise, she explained that some Caottal-uran mantics were the product of a semisecret group known as the Sanslova, who practiced a unique blend of mancery and alchemy.

According to the sacrist, their true danger lay in their ability to gather and share information swiftly over great distances. Elweyr, more circumspect than usual, simply nodded, but Druadaen had the impression that he recognized their name.

Padrajisse was equally blunt in dismissing whatever role she might have had in settling the matter of the poisoned Outriders, claiming that she merely wished to "prove useful" before sailing home. She did not sound eager to return to Corrovane, but she seemed even less sanguine at the prospect of remaining in Crimatha. Or anywhere in Far Amitryea, for that matter.

Druadaen had mentioned that the captain of the *Atremoënse* intimated that she might welcome the prospect of joining them in their travels through Crimatha. Her first response was a dry grunt. Her second was hardly more reassuring. "Why not?" she had muttered as she rose to return to the temple hosting her in Treve. She flatly refused the group's offers to escort her, dismissing the notion that the Kar Krathauans might be lying in wait along her route.

The group ate their meal in comparative silence, other than a few trenchant observations on the sacrist's demeanor. As they returned to the *Swiftsure*, they decided to seek an early meeting with Talshane. Perhaps he might offer some perspective upon her singular behavior.

They arrived at the fortlike consulate while the rest of the city was still waking, peering out windows to check the dove-gray skies for hints of the day's weather. Druadaen was the only one who was not surprised to discover the Dunarrans already up and active. Two guards made brisk patrols around the crenellated parapet of the roof wall. Messengers, both mounted and afoot, were already being dispatched and received. After a brief wait, Druadaen and his companions were ushered in through the main entry—a small portcullis—and led to a windowless room. The doors closed firmly behind them.

"Be seated." The words were part offer, part order, and had been spoken by a man standing before a wall map at the far end of the room. The cartographic conventions were standard Dunarran, but several peripheral sections had been replaced. They were field draftings, signifying frontier areas that had been recently surveyed in greater detail by Outriders.

The man gestured to a ring of chairs which were, by either chance or design, in just the right quantity for their group. Probably several decades older than Druadaen, he would not have appeared so except to another Dunarran, or possibly, Iavan. Still, he was relatively young to be a station chief, particularly for Shadowmere: the nexus of all Outrider and Courier activities in Far Amitryea. Rather than asking them to explain who they were and their business, he swiftly synopsized his surprisingly complete information on them, then extended an open hand toward Druadaen. "I believe you have something for me."

Druadaen passed him the secure pouch. He opened it, glanced inside, studied one item intently, then resealed and set aside the pouch. "So," he said, a smile trying to push up one corner of his mouth, "you had quite a first night ashore, as I hear it."

Druadaen's companions stared at him. He held up his hands in denial. "I did not—"

"Outrider Druadaen sent no advance report," Talshane explained to the others. "I received a full, if unofficial, account from Senior Sacrist Padrajisse."

"When?" Umkhira blurted out.

"About an hour ago," he answered. Seeing their looks, he amplified. "She's a very early riser. And seems to require very little sleep." He scratched an ear. "She became a bit of a legend among the Outriders here."

"She is certainly unique," Druadaen agreed with a small smile.

Talshane answered with one of his own. "Ah, there's the Courier in you. What's your unofficial motto, again?"

Druadaen recited it with a rueful smile: "'Tact unto death.'"

Talshane's smile widened. "That's it." He glanced around the group. "Not a lot of them will admit to it, you know. Makes them sound..."

"Irresolute?" S'ythreni asked impishly.

He laughed. "Something like that. Now, Druadaen, since you've discharged your dogsbody-duty"—Talshane glanced at the hide dossier—"maybe you'll tell me who you annoyed back home?"

"Sir?"

"Well, someone was irritated enough to send you halfway across the world to deliver routine messages."

Druadaen sighed. "I don't even know who gave the order, let alone *why*."

Talshane grinned. "A common refrain. I hear the same from at least half of the others that are sent out here on similarly pointless errands."

"Told you so," Elweyr muttered sideways at Druadaen.

Talshane nodded. "You seem well informed, Master Elweyr. Of course, your years as an alchemist in Menara certainly afforded you ample opportunities to see how the Consentium operates. Which reminds me: Senior Archivist Shaananca sent along a request"—he tapped the secure pouch—"to help locate your parents. I shall start that process as soon as I return to Shadowmere."

Elweyr looked wary and stunned, showing no sign that he might respond. Before his odd silence could become uncomfortably long, Druadaen shifted to the reason for their visit. "We are eager for any advice you might have about working with Padrajisse. We will be traveling with her soon."

Talshane grinned. "So she mentioned." His smile became meditative. "Frankly, she's still something of a mystery to me. But she is utterly reliable and utterly determined. She is also utterly candid, to the point of not merely insulting others but injuring her own hopes."

Ahearn's frown was more sad than concerned. "Sounds as though you've a specific instance in mind, Master Talshane."

"Just 'Talshane,' if you please. No, I'm not thinking of any single instance so much as comments and accounts that came to me unsolicited."

"From whom?" S'ythreni asked.

Talshane shrugged. "Colleagues in Shadowmere, some in her own temple." He leaned his elbows on the arms of the chairs, regarded them over intertwined fingers. "Are you familiar with her god, Thyeru?"

"One of the Helper pantheon," S'ythreni murmured, as if she wasn't sure. "The deity of law and oaths."

Talshane nodded. "Padrajisse was determined to become a sacrist before her epiphanesis. She was encouraged by her paternal grandmother, who was from one of the high orthodoxy sects that prevail in Mihal'j."

When only Druadaen showed some hint of understanding Talshane's implication, Elweyr explained: "Although worship of the Helper pantheon is considered strict in Corrovane, it's permissive compared to the Desert Orthodoxies."

Talshane nodded. "Padrajisse wasn't exactly a pariah in her youth, but she didn't rise up through the ranks as quickly as her skills warranted. According to her fellow Thyeru sacrists, she's the oldest person ever to set out on a first pilgrimage. And of all places, she chose Shadowmere."

"Why do you say, 'of all places'?" Umkhira asked. "Is Shadowmere a very holy place for her god?"

S'ythreni cocked her head. "From what I've heard, Shadowmere isn't associated with *anything* holy."

Talshane opened his hands into an explanation. "An old legend claims that the original patron deities of Shadowmere were twins: one the god of swords and one the god of betrayals. But, despite being immortal, their names will remain forever unknown, because within an hour of their birth they always kill each other. Over and over and over again."

S'ythreni sounded both sardonic and amused. "I suspect their temples were a bloody mess. Literally."

"I doubt any temples were ever built to those gods," Talshane said with a shrug. "But the legend captures the character of Shadowmere, and Padrajisse made her pilgrimage there to change it."

"Sounds like she was spoiling for a fight she couldn't win," Ahearn mused.

Talshane sighed. "She accrued a fearsome reputation among the foes of Thyeru. But she accrued an equally fearsome reputation among the other Helper sacrists in the city."

Umkhira frowned. "So in defeating many enemies, she made even more among her friends."

Talshane nodded. "In Shadowmere, you either learn how to walk a very fine line—or you may lose your legs." He leaned back, a melancholy look on his face. "So when they learned I was heading down here—"

"—they sent her along to 'help,'" S'ythreni concluded.

"I suspect that was their thinking. But rest assured: she will be a good comrade, whatever lies before you." He looked around the circle. "But you haven't mentioned what brought all of you here to Far Amitryea. Now he"—Talshane pointed at Druadaen—"hardly had a choice. But since the rest of you look like fortune-seekers, whatever he means to do next must sound profitable. And that would be . . . ?"

Druadaen's four companions looked away, embarrassed. He shrugged and sighed. "Giants," he said. "I'm looking for giants."

"Are you now?" Talshane's eyes may have twinkled as he leaned his chin into a palm.

Druadaen stared. "Padrajisse told you." He shook his head; she had assured him she wouldn't mention his quest.

Talshane grinned amiably. "Well, don't take her to task for it. She was quite sure that I already knew."

"Why?"

"Well, because you were in Treve to deliver a secure pouch, she thought all your business here was official and that I'd already know about it. Including your 'mission' to locate giants."

"Here?" laughed Ahearn. "Why? Does she think there are giants wandering about the streets of Treve?"

"No," Talshane admitted, "she thought you were talking about the ones just south of Crimatha." The room was suddenly silent. He smiled at Druadaen. "Sometimes fortune smiles on seemingly forlorn enterprises. You see, if you had met me in Shadowmere, I would have sent you here, anyway."

"So...there *are* giants here?" Ahearn asked incredulously. "Well, near-abouts, at least?"

Talshane smiled and nodded. "About fifty leagues to the south. Apart from the far wilds of Northern Omthrye, it's the only part of Far Amitryea they're known to inhabit."

Druadaen glanced toward the map on the wall. "Fifty leagues is well over Crimatha's border, isn't it?"

The station chief shrugged. "Crimatha is bounded by land that has slipped back into wilderness. So its borders aren't as fixed as our cartographers would like. If King Arvanak agrees to protect an area's farmers and they agree to pay taxes to the Crown, then you are in Crimatha. Otherwise, you're not.

"Now, let's take a look at those maps. Recent events acquainted me with the northeast hills and forests, but I'm sure I can find a few Outriders who are familiar with the southwest. And maybe they can point to some likely places to find giants...or at least, show you places where you won't."

CHAPTER THIRTY-FOUR

Two days after they'd followed a winding stream across Crimatha's uncertain border into scattered farms and copses, S'ythreni gestured for Druadaen and the others to halt. She reined in her horse, shielded her eyes, and pointed ahead. As Druadaen stood in his stirrups to get a better view of the forested hills that were rising into view over the horizon, she offered a confident announcement: "Smoke."

Druadaen prided himself on having keen eyes, and he was sure that Ahearn's were at least a match for his own. But when no one else was able to detect what she clearly could, S'ythreni smiled crookedly and told them: "Trust me."

Druadaen nodded, glanced at Ahearn. "It's still a long ride off if we can't see it, but we should not assume that whoever lit that fire hasn't moved closer since doing so."

Padrajisse urged her horse forward to stand with theirs, agreeing with a curt nod. "If the fire has been burning for a day or more, those who set it may only be a few leagues in front of us now." She glanced at Ahearn, her gaze as intent and expectant as a falcon's.

He nodded. "Very well. Time for a meal, then. No fire, though. S'ythreni, you keep an eye on the horses, yeh?"

S'ythreni started grumbling about having to watch over the horses yet again. Which was ironic, since she clearly preferred the company of animals to that of humans. But then again, nothing could compete with her fondness for the one thing she embraced at every possible opportunity: griping.

"I'll see to the horses," Druadaen said to S'ythreni. "You should rest."

She turned a surprised smile upon him, patted the nose of her mount, began poking around in her saddlebags for some of the biscuits and smoked meat they'd brought from Treve.

The routines of leading the mounts down to the stream, checking their shoes, and making sure they didn't graze on sourgrass were calming, familiar. The south of Crimatha reminded him of the wilder parts of the Connæaran border. Broad-leafed trees vied with firs to dominate the forests. Meadows rolled like green carpets toward hillocks at almost every point of the compass. Sweetgrass was the rule and sourgrass the rarity. Flocks moved like wooly clouds through glens before drifting up their slopes.

Those pleasant vistas had begun ten leagues north of the border and ran on until flattening into the storied Aswyth Plain. That was where Talshane's guide had bid them safe travels and turned about to begin collecting new advice pouches along the main road back to Treve.

It was hard to envision the broad, overgrown Aswyth Plain as the site of great battles that had ultimately restored rights to commoners and become the foundation of the realm of Steelring: the ancient name for the mountain-girdled western extents of South Omthrye. As centuries passed, time and strife had caused Steelring to contract back into the coastal province from which it had originally grown: Crimatha. And as the high-water mark of human settlement receded, the once-extensive farmlands and cities of Aswyth Plain became a great sward once again. It was now dominated by wooded vales and sun-bleached remains of castles and capitols, protruding up from the ground like the time-rounded teeth of buried gods.

"'Ey now, Dunarran! What's got you lost in daydreams? Remembering books or finding giants?"

Druadaen started at Ahearn's merry cry, gathered the reins of the horses and led them back.

The group was standing in a line, staring at the horizon. The fire that only S'ythreni's eyes had been able to pick out was now ominously visible. "Well," she said with forced brightness, "*that* certainly doesn't look promising."

Then she glanced at Druadaen and rolled her eyes histrionically. "Wait! What *am* I saying? Actually, since we're trying to find giants, that looks *very* promising." A beat. "Because we're all insane."

Just over an hour later, they spied a scattered group moving toward them at a steady trot. Along with the others, Druadaen's hand went toward his weapon. But S'ythreni shook her head: "Don't bother."

The reason for her diffidence became clear soon enough; the approaching figures were not Bent, but farm families, carrying the belongings that practicality or attachment dictated they could not leave behind. Upon spying Druadaen and the others, they came to a halt, then surged forward again, shouting, waving their arms desperately.

"As if we don't see them," S'ythreni muttered, which earned a stern look from Padrajisse.

The refugees started crying out as they came closer:

"Where have you come from?"

"Were you sent by the Crown?"

"How many more of you are there?"

"They're right behind us!"

That last comment earned a squint-eyed assessment of the horizon by S'ythreni, who concluded it with a shake of her head.

Only Ahearn and Padrajisse seemed to expect what came next: the close crush of almost five dozen desperate, exhausted people, several of whom started weeping spontaneously. One or two made abortive grabs for the group's saddle-slung weapons, raging at the Bent who'd destroyed their homes, vowing to avenge family, friends, and in some cases, pets and even possessions.

Those who had lost family and friends were ominously the least loud yet the most focused. Druadaen was quite certain that, had those particular refugees been furnished with weapons, they would have immediately headed back toward the sites of atrocity. They no longer feared for their own lives; their eyes mutely proclaimed that they had accepted—perhaps welcomed—their own death as the price of slaking their thirst for vengeance.

Others attempted to hand up bribes, messages, even wailing

toddlers...until one thin, towheaded boy pointed at Umkhira and shouted, "Bent! Bent! They ride with Bent!"

The crowd surged back as impulsively as it had swamped them. But now, fear was growing. And on a few faces, Druadaen watched as their desperate rage at the murderous raiders behind them was transferred to the small group of riders that they handily outnumbered. One of them, reddening with fury, drew a dagger, started forward—

Padrajisse lifted her sword sharply; dazzling white light blazed forth from it, blinding despite the daylight.

The boldest of the rage-fixated refugees stopped. The rest shrank back, and the fear in their eyes was not at the threat of imminent death, but divine wrath.

"Hear me!" Padrajisse cried—and it seemed certain that even the deaf would have heard; some unseen invocation had made her voice as loud and piercing as a thunderclap. She stared around, as severe as a graven image, until even the children stopped whimpering. "We are here to help, not harm. But we are not here in answer to a summons. We were traveling upon Aswyth Plain on our own business."

"You're not sent by the Crown?" a voice wailed in despair.

"We are not, but we presume to act with the blessings of King Arvanak. Among us are allies of Crimatha—Corrovani and Dunarran—who shall ensure that swift justice falls upon the necks of your attackers. Now: Who among you has served in the hosts of King Arvanak?"

Two men raised their hands.

Padrajisse appraised them solemnly, unrushed, and then asked the younger, "You—and *only* you: tell me the nature of the Bent that attacked you, and their numbers."

The man breathed deeply and stared at the ground, hands on hips. Druadaen had the impression that it might have been the first time since fleeing his farm that he'd had the time or presence of mind to reflect on what had actually occurred. "It were yaps, Sacrista, maybe fifty of 'em. I saw a few kaghabs, too, I think. Mighta been the yaps' captains; might just have been there to share in the loot."

Padrajisse frowned in response to this news. "I do not know these breeds of Bent."

Umkhira spoke loudly, as if daring any to challenge her right to do so or her identity as one of their rescuers. "These 'yaps' call themselves hyek, and while Bent, are not an urzhen species. Kaghab is the common word for kagh gaban. They are large relatives of the ur gaban and are fearful in battle."

"I can attest to that," Elweyr muttered. "I saw one tear a wheel off a cart with his bare hands."

The older of the two soldiers hobbled toward Umkhira, the long run having apparently taken a heavy toll on his joints. "And what manner of Bent would you be, then?" he asked. "*Darger*, maybe?"

Druadaen tensed; he saw Ahearn holding his breath. But Umkhira regarded the man with a curious frown. "Are you unaware that we ur zhog consider that term a slur?"

"A slur?" He was genuinely confused. "You'd prefer HalfBent?"

She sighed, clearly resigned to accept that he used the term out of ignorance, not malice. "I am ur zhog; a Lightstrider."

He blinked, then shook his head. "Well, y'are whatever y'say y'are, I suppose. Me, I've never heard of your kind. But if ye're here to help us, then ye're welcome as the rest of your band." He sized them up, frowned dubiously. "How long do you think it will be before the king's host gets here?"

"That," intruded Padrajisse, "will depend upon how soon you cross the border and send word. In the meantime, we shall learn the precise numbers of the Bent and both injure and delay them, if our numbers are sufficient for that task."

"Where's the army when we need 'em?" shouted a wild-eyed woman clutching two children.

"Until they know they are needed, they are where you'd expect: in their garrisons. Although many of Crimatha's forces have been fighting against raiders that have roved along both sides of the Landskye border."

A dour man shook his head. "Ah, they get all the help, up there."

Which, to Druadaen's ear, was simply a local version of the universal gripe heard in every corner of every kingdom: that the Crown paid less attention (and yet sent more tax collectors) to their own region than any other. But in this case, the complaint was singularly ironic; the locals had yet to declare allegiance to King Arvanak. Druadaen held up a hand. "In advance of help, we must achieve what we can. And our greatest need is to learn whatever we can about the attackers."

"They're Bent," said the fellow who had reported their type and numbers. "What more do you need to know?"

"Can you tell us where they came from?"

"The Thurial Mountains," answered another. "The tribal markings were on their shields."

"And are they more likely to attack at this time of year?"

"Bent are likely to attack at every time of the year," muttered a very flushed man of considerable girth.

A woman with a shock of white hair and sky-blue eyes shook her head. "No, Jeram. It's not common to see yaps before the first crops are in. Makes me wonder—" And she was suddenly silent, looking down.

When she did not resume, Ahearn called to her, "What do you wonder, Grandmother? Don't be keeping secrets from us, now!"

She ducked her head, shook it once.

Druadaen saw that most of the refugees had also directed their attention elsewhere. Anywhere but upon the group, in fact. "Did something unusual happen before the hyek fell upon you?" he asked.

The old woman looked up, scanned the people around her. "Will none of you say?"

"Please tell us," Druadaen urged.

The older man who'd asked if Umkhira was a *darger* shrugged. "If we tell you, you'll turn tail, sure as I'm breathing."

"Try us," drawled S'ythreni. "You have no idea just how foolhardy we can be."

"Well, last moonphase, several of us lost sheep, goats, pigs."

"To what?"

"Well, it's not like we ever saw 'em. They came at night, y'see."

"Aye, an' what else would leave such a footprint?" the old woman almost shouted.

The younger of the two former soldiers sighed. "It was a giant, if you must know. Could be more than one, but I doubt it."

"Well, why didn't you say so?" Druadaen's enthusiasm was not dimmed by the strange looks elicited by his eager smile. "Where are they?"

The two ex-soldiers and the old woman all pointed at a particular section of the wooded hills on the southern horizon. "It's where they usually come from," she added. "And when they do, Bent follow in after 'em like locusts. If there's any time when we're likely to be weak, that's it."

The older soldier sucked his teeth with a look of resignation. "And now you're going to turn around, ain'tcha? Probably after telling us that 'you'll be back' with a larger force." He said it with the quiet bitterness of having endured at least one such broken promise.

"No," Druadaen said with a smile, "after we've chased off the Bent, we'll take care of the giants. Ourselves."

Wide-eyed stares were the unanimous response to his assertion. The soldier looked at the group doubtfully, as if recounting them, just to be sure. "No unkindness meant, but are ye sure yer up to the job?"

"I guess we're about to find out," muttered Elweyr. "Now, what's the best way to approach your farms without being seen?"

Druadaen crossed his arms as he surveyed the source of the first smoke they spotted: a ravaged farm. To both the east and the west, fainter telltales of fires climbed toward the late afternoon skies. "Either the hyek band that struck the refugees has split up, or there were others spreading out across the plain at the same time."

"The latter, I think," S'ythreni said, shielding her eyes against the sun with both hands as she surveyed the farm buildings. "I've counted almost three dozen hyek, so far. And two kaghabs."

"Agreed," Padrajisse said firmly. "Bent are dangerous, but they are rarely organized."

"Well, no matter how many of them are elsewhere or how busy they've been," Ahearn muttered jovially, "we have a count of those here and the sun is making haste to the horizon. So we'd best have fewer words and more deeds. Night is no friend to us, but quite congenial to the Bent."

Padrajisse nodded at him. "What is your plan, Ahearn?"

The swordsman swung into his saddle, glanced up and down their line. The horses stood in a shallow gully that brought the riders' eyes just level with the top of the unharvested wheat. "These yaps are in two separate groups, both near the burning house. We're six on horseback, and with a sacrist and a mancer for good measure. So the plan is simple: first we ride down one group, then the other. And we have mancery and miracles to dispatch any that remain!"

Padrajisse stared at him a long moment before examining the

expressions of the others in the group. "Do none of you find this strategy... wanting?"

"Well, now," Ahearn said in an almost gentle voice, "it may have slipped past in all the initial palaver back in Treve, but I *am* the one who leads us in battle. It's agreed."

Her stare rotated back to him; if she was aware of how atypically deferential Ahearn was being, she gave no hint of it. "It was not agreed to by me."

"With pardons, Sacrista, you *were* told. And where's the problem with what I propose? Bent won't stand before a charge, and once we're through 'em, they'll be scattered. Easy to pick off by blade or bow." He smiled. "Or by a touch of otherworldly power, yeh?"

She shook her head. "Have you considered the weapons they bear?"

"Eh? What of them? Axes and halberds. A few overlong pig-stickers, as well. Naught odd about that."

Padrajisse sighed, turned toward Druadaen. "You see the point of my question, surely."

Druadaen shrugged. "I may."

"Well, then please enlighten me," Ahearn muttered tightly. He was beginning to sound annoyed now that Padrajisse had brought someone else into the debate. Or maybe it was because she had specifically brought in the party's other leader. Either way, Druadaen was coming to a deeper appreciation of why she might not have been welcomed in other groups. Particularly those within her own temple.

He leaned over the neck of his horse to look along the line. "Who—other than you, S'ythreni—have learned how to fight from horseback?" Padrajisse nodded deeply at his inquiry.

Ahearn frowned, but now that the discussion had widened so that it was no longer implicitly focused upon his competence, his tone became more amiable. "Well, with the exception of our not-green lass, all of us, I warrant."

But Padrajisse replied before Druadaen could find a more tactful way to convey what she delivered as an impatient rebuke. "He did not ask how many of you have *fought* from horseback. He asked how many of you *learned* to do it."

Ahearn snorted. "Well, that's just the way Dunarrans ask questions—particularly *our* Dunarran, gods love him. Always talking up book-learning and training over practical experi—"

"No, his question was precise and pertinent," Padrajisse interrupted sharply. "If the hyek know how to use those longer polearms—and I suspect they do—then untrained horsemen would be ill-advised to ride against them."

Ahearn frowned. "I mean no disrespect, Sacrista, but a rabble of lightly-armored Bent rampaging about a farm are not about to come together and stand us off with a thicket of spears."

"No," Druadaen agreed, "they most certainly won't. But those long 'pig-stickers' are billhooks. They can cut you out of your saddle if you're not careful." *Or not trained.*

"And even if you dodge the blade," S'ythreni followed, "with one turn of the wrist, they can catch your shoulder with the hook as you ride past." She shrugged. "Getting pulled backward off a galloping horse has killed many a *trained* rider."

Despite a glower, Ahearn drew a deep breath. "And what's your answer, then?" He stared at Druadaen, angrily but also as an appeal. "To wade into them on foot?"

"No," Druadaen answered, "you are right: that would certainly be foolish. But cavalry often has better options than a headlong charge."

"Well, then, Outrider," Ahearn said, exchanging shrugs with Elweyr, "what do you have in mind?"

CHAPTER THIRTY-FIVE

Watching S'ythreni ride, Druadaen had the distinct impression that she would have been just as capable without a saddle. If not more so. But the reverse was true of Padrajisse, who, although trained, always sat her horse as if she were on a parade ground.

Never was that more evident than when they had to lay low along their mounts' necks as they approached the burning buildings. They remained in the lee of a tall, thickly tangled hedge that lined one side of the paddock, its grass stained black-red with the blood of bludgeoned goats and axe-hewn sheep. But Padrajisse kept forgetting to lay forward on her mount, even though Druadaen whispered patient reminders that the success of their plan depended upon it. She dutifully complied—and forgot again within the span of a minute.

S'ythreni edged forward until her horse's nose was almost in the tail of Druadaen's. "Tell me why we're doing this, again?" she muttered.

Druadaen sighed. "Firstly, to help the refugees we encountered earlier today."

"Well, see, there's a problem with that. All the ones who survived are leagues away and running for the border as fast as they can. And the ones left here . . . well, they're beyond helping." She raised her head enough to peek over the hedgerow. "Same for this farm, from the look of it. I suspect the others are no different."

"Still, it is the right thing to do."

"Right does not mean profitable or even survivable."

"That is true. But this is also the smart thing to do."

She sneered. "You are hoping to extract information on the giants from hyek? Really? Did you fall and hit your head when I wasn't watching? Because that is a very foolish idea."

"My head is quite intact, and no, I don't expect to gain any useful information from the hyek."

"Then how is this the smart thing to do?"

He turned so that she would see that he was losing patience. "Would you rather go up-country to seek giants having left all these Bent *behind* us?"

She frowned, glanced aside. "Well," she muttered as she let her horse fall back from his, "our actions here are only sane in that they make your *insane* plan safer. A bit like bringing a pillow to break a fall from a cliff, if you ask me."

"But I didn't ask you." He reined in his horse. "We are at the limit of cover. We must be silent."

The other two drew their own mounts to a halt, looked over the top of the hedge carefully.

Not a great deal had changed since they'd split off from the others half an hour earlier. The hyek were still in two rough groups. However, they had drawn further apart. The first, and larger, group remained close to the burning house with occasional forays into the barn, which had also started smoking.

The second group had wandered further north into the fields, searching for . . . something. They occasionally burst out with great yells and howls, but those invariably faded into disappointed snarls and, eventually, silence. They were now within two hundred yards of where Ahearn, Elweyr, and Umkhira were crouching, having left their own horses tethered in the gully about a hundred yards behind them.

Advancing closer to the Bent had seemed essential when Druadaen's group had split off to creep up along the enemy's flank, concealed by the hedge and often blocked by the barn, the house, and the smoke. But halfway through that wide movement, the second group of hyek had become intensely interested in the northern field and had been drawing closer to Ahearn's group. Tall and rangy, hyek were significantly faster than humans, so it was becoming increasingly likely that if Ahearn's group had to flee, they would lose any footrace back to their mounts in the gully.

Which was not something Ahearn had specifically foreseen, but his general misgivings over Druadaen's plan now sounded ominously proleptic. When tasked to lead Elweyr and Umkhira into bow range, the swordsman had looked askance. "Dividing forces in front of the enemy, Dunarran? Not in your rule books, I'd wager."

"It's only 'in front of' if they see you. Which the hyek clearly have not."

"You're gambling a lot on that," Ahearn retorted, "including my very pretty neck."

Druadaen nodded. "There is always danger in luring out an enemy. But with Elweyr's abilities, you should have enough time to retreat, remount, and withdraw, if the plan doesn't work."

"And if it doesn't," Ahearn insisted sharply, "then we'll try it *my* way."

Druadaen had shrugged and offered a single nod. He did not point out that Ahearn still hadn't advanced any tactical solutions other than a direct charge. Or that if Druadaen's plan did not work, there wouldn't be the time or opportunity to try a new one. The only option would be swift flight.

But even that looked questionable, now. S'ythreni had dismounted and kept trying to wave at Ahearn and the others from the side of the hedge away from the hyek. After several tries, she turned, frowning. "I don't think Ahearn's group can see us."

Druadaen risked a peek. "It's the smoke," he agreed. "The drifts that hid us as we approached have started shifting."

Padrajisse sounded concerned. "Toward Ahearn?"

"Not directly," S'ythreni muttered. "They're spreading slowly into the field between us."

The sacrista frowned. "So Ahearn's force can still use their bows against the hyek but are unable to see that we are in position."

Druadaen nodded. "Which means they can't tell when it is safe for them to begin their ambush."

S'ythreni swung up into the saddle, squinted into the drifting smoke—but quickly rose in her stirrups to look beyond it. "Well," she muttered, pointing with her fine chin, "we have a new problem."

Druadaen followed her gaze. Another half dozen hyek were rising above the crops, farther off than the ones approaching Ahearn. They were still well out on his right flank, and their maws were soaked red.

S'ythreni answered his question before he could ask it. "Ahearn and the others haven't seen them."

Druadaen nodded. *Because they are watching for us on the opposite flank and keeping an eye on the hyek to their front. So much for my fine plans.* He turned toward Padrajisse. "I presume that the bestowals of Thyeru will not reach so far as either of those groups of hyek?"

She shrugged. "The few miracles that could would be weakened by the distance and achieve little."

"Is it possible to send even a brief message to Ahearn or those with him?"

"It would be had I linked with any of them. That step was not taken."

Druadaen nodded, all his attention focused on holding back the question trying to push open his mouth into a shout: *And why do you only tell us about that* now? Instead, he turned to S'ythreni.

She was already shaking her head as she returned to her horse in a crouch. "The range is too great to shoot accurately—or quickly—enough to do much good." Once beside the saddle, she threw back the strap that kept Ahearn's longsword snug in its sheath. "It seems we'll be making a cavalry charge after all." Ahearn had loaned her the blade inasmuch as he intended to use either his bow or bastard sword.

Druadaen sighed. "Agreed. We can no longer wait and hope that Ahearn's and Umkhira's arrows will attract the attention of the first group of hyek while we near their flank. We must intercept them, now."

Padrajisse nodded her understanding. "Once the others need not watch those hyek, or for our signal, they are more likely to see the new group approaching from their other flank."

Druadaen tightened the straps on his shield and held the sword low and well out to the side; raising it was the universally recognized sign that the charge was imminent. *If only we'd had some way to reach Ahearn's group...*

Just as he was about to raise the sword, both Umkhira and Elweyr started as if struck. The thaumantic turned directly toward him; impossibly, he seemed to know right where to look.

S'ythreni waved vigorously. Elweyr waved back.

At that same moment, Umkhira, who'd turned in the other

direction, caught sight of the new threat on their other flank. She pointed them out to Ahearn. After a moment's consideration, he gestured for Elweyr to watch the closer group to their front, and then he and Umkhira began loosing arrows at the half dozen which had appeared unexpectedly to their right. Hyek responded to the attack with surprised and outraged howls, turning to and fro as they sought the archers who were beginning to score hits on them.

That noise attracted the attention of the larger group of hyek that had been wandering closer from the south. Their reaction was pure outrage; some shouted urgently at the last cluster of hyek near the buildings while the rest coursed unevenly forward, snarling what were presumably curses and mortal threats.

Druadaen nodded to S'ythreni and Padrajisse, but only half-lowered his sword, urging his mount into a forward trot rather than spurring it into a charge.

As he'd anticipated, it took the main body of hyek several seconds to reorganize themselves, locate Ahearn and Umkhira, and begin moving toward them, their flank threatening to overrun Elweyr where he crouched, waiting. As their howls grew louder and they charged, Druadaen lowered his sword the rest of the way, leading the other two in an arcing sweep that brought them onto the Bent's rear flank.

As fast as the hyek were, the three horses closed the distance in seconds. Druadaen, riding with sword held back and ready, was wondering if they would sweep right through the Bent before being spotted when one of the rearmost turned. He might have done so to see if the group back at the farmstead was moving to join them, or he might have heard the thudding of hooves to his rear. Either way, his eyes went wide, and he started a shrill shrieking that reminded Druadaen of the high-pitched alarm cries of foxes. Druadaen crouched lower and put the spurs hard into his mount's flanks.

The remaining twenty yards went past in a blur, during which the hyek who'd seen them kept screaming to get the attention of his charging, roaring mates. Who finally broke stride and turned just as the three riders swept through them.

As with most charges, the carnage was so swift and savage that it was as much a matter of trained reflexes as intent. Druadaen lowered his sword as he neared the first Bent, then cut upward, coming up beneath its rising weapon arm. Its axe flew away, its blood sprayed, its shout of rage became one of agony.

But Druadaen was already using spur and knee to urge his mount slightly to the right, bringing him in line with another of the hyek as he let the sword's upward momentum carry it from his right to his left. As he came alongside the Bent, he rolled his wrist, then elbow. The inertia brought the sword around smoothly into an overhand cut back to his right—which bit deep into the top of his target's shoulder.

Motion to his left—high and narrow—prompted Druadaen to raise his shield and angle it outward. A billhook slammed down against it, just where his left shoulder had been exposed an instant earlier. The impact was bone-jarring, but the angle of the shield not only caught the heavy head of the weapon but sent it sliding away. He pulled his mount into a half caracole; now he was facing his attacker, who was still trying to muscle the unwieldy weapon around into a useful position. *Apparently,* thought Druadaen as he spurred his horse toward him, *this tribe hasn't dealt with* trained *riders before . . .*

After that exchange was over, and yet another came to a similarly grisly conclusion, the tempo of the melee changed enough for Druadaen to rein in and glance around. The five surviving hyek were fleeing, two staggering as they went. Seven were motionless on the ground, two more crawling for cover into the nearby crop rows which had not been crushed by the combat. S'ythreni was following the routed Bent at a canter: just enough to keep them running away as hard as they could. Padrajisse was leaning over in her saddle to examine a wound high on her mount's left haunch. She saw his gaze. "A long cut, but shallow. It can wait until we are done here."

Druadaen nodded, turned toward Elweyr . . . but he had closed ranks with Ahearn and Umkhira. His arms were lifting in a gesture that often signified he was weaving a very ambitious thaumate. The half dozen hyek bounding through the crops almost all had arrows sticking out of them already but showed no sign of having any intent other than closing with and slaughtering their attackers. As with the group broken by the charge, there were no kaghabs among them. Which was welcome, but also worrisome.

"Druadaen." S'ythreni's voice was low and her tone was not encouraging. He turned.

The hyek that had been among the buildings were now moving toward them at a trot. But they had increased in number. And would continue to do so, Druadaen realized: as he watched, another half dozen emerged from the house that he and the others had thought was actively burning. Judging from all the Bent coming out, it was merely smoldering. And it held one last surprise for them. Or, more aptly, two more surprises: a pair of kaghabs stooped under the scorched lintel, carrying battle-axes as if they were just outsized hatchets.

S'ythreni's voice did not often sound tense, but it did now: "What do we do, Druadaen?"

What, indeed? he wondered. There was almost a score of hyek in addition to the kaghabs, all heading toward them at an accelerating lope. Druadaen had no tricks left, no flanking moves or other deceptions with which to acquire an advantage. The choices were stand and fight or turn and run.

Druadaen looked over his shoulder. The less powerful bows of Ahearn and Umkhira continued to feather the leather armor and limbs of the attackers who should have already crashed headlong into them. But Elweyr was apparently using a thaumate similar to the one he had against the forces of the Unnamed Shaman and again against the creature at the Back Door. Now, as then, the Bent were moving as if burdened under immense loads. Slow and close, Ahearn and Umkhira continued to fire shaft after shaft into them; one fell over, as he watched. But the rest were coming on, and soon his friends would have to toss aside their bows in favor of sword and axe and the hope that they would prevail over five weakened, but very large foes.

Still watching that strange combat, Druadaen shook his head. "We cannot flee; Ahearn and the others would not make it to their horses in time, particularly not if Elweyr has to allow his thaumate to fall." He turned his horse to face the oncoming hyeks and kaghabs. "We must cover them until they finish the ones behind us."

"You hope," S'ythreni added, but she, too, had turned her horse toward their enemies.

"What is your plan?" Padrajisse asked.

Druadaen shrugged. "We have no choice. We must fight."

"We might," Padrajisse amended. "But for the nonce, have one slight measure of faith, Outrider."

"But, Sacrista—"

She cut a dismissive hand in his direction. "Do not distract me." She urged her horse to take a few steps forward; as it did, she appeared to be on the verge of entering a trance, rather than a battle.

The hyek and the kaghab leading them were less than seventy yards away.

Druadaen and S'ythreni exchanged looks and readied their swords. They were unwounded and still fresh. There was a chance, albeit a very slim one, that they might yet survive, but...

Padrajisse sat her horse slightly stooped and still. Druadaen could not see her face, but she was muttering. Whether the words were prayers, supplications, or curses, he could not tell. Druadaen was about to draw his horse alongside her, to cover her by countercharging the Bent when they reached twenty yards, when S'ythreni hissed at him.

"You might ruin her god's miracles just like the shaman's," she whispered.

Which, he allowed, was a very good point. So instead, he made sure his dented shield was tight on his arm and, not for the first time, wished he had his father's sword. He put a calming hand on his mount's neck, which was becoming increasingly restive as the wild sounds and distinctive carnivore scent of the Bent came nearer.

He lifted the reins to countercharge—

Three of the hyek fell headlong, shrieking in panic. Most of the others, including the kaghabs, stopped as if lost. Only the four rearmost kept coming but slowed as they arrived in the midst of their fellows who were now stumbling about uncertainly, arms outstretched—and utterly blind.

Druadaen almost spurred his mount, then reconsidered. "Will attacking them shatter the pattern in which they are caught?"

"The miracle," Padrajisse corrected sharply, "shall not fall. But nor will it last long. Whatever we mean to do, we must do now." She prepared to dig her heels into her horse's flanks.

But she stopped, staring as Druadaen sheathed his sword and swung out of his saddle to ready his bow.

With a fierce grin, S'ythreni did the same, but was cocking her crossbow. "I shall see to the kaghabs." Druadaen agreed with a shrug.

"This would be the moment to charge," Padrajisse muttered loudly, "since we *are* all trained to fight from the saddle."

"Yes," S'ythreni called to her, "but why not feather them from here? Besides, the Dunarran and mancery don't always get along."

"The bestowal you see before you is not 'mancery,'" the sacrista muttered angrily. "It is the living favor and will of Thyeru." But rather than pressing the point, she glanced sideways at Druadaen, who saw a hint of concern in her face.

Just before he drew the bowstring to his ear and released the first shaft.

Druadaen walked alongside Padrajisse's mount as she urged it toward the litter of Bent bodies. Most were completely still. A few still moved feebly. S'ythreni ran ahead, longsword back in her hand. She walked a distant circuit around the dead and dying, studying them carefully.

"There was more than archery at work here, Outrider," Padrajisse said stiffly.

Druadaen knew what she was referring to but said nothing. After all, what *could* he say?

"Was it divine providence that the aeosti's first two targets were kaghabs, and that, in each case, they fell dead within seconds? Convulsing?"

"I could not say," he answered. Which, strictly speaking, was true.

"It is strange beneficence, if so," Padrajisse continued archly. "For the aeosti's subsequent quarrels were nowhere near so singularly mortal. Even though the hyek should have been much easier to kill."

Druadaen saw the statement for what it was: conversational bait trailed in potentially contentious waters. And the reason was not merely plain, but predictable: those Helper deities that were most concerned with compassion, integrity, and justice typically declaimed the trade—and tools—of assassins. And unless the two kaghab had both suffered mysterious yet fatal seizures in the space of a single minute, there was only one reasonable explanation for their sudden demise: poison on the arrows which had struck them.

Clearly, S'ythreni had either acquired some while she was with the others in Menara or, more probably, had kept back a vial or two of what Elweyr had passed out before the attack upon the Unnamed Shaman. It was also possible that she had palmed some from the many bodies she had searched during their time in the Under. Whatever the source, the toxin was so swift and powerful that it had not escaped Padrajisse's notice. And her deity, Thyeru, was, after all, the pantheon's god of law and oaths.

After several seconds of silence, she drew her mount to a halt. "Well? Have you no speculations of your own?"

Druadaen turned. "I have many speculations, Sacrista. But they are secondary to my one great certainty."

"Which is?"

"Which is that however S'ythreni's quarrels slew those kagh-abs, we are probably alive because of it." He turned back to look at S'ythreni.

Who, having finished her survey of the bodies, sheathed Ahearn's longsword with one hand as she drew her own shorts-word with the other. She then slipped quickly among the fallen Bent—but not to search them for valuables, as Druadaen had expected. She went between those who were still alive, moving with the grace and long strides of a dancer, plunging her shorts-word into the front or side of each one's neck.

Druadaen started. Despite months together, he'd never seen her—or the others—so blithely dispatch wounded adversaries. In the Under, every battle was a fight to the finish; the wounded were still dangerous, and an immediate coup de grace was the only way to be certain that they did not rise up and attack from behind.

She noticed his stare when she returned. She shrugged. "Did you plan on taking them prisoner? All the way back to Treve?" she asked.

Druadaen shook his head.

S'ythreni noticed the sacrista's pale face and withering stare. "And do you mean to ask your god to heal all of them?"

"I would," Padrajisse replied sharply, "rather than massacre thinking beings as you have."

S'ythreni shrugged. "Yes," she agreed, "the same 'thinking beings' that came here and did quite a lot of *their own* massa-cring. I'm afraid I do not share your delicate scruples, particularly beyond the safety of city walls or border garrisons."

Padrajisse grunted as if she had been the one slain.

"Well, *that* was exciting!" Ahearn's voice announced from behind. Druadaen admired his ability to sound sardonic and merry at the same time. "Just about done tidying up, are we?"

"'Tidying up'?" Padrajisse repeated, aghast. "Is that what you call this callous execution of the fallen?"

"Why yes, yes I do, an' it please you, Sacrista. Because that's nicer than they'd have done to us, I assure you. Or would you rather leave them to die slowly in the fields?"

"Yes, I would. Providence might see fit to spare them or send them some other swift end. But it is not incumbent upon our hands to finish such work. We did not come to kill, but to prevent them from doing so."

Ahearn cocked his head as Elweyr walked up behind him, Umkhira trailing. "I've no wish to debate such points with one so learned and whose ears are so attentive to the words of the gods. But as a simple man of mortal means, I can only act as I've learned in many fights against the Bent; if you don't finish them, you are giving them another chance to finish you. Because you may bet your gold and garters that they won't rest until they do. So if it's a matter of choosing between their fate and my comrades' safety—well, there isn't really a choice to be made, then, is there?"

He turned to the two behind him. "All well, then?"

Elweyr nodded. "And you?"

"Hardly a scratch," Ahearn announced loudly, despite a very visible gash on his left leg. "And you, Umkhira: you seem completely unharmed."

The Lightstrider nodded.

Then she fell over.

CHAPTER THIRTY-SIX

In a moment, the group had gathered around Umkhira, who was barely conscious. Ahearn was asking her what was wrong, more loudly and slowly with every subsequent query. Elweyr stood and began scanning the horizon. S'ythreni, like Druadaen, was inspecting her for wounds.

They found the probable cause at the same moment: a puncture on the side of her right thigh. It was leaking a clear serum rather than bleeding, and the sides were not merely raw and swollen: they were ringed with what looked like blisters or pustules.

Padrajisse pushed between them, glanced at what they had found, and looked at Ahearn and Elweyr. Discovering that the latter was presumably scanning the horizon for potential foes, she focused her inquiry on Ahearn. "Where is the blade that struck this blow?"

Ahearn stared at her as if she might be more than a bit mad. "Sacrista, we *were* a bit busy, y'know."

"Be that as it may, she will be dead if you cannot find the weapon. Of the three poisons this might be, none give us much time."

"Well, what kind of weapon am I looking for?"

"The wound is from a dagger thrust," Druadaen told him. "Or maybe a sword point."

"Dagger," S'ythreni and Padrajisse chorused in similarly certain tones. Druadaen stepped back from Padrajisse and Umkhira and hurried back to the site of the Lightstrider's desperate melee against the hyek. S'ythreni was a moment behind him.

The ground was a tangled mess of stomped and crushed corn, hyek corpses so filled with arrows that they resembled grotesque pin cushions, and pieces of shattered weapons and gear. Still, the pattern of debris told the story of the engagement.

The hyek had come within a dozen yards of the three defenders when the tracks of their charge—indicated by the long stride between each footprint—became a close shuffle. That was the point at which Elweyr had completed the thaumate with which he had so profoundly slowed them.

But beyond there, it was harder to reconstruct the course of the melee. The tracks of the attackers resumed on a crisscross course that made no sense until Druadaen realized that they had not all been freed at once from whatever burden had slowed them; they had been released one or two at a time. And they had run in different directions because, in the intervals, the defenders had changed position.

That change of position had routinely included falling back and at the last site of combat, it appeared that three had been released— or the mancery had faded—all at once. The resulting tracks were unreadable; not only did it become impossible to sort out individual paths from the multiple overlapping footprints, but the dodging and feinting of the melee had obliterated a large portion of them.

"What are you doing?" S'ythreni muttered.

"Looking at how the battle unfolded."

"What? Why?"

"In order to determine where that wound was inflicted upon Umkhira."

Ahearn barked out a bitter laugh from where he'd started searching among the rows of corn. "Half philosopher, half fool, just as the saying has it."

Druadaen kneeled down at what looked like the rearmost limit of Umkhira's fighting retreat. Her prints were thick there, and fortunately, her boots left distinctive marks. They were not so well-made as those belonging to the humans, but not so crude and irregular as the ones worn by the hyek. There were broken Bent weapons and a riven shield—Umkhira's—on the ground. He scanned the enemy bodies. Of the two that were close enough to have fallen fighting the Lightstrider, one still held a crude, heavy sword. The other one's weapon—an axe—had broken, the haft riven almost its entire length. That hyek would have needed to draw a new weapon. And sure enough, just a foot into the flattened corn, Druadaen saw a dull glint of low-quality iron.

He fished it out of the saw-toothed stalks carefully; some poisons were able to pass directly through the skin. He stood. Ahearn and S'ythreni were staring at him.

"Is that—?" began the swordsman.

"I think so," Druadaen answered, holding it out. "Here: take it to Padrajisse. Run."

"You're not coming?"

"I'm not done."

"Why? What are you—?"

"Go. Time is short."

Ahearn ran off. But S'ythreni was in a squat, scanning the ground. "What are we looking for?" she asked.

He smiled at her. "The best way to flip this dead hyek on to his back."

She joined him at the blood-slick corpse. "And why are we doing that?"

"You'll see. For now, just get a good grip on his arm."

As Druadaen and S'ythreni approached, Padrajisse looked up. "The dagger must only have been tainted at the tip. There is no longer any sign of it. So I remain unsure which poison this is. I fear that—"

S'ythreni held out her hand. "Try this." It was the dagger's scabbard, taken from the dead hyek's belt.

Padrajisse's eyes widened as she grabbed it and looked inside. In a moment, she had her own blade out and was sawing through the surprisingly well-made sheath. As it opened like a rent peapod, a light green dusting was revealed at the very end of its inner surface.

The sacrista began rummaging hastily through the shoulder bag Elweyr had fetched from her horse. She glanced at him. "You are an alchemist. Can you help?"

He shook his head. "I am not so familiar with antidotes as I am with other...compounds."

Padrajisse, who selected a small vial from among dozens of others, turned her head toward S'ythreni. "Do you have knowledge of the poison?" When the aeosti shook her head, surprised at the question, the sacrista explained. "You knew where to look for this: that it would be compounded as powder kept from the open air, rather than mixed into an oil."

S'ythreni just shrugged.

Padrajisse seemed to forget her in the same instant, her focus narrowed to careful application of the antidote.

Ahearn leaned sideways. "I thought there was a...a miracle for poisons," Ahearn whispered toward Elweyr.

The thaumantic nodded. "Yes, but I don't think it works on all poisons. Besides, while the three of you were off searching for the dagger, she invoked something that slowed Umkhira's breath and heartbeat."

Druadaen had seen that bestowal used during the most hair-raising of his assignments as a Courier. "It slows the body's processes. It gives a physician—or other sacrist—more time to intervene. But while that miracle is functioning, the sacrist who invoked it may call for no other."

"You know more than most, Outrider," Padrajisse muttered, leaning back, her eyes closing for a moment. The wound started bleeding more profusely, but Umkhira's eyes opened. "I...what happened?"

"You were poisoned," Padrajisse said flatly as she repacked her physician's bag. "You may thank the graces of Thyeru for your return to health...as well as your sharp-eyed and quick-witted aeosti friend."

"Companion," corrected S'ythreni.

Padrajisse rose; by her lack of reaction, it seemed she either had not heard the aeosti's emendation or simply did not care. "If you can, Lightstrider, you should walk about. It will speed the spread of the curative, eliminate the last vestiges of the poison more rapidly."

Elweyr, waiting with bindings in hand, looked at the wound. "It's bleeding more heavily."

Padrajisse waved a dismissive hand. "It is more important that she start walking, but she may hold wadding to staunch the flow as she moves." She bent down and picked up the remains of the small scabbard.

Ahearn looked over her shoulder at it. "That's too small and too fine to be Bent-made."

She nodded. "This is not their manufacture. It is Caottaluran. Very sophisticated, very expensive. There is a small reservoir near the bottom. When the blade is sheathed, it slips past that reservoir: closes it more tightly, in fact. But when drawn, the movement of the blade opens the reservoir, causing its tip to be lightly dusted.

The poison remains inert there until in contact with blood or some other fluid of a living creature, or is washed off."

As Umkhira took a wad of wrappings from Elweyr with a nod, Ahearn frowned and folded his arms. "And what in the name of every avatar do the Caottalurans mean to achieve out here?"

"I don't know," Elweyr muttered, "but we should report this to Talshane."

Padrajisse shrugged. "I suspect he already knows. We encountered similar signs of their meddling when we rode to the aid of the Outriders in the unclaimed lands between Crimatha and Landskye."

Druadaen frowned. "Could it be that these are all pieces of some greater plot?"

"Not as you mean it. The Caottalurans are certainly known for sophisticated and intricate scheming, but they also understand the more general value of spreading terror and dread among one's enemies." She glanced at the dagger. "Imagine farmers reporting magically lethal blades . . . and the panic that would ensue."

S'ythreni rolled her eyes. "Would anyone be so gullible?"

She shot a hard stare at the aeosti. "It seems that you had no more precise knowledge of this poison than anyone else. And farmers have neither eyes trained by close combat, nor experience of tainted blades, and so may not even imagine that poison is at work—particularly not a poison that is so swift and invisible as this one.

"So it does not require gullibility to attribute this to mancery. Indeed, many of the borderers who suffered along with the Outriders were halfway to that very assumption."

S'ythreni's slightly open mouth closed sharply.

Umkhira, who had started walking a slow circuit around the others, bowed her head in Padrajisse's direction. "I thank you and your god, Priestess. Indeed, I thank you twice."

Padrajisse looked perplexed. "Twice?"

The Lightstrider nodded. "For saving me from the venom, and earlier, for saving all of us."

Padrajisse frowned. "I do not understand."

Elweyr shrugged. "If it wasn't for you or your god communicating your location just before the attack, who knows how it would have turned out?"

"But I did not pray to Thyeru for the succor of a summons. Indeed, Druadaen asked if I could, but that is not possible unless a bond of summons has been created beforehand."

Umkhira stopped. "Then how did I know where to look, to see the group of hyek that had appeared to our right?"

Elweyr was nodding slowly, carefully. "For me, it was a sudden awareness of your location. And not a vague, general sense that you'd arrived at the anticipated position; I knew *exactly* where you were."

"Well, Sacrista," reasoned Ahearn none too confidently, "it seems that either your god saw fit to smile upon us unasked or we have been the beneficiaries of yet another of the universe's unanswerable mysteries."

S'ythreni stared at him, then at the general nodding his summation evoked. "Really? You consider this a mystery?"

"And do you have the answer?" asked Padrajisse, who had been one of those nodding.

"I might."

Umkhira crossed her formidable arms. "And it is?"

S'ythreni pointed at Druadaen.

"Him?" squawked Ahearn.

"Me?" exclaimed Druadaen.

"No, fools." S'ythreni jabbed her index finger at his wrist with precise intent. "The velene. That's just the kind of thing legend says they can do."

Ahearn looked wonderingly at Druadaen. "Did the metal beastie come alive, then?

He shook his head. "No."

Ahearn shook his head. "Then how in the hundred hells do you know—?"

"Stop," ordered S'ythreni. She waited until all their eyes were on her. "You all understand that I keep using the word 'legend' for a reason, yes? Because no one really *knows* that much about the velene. I suspect we've never known much about them at all. Not even the Uulamantre, the eldest of the Iavarain." Looking suddenly away, she sheathed her shortsword. "At least none that I get to speak with."

Druadaen was convinced that behind her final mumbled qualifier lay an Archive worth of revelations about S'ythreni and the Iavarain in general.

Her head snapped up. "Movement," she muttered, pointing into the rows of corn through which the first group of hyek had been making such uneven progress.

"One of their wounded?" Ahearn asked, bastard sword suddenly in both hands again.

"Possible," Umkhira muttered. "I shall see."

"Why you?" S'ythreni hissed.

"Because," the Lightstrider hissed back, "I am 'Bent,' am I not? And wounded. I may be able to approach where you would not." And she was gone, the blood-clotted wadding dropped behind her.

Ahearn cursed silently, stared when Druadaen took a knee. "What're yeh doing?"

"Umkhira is our eyes out there," he answered. Then he pointed at S'ythreni. "And she's our ears right here. We humans, standing, trying to detect something they haven't?" He shook his head. "All we are doing is helping our enemies find us."

Ahearn fretted, but ultimately crouched down along with the rest. Padrajisse smiled grimly.

A minute passed, perhaps two...

S'ythreni tilted her head, then turned a worried look back at the sacrist. "That poison, or the antidote: Could it cause the victim to become, well, deranged?"

Padrajisse frowned. "I do not believe so. Why?"

"Because Umkhira is...I think she's *singing*."

Either because the aeosti mentioned it, or the Lightstrider's voice became louder, Druadaen could now hear it: a faint, melancholy melody.

Even Padrajisse joined in the unanimous exchange of surprised looks.

The singing stopped.

Ahearn held his sword ready. "Do you think we should—?"

Druadaen held up a hand a moment before S'ythreni shook her head. "Someone coming."

"Umkhira?" Ahearn asked.

"I'd say if I knew," the aeosti snapped. "Maybe, but the tread sounds heavier." She drew her shortsword. Ahearn was poised to lunge.

Druadaen nodded to Padrajisse, who readied herself. Then he met Elweyr's eyes and glanced toward the crop rows behind them. The thaumantic nodded and turned to watch their rear.

"We are coming to you," Umkhira said in a very slow, calm voice.

"We understand," Druadaen answered before Ahearn could reply with something both tense and jocular.

S'ythreni used her shortsword to indicate a particular point in the wall of corn.

Crackling of green shoots emanated from that area. Deeper in, half-formed ears waved and rustled. "We approach," said Umkhira.

The tall green stems parted and she emerged, carrying a very young girl in her arms. The child's knees, elbows, and hands were covered with dirt and what might have been dung. So was her face, but there, tears had cut clear rivulets down to the bottom of her full cheeks. Her eyes were wide as she looked around at the group, shrank back as she saw the weapons, but in her eyes was recognition: the armed people were of her own kind.

Druadaen heard Padrajisse release a long, shuddering sigh. He glanced over, saw her eyes brightening, her mouth working to make the words. "You hold her as would a mother," she choked out.

Umkhira smiled. "Among ur zhog, children are the responsibility of one hearth, but welcome and cared for at all of them. And shall I tell you how we know if another species can be reasoned with, appealed to?"

Padrajisse nodded.

"That they sing sleep-songs—lullabies, I think you call them." She put her nose against the child's ear; the little girl visibly relaxed. "I let that speak for me before I showed myself. And she understood. Even though I am what she has been taught to fear."

Druadaen swallowed, stood.

The little girl's eyes followed him. They were hazel: the color Heyna's had been. He smiled and she smiled back, fear and hope vying in her face. Probably the look that had been on his own face when Varcaxtan had lifted him out of the root cellar in Connaear so many years ago.

He turned toward S'ythreni, waited until she noticed and met his eyes, surprised.

"This," he said.

"This . . . what?" she asked.

"This is the answer to your question."

"My—?"

"This is why fighting here was the right thing to do."

Ahearn drew in a long breath, clapped a hand down on Druadaen's shoulder, was about to say something. But eyes suddenly wet, he only nodded, turned, and walked away.

CHAPTER THIRTY-SEVEN

The next day, after a night of listening to the Bent winding horns, the hyek faded back toward their warrens in the southern hills. Whether they left because they had taken all that they wished or were unnerved by the unexpected silence of the horn of one of their larger groups, would never be known.

However, as was their wont before withdrawing, they put the torch to everything that would burn. But because both crops and roofs had been gently soaked by rains the prior week, their efforts were only moderately successful. Still, smoky smudges hanging above the steadings of Aswyth Plain announced their departure to all who'd survived their attacks.

So it was no surprise that, shortly after breakfast, S'ythreni spotted another group of refugees moving from east to west, just beyond the small river that marked the northern border of the despoiled farmlands. Hoping that someone in that group would know the girl or how to return her to any surviving family members, Ahearn, Elweyr, and Padrajisse mounted and rode after the refugees, the little girl seated in front of the swordsman.

Before they did, Umkhira said her farewells to the child, who touched the Lightstrider's wide, pronounced brow with gentle fingers. As her escort cantered northward, she waved a spread-fingered goodbye from around Ahearn's broad torso. After that, Umkhira seemed weary or melancholy or both. Druadaen suggested more rest might be in order, and, for the first time in his knowledge of her, she admitted that she did not feel as strong as usual. She went into the dark of the unspoiled root cellar and, if snoring was any indication, was asleep within five minutes. Druadaen remained on guard at their camp while S'ythreni vanished into the fields to find the trail of the giant that the first group of refugees had reported.

She was back within half an hour. Not surprisingly, the giant's movements around the farm were easily found and followed. It had smashed a wide swath through the corn and had done much the same to the surrounding vegetation when it reascended the slopes from which it had come.

Druadaen had not been looking forward to his next duty. Because S'ythreni had far better eyes, her new job was comparatively easy: sit atop what was left of the roof and keep watch. Lacking her keen vision but possessing a great deal more strength, Druadaen's task was to gather the bodies. Moving the hyek corpses was physically taxing, whereas finding and recovering those of the farm family was heartrending. Still, it had to be done and had he been a Legior, it would have been a frequent task—assuming he would have ever seen war at all.

He was about to get the furthest of the hyek corpses, when S'ythreni called out to him. "Dunarran."

He turned. "Yes?"

"Yesterday...what made...I mean, why...?" She shook her head angrily. "You lied to the sacrista. You told her that *I* knew to look for the poison scabbard, that I found it. I didn't ask you to lie for me." She became angry. "I don't want *anything* from you."

Or from anyone else, he seemed to hear like an echo following her words. "Actually," he pointed out calmly, "I did not lie at all. Nor did you. You simply handed her the scabbard. It was she who assumed that you were the person who found it."

"Well, yes...but it was a reasonable assumption."

Druadaen shrugged. "It was an assumption, nonetheless."

"But why do that? I don't need your—"

"Yes: as you made explicitly clear just now and over the months before, you need nothing from me. But Padrajisse knows you used poisoned bolts on the kaghab. Of which she disapproved. Powerfully."

"I neither court nor care about her approval."

"Which you have made equally clear. But all of us must work together, must trust each other, must feel ourselves part of a fellowship. Having you help her save a life through your knowledge of poison seemed likely to balance her judgment against your using it."

"That hardly means she's 'forgiven' me."

"True. But it means she must also consider this: if you were not acquainted with the use of poison, Umkhira might have died." Druadaen shrugged. "I believe that has tempered her feelings toward you. At any rate, it was worth a try." He started away to begin the exhausting work of dragging bodies.

"Dunarran!"

He turned back to her. "Yes?"

"I...I understand you were trying to be helpful. I appreciate that."

Druadaen managed to hide his surprise. "I was happy to help; I expected no thanks."

"And you won't get any next time!" S'ythreni snapped. "Your good intentions are no excuse for meddling in my affairs." She stamped up the ladder to the roof.

Druadaen watched her do so, wondering if she realized that, despite her denials, she had just obliquely admitted to thanking him.

Somehow, that made the prospect of dragging around fallen hyek slightly less onerous.

Ahearn and the others did not return until the sun was well progressed toward the western horizon. After being sent from one group of encamped refugees to another, they ultimately found some of the child's relatives: the family of her maternal aunt. There was no word on the child's own mother, but the three riders had the unpleasant task of describing the four human corpses they'd found scattered about the farm but had refrained from showing her. The aunt's family listened and confirmed that the dead were the little girl's father, maternal grandfather, and two oldest brothers. Saddle-sore and melancholy at having had to transfer such terrible news in the same act as restoring the child to what might be her closest remaining family, Ahearn and the others were quiet upon their return and remained so for most of that evening. As night fell, two other relatives of the little girl's family returned to survey the farmstead, deemed it salvageable, professed regret at having nothing with which to pay the fellowship for their help.

Druadaen waved off their concern, inquired if they meant to remain there for the foreseeable future. When they responded in the affirmative, he explained that they would be doing the group a great service to mind their horses while they tracked the giant into the hills. Eyes wide, the two men agreed and left abruptly.

"Careful now," murmured Ahearn with a smile once they were out of earshot, "you'll scare off all the farmers with that wild talk."

Druadaen shrugged and smiled back. "And still, they accepted the request."

"Yes," S'ythreni said, "since they have every expectation that we won't be coming back for those horses. We'll be too busy getting digested by giants."

They set out upon the giant's trail before dawn, proving in practice what S'ythreni had suggested: that anyone could follow its progress even on a moonless night. Shortly after leaving the croplands, the giant had entered the light woods near the base of the hills that led up to the Thurial mountain range.

As the trees and low undergrowth became thicker, it became just that much easier to track the immense creature. It wasn't even essential to be able to see its yard-long footprints and the crushed fronds on the forest floor; bent saplings and snapped low-hanging branches produced a gap in the canopy that shone down upon them like a road fashioned from twilight.

Shortly after dawn, the path ended at the base of a stream that cascaded down from rocky heights. It was the work of a moment to see why: the giant had ascended here, using the boulders in and around the cataract as if they had been a stone staircase. It also became apparent that the giant could not leave the side of the watercourse without leaving clear marks. Where it had stopped to eat a meal, the hooves and horns of a sizeable goat were strewn about a flattened patch of stream-hugging grasses. The ram's well-gnawed skull had been perched on a rock, looking downhill at them with empty sockets as they ascended. Umkhira inspected the remains and announced that they were about a week old. The group pressed on.

They didn't come across another departure from the winding

stone stairs until the sun was beginning to set. Several trees had been pushed over in a clump which had the distinctive shape of a large biped crushed into its center. "Sleeping mat," Umkhira commented confidently as the shadows lengthened. "This giant is traveling much faster than we are." That simply reinforced their tentative conclusion that despite their quarry's apparently casual progress, it had still covered as much ground in a few hours as they had in the course of a daylong forced march that left all of them spent.

Ahearn strolled about the site, finding a few more bones tossed into nearby bushes. "Seems as good a place as any to make camp. These fallen trees will provide an extra brake against the wind."

Umkhira frowned. "Druadaen's readings suggest that giants may be followed by Bent, or other creatures that mean to feed upon their leavings."

Ahearn smiled. "Aye, and they are ahead of us, too." He held up a cracked bone. "Split with a blade. I wouldn't be surprised if we find some of their scat about."

"Who could tell?" S'ythreni said, raising the back of her hand to her nose and pointing deeper into the woods. When the others looked at her, puzzled, she explained. "Don't go in that direction...not unless you want to conduct a detailed study of a giant's digestive leavings." She stared at their lack of reaction. "Really? None of you can smell that?" When the others shrugged, she shook her head and pulled her sleeping roll free of her pack.

Although Umkhira assured them that the Bent who'd sifted through the giant's leavings had not been at the site for several days, they nonetheless decided against having a fire. No reason to take the chance that the Bent might see it and return. Or worse yet, that they might warn the giant, although Umkhira and Druadaen both agreed that was unlikely. Both the folklore of the ur zhog and the accounts in the Archive Recondite asserted that whatever cooperation occurred between the Bent and the giants was opportunistic rather than planned.

Ahearn nodded approval. "Well, if a Dunarran and a Light-strider come to the same conclusion, that's as close to a certainty as one gets in this world. Now, then, let's remedy something that got us in hot water the other day."

"Such as?" Padrajisse drawled.

"I'm glad you asked! I've spent the better part of our hike thinking how useful it would be if you, eh, 'bonded' with all of us. I think that was what you called it, but whether that's the right term or no, it certainly would have helped our battle plans go more smoothly!"

"It is the correct term, but I cannot create so many bonds."

"Why not?"

Elweyr nudged him. "Hssst. Enough of that. Don't put a sacrist on the spot."

"I'm not!"

"You are when what you're really asking is, 'Why won't your god give you more power?'"

Padrajisse waved what might have been dismissive gratitude at the thaumantic. "The answer, Master Ahearn, is that many factors bear upon how much we may impose upon our deities. Once established, any bond to another entity remains a constant, albeit small, drain upon a deity's attention and beneficence. If any consecrant overreaches for such favor, the deity usually reminds us of our place by withdrawing what blessings exist and turning their face from us for several days."

"Well then, how many can you give us, do you think?"

"Gods and garters," Elweyr almost growled, "do you think you're ordering eggs, Ahearn?"

The swordsman stared at his friend in both confusion and surprise. He seemed about to say something but then turned back to Padrajisse and waited.

Who shrugged. "I think I can risk two. I will start immediately. Do not disturb me until I am done." She turned toward Druadaen, closed her eyes, and held her hands out in his direction, palms up. Almost immediately, she frowned, then her eyes opened sharply. "That is very strange."

S'ythreni rested the tip of her long, fine index finger upon her chin. "Told you."

"So you did," Padrajisse allowed. She frowned at Druadaen. "And you have no idea what causes this . . . this disruption of miracles and mancery alike?"

Druadaen shook his head. "None," he admitted. "Unless . . . could it be some kind of, well, curse?"

She started. "A permanent curse? Put upon you by what powerful foe?"

"Not by a foe." Druadaen felt old fears rise. "I have wondered if it could be connected to my rejection at the epiphanium."

Padrajisse's eyebrows rose. "It sounds as though you have a story to tell me."

Druadaen looked uncomfortably around the group, all of whom leaned closer. "To date, I have left this as a . . . private matter."

Padrajisse nodded. "Understandable. But if these companions are willing to join you in your search for giants, perhaps you owe them an accounting of this part of your past. It seems a reasonable way of honoring their willingness to travel with you out of loyalty."

That's not why they're doing it, but . . . And so Druadaen told them the very abbreviated version of his invitation to, and baffling rejection at, the epiphanium of Amarseker.

Padrajisse sat silently for several long seconds after he was done telling the tale.

"Well?" he asked. The others leaned toward the sacrista, interested, attentive.

"I do not think your nullification of miracles or mancery is the act of any god of the pantheons you sought. And of them all, Amarseker is the one least likely to act in such a contrary and capricious manner. Even more so than my own lord and Creedgiver, Thyeru. But what causes the phenomenon—that I cannot say. Now, I would have you answer a mystery for me. This velene of yours: Is it living or not?"

"It is not mine," Druadaen averred.

"How do you know?"

He shrugged. "In addition to being told as much by those who would know, it is unresponsive to me."

"Unresponsive? In what way?"

Druadaen leaned back. "When I think, or voice, requests, it always ignores them. Or does not hear them. Either way, if it does not respond to my will, how could it be called 'mine'?"

Padrajisse turned toward S'ythreni. "You seem to have deeper knowledge of it, so I shall put the same question to you: Is it a living creature or otherwise?"

The aeosti shrugged. "I don't know. I'm not even sure Shaananca did."

Padrajisse straightened. "Shaananca, Mentor of the Ar?"

Druadaen managed not to react to the fact that the sacrist knew of his guardian not in her role as the Consentium's Senior

Archivist, but as a Mentor—rather than a Guide—of the Ar. Whatever that was.

"Ay-eh, that's the Shaananca he knows," Ahearn confirmed with a smile. "You're acquainted with her?"

Padrajisse shook her head. "I have never met her. My familiarity with her is restricted to her name—and position—alone." She glanced at Druadaen out of the corner of her eye. "Why did you not say from the first that you are on a mission for her?"

"Because I am not."

"Y'see, now," Ahearn said through a widening grin, "Shaananca's too wise a magic auntie to send her nephew off looking for giants to kill 'im. That's all his doing."

Padrajisse never even turned her eyes toward the swordsman. She leaned toward Druadaen, as if closer study would solve his mysterious origins and intents. "And how did you assume such a strange quest?"

"With respect, I'm not sure I've assumed a 'quest.' I'm just trying to answer questions. An increasing number of them, it seems."

Padrajisse seemed both mollified and disappointed. "Questions regarding what?"

Druadaen drew in a breath, took a moment to consider how to give the most coherent and yet concise explanation of the strange inconsistencies he'd found regarding the urzh and their recovery and impossible resilience to staggering casualties, the fossils which sages said could not have formed in the time that the world had existed and, just now, the apparent physiological impossibilities of the species known as giants.

He had just begun enumerating the confounding details of their anatomy when Padrajisse sliced her hand, edge first, through the air between them. "I have heard enough. You seek to explain the will of the gods. It cannot be done. You would be wise to put your faculties to a better purpose." She considered him solemnly and perhaps with a hint of sympathy. "Of course, being denied epiphanesis might put any active mind on such a path as yours. You no doubt hunger for answers to so many of the questions that the embrace of a deity and its creedland renders moot."

Umkhira nodded. S'ythreni seemed to be trying very hard not to roll her eyes. But Ahearn and Elweyr exchanged brief uncomfortable glances. Druadaen never asked other people about the creeds to which they belonged; his own disappointments had schooled him in why others might wish to keep such matters private. But there was something in the two men's reactions which suggested that they were not in complete agreement with Padrajisse's assertion.

Perhaps she sensed the generally tepid reaction to her words because she added even more emphatically, "Each creedland provides answers. I am told that even the Great Tract does. And who may say that any of them are entirely correct or entirely incorrect in the lens they hold up to reality?"

Umkhira started. "I am surprised to hear a thinski...er, human say that. Seen from without, your society's temples all seem convinced that they are the sole possessors of the truth of the world around us."

Padrajisse shrugged. "Many claim just that. And those which do are often at war with others who make equally absolute claims. Yet even that is part of the greater equilibrium between the gods."

S'ythreni raised an eyebrow. "How so?"

"Is it not obvious? Creation itself reflects the properties of its creators—the deities—naturally enough. So the wars between, and also within, thinking creatures must correspond to similar variations among and within the individual gods. Some are absolute and unyielding; others are flexible and tolerant. Some espouse altruism and modesty; others encourage gain and vainglory. Such contending forces exist within each species and within the heart of each individual. How could it be otherwise, since we are but the ripples of the creation which arose from their power, and so, took its shape from their spirits?"

Umkhira frowned. "This is a strange speaking from a human priest. Most only pronounce, declare, and declaim, regardless of what they value."

S'ythreni smiled at her. "We may not have much in common, Lightstrider, but we share this experience when it comes to human temples. But, in fairness, Padrajisse is a sacrista of a Helper deity; you will hear temperate words much more frequently among them than others. And some would say Thyeru's consecrants are among the most open-minded and just." She turned toward Druadaen. "Others would say it is Amarseker."

Umkhira's frown had not lessened. "Yet they are not among the greatest deities of that pantheon, are they?"

Padrajisse shook her head—sadly, Druadaen thought. "No. We of Thyeru consider those in the Creedlands of Amarseker to be close kin because we both walk a very hard path. We follow precepts rather than laws, must measure and decide upon our deeds. In other temples, there is more reliance upon universal rules than personal reflection.

"Still, there are many commonalities which run through all creeds. Indeed, even those who choose to rove rootless in the Great Tract"—Ahearn shifted uncomfortably at the forced toleration in her tone—"show their common origins with all others. Similar observances are always on the same days of the same moonphases. All have a rite that we call epiphanesis. And in all, if a transgression is great enough, an offender is—" She stopped, eyes wide as she realized the conclusion toward which she was headed.

"An offender is banished to the Wildscape." Druadaen finished for her. He shrugged. "You do me no injury saying this. It is simple truth, and every night reminds me of it. So that is why I cannot help but wonder if my disruption of both the mancery and miracles is a curse."

She shook her head sharply. "No. I cannot believe it. Not of Amarseker, anyway." Her eyes fell. "But what it might be? That I cannot say any better than you."

Ahearn rose and stretched. He looked up into the deep blue dusk from which stars were beginning to emerge. "There's more mystery than certainty in this world, I always say. Not much comfort in that, except that you can rely on it being true." He rubbed his arms against the upland chill. "Time for a warm bedroll. If it's all the same with you, I'll take the middle watch."

CHAPTER THIRTY-EIGHT

Weary and cold, Druadaen hardly remembered slipping into his own bed roll, shortly after midnight. As was often the case when he bivouacked beneath the stars, sleep came swiftly and started out dreamless—

—Until, with great suddenness, he was looking down on his own slumbering body, wrapped tight into his bedroll against the brisk air. Padrajisse was on one side of him, Umkhira on the other. As his dreams so rarely were, the scene was as hard-edged as reality itself—except that he heard murmurings. He tried to walk toward the sound, but instead, its ebb and flow seemed to lift and draw him to its source...

The next moment, he was just beyond the edge of the clearing the giant had made in creating a bed for itself. Within the intact tree line, he stood—or floated?—only a few feet away from Elweyr, S'ythreni, and Ahearn. The latter was shaking his head. S'ythreni was looking away from him, somehow managing to look bored and exasperated at the same time.

"No," Ahearn said slowly but firmly, "I still say he did the right thing by bringing us here. It takes us in good direction."

"Well, it's not a good direction for money," the aeosti tossed over her shoulder.

"Not right away, no, but his connections are a kind of currency unto themselves."

"Perhaps, but we can't eat it or spend it. And in the meantime, his 'connections' indulge his pointless questions and make it possible for him to come all the way down here...just so he can almost get us all killed. And for what? Those Bent didn't have even thirty billon marks between them, and I'd lay odds that some came from the farm. And you know if there's any doubt, he's going to make us turn them over to whatever is left of the family."

"And is that so bad a thing to do?"

"That's not my point. I'm not concerned with whether we keep thirty marks or not. I'm concerned with taking jobs that have no profit. There wasn't a weapon or piece of equipment on the Bent that's worth the weight of carrying. Again. And now it turns out his 'power' to disrupt mancery and miracles may be a curse, instead."

"The sacrista said it's not a curse."

"No, she said she *doesn't know* what it is. And even though she insists there's no connection, don't you find it suspicious that a god rejects him on the very day of his epiphanesis? I am not sure I want to be standing beside him when the skies open up to tell him *why*. Besides, why didn't Good Sir Integrity share that story until now?"

"And just when is the right moment to share such a thing? And with such a lot as us?"

S'ythreni started. "What do you mean, 'such a lot as us'? I will consign my soul to the forests and seas, right now, if you try to convince me that we're not 'good enough' for him."

"No, my foolish, darling Iava. I'm referring to our constant foolery, particularly in the face of anything we're expected to revere."

Elweyr rubbed his palms together. "And how does that justify his decision to withhold the story of his failed epiphanesis? His curse has almost killed us at least three times."

"Now don't be getting sly on me, Elweyr. You know full well that the fellow didn't realize he put spells awry until you told him so under Gur Grehar. But after that, well, wear his boots for a moment: Would you be in any rush to share such a strange and sobering tale with three rough-mannered fortune-hunters who refuse to take anything seriously? Tell me honestly, now: What do we three *not* make light of?"

S'ythreni sneered. "He might be improved by learning to make light of a bit *more*, if you ask me."

"And I'd agree. But that might be hard for a fellow—an orphan, no less—who grew up after being turned away from his epiphanesis." Ahearn shook his head at the notion. "Have you ever heard of such a thing?"

"No," murmured S'ythreni. "That is not our way."

Elweyr shrugged. "And like you, Ahearn, I was never put before a dreamguide to become an epiphane."

"Aye, but that doesn't answer my question. A youngster being turned away so abruptly: it's just not done, is it? An epiphane is invited by the deity itself, yeh? So the good-faith assumption is that, all things being equal, a young lad or lass is welcomed into that creedland. But our Dunarran arrives full of hope, only to be told 'away with you' and 'don't bother trying any other temple'? Nasty damn gods, if you ask me."

Elweyr tilted his head. "That doesn't quite make sense, actually."

"Ah, the words of the sacrista herself, now. Is this a further sign of your silent reverence for her?"

"Don't mistake respect for reverence, Ahearn. And no, I don't give a fig for what comes out of Padrajisse's mouth, except for when its accurate. Like her summation of Druadaen's situation. I don't know much about gods in general or the Helper pantheon specifically, but is it plausible that its patron deity of *justice* would have him made an epiphane only to turn him away? It makes no sense. Worse: it is exactly the opposite of how Amarseker is said to behave."

S'ythreni straightened, eyes bright. "Unless that's exactly *why* Amarseker brought him to the epiphanium."

Ahearn started. "To make a poor, well-meaning stripling of a boy miserable? Gods, S'ythreni, that's a more cynical ploy than I thought even you could imagine."

"No, no; I don't mean that Amarseker wanted to hurt him." She leaned forward, as if she were tracking the ideas as they came out of her. "What if Druadaen's rejections by the other temples was exactly what caused Amarseker to take pity and find a way to talk to him, to save him further misery by warning him that he would not be welcomed in *any* creedland?"

Elweyr started rubbing his palms together again. "But that's not what Druadaen told us."

"He was thirteen," rebutted S'ythreni. "And he was terrified. And in the end, he was crushed. I'm not sure that even at *my* age, it would ever occur to me that Amarseker was trying to help rather than hurt me. Although, I wouldn't be surprised if the god itself was bound not to share that information."

Ahearn crossed his arms, frowning. "Why do you think that?"

"Because if providing an answer wasn't a sensitive issue, why didn't any of the other gods simply tell him that he should abandon his attempt to find a creedland?"

Elweyr nodded. "Yes. It's almost as if Amarseker crossed a line the others weren't willing to, although why gods would have such trepidation is...well, it's imponderable."

S'ythreni nodded back. "Exactly. Which makes Druadaen just that much more risky as a companion, and why it could be suicide to embrace him as a friend."

Ahearn's frown had deepened. "Leaving aside all the fine and futile speculations upon the deeds and reasons of deities, let me be sure I'm understanding you, High-Ears. Are you saying we should forsake the fellow?"

Her eyes widened. "'Forsake' him? If by 'forsake' you mean 'abandon,' then no: we're partners and we have an agreement. We see this out. But we are *only* partners, not kin. So to part ways afterward is not 'forsaking' him; it is simply a business decision. One we should consider very carefully."

Ahearn shook his head in disappointment. "Well, I suppose I shouldn't be surprised. It's clear you haven't liked him. Not from the start."

"And why do you say that?"

"Well, look at how you treat the fellow!"

"Ahearn," Elweyr muttered as S'ythreni smiled faintly, "how is that any different from how she treats *us*?"

The swordsman frowned. "Well, now that you mention it... But see here: whatever sass and sniping you may aim at us, you've never made any noise about parting ways."

"That's because as far as I can tell, you two don't have any cosmic mysteries hovering around. Mysteries that could get me killed."

"As if our trade makes us strangers to peril?"

"Yes, the peril that we assess and then accept or decline in the pursuit of our goals. We may not have perfect foresight, but our futures—together and separately—are the product of our own *choices*.

"But traveling with a mancery-smothering Dunarran orphan who was inexplicably turned away by the god who should love him best of all?" She shook her head. "That is one mystery nested inside another. And we have no means of assessing the danger we court by associating ourselves with it. So of course we're not strangers to peril, Ahearn; we survive by being able to measure and decide just how much of it we're willing to accept. But we have no way to do that with Druadaen." She looked down. "Which I regret."

Ahearn cocked his head to the side, smiled, opened his mouth to speak—

—And Druadaen snapped upright from his bedroll. He hadn't had a dream like that—so lacking the Wildscape's transmogrifications of time and place and even persons—since shortly after they had set to sea from Araxor aboard the *Swiftsure*. It was so extraordinary, so believable, that he momentarily wondered if it was not a dream but a vision. He rubbed his already sagging eyelids, and they opened long enough to show him that—just as at the start of his dream—the only two other people present in their camp circle were Umkhira to one side and Padrajisse to the other. But only Ahearn was supposed to be awake for the middle watch, although he might well have wakened at least one of the other two. Still, it was suspiciously akin to the scenario that he'd seen in his dream...

But it was also true that one's mind remained aware even as it slept. So the odds were infinitely greater that the watchful part of his sleeping mind had noted the departure of Elweyr and S'ythreni and incorporated them into his dream. It was certainly not as strange (not to say bizarre) as his chaotic runs through the Wildscape, which grabbed and warped and fused recent elements from his waking existence into a collage at once strange and unnerving.

Still, this dream had seemed *so* real...

The next morning's journey further up the stepped falls of the cascade began as a long, uninterrupted climb, for no other reason than the giant had not stopped along that stretch. If anything, the signs they found suggested that it had bounded up the rocky staircase in great leaps, or as Ahearn put it, "two stairs at a time."

When they finally noticed a wide clearing in the forest canopy near a small waterfall, they hoped that they would find another place where it—and now they—could rest. What they hadn't expected was the singular sound that occasionally rose above the constant rush and crash of plummeting water: harsh voices, speaking in Undercant.

The Bent were so busy squabbling and shouting to be heard above the cataract that they were not aware of Druadaen and his companions until hit by a volley of arrows. And one quarrel. Loosed from under thirty yards, all but one of them hit their marks. Druadaen rapidly drew again to the ear as the survivor—a haggard ur gabar, from the look of him—fled into the trees. He disappeared behind a cluster of close-grown firs, but Druadaen waited, aiming just beyond the farthest pine bough—and loosed again as the wiry little Bent ran back into the open.

The gabar's shriek was short, as if permanently pinned in its throat. The shaft hit him just above where his neck joined his body.

Umkhira ran ahead, turned a mercy knife upon the two that were still thrashing, and surveyed the scene. As Druadaen and the others approached, she gestured around at the bodies. "A lame hyek. A small HalfBent. Two escaped urzhen slaves, one missing his tongue. And the ur gabar. All half-starved. They were fighting over that." She pointed to the scant remains of a lamb and then raised her finger to indicate a long, wide gap in the forest. The ground beneath the gap in the trees was hard-packed; a few immense footprints had been captured in now-dried mud. Umkhira pointed at them. "Those are the only tracks the giant made going away from this place. It has left the falls."

Ahearn leaned on his unstrung bow. "Looks like he's headed off home, now."

Elweyr glanced at the corpses. "And these were the rats that lived off his leavings."

Umkhira nodded. "It is not surprising. They were all outcasts from their tribes, although for different reasons." She studied the rugged highlands into which they had ascended. "We seem to have come to the start of falls." She nodded up at a cluster of white frothing streams that rolled down through channels worn in the rocks above. "Those three small waterways: they are what flow into the wide basin here, just beyond the lip over which the narrow water flies." She finished by pointing at the source of the gushing cataract.

"Meaning?" Padrajisse asked, panting from the morning's long, upward hike.

Umkhira shrugged. "Another reason this is a likely place for it to make a home. The pool holds enough water for all its needs." She frowned. "Actually, it is enough water for the needs of *several* giants."

Ahearn rolled his eyes. "Well, isn't that a cheery thought." He secured his bow, drew his bastard sword with both hands. "I guess there's nothing for it but to see if the great pillaging pillock is at home." Together, they started upon the widest footpath any of them had ever seen.

The giant's lair was located at the end of the footpath, or rather, the stone shelf that extended onward from it. Trees clung tenaciously to either side. A sheer rock face dropped steeply to the left; another rose just as steeply to the right. The lair was situated at the point where the shelf ended: a wedge-shaped cleft in the rocky shoulder of the slope. It could also have been described as a shallow, wide-mouthed cave: exactly the kind of den described by the majority of the accounts Druadaen had perused in the Archive Recondite. But instead of having a peripheral population of cooperative Bent, the approach was completely undefended and unpatrolled.

Except for cats. *Big* cats. Some might have been bobcats or hybrids between them and domesticated varieties. But whatever their origins, none of them were smaller than spaniels.

They did not behave like feral felines. The half dozen of them—or maybe more; who could ever be sure with cats?—were all lounging in the general vicinity of the overhang. Most rose when Druadaen and his companions approached but did not spring up in alarm or with the fixed gaze of big cats about to attack. Two retreated until they were beneath the overhang, their tails fluffed out like pipe cleaners. Another one let out a long, low, whining yowl: the classic sound of a tomcat encountering a hated rival in a midnight alley. Two others stood, stretched, hissed hoarsely, unwilling to give up what were obviously favorite spots on favorite rocks. And one simply looked over at the approaching bipeds before laying its head back down.

"This," Elweyr muttered, "is very strange."

Umkhira nodded. She glanced at Druadaen, who also nodded. They resumed a slow approach.

The cats all departed eventually, but more out of irritation than fear. They reluctantly gave ground, a few hissing, spitting, and then running, but just as many simply yawning and padding over the lip of the downside slope.

Ahearn muttered, "They're just damned big barn cats."

Which was the conclusion to which Druadaen had come, having known a few barns and their cat populations in his youth. Like them, the only thing they had in common was that they all grudgingly tolerated each other's presence. No, definitely not wild cats.

As the last and largest slipped over the slope toward the forest below, Elweyr muttered, "Hope this giant doesn't have dogs, too."

"From your lips to an avatar's ears," Ahearn said through a soft exhale. "Let's go find out."

Druadaen held out an arm before the swordsman could advance on the small rise that led up to the space beneath the overhang. "Wait." Moving slowly, he edged to the downhill side of the narrowing rock shelf and peered over.

No sign of the cats. But at the base of the slope there was a small glen, not much more than a notch among the trees—where a flash of white caught his eye.

A bone. And now that he looked more carefully, he saw bleached hints of others protruding from what looked like a pile of—

"Ah," sighed S'ythreni, who was peering around him, "I believe we've found the privy."

"Yes," Umkhira agreed, having come up on the other side of Druadaen. "But more than that, I think."

Druadaen glanced beyond the offal, following the Lightstrider's gaze, and was surprised to discover a thatch of bright yellow stretching away from it, winding out of the little glen.

"Sunflowers?" Padrajisse breathed in doubt and wonder. Apparently, everyone had come to stand on the edge of the slope, which was not a wise tactical choice, but Ahearn tended not to think about such minutiae.

"Quite the odd contrast," Elweyr muttered.

"But it is not odd at all," Umkhira said. "See how the slope runs down through the glen?"

"Yes," Padrajisse said, frowning, "and so?"

Druadaen saw it suddenly, remembering one of those pictures which, if you changed the focus of your eyes, the scene altered. Whatever had been discarded, or excreted, down the slope into that tiny glen had ultimately become rich soil, which rains had washed further down the gentle dip into the notch. That was the fertilizer that had allowed the sunflowers to flourish, which would otherwise have had no chance taking root on the rocky hillside.

"Those flowers: they are not there by chance," Umkhira said thoughtfully.

The Corrovani sacrista reply was indignant. "You assume it *meant* to create this strangely fortuitous arrangement? Come now; do not ascribe intent to the actions of a creature that can barely be called sapient!"

Umkhira smiled as she leaned to look past Druadaen. "Servant of Thyeru, see how the notch between the trees lies? It follows the path of the sun so that the light may shine on the flowers from shortly after dawn until the hills behind us block its rays."

"Wait," muttered Ahearn. "Are you two actually saying that this giant *means* to grow these plants?"

Druadaen's answer was a smile...as he sheathed his sword.

"Are you mad?" gasped Ahearn.

"No. And I think you would do well to put up your own blade."

Ahearn's chin came out. "I will not. So maybe the giant likes flowers. Well and good. Doesn't mean it wouldn't like to gnaw on my thigh bone even more."

Well, there's no arguing that, Druadaen allowed with a shrug.

But as he did, Umkhira slung her axe across her back and said, "Come, Druadaen. We shall seek the giant together. Perhaps, if it, too, is familiar with Undercant, I might help you communicate with it."

The others followed a good ten paces behind, shaking their heads and muttering darkly about the imminent demise of their friends.

One of the many things that Druadaen had learned during his time in the tunnels of the Gur Grehar was that lairs were almost always musty and rank with body smell. Whether that was the sweat of the Bent or the secretions and oil and shed-skin stink of wild creatures, one or both of those scents invariably marked where they slept, regardless how the odors varied by species.

Here, there were none.

Nor was there the usual litter of bones and half-chewed pelts. No spoor whatsoever. He looked left toward Umkhira, who met his surprised look with one of her own. To his right, Ahearn advanced in a wide stance, sword ready in both hands. If he had noticed anything ominous, he gave no sign of it. Once under the jagged chin of rock that protected the cleft from the elements, they paused, examining the area carefully.

Along one side of the curving rear wall were unusual lengths of dried venison, as if after having been gutted, the meat of the animal had simply been stripped off the larger bones in one great yank. They reminded Druadaen of skinned rabbits, hung near the fireplace of borderers and farm folks. And judging from the row of empty wooden pegs stretching away from those that still had a carcass secured to them, a once considerable supply of meat had been considerably diminished.

The area in front of them, and the other side of the rear wall, were given over to the tidiest pile of junk that Druadaen had ever seen. Old doors and barrels propped up against tree trunks and fire-scored roof beams. Sledgehammers leaned against various weapons which had probably belonged to others who'd met their ends doing exactly what the three of them were doing now. Except...

The barrels had lengths of rope strung across their openings: carrying handles for containers that would be just the right size for a giant's bucket. The bark-stripped boles and beams were either parts of a skinning—and maybe drying—rack or pieces of a travois. The door had clearly started out as a fixture on a castle or a fortified outpost but had since been fitted with either oxen tack or a horse's girth strap across the back to create a serviceable shield. The two-handed battle-axes would have been merely outsized hatchets for a giant, but then again, for them, most trees were the equivalent of saplings. The trimmed bole of a young oak with a shillelagh-cut head—obviously a club—lay across the tops of a half dozen sea chests from which mice were scattering: makeshift grain bins, apparently. And the sledgehammer was just that, although it would look like a toy in a giant's hand.

But the great sword did not seem to have a purpose other than the one for which its human smith had intended it: a weapon. And although it would seem akin to a narrow huntsman's sword when wielded by a being at least ten feet taller than either Druadaen or Ahearn, it would certainly be capable of cutting either of them in two at a single blow.

The only strong scent in the wide cave came from the edge of the overhang farthest from the dried venison: pine pitch. A bucket—well, barrel—of it stood a few feet back from a firebreak comprised of boulders.

Ahearn leaned away from his ready blade to whisper, "All the comforts of home, hey? I wonder if he's got a—"

"*Shhhh!*" Umkhira hissed. "Listen."

They did.

"Do you hear that?"

From the dark alcove at the center of the rear wall, there emanated a deep susurration.

"If the earth itself breathed," Umkhira said quietly, "that is the sound it would make."

Ahearn smiled. "I'll bet whatever you like that we're not hearin' from any elemental force of the rock and soil." He started forward, sword raising up over his shoulder...and bumped into Druadaen's outstretched arm.

"Firstly, we came to converse, not kill. Secondly, I am the one who brought us here; it is only right that I should be the one who meets what awaits us."

"Well," Ahearn sighed, "You need to swap the order of those two points to put the most worthy first. But otherwise, I'm in agreement...and right behind you." He smiled. "You mad bastard of a Dunarran."

CHAPTER THIRTY-NINE

The giant was, in fact, sound asleep.

However, they were quite surprised to discover something they had never considered: that it was female. If the long deer hide and bedsheet smocks hadn't been suggestion enough, one look at her face would certainly have sufficed; it was broad but surprisingly fine-featured and framed by tumbling curls of light brown hair.

Ahearn stopped as if frozen by mancery. "Now what?"

Druadaen felt a frown forming. *Now what, indeed?* He'd experienced the same reflexive pause when he'd first discovered the sex of the blugner they'd fought in the Gur Grehar. It made little sense, really; the prohibition against killing women and children was not observed among most underkin and, truth be told, not often enough among humans, either. But that discovery had come after a life-and-death battle during which, had he known the sex of the blugner, it would have been nothing less than suicidal to scruple over it. But here...

"What is your plan?" Umkhira whispered.

Druadaen shook his head. He'd envisioned giants as large, angry, brutish creatures that would only respond to mortal threat. A crossbow held to one temple with their body soaked in oil and a burning torch ready to hand had been one set of precautions he'd contemplated. Having Elweyr and Padrajisse stun or daze the being had been another. And the latter might still work, but...

"My plans do not suit this situation. We must find a way to wake her gently."

"Gently?" Ahearn looked at his sword. "Share your wisdom."

Umkhira was frowning. "If only there was a way to bring her around slowly..."

Druadaen stared at the Lightstrider, then smiled. "Thank you. That is exactly the plan we needed."

Her frown deepened. "Do you mock me? That was no plan; that was a wish."

"But it was also a plan. One you've already demonstrated with great success."

"Me? I have done nothing of the sort!"

"In fact, you have, just the other day."

Ahearn rolled his eyes and muffled a moan. "Oh, fer bogsakes. You mean to *sing* to it?"

"To *her*," Druadaen corrected. "And yes, I do." He thought. "But from beyond arm's reach."

"You'd be meaning *her* arm's reach, a-yeh?"

"Yes."

"And do you think she'll even hear us from that far away?"

Druadaen shrugged. "I do not know. But this seems an excellent time to find out."

However, his simple plan ran into an immediate snag: they could not decide on what to sing. Although they all spoke Commerce, none of them had grown up with the same songs. As they debated and compared tunes, their whisperings became annoyed mutters.

The giantess stirred. She quieted, but her breathing did not slip back into the same, sonorous drone as before.

"I have refrained from suggesting it," Druadaen murmured quickly, "but there's at least one song we all know."

"There is?" Umkhira asked.

"Which one?" insisted Ahearn.

"The one the sail handlers sung on the *Swiftsure* almost every day."

"*That* song?" Umkhira almost recoiled. "It was very lively. And vulgar."

"So we will sing it more slowly," Druadaen replied. "And we will...uh, well..."

"And we'll sing it sweetly," Ahearn concluded with a smile. "Like every word is a drop of musical honey from the purest lullaby."

Umkhira's eyes seemed ready to start out of their sockets. "And just how should one sing those words in such a tone—?" But Ahearn did not wait; he lifted his chin and put his voice to the task.

And to their surprise, he not only managed to make the rapid, ribald lyrics sound like a slow, cheery campfire song, but did so in a rich, mellow bass that would have been the envy of most court minstrels.

Druadaen added his serviceable baritone and Umkhira her soft, if rumbling, alto.

For a full minute, there was no response. Then the immense body under the blanket—actually, multiple bear hides stitched together—shifted, rolled away, then began to roll back in their direction.

"Be ready!" Druadaen whispered.

"For what?" Umkhira wondered.

"For . . . anything!" he replied.

But once again, what happened was arguably the one thing they were not ready to respond to. The giantess's eyes opened lazily—they were a rich chocolate brown—and slowly closed.

—and then opened wide with an audible slap of skin hitting skin. She jerked forward . . . but not to attack. Rather, she grabbed the bear-hide blanket to her with a panic of startled virtue that recalled young girls reacting to unexpected intrusions upon their bedchambers.

"We mean no harm," Umkhira said in Undercant.

"Then don't use the language of vermin!" the giantess burbled in passable, but very slurred, Commerce. She squinted hard at Umkhira. "Oh. Pardons." She straightened. "Yet you intrude. With weapons ready." She licked her lips.

Ahearn brought his sword to readiness again.

But Druadaen had been watching more closely. She had licked her lips, yes, but they were cracked and almost gray. "Are you . . . thirsty?"

"For our blood, maybe," Ahearn muttered.

He hissed the swordsman to silence as the giantess put a hand to her forehead. "I am . . . I need . . ." She swayed. As she did, one of her hands lost full grip on the blanket of many bearskins and her torso was revealed.

Despite her pale and drawn cheeks, her body was bloated.

"Are you well?" Druadaen tried again.

"I am well enough to defend myself against littlings." She started the reply as a growled threat, but it ended as a long, shuddering sigh of pain.

Umkhira was frowning. "You are ill."

"I do need water," she groaned. "If you have come to kill me, I will fight as best I may. If not, then please—bring my water from without."

"Where is—?"

"Next to the hearth."

Druadaen considered. That would mean it was in one of the barrels. It would take two strong persons to move it. He turned to Ahearn . . .

But Umkhira spoke to him before Druadaen could. "Come, swordsman. Let us fetch water while the Dunarran speaks to the giantess." Druadaen moved to stop her, but the Lightstrider shook her head with a smile. "I am every bit as strong as you. Stronger perhaps."

He smiled back. "Send in Elweyr, if you would. With all our rations."

Shortly after she exited with Ahearn, the thaumantic edged cautiously into the alcove. "I do not mean to intrude," he muttered.

"Well, whatever you mean, intrude is what you have done. All of you." The giant's eyes seemed to lose focus for a moment. "Tell me: Why are you here?"

"To speak with you."

She raised her eyes to the rough rock overhead. "Surely, I am walking in the Great Tract."

"No, we are really here to speak with you."

A great sloshing announced Ahearn and Umkhira's return with a sizable barrel of water.

Her eyes opened wide. "Dream or not, that is very welcome." She leaned over, carefully avoided touching them, and swung the barrel up to her lips.

As she finished, Elweyr held up the pack into which he'd put their rations. "We come with a gift, as well."

"Littling food?" Her eyes became clearer, almost seemed to twinkle. "Oh, that would be wonderful!" She took the pack delicately, removed the wrappings, and ate whole meals as if they were small appetizers. After finishing, she smiled—and then clutched her stomach. Which was suddenly bubbling and gurgling like boiling tannery vats.

She leaped out of the bed with surprising alacrity, bear skins flying apart and falling everywhere as she bolted out of the alcove and leaped down the slope.

"Well," commented Elweyr, "that certainly went as planned."

CHAPTER FORTY

When the giantess reappeared over the lip of the footpath, she waved away solicitous inquiries. She staggered into her alcove and collapsed facedown on the bed.

Where she slept for five hours, snoring so loudly that all animal noises in the region were stilled. However, when the snoring stopped abruptly, she called out to the group and invited them to return.

She was sitting up this time, the bearskins in a rough pile beside her bedding: cowhides over dried bushes. Her face was less drawn and her body less bloated. "Be seated," she invited, speaking Commerce quite competently, but slowly, as if reacquainting herself with its sounds and structures. She turned toward Umkhira. "Why did you address me in Undercant?"

Druadaen answered. "That was my doing, mistress. The books of our learned scholars presumed it was the language you were most likely to know."

"Do they think we have no tongue of our own, or would settle for so limited a language?"

"I cannot say what they thought."

"Well, it appears they thought we were stupid. And that would make them stupid for thinking so."

"Well," Ahearn said carefully, "it's hard to be sure about such things in advance. And truth be told, you sounded a bit like a drunken sailor when you awoke."

"Yes? And just how articulate are you when you first rise?"

"Articulate? You know that word?"

"You are surprised? Well, I'm equally surprised that one of *you* learned it." She considered them. "Although I must admit, you have far, *far* better manners than any other littlings I have known in...oh, a very long time, now."

"How long?" Druadaen asked quietly.

She looked at him quickly. "So you *did* come to talk. I hear that searching tone. What is your name?"

And so they went through the introductions, with more politesse than many human gatherings Druadaen had attended. The giantess's name was Heela and she ended by apologizing for her sprint down the hill. "As you gathered, I have not been well."

"Something you ate?" Ahearn wondered aloud. Every eye gored him. "What?" he asked. "Wasn't that the complaint?"

Druadaen did his best not to notice the swordsman nor the rest of their fellowship's reactions to his explicit and tone-deaf frankness. "Perhaps you were injured recently?" The giantess's blank stare compelled him to become more direct. "Perhaps during a recent...trip to the human farms?"

She frowned. "No."

Druadaen heard the evasive tone. "Perhaps during your return here?"

"So you followed me," she sighed. "I cannot deny it. I was there."

"And was there any...eh, violence that—?"

She jumped to her feet; the rock under their feet shook slightly. "Whoever told you there was violence lies!" she shouted, her voice booming back at them from the stony sides of the alcove.

"Tell that to the dead farmers," Padrajisse pronounced darkly.

"Dead—?" Heela closed her eyes but not in time to keep two gill-sized tears from squeezing out and then rolling down her still-hollow cheeks.

"You had no hand in the attack?" Druadaen asked.

She shook her head. "I went at night. Just so that I would not be seen, not meet the humans."

"So you could steal," Padrajisse amended in a stony voice.

"Yes," Heela sniffled. "So I could steal."

Her frank admission and regret even silenced the moralistic sacrista.

"Why do you steal?" Druadaen asked softly.

Heela waved a massive palm at the sky beyond the overhang. "The usual reason: to get enough to eat. But this season—it was different."

"Different in what way?"

Tears flowed freely; they made sounds like shot glasses being emptied upon stone. "I lost my child."

Umkhira started forward, hand outstretched. "To disease? To enemies? To—?"

"To the fate that has us lose so many children. To the curse of our own bodies."

The group was suddenly very silent.

Druadaen rose and sat closer to her. "We do not understand. How is it that your bodies cause you to lose so many children?"

"Truly, you cannot reason it out?"

Druadaen shook his head, offered a rueful smile. "You said it yourself: our scholars can be stupid. I suppose I am no smarter than they are."

She sighed out a few last tears, nodded. "If you are stupid, at least you are honest." She wiped her eyes. "I suspect your scholars think us stupid because the only time we encounter littlings is when we are first awake and ravenous. Or after, when we are torpid from overeating."

"Wait," Elweyr said, "you hibernate? Like bears?"

She laughed sadly. "Like bears? How I wish that was true. A bear sleeps through a few months of winter, but we are only fully *awake* for a few months out of the year."

Druadaen nodded. "So when you awake from your long sleep, you are half-starved."

"And only half-aware," Heela finished. "Yet if we do not find food quickly, we are finished. We have a quick rush of vitality, but once it fades, we are too weak to move. So we must get food quickly. And a great deal of it."

"So that's why you kill all the farmers' livestock," Padrajisse supplied.

Heela shook her head. "We only take a few of their animals. Just enough to keep going long enough to get back to our homes."

"So, you are not primarily meat-eaters?"

Even as Heela shook her head, Druadaen felt pieces of a puzzle begin to fall together, as if of their own accord. "That's why you took so much of the corn," he said aloud. "Because it fills you quickly and is rich in sugar."

She nodded. "But it is difficult to digest when uncooked." She glanced at the downhill slope with shamed furtiveness. "But when I woke this year, I had less time than usual. So I had to eat as much as I could as fast as I could."

"Because of your child?" S'ythreni asked uncertainly.

"Apologies. My words were not clear. I did not lose a child; I lost an infant." When the others did not understand the distinction, she added, "My *unborn* infant."

In the silence that followed, the story of her loss unfolded before Druadaen as if Heela was telling it herself. She had come to term before hibernating. Which had been dangerous: whereas a human could keep eating right up until birth without interruption, the giant had only a few months every year to eat enough to maintain a healthy weight. "So you were extremely weak this year because you miscarried just before hibernating?"

"Yes. And because winter was about to set in, there were no crops in the fields. So I could not get food without breaking into your buildings. And that leads to a fight, which is neither right nor wise."

"And none of your kin could hunt for you?"

"Hunting is slow. We have little luck ambushing game. Besides, what few kin I have were already gone when I lost my infant-to-be."

Umkhira's eyes were wide, her voice angry. "Your kin departed *before* you gave birth?"

"Yes; *they* had to, or we would all have perished." She saw the confusion on Umkhira's face. "We giants must live alone. Because if a group of us were to awaken—ravenous and desperate—in the same land, we would strip it bare. You littlings would have no choice but to kill us all, despite your fears."

Ahearn had rested his sword on his shoulder. "It's a wonder you ever have babes at all."

Heela nodded. "It is not something we do lightly, because it requires so many to help. Great amounts of food must be put aside for when the mother can no longer feed herself. The mother and father must be of different clans, so they must meet and then make sure that they are awake for the same few months in the following year." She shrugged. "It is rarely successful unless one or both clans come together to make it possible."

Druadaen nodded. "Another thing the scholars did not understand."

Elweyr looked sideways at him. "What do you mean?"

"Many of the accounts indicated that when more than one giant is reported raiding in an area, it means that more show up." He glanced at Heela. "They thought it meant you were waging war against us, trying to drive off humans or any other races that had settled on your lands. But in fact, it was a clan gathering to help prepare for a pregnancy. But that means..." He stopped, reflected. "It means that a clan adds a new child only every ten years. Or longer."

"Much longer," Heela added. "We are lucky if a clan adds one to its number every thirty years."

Umkhira's eyes looked unusually shiny. "You must want to be parents very much. Twins must be a cause for great celebration."

Heela's eyes closed tightly. "No. They are a death sentence. No mother among us has ever survived a double-birth. And very few of the infants do." She sighed and opened her eyes. "Fortunately, they are very rare."

"It seems there is an obvious answer to your dilemmas," Padrajisse announced. "You must start your own farms. You could gather as clans and hibernate in shifts. How would that not answer your woes?" It was significant that even Ahearn, for all his over-hasty suggestions and deductions, looked away in sympathetic embarrassment as the sacrist offered her solution.

Heela looked at her almost pityingly. "That would be a fine idea, if the world was sized to us. But it is not. Where is corn and wheat that is sized as we are? And even if such plants existed, where is the soil deep enough to grow them? And how do we learn the skills and ways of farming, and fashion the needed tools, when we are alert only three or four months out of every year?"

She shook her head. "It is the same problem with every craft we observe among littlings and yearn to possess for ourselves: it takes so much of our time to find game—or take small measures of your crops or livestock from widely separated farms—that it is all we can do to sustain ourselves."

"And your Bent vassals bring you nothing?" Padrajisse wondered.

Heela stared at her. "Vassals? You think they serve us? Or that we would accept them as allies?"

"Well, it is widely known that they raid with you!"

Heela frowned. "Really? Is that what you *know*? It is certainly true of some of us, but after all, every race has individuals who are an embarrassment to the rest."

"So the Bent that set upon the farms on the near reaches of Aswyth Plain are not your allies?"

Heela's laugh was so loud and bitter that the whole fellowship flinched. "Allies? They are parasites and carrion-pickers. They follow in our wake to fall upon already-terrified farmers and then scavenge from our leavings. The one way they are useful is all the noise they make when fleeing from attackers. They warn us that littling soldiers have arrived, much as your watchdogs tell you when we approach." Her look was wry. "Apparently the underkin never got the chance to do so, this time."

S'ythreni's smile was small but sly. "We were careful to make sure they didn't disturb you."

Heela glanced at her, then shrugged. "I am well rid of them. Sometimes, they purposely lured small patrols up here."

"Why?" S'ythreni asked.

"Because when littling soldiers find me, they try to kill me. Some always die before the rest run. The Bent strip the corpses. The equipment is always better than what they craft for themselves."

Padrajisse nodded solemnly. "Urzhen—present company excepted—would always rather risk their lives than learn a productive craft. Even weapon-making."

The giantess cocked her head; Druadaen could hear tendons stretching like crossbow strings. "It is peculiar how you know so much about them yet understand so little. Their every contact with human weapons is a moment of glee."

"Of course," Padrajisse agreed in a stubborn tone. "Because they are more effective."

"Yes, but also because wielding them is delicious revenge. Every time they hold even a mediocre human sword, they are reminded of the most frustrating truth of their existence: that no Bent has ever created such a fine tool. Only a few of them have the patience and the fine, clever fingers required to craft one. And since cursing the universe for their lot is pointless, they curse you instead. They curse your skills, your learning, your craft."

She leaned back. "If you do not understand this, you do not understand the urzh and those like them." She looked at

Umkhira. "Ur zhog are different, but they still feel some of the same impatience."

Umkhira stared. "You know my kind?"

"I do, Lightstrider."

"But how?"

"Giants live a very long time."

"So my kind were once here?"

Heela nodded.

"And what became of them?"

"They were destroyed."

"By...?" Umkhira's voice faded, but her glance around the group made her intended question clear: Had the Lightstriders been exterminated by humans?

But the giantess shook her head. "No. Not by them. By the other urzhen."

Umkhira's eyes were wide. "Were we competing with them?"

"No."

"Then why—?"

"Because you Lightstriders are too much like *them*." Heela pointed an immense finger at the rest of the group. "And yet when the urzhen of the Under look in your face, they see so many of their own features staring back. They envy you. And so they resent you." Heela shrugged. "We understand this envy because we experience it ourselves. But with us, it happens when we look at *you*." Her gaze moved from one human face to the next. "We see faces and bodies that are almost exactly like ours. And yet, all that you have, we are denied. All the skills that our size prevents us from learning, you command with ease."

Ahearn's tone was reflective. "Now that's a strange thing to hear, since no small number of us wish for the size and strength of giants."

Heela shook her head. "That is because you have no idea of what you would lose."

"Such as?"

"You wish a list of our envies?" She sighed, looked up at the rough, primordial roof of her cave. "That you keep useful animals the year around and train them to do your work and follow your commands. That you dig in the ground, wrest metal from it, and then fashion the ore into cunning tools and weapons. That you learn to record and share your thoughts as marks upon parchment.

That you make art of so many shapes and kinds. That you sail upon the seas and see every part of this world. But above all, that you fill your doll houses with comforts and devices that allow you to not merely survive, but to enjoy your lives in the company of your own families. All year long."

She shook her head. "Many giants brood upon these things. Many come to hate you for possessing them. Some of those go mad with jealousy. So they destroy what they cannot have. They take more than they need. They inflict the pain that they feel upon littlings...and come to hate themselves for doing so." She looked up. "We are not a savage race. We are not hateful. But we are trapped in bodies that do not belong in this world, for clearly, your gods are the ones that shaped it."

Padrajisse straightened stiffly. "You may be without deities, but you clearly know and walk in the Great Tract. So you also know that creation unfolds at the behest and inspiration of both powers. Giants are not—"

"Are not what, Priest?" Heela rose, her hair grazing the rock overhead. "Will you now tell me that giants are *not* made so large and so loud that we terrify all other creatures? Or that our needs for so much sleep and food do *not* prevent us from knowing the wider world? Or that we do *not* lack animals and plants large enough to meet our needs as most do yours? Or that therefore, theft is *not* our only means of survival? And so, makes us hateful to every thinking species—including our own?"

Padrajisse rose. She bowed to Heela. "I did not mean to give offense. Clearly, I have. Accept my apologies. I shall wait without." She turned and left the alcove. The sound of her hobnail boots was audible until she had gone beyond the overhang.

Druadaen sighed. "I regret that our first meeting has been so contentious."

Heela shrugged. "Actually, this is the longest conversation I have ever had with littlings. And the most pleasant. Far more so than the last one."

Ahearn's eyes were wide. "Gods save us, how much less pleasant did that get?"

Heela considered. "Well, by this point, half of them were dead. Now, you said you came to talk to me."

"We have."

"'We'?"

Druadaen felt he might have blushed. "Well, *me*."

"And what has made us objects of such interest to you?"

"I have read every account of giants that I could find, and although many describe how you fight and how you may be killed and where you might—*might*—be found, almost none describe how you live or what manner of being you really are."

"And what would you do with such knowledge?"

"It is part of a greater inquiry."

"Which is?"

"To better understand the many impossibilities of this world, of which your anatomy is one of the most puzzling."

"And what would your king do with such information, do you think?"

"My country has no king or autocrat. But I cannot say the ends to which my knowledge might be put. If not now, then later.

She nodded. "You are honest and curious. That makes you more dangerous than a hundred littling blades. But come, I shall tell you what you wish."

"I thank you." Druadaen knew he should leave it at that, but... "If I am so dangerous, then why have you agreed to help me?"

She smiled. "Because"—her eyes twinkled—"you are honest and curious."

CHAPTER FORTY-ONE

Druadaen guided Heela to the broad expanse of rock that ringed the pool from which the cataract began its descent down the hill. She sat, gathering her bathing garment around her as tightly as modesty would allow. "Will I have to remove it?" she asked him.

He shook his head, smiled. "No. I can determine its weight and volume separately."

She smoothed the garment, a shift made from an old campaign tent and a small sail. Her cats ambled toward her, two rubbing against her legs.

S'ythreni smiled. "I thought you said all animals ran at your approach?"

Heela answered with a smile of her own. "From what I have seen, cats follow only one rule reliably."

"Which is?"

"That they follow *no* rule reliably."

S'ythreni laughed. "Now that is an axiom I shall remember."

"You should. It is one of yours."

S'ythreni's brow furrowed. "Mine?"

"It is an Iavan saying. A very, very old Iavan saying. I think your word is Uulamantrene?" Failing to notice S'ythreni's dumbfounded gape, she turned back toward Druadaen. "Shall I get in the pool now?"

"Not yet. I must ready my measuring devices."

She stared at the contraptions he had made, with Elweyr's ready assistance, out of shields, beams and a single, smoothed length of pine. "It is very strange."

He smiled. "You are very kind to have loaned us all these parts." He adjusted the cradle which straddled the mostly flat rocks that flanked the natural spout from which the cataract rushed forth.

"I had no reason not to loan them to you," she replied. "Particularly when you offered to repair or restore so many of my tools."

Ahearn looked up from rebinding the wider grip that Heela had added to one of her human battle-axes. "Ah, fixing things for you just makes it clear that our species are more alike than different."

"Why?"

"Well, you're just like a human wife, aren't you? 'Fix this, do that!'"

Heela laughed uncertainly; her existence was utterly without parallels to human domestic life. But Umkhira raised an eyebrow. "If that is truly what your wives say, then you have strange wives."

Druadaen looked up from ensuring the four round shields were firmly secured to the pine shaft, each one fixed at a right angle to its length. "Ahearn, Umkhira: a hand, if you please."

They put down their mending and sharpening tasks and helped him set the pine in fat-greased brackets on both sides of the cradle: the axle was secure. As they closed the top of each bracket, Padrajisse looked at the strange device as if with new eyes. "I have seen such a machine before. On one of your ships, Dunarran. But it was upright and measured the wind."

Druadaen nodded. "An anemometer. The number of rotations in a minute tells you the speed of the breeze. Here, we lay it on its side to measure how much water leaves the pond every minute."

Heela frowned. "I thought you determined that yesterday, when you tested the device."

"I did, but now we will see how much more water empties out when first you lay down in the pond."

Her face brightened. "And that is how you shall know how much I weigh!"

"More or less."

"So all I have to do is sit in the pool?"

"No, you must lay in it, with just your head above the water. And I will need you to keep one wrist close to the surface."

Heela's frown was one of perplexity, not disapproval. "You already determined the speed at which my heart beats."

"Yes, but that was yesterday, on land, and at a higher temperature. It may change today."

"And what is the importance of that?" asked Umkhira, who had gone back to hammering a metal shield into a shape that would make it a useful serving dish.

"Determining Heela's weight is only part of the process whereby I may estimate how much blood her heart is pumping every minute."

S'ythreni's smile and tone were akin to those with which older siblings simultaneously tease and indulge the pet projects of younger ones. "And all of that tells you...what, exactly?"

Druadaen smiled back at her. "Are you really sure you want that explanation?"

"Gods no!" she laughed, returning to the tedious job of restitching the blanket of many bears.

"Well," said the giantess, shooing away one of the more insistent cats, "what *I* would like to understand is why you are doing this at all."

"He means to find out if you exist," Ahearn snickered. "He's quite sure you can't."

"Ignore him," Druadaen muttered with a grin, "although there is something in what he says. It's hard to understand how your body functions without a faster heartbeat. Somehow, enough blood is reaching your extremities, even though your pulse is much lower than the largest titandrays."

"Ah. The great beasts of legends." She nodded sadly. "They are no longer found on Far Amitryea."

Padrajisse was frowning at the giantess's flank. "Mistress Heela, how long have you had this injury?"

"An injury? I did not know I had one."

Padrajisse uttered a concerned grunt. "You seem to have a seeping wound," she said gravely, "just above your hip. With your permission, I would examine it. And treat it, if I can."

Heela shrugged her acquiescence as the sacrista shot a concerned look at Druadaen.

He rose from adjusting the twine and take-up spool of his makeshift flow meter. "Heela, may I join Padrajisse?"

"I suppose so. What manner of injury is it?"

"A cut in your side. Ragged." Padrajisse answered, as she held aside the giantess's shift. Approaching, Druadaen studied the puzzling rent in the massive torso. It was almost entirely bloodless and did not resemble a laceration. It appeared more like a slit in a pouch packed with thick, almost caked lard. "Heela, you do not feel any pain?"

"Where you are? No. That is the part of our bodies where we store slumber fat. It has almost no feeling. Is the injury deep?"

Padrajisse was frowning at the ragged edges of the wound. "It is difficult to say, but there is no blood showing. But will a wound on your side heal without care?"

Heela thought for a long moment. "I cannot say. The cut you describe is the kind we get when running through trees, stumbling and focused on nothing but food. Usually they heal, but sometimes they do not." She paused. "Does the wound have a bad smell?"

"No. At least, not yet. But with your permission, I would close it."

"Will your god allow you to use its power on me?"

Padrajisse's smile was more like a grimace. "Probably, but I need no miracle for this work. You may feel a pinch or two." She glanced into her physician's pouch. "Umkhira, do you have another of those large needles?"

Umkhira raised an eyebrow. "They are iron nails, but I do have one other. Here. I shall make a fire to purify it."

"Many thanks, Lightstrider. Druadaen, I have seen that you keep a clean blade in your pack."

"I do, Sacrista."

"Do you see the outer margins of the fat, where it has dried?"

"Yes."

"These concern me. Please remove that part until you get to a softer margin."

Druadaen produced the knife, approached, then hesitated.

"Why do you pause, Dunarran?"

"I am no surgeon, Sacrista."

"If you can cut the rind off soft cheese, you can easily do what I have asked. Besides, you wished to study giants closely." Padrajisse probably meant her tone to be jocular, but it came out as darkly ironic. "You may now study one more closely than any human in living memory. Perhaps ever."

Druadaen nodded, beginning to realize that this was indeed a singular opportunity to learn about giants, but not as the sacrista meant. Shifting the knife to his left hand, he dug in his bag with his right and found one of the empty vials he always brought on his travels. "Heela," he began, "I have an unusual request..."

By the time the sun was settling behind the higher slopes to the southwest, the fellowship had built a roaring fire. Its leaping flames were quite high, thanks to a judicious application of the pitch that Heela harvested every time she happened to break the heavy branches or even boles of suitable trees. Umkhira's and S'ythreni's hunt had been successful and Druadaen discovered his mouth was watering at the smell of venison. Having given all their rations to their host two days ago, the group was in dire need of a good meal.

Druadaen smiled as the fire warmed his face and he mused at the aptness of characterizing Heela as "their host." Whereas almost every step along their path had been more difficult than anticipated, this one—meeting a giant—had ultimately proved to be a happy surprise. Instead of coercing her compliance through an array of lethal threats, willing cooperation had arisen from conversation, compassion, and a willingness to let mutual curiosity become greater than mutual fear.

Ahearn rose to test the readiness of the meat. Anticipating greasy fingers, Druadaen carefully packed away the last of the day's notes. He secured the sheafs in one of his last tubes, which he then stored neatly within the remarkable self-sealing pouch he had been given by Aji Kayo.

"So, friend Druadaen," Heela said, watching his packing with interest, "what have you learned?"

He shrugged. "I won't know until I have a quiet—and safe— place to consult the books I left back in Treve."

"Surely you must have guesses, though?"

"Oh, now you've done it," Ahearn laughed. "You've asked our very own Dunarran foo—er, philosopher to share his guesses and hypotheses."

"So?"

"So, now we'll be stuck here listening forever. Which will force us to decide between the only two options we'll have, at that point."

"And what are they?"

"Why, to cut out his tongue or cut off our ears."

Heela was aghast until even Druadaen himself had to grin. Padrajisse may have as well. Or she may have experienced a sudden uprush of bile. It was impossible to tell which.

Heela finally laughed tentatively, looking around the fire as if she had come to doubt the sanity of littlings all over again. "Jests aside, you became increasingly interested in your measurements as the day went on. Why?"

Under other circumstances, Druadaen would have continued to defer answering. However, as the group was leaving on the morrow, this was the last opportunity to satisfy her understandable curiosity. "Unless I am very much mistaken, a purely natural biped of your size, and with your heartbeat and approximate mass of blood to circulate, should barely be able to stand up without becoming faint. Or unconscious."

"So," Heela said with a nod, "we are, as our legend tells, a creation of gods that meant us to exist as we do: forever stunted by our size. Why else would they make us as we are?"

"Which I must politely dispute," Padrajisse said as she rose to help cut the venison. "As to the reason you were made as you were, who can say? The gods are the gods and their ways and powers are as unfathomable to us as ours are to ants.

"But like all things, you serve a purpose in that consensus of powers which we call creation, whether or not it is obvious to you or any other being that inhabits these mortal coils. And that purpose would not simply be to exist in misery.

"However, we are in full agreement on one point: that you are indeed a supernatural creation of the gods. And whether they fashioned you so that your body is a miracle that now works without their further intercession, or whether their constant touch is what sustains you against natural laws, that is merely a difference in the manner of their involvement. Druadaen's measurements prove only one thing to me: that every beat of your heart is proof of deity's impress upon your origins and being." She moved around the group, passing out the steaming meat.

"It is strangely pleasant," Heela mused, "to have such disagreements." Padrajisse was not the only one who stared at her in perplexity. "You see, I have rarely spoken to littlings before. But never have I been able to converse and laugh and even debate with them." She sighed. "It is a shame there cannot be such concourse between our peoples. But what would be the basis of it? What common goals do we share? What do we have that you would ever want?"

"Well," mused Elweyr, "there's the pitch."

"What about it?"

"It's fairly valuable. Needful for many things." He shrugged. "It's not as valuable as silver, or gold, or even copper. But there's always demand for it, and you get it simply by moving around," he finished with a smile.

"But would the farmers of Aswyth Plain have any interest in it?"

Ahearn's eyes glittered. "Not for themselves, no, but no farmer ever lived five seasons who did not find a way to sell or make use of everything that comes to hand. And in the case of pitch, they can store it until they go to market. Or traders come to them."

"Traders do not come here often. The roads to this place are few and poor."

"Well," said S'ythreni, "maybe you could help with that, too."

Heela shook her head, partly in perplexity, partly in denial. "I have no knowledge of roads, and I am not skilled with tools."

"Well, are you skilled with walking?"

"I do not understand."

"Do you not?" The aeosti smiled. "If you spend a day walking back and forth on a stretch of their roads, it will be flatter and harder than the streets of Treve."

Heela was frowning and smiling hopefully at the same time. "And if I . . . if we giants . . . could do this for the littlings, would it really be worth enough for them to give us the food we require?"

Druadaen considered. "If it keeps you from stealing it and destroying even more in your raids, perhaps so. But if you also became their friend . . . well, that is a value unto itself." Ahearn nodded agreement with a shrewd smile.

"Again, I do not understand."

Druadaen folded his hands. "If you become the farmers' friend, then you will have the opportunity to explain that the Bent are not your allies and do not act at your bidding. You might even offer to warn the farmers if you see signs that the Bent are gathering for a raid."

"Or," urged Padrajisse cautiously, "you might invite the nearby families to light a signal fire in the event they are already beset by underkin."

She brightened. "I could run down the hills and scare away the Bent, just as I have scared the farmers in the past. Yes, that might work."

"Might." S'ythreni sighed. "Littlings have short memories and greedy hearts." She looked around the group. "Mostly."

Heela nodded. "I am not convinced that such agreements could ever be struck with the farmers, S'ythreni, but any hope is an improvement over present conditions. I shall try these things, and if they succeed for me, then they may help others of my kind." She held out a careful hand toward each of them. With each, she touched palms. "I shall remember our conversation and keep your faces and words close in my heart."

She yawned. "Now my eyes grow heavy again, but I believe I shall sleep more peacefully than I have in many a decade. And that means I may not awake before you depart. So before I seek the comfort of my restitched blanket of many bears"—she smiled at S'ythreni and Umkhira—"tell me: What may I give you in return for the hope you have given me?"

They looked at each other. Over the past three days, they had seen everything Heela possessed and had repaired over half of it. It was of no value to anyone but her. And as they had gleaned from her stories, giants neither used nor coveted precious metals or gems. The sensible ones realized they had nothing to buy, whereas the blindly covetous ones quickly discovered how often they dropped and lost such small objects.

When no one responded, she turned toward Druadaen with another yawn; it blew his hair back as if he had been standing at the prow of a ship sailing into the wind. "You," she said, "are always asking about the past. So maybe I can tell you of earlier days, either the ones I have lived in or have heard about. We giants do live a very long time if we are not untimely slain. And while we do not have archives such as the one you have mentioned, we do have long memories, too. So what we lack in present knowledge, we may make up for in telling you of older days. Or even old acquaintances."

Druadaen straightened. "Acquaintances such as...?"

"Other creatures that live a very long time, naturally. But I doubt there are many of those left."

S'ythreni picked venison daintily off a bone. "Why do I suspect that very few of those acquaintances die of old age?"

"Because you are aeostu and you know the way of such things. Still, there are things in the world even older than you."

Druadaen took a guess. "I suspect that the long-lived beings of your acquaintance also spend a great deal of time asleep."

Heela nodded. "How did you know?"

"Because if they do not die of old age, it means they must die from killing each other—which makes little sense—or from having to find food regularly and come into contact with 'littlings.'"

She nodded. "So you understand."

"I'm starting to," Druadaen answered hopefully. "So I presume our best chance of talking to an ancient being is to find one that spends a great deal of time asleep. Like you."

She shook her head. "Even more than us. Waking every year still makes us easy to find and predict. No, the more a species sleeps, the more likely some of those old acquaintances are still alive." She thought, nodded to herself. "You need to speak to dragons."

Druadaen thought he might swallow his tongue. "Dragons," he repeated in a croak.

"Yes," she said. "Not that I am personally acquainted with a lot of dragons—"

—he managed not to blink: *not a* lot *of dragons?*—

"—and most of those I knew have probably fled to North Omthrye. Not enough room for them down here, anymore. But I have suspicions where a few others have gone, and where their kin still lair."

"And how long do dragons sleep?"

"Long enough to digest a whole town, I suppose," Ahearn mused, deftly picking his teeth with his dagger.

Heela ignored him with a small smile. "They seem to sleep longer as they grow older. Or larger. Or both. I am not really sure. Some are said to sleep for decades."

"Well," said S'ythreni far too brightly and with far too wide a smile aimed at Druadaen, "I guess we'll just have to ask them when we drop in for tea."

Heela had not yet learned to discern the aeosti's arch irony. "I do not know how they would feel about such questions. Dragons are cagey folk—"

—Wait: Dragons are "folk?" Really?—

"—so I don't know if they would answer you. Or consider it polite for you to ask. But I suppose the only way to find out is to try." She rose and stretched. "Now, if you will excuse me, I am going to take your scraps and throw them down the slope. That will keep the cats from bothering me while I eat and tell you what I know of dragons." She picked up the hopelessly battered shield that had been pressed into service as a bone dish and walked toward the far side of the footpath, making the same *psss-wsss-wsss* cat-summoning whisper that Druadaen had heard in human cities and farmlands since he could remember.

As soon as she was out of earshot, S'ythreni made a whisper of her own. "So let me guess: Now you mean to go have a chat with 'not a lot' of dragons?"

"Well," Druadaen answered with a small smile, "I suspect just *one* would do."

CHAPTER FORTY-TWO

They returned to the farm where they had left their horses and by the time they had paid for that and purchased what little of the remaining food the shattered family could spare, they had fewer billon marks in their pockets than when they had crossed the southern border of Crimatha.

The farmers goggled at the news that they would soon be visited by a giantess who wished to be a helpful friend rather than misunderstood foe and who would be congenial so long as they refrained from doing anything untoward. Such as attacking her with spears or flights of arrows. They waved limp hands in farewell, still reeling from the notion that a giant would come in daylight, solely for the purpose of chatting with them.

Toward the end of the day, Umkhira pointed at a stretch of woods that was miles away from any habitation. "We should seek game."

"It will delay us considerably," Padrajisse observed.

The Lightstrider shrugged. "The food we acquired last night will last us two days at most. By then, we will be in thickly settled farmland. There will be no place to hunt and we have no money to buy food."

S'ythreni glared at Ahearn. "So far, this 'profitable trip' to Far Amitryea has been a dismal failure."

Before he could respond, Elweyr turned to her. "I wonder if the farmers of the region would agree."

She frowned. "Well, I suppose not. Although when the giants come, I wonder if they'll remember to greet her with fair words instead of sharp spears and arrows?"

Elweyr shrugged. "We can't control everything."

Ahearn sighed. "Can't control anything, really. But one does what one can."

"Now there is sense spoken by a swordsman," Padrajisse pronounced. "Let us be equally sensible and seek game in that forest, as Umkhira suggests. It is a long road back to Treve."

"And beyond to the rest of Far Amitryea and the dragons in its Uplands," Ahearn added with loud enthusiasm. "I'm eager to see the whole place!"

And plunder it, Druadaen added silently. But he smiled at the swordsman's ebullience, in spite of himself.

S'ythreni had leaned over the neck of her horse to glare at Ahearn again. "Really? We are truly going off on a wild-goose chase—well, dragon chase—across this gods-forsaken continent? Based on memories and rumors that are centuries old? You heard Heela: most of the dragons have left. Or said they intended to."

"And by now, I warrant they are all safely dead," Elweyr added.

"Not all," Umkhira said with what sounded like grim finality.

"According to whom?" S'ythreni snapped.

"According to Aji Kayo," Druadaen put in sharply. S'ythreni stopped with her mouth open. Druadaen nodded. "It seems you know him."

"I know *of* him," she muttered. "Is he still alive?"

"He was, just before we left Tlulanxu."

Elweyr waved a hand. "Well, even if a few dragons are still alive, I'm sure they're very hard to find." His hands were gripping the pommel of his saddle so tightly that they were white. "Which means we all get to live that much longer."

"Actually," mused Ahearn, "I think I know someone who knows where to find them."

Elweyr sighed, glanced at Ahearn. "You just had to say that, didn't you?"

Umkhira frowned. "What are you two talking about?"

Padrajisse raised her chin. "They are talking about me."

"You? And what do you know about dragons in Far Amitryea, Sacrista?"

"Only that it has few, if any, remaining."

S'ythreni sounded both sardonic and nervous. "And you know where they are, then? Maybe you have their address?"

"Not precisely," Padrajisse answered with a stiff spine and tone, "but several are still said to exist among isolated peaks beyond the northeastern end of the Thelkrag Kar."

Umkhira shook her head as if a fly were trapped in her ear. "But...The Thelkrag Kar is a mountain range back on Ar Navir."

"Correct. The northern half of the range is in wildlands. The southern half is within the borders of Kar Krathau."

"Wait," interrupted S'ythreni sharply." Isn't that the home of those soldiers we almost fought in Treve? The nation that is Corrovane's hereditary enemy? *That* Kar Krathau?"

Padrajisse's reply to the aeosti's histrionic sarcasm was haughty. "To my knowledge, there is no other 'Kar Krathau.' And you may both recall that its sigil is a great serpent." When Umkhira's face showed no such recollection, she added. "Surely you saw it on their livery."

"Well, yes, but..."

"But you thought it was simply fierce symbology. I assure you: it is more than that. Their oldest legends are filled with the affairs of dragons."

S'ythreni rolled her eyes. "Oh, this just keeps getting better."

Elweyr's voice was low and cautious. "'Affairs of dragons'... you mean, the Kar Krathauans routinely killed them?"

"There are reports of that, too. But I did not mean 'the affairs of dragons' as a euphemism. Kar Krathau's ancient kings are said to have had converse with various direkynde, dragons being first and foremost among them."

"And now?"

"No one knows. Or perhaps, those who know will not say."

"I could understand why," Elweyr muttered.

"They would be called liars and madmen," Umkhira agreed with a sharp nod.

"Or worse." Elweyr looked from one puzzled face to the next. "Well, think on it: How much would *you* trust anyone who confers with dragons?"

"Or with whom dragons are willing consort. I'm not sure which is a more ominous sign," Umkhira pointed out. She glanced at Druadaen. "Are you sure you wish to seek out monsters that seek the company of Kar Krathauans?"

He shrugged. "You make a good point. I would certainly prefer to speak with creatures that sought out the Iavarain." S'ythreni's small smile was both annoyed and grateful. "But since there are no such dragons, I must seek the only ones of which we have word."

"Which means we're headed back to Ar Navir," Ahearn concluded through the gust of a great sigh, "rather than seeking our fortune here on Far Amitryea." He made a *tsk* sound. "Well, there's nothing for it, I suppose. I tell you true, I never thought I'd spend more time a-sea than most sailors!"

Druadaen doubted that he appeared any less surprised than his companions. He—and apparently, they—expected that Ahearn would be the one most likely to complain about having to leave Far Amitryea's legendary lost cities and ostensible treasures. But mysteriously, he had accepted it with a shrug and a wisecrack. It was a surprise, to be sure, but very welcome indeed.

They rode toward the woods in silence.

Except for Elweyr's and S'ythreni's intermittent grumbles.

Game in the modest forests of Aswyth Plain proved moderately plentiful but not prodigious. So, by the time the fellowship dragged into Treve almost a week later, they were not only unwashed and tired, but so hungry that their stomachs were growling at each other with far greater frequency than they were.

Happily, when they stopped by the Dunarran station house to return the horses, Talshane had not yet returned to Shadowmere, but instead, heard of their return and sought them out for a report on their activities. In the first moment, his eyes—and nose, apparently—told him that baths and a meal would be a welcome show of gratitude—and fair trade, besides.

Over a savory stew in which mutton, potatoes, and currants figured prominently, they learned that Captain Firinne's *Swiftsure* had just returned from her errand to Shadowmere the day before. The prompt dispatch of a messenger alerting her to the group's return produced a prompt reply in which she offered them working passage back to Ar Navir. Inasmuch as such intercontinental transits were rare and usually quite expensive, it was a singular piece of good fortune. It also meant that the fellowship would not be sundered by parting from Padrajisse, now that they were all returning not merely to the same continent, but the same region upon it.

Upon taking their leave of Talshane, none disputed Ahearn's happy assertion that returning to Treve had meant, at last, a return to good fortune, and he pronounced it as an omen of fine things to come when they reached Ar Navir. S'ythreni did not exactly disagree, but sardonically asserted that she'd wait and see, since the only luck they seemed to possess was of the bad variety. Ahearn challenged her to reconcile that with the fact that three hours in Treve saw them fed, clean, and furnished with a ride to exactly where they wished to travel. The aeosti offered a predictably sly reply: that this was, of course, the exception that proved the rule.

So the following dawn, it was something of a surprise to Druadaen when, having ascended the companionway to the *Swift-sure*'s deck, he discovered Ahearn already fully awake and quite morose, even though Raun was still fawning over him in fits of canine ecstasy, undiminished from the day before.

The immense wolfhound broke away from his incessant cir-clings and nuzzlings long enough to briefly jam his muzzle into Druadaen's outstretched palm, and then leapt back to Ahearn as if discovering him newly returned, all over again.

"A fine day," Ahearn announced unconvincingly.

"It is," Druadaen agreed, "but not cloudless."

"No?" Ahearn asked, looking around. "Haven't seen one."

"You wouldn't. It's the one right over your head."

Ahearn smirked and smiled. "True enough, I suppose." The frown returned quickly as he ran his hand along the dog's spine. "I've been thinking. About when we return to Ar Navir."

"What about it?"

"Well, I can't help but feel that it's been no kindness to Raun, waiting on us as we charge about on horses he can't pace and chasing down giant creatures he can't fight."

So you're finally realizing that? But Druadaen's own experience immediately had him repenting that thought: *You wouldn't have felt any different, if you'd ever had to leave Grip, or Shoulders, behind for their own good.*

Possibly misinterpreting Druadaen's silence as disapproval, Ahearn was quick to add, "And then there's the cost. If Captain Firinne and then Chief Talshane hadn't been so good as to give him a home while we were out galivanting after giantesses, I think we'd have spent far more coin on his care than we made. Not that we made anything at all on our sorry southern foray."

Druadaen heard the almost histrionic tone of Ahearn's concluding gripe. "'Sorry foray'? Really?"

Ahearn glanced sideways and couldn't help grinning. "Ah, you're coming to know me too well, you are. Catching me at playing brusque and bothered. So I guess that means we must now either part ways or stick together like glue." Seeing Druadaen's mute surprise, he added, "Well, it's only common sense, isn't it? Once you become predictable to another feller, that either means he's going to eventually bring you the worst kind of harm or the best kind of help."

Druadaen could feel that his smile was lopsided. "There's rarely a middle course for you, is there?"

"See? There you go again, knowing me far too well for your own good—to say nothing of mine!" He folded his hands as he let them slide out beyond the gunwale, and his tone became more serious. "But, jolly talk aside, it's the way of the world, isn't it? At least for people like us. It's the way we have to live, if we're to survive."

Druadaen frowned. "That could mean many things... and I don't know which you intend."

Ahearn shrugged as he stared out over the timeworn towers of Treve. "In this line of work, you have two choices. One: you stay light on your feet and keep your associates at a distance where you can watch for their hand in your pocket or holding a knife at your back. Or two: you become siblings of the sword. That way, you know you're safe, because your mate's back will always be right up against your own, come what may."

Druadaen smiled. "So we're mates now?"

Ahearn rolled his eyes. "Gods help me, but it seems so. What a fate I've come to! Shackled to a bookworm Dunarran who doesn't appreciate manly obliquity between two brothers of the sword." But he was smiling as he said it.

"I'm sure you'll correct my deficiencies in time."

"Ye're not a very promising pupil," he sighed. "Even so, I'll give it a try. But by guts and gabars, the mere thought of tutoring a Dunarran to be a suitable comrade makes me wobbly. I'd best get a stiff drink before breakfast to fortify myself for such a trial." He was halfway to the companionway. "Well, are you coming or not?"

PART FIVE

CONUNDRUM: DRAGONS

Journal Entry 188
13th of Last Remembrance, 1798 S.C.
Araxor

As journeys go, our return across the Great Western Ocean was remarkable only for its interminable annoyances and delays. We were twice becalmed for days, endured a grippe which made its way through most of the crew, and discovered that half our potable water was infested with almost invisible sea worms. Although not uncommon in the tropics, these parasites are rarely encountered elsewhere and are almost unknown in Far Amitryea. Captain Firinne suspects that the Caottalurans who had made so much trouble in Crimatha might have had a hand in contaminating the water we took on in Treve. It would also have been well within their capabilities to have insinuated some grippe-bearing rations into the ones acquired for the crossing. In consequence, the company of the *Swiftsure* was especially glad when the shore of Corrovane hove into view over the eastern horizon.

I probably found the monotony of the voyage comparatively easy to endure because I had no shortage of work to occupy me. On the one hand, I had my various notes on Heela to compile and assess. On the other, rereading the tomes on dragons and direkynde that Aji Kayo gifted me might now mean the difference between life and death.

I initially expected to finish and seal away my observations from our time with Heela a few days after sailing out of the Earthrift Channel and back into the Great Western Ocean. But the findings were so extraordinary that I examined and double-checked them multiple times, assuming that they were artifacts of my own error. But after doing so, and even when assuming that every estimate and measure was either fifty percent too great or too small, it made no difference to the final outcome.

As Ahearn had joked, I presumed that Heela cannot possibly exist. Or, more precisely, not without the aid of wholly unprecedented anatomical structures or, as Padrajisse had insisted, the constant intervention of miracles or mancery.

Even allowing for the crudity of the measurements I devised and the instruments I assembled, there is no way to explain how enough blood circulates through her body to maintain her observed levels of activity. Furthermore, she has none of the compensating anatomical adaptations present in all other supragants. Therefore, something other than nature must be at work. Which was a significant enough discovery for my purposes. But as I was completing my research, I stumbled across an unlooked-for revelation that not merely supports my conclusions but is an unprecedented exception to all known natural science. And I found it in the strangest place of all:

Heela's fat.

From the outset, I knew it might have properties quite different from those of other creatures. I was guided in this by natural philosophers who have measured how identical masses of fat from different species release more or less heat and also burn at different rates. And although I had not foreseen having any reason (let alone opportunity) to examine the fat of a giant, happily, I was not without the resources to do so: Elweyr kindly loaned me the necessary implements from his traveling alchemy chest.

I had expected that giant fat might be among the most energy-dense out of all species. And it did indeed burn quickly, cleanly, and quite hot. Upon finishing those measurements, I put the glass lid back on the crucible to extinguish the flame. Several minutes elapsed before I noticed that the cover was now opaque. On closer inspection, I saw my mistake: the alembic was filled with dense vapor. Thinking that the fat had smoldered for a while because I had failed to seal the alembic completely, I lifted the lid to release the smoke and reseal the container.

The fat burst into flame: instantly, vigorously. Curious, I replaced the lid, ensuring a tight seal. The flames died down, but, on closer examination they were still not fully extinguished.

I will skip over the many dull methods I employed to confirm what I had discovered by pure chance: that giant fat either releases its own supply of air as it burns, or something else maintains its combustion. I have no theories about how this could be nor how such a unique adaptation to hibernation came about. And I have no way of knowing if or how this phenomenon might enable some of the other inexplicable functions of a giant's body. But I do know this: if the only way to explain one violation of natural law is by attributing it to yet another violation of natural law, it deepens the conundrum of how such a creature can exist at all.

After concluding my work on giants, I turned to a much closer rereading of the books given to me by Aji. I also began to wonder if he is some kind of seer; among the dozens of tomes I know to exist on the species collectively referred to as direkynde, he chose the ones that make especially detailed studies of what is known of dragons.

Like other direkynde, they are rare, breed seldom, and when they do, produce single or very few offspring. However, whereas most are relatively wary of sapient species, dragons are less so, given their ability to quickly fly over great distances. This allows them to attack from, and then retreat to, lairs nestled high in mountain crags that are all but inaccessible to the foolish few who pursue them. It is no doubt why the old adage warns against hunting them (and other direkynde), by reminding would-be heroes that, "monsters are meant to be killed by other monsters."

I read what I just wrote and must admit that, of all our fellowship, S'ythreni is certainly the most sane. It is she who persistently reminds the rest of us that seeking one of these legendary embodiments of total ruin is a madman's quest. And I cannot dispute her assessment.

However, I have also realized that one of the few places where I might hope to find the reasons and mechanisms which underly the inconstancies of this world is in the presence of a dragon. Or more specifically, in their memories. They are the last species whose lives may reach back to ancient times and perhaps the very origins of our world, and so, may know with authority what modern tales and tomes may only recount as shadowy myth and legend.

I finally put aside Aji Kayo's books the day Corrovane rose over the eastern horizon. As we made for the city from which we had departed Ar Navir—Arathor—I asked to meet the fellowship over dinner. This was not difficult to arrange. Even Padrajisse, who is hardly a congenial person, has come to accept us just as we accept her. Ours is an unusual group, one that defies and transcends commonplace presumptions as to the peoples and species that can forge bonds which transcend (or ignore) their differences. So it was with considerable regret, and no small amount of personal trepidation, that as we sat down to our dinner, I broached the topic that was sure to be a surprise, albeit a relief, to them all.

"I consider, and call, all of you friends," I began. "And so, to be faithful to that most precious of—"

"Oh, by all the Bent that have ever been bent," Ahearn groaned, "here it comes."

I refused to let the solemnity of the moment be lost. "I cannot, in good conscience—"

"No," interrupted Elweyr, clearly bored, "we're not going to leave."

"But I—!"

"You," intoned Padrajisse, "are a person of high principles and high intelligence, but apparently very little common sense. It would be suicide for you to seek a dragon on your own."

"Well, assuming you are right, then I don't intend to commit homicide by dragging all of you along with me!"

"'Dragging' us?" S'ythreni scoffed. "As if you could. Listen, Dunarran, we can cut and run at any moment...but what if we *do* find a dragon? And what if it's old and decrepit? Or asleep? Or both? It could be the treasure of a lifetime. And like giants, I live a *very* long time."

Padrajisse did a poor job of hiding one of her rare, vinegary smiles.

S'ythreni shot a sideways look at her. "Does that amuse you?"

"Actually," mumbled Padrajisse through what threatened to turn into a sputter of laughter, "I am amused at *you*."

"Really? I'm so glad that I can be witty even when I'm not trying to be."

Umkhira leaned forward. "Be unconcerned, aeosti; we do not expect you to profess fondness nor friendship toward Druadaen. Or any of us, for that matter. But it is often entertaining to see the lengths you will go to deny those feelings."

S'ythreni is not often speechless, but she was at that moment and for most of the dinner that followed. After I was assured, scolded, and parodied by the very persons I meant to keep from sharing my fate, they freely admitted that they had a running bet on when I would finally make my "you must leave me!" speech, as they called it. Ahearn had won, explaining to me that, "I knew you wouldn't be able to bring yourself to do it until the last possible moment."

"Well," I replied, "I am surprised, but gratified, that it was you who anticipated I would be so reluctant to compel us to part ways."

He glanced away. "Well, now... I didn't say *that*, exactly."

I think I frowned. "Then who—?"

"I thought it likely you would not do so at all," Umkhira said quickly.

I wasn't sure how to take that. "Did you think I lacked the courage to go alone?"

She shook her head very sharply. "No."

"Then what—?"

"Among my people," she interrupted, "it would be an affront to do what you have done."

Ahearn leaned back with a smile and a shake of his head. "Hard to know who's crazier: a Lightstrider or a Dunarran. What do you think, Elweyr?"

"I think I want to finish my fish in peace."

Umkhira had become more accustomed to the jibes and jests of humans, but this time, she was on the verge of becoming her original, more prickly, self. "There is nothing 'crazy' in assuming that a true friend shall not send you away just as great danger looms ahead. Why would they do so unless they secretly believe your honor, your loyalty, or your courage are wanting? Because what is the value of such bonds if they do not hold firm in the face of such threat?"

I smiled. "I assure you, Umkhira, I meant no insult."

She smiled back. "I know this. I also know you prize this fellowship. As do I. As do we all. And it is the way of your people: you wish to ensure that your own choices do not risk the lives of your friends. You mean it as a kindness—and among you, perhaps it is, since most humans provide for themselves and their families by growing, making, or selling things. We do not. And so we are different."

"Different in what way?" asked Padrajisse, puzzled.

"We are more like your armies," she answered. "We live by

the hunt, by foraging in wilderness, and by raiding. If we are to survive, we must stand together like your soldiers in war. If we do not, we die."

"Well," S'ythreni said, "I never thought I would see the day when a Corrovani sacrist was *less* earnest than both a Dunarran and a Lightstrider." She shook her head. "That's the real reason I travel with all of you: the chance to watch the laws of the universe being broken right before my eyes. Over dinner." She grinned at me. "You should try it; it's a great deal less taxing than global quests."

I assured her I would take it under advisement. However, that did not deter me from meeting with Captain Firinne the next day to review the route to our final destination.

The captain had generously offered to deliver us to what she believed was the closest, swiftest, and most inconspicuous approach to the mountains where the dragons of Kar Krathaun legend reputedly had their lairs. Although she normally retraced the same course to and from Dunarra, her role as the captain of a Courier vessel gave her considerable latitude if a different route promised access to infrequently visited sites. It was dubious to assert that the new itinerary rose to that standard, but the small smile she wore as she listed its modest benefits suggested her true motivation: she knew that we were penniless and had no reasonable prospects for a second working passage in that direction.

She extended an additional kindness to Ahearn when he approached her with the face and posture of a brokenhearted schoolboy and asked—as if each word was being torn from his heart—if she would consent to take Raun back to Menara. Or, more specifically, to the cottagers who lived just east of that free port. She agreed, observing that it was good fortune indeed that time with the velene had apparently cured him of his seasickness. Those of us who were more familiar with powers of the deep silver object/entity/both/neither were less sure it had wrought such a permanent change, but we were not about to disabuse her of that happy belief.

The captain's new plot had the *Swiftsure* navigating north to the Channel of Glass by way of the Tashqend Strait. Together, they separate the mainland from the peninsula that is dominated by Corrovane, Old Kar Krathau, and the mad clutter of independent cities, towns, and duchies that lay between them.

But no sooner had we finished planning for that journey than news-criers appeared on Arathor's wharves, warning captains that any who meant to travel to the Channel of Glass now did so at considerable peril; frictions were on the rise between Kar Krathau and the Channel Cities, Rhuutun and Asak-Cor.

So instead, we shall round the long sweep of Corrovane's southern coast, enter the sheltered sea known as Pelfarras Bay, and go straight across to the realm of Vallishar. Happily, not only does this new course still support Captain Firinne's rationales for her generous detour but adds an even stronger justification: an opportunity to refurbish the copper plates which line the *Swift-sure*'s hull from waterline to keel. Vallishar's walled capital and first port, Marshakerra, is the collection point of most of the nation's plentiful copper and is also home to masters in various related crafts, nautical and otherwise. Few captains that enter her bay fail to avail themselves of the city's expert plating services. *If* they can afford them. But as the saying goes, when there's enough copper on hand to line a hull, most captains will use it to retire and most owners will hoard it in a counting room.

From Marshakerra, we shall travel fifty leagues up the Serpent River to the point at which it crosses the Kar Krathaun border. We have no detailed knowledge of the lands beyond that point, other than that they are sparsely settled and that the current grows more swift and cold the further one follows it to the north. When we reach the highlands where its headwaters join, we will have reached the skirts of the eastern mountains of the Thelkrag Kar.

And only as I wrote that do I finally think to wonder: Did the Serpent River get its name from the snakes which abound along its shores, or the dragons that legends place among the peaks brooding just beyond its source?

CHAPTER FORTY-THREE

The boatman glanced behind him, as if he feared that a mass of riders might appear on the plains between them and the distant and irregular bump on the horizon: the Vallishan city of Natnusarn. When he turned back, he did not look directly at Druadaen or anyone else in the group but stared at the white-flecked surface of the Serpent River instead. "That's not a lot ye're offering."

"It seems a fair sum," Elweyr said calmly. "We asked around in Marshakerra when we debarked, and then yesterday when we arrived in Natnusarn. We've offered you half again as much as hulls on this stretch of the river get for passengers. Or so we're told."

The younger fellow standing behind the captain of the boat smiled slightly and shrugged. "But you see, the cost is not just for passage."

"No? Do you provide entertainment, too?" Ahearn asked sardonically as he eyed the worn, flat-bottomed cross between a barge and lighter.

The captain looked up quickly. "The only entertainment there'd be is angry soldiers chasin' us with swords and spears. Not my kind of amusement, frankly."

Umkhira crossed her arms. "Whose 'angry soldiers' would those be?"

The captain looked no less stunned than if Raun had spoken. "Do I really have to answer...'it'?" he asked the rest of the group.

S'ythreni stepped forward so quickly that she was nose to nose with him before he could gasp. "Yes. Yes, you do," she whispered with the smile that always made it necessary for Druadaen to suppress a shiver.

But he put a hand on her shoulder and drew her back gently. "Captain, we are a fellowship, and you either address—and treat—all of us equally, or we shall bid you calm waters and take our leave."

The grizzled riverman shook his head, glanced at the younger man behind him. "Do you reckon we have to take 'em, Jaffet?"

Jaffet schooled his face to patience. "We need passengers as well as freight. Assuming you mean to keep running this boat."

The captain chewed at irritated gums with yellowed and incomplete teeth. He stared at the shabby hull with a look that Druadaen had seen on the faces of boatmen the world over: resentment fused with dogged determination, but running beneath both was desperate attachment, the kind which a beleaguered parent might feel for a wayward child. The captain would probably have scuttled the boat himself if he could have afforded—and been able to bear—doing so.

He turned back the group, eyeing them suspiciously. "Well, if ye step on my boat, you know I'm in charge, aye?"

They nodded. "You come well recommended," Padrajisse added.

He glared at her, then faced Druadaen and Ahearn frankly. "Recommendation or no, I can't say I welcome your custom. Wouldn't take your coin at all if I didn't have to."

"I feel so very welcome," S'ythreni almost purred.

"And well you should, since I'll be risking me life to carry you up this river."

Druadaen raised a doubtful eyebrow. "Surely, that is an exaggeration." The younger man looked away, tried very hard not to smile.

But the captain chewed at his gums a bit more and then stared hard at Druadaen. "First things first: our chances of staying alive are rosier if *she* can keep quiet." He jabbed his finger at Padrajisse without looking at her.

The sacrist looked too aloof to be offended. "You do not like my frankness?"

"I like your frankness just fine. It's your accent that makes me worry."

"Ah."

"Yes: '*ah.*' Corrovani have no friends in the court of Grand Potentate Ralyk Kartitham the First." He barely stopped himself from spitting.

Druadaen found it interesting that any of Vallishar's rulers bothered to number themselves; it was almost unheard of that any family stayed in power long enough to put a second person on the rather gaudy Vallishan throne. "So, no friends in court, but what about out here?"

The captain shrugged. "More, but still not many. Nothing personal, o' course. But being a friend to you lot is being no friend to myself, if you catch my drift."

"We do indeed," Ahearn assured him with a hand on his shoulder. "And fear not, I shall do the talking."

"Enough for all of us," Elweyr added, and returned his friend's affronted glare.

The man carefully removed the swordsman's rough hand from his sloping shoulder and glanced almost shyly at S'ythreni. "Ah, eh...mistress, you might want to cover those lovely, fairy ears of yorn."

"And I might want to cut yours off for even making that suggestion."

"I make it for your own good," he protested, holding up both palms in warding. When he saw that his plea for reason had no impact, he widened his appeal. "It's for the good of all of us, really."

"Why?" Umkhira asked. "Are Iavarain thought to be close allies of Corrovane?"

"Well, not anymore, but the legends tell of just that, don't they? An' sure but it's certain that you've no truck with the Kar Krathauans, nor they with you."

The young fellow Jaffet added over the boatman's round shoulder, "And if you aren't friends of that grim folk... Well, they do tend to see the world in absolutes."

S'ythreni's mouth was a grim slit. "Very well. I shall comply. At least until we reach open country."

"I'm very grateful, I'm sure, Mistress Fairy." He looked around the group, a sudden pang of what might have been conscience distressing his features. "You're sure you want to cross over into Kar Krathau? It's not as if—"

"Uncle," muttered Jaffet, "if we don't have passengers—"

"Hush with you! I've run this boat for twenty-three years and know when we need coin and how much. And stop callin' me yer uncle. We're barely related."

"But mother is your cousin—"

"Second cousin, and right now, I'm wishing she wasn't." He turned his back on the fellow. "If you've not been to Kar Krathau, you should know this for your own good: they'll take even less kindly to you than Kartitham's swells and toadies would."

"We are quite aware of that. And if we could follow a different path, we would. But current conditions made that impossible."

"Ah!" said the captain. "You mean that fuss up around the Channel Cities. Still going on, I hear. Well, if go you must, then we must be going. Now. The longer we stand here jabbering, the greater chance that someone will take notice and take word to them what might wish to spoil your trip."

Three days into the unspoiled trip, the captain's self-styled "nephew" approached the group during a relatively peaceful moment and asked who, exactly, had recommended their boat.

Ahearn kept his face genial, but his tone was cautious. "And what's it to you?"

Jaffet shrugged. "Well, if I don't know who did us that kindness, I can't very well buy him a drink."

Umkhira frowned. "Could that not be seen as a bribe? An encouragement to continue and even increase the praise he shared?"

"Possibly. Although in Vallishar, you'll find that bribes usually precede the favor they purchase." Even Umkhira smiled at that. "As I say, it's just to offer thanks, really. It doesn't often happen that you are recommended by people you don't know."

Umkhira's smiled faded. "Is everything so driven by money in your land?"

He shrugged. "Isn't it everywhere? It would be nice if it was otherwise...but it's not."

Ahearn's eyes were hard. "Given your 'uncle's' recommendations against crossing over the border, maybe it wasn't a 'friendly' tip, if you take my meaning."

Jaffet blinked. "So, they were hoping that by taking you over the border—?"

"That you and your 'uncle' would wind up as food for the

fishes," Ahearn said, laying his index finger alongside his very straight nose.

The nephew looked like he was on the verge of vomiting.

"Pay no heed to the swordsman," Padrajisse muttered in prim indignation. "He sees schemes in everything. No doubt because he has no shortage of his own."

"That doesn't mean he's wrong, though," Jaffet mumbled in distress, "particularly when it comes to the vipers who control the river traffic in Marshakerra. Gods, I thought I was helping my uncle—well, my relative—when I encouraged him to sell you passage. But I might have signed his death warrant." Then he had a further thought that opened his eyes even wider. "And mine!"

"I doubt it," Elweyr said quietly, calmly. "We're almost sixty leagues over the border. Haven't seen a patrol. There's no boat shadowing us—"

"How would you know?"

"Trust me: I know. And that bridge we just passed—the only one over the river, yes?—didn't even have guards on it." Elweyr shook his head. "Ignoring the fact that the people who recommended your boat are known to a captain we trust, it's hard to see how their suggestion could be the start of a plot to attack you. We're too far away from the border now, and there's no sign of anyone following us. If they intended this to be a dangerous voyage for you, I suspect they're leaving the danger to chance encounters with Kar Krathauans and river pirates. Assuming there are any."

"But rest assured," Ahearn followed quickly, "that whatever threat might arise—whether by intent or by chance—we are more than capable of dealing with it." Druadaen may have been the only one of the group not to roll his eyes.

Jaffet nodded but was still scanning the shores nervously. "My thanks. And to answer your friend's speculation, there *are* river pirates, but they tend not to operate this far north."

"Why?" asked Druadaen. "In the past hour alone, we have seen far fewer farms and riverside...cottages." He had almost used the far more accurate word *shacks*. "Usually, pirates make their bases in just such remote areas."

"With all respect, that's as might be elsewhere, but on this stretch of this river, there's nothing a pirate would want north of the bridge."

Elweyr's eyes were carefully blank. "I heard one of the oarsmen calling across to the last boat we passed, about half a mile after the bridge. If I understood the dialect correctly, he said he was taking a cargo of copper downriver. That sounds fairly valuable."

Frowning, Jaffet asked, "Do you remember the word he used for 'copper'?"

"There's more than one?" S'ythreni asked.

Elweyr frowned until his memory cooperated. "*Fadanig*."

The nephew's nod suggested that was the answer he had expected. "That is the word for copper ore straight from the mine. Before any smelting. A great deal of work before the metal can be separated from it." He shrugged. "And pirates don't like work." He looked admiringly—enviously?—at Elweyr. "You have an excellent ear for languages."

Elweyr waved a dismissive hand . . . which elicited a proud bellow from Ahearn: "That's because he speaks 'em all or seems to! Has his nose in a book every bit as much as the Dunarran!"

So much for not mentioning my origins, Druadaen thought. *Then again, as the fellow's uncle pointed out, traveling up the Serpent River with a Lightstrider, an aeosti, and a prickly Corrovani sacrist are more or less a guarantee that everyone we pass will stare at and remember this boat.*

However, although slightly surprised by Ahearn's revelation, Jaffet was more fixed upon Elweyr. "Are you a scholar, then? A linguist?"

Before Ahearn could answer, Elweyr said, "Yes." His tone was so flat that even Ahearn understood that further commentary was very much *not* wanted.

But the "nephew" was undeterred and began pointing out how the language had changed as they crossed the border, which increased as they drew further away from Vallishar's heavy Ballashan influences. Kar Krathaun owed more of its vocabulary and structure to Yrsyr and a good number of bastardized Amitryean loan words.

When he had finished, only Elweyr was actually listening to him. Druadaen had kept half an ear on the conversation but had been watching the changing banks and terrain beyond. The eastern side of the river now appeared uninhabited.

"So," Elweyr said a few moments after the bright-eyed "nephew" had concluded, "are you a scholar also?"

That elicited a radiant—and surprisingly full-toothed—smile. "No, but I hope to be. Someday soon."

Druadaen saw the careful nods of the rest of the group, knew that they meant the same thing that his own polite smile did: this fellow was well into his twenties and for him to leave his livelihood as a second mate on a riverboat for a life of scholarship would require a miracle.

"Well," Elweyr started with miserable awkwardness before stopping and beginning again. "Well, I hope you shall find a way to start upon that path. Soon." His concluding smile was as brittle as his nod was stiff.

Happily, Jaffet either took no note of Elweyr's discomfort or blithely ignored it, discoursing instead on the region through which they were passing. After warning them all that he had rarely come so far up the Serpent River, he proceeded to provide a wonderfully detailed overview of it. Including that it was almost universally suspected that the Kar Krathaun protectorates to the north sent agents to purchase the bronze weapons crafted along Vallishar's border, which were then sent up-country until, just before the so-called Last Ford, they were covertly ferried across to Bent parties on the eastern shores of the Serpent River.

Which, Druadaen realized, was why the right bank was unsettled. Although the Bent chieftains no doubt understood they were not to attack humans within the borders of Kar Krathau or its allies, their warriors were probably far more likely to disregard—or simply forget—that prohibition.

So it was understandable when, two days later, the captain told them that he could no longer anchor overnight in the shallows on the east bank; they'd have to make camp on the west. Jaffet nodded forlorn agreement behind him.

"Why change now?" Padrajisse asked with a hint of impatience.

The captain pointed upstream toward the forests and rugged country that ranged across the northern horizon. "Because we are nearing Bent country, Sacrista. And tomorrow, we'll reach Last Ford. End of our journey together, and a little too close to their roving for comfort. Desperate ones hang about the shallows, wait to waylay those such as us. And sometimes they get impatient and wander down the eastern bank, scouting for a likely mark."

Ahearn's eyes narrowed. "Now, I'm not liking this a bit, Captain. I still say we're safer on the eastern bank."

"Are you mad?"

"Well...that's a different topic. But I'm smart enough to see that we have an ur zhog in our group, and she has more chance interceding for us on the east bank than we have any chance reasoning with the gray-armored grimboys on the west."

Jaffet looked at his uncle. "He's probably right," he muttered.

"Boy, I'll not have you taking sides against me! I'm your uncle, godsdammit!"

"Wait: you told me not to call you my unc—"

"Be drowned for a darger, you!" the uncle swore, forgetting there was an ur zhog standing only a few feet away. "If I say the danger is greater on the eastern bank, you can trust my blood and years that I'm not mistaken."

"Captain," said Druadaen calmly.

The man whirled back to face him, face as red as a boiled lobster.

"Captain," Druadaen repeated in the same tone, holding the other's gaze steadily.

The older man calmed down. "You've a piece to speak?"

"More of a question, actually. How often do the Bent come this far south of the ford?" When the captain looked away uncomfortably, Druadaen followed with, "Come, I don't mean to pin you down. Just a round number: How many times a year?"

The older man didn't meet his eyes. "Two, maybe three times."

His "nephew" raised his eyebrows. "Three times?"

"Well," the captain spat, "it's happened. Once. Or so they say."

Druadaen nodded. "Let us say three times a year. And how often do Kar Krathaun patrols check this part of the river?"

The captain looked away again; his muttered words were inaudible.

"What's that?" Druadaen asked.

"At least once a moonphase," Jaffet provided. "Sometimes every week."

"I see. Thank you," Druadaen said calmly. "So let's say just once a moonphase. That makes approximately twenty-five times a year. Which is to say it is at least eight times more likely that we will have an unpleasant encounter on the western bank than on the eastern."

"But...but, on the east...Damn it, man: they're Bent! Don't you understand? Not Lightstriders like her. They're Rots and even Reds!"

"And I can set markers that are common among all our peoples," Umkhira replied. "They will be well beyond the limit of our camp, so any urzhen will see them in advance and know to avoid us or that we mean *h'adzok*."

"*H'adzok?*" he echoed, baffled.

"That we are a camp of truce. That we do not consider them foes and that our presence is not a challenge. Although if the information shared by your—er, relative—is accurate, it is they who would be walking unannounced in the lands of their ally, Kar Krathau. So only lawless outcasts would ignore those markers. And only if their need is so great that they cannot afford to heed them."

Druadaen looked back at the captain. "Do you have further objections?"

"And are you really going to argue with well-armed customers who have only paid half their fare?" whispered Jaffet.

The older man chewed savagely at his gums. "It'll be the death of us all, I wager, but I see I'm the only sane soul on this wretched boat." He glanced at S'ythreni in what looked like a last bid to find an ally.

But she shrugged. "Sorry to say so, but I agree with the others."

He shook his head. "Ye're fools, every sodding one of yeh. Maybe I'm just getting skittish in my old age, but damn if we're not safer among our own kind. Broadly speaking, that is. Sweepman, a point to starboard and make for the eastern bank. Let's look for a likely place to make camp for the night."

CHAPTER FORTY-FOUR

Whether they had similar misgivings, or simply wished not to aggravate their employer, all three of the boat's crew slept aboard, as did their captain. Jaffet clearly had no desire to do so—the boat was cold, leaky, and routinely beset by the insects that gathered in the shallows—but whether out of loyalty or obligation, he too decided to bed down among the crates and barrels that would be off-loaded at Last Ford come the morrow. But before retiring, he shared the evening meal with the group, helped bank and keep the cook fire going, and helped smother it to embers when it was time to turn in.

As Jaffet walked back to the long plank that traversed the distance from the shore to the square-bowed boat, Druadaen stood and stretched. "Same watch rota?"

Ahearn nodded.

Padrajisse did as well. "I almost nodded off last night. I shall endeavor to do better."

Which sounded like a fine idea to Druadaen. Of the three two-person watches, the first, or "dusk," watch was arguably the weakest in that both of the sentinels—he and Padrajisse—were dim-eyed humans. Umkhira patrolled the perimeter during the "night" watch, and S'ythreni remained peering out over her crossbow during the "dawn" watch; the chance of being surprised was low indeed when they were awake. Most enemies waited until the deeper darkness of true night before attacking, so they hoped that the first watch had less need of better eyes—and, in S'ythreni's case, better ears, too.

Druadaen still felt half-blind as he walked the perimeter in the near-dark, and his mood was not improved by discovering that he could still make out some embers through gaps in the stone wind-break with which they had also meant to screen the firelight. He whispered his discovery back to Padrajisse, who muttered inaudible deprecations as she quickly snuffed the last of them out.

Yet, despite Druadaen's misgivings, that was the only significant event of the watch, and when it ended, he was ready and eager to crawl into his sleeping roll as soon as Elweyr had rubbed his eyes enough so that they stayed open. Umkhira merely smiled indulgently and rose into the darkness, as ready as if she had never slept. *And maybe she hasn't,* Druadaen hypothesized as he became drowsy, hoping that if he did dream, he would not remember it.

In Druadaen's dreams, Umkhira cried out, "Attackers!" But in that same instant, he realized: *I'm not dreaming!* He jerked upright against the resistance of his cuirboulli chest armor, just as Umkhira shouted the warning again.

Outrider training took over. Druadaen dropped back to the ground, spun out of his sleeping roll toward his weapon, adrenaline already surging. Every second counted. He scanned the camp...

And in the first second, saw Umkhira's silhouette in the dim moonslight, bow in hand, drawing it to her ear as she sucked in another great breath...just as the arrow slipped from her suddenly trembling fingers. Her third shout was barely a strangled croak and as she began to stagger sideways, Druadaen saw a short arrow—the kind made for smaller bows—protruding from her side.

In the next second, he rose into a crouch. Ahearn was up, S'ythreni already over her crossbow, and Elweyr was rising. Padrajisse was doing much the same as Druadaen had: staying low as she reached for her weapon. But unlike him, no training had ever accustomed her to sleeping in armor.

Druadaen completed his sweep during the third second, detected movement around the boat behind them. One figure was already running unevenly up the bank: almost certainly the captain, judging from the gait and size. Druadaen saw as much as heard the activity on the boat itself, saw shadow figures that might be about to follow. Or flee.

Druadaen rolled up out of his crouch, longsword in hand. He couldn't see the attackers, although as Umkhira toppled over, she was clawing her large hand toward the southeast.

A thin whisper cut through the air between Druadaen and Elweyr, who started as an arrow narrowly missed him...and hit the captain as he charged up behind. The boatman howled, the shaft sticking straight out from his midriff, and fell forward. A sharp snap and louder howl foretold a grim outcome: his fall had broken the shaft and likely driven the arrowhead deeper into his gut.

Druadaen rose into a low sprint toward the perimeter. Behind, S'ythreni uttered a curse and warning to Ahearn, who had also charged outward from the campfire, probably thinking the same thing as Druadaen: *Are they Bent? Or do they have some other way to see us?* Either way, the Outrider and the swordsman had the same job: intercept attackers before they could get to the mantics. Which would also take them away from any light or heat that might have silhouetted them for archers in the darkness.

Druadaen was about to shout at Padrajisse to confirm that she would soon invoke the miracle they'd arranged for such situations when a rough *pop!* sounded near Elweyr: an arrow was protruding from the flap of armor that covered the mantic's thigh. He half fell to his other knee; the arrow had pinned the leather tasset to the flesh of his leg, and he was already rummaging frantically in his alchemist's pouch.

Ahearn, a charcoal-on-blackness shadow, roared a wordless challenge at some adversary pounding closer on that flank. A moment later, steel clashed on steel. As it did, Druadaen heard the slap of a crossbow and a satisfied snarl from S'ythreni. As if responding to her, a body still out in the darkness fell with a distinctive *shhrruunk*: mail armor hitting the loam.

Probably not Bent, then. Few of them had human armor. Druadaen glanced toward Padrajisse to see if she had started her invocation—just as the circlet on his wrist uncoiled into the dragon-shaped velene and flew like a silver bolt of moonlight toward Umkhira. From the corner of his eye, he saw Elweyr gulping down the contents of a vial, hand quaking as he did.

"Padrajisse," Druadaen shouted as he swung back to face out into the darkness, "when are you going to—?"

"You are blocking Thyeru's miracle, Dunarran!"

By the hells, I'm *what's keeping her from invoking it!* In the rush, he'd forgotten to make sure he was out of the path of her intended effect. He darted toward the left flank, shouted, "Moving!"

"I am not blind," she answered, the instant before she raised an empty hand toward the sky.

Six dim silhouettes shone dimly in the darkness south of the camp. It was as if their bodies were covered with the algae that glow in the wake of passing ships.

They were in two groups of three. Of those closest to Ahearn, one was already on the ground, the illumination already fading, S'ythreni's bolt protruding out of him like a dark stake. The other two were engaged with Ahearn, who was giving ground slowly. S'ythreni was racing toward them.

The other three enemies were in front of Druadaen about sixty yards away, two well out in front of the third. That one was an archer or perhaps a mantic. He swept a brief hand gesture through the air.

Behind, a loud gasp burst from Padrajisse, but cut off sharply, as if the air had been prevented from leaving her throat.

Definitely a mantic. Druadaen started toward the two who were out front. He drew his long-quilloned dagger in mid-stride and spared a glance toward Ahearn.

Druadaen had never before seen Ahearn facing a swordsman of his own caliber, and only S'ythreni's entry into the melee kept him from being overwhelmed by the two attackers—until the smaller of the two swung wildly, stumbling.

As Druadaen closed through the final yards, the moonslight revealed details of the two men who were crouched in readiness. They wore loose-fitting clothes, light armor, large bucklers in their left hands, wickedly curved swords in their right. The weapons were the shape of sabers but as light-bladed as shamshirs. Oddly, their very tips did not glimmer like the rest of the blade. They were both dull, as if covered in dust—

—or a powdered toxin, Druadaen realized suddenly. *Like the one carried by that hyek raider on Aswyth Plain.* He felt other factors rush in to support the possible connection:

—The two protectors' clothes and armor recalled the kind favored by Caottaluran *haideqs,* or bodyguards.

—As on Aswyth Plain, the coating on the sword-points was so fine and thick that no light reflected from the metal beneath.

—And while swords often get smeared with dust or mud, the

two toward which he was charging weren't dirty: they'd been carefully treated, the substance ending in a straight line about three inches below the tip.

All of which explained their almost lazy stances: *They're going to hang back and wait for an easy opening, because one flesh wound and I'm done.*

But that told Druadaen how they intended to fight and the outcome they expected. Which made them predictable.

Druadaen charged harder. The mantic behind the two of them seemed annoyed, gestured.

Druadaen felt a tingling pulse in the air that was gone the same instant he detected it.

The loose-limbed posture of the mantic snapped into rigid alertness as he tried the same gesture and then took a step back.

As Druadaen closed through the final yards, swerved out to the flank, and bellowed, "Elweyr!"

Either the thaumantic had already been in the process of producing the thaumate, or had been jarred into action by Druadaen's shout, but the effect was the same: the smaller of the two haideqs wobbled and staggered back unsteadily. The other glanced behind but did not discover his master calling forth further mancery of his own; rather, he was stepping backward, each pace faster than the last.

Druadaen ended his sprint with a leap, his parrying dagger out and ready, his longsword back, hilt level with his waist. The larger haideq turned back to meet him, raising his buckler and aiming a hasty cut at the Outrider's head; he'd apparently forgotten that even the shallowest cut on an arm or leg would end the battle.

The fellow's surprised haste was what Druadaen had been watching for. He caught the sword in his dagger's quillons and rolled his wrist hard, snaring the blade. He pulled on it, the man resisted—and Druadaen let the blade go as sharply as he'd caught it.

The sudden release caught the other by surprise, the haideq staggering back before he could stop pulling—or recover enough to reset his buckler.

Druadaen's thrust came from his hip as well as his shoulder. The longsword's point punched through the haideq's light leather armor, breaking ribs and transfixing the lung behind. Druadaen twisted his wrist as he pulled the blade free.

He spun away from the falling, mortally wounded man,

discovered the smaller haideq just shaking off whatever thaumate Elweyr had used upon him. The turn had also given Druadaen a brief glimpse of Padrajisse, now free of the mantic's power and sprinting—long-legged and gaunt—toward Umkhira.

The second haideq's disciplined and economical movements confirmed Druadaen's initial impression: this one was older and better trained. Also, he clearly remembered the dust on his sword; he gave ground generously, watching for Druadaen to become impatient, incautious. So Druadaen obliged.

After a few abortive passes that the haideq warded off with deft parries, Druadaen let slip a few curses, increasing the pace of his cuts until he finally brought his longsword all the way back over his shoulder for a savage strike...and as he did, his left guard dropped as if momentarily forgotten.

The haideq saw the opportunity: his adversary's left leg was forward and his turning flank was exposed. The smaller man's lunge was like a dance leap, the tip of his sword licking out toward lightly armored flesh—

Just as quickly, the parrying dagger in Druadaen's left hand shot up again, but not back into a guard position. It angled into a swift intercept that caught and ran along the other man's sword until it racked back against the dagger's wide quillons. Another quick blade-wrapping twist trapped it there. The haideq tried pulling it back, but, realizing the danger from the longsword, abandoned his weapon, allowing it to fall as he brought his buckler up against Druadaen's incoming blow and grabbed for the dagger on his belt.

Druadaen let his longsword come down in the expected over-hand cut, but not quite as hard and swift as he could have; instead, he dropped his elbow as the blade's arc reached its midpoint. That jinked it suddenly lower—and straight into the haideq's left leg, just above the knee. The man crumpled, still grabbing after his probably poisoned dagger while screaming in rage and pain. Druadaen finished his opponent with a back cut that bashed aside the weakly held buckler, then scanned beyond the bodies of the two dead haideqs; the presumably Caottaluran mantic was a rapidly dwindling figure in the slightly increased moonlight.

Druadaen's first impulse was to give chase. Not simply because he was faster than his fleeing enemy, but because the Caottaluran was almost certainly the one who had organized this ambush; he'd known who had instigated it and why. Druadaen started to step in that direction...but the clashing of swords had not abated back where Ahearn was fighting. He turned and ran toward the shadow figures still struggling there.

As he closed, he glimpsed Padrajisse kneeling over Umkhira, and beyond her, Jaffet charging up the bank toward the camp. But his attention was upon the ferocious melee between two very different but closely matched swordsmen.

Ahearn's opponent was very broadly built, and Druadaen could see military training in the way he used his slightly curved broadsword: consistent, economical, patient. However, that training apparently made him more predictable than Ahearn, whose greater agility favored his polyglot style and habit of watching for split-second opportunities.

S'ythreni was maneuvering, trying to get behind the broadswordsman, dart in for quick strikes against a leg. But again, his training was up to that challenge; he gave ground, turning away from her. And as Druadaen charged closer, she lunged a bit too far and his broadsword flashed out at her.

She had to leap backwards so abruptly that she staggered and nearly fell...just as Jaffet ran past her, charging toward the melee with dagger drawn.

Druadaen sprinted even harder. *That fool will get himself killed—*

Or so he thought until Jaffet's charge brought him directly behind Ahearn.

S'ythreni saw the move as she was regaining balance and took a desperate leap to intercept the boatman.

Her reaching shortsword clipped Jaffet in the back as he dove to backstab Ahearn. Instead of plunging into his target's kidney, the boatman's stiletto faltered downward and pierced the leather protecting the swordsman's buttock. He emitted a bark of pain, and Druadaen realized that he would not get there in time to block the enemy warrior while Ahearn struggled to keep his footing and recover from the surprise.

But his square-shaped adversary was unable to take advantage of Ahearn's sudden vulnerability. In trying to land his cut on S'ythreni, the enemy swordsman had also overextended, tracking so far after her that he was in danger of falling. He twisted sharply at the waist in order to both straighten up and bring his shield around to block the anticipated attack of his adversary's hand-and-a-half sword.

Ahearn might have been able to dispatch him then, had the stab into his left buttock not made him stumble. Growling, he recovered an instant before his foe and pushed forward, attacking. He wasn't fully ready, so the blows were wild, but the flurry was so fast that it drove his enemy back, the bastard sword seeking the man's helmeted head.

But his mail-clad opponent gave ground, thereby buying time to regain a secure stance and get his shield back into position against the swift, high cuts. As the warrior ended his brief retreat, Druadaen could read the steadiness of his head as if it were straight out of his old training manuals: the broadswordsman was preparing to go back on the offense, was assessing the tempo of his opponent's blows. And as Ahearn drew back for another swing, both arms raising his bastard sword over his right shoulder, his mail-armored opponent drew back his broadsword, hidden behind his shield...

But that carefully timed attempt to put a heavy thrust into Ahearn's midriff had a cost: committing to a solidly planted stance that indicated his intentions...which was apparently what Druadaen's comrade had been waiting for.

Ahearn's last high cut was a subtle feint; it made lighter contact as it grazed across the top rim of his enemy's shield. As it did, Ahearn slipped slightly further to that flank, his sword coming around more swiftly as a result of his checked swing. The attacker, shield up to protect his head and shoulders, did not see that change of position and attack in time; he thrust hard for Ahearn's torso—which was no longer where he expected it to be. And as his sword came out beyond the protective plane of his shield, Ahearn brought his own blade down in a forceful chop from the side.

The man's chainmail sleeve saved his hand from being cut clean off, but the wrist was half severed. Blood sprayed. The man staggered to the side, away from his enemy, then slowed, and finally fell to a knee. He never uttered a sound.

Druadaen skidded to a stop next to Ahearn, who waved off his concern as S'ythreni darted back to her crossbow. "I thought you might not get out of that fight alive," Druadaen said, panting from the sprint.

Ahearn grinned through a wince. "Thought the same thing a few times. But here I am!"

The crossbow slapped. A quarrel whined away into the darkness.

Druadaen shook his head, looked at S'ythreni—the instant before they all heard a distant yelp.

She stood, satisfied. "Live by the vial, die by the vial," she pronounced.

"What do you mean?"

"I mean he just got a dose of his own medicine. Well, toxin." She returned Druadaen's stare. "Well, you don't think I discarded the remaining doses we found in that hyek's scabbard, do you?"

Druadaen stared into the darkness and shook his head.

She seemed to read his mind. "We couldn't give him enough time to use more mancery, even though it would have been helpful to . . . to 'speak' to him. He's a Caottaluran mantic, I'll wager, and they are masters of spying and evasion. Once he felt safe enough to stop running, he'd likely have brought an effect that would keep us from finding him or his trail. And then he'd not only make good his escape but live to make a report."

Druadaen nodded. "I know. But it's regrettable."

"Agreed," S'ythreni muttered, "but you and I have different regrets." The icy edge in her tone left Druadaen with little uncertainty of why she would have liked to take the mantic alive.

Padrajisse's voice reached toward them. "The nephew is wounded as well?"

"Not a nephew and no friend of ours," Ahearn shouted.

"Indeed?" she replied, approaching. Beyond her, Umkhira was sitting up, head in her hands.

"Jaffet tried stabbing Ahearn in the back," S'ythreni muttered, her eyes intent on the groaning boatman.

"Roll him over," Padrajisse said. "I must inspect the wound."

"You mean to aid him?" S'ythreni hissed.

"I do. Druadaen, will you help me move the patient?"

He did, glancing at the aeosti. "Very possibly he'll be our only source of information. One of the haideqs might still be alive, but he'll be dead before dawn."

"This one interests me more, anyway," Elweyr said, pushing into the group.

Druadaen moved aside for him. "Glad to see you're alive."

"I wouldn't be if it wasn't for her," he replied gruffly, nodding at Padrajisse.

"And your own mastery," the sacrista added. "That antidote you took; I am unfamiliar with it."

"Slows all bodily functions. Gave me more time. Which is to say, it gave *you* more time. Do you know what they put on the arrows?"

"Hyprine," she answered confidently. "It has distinctive effects. They are counterintuitive."

"In what way?" Druadaen asked as she expertly cleaned Jaffet's wound.

Padrajisse's voice revealed a new side of her: the detached didact. "Hyprine derived from our own liver works to thin our blood. It has few, but important, medical uses. More commonly, it is used by assassins, since it increases the rate of bleeding from any wound and leaves no unusual residues.

"But when the hyprine is derived from certain supragants"— she gestured at Elweyr's bandaged leg—"the bleeding is not only much more rapid, but apparently startles the body. It releases a rush of the substance that causes blood to thicken and clot. Far too much of it. And not just at the site of the wound but throughout the body."

"So," Druadaen speculated, "seizures? Fits? Sudden death?"

Padrajisse nodded. "All of that and worse. Examination of those killed by hyprine shows immense clotting in the arteries, but more importantly, in the smaller vessels that govern our organs and release of special humours, such as adrenaline."

She studied Jaffet's wound more carefully. "It is a terrible death. Convulsions, derangement, agony. It can go on for hours or be as swift as those seizures which kill the elderly in an instant. It never follows exactly the same pattern, though, since the action of hyprine differs according to each person's anatomy, as well as the particulars of how it is introduced into the body."

Druadaen glanced from Elweyr to Umkhira. "Is she more susceptible or was there more on the arrow that hit her?"

Elweyr shook his head. "No, *I* just got lucky. The arrow went through my armor; that always scrapes some off. It also didn't go in very deeply. But I'd still have been dead without Padrajisse."

"It was not all me," the sacrista objected as she considered the wound with a frown. "Much had to do with the time saved by the intercession of the velene." Her eyes seemed to brighten. "You should have seen it," she said to no one in particular. "When I reached the Lightstrider, the creature or artifact or—well, the velene was straddling the wound. The bleeding had almost stopped."

"It healed her?" Ahearn's tone was that of a wonder-struck youth.

"No. It slowed the movement of not only the blood, but all the fluids near the wound."

Druadaen nodded. "Including the toxin."

Padrajisse nodded. "It also seemed to make Thyeru's curative miracles more effective. I have never seen such rapid reknitting of muscle and skin. So I was able to move to Elweyr that much sooner." She smiled. "It was a blessing to see the power of the velene."

"Speaking of which," Druadaen said with a frown, "where is it?"

Padrajisse was studying Jaffet's wound again. "It did not return to you? Then I do not know. It flew off once I was done with Umkhira."

"You keep staring at his wound," S'ythreni muttered. "Is it mortal?" Her tone added, *please say "yes."*

But Padrajisse did not answer her directly. "It will not heal on its own. The cut is deep and has touched organs. But I am unsure if Thyeru will bestow healing upon this one, after his treachery. He is the god of law and oaths, so I am loath to ask, since I do not know the answer I might receive."

"Then let this answer be enough," Jaffet muttered as his hand moved quickly toward where Padrajisse's leather tassets were gapped by her kneeling position. Something flashed into her thigh.

"What did you do?" S'ythreni screamed.

But Jaffet ignored her. Raising his head to stare into the sacrista's shocked and terrified eyes, he chuckled and taunted, "Physician, heal thyself."

CHAPTER FORTY-FIVE

For a moment, no one moved. Padrajisse closed her eyes.

Then S'ythreni stamped her boot on Jaffet's hand: an even smaller stiletto popped out of his fingers. It had two fine metal tubes running out of the hilt on to the blade: crafted specifically to deliver poison. She held it under the boatman's chin. "You womb-souring animal! You have one chance to tell me what was in here."

He glanced at Padrajisse. "See for yourself."

The sacrista's face was twitching. Then one side of her mouth sagged, and she bucked backward. She tried hard to remain silent, but a shuddering groan erupted from her, an animal sound which seemed to come up from the bottom of her belly. Umkhira staggered over and, along with Druadaen, held the spasming sacrista as still as possible.

S'ythreni pushed the knife tighter against the nephew's throat. "Tell me where you keep the antidote."

Jaffet's only reply was a laugh.

"There is none," Elweyr explained in a gravedigger's voice.

"Then how did she save you from—?" She fell silent when she saw the look on her friend's face.

"S'ythreni, *oa menessë*: she is a sacrista. How do *you* think she did it?"

The brutal irony—that she who had rescued two of them from the certain death of hyprine was now powerless to save herself from its ravages—seemed to pull all color out of the aeosti's face. Dagger quivering dangerously in her hand, she stuck her face into Jaffet's and shrieked, "You imbecile! She was saving you!"

The boatman sounded increasingly weak. "Why? So my mentor's family can track me down and kill me over the course of days? No, I am no coward. I will die quickly."

S'ythreni blinked, then nodded. "Here," she said, "let me help you." Faster than Druadaen's eye could see, her right hand swept in, shortsword held in an overhand grip. She rammed it down into his heart.

"S'ythreni, he was—!"

But she rose in one motion and strode away, one hand held up to stop any further words from Druadaen or anyone else.

Padrajisse writhed. Her eyes flew open; they were staring in different directions. She tried to control her motions, shuddered as if an animal inside was trying to get out. But the sacrista lost that final struggle for dignity: her body wrenched so hard that bones cracked. Then she howled and soiled herself.

The end came shortly after: one abrupt but sustained spasm of boardlike rigidity and then complete collapse, as limp as a bag of old rags.

Druadaen and Umkhira exchanged glances. He wondered at finding nothing odd in seeing only pain and deep mourning in her ur zhog eyes. They nodded to each other, eased Padrajisse's corpse to the ground, and then he passed a hand over her face to ensure that she would not go into Thyeru's Creedland while staring at the world she had already left.

Rising, they found Ahearn standing over the broad warrior he had bested, holding the slightly curved broadsword appraisingly. One glimpse confirmed Druadaen's suspicion: the weapon and the man's armor bore a brass badge stamped with the outline of a dragon in flight. "So, Kar Krathauans."

Ahearn nodded. "Hardly a surprise. But odd to find them on this side of the river."

"Odder still that they knew where to find us," Elweyr observed as he joined them.

Druadaen nodded, glanced back at Jaffet's corpse. "It's easy to see how they knew to ambush us here. But *why* they did? There's a troubling mystery."

Ahearn used his toe to poke the terribly pale soldier, who had used his baldric to cut off the flow of blood to his wrist. "Here now, you. My friend finds your actions mysterious. A thorough answer might change my opinion about putting a proper binding on that little scratch I gave you."

The Kar Krathauan looked up balefully, then leaned over and very deliberately spat on Ahearn's boot.

"Ah, I was afraid you might say that," the swordsman sighed sadly. "You might want to reconsider your answer, seeing as how it's unwise to disappoint us. Apropos of which—" Ahearn's spittle-covered boot flashed up and caught the man full in the face. The cause of the resulting crunch was evident as he fell back; his nose was not merely broken but flattened.

"Now, see," Ahearn mused philosophically, as he held out a hand to restrain Druadaen, "my friend here—the one whose delicate sensibilities are troubled by your mysterious actions—wants me to give up trying to convince you that cooperation would be best for all concerned." He paused. "But I am a rather hardheaded man, and I'm as impatient as I'm stubborn." He crouched down. "So, mate, what'll it be? Cooperation or more persuasion?"

Druadaen pulled the swordsman back, discovered that despite his terrifyingly jocose demeanor, his muscles were taut to the point of quivering. "Ahearn, he's a Kar Krathauan. He's not going to share anything. He's sworn to that on his honor and that of his family."

"Is that a fact, now?" Ahearn mused, his muscles relaxing.

"Listen to the Dunarran," the Kar Krathauan said through a split lip. "He knows whereof he speaks."

Ahearn turned to the bloodied soldier. "See, my friend here *is* a nice fellow, isn't he? But I'm not. So start talking."

The man raised his chin defiantly. "Go to the last hell."

"Oh, I'm sure I will—and I'll see you there." Ahearn swept the man's own sword across his neck with a sudden sureness that surprised not only Druadaen but Elweyr.

When Druadaen finally found his voice again, he shouted, "By the gods...why?"

"*Why?*" Ahearn laughed as if it were the stupidest question he'd ever heard. "Because you'd have argued against it like a hand-wringing consecrant of Asheen the Pacifist."

"Yes, because both mercy and justice demands no less when

the lives of another come to rest in our hands alone. But we also needed information."

"And it was you who pointed out that he wasn't going to give it to us. And yeh, information is valuable, but not if it costs us our lives."

"What do you mean?"

"I mean you couldn't afford to let this one leave the field alive. You've got the right of him, and you saw him bear it out. Kar Krathauans may be flesh and blood, but they have souls of stone and wills of iron. They'll report to their captains or die trying. So it was either kill him now—as he'd wish—or later, after you came to realize that even if you *did* allow S'ythreni to play mumblety-peg about his bollocks with her dagger, he'd still not say a word. And we'd be that much closer to dawn and discovery."

Druadaen struggled to find a rebuttal, a reason that Ahearn was wrong—*had* to be wrong—but given the circumstances, he couldn't find one.

He discovered the swordsman's hand on his shoulder. "You're a good leader. Mostly. But you need to leave your blasted Legion behind. Not the training, exactly, but the purpose."

"What do you mean?"

Elweyr nodded. "He means they're trained to fight wars. That just as they trained you to fight, they trained you to obey rules. And those rules don't apply out here. Because this isn't war; this is just killing."

Druadaen felt a chill run through him. It wasn't in reaction to the cool night air, or even the grim picture Elweyr and Ahearn were painting; it was because they were right and he'd resisted seeing it plainly for this long. Until now, when he could no longer avoid seeing the unvarnished truth of what they had to do in order to survive.

Ahearn patted him once on the shoulder and leaned toward the dead man. "Now that *that's* settled, I think I'll just claim my part of their goods right now." He reached down toward the corpse's pale neck.

"What are you doing?" Elweyr asked suspiciously.

"Getting what I won at the risk of my life, I'll have you know! He's not the type to wear jewelry, I reck, so that bauble about his neck is a graced amulet, for sure!"

Elweyr's voice became almost clinical. "Are you sure it's manced?

Ahearn pulled the heavy chain from the body's neck. "Eh-hah, aren't you? If there's not a bit a mancery in it, then what else was keeping you from slowing him down?"

"You mean in addition to the hyprine sprinting along my veins? Oh, not much I suppose." His tone was no longer sardonic when he ordered, "Give it here." Seeing Ahearn's reluctance, he rolled his eyes. "Damn you, I don't want it for myself. But I do want to see if it's safe for you to keep."

Ahearn frowned but dropped it into his friend's palm.

They waited as Elweyr turned it over slowly, eyes half-lidded.

"Well," asked Ahearn testily, "is it graced?"

"I'm not sure yet."

"Well, hurry up, blast you!"

After another few moments, Elweyr held it away from him, studying it before he nodded. "Now I'm sure." He turned and hurled it into the river.

Ahearn looked like a child whose new toy had been flattened by a passing wagon. "So it wasn't manced?" he almost wailed.

"Oh, no; it was."

Misery rapidly became rage. "It was? Then why in flaming—?"

"Because," Elweyr interrupted in a tone of rebuke, "some enchantments come with a cost. And theirs almost always do," he emphasized, jerking his head toward the corpse. "Besides, some artifacts alert their creator if they change hands without consent of the one upon whom it was bestowed, or those who received it from a rightful owner."

Ahearn actually kicked the ground with his boot. "Well, we still could have sold it for—"

Elweyr shook his head. "There are some kinds that can be tracked even if they're not worn. Besides, if you plan to sell it for something other than a piece of jewelry, then you plan on selling it to someone who knows what it is."

Druadaen nodded. "And that is also someone who knows that they'll see Kar Krathaun gold in their palm if they just point their finger after us."

Ahearn glanced from one to the other, then stomped away— and almost tripped over Jaffet's body. He snarled as he stumbled, which clearly irritated the wound in his buttock. Then he began to grin. "I always said that mouthy bastard was a pain in the—"

"No," Elweyr said shaking his head in an attempt to ward off the dismal pun. "Just...no."

After searching for the velene and fearing it lost—or that it had abandoned him—Druadaen was startled to discover it perched upon the bloody chest of the first haideq he had defeated. Along with the others, he was even more surprised to find the fellow still alive; a near-miracle, given his wound. Druadaen nodded to himself; Padrajisse's assertions about the velene's curative, or at least sustaining, powers had not been exaggerations, apparently.

But when he extended his arm, the velene stared without moving; it had no intention of returning to his wrist just yet.

Umkhira, who was walking with the aid of an oar, nodded. "It means to keep him alive. At least, for now."

Ahearn nodded. "She's right. Seems yer silvery pet made sure there's someone left to answer your questions."

The haideq was not cooperative at first, but it seemed that the velene was doing more than controlling bleeding internally and externally; it was also reducing the pain much as it had reduced Raun's seasickness. After several agonizing attempts at refusing to cooperate, the haideq shared what he knew. Which proved to be relatively little.

"We weren't trailing you as you mean," he said, his thick Caottaluran accent mixed with something else: T'Oridrean, maybe. "We just received information."

"How?"

"Through our *zhedrayam*."

"'Master,'" Druadaen translated for the others.

"Not exactly," Elweyr corrected. "Not if his *zhedrayam* was Sanslovan." A surprised sideways glance from the haideq confirmed that had been the case. "In that mantic order, there is a strict hierarchy which coordinates members of many skills and aptitudes. Sanslovan haideqs are sworn to defend the life of their mentor—a mantic—unto the loss of their own. At least until they have completed their probationary period in the order and become *hazhadam*: independents or 'self-masters.'"

Druadaen nodded, tried not to appear as impatient as he felt. "Valuable knowledge, but again, haideq: From whom did your *zhedrayam* receive word of our whereabouts?"

The haideq started to shrug, remembered the pain waiting

just beyond the limits of his immobility, shook his head instead. "I don't know. Only my master knew that."

Druadaen tried a different tack. "Do you recall when he received word? Or where?"

The increasingly pale man nodded faintly. "On our way here."

"What?" exclaimed Ahearn, rubbing the inexpert bandage that had been applied to his posterior. "That's madness! They sent you after us before you knew where we were going?"

"We were sent even before we knew who we were to ambush."

"Is he deranged from blood loss?" Ahearn asked of the others.

Elweyr shook his head. "No, I think not. And I think I am beginning to understand how this was arranged. Tell me, did your *zhedrayam* tell you of the plans in the evening or in the morning?"

"The morning."

Elweyr nodded. "So he received messages during the night. When he was asleep."

"That is their way, usually. He dreamspoke with whichever senior Sanslovan wished this done." The haideq considered, frowning bitterly. "But it seems their dreams are not always so clear."

"Why do you say that?"

The bodyguard's eyes cut briefly toward S'ythreni. "The aeosti. We were told there was one among you, but when we observed you from the bank, we saw none. Even my *zhedrayam* thought there had been a mistake, a misunderstanding, although he said that it should not be possible. We looked carefully but her head was always covered, and she does not—well, does not look like an Iavan."

"What do you mean?" Druadaen asked, holding up a hand to keep S'ythreni from breaking in.

"In my travels with my *zhedrayam*, I have seen parties of Iavans from Alriadex and sometimes from Mirroskye itself. They are never equipped as men. All their clothes and gear is ... is different. Strange."

"What brought you to Kar Krathau?"

"We had no reason to come here, except to find you. We were in Vallishar. At court. To help the Grand Potentate." He laughed sharply; blood spattered out on his lips and chin.

"You found your work for him amusing?"

"No. But it was laughable that the Grand Verdigris never

realized that working for him was a way to work for ourselves. We lined our pockets with spoils whenever he called upon my master to settle matters in which he himself could not afford to be implicated. And all the while, we worked as intelligencers for Rakuur."

"Rakuur?" wondered Umkhira.

"Sovereign Overlord of Caottalura," murmured Elweyr, who turned toward the dying armsman. "Did the Grand Potentate approve your mission here, or was it unknown to him?"

But the haideq's only answer was a long, final sigh.

The velene rose slowly and lifted its head, silver eyes regarding Druadaen, who extended his hand toward it. It ran up his arm, flowed around his wrist, and was suddenly a featureless bracelet again. "Well, it seems that when we have finished our business in the Thelkrag Kar, we shall not be returning through Vallishar."

S'ythreni glanced at him. "Because we can't be sure what kind of reception we would get from its Grand Potentate?" She shrugged. "I am simply happy we need not pass through that sewer again."

"It's a long way around to the next country on the littoral," Elweyr pointed out.

Druadaen glanced at the riding boots of the two haideqs. "Well, at least we won't have to walk. Let's follow their tracks."

CHAPTER FORTY-SIX

It took them almost an hour to discover the attackers' camp. It would have taken longer if one of the Caottalurans' restless mounts had not whinnied.

Their attackers had bivouacked in the lee of an unusual terrain feature: a low notch between stone outcroppings that were hidden in the midst of a small but thick copse of *sartszan* firs. But because those trees could thrive in the same soil as the sourgrass that surrounded them, it was not likely that shepherds or riders would ever venture beneath them and thus stumble across the notch's small oasis of sweetgrass and potable water.

Ahearn grunted when he saw the six tethered horses. "Billon to buttons it was the Kar Krathauans who knew of this place."

"Well," S'ythreni agreed in a tone that made it obvious she did not consider that news a revelation, "it is within their territory."

"Aye, but that's not the importance of it." When the aeosti just stared at Ahearn, he added, "It means that whatever orders that haideq's sorcerous master received, he didn't plot our demise on his own. Someone from this side of the border was in on plotting the ambush. Possibly from the very start."

Elweyr nodded. "This notch was the perfect spot from which to stage it. It's near the furthest eastward curve in the river, concealed their mounts and cook fire, and is only a two-mile march from where the captain usually stopped before finishing his upriver run to Last Ford." He looked around the campsite. "And since there don't seem to be any settlements on this shore, only Kar Krathaun patrols would know about it. So it seems some of them wanted us dead, also."

"Or possibly just the sacrista," Druadaen added. "The enmity between her nation and theirs runs long and deep."

"Either way," S'ythreni objected, "how did they know we were coming? Gods, they even knew there was an aeosti with you."

"They knew more than that," Elweyr muttered.

"What do you mean?"

"He means that they knew about me, as well," Umkhira muttered from where she was resting against a fallen tree trunk. Druadaen was impressed that she could already stand, let alone walk. "It was not chance that they began their ambush during my watch."

Ahearn nodded. "Eh-yeh, because if they attacked when no moon was up, and they could get you first, they knew we'd be night-blind."

She scoffed, but not at him. "They need not have bothered. I was yawning like a pampered stripling when they shot me." She shook her head. "Six human bodies and I didn't see one of them."

Druadaen smiled. "I doubt you're to blame for that, Umkhira."

She frowned. "What do you mean?"

"I mean they knew a Lightstrider was going to be on one of the watches. So they took measures."

When her frown deepened, Elweyr clarified. "*Mantic* measures. Tell me, when did the weariness and yawning start?"

She sighed. "Right before they..." Her voice tapered off. "Mancery, you think?"

"Mancery, I *know*," Elweyr emphasized. "You never lose focus on watch. Hells, I don't know how you do it. But I *do* know what they did."

"Made me weary when they started to approach?"

"At least that. Possibly affected your vision, too. They may also have a way of concealing their body heat."

"Mud works," Ahearn offered.

"So does mancery," his friend retorted archly, "which seems more likely, since there was no mud on them. Besides," he added, gesturing toward the killing ground almost two miles north of them, "this *all* reeks of Caottaluran mancery. They prefer *manas* constructs that confuse others and conceal themselves."

"So you believe they waited for my watch, to make me weary and inattentive so that I would—?"

"—would be an easy target for their archer," Druadaen added. They had found a horse bow near the haideq that the velene had kept alive. "And we can be fairly sure of what was in the empty vials we found near them."

S'ythreni nodded. "A philter that made their eyes the equal of Umkhira's. Or mine. At least for a while."

"That's how they were able to aim their arrows and coordinate their attack," Druadaen added with a nod. "Their archers might have picked us off one by one if you hadn't shot back and killed the close one outright." He smiled at the aeosti. "You certainly ruined their plans."

"I excel at that," she agreed sweetly, then turned toward Elweyr. "You seemed to know what that haideq meant by 'dreamspeaking.' I've never heard of that."

Elweyr nodded slowly, began to sort through the kit he found near the only fur-lined sleeping roll in the camp. "The first night we met Padrajisse, she mentioned how Sanslovans are known for being able to share information over great distances."

"I recall," S'ythreni nodded. "And they do this when they're sleeping?"

"No, they're not actually sleeping," he answered as he checked a small chest not unlike the one in which he kept his own alchemy equipment. "They are in a mutual trance." Finding the chest untrapped, he opened it. "They enter those trances by drinking 'teas.'" He reached into the small coffer and produced a narrow silver tube that was fitted with a plunger. "The process is an offshoot of alchemy called intinctamancy."

"Called...what?" Druadaen realized he was squinting at the strange word, as if that might help him understand it better. The rest of the group seemed to be having similar reactions.

"Intinctamancy is not really a mantic discipline," Elweyr explained, "just a different way of creating their effects. The infusions or 'teas' induce trances which reportedly increase the mantic's focus and the clarity and depth of *manas* they can build into a construct."

"Well," Ahearn exclaimed, "that has to be a great, steaming melder of a lie, now doesn't it? For surely, if their dainty brews were full of such power, they'd rule the world...er, wouldn't they?"

"They might," Elweyr answered seriously, "except that a mantic in a trance state is a *helpless* mantic. They may be seeing and exerting influence upon distant persons and events, but they have no awareness of their immediate surroundings."

Druadaen glanced at the two haideqs' bedrolls, one on either side of the Sanslovan's. "So they have personally death-sworn warriors who watch them around the clock."

Elweyr nodded. "Regardless of their different disciplines, it's said that almost all Sanslova are proficient enough at somnomancy to be able to suspend themselves on the edge of a dream state and touch other minds, share experiences, or even witness events across great distances."

Umkhira's eyes widened. "So you believe the Caottaluran cur who insulted us in Treve contacted the one here?"

"Well, if it *wasn't* him, then who else have we met who would not only wish us dead, but knows our numbers, our skills, and that we might show up in the general vicinity of Corrovane? And how did they know what the assassins did *not*: that there was an aeosti with us?"

"By the Great Bole," S'ythreni swore, "it must be! Whoever dreamspoke to the ambushers *knew* I was with you, even when the worm-whelped mantic and his assassins were certain it was a mistake. No," she finished with a sharp shake of her fine head, "that cannot be coincidence."

"Still," Ahearn mused, "while I will certainly nurse a grudge as readily as the next oaf, that little dance in Treve was quite some time ago."

"Caottalurans have long memories," Elweyr said with a shake of his head, "particularly when it comes to slights and exacting revenge for them. And the deeper we look, the more connections we find. Unless they are all coincidences."

"Connections such as . . . ?" Ahearn asked, crossing his arms.

"Well, tonight we were attacked by Caottalurans *and* Kar Krathauans, just as we were in Treve. And the Caottalurans had more of the toxin that almost killed Umkhira on Aswyth Plain. And lastly, we have to consider that they might have been behind what happened to the food and the water on the *Swiftsure*, particularly since that suggests they could have known not only when, but on what ship, we would be arriving back in this part of the world."

Ahearn was still frowning dubiously. "Just so we don't go racing away on the backs of presumptions, we don't actually *know* that the feller in Treve was a Sanslovan, now, do we? As I recall, poor Padrajisse merely pointed out that *some* Caottaluran mantics were part of that scurvy sect, yeh?"

Druadaen nodded. "You're right. I wasn't sure myself until I searched the mantic's body and found this." Druadaen produced the dagger that he'd taken from the man's belt, drew it slowly from its scabbard. Not only was the thin, curved blade identical to the one that had been waved at him in Shan's Shanty their first night in Crimatha, but its ornamentation explained why it had gleamed like a moving snake: it was marked with the intaglio imprint of a viper. The serpentine shape emerged from the grip, twisted between the quillons and finally stretched a wedge-shaped head out onto the tang, eyes staring toward the point.

Ahearn stared at it, then shrugged. "Aye, one and the same. I suppose they have a secret handshake, too. Now, let's see about making their ill-gotten gains *our* ill-gotten gains."

Of the six horses, two of the Kar Krathaun mounts were part percheron and trained for war. The other horses were lighter of frame but in equally good condition. The Caottaluran tack was lighter and flexible, whereas the Kar Krathauans' was as sturdy as that used by the Ord Ridire, if less handy. However, both mounts and tack bore distinctive brands and marks; anyone with knowledge of them would immediately know how they'd been obtained.

The purses on the slain proved light, but each of the six had considerably more secreted near or in their kits at the camp. In addition, the mantic had two cunningly hidden gems, probably intended to facilitate rapid escape or a fast and impressive bribe. The two Kar Krathauans not only had stamped coins of the realm, but two small gold ingots, again stamped.

"Dare we take them?" Umkhira wondered.

Ahearn forced a characteristic grin to his face. "They are thin and gold is soft metal. There's nothing on those little beauties that a stout hammer won't fix."

As Ahearn was putting that assertion to the test, Elweyr found two books in the Sanslovan's gear. One was focused on their somnomantic practices. The other was a strange combination of training manual and history that afforded him a more detailed overview of the organization and methods of the notorious Caot-taluran mantics. He also discovered various vials and ampules in a pouch not unlike his own and a ciphered codex that indicated what each was. He took one look at the cipher and put it aside; it would require detailed study.

It took half that time for Druadaen and the others to determine that almost every item of their attackers' gear was superior to theirs. Some of it was quite excellent, and the Kar Krathaun items were once again distinguished by their sturdiness and efficiency. In the end, the only things they did not load on the horses were several bottles of liquor that they dared not trust.

But for Druadaen, the most valuable find was a hide tube, coated with gutta-percha and filled with maps. Almost two dozen of them.

Half had apparently been prizes, judging from the stains and rips. One was particularly grim; a map issued to Outriders several decades ago. The others had been drafted by Kar Krathauans, and if their precision was slightly less than that of Dunarran charts, the local knowledge reflected in the renderings and notes was invaluable. This was especially true of an older and smaller map which showed the immediate region in great detail. It even featured a mountain labeled with a name that Heela had mentioned: the Last Scarp. A footnote indicated that its original moniker had been the Final Talon. It even included a sketch of the peak.

Druadaen studied the drawing intently. If the image was accurate, the Final Talon was the strangest mountain he had ever seen. At some point, one entire side of its peak had apparently been sheared away. What remained was black, jagged stone that prevailing winds and weather had eroded so strongly that it had become concave. As a result, the top now overhung the missing part, curving over in a distinctive claw shape that had made its name a near-inevitability. However, a small footnote to *that* footnote claimed that during the ages before humans rose to preeminence, it had been referred to as the *Dragon's* Talon, ostensibly because it had marked the beginning of the great wyrms' domain.

As they led the horses away from the camp, Druadaen showed the map to the group. Although suitably impressed, they were more focused on deciding which, if any, of their attackers' weapons or armor was safe to keep. The final decision was that the Caottalurans' equipment could be retained, but the Kar Krathauans' could not.

Sorting out the aftermath near the boat took much longer because, after searching the bodies, there remained the thornier issue of what to do with them. The debate was spirited. Some wanted to honor the dictates of Padrajisse's deity by reducing her corpse to ashes and so, proposed that as a universal solution. Others cautioned against the risks of attracting attention with a pyre, suggesting burial instead. But the advocates for cremation pointed out that graves were easily found and opened, if not by searchers then by natural scavengers.

Druadaen seated himself and let the debate go on until it was clear that it was no longer an attempt to find the best answer, but simply an argument and test of wills. He stood up and said very loudly, "We do not have the time for this. Not the debate, not the building of bonfires, not the digging of graves." They fell silent, staring at him in an unpromising mix of surprise and disapproval. "You will not like what I am about to say, but let me finish before you state your objections.

Elweyr was the first to sit. The others followed a moment later.

Druadaen pointed calmly to the west. "The maps we just found show a Kar Krathaun outpost five leagues in that direction. It is probably home to their local patrols. Some of those patrols come to this side of the river, judging from their camp.

He pointed to the three Kar Krathauans' corpses. "Unless they were here strictly as hired swords paid by the Caottaluran, we must expect that within a day, maybe two, their outpost will send out riders to determine their whereabouts and condition.

He waved his hand at the rest of the dead. "So the real question is, what do we do with *all* the bodies? If we leave them here, it makes no difference whether we bury them or not: they'll be found and we'll be pursued—swiftly and with determination. A fire might destroy some of the remains but will surely attract Kar Krathauan attention that much sooner.

"So we have one—just one—hope of escape. We must take the bodies with us upstream, capsize the boat so it appears to have been wrecked, and affix weights to the bodies in the hope they will stay submerged, at least for a few days."

Druadaen saw questions arising, held up his hand. "The maps show a sizable tributary running down into the Serpent River two miles south of Last Ford. It comes out of the high ground as rapids but then spreads out to form a large, deep pond. That's where we sink the bodies. Then we go up the tributary until we reach rapids fierce enough to wreck the boat. Once we are sure that it has been destroyed, we strike east at best speed."

Druadaen sat down. "If we are fortunate, the local patrols will not come across any of the remains, or at least not suspect what they truly signify. If they do, then every day we have traveled reduces the chance that they can find our trail and pursue us." The anger in the group's eyes had transformed into something more like bitter resignation.

Elweyr frowned. "What about the three boatmen? There's no sign of them. We can't know when or what they might tell others."

Druadaen nodded. "That's just one more reason why we cannot afford to waste a moment. They probably fled to the opposite shore. They might not have reached it. If any of them did, they were probably exhausted, and are now hoping they won't be found. If they are, they could be held and questioned for weeks.

"However, we have to assume the worst: that they have already been found or will actually head for the outpost to report what happened." He looked around the group. "That means we don't have time to get any sleep. We must finish here and head upriver. Let us be swift."

CHAPTER FORTY-SEVEN

Although there was much to accomplish before they could get underway, at least the tasks were straightforward.

A quick inventory of the crew's personal effects produced nothing remarkable, but that made it suitable for trade. The boat's purse contained only a few dozen billon marks, and just by weighing them in his palm, Ahearn could tell that they had been cast from a highly debased alloy, clipped, or both.

Other than some new ropes, cordage, and tarps, the boat's chandlery was useless. The cargo was mostly bolts of fine cloth and worsted, some suitable for bandages or packing wounds. The balance was iron nails and tools: useful for weighing down the bodies, but not much else. Small casks of Mihal'ji dried fruits and hot spices were an unexpected treat but the most helpful find were sacks of spelt and small casks of salt pork and hard, spicy sausages: all good rations for the journey ahead.

They were finally ready to prepare the bodies just after the sun cleared the horizon. They began with Padrajisse. Umkhira opined that her gear should be sunk with her, insisting that it was the closest equivalent to burning her possessions with her.

But Elweyr shook his head. "No, she would want us to take what we need and then return her most personal effects to one who would do her honor."

Umkhira frowned but nodded. "If we are to convey her

personal effects to those who wish to remember her, should we keep something of her, as well? A lock of hair, perhaps?"

Elweyr shrugged. "The Helper gods, or at least the ones most closely aligned with the Ar, feel that the remains of the dead are no longer distinct from other matter. So when the *anima* that we knew as Padrajisse departed"—he touched the wrapped corpse gently—"this body became an object, no more or less worthy of reverence than any other."

Druadaen frowned. "Elweyr, how is it that you know so much about the Ar?"

Elweyr did not seem to hear him. "We should prepare her, now."

The differences between readying her corpse and the others were small: each of the fellowship attached one of the weighted sacks and spent a moment with her. The other bodies were prepared without ceremony, although the captain's was handled less brusquely, and Ahearn made a point of personally wrapping the Kar Krathauan he'd slain. But when they finally got to Jaffet's corpse, they frowned and hung back.

"Wish we could leave this one for the vultures," Ahearn muttered.

S'ythreni shook her head sharply. "No. They'd just vomit him up."

Elweyr sighed. "I've got to confess, I never suspected him of double-dealing."

Umkhira huffed. "His greater dishonor, that he could lie so very well that all of us were misled."

Druadaen nodded. "We even believed his dreams of becoming a scholar."

Elweyr cocked his head. "That might have been true, actually. His long discourses on local history and love of languages weren't feigned."

"Meaning?" S'ythreni's head tilted to match Elweyr's.

"Meaning that I suspect the Caottaluran wasn't just paying him with money, but with the promise of sponsorship, of becoming a scholar or alchemist for the Sanslovans." He paused. "Assuming that his 'mentor' wasn't simply lying."

S'ythreni smiled coldly. "Now *that* would have been the crowning irony."

"No," Ahearn muttered. "There's a greater irony here."

"Which is?"

"Which is that we've traveled half the world to win a fortune.

But do we find it as we meant to, won through daring battles with legendary foes?" He gestured at the wrapped bodies around them. "No. Our great treasure comes from a bitter end to as dull a trip as was ever taken on a rundown riverboat. Hells, it isn't even a proper treasure; it's just scraps and leavings, stripped from these blackguards just as they stripped it from others. The only difference is that we paid for that dubious privilege and paid dear." He glanced at Padrajisse's wrapped remains. "Yes, I've wanted to find a fortune... but never this way."

Elweyr's voice and face were solemn: "Beware what you wish for—"

"'—because you just might get it,'" Ahearn finished, spitting as he did. "Quote me no tired axioms this day, friend. It's not yet time for breakfast, and I've already had a bellyful of tutoring from Dame Fate." Shaking his head, he stalked to the stern of the boat and busied himself clearing it so that the sweep's play was full and free.

As they finished arranging the cargo to better balance the hull, S'ythreni stood up, rubbing her lower back. "Well, since anyone who finds our trail is likely to be sane, we don't have to worry about them pursuing us for too long."

"And why is that?" Umkhira asked.

"Because sane people will run away the moment they realize we're heading toward a dragon's lair."

Elweyr rolled his eyes.

Druadaen shrugged. "She has a point."

"She usually does," the mantic allowed with a sigh. "About time we ride north and you and Ahearn start upriver." Umkhira, who remained wary of boats, quickly hopped over the side and waded to shore. S'ythreni and Elweyr were right behind her.

As they neared the horses, Ahearn grunted. It was the first sound he'd made since going aft to check the stern oar that was the boat's sole means of both propulsion and steering. "Well," he muttered, staring at the bank behind, "*this* is a fine farewell present." Those on the shore returned to its edge for a better view of the spot at which he was frowning.

The climbing sun's shadows had shortened enough to reveal a drowned man tangled among the water lilies clustered beneath a low-hanging tree branch.

"One of the oarsmen?" Umkhira asked.

Druadaen nodded. He stripped off his harness and baldric, lowered himself over the low transom, and waded into the shallows to retrieve the body.

"Was he wounded?" S'ythreni called after him.

"Not that I can see," Druadaen answered as he rolled the corpse over. He began towing it back to the boat.

"You mean...he drowned?" Umkhira murmured in disbelief. "Here? There is almost no current, and the water is barely above one's head."

Ahearn spat over the side. "Are his shoes still on?" he asked Druadaen.

"Yes."

Ahearn shook his head. "Ah-yeh, drowned. Probably the first time he was in water over his knees." When he saw their stares, he nodded sagely. "Trust me; I've seen it before."

Umkhira sputtered. "But why...why would anyone work on a boat and not learn how to swim?"

Druadaen pulled the corpse around so that he could lift its feet over the transom. "I saw the same thing during my travels as a Courier. But I was warned not to ask about it; the topic was known to embarrass and insult the river folk."

Ahearn shrugged. "Ignorance is passed on just like knowledge. If parents don't know how to swim, it stands to reason they can't teach their children, either. Like as not, the only wisdom they have to offer is 'Don't fall in!'"

"That sounds like the voice of personal experience," Druadaen observed.

Ahearn nodded. "'Twas the advice I was given as a lad, until I came under the wing of a boatman who felt differently and taught me to swim. The hard way, I might add."

S'ythreni looked confused. "But you didn't grow up on a boat."

"Oh," Ahearn twinkled, "didn't I, then?" He stood to the sweep with an easy familiarity. "Dunarran, I seem to recall you have a passable familiarity with ships?"

Druadaen smiled. "Passable. Here, let me help you man the sweep."

"About time you offered. Let's be off."

The current became less swift as they moved further northward on the Serpent River. After a vigorous rush downhill from its source in the eastern foothills of the Thelkrag Kar, the river slowed and widened as it reached the flatlands. According to the maps, it became so broad at Last Ford that the banks, although a hundred yards apart, were joined by a wide bar of sand and rock that was never more than three feet beneath the lazy current.

Two miles south of that landmark, they sculled close along the eastern shore and entered the tributary. After only a hundred yards, the banks pulled away, revealing the pond. They headed toward the deepest waters and, once there, checked the bodies to ensure that the weighted bags would neither tear nor come loose. That done, they began carefully putting them over the side. When it came to the hapless captain and particularly Padrajisse, they were not only even more careful, but gentle.

Ahearn glanced at Druadaen as they prepared to let the corpse of the Corrovani sacrista slide into the dark, still waters only fifteen yards off the pond's northern shore. "Have any words, mate?"

Druadaen quirked a rueful smile at Ahearn. "I seem to recall a conversation, at the start of our travels, that whereas I was to be the owner aboard, you were to be the captain. Last rites are a captain's duty, in the absence of a consecrant."

Ahearn's smile was a match for Druadaen's. "Fine time to bring that up. Well, leave a Dunarran to remember every little detail of every agreement." He stood straighter and said to the open sky, "Thyeru, I'm not of your creed and know little of you. But I know this. Padrajisse of Corrovane was your good and faithful daughter, and to us, a good and faithful friend. Any flaws she might have had"—he seemed to push away a small, sad smile—"are surely of no account when tallying the balance of her soul. I assume she's already in your creedland. But if she's not, then know this: that when Ahearn dies on an enemy sword and goes to the Great Tract, he'll hop the divide between it and your creedland to hold you to account." His chin jutted defiantly at the sky for one more moment. Then he nodded to Druadaen, who tipped the plank upon which her corpse rested. It slid into the water, ripples painting a pattern of shining concentric rings upon the surface before stillness returned, and it was as if she had never been.

Without speaking, they returned to the sweep and brought the prow around to aim at the white waters rushing into the pond from a low ravine to the northeast. As they drew closer to it, Ahearn started humming a melody that sounded like a highly simplified sea shanty. When Druadaen asked him what it was, he grinned. "A song from my youth. Not so fine and poetic as what I've heard on the big ocean-crossing brigs you're accustomed to. Riverboat work is, as y'may have noticed, repetitive and wearying." He chuckled. "The songs follow suit."

Druadaen smiled. "You seem happier since you threatened Thyeru over the fate of Padrajisse's soul."

"Well, it's a bracing thing, engaging in a bit o' high-stakes heresy before lunch." His stomach growled audibly. "Or before breakfast, too, as my gut is quick to remind us."

"We could stop for a—"

Ahearn shook his head. "Nay. You've the right of it when you say we've no time to waste. Besides, I'm not in the habit of taking orders from my stomach . . . or anything or anyone else, for that matter. And strange as it feels, there's some comfort to be had in old habits, old routines," he finished with an almost languorous pull at the oar.

"Your spirits do seem to be much improved."

"And why wouldn't they be, with the bodies—friends and foes alike—overboard and off of our hands."

"And yet . . ." Druadaen left the presumed caveat dangling.

"And yet," Ahearn obligingly completed, "this work puts me in mind of my youth. I had more than a bit of experience doing this, you might have sussed by now."

Druadaen grinned. "Did your family work a riverboat?"

"Not that I know of. Don't remember much about me mum or da. Not much more than that they met unfortunate ends. Gaeltaghdan merchants they were. Which is to say, explorers and wanderers as well as speculators after new goods. So, they never got around to encumbering me with siblings."

Druadaen managed not to roll his eyes. Not because of Ahearn's story, which was sad and poignantly familiar, but because Druadaen could hardly believe that one of his earliest theories was now confirmed and incarnate in the swordsman: fate had created yet another hero-orphan. Impossible. Absurd. If this was the universe's idea of a side-splitting joke, he was not amused.

"Best I can recall," Ahearn continued, "we were on the Ryepare River when I lost them. Rather than put me off at the nearest town to fend for meself, the captain took me on as crew." He laughed. "Think of it; a four- or five-year-old working as a crew hand on a riverboat! At that age, I was a mouth to feed and not much more. But I was big for my age and not entirely stupid, so I learned the life and became relatively useful.

"And reliable. As you may or may not know, hands on riverboats are a notoriously fickle bunch. It's rare for any of 'em to stay with the same boat for more than a few years. So by the time I was starting to scratch at the first hairs on my chin, I was the closest thing Captain Lartan had to a son. Or maybe a family at all."

He worked the sweep a little more slowly as they approached the ravine that framed the rock-strewn mouth of the tributary. "Might still be there now if we hadn't been set upon by a nasty bunch what called themselves the Riparian Reavers. They killed the captain and took the boat. And me with it. I was thirteen and it's likely they would have fed chunks of me to the fish 'ceptin' for the fact that I was as good as any of them at handling a boat. And I'd learned figures from Captain Lartan and the trick of reading as well, so I was part of their 'loot,' I suppose.

"Their leader was a grizzled, one-armed fellow who was as shrewd as he was tough and had an eye to grooming me to their crew. But he met his end in a fight he shouldn't have lost, along with his right-hand man. The new captain was wild, unpredictable, and had little use for the way we'd made most of our coin during my time with 'em: selling what cargos we took in markets where the merchants' chops wouldn't be recognized. And as the dead captain had taunted this new one about not having half the brains of a boy—meaning me—he was determined to put me in my place. Which, to his mind, was in his cabin and beneath his smelly, greasy body."

Druadaen had almost forgotten to mind his half of working the sweep. "What did you do?"

Ahearn timed a shrug so it blended into the pull and push of the stern oar. "Squirmed away, I did. Pots, plates, forks went every which way. Including a knife, which went straight into his eye when he came at me again. The crew were hammering on the door, so I cried out that there'd been murder, let 'em all come rushing in ... and went over the side."

Ahearn saw the winding path of open water that the maps had indicated, shifted the oar sharply and pushed through a crosscurrent to get further upstream. "That happened up in Eld

Shire, and I'd just turned fourteen, I think. Came ashore with nothing but the rags on me back and the will to survive. Not proud of the corners I cut to do so, I'll admit. But by the next year, I'd become acquainted with enough of the locals that I became a... well, I suppose I was the 'indentured lackey' of a band of roughs who made their living hunting and bountying. But by sixteen I was large enough to best most of 'em in tests of strength, so I was raised up and made an equal."

He shrugged. "Learned some skills. Learned to kill Bent. Learned not to care about very much at all except gold and my next meal. Being in Eld Shire also put me near more books than I'd ever seen, and so I became the band's agent, selling and buying and seeing to our needs. I knew the Ryepare River, from Eld Shire to Taunarisha, better than the back of m'hand. Saw Menara, had visions of being a rich man in a fine house who never had to wash blood off his limbs to become presentable."

"And then you got lost in the tunnels of the Gur Grehar?"

He nodded. "And by lost, I mean, the only one who survived an ambush. Once again, made away by swimming, but this time in an underground stream, no air pockets to be had. Thought I was as good as dead just before I came up in a cavern—and found meself face to face with a tribe of Bent." He shrugged. "You know the rest, more or less."

Druadaen saw movement at the upper limit of his vision. At the lip of the ravine's overhang, a silhouette on a horse waved to him: Elweyr. He waved back, pointed upstream. The silhouette receded, angling in the direction he'd pointed.

"Mind the oar! Keep us moving ahead, but slowly!" Ahearn shouted. He grabbed a heavy boat hook and ran, sure-footed despite the chop, to the bow. Once there, he pushed the prow away from a series of potentially hull-gutting rocks. When they were in comparatively clear water, he turned and scanned the stretch of the tributary now behind them. He waved to Druadaen, shouted, "Time to go!" and leaped to a rock that led to others which in turn led to the bank.

Druadaen sprinted forward, stumbling; just because he had sea legs did not mean he had what the boat's captain had called "river feet." But the skills were comparable enough that he got to the bow just as Ahearn swung out the boat hook to help him lunge to a nearby rock.

"A little warning would have been helpful," Druadaen muttered sharply as he landed awkwardly on the froth-ringed boulder.

"And where'd be the fun in that?" Ahearn countered with his very white smile. "Besides, I didn't see a way off until the moment I hopped. And you'll be happy to see we made a good job of it. Look."

The water to either side of them, accelerating as it battered and bashed its way through a maze of boulders, caught the boat and spun it around, pushing the prow downstream. Gathering speed, she glanced off one rock, miraculously missed a second, but hit the third almost dead-on. Her prow sundered with a lightning crack. Wood groaned and squealed as she rode over the rocks. It didn't put a hole in her bottom, but several strakes split and gapped, and her stempost began listing to port: a sure sign that it had partially detached from the rest of the bows.

Dunnage tumbled into the roiling water. The drag on the stempost tugged it away from the hull, made the whole boat sag to port. She tried to right herself, but the water, pinched by the stone-fanged notches through which it flowed, was so choppy and wild that she couldn't find her natural balance. Instead, the wild currents pushed her relentlessly forward.

For a moment, she seemed steadier—just before cracking straight into a high, rounded boulder. The impact didn't reduce her to flinders, but the prow came away with a shuddering groan of wood. Water rushed into the widening gap that had been her bow, just as she spun free of the boulder and was driven into a skirmish line of jagged rocks.

The abrupt arrest of her progress pulled her apart at her weakest point. As her dragging prow dug low in the water and caught against a stony mass beneath the fuming torrent, the following current slammed into her suddenly motionless stern. The entire transom came out of the water, flying up fast, hard, and high.

The boat half turned in midair. The remaining dunnage was flung out of her with the force of an explosion. She came down keel-sideways, landing on the rocks with a splintering crash. Although still hanging together, the shattered hull began pulling itself apart as it jounced down toward the next set of rocks, which awaited her like frothing gray molars.

"As I foretold," Ahearn pronounced proudly, hands on hips. But there was a mournful bend to his brow.

Druadaen stared at him. "Why the sad look?"

He sighed. "It is ever a melancholy thing, witnessing the death of a boat. Particularly if you're the one who murdered it."

Druadaen put his hand on the swordsman's shoulder. "Yet, you've done it so convincingly, that it might be what saves our lives." He looked up at the crest of the ravine, saw figures waving, and heard the distant whinny of an impatient horse. "As you said, Ahearn: 'Time to go.'"

Journal Entry 192
12th of Ashes, 1798 S.C.
Kar Krathaun borderlands, south of the Thelkrag Kar

There are clouds approaching from the west, and if they bring rain, it could be several days before I have a chance to open this journal without courting disaster. More than a few old entries have already been lost to unexpected ocean spray or sudden rain. Yet if I delay recording this strange observation, I might forget to.

We made good progress away from where we "murdered" the boat, as Ahearn put it. His regret at destroying it was a strange contrast to his normal bluster, particularly since what he recounted of his youth aboard a riverboat seemed an unlikely wellspring for melancholy reverie. But he had a greater surprise in store for me, this day.

When dusk ended our ride away from the Serpent River, Ahearn took it upon himself to count out the gains we had realized as a result of the ambush. Having started out as the sole leader of our fellowship, it continued as his prerogative and his duty to apportion the coins into equal shares. I never thought much about it, and it seemed a task to which he was eminently suited. After all, he has never been less than forthright about his interest in money, and the more of it, the better. But prior to this evening, I had always been otherwise occupied or distracted when he set about dividing the gains and then packing his own portion of them.

To say that it is a singular ritual is a profound understatement. First, he scrupulously sorted all the coins by metal, then into approximate categories of size. Each of those divisions he then split into five equal parts. Somewhat surprisingly, where a category of coin was not divisible by five, he took the lesser portion for himself.

Once he had finished sorting all the coins into our five shares, he bagged the other four piles and then turned to his own. He methodically counted out two coins into a pile that was just beyond his lap, and then put one into a second pile barely within reach. When that process had been repeated for all his coins, he neatly stacked those coins in the larger pile, and arranged them until each stack was roughly uniform in width, but also equal in height to the others.

He then transferred them to the center of a square of old tarpaulin, wrapped them together, and bound them tightly until they resembled an irregular brick. He put that block of coins carefully, almost delicately, into his most secure saddlebag, whereas the smaller pile of coins he swept carelessly into an inferior bag. A few scant outliers are the only ones that wound up in his purse.

I am the first to admit that Ahearn is much more than what he at first seems: a simple swordsman full of grand gestures and bravado. And I am quite sure that I have yet to discern all that he cunningly conceals behind that soldier-of-fortune facade. But simply realizing that there is more to him than meets the eye still does not explain his fastidiousness in dividing our gains and the peculiar way he stores his own share of them.

I have seen greed, and initially, I thought his constant focus on profit might be a symptom of it. But if he had been infected with that soul-rotting malady, he would have stinted *others* when determining the shares, not himself. And while the meticulous packing of his own coins reminds me of a miser's fetish, Ahearn neither hides his money nor hoards it. Indeed, he is the first to put forth coin when it is advisable and is not only open-handed with his friends, but infirm beggars as well.

However, after the prior night's interrupted sleep, I am deficient in both desire and mental energy to do more than take note of his peculiar habits when handling money. But it requires no special effort or insight to suspect that there is an untold story behind it. Perhaps talking about the hardships of his early years rekindled old habits of how he had to count and store his money on a boat filled with river pirates. However, that is but a guess and what I actually *know* of Ahearn's history would not even fill one page of this journal. Besides, he has a marked tendency to make light of and lampoon the very topics that might naturally lead to a discussion of one's past.

Which leads me to believe it is a rich repository of singular, if not necessarily flattering, stories.

CHAPTER FORTY-EIGHT

Whether it was a result of the swiftly executed escape plan or luck, Druadaen never spotted any pursuers behind the group. More significantly, neither did S'ythreni.

However, it was certainly sheer good fortune when, just a day into their flight northeast toward the border of Kar Krathau, light rains set in: enough to wipe away any tracks their horses may have left on the increasingly rough ground.

The third day of their flight from the Serpent River dawned clear and fresh. Without a single cloud in the sky, the steep massifs of the Thelkrag Kar loomed gray and stolid to the north. After a few minutes with the Kar Krathaun patrol map, Druadaen confirmed that they had crossed the frontier early the previous day. This meant that the time had come to head directly north, orienting on the peaks that would guide them to their destination: the Final Talon.

The change in weather also meant it was safe for Elweyr to begin studying the code with which the Sanslovan mantic had labeled his various vials and powders. Rain was a threat to all but press-struck tomes, so he was reluctant to expose the small, leather-bound codex to the elements.

The only worrying part of the countryside that rolled out before them was that it wasn't as unpopulated as they had expected. Although there were no roads, every new vale and stretch of grassland seemed to reveal a steading of settlers from Kar Krathau. Some were as small as a pair of cabins, some much larger, but without fail, their buildings reminded Druadaen of what he had seen among the bordering communities of Connæar: heavy construction, over-hanging second stories, and windows that were as narrow and tall as archery slits in a fortified tower. Clearly, intrusions by Bent were part of life on this frontier, too.

Although steering clear of the settlements, they came close enough to catch occasional glimpses of the inhabitants. Their dress was unusually long beneath the waist, usually covering the leg down to the ankle. Women and men wore much the same garb: typically some variation of heavy worsted or hide breeches and equally heavy and rugged tunics. Dyes were either not abundant or unwanted, since most of their garments had only the natural colors of their source materials.

The soil was stony and did not favor farming, so herding and hunting seemed to be the primary livelihoods, both of which demanded the excellent riding skills that the group witnessed among them. And although the inhabitants were not exactly dour, it was difficult to imagine any of them indulging in a lively country reel. However, despite the challenges of the terrain and location, they nonetheless appeared healthy, prosperous and determined: the very picture of somber Kar Krathaun industry.

As they left behind a steading large enough to be deemed a village, Ahearn recited the axiomatic simile, "As gray as Kar Krathau." He shook his head. "And all this time, I thought they meant the mountains."

S'ythreni chuckled, glanced back at the inhabitants toiling in their drab garb. "I must give credit where credit is due, Dunarran. Your quest has shown me yet another impossibility."

Druadaen gamely played the straight man. As usual. "And what might that be?"

"That there can indeed be a hell on earth. If it were possible to die of dullness, it would be epidemic here."

Ahearn shrugged. "Yet, they all seem well fed. And I've yet to hear the sound of a child being beaten." Umkhira started and stared at his addition.

S'ythreni's rejoinder was a dismissive sigh.

Ahearn was not deterred. "And we've not seen a single burnt building or ruined steading. So despite the wildness of the area, it seems they are safe here."

S'ythreni shrugged. "*Eshfeth ana so'u alva.*"

Ahearn stared.

Druadaen leaned toward him. "'Every bird to its own nest.'"

"Ah. Well, maybe so, but you have to admit they're born of hardy stock. Tough fighters that ask no quarter."

Umkhira frowned. "Do you so respect Kar Krathauans?" When Ahearn nodded, her frown deepened. "Then why did you not treat the warrior you defeated with honor?"

"He spat on me boot!"

She shrugged. "You attempted to use threats to compel him to break his oaths to his people."

Ahearn considered. "A bad business, that. Because no matter what I did or said, it was always going to come to that same end. He simply knew it before me. And hastened the inevitable." He turned back and looked at the low, dark buildings. "Whatever you might say about 'em, you can't claim they're without honor."

"No," agreed Druadaen, "you certainly cannot. But let's not tarry here. I suspect their eyes are as keen as their swords."

At dusk, they topped a rise and spied a gnarled tip of black rock scraping its way above the closer peaks of the Thelkrag Kar: the Final Talon.

"Doesn't look like horse country ahead," Ahearn observed soberly.

Druadaen shook his head. "No, it doesn't, but we'll travel mounted as far as we may."

Elweyr was already off his horse, eager to use the last of daylight to continue his attempts to crack the Sanslovan's cipher. He had done the same thing the prior night, explaining that he was getting close, very close.

Druadaen and the others were happy to leave the mantic to his work. Some of the philters and draughts were likely to prove useful, and, as Ahearn observed, one wanted all the advantages and options possible when preparing to meet a dragon.

So Druadaen and the other three set up their camp in a small copse. It was the last one before the land flattened into the great plain that ran northward until rising to become the foothills of the Thelkrag Kar. The nightly routines—scouting their surroundings, making and tending a cookfire, readying food, arranging watches—all went past without Elweyr ever rising or even looking up. Perhaps, Druadaen reasoned, Elweyr would at least stop to sup from the plate they'd left for him.

Not a morsel had been touched when, three hours later, Druadaen walked wearily to Ahearn and shook him: change of watch. As the swordsman rose slowly, Druadaen removed his baldric, laid his weapons within reach, and spent a moment wondering how the mantic could go almost a whole day without eating. Then he lay down and waited for sleep to arrive, hoping it would not be accompanied by dreams when it did.

As they often did, the nightmares of the Wildscape only beset him after his body's thirst for rest had been slaked. In them, he was lost in mountains that were made of fossilized shadows, where dragons with the heads of tigers fought against tigers with the heads of dragons. Which, it turned out, was all taking place in an immense terrarium, ringed by faces of such great age that Druadaen could not tell if they were looking into it from a tomb or the terrifying reaches of infinite space.

He was in the middle of wondering if there was actually any material difference between those two vantage points, when the entire scene vanished. It did not transmogrify or fade; it was simply gone...and in its place was their camp.

Once again, just as he'd experienced the night before they'd reached Heela's cave, the sights and sounds were unusually crisp and real—and he could see himself asleep below, as if staring down from the top of a tree. Umkhira was sleeping to one side of him and Elweyr to the other. As he watched, Elweyr rolled over slowly, spent a moment watching the other two figures, then rose quietly and passed into the surrounding trees: the very trees in which they had made camp. But there was no sign of Ahearn or S'ythreni standing their watch.

As before, Druadaen felt like a ghost tethered slightly behind and above Elweyr until the mantic emerged into a small clearing; two large trees had fallen at right angles to each other, crushing everything that had been beneath and between them. Ahearn and S'ythreni were already there, both carrying their weapons at the ready, but without any sense of urgency. Just watchfulness.

"You're late," S'ythreni muttered through a suppressed smile. "As usual."

"It's part of my charm," the mantic countered. "Anything moving out here?"

"Not that we've seen," Ahearn commented.

"Or heard," S'ythreni added before hefting her crossbow. "Still, better safe than sorry."

There was a long silence. Each of the three seemed to be studying the others.

"Well, here we are," Ahearn said gamely. "In sight of a dragon's aerie, if legends hold truth. So: Do we go on or not?"

Elweyr sat on the bole of the larger of the fallen trees. "Is there really any question? Druadaen has been as good as his word from the moment he joined us. I'm not sure I'd like what it says about us, or at least me, to split away from him now."

"It would say that you—that all three of us—are *sane*." She sighed and sat on the other fallen trees. "But we're not, are we?"

Openly surprised, then openly relieved, Ahearn leaned back into a muted laugh. "Why, High-Ears, are you taking a shine to the Dunarran?" Her outraged stare wrung an emendation from him. "In a sisterly sense, that is."

She rolled her eyes but smiled. "I suppose I have 'taken a shine' to him. As much as I can to any human. And I have to admit that he does ask interesting, if totally unprofitable, questions."

Elweyr nodded. "I can tell you the moment I realized that he and his quest might not be *entirely* insane."

"Aye?" said Ahearn, smiling. "And when was that?"

"It was one of those long days on our voyage to Far Amitryea. We were nearing the end, already between its north and south halves, and had just started crossing the Sea of Marthanlar. So foggy you could barely see the end of the yardarms. We were on deck together and I asked him why he didn't just accept what the rest of us do: that the world's contradictions were put here intentionally by the gods. Either to test or tease us or maybe as thought puzzles."

S'ythreni leaned her chin into her hand. "And what did he say?"

Elweyr looked up, remembering. "'Such a design is not simply inelegant; it is inconsistent and arbitrary.'"

"Er, yes, I remember him saying something similar to that," Ahearn acknowledged with a frown. "But I confess I may have, er, missed some of the finer implications."

Elweyr smiled. "Almost every mantic or sacrist worth their

manas has detected the inelegance he was referring to. There's the natural order that governs almost everything in this world, but then there's the supernatural order that we traffic in. And the point at which those two 'orders' overlap is... well, it's orderly, but it's not *logical*. That's what Druadaen meant when he was calling the design of the universe inconsistent *and* inelegant. Because while the supernatural order has rules, they don't really follow any pattern or paradigm other than it requires more power and concentration to generate greater effects."

S'ythreni nodded. "Unlike the natural world, where one principle leads to the next."

"Ah," Ahearn said, brightening. "Such as the way species are shaped by their surroundings and continue to be so as circumstances change."

Elweyr nodded. "It's a dividing line that we alchemists encounter early in our training. The first compounds we learn to create are called 'natural formulations.' They require no mantic skill or command of *manas* whatsoever. Gathering the ingredients and processing them into draughts can be carried out by anyone who has been taught what to look for and what steps to take. And there is an underlying logic to the transformations and the interactions of the different agents and reagents. It is often very subtle, but it is there, and the more you learn about natural formulations, the more you become aware of the consistent patterns that exist among them.

"But *alchemical* formulations are an entirely different matter. There are specific rules for creating all the philters and draughts. And if you follow them correctly, they always produce the same results. But nothing from any one formula provides much insight into any other formula. The substances and procedures for each are... well, like Druadaen says, they are arbitrary. Unlike natural formulations, there's no underlying logic to them, so discovering them is dependent upon trial and error... and maybe the instincts of a gifted master. But there's no point to using consistent methods of observation and hypothesis, because that won't give you any understanding of how and why the ingredients work together." He stared up into the star-strewn sky. "I have to admit, it always bothered me a little."

Ahearn frowned. "You mean, that there's just no way to learn what makes them occur?"

"Well, that too, but I mean the bigger issue behind it. One part of our existence obeys laws that make increasingly more sense the more you learn. But the other part is...well, it just *is*. It never changes and we have no way of learning how or why it trumps the natural order. It's...it's not accountable." He sighed, lifted a helpless palm. "But who has the time to wonder about such things? Particularly when you're a starving apprentice with a craft to hone, a living to make, new thaumates to learn? And then, once my circumstances became even more, well, 'lean'..." He finished with a shrug. "Questions about the nature of the universe seem very extraneous when all one's energies and focus must remain upon paying for day-to-day survival."

"Temples and tarts," Ahearn muttered through a smile, "you almost sound like the Dunarran, when he's holding forth about his quest!"

Elweyr shrugged. "As S'ythreni says, he asks interesting questions. But I think we have a more pressing one that needs answering as quickly as possible."

Ahearn nodded. "The river ambush?"

Elweyr nodded. "I find it hard to believe that the Sanslovan from Treve is behind it. Or, at least, that he's the only one."

"It's a fair question, I'll grant you—but you said it yourself: they have long memories and a taste for revenge."

"So they do, but the more I think about it the more implausible it seems. I mean, even if that Sanslovan is the one who set it all in motion, how did he gather all that detailed information about our group?"

S'ythreni leaned forward in mock terror. "Maybe there's a traitor among us!"

The mantic shot her a hard glare that took the aeosti aback. "If I thought that was possible, I would already have acted upon it."

Ahearn shook his head. "And consider our only three suspects: an honor-obsessed ur zhog, a sacrist of Thyeru, and an earnest Dunarran on a quest." He shrugged. "So let's be frank; the three people in our group most likely to bend the rules for their own purposes are *us*. Or at least, we were."

S'ythreni smirked. "Your words are a great comfort."

"Well, you can choose which is the greater comfort: that the other two in our group are not turncoats because they're plainly more trustworthy than we are, or that we have managed to attract the attention of enemies who are as dogged as they are shadowy." He shrugged. "Me, I'll take the secret enemies. New foes are a daily likelihood in our line of work, but faithful mates? They're a real rarity."

Elweyr nodded, but was frowning, too. "But none of that answers how and why one Caottaluran's grudge could grow to involve so many people: the nephew who was suborned; the people he bribed in Marshakerra to recommend his 'uncle's' boat; and the Kar Krathauans who helped the mantic and his haideqs ambush us. Beyond the expense, that requires a great deal of very troublesome coordination. Something's missing."

S'ythreni tilted her head. "I wonder . . . could it be that the Sanslovan we shamed back in Crimatha is some kind of princeling?"

Ahearn shook his head. "The Kar Krathauan in charge of the ship's troops was not a man to be trifled with, nor would he have agreed to babysit an aristocrat's spoiled spawn. He spoke hard words to that mantic and was ready to leave the prat to his fate if he flung more insults or spells."

"Well, *tried* to fling more spells," added Elweyr with a hint of slighted pride.

S'ythreni had been nodding at each of Ahearn's assertions. "So if the Sanslovan in Crimatha hasn't the personal or familial power to carry it off from half the world away, then what do you think set it in motion?"

Ahearn sighed. "Druadaen."

The other two blinked.

"Impossible," S'ythreni scoffed.

Ahearn held up a hand. "Peace, High-Ears; you didn't ask *who* set the ambush in motion, but *what*. And I'll answer your question with one of my own: What is it about our merry band that could make it such a target?"

"Ah," said S'ythreni. "Yes. Druadaen. As I've said from the start."

Ahearn nodded vigorously. "I would bet silver against salt fish that he, his high-placed connections, or his questions have brought us close to something larger than we bargained for."

S'ythreni and Elweyr looked at him. "Larger than *we* bargained for?" she asked.

"Oh, very well; yes, you were right in your misgivings, High-Ears. All the things that made it potentially profitable to travel with him also made it dangerous to travel with him. And it seems we got all latter and none of the former."

Mollified, S'ythreni asked, "But still, how would trading harsh words with one Sanslovan lead to such an expensive and carefully crafted ambush half a world away?"

Ahearn's head tilted forward toward his folded arms. "I'm thinking that the problem with Druadaen's travels isn't that he's on a fool's errand so much as it's opened up old, forgotten caves that should have been left that way. Because in one or t'other of 'em, we brushed against the web of a very large spider. And now that spider has become interested in us."

"Interested enough to find out if we'd make a good meal," S'ythreni added.

"Perhaps, but I'm thinking that the interest isn't coming from its belly but its brain. That it's not hunting us out of hunger but precaution. Maybe even protection."

"From us?" S'ythreni's laugh threatened to break through her incredulousness.

"No: protection from Druadaen." Seeing their looks, he held up a hand. "I don't mean him, personally. I mean what he knows. Or maybe what he's searching for."

Elweyr sat straighter. "You mean that someone, or something, doesn't like the questions he's asking. If that's true, then—"

A long warbling cry seemed to wind out of the trees behind them.

Their weapons were up in an instant. Ahearn glanced at S'ythreni. "See anything?"

She shook her head. "No. I'm not sure it even knows we're here."

"What do you think it is?" Elweyr whispered.

She smiled. "Only one way to find out." She leaned her crossbow carefully against the trunk she'd been sitting upon, then started for the trees.

"Might need that!" Ahearn hissed after her.

"Snags on the undergrowth." She muttered something else about staying fast, silent, and alive as she disappeared into the fronds and bushes between the trees. A moment later, a second warbling cry arose, closer and much, much louder.

So loud that Druadaen jerked out of the dream, suddenly awake...just in time to hear the warbling cry from his dream dying out.

Dying out in the waking world.

He pushed away the shock and nausea, grabbed his weapons, saw Umkhira had already unsheathed hers...and that they were the only two left in the camp. No sign of Ahearn or S'ythreni, who shared the late watch. And Elweyr's sleeping roll was empty.

No. It's just a dream. It has *to be. How could I see and hear—?*

And then the warbling cry sounded again, and he was bounding after Umkhira into the bush.

Except she had veered toward a game trail that would lead them away from the clearing with the two downed trees. "This way," he hissed after her, thinking, *Please let me be wrong. Please let it have just been a dream—*

But when he emerged into the clearing, Ahearn and Elweyr were just where they'd last been in his...dream?...crouched and weapons ready. And then, hitting him like a blow from an invisible and soundless maul, he saw the final, impossibly specific proof that his dream was not, in fact, a dream:

—S'ythreni's crossbow, leaning just as she'd left it, propped up and ready against the fallen tree trunk on which she'd been sitting.

Druadaen's body pulsed with a flash of fever. Sweat suddenly sprang from almost every square inch of his body, clammy and slick. S'ythreni slipped out of the bushes, shortsword black with blood, saw them all, but her wondering eyes went to Druadaen. And they seemed to be asking, *Why are you here? What do you know?*

"Well," whispered Ahearn, "what was it?"

She wiped dark, nonreflective ichor off on a nearby plant. "A giireyza." She glanced at Umkhira. "But just a small one." Her gaze went back to Druadaen. "Are you...well?" Ahearn and Elweyr turned, startled to see him, the color suddenly draining out of their faces.

"I—I am well. But the creature's calls—they alarmed me." He licked dry lips. "I was dreaming," he said. And realized that he had simultaneously lied and told the truth.

He nodded reassurance to the others, turned, and hastened back to his sleeping roll. He pulled it up to his chin, closed his eyes, and resolved to sleep—to just sleep: that and nothing else.

Except when the dawn came, he hadn't slept at all. And it was a distinct possibility that, during all those hours, he hadn't even blinked.

CHAPTER FORTY-NINE

The next day's pace slowed as the ground became increasingly rugged and the Final Talon scratched its way higher over the other mountains and into the blue sky. But Druadaen hardly noticed.

He was slightly more aware that the group was unusually quiet. Except Elweyr, who triumphantly reported that he'd cracked the Sanslovan's code and had deciphered the labels on all the vials in his alchemical treasure trove.

But Druadaen only half heard the details. For the first full hour of their slow ride toward the mountains, he had struggled to make sense of the previous night. And now that he had, it was imperative that he sort through the realizations, the consequences, and address them as quickly as possible.

Leaving aside the many questions raised by his apparent ability to see distant reality in place of dreams, Druadaen's unintentional eavesdropping had produced several unpleasant but important realizations. He had always known that Ahearn, S'ythreni, and Elweyr had reservations about working with him and were tentative about the future of their fellowship. He had begun with enough reservations of his own. But time and shared peril had eroded a great deal of his skepticism. Happily, it had the same effect upon theirs: more so, since their attitudes had changed from an initial readiness to abandon him to last night's final resolve to stick with him, come what may. Ultimately, then, time together had changed their attitudes to a far, far greater degree than Druadaen's.

But that paled beside the ugly revelations, the ones that revealed how jaded his companions had been. That their true attitudes toward him had not merely been uncertain, but dismissive and denigrating. That their hypocrisy had been fueled by pure mercenary opportunism. That they had remained with him because he might bring them to the attention of persons of wealth and power—which was to say, *useful* persons. That, in brutal summary, he had been nothing more than a means to a very meretricious end.

And that was not the worst of it, because the most alarming failure was his own: failing to recognize their true motivations. Which meant he could not be sure that he'd detect other lies or half-truths they might tell in the future. Leaving him with a crucial and fundamental question: How could he ever trust them, now?

At another time and place, his instinct would have been to confront them or simply declare their association at an end. Unfortunately, he happened to be in wilderlands, just beyond the border of an enemy country, traveling to find a dragon in its lair. And given how far he'd come, and how close he might be to the cornerstone of all the answers he sought, he was unwilling to allow a few petty dissemblers to ruin such a singular opportunity. But how best to move forward?

If he openly confronted the three about their duplicity, there were two ways in which that was likely to cause the group to fracture instantly. One was that they might try to reject or deny his accusations, which would leave them all at an impasse. But the other was even less promising: once he explained *how* he had learned of their deceit, why would they—why would anyone—remain with a person who not only possessed the ability to eavesdrop upon them, but could not control when and where it happened?

That dubious "ability" raised a host of unrelated issues as well, not the least of which was the realization that the exchange he had seen between Shaananca and Alcuin was real, and that it had profound ramifications upon not only his own situation and fate, but the security of the Consentium. But those and other internal debates had to be put off until time and circumstances allowed. Right now, he had to decide if he could confront the three without driving them off, but without doing to them what they had so often done to him: lie.

As they topped a small rise, the Final Talon reared into view again, as if challenging him. Challenging him to act, because before they went any further, any closer to so fateful a destination, Druadaen needed the answer to a question even more urgent than the ones he hoped to ask a dragon. And he needed that answer right away.

"Umkhira," he called ahead, "do you still have those antelope in sight?"

"I do!" she answered eagerly. For the past two days, she had kept to the front of the group, hoping that there might be enough time to bring down some game with which to supplement the dry rations they'd salvaged from the boat.

"Then we'll check our path forward while you get us some fresh meat!"

She smiled broadly and wheeled her horse down toward the small herd they'd spotted a few hundred yards away.

S'ythreni cleared her throat. "You are quite aware that with my eyes, I could have told you—"

"And *I* am telling *you*," Druadaen interrupted, turning his horse and facing them directly, "that right now, I want your attention, not your eyes."

Ahearn leaned back. "Hey-ah, now Druadaen, what's amiss with y—?"

"I want *your* attention, too, Ahearn. All of you."

They stopped and stared at him.

He rested his hands on the pommel of his saddle. "We part here."

For two whole seconds, they simply gaped at him. Then they burst into protestations of "What?" and "But that's—!"

"That was a statement," he interrupted, "not an invitation to discussion. But since that wasn't clear, I will rephrase: I am going on without you."

It took them a few more seconds to realize that he was neither joking nor insane; he was deadly serious.

"Why?" Elweyr asked finally.

He stared at them, one at a time. "Do I really have to say?"

They looked into his eyes. Then they looked at each other.

When they looked back at him, their eyes had changed to those of snared rabbits. They knew, now. Knew that *he* knew. They didn't even bother to ask how; they didn't have to. His look told them that, after last night, their secrets were secrets no longer.

Ahearn put out a hand in appeal and put forth his best temporizing voice. "Now, Druadaen, you have to understand—"

"No. *I* don't 'need to understand' anything. But *you* do. And then you must make it clear that you *do* understand. Or we have no further reason to speak."

"Certainly. Yes," Ahearn said. Elweyr nodded. S'ythreni was still so surprised that only her friend's bobbing head reminded her to set her own into matching motion.

Druadaen looked at each of them again. He waited a moment, then: "Never lie to me again. Ever. About anything. If you do, we are at an end. Do you *understand* that?

Ahearn was about to speak but S'ythreni poked him. They just nodded.

"Good. Now you have a choice to make. If you come with me, you are promising that you will never lie to me again. If you can't make that promise in good conscience, then take your horse and your shares and leave." He stared at them. "I'm waiting."

They looked at each other sheepishly. It was Ahearn who explained. "Er... we mean to go with you. We're just waiting for you to, well, start going, again." He nodded toward the mountains ahead.

Druadaen rolled his eyes. Then he turned his horse and urged it in the direction of the Final Talon.

And smiled as he heard three sets of prompt, following hoofbeats.

A night of camping upon the open plains left all of them eager to press on. In none of their earlier travels had they ever been so exposed and so far from any refuge or retreat. And never had the group been so quiet.

But the next day, Ahearn's banter proved to be irrepressible. "Why, it's almost as if these plains are the perfect front yard for a dragon!" he observed with histrionic surprise as they climbed back into their saddles. "With a good pair of eyes, you could see anything coming from miles away and at least a day before it reached you. And with a good pair of wings, you could fly out and catch them in the open." He smiled grimly. "Just like our current circumstances. My, what are the odds of *that*?"

"I don't know," S'ythreni muttered, standing in her stirrups, "but I think the odds are good that we'll find out soon enough."

"Why?" asked Elweyr in a cautious tone.

She pointed forward. "Because this is where everybody else learned the answer to that question."

With the shadows of clouds scudding across the wide green carpet of sweetgrass, Druadaen could not immediately force his eyes to focus upon what lay before them. Then the last of the streaming patches of darkness sped past and the sun shone brightly.

The plain was littered with bleached bones and half-intact skeletons. Most were of larger animals: elk, sheep, cattle, and horses. But there were also a variety of two-legged remains, as well as a smattering of rusted weapons and shredded armor which left little doubt as to how the owners met their various ends.

"Well," breathed Elweyr, "this certainly looks promising."

S'ythreni leaned forward to look at Druadaen. "You are still certain you wish to go forward?" He met her eyes. She sighed. "Of course you do." Leaning back, she added, "Why did I even bother to ask?"

They urged their mounts toward the field of death.

Upon entering the outer edges of the scattered remains, Ahearn pointed out one of the more withered skeletons. "Urzhen. Rot, if I'm not mistaken."

Umkhira sighed. "You are not. There are Red amongst them as well."

S'ythreni nodded. "It's quite a gathering of the realms, really. And historical, too. That half-chewed shield is First Consentium auxiliary, the armor next to it is Iavan sheath, and the sword in the hand of the thin brown skeleton just beyond them is Ballashan, Late Empire." She settled back in her saddle with a resigned grunt. "At least we can console ourselves by knowing we're to become part of a very august collection."

"And even here, there are grave—or barrow—robbers," snarled Umkhira, gesturing into the distance with her axe. "See there? The low ridge of fresh dirt?" She shook out her reins, got a better grip on the axe. "But to desecrate the fallen *here*—well, they have courage uncommon among their ilk."

Druadaen held up a hand, focusing on the fresh soil she'd indicated. "I'm not sure you are correct, Umkhira."

"You think they are less than bold, digging among the dead in this place?"

"No," Druadaen answered, "I do not think they are grave robbers at all."

Elweyr nodded. "I haven't seen a burial site yet. I'm not even sure this was where the killing was done."

Ahearn looked around quickly. "Ye're right. It makes less than no sense that any dozen armies brought so much livestock with 'em. Besides, half the horses are unshod and there's no remains of barding or heavy tack on any of them."

Umkhira frowned. "So . . . ?"

"So," muttered Druadaen, "this isn't a battlefield. This is a killing ground."

"For the dragon?"

"No," answered S'ythreni in a tight voice, pointing at another low heap of dirt, "for its spawn."

A distinctly reptilian nose popped up from the soil, questing. Then the whole head emerged in profile; a single thin-irised eye rotated toward them and assessed. It reminded Druadaen of swamp lizards he'd seen during his single fateful visit to Solori. And since it was coming up out of the ground—

"Dismount!" he shouted, swinging rapidly out of the saddle.

They followed his lead, Ahearn asking, "Isn't this the moment we want to be higher than 'em?"

"No. Get ready."

"Wha—?"

Before Ahearn could finish his question, the creatures' actions answered it. Four more of them appeared with little warning, two writhing up through cattle skeletons that concealed the entry to their burrows. They were low to the ground and moved in the same sinuous slither-crawl as the ones Druadaen remembered from Solori, but whereas those were slightly larger, these were more heavily built, and their hide looked more rugged.

Ahearn was already standing beside him. "You seem to know a bit about these beauties, so—?"

"They're likely to come in pairs. Don't use a shield; one will just grab it and hang on while the other chews a limb off. And if they seem to give ground, watch out for the tail."

"Okay," shouted S'ythreni, "so that's how they kill us. What about us killing them?"

"Hold fast; they'll charge. You want that. Makes their head vulnerable. Get a leg, otherwise. Body wounds won't stop them in time."

And then there was no time left to do anything but try to make sure the horses stayed back and to keep a rough line in front of Elweyr.

Whose first thaumate probably saved them all; the three in the lead suddenly slowed, as if forcing their way through cold mud, heads straining to reach the four bipeds that were so close they could smell them...

Which was the last sensation any of those three experienced. Swords and axes flashed fast and hard and laid them all out, their heads cleft or pierced. More flowed toward them, but in ones and twos that the group was able to surround and bring down quickly. When a total of six lizards lay in front of them, the seventh paused and considered the difficult and death-strewn ground before it. Then it considered the rear leg of the closest of its slain fellows and began gorging on it.

Ahearn and Umkhira made to move forward, but Druadaen called them back. "To the horses. Keep distance. Use bows," he shouted.

A minute later, having retreated fifty yards, Druadaen and S'ythreni sheathed their swords and strung their bows as Umkhira and Ahearn each guarded a flank. The air began to hum with arrows and quarrels, and the first target upon which they concentrated their fire thrashed, almost pirouetted on its tail, and fell back, legs kicking spasmodically. The others looked up stupidly and resumed gnawing into the bellies of the dead.

But the next one they hit—the largest—snarled, reared up, and began scrambling toward them over the other bodies, hissing like a monstrous snake. The smaller ones ventured after it, but cautiously.

Their prudence saved them. By the time the leader reached Umkhira, it had half a dozen arrows and quarrels sticking out of it, one in its head. The Lightstrider did not so much attack the half-blind and staggering creature as she provided a merciful coup de grace. Whether out of experience or instinct, she took one menacing step toward the others. They spun and sped back to their burrows.

They looked at the slain reptiles, then each other, panting but very glad to be alive.

"Tell me, Dunarran," Ahearn exhaled mightily, "you've read a few books on the great wyrms, haven't you?"

Druadaen drew a deep breath before replying, "I have."

"Do they say anything about how dragons react when you kill their young?"

After recovering as many arrows and quarrels as they could, they rode back to the edge of the bone-field in an attempt to follow it around to the other side of the plain, rather than pressing on through even more dragonspawn.

However, upon finally discovering open ground a mile to the east, they also had a better view of the entirety of the death-ground. It was not, as they had initially believed, a rough oval. It was wedge-shaped, the sides narrowing as they drew closer to the foothills just a few miles to the north.

"That's odd," Umkhira murmured.

"It is indeed," Druadaen agreed, projecting the point at which the death-ground's two converging sides would meet.

Elweyr's comment matched Druadaen's observation. "The narrow end of that pie slice does not lead to the Final Talon." His finger traced the segment of the horizon that separated those two points. The Final Talon was decidedly further to the west.

"But does that matter?" S'ythreni wondered. "We don't know that the dragon, if there is one still alive, flies to this place."

"Strange the bone-field would be shaped that way, then," Elweyr replied.

Umkhira nodded. "The shape is not the doing of the dragonspawn. The spoor of burrowing animals always spreads out in a circle. So do their young, as they dig new dens."

Druadaen frowned. "The more I look at all the bodies, and how no two of them had the same equipment, the more I start to wonder if the dragon doesn't just come out here to attack, but to drop what it's killed elsewhere. To feed its young."

The others stared out at the field again, except Elweyr, who was nodding. "It's the simplest answer. Some of those skeletons, particularly the cattle and horses, don't look like they were torn apart so much as they were shattered. As if they were smashed by a hammer, or—"

"—or dropped from a great height," concluded S'ythreni in a murmur. "Yes, but that would also mean the dragon is not flying here from the Final Talon. At least, not directly."

Druadaen aimed his finger at the point where the two converging sides of the wedge intersected; it rested upon a high, stony hill. "Unless it takes the same indirect route from the Final Talon every time, that hill would be the dragon's logical point of departure.

S'ythreni sighed. "And that's where we're going, then?"

Druadaen nodded. "That's where we're going."

"Well," Ahearn pronounced, "at least it will be a death and a deed worthy of song!"

Elweyr stared sideways at him. "It's not as if anyone will ever know we were here. Or up there."

"Elweyr, you are my friend and my brother, but I must tell you true: sometimes, you are a very depressing person. Now, let's be about becoming the stuff of legend! Druadaen: lead on!"

CHAPTER FIFTY

By the time they had ridden close enough to discern the large dark opening in the side of the hill at which the bone-field pointed, there was little doubt that they were approaching a dragon's lair.

Although Druadaen's books rarely spent more than a few words on the approaches to such a cave, one didn't need to be an expert to discern the unmistakable signs of a great wyrm. The slopes leading up to it were barren except for dead trees that were either splintered, severely scarred by fire, or both. There were no bones or other signs of slaughter, but Druadaen's tomes had been a great deal less uniform on that point than legend. As a rule, campfire tales of dragons took their cues from the most lurid and horrible accounts. But the cave opening was certainly wide and high enough.

Ahearn shook his head and glanced at Druadaen, whispering, "So, dragon scholar, I never thought I'd have the reason, or foolishness, to ask such a question, but how do we go about this?"

Druadaen had ruminated upon the options many times, but he, too, was somewhat distracted by the realization that he was actually standing in front of a dragon's lair. Fortunately, rote recitation provided the answers until his brain finally caught up with his tongue. "Firstly, remember: we are not here to kill it."

"I know; we are here to talk to it. Might not share your interest in having a nice chat, though."

"Then we'll leave if we can."

"You mean 'run like rabbits,' I think," S'ythreni amended.

"If we have to fight, don't use bows and crossbows. If you stand still long enough to aim, let alone ready another shot, you are probably dead. Besides, even a crossbow such as S'ythreni's is not likely to pierce a dragon hide."

"Is anything?"

Druadaen nodded at Elweyr's despair-tinged question. "Heavy weapons may smash through. The point of a very strong sword can reportedly be thrust between the scales. Still, weapons are your last resort. Stay light on your feet. Drop anything that might encumber you, particularly shields and any awkward or heavy parts of your armor."

"Why?" asked Umkhira. "As this day neared, I have longed for a suit of the smooth, bright plates that is made in human foundries."

Druadaen shook his head. "Even if steel could resist its teeth or claws—and no one has lived to claim that—the force of its jaws and its blows is enough to kill you outright. So keep moving and keep to its flanks if you can."

"Unless you want to become a living torch, that is," Ahearn added.

Druadaen shook his head again. "It's not just the flame you must avoid—and not all possess that ability, apparently. It's their eyes."

"Their eyes? What do they do? Spray tears of acid?"

Druadaen forced his tone to remain level. "No, Ahearn. The gaze of a dragon is said to mesmerize mortals. And if you are mesmerized, then you are not moving. And if you are not moving, you are as good as dead."

The swordsman's jocularity faded. "I can follow that logic."

"Good. I will lead. Let's go."

They approached quietly and carefully. There was no sign of movement nor the faintest sound. Once within a dozen yards, Elweyr called for a halt and suggested that he scout out the entrance using one of the Sanslovan's philters.

He stripped, drank the contents of the vial, and over the course of a minute, his skin began to mimic that of a chameleon, blending into the gray and brown of the hillside. He crept forward and after he'd made ten yards' progress, only S'ythreni's eyes were sharp enough to detect him until he finally slipped inside the cave. Umkhira reported that she couldn't see the heat of his body.

A quarter of an hour later, S'ythreni squinted, sat straighter, announced, "He's coming back."

Once within fifteen feet, Elweyr was visible again, albeit barely so. Ahearn whispered, "Did you see it?"

"You mean the dragon? No. But I saw something much better. Coins of every kind, scattered everywhere. Fine weapons and armor, too. There was a lot of rubbish mixed in, but the whole hoard is right in the open, ripe for the taking."

S'ythreni and Ahearn exchanged looks. "Elweyr, you know our motto."

He nodded impatiently. "Yes, if a thing looks too good to be true, it probably is. But there's no sign of the dragon. No remains of his prey, nothing. Maybe he's been dead for years—decades—and no one has had the nerve to come this far into his domain. Or maybe they didn't notice the shape of the bone-field and went to the Final Talon instead. What I do know is that we are fifteen yards and fifteen minutes away from the end of all our troubles—and the beginning of a life of ease, if we want that. Because a few full bags mean we will never again *need* to do anything we do not wish to."

Druadaen and the others exchanged looks. "This discovery has made you unusually ... optimistic." The word he'd wanted to use was "hasty." Or maybe "incautious."

When no one disagreed with Druadaen's characterization of his behavior, Elweyr looked around the group in annoyance. "Really? We come all this way, and now you're afraid to cross the threshold because there *isn't* a dragon to fight?" When they just kept looking at him, he folded his arms. "So I guess this means we're going to wait for the dragon to *come back*?" He glanced up at the sun. "How long should we give him?" he wondered in an archly sarcastic tone. "An hour? Two? Because it would *certainly* be foolish to just dart in there now, fill a few bags, and leave."

Ahearn sighed, glanced at Druadaen. "He has a point, you know."

"He has become drunk with lust for gold," Umkhira countered. She looked at him frankly. "Elweyr, this is not like you."

"You're right," he admitted with a nod. "This is a different me. This is the me that is tired unto death wondering where and how we're going to turn up our next meal, our next room, our next pittance of coin. And the only thing stopping us—all of us—from freeing ourselves from that worry and want is the fear of entering an abandoned cave filled with treasure. And every minute that passes increases the possibility that *something* will ruin this opportunity."

"You mean, something like the return of a dragon?" S'ythreni asked facetiously.

"Maybe. But in the time we've spent debating this, we could have been there and gone."

Druadaen looked around the group. S'ythreni and Ahearn were looking toward the cave with wistful longing. Umkhira met his eyes, shrugged, glanced away.

Druadaen frowned. They had all been willing to remain with him to meet a dragon. But if the dragon was not here—and neither the cave nor the hillside showed any sign that it had been recently—then he could not in good conscience become a door guard for an absent dragon that might very well be dead.

He sighed, looked around at them. "I will lead the way. If the dragon returns while we are there, I will bear the responsibility for our intrusion."

"Not sure a dragon is going to care about such niceties," Ahearn commented with an eager glance back at the cave.

"Probably not," Druadaen agreed. "But it may stop long enough to talk when it sees I am without plunder."

"Wait," S'ythreni said sharply, "do you mean you are not going to take any of its hoard?"

"That is correct. I came here to meet and speak with a dragon. I will not abandon that. If it returns, I will expect you to drop what you have taken." Noticing their reluctance at meeting his eyes, he added, "Do you really think you have any chance of escaping if you try to keep it?"

They shrugged. Ahearn added, "If the monster finds us rooting like so many swine around its larder, I don't think anything you say or do could keep any of us alive. Including yourself."

"Again, probably true. But even though I am at loose ends, I remain an Outrider of Dunarra. Besides, my journey has not been to seek treasure but knowledge. So I will keep my troth with both."

The others shrugged. Druadaen stood, reflected that although there had been no shortage of grief and mischance, he had enjoyed his life and had accrued no regrets in his living of it. "Follow me." They did.

He stopped at the mouth of the cave. As Elweyr had reported, it was—or had been—the home of a dragon, but there was no sign of it nor any hint that it had been there recently.

The group had arrayed themselves in a line centered on Druadaen. They alternated between staring at the scattered coins and him. He nodded at no one in particular. "I shall remain here."

The original three of the group sprang forward, emptied rucksacks at the ready.

Umkhira came to stand beside him. "I suppose I would be foolish not to take some as well, but I am loath to leave you here."

Druadaen smiled as the scudding darkness of a cloud passed before the sun and the light in the cave dimmed. "Do not be concerned," he said. "If we are discovered in here, I doubt it will matter where anyone stands."

"That statement," said an impossibly deep, almost metallic voice, "may be the truest thing any human has ever said in my presence."

Druadaen did not start away like Umkhira; he was too busy noticing that the shadow of the passing cloud had not moved on.

Because evidently, it had been the shadow of the dragon that was now standing behind him.

CHAPTER FIFTY-ONE

Druadaen resolved not to turn hastily. That could be mistaken for a prelude to attack or flight. Fortunately, the voice seemed unhurried. Probably because sarcasm is best when each of the barbs is delivered slowly, separately.

"You are all so predictable." A dragon-snort ruffled Druadaen's hair with the force of a sea breeze but an odor that recalled both iron filings and the air after a lightning strike. "For some reason, all your species invariably expect to find me lying on my 'hoard,' just waiting—or better yet, sleeping—as you creep in to slay me. All carried out with righteous words spewing from your lips and greedy hearts pounding in your chests." It paused; Druadaen was grateful for the moments he'd had to think.

"Really, now," the majestic voice continued, "could any creature be as irremediably stupid as that and survive for hundreds of years? I can't see it, personally. But I want to see you, *intruder*... before I send you to whatever indifferent doom awaits your kind."

Druadaen turned and beheld the dragon... and in that moment, his growing fear transformed into surprised curiosity.

The great wyrm was not as usually depicted. Instead of a long snout and equally long jaws reminiscent of a saltwater crocodile, its head was surprisingly compact and fixed on a thick, sturdy neck.

It leaned back, hornlike eyelids narrowing. The dark purple irises were fixed upon Druadaen, but more in surprise and curiosity than menace. "Are you well, staring at me thus?" The wide, flange-like spines of its crest unfolded, rising as the dragon glanced at the rest of the group and asked, "Is this one, eh, 'simple'?"

Umkhira raised her chin in reply. "He is not. And he is the only one who refused to take any of your treasure."

One of the dragon's eyelids lifted, creaking like wet rigging. "Is that so? Well, he is either an utter dolt for risking his life without intending to gain from it, or he is among the cleverest two-legs I have ever met. And," he growled, "as for my 'treasure,' that may be the most amusing misperception your breed has of mine."

Ahearn cleared his throat carefully. "Then what is this I'm standing in? Rubbish?"

"Yes," the dragon answered blithely, "that is exactly what it is." When the three fortune-seekers goggled at the wyrm's answer, it held up a single didactic claw. "Think on it: What use does a creature like me have for baubles such as gold and gems? They are all so tiny that my breed can't even hold them. Assuming we had any reason to do so."

"That doesn't explain your impressive collection of fine armor and weapons," S'ythreni rebutted cautiously. "I see several that are unique. Objects of legend."

The dragon actually shrugged. "I wouldn't know."

"You may trust her assessment," Druadaen said. When the dragon turned toward him, he explained, "I am familiar with the markings on some of the shields, from depictions in books and scrolls." Many bore impresas associated with revered heroes who had disappeared over the past two millennia; as such, they were a de facto collection of obituaries.

The dragon's expression was one of bored indigestion. "What you call relics I call the useless spoor of those who came to kill me. And why? Because they all believed that as a dragon, I surely had a vast trove of wealth and artifacts."

"But you do," Elweyr said, staring at the evidence that was all around his feet.

"And where do you think all of it came from?" the dragon snapped impatiently, the crash of its vocal cords echoing off the walls like blades crossed in a swordfight. "From the ones who came *before* them. Who died and left behind the armor and wealth they—and their lackeys—were carrying at the time. And so on and so forth—ad nauseum, ad infinitum—until I'm wing-deep in their rubbish." The dragon glowered at the accumulation, but then its irritation evolved into a sly, serrated smile. "The irony is delicious, don't you think? That you are the ones fueling the myths and the greed that keep bringing you to your doom?"

Hearing an angry grumble rising from Ahearn, Druadaen asked loudly. "How frequently do such treasure-seekers disturb you?"

The dragon had to think a moment. "Not often, anymore. They used to be as thick as fleas on a dog's back. Or so it seemed. But one is either vigilant or one is dead." The great wyrm reflected. "Probably why so many of my kind are dead."

"When did you become aware of us?"

"Early yesterday." It smiled. "The plains are most convenient for seeing intruders at a distance."

"I told you so," Ahearn said to the others in a tone of rueful triumph.

Druadaen kept his focus on the dragon; as long as it was talking, they still had time to figure a way out of their predicament. "Why did you not attack us at that time?"

The dragon may have stifled a yawn. "Why should I? Either you were going someplace else, or you would ultimately deliver yourself here. All I had to do was leave before dawn, hide on another hill, watch you approach, and then glide to where I stand now, blocking the only exit." This time it did yawn. "A model of convenience."

"And most elegantly reasoned," Elweyr muttered through softly chattering teeth.

"Well, it should be," the dragon asserted, flipping a dismissive paw at the compliment. The scales on its forearm clattered softly, like an array of linen-wrapped castanets. "It's how I've trapped all your predecessors. As you can see." Its gaze traveled over the valuables in which they stood ankle-deep. "Which reminds me: it is time to resolve the matter of your trespass and attempted robbery. Which, of course, means that I must devour you. However, before doing so and adding your accoutrements to my collection of rubbish, I am willing to exchange a few more words with the doomed."

"We are grateful," Druadaen replied, even as he heard the group starting to move carefully. The dragon's eyes defocused, apparently tracking them all simultaneously. Adopting a thoughtful, heads-down posture, Druadaen folded his hands behind his back; a palms-down gesture brought their movement to an end. "And, we are flattered."

"You shouldn't be," the dragon snapped. "I am merely bored. Although, if I find you sufficiently diverting, I may allow some of you to exist for a bit longer. And if any of your sovereigns or relatives show up looking for you, I suppose I might consider ransoming you. Which would be wonderfully amusing."

"Why?"

"Well, since neither you nor treasure are valuable to me, exchanging you for gold would be like trading nothing for nothing. A deliciously pointless exercise, don't you think?"

"So you would keep us as your hostages, then?"

"Hostages?" The immense, square-jawed head flinched back. "Such a thuggish term. Let us rather say it would be welcome if your rescuers were to conceive of themselves merely as your *fidejussors*."

"As fee-day whats?" asked Umkhira, her confusion veering toward annoyance.

Druadaen and Elweyr had their mouths open to answer, but Ahearn beat them to it. "A *fidejussor* is one who stands in obligation to pay the debt of another." The rest of the group stared at him. "Well," he explained with a blush, "I do *read*, y'know!"

"Another impossibility become reality," S'ythreni muttered.

The dragon watched the exchange with an expression that, had its face been human, might have been amusement. "Individually, I find your company rather unpromising. But collectively, you are somewhat diverting . . . albeit unintentionally so." He stretched, reclined across the mouth of the cave. "Let's play a game."

"Does it involve getting eaten?" Ahearn asked quickly.

"Only if the player asks stupid questions," the dragon shot back. "Come now. Here's how we play: you explain why you came here and why you thought it was acceptable to kill me in my own home. Then I will laugh at, and merrily dissect, your pitiful attempts to justify your homicidal intents. Who wants to go first?"

Druadaen took a step closer to the dragon, who muttered, "Why am I not surprised?" In a normal tone: "Yes? Now don't rush; make it a really *good* excuse!"

"I cannot play your game. But I do want to assert that in coming here, we did not want—nor mean—to kill your young."

The dragon shook its head; its folded crest rattled like a dozen loose shields in a rolling barrel. "Kill my young?" The great wyrm looked sideways at the others. "So, he truly *is* simple?"

Druadaen pressed on. "On the plain, earlier today, we either slew your young or...or creatures that are in your service."

Its midnight-purple irises widened. "Ah! They are neither my spawn nor bound to me in any way. They are...well, convenient scavengers. Nothing more."

"Scavengers?" echoed Umkhira.

"Do I not speak clearly? Yes, they are *sca-ven-gers*, ur zhog. It is where I dispose of the carcasses after I have fed. Like me, the reptiles there sleep a great deal, but wake when they detect movement. Or a body dropping to the ground from a hundred feet. They are very thorough and strip everything to the bones. No waste, no charnel smell." It breathed deeply from a gust blowing past the entrance to the cave. "I do love living in the mountains! The air is so fresh."

"So..." Elweyr hazarded, "the plain is *not* your killing ground?"

"No, but I *do* like that term. 'Killing ground': it certainly sounds ominous—and off-putting—doesn't it?"

Instead of smiling, Ahearn folded his arms. "It is also perfectly placed to give you an opportunity to observe the skills of your potential attackers, as well as any tricks they might have up their sleeves."

One armored eyelid lifted slightly. "So, the well-equipped butcher's assistant is not as slow as he looks. Refreshing. I can usually predict the mental acuity of swordsmen simply by looking at their favored weapon."

"Oh?"

"Yes; their intelligence is inversely proportionate to the length of their preferred blade."

S'ythreni smirked. "Really? Because that would make anyone with a shortsword a genius." She looked at the weapon she was holding. "Which I assure you is not the case."

The dragon glanced at the blade. "Yes, that would be a logical deduction. But you've a quick wit and a clever tongue. So how does that make you less than perspicacious, aeosti?"

She stared at the wyrm. "You might not have noticed, but I've entered a dragon's lair armed with a pair of *shortswords*."

The soft rumble in its throat might have been a chortle. "Well played. And intriguing. Tell me: Why march to suicide? You are Iavan. You could have slipped away at any time. And generally, your kind has almost as little use for wealth as my own breed."

"I'm not here for treasure."

"No? Hmmm... what of you, Lightstrider? You come from a covetous species."

"No more covetous than others," Umkhira shot back in annoyance. "And among my people, I am not one of those cursed with greed. I am here because honor demands no less." She glanced at Druadaen. "I am his comrade and friend."

The dragon's eyes followed hers then shifted to look at Ahearn and Elweyr. "Certainly the two of *you* came along for as much coin as you could carry off?"

"At first," Ahearn admitted with his chin up, "but as time wore on, I had... other interests."

"Such as?"

Ahearn cut a quick glance at Druadaen, then shrugged. "Well, he's my mate, isn't he?"

The dragon settled into a more relaxed pose. "Fascinating. I do believe you are telling the truth. Or you are all profoundly self-deluded. Or both. Just how long have you been journeying here to encounter final oblivion?"

The dragon might reasonably have regretted the response the question elicited: a four-voiced, tumbling account of the travels and tribulations they'd faced over the course of their thirteen moonphases together. But instead the wyrm listened and studied them as they spoke, and also, more slyly, how they reacted to each other. "Singular," the dragon breathed at last. Then its eyes shifted back to Druadaen with an almost metallic click. "And you have nothing to add?"

Druadaen shrugged. "They have told our story admirably."

"Perhaps they have. And perhaps your revoltingly earnest demeanor is not feigned but genuine. But it is your strange quest— which your companions have only alluded to in general—that seems to have bound them to you. That holds you all together. So, tell me: Exactly what is it that you are seeking?"

Druadaen considered. "My friends have conveyed the basics quite well. I could expand upon the details, but that, well, that would take a good deal longer."

The dragon adopted a posture of sybaritic repose. "We have

nothing but time. Well, maybe not you, but a few days or years more or less mean nothing to me."

So Druadaen explained, including the other anomalies that he had encountered during his years in the Archive Recondite but would have no foreseeable opportunity to investigate. As he spoke, he became aware that the other four had not only come alongside but were staring at him.

When he finished, Elweyr said, "You know, when you present it all at once..."

"You think disturbing thoughts, Druadaen," Umkhira murmured. "But necessary, I think."

Ahearn smiled proudly, nodding, and looked at the dragon. "So, what do you say to *that*?"

"I say," it said calmly to Druadaen, "that I cannot decide which is more intriguing: the contradictions you have unearthed, or the nature of a mind that would dedicate itself to such a project. Or, the possibility that you are the most gifted liar I have ever met."

"You think all that could simply be the foundation for a *lie*?" S'ythreni asked, incredulous.

The dragon glanced at her. "I said it would make him the *most* gifted liar I have met...and I have met more liars than you could possibly imagine. But if I have learned anything, it is that all natural laws exist to be defied and all limits exist to be exceeded." It rose up on its forelegs. "I allow that it is very likely that you are telling me the truth. But I require proof."

"I would provide it, if I had any with me."

"As it so happens, you do. Now," said the dragon, lowering its head so its eyes bored directly into Druadaen's, "tell me again, this time just in general terms, what you hoped to accomplish by coming here."

Druadaen began...but hadn't uttered three words when the dragon's head popped up again. "This is very odd."

"What?"

"With rare exception, I can read thoughts with greater ease than you—yes, even *you*—can read a book. But..." The dragon drew up to its full height. The others shied back, but Druadaen was strangely certain that this was not a posture of threat. It was a formal stance.

The dragon's voice was studied and serious. "Human, if you are willing, I would touch your mind."

"I'm not stopping you."

"No, not exactly, but"—for a second, the great wyrm looked as though it was about to make a confession—"but you must... must *permit* me."

Druadaen stared. "How?"

"As if this is a thing one being can teach another? It is a simple act of will, but I suspect you are more stubborn than you know. Now, relax and relent. And swiftly: my patience is wearing thin."

"Don't rile him, Druadaen," muttered Ahearn. "He might start by roasting you, but odds are good he'd fricassee the rest of us for good measure."

"Indeed I might," the dragon boomed, "but I will not be the one to start that process. Not with your unusual friend, at any rate."

Druadaen stared again. "Why?"

"'Why' yet again?" The dragon shook its head. "You really must expand your repertoire of questions. 'How' or 'what' are perfectly serviceable. 'Where' and 'when' are a bit pedestrian: information that could be gleaned easily enough through observation. But as for *why* I will not incinerate you? Do not get any lofty ideas about yourself or my opinion of you. The reason is so much more basic than that."

"And it is?"

"That with every passing minute, you are proving to be the most peculiar visito... er, victim I have had in a very, very long time. Now, try again: allow your mind to be open to me." The dragon peered at him. "I'm waiting."

"I'm trying! But it is not something I know how to do."

"Do you not feel a pressure against your thoughts, your consciousness?"

"No."

The dragon frowned. "This is most troubling."

"Hah!" laughed Ahearn in vicarious triumph. "The Dunarran's so stubborn that he can even mangle the mancery of dragons! Hey-ah, mate; that's a tale to tell!"

"Be still, you steel-waving fool! What I am attempting is not mancery." The dragon's eyes, still fixed upon Druadaen, narrowed. "This impediment, whatever it is, leaves you unknown to me. And what is unknown I may not safely trust."

Elweyr's voice had a tremolo of fear in it. "As old as you are, is it not also appealing—intriguing!—when you encounter something new? Something different and interesting? Like my friend?"

The dragon's frown was mighty. "Do not try to manipulate me, human. I am all too aware that curiosity is my species' weak spot. That is exactly why I may not indulge it. And you may rest assured that if there was some other way to determine your friend's true intents, I would already know everything—"

In a quicksilver flash, the velene was sitting alongside Druadaen.

"—or maybe I wouldn't," the dragon finished, leaning away.

CHAPTER FIFTY-TWO

S'ythreni's tone was more careful than usual. "You were saying something about having seen everything before?"

"Indeed I was," the dragon murmured. "Indeed I was."

Ahearn uttered a satisfied huff at that response, but Druadaen did not hear concession in the dragon's tone. It was a mix of wonder and surprise.

"Well," it said, stirring, "there is always value in novelty."

"By novelty, do you mean the unknown?"

The dragon stared at Elweyr briefly. "If that is what I meant, human, then that is what I would have said. This...is merely a novelty."

Unless Druadaen was quite mistaken, the dragon's use of the word "merely" had been profoundly forced.

The velene swished its mirror-tail once and, in a leap, was back on Druadaen's wrist and reformed into a bracer. All in one fluid motion.

"Singular," breathed the dragon, staring at the bracer. Then it looked up and frowned. "Why are you all still standing? It makes me weary, just looking at you. There, yes, sit; that's better. More comfortable for you, less irritating for me."

Umkhira frowned. "Are we still hostages, then?"

The dragon sighed. "Directness is not merely useful; it is a great good." He glanced at the Lightstrider. "However, one can always have too much of a good thing." He turned back to Druadaen. "Such as books. I suggest a new game. You regale me with all the facts you have learned about dragons while studying in your archive, and I will try to keep from dying of laughter."

"Well," Druadaen began with a shrug, "except for the ones that are strictly devoted to anatomy, they assert that all of you are..." He stumbled on the word. He didn't *think* it would be suicidal to utter it, but still...

"We dragons are all what?" the great wyrm pressed. "Erudite? Witty? Charming? Immortal? Imposing?"

"No. Evil."

Instead of a swift death, Druadaen received a choice look. "How amusing; some of my cousins have said the same about your breed. All of your breeds. But in fact, few creatures are inherently evil. Savage? That is a different matter. But I suspect our species have good and evil in equal measure."

S'ythreni leaned forward, mischief in her eyes. "And *are* all dragons witty and erudite and immortal and imposing?"

"You left out charming."

She laughed, but Umkhira was frowning. "Is all of that true?"

The dragon snorted. "None of it."

"None?"

"None." It sat back on his haunches. Its crest flattened, the tail slid along the floor with a grating hiss as it gathered beneath the heavily muscled body. "Shall I tell you what I find most irritating about my own breed?"

Druadaen noticed that Ahearn was apparently preparing to answer in the negative, so he asked hastily, "Your breed? Irritating? In what way?"

It snorted; a wisp of vapor—or smoke?—may have escaped one nostril. "Although we count centuries the way you count years, most of my kind remain as dull-witted and unimaginative as they were in their youth. They *do* acquire patience; a dragon which does not learn that lesson does not live very long. Your breeds see to that. But an appreciation for reflection and wit and the rich variety of this existence?" The great wyrm shook its head. "It never quickens in them. You would think after a few centuries of grabbing heifers and terrifying unwashed storekeepers and mud-covered dirt scratchers, they'd grow tired of it. It's all quite monotonous, really.

"But no: as among your species, the majority of mine remain content within their narrow round of existence. Me? I cannot imagine enduring so limited a life. Why, just considering culinary variety alone, the willingness to settle for the limited fare of these lands"—he glanced sourly at Ahearn and Elweyr—"is quite beyond my comprehension."

As Elweyr gulped audibly, Druadaen nodded. "So, you *do* eat our kind?"

"Eat your kind?" The dragon shuddered. "Some do, I suppose. But me?" Its great, horned brow furrowed. "Well, if I was starving, perhaps."

"Oh?" Ahearn replied in a tone of injured pride rather than relief. "And what makes us such inferior fare?"

The dragon looked at him from the corner of its eyes. "You really want to know?"

"I do!"

"Well, firstly, you are to be congratulated for being bold enough to ask that question. Unfortunately, your boldness seems to be inversely proportional to your common sense. Ah, well, it is often thus. But, as to the matter of consuming your kind:

"Firstly, you are very small: a morsel barely worth the work of catching. And you *can* be very difficult to catch, particularly once you get into tunnels, or basements, or other tight places. All that work and then almost no reward? Intolerable."

"So which of us are most easily caught?" Elweyr asked in a voice at once horrified and fascinated.

The dragon looked at the roof of the cavern as if trying to summon memories from it. "Well, let's see. The old ones." The wyrm made a face. "Stringy. And they taste...odd. Then there are the heavy ones. They are particularly likely to be caught because many of them cannot reach—or fit into—those tight places where the rest of you take refuge."

Ahearn scowled. "So you like your humans on the plump side, eh?"

The dragon recoiled. "I did not say that I *prefer* them. I said they were easy to catch. Unfortunately, they are...not pleasant to eat. Unless one has a taste for uncured bacon. Now, *actual* bacon, particularly after it has been seared...!" He snapped out of his dreamy distraction. "Let's see, which others are easy to catch?"

Ahearn's scowl became almost rageful as he put his hand on

his sword hilt. Suddenly, terribly, Druadaen was sure that it was not a bluff. "Wyrm," the swordsman said in a low tone, "whatever you say next, do not tell me that you prefer to catch children."

The dragon, already surprised by the suicidal boldness of the swordsman's reach for his weapon, started. "Hunt children? What do you think I am? A monster?"

Elweyr shrugged mildly. "Well, actually..."

"Ah-hrm. A poor choice of words on my part. Allow me to rephrase: Do you think I am an *idiot*? Firstly, nothing enrages any worthwhile species like the killing of its young. I assure you, all of my kind understand this quite well. Better than you'd think, I suspect.

"But a creature that demonstrates a *preference* for slaughtering pups, or spawn, or kids, or kittens, or children?" It shook its head. "Despite the many terms different breeds have for their young, the destruction of them is always the same to those who gave them life. They invariably resolve to slay such a monster at any cost. Including their own lives."

Elweyr frowned. "But there are many accounts of dragons taking particular delight in slaughtering and eating humans. Whole towns of them."

The dragon released a long sigh that carried out a few more wisps of vapor. "Well, what family is without a few bad eggs— literally? You have an expression for similar troublemakers among your own kind. I believe you call them hotheads." The dragon cast a sideways glance. "Of course, among us, that too can be taken literally."

Umkhira folded her arms. "So if you do not prey upon our races, what do you eat?"

The creature's dark purple eyes narrowed in remembered delight. "Ah, cattle. Oh, horse will do, and sheep are acceptable, although one coughs up wool for days. But cattle. Particularly lightly broiled. I do not know why one of my breed would willingly dine on anything else." It laid its chin upon folded paws. "But kine are hard to come by, now. Not without raising the countryside to arms."

Elweyr raised an eyebrow. "I find it hard to believe that a rabble of farmers and herders would give you any pause."

"No, they would not, but the army that comes after them is a different story. How do you think my breed is so diminished?

That we succumbed to 'old age'? No: it was fury. Our fury, for the most part. Fury at the memory of these plains when they were dark with wild herds of all sorts of delicious ruminants, when we hunted and fed without fear of reprisal." The wyrm shrugged. "Over time, resentment against the various species which wrought those changes has made many of my kind, well, 'hotheaded.'"

"So," Ahearn summarized with ill-disguised satisfaction, "once a dragon is finished with the common folk, the army comes out and finishes him."

The dragon shrugged again; its scales popped, creaked, and cracked. "It is suicide for my kind to start that cycle. And I suspect that is the intent of almost half of my kin who have succumbed to the temptation. Because the alternative is to fly farther and farther in search of less and less prey. In time, one must spend all one's days asleep, lest one starve."

Druadaen considered the dragon's quandary and then wondered aloud. "What about mountain goats?"

"Adequate, but a bit gamey. Oh: You mean why don't I *hunt* them?" Druadaen nodded. The dragon shook its head stiffly. "Do you have any idea how hard they are to catch? Leaping from rock to rock, and then stupidly plummeting into crevasses—from which I cannot safely escape by flying, mind you.

"Also, soaring about the mountains in search of prey is easily the most effective means of panicking the local settlers, who presume it signifies that I am preparing to wreak havoc upon them." It snorted. "As if I would parade myself across the clouds to announce my intents! Either way, though, you will appreciate that hunting mountain goats brings far more trouble than it is worth."

Druadaen almost rejected the idea that came to him; it was just too simple. Or was that its best feature? "What if we could save you the bother of hunting them yourself?"

The dragon raised one eyebrow. "Clearly, you have a proposition in mind."

"I do."

"Well, speak plainly and don't keep me waiting. Otherwise, I might get bored and eat you after all." It shuddered. "Despite the taste."

CHAPTER FIFTY-THREE

Druadaen sighed. "Could you please stop chewing for a moment?"

"Again?" the dragon asked pettishly.

"I haven't finished measuring your jaw."

The creature's sigh blew Druadaen's hair straight back. "Oh, very well." No sooner had the splintering of bones and scissoring of meat stopped than it glanced sideways at where the group was roasting the last of the goats for their own consumption. "It's so hard to decide: Cooked or uncooked? They both have their own particular gustatory appeals."

Druadaen finished reeling out the marked cord with which he had taken the dragon's various measurements. "Then why don't you, er, cook more of the ones we bring you?"

"What? When you can do it for me? And so very, very nicely, too. My method sears the outside but leaves almost everything else completely raw. Which is delectable, but when one desires cooked meat, slow roasting is vastly preferable."

Druadaen nodded absently, stepping back. "And you are still unable to resume your own, er, incendiary exhalations?"

The dragon's eyes rotated toward him. "As I told you, that is not something I can perform for very long or very frequently. It will be some time before I could hope to do so again." It seemed miffed. "Perhaps you would be more impressed if I demonstrated it upon *you*?"

Over the last few days, Druadaen had grown accustomed to the dragon's preferred form of banter: dire-sounding threats based on the wildest legends of its propensities. He smiled. "I do not require personal immolation to be impressed."

The dragon huffed. "But you were *un*impressed. And do not dissemble; I can tell when I disappoint."

"Well," Druadaen explained reasonably, "you yourself have said that almost all stories regarding dragons are just that: stories."

"True," it mused, mollified. "But it rankles me when I under-whelm humans."

"I understand," Druadaen nodded, waiting for the mouth to become still before measuring and counting the cutlass-sized and -shaped teeth. "I'm sorry that my inquiries are annoying. It is just that I was unable to learn very much."

"What is there to learn? I breathe fire. Sometimes. And not at the volume or temperature that your ludicrous legends depict. Burning down whole cities with a constant gush of metal-melting flame?" It snorted. "Not even the greatest of my breed would have claimed such absurd abilities. And they were pathological liars. Among other things." It sighed. "But what *have* you learned about my underwhelming ability to breathe fire?"

"Well, it's clear you don't actually *breathe* fire." Druadaen moved to the nostrils. He stared, then decided, in this one regard, to skip measurement and rely upon an estimate.

"As I told you," the dragon said testily, "the sensation is reminiscent of when your kind regurgitates bile."

Druadaen stopped. "How do you know what that feels like? Were you reading the mind of someone when it happened to them?" Not unlikely; looking into an angry dragon's eyes could certainly cause all kinds of spontaneous emissions and excretions. "Or are you able to read memories, as well?"

The dragon raised its head. "You must allow me some secrets, human. Without some measure of mystery, there can be no measure of majesty."

"Is that a saying among dragons?"

"Well, having just said it, I suppose it is, now. But I will have the unpleasant truth of your observations about my underwhelm-ing pyrotic exhalations."

Druadaen raised an eyebrow. "Actually, that term is very accurate; they are pyrotic." Seeing the confusion on the great wyrm's pronounced, horned brow, he expanded. "Whatever you expel does not ignite until it is beyond your mouth."

"Well, thank goodness for that! It is unpleasant enough as it is!"

Druadaen nodded. "I cannot tell what the means of ignition is, but I noticed a familiar odor just beforehand."

A pause. "Well, you see, human, when one eats a great deal of raw meat, one's breath is sometimes—"

"No, no: this was the scent of what you were expelling. It smelled vaguely like linseed oil."

"That seems odd. And you seem to attach significance to it."

Druadaen shrugged. "Rags soaked in linseed oil have been known to combust spontaneously."

"So you are saying that dragon flame is indistinguishable from a crude agricultural byproduct?" There was far more injured pride than anger in its voice.

"No. I think that is what ignites whatever else you exhale, which I suspect is a gas of some kind. But as I have no way to sample it—"

"Just as well, perhaps," the dragon huffed, rising up. "Each revelation about my 'pyrotic exhalations' is more depressing than the last. At least I will make a good show of flying. And while I'm at it, I will retrieve that goat you could not reach. Are you ready to make your observations?"

"I am," said Druadaen. But having studied the dragon's body in great detail over the past two days, he was filled with misgivings that he might once again have to share "underwhelming" results.

Regardless of how it was accomplished, a dragon aloft was a breathtaking sight. But the process whereby it became airborne *was* somewhat underwhelming, even though Druadaen had been prepared for that. After all, a body weighing several tons but equipped with wings proportionally no thicker than a bat's, wasn't going to launch effortlessly into the air like a sparrow. Or, if it did, then it would be the most profound violation of natural law Druadaen had yet witnessed.

Instead of taking wing and immediately soaring, the dragon exited the cave and started scaling the hill, ascending with a wide-limbed crawl. Once at the summit, the great wyrm turned toward another hill, lifted its head and closed its eyes. It held that pose of arrested readiness for a minute, then another.

Druadaen had begun to wonder if it was possible for a creature to forget how to fly when a breeze blew up the hill from the plain...

The dragon transformed itself in an instant; its wings spread, and its body seemed to grow. But that was just a momentary illusion caused by the sudden unfolding of webbing that that ran from its upper arm to the midpoint of its body. With a prodigious leap, the dragon caught the breeze rolling up the slope and was suddenly soaring with deceptive ease, appearing to float in midair as it ascended.

As the breeze began to fade, more webbing appeared. These new flaps ran from beneath its ribcage to the front of its haunches, and also from the rear of its legs out to the end of the tail, widening it into a serrated stiletto silhouette. All these folds and webbing now worked like lateen sails, tilting and angling to catch smaller gusts and updrafts until the dragon reached the top of the next hill.

Druadaen discovered his mouth had gaped open in wonder. Not at the power of the flight—it was more a matter of strength-assisted gliding—but at the extraordinary elegance of the body's design and the creature's use of it.

He started when Ahearn's voice arose unexpectedly behind him. "I'll never admit it where he can hear me, but that scaled bastard is one magnificent creature."

The dragon turned toward them. "So kind of you to say!" he bellowed, and then roared with laughter.

Ahearn stepped forward abruptly, as if he meant to charge at the chortling dragon, which leaped again and soared toward an even higher hill. "Well, that proves your theory, Dunarran."

"What does?"

Ahearn shook his head angrily. "No natural creature could hear me from that distance. Impossible, particularly with the wind."

Druadaen nodded, but more to himself, as he observed a different violation of natural law: that now, even as the dragon beat its wings, there was no sign of them ripping or that the long bones upon which they were extended showed any sign of bending, let alone breaking.

Having a reasonable estimate of the dragon's weight, and an even more precise estimate of the area of the fully extended wings, he knew roughly how much air needed to be moved, how quickly, for the creature to fly actively. But even without that exertion, he knew how much stress was on those wings and those bones simply to remain in place as rising currents carried the immense weight of the dragon upward. And the moment had come when they should have collapsed, cracked, or torn under the strain.

But it didn't happen. Not on the dragon's quick flight to the new hill, or on the longer, soaring transit to the closest mountain of the Thelkrag Kar. And upon its return, when it swooped down to claim the goat that had slid down a sheer face after being felled by Umkhira's arrows, the dragon banked hard, webbed extensions flaring and wings angling to bite into the breeze. Without even bothering to land, it opened its maw and caught up the carcass: effortlessly, swiftly, without landing or wasted motion.

As the dragon swooped down toward the top of the hill on which he waited, Druadaen was once again able to see its face: rapturous glorying in the power and freedom of its flight and a hint of regret that it would soon be earthbound again. It landed and set about devouring the goat, pulling it apart, more by wrenching back with its neck than shearing the meat with its jaws. Its heavier foreparts, stronger neck, and shorter gullet made far more sense than the almost serpentine shapes attributed to the wyrms of legend. This dragon could quickly reduce and consume an entire mountain goat in mere minutes. Longer, narrower jaws would not have had the viselike grip nor the ability to dismember prey so easily. And it was anyone's guess how long it would take for the meal to work its way down a snakelike throat, to say nothing of the difficulty of bones jamming sideways, or against each other.

When it had gulped down the last of the goat, the dragon spread its wings and almost floated down toward the apron of cleared rock that was the threshold of its cave. It landed without raising the faintest puff of dust. It smiled at Druadaen, who had the sudden impression that its gore-coated maw was equal parts bulldog and bull shark. "Are you underwhelmed *this* time?" He didn't bother to look at Ahearn but added, "You do not need to answer, steel-waver. Your unsolicited opinion is already a matter of record."

As Ahearn fumed, Druadaen shook his head. "It was magnificent. But it made me wonder..."

"Yes?" prompted the dragon with a warning in its tone.

"Just before you returned, I saw the look on your face. If you enjoy flying so much, why do you not do it more often, up in the mountains where no one could find you?"

"Because your species—indeed, all two-legs—are always watching. And because they presume that flying is a precursor to depredations by my breed."

Druadaen frowned. "I am sorry if my request to see you fly put you at risk. I—"

The dragon raised a stilling paw. "No more. It was my choice, and not one I made out of kindness. The food you brought saved me the necessity of risking a long, vitality-sapping flight, scanning the wilderness for free herds. And all it cost was showing you a few paltry lifts and swoops. And wounded pride." When Druadaen stared in perplexity, the dragon clarified. "I am reduced to performing circus tricks for my supper." It spat out a bitter laugh. "Behold the mighty dragon and despair!"

It glanced south. "It was a very short flight and away from the plains, so hopefully your kind has not been agitated." He released a great sigh before walking regretfully into the cave. "Come. I do not wish to tempt fate. And don't lag; I won't step on you."

Druadaen entered alongside the great wyrm, wondering if it was another violation of natural law that a creature as large as a house—and twice as long, counting the tail—could have such an extraordinarily precise sense of its closest surroundings and similarly precise control of its movements within them.

"Your question about flying," the dragon rumbled as the cave widened out, "touches on a sore point between our species."

"Because it attracts angry settlers and possibly armies?"

"Well, that, too...but there is a more basic concern." It gestured toward a rock suitable for human seating as Ahearn wandered in behind them, silent and sullen. "Flying rapidly depletes my breed's vitality, makes us very hungry."

"Understandable."

"Therefore, if we fly, we must eat a great deal. More than one or two sheep or goats, at any rate."

"So...cattle, horses?"

Its nod was shallow. "But even those of us who are large enough to take such heavy prizes to our lair cannot do so profitably."

Druadaen nodded, understanding. "Because flying with that extra weight costs more energy than you get from consuming them."

"Precisely. So we must eat our kill where we find it."

Ahearn tilted his head. "Well, then, yer damned if you do and damned if you don't. If you can't afford to risk hunting across the wilderness, you've no choice but to raid livestock and stay while you gulp it down. Which brings out locals with pitchforks."

The dragon glanced at him. "I may have to revise my unflattering opinion of you, steel-waver. You are correct. There is no way for me to secure enough food."

"How long can you survive this way?" Druadaen asked in hushed tones.

"Well, I have managed for two centuries so far."

"Two centuries!"

"Yes. Because, like the giant you met, I enter torpor when I have insufficient food. The difference is that I may remain in that state for a very, very long time."

"Years?"

"Decades. Possibly more. I do not want to risk discovering the limits." The dragon extended its wings like an athlete stretching muscles after a long event. "Now, let's return to a happier subject; you were explaining how seeing me fly was a transformative experience."

"Well, I'm sure it was..."

"But?"

Druadaen shrugged. "But, given your weight and anatomy, you shouldn't be able to fly at all. Not even glide. It is physically impossible."

"Well, *I* could have told you that. And without all the infernal poking, prodding, and measuring."

"And doesn't that bother you?"

"No. Why should it?"

"Because fundamental parts of your existence defy natural law."

The dragon waved a blithe talon. "And what of it? If one starts asking such questions, there is no end to them. For instance: How do I contact your mind—well, not *yours*, but others? What are these powers that your breed calls magic and why do they work? And are you any closer to resolving the conundrums you found when examining the Bent and giants?"

The dragon daintily picked at its teeth. "The world is filled with mysteries for which we not only lack answers—and probably always will—but for which we cannot even form adequate questions. As a dragon, understanding the limits of logic is a birthright." It paused. "Well, 'birthright' is not the proper word. In fact, the term is hilariously and ironically misleading when applied to us."

"How so?"

"Because dragons are not born."

"By all reports, you lay eggs."

"That is correct. But you miss my meaning. So I shall rephrase: we do not have offspring."

As the rest of the fellowship entered the cave, Druadaen tried to reconcile what the dragon told him with what he had read. "But there are accounts of how dragons must mate while in flight in order to—"

The dragon jumped up. "We do *what*?" it roared.

"Mate," Druadaen said as evenly as he could. "While flying."

Its purple eyes closed as it raised a heavily scaled paw to cover them "Only a human could conceive of such a perversity," the dragon groaned.

Druadaen scratched an ear. "The stories originated with another species, I believe."

Two of the vast claws parted, revealed a searching violet eye. It roved until it found S'ythreni. "Ah. I should have known. A fabulation of the Iavarain. Before their fall, they were almost all hopeless, if debauched, romantics."

S'ythreni appeared to be readying a retort but abandoned the effort with a wave that seemed to be more a gesture of admission than futility.

Druadaen rose. "So do you rely upon self-fertilization, then?" When the dragon shook its head with a look of disgust, he put out his hands in an appeal. "So how do you reproduce?"

"We don't."

"But the eggs—"

"The eggs are not our *offspring*. They are *us*."

Druadaen glanced at his four companions. They looked every bit as confused as he felt. Maybe more so. "When you say, 'they are us'—"

"I mean exactly that!" The dragon glared at them all. "Those eggs do not contain young, do not promise a new generation and increase of my breed. Each contains a new body for the dragon that laid them, should it perish."

Druadaen stammered. "B-but, that would mean that—"

"That we are our own beginning and our own end." It shrugged. "And now you have the ultimate violation of natural law to add to your collection. You're welcome." It preened. "It is integral to the majestic nature of dragons to be the acme of all things. Even contradictions."

Druadaen was the first to regain his voice. "But...how can that be?"

"I do not know; it simply is."

"No, no; what I mean to say is, how could such a species even come into existence, how could it start? And how would it increase in number if it produces no new beings?"

"Your deductions follow as inevitably as night does day."

"But it is quite impossible!"

"As I told you at the outset, my breed's consciousness is shaped by the understanding that there is no logical explanation for us. Or rather, if there is, it lies beyond our scope, just as we seem to lie beyond the limits of what your book-clutching philosophers call 'the natural order.'" The dragon waved a paw at the world around them. "We have a saying, 'Which came first, the dragon or the egg?' You have a similar saying about chickens, I believe."

"Yes, but that is a metaphorical question. In your case, the quandary is literal. The first of your bodies must have come from an egg. But where did that first egg come from?"

"Who knows?" Its mouth curved in a sly grin. "Maybe it's the result of... *magic!*" The serrated smile persisted.

Druadaen saw the mischievous look. He smiled back. "You don't believe that."

"Not for a second," the creature confirmed with a chortle that sounded like the start of a landslide. "But I do believe—I *know*—this much: to dwell upon such things invites madness, if done for too long. And since I live a very long time, I could go very, very mad. Not a good outcome for my species or yours, I'm sure you'd agree."

The dragon dusted off its massive thighs; that smoothing of scales released a shower of smaller coins that had become trapped between and beneath them. "Well, I suppose you certainly will have a great deal to write about when you get back to your archive."

Druadaen shook his head. "At this point, I'd hardly know where to start.

The dragon nodded slowly. "That might be fortunate, in a way."

"I don't see how. I wouldn't be standing where I am now if those who came before me did not record what they knew so that I might build upon it."

The dragon folded its paws. "My, but you set great store by these books, don't you?"

Druadaen tried not to resent the facetious tone. "They have been useful enough so far."

"Have they? Hmm...shall I tell you what I have observed about *all* your species' books over these many centuries?"

Druadaen crossed his arms. "Please do."

He wondered if the dragon's raised chin and finger were an unintentional reprise of academic posturing or actually meant to lampoon them. "If there's any one thing that can be said for most books," the dragon began with a pedantic flourish, "it is this: the more their authors claim complete authority in a subject, the less they actually have. And since so many of your own investigations arose from old tomes filled with old observations scribbled by old men, let us begin by considering books which purport to deal with legend—I beg your pardon: 'history.'

"Firstly, the more distant the epoch, the less a modern observer may hope to accurately and adequately represent not merely the events, but the mentality, of those days. And this is because their understanding of both are ineluctably shaped by whatever accounts they themselves have found in archives: accounts written by people who simply happened to live during those times.

"Scholars assume that these accounts are extremely reliable and accurate, but just how accurate is that assumption? After all, who is most likely to take the time and trouble to record contemporary events? Why, those who have something to gain by doing so. Only a very few will be motivated by the desire to preserve knowledge, since there isn't much money or fame in it."

"B'gods," Ahearn muttered, leaning toward Druadaen, "he talks just the way you do. Worse, even."

The dragon continued without pause. "Now, who is most likely to gain from such scribbling? Why, someone who can accrue power or money by crafting an account that convincingly presents one side in a dispute or conflict as being superior, or innately preferable, to the other."

Druadaen sighed. "So you believe that the accuracy and

objectivity of authors is made suspect by their personal motivations?"

"How could it be anything but? I have seen this phenomenon play out countless times. Let us say a historically faithful account is written. It may be rescribed once, maybe twice, but ultimately, the copies go up in flames during the next of your species' frequent upheavals. It is a rarity for any to remain after but a few slim centuries. Meanwhile, innumerable partisan diatribes from the same epoch endure because their reproduction was as prodigious and rapid as that of flies breeding in dung. An apt metaphor, actually."

Druadaen smiled. "For one who finds little of use in books, you seem to have made quite an extensive study of them."

The dragon's slow, answering smile grew very broad. "Ah," it said in a sly tone, "you have caught me." Druadaen nodded and discovered that it was impossible to see all those teeth and not think of being eaten. "And catching me out demonstrates what may be the best value of books: that if read properly, they do not fill the reader with fixed ideas, but rather, create a habit of interrogating them. And how can true change occur without that skill?"

A delighted grin had been slowly spreading across Ahearn's broad face. "Well," he said loudly when the great wyrm had finished, "I didn't expect to hear good, ordinary sense from such an extraordinary creature, but this has been a journey of many surprises. I am with you, wyrm; whatever value is to be found in books is vastly overrated. Action! Action is what is wanted!"

"That is not what I said," the dragon sighed, closing its eyes.

"How not? You told my mate here to act more and read less!"

"No, I am merely intimating that if he means to change what your species knows—or what it *does*—then it would be unwise to rely too uncritically on books, or to assume that greater antiquity implies greater accuracy. Or honesty."

"And how is that any different than saying a bloke mustn't let books or endless cogitation get in the way of what makes change happen: action?"

The dragon's voice took on an edge of irritation. "You mean well-reasoned 'action' such as yours? Murdering thinking beings in their warrens for the bounty on their heads or thumbs? Seeking 'great beasts' to slay for their presumed treasure? Roaming around the world with no greater goal or purpose than collecting the rubbish you see around me here?"

Ahearn was no longer smiling and had become quite red. "Well, then what's your idea of action?"

"Oh, I don't know. Maybe going to an uncrossable river and building a bridge. Going to an orphanage and being kind to a child. Or better still, going to a high mountain and learning to fly."

"'Learning to fly'? I don't have wings—or haven't you noticed?"

"I noticed. But I was hoping you wouldn't. At least not until you had taken that first, elucidating leap."

Ahearn crossed his arms and half smiled, half snarled. "Into the revelations of the great beyond, eh?"

The dragon glanced at him. "Despite your innumerable flaws, you do have a gift for banter. For that, I will overlook much. Now, all this chatter has tired me. I have fed adequately and exerted myself. I shall sleep. So should you."

"Why?"

"Because you are leaving tomorrow." Seeing their surprised looks, the dragon explained, "I am ensuring that you observe proper etiquette by not overstaying your welcome. You may thank me when I wake."

CHAPTER FIFTY-FOUR

From the first day at the cave, the fellowship had agreed that the only plausible threat when spending a night in a dragon's lair would be if the dragon itself decided to attack. In which case, you might as well die in your sleep. So they had reduced their watches to one person instead of two and enjoyed both more and deeper sleep.

Therefore, it was doubly startling when S'ythreni shook Druadaen awake. She didn't bother to whisper. "There's a large group on the plains. Settlers, from the look of them."

The others were rising as Druadaen buckled on his baldric. "How many?" he asked.

"And how far?" the dragon added, opening one eye to watch the humans ready themselves.

The aeosti had returned to the cave's rough apron, staring out over the plain. "Just over fifty, I think. Three are mounted. They stopped to camp about five miles south of the killing field."

"Well," sighed the dragon, "it seems some cow-lover saw my brief aerial display." It shook its head. "They grow more panicky by the month."

Druadaen shook his head. "I am truly sorry."

The dragon snorted. "I could not have gone much longer without leaving to gather my own food. And that would have entailed activities these herd-tenders would have found far more alarming,

494

I assure you." It stretched and rose. "No, detecting and reacting to me again after these many years was an eventual certainty."

"And what will you do?" asked Umkhira, who joined S'yth-reni at her post.

"*That* is far from certain, Lightstrider. But it shall surely be fateful."

Druadaen, head tucked as he thought, crossed his arms. "Do the settlers know of this lair?"

"No. They have only encountered me on the 'killing field.' They seem to presume, as their legends tell them, that my kind all lives far up in the mountains."

"At the Final Talon."

"Well, the *Dragon's* Talon, but yes. When we had plentiful game and little to worry from two-legs, those peaks were our home. But this time they are sure to find me here."

"Why?"

"Their path into the mountains passes near the base of this hill. They will surely notice the tracks and spoor of your mounts." It shrugged. "Now, I have but two choices. I can abandon this place and take refuge in a smaller, meaner cave I have already prepared. Or I shall fight and die here, and hope to be reborn into one of the eggs I have hidden at the other lair."

Druadaen nodded, head still down. "And where is this other lair located?"

The dragon tossed its powerful head to the east. "A long morning's ride. Or a long day on foot. Why does that matter?"

"Because I believe we can lead the settlers away from here and toward your other lair, instead."

The dragon's brow crackled as it furrowed. "How? You would do a very poor imitation of me, I think."

"That is true. But I suspect Ahearn could deliver an excellent impersonation of a heroic dragon hunter."

The swordsman blinked. "I could?" Then he smiled broadly. "Why, yes: I could!"

Druadaen nodded. "His accent is not from this region, but nor is it so unusual to be considered exotic or memorable. He grew up in Clearwall and Eld Shire, so the settlers will presume him to be exactly what he is: a Midlander. I, however, will conceal my accent by being his silent servitor."

"Oh," Ahearn exclaimed grandly, "I like *that* part!"

Druadaen smiled before he could stop himself. "We shall intercept the settlers, tell them we are tracking the dragon to its lair, and warn them against crossing the killing field. After all, the dragon is not only reputed to watch it, but its young are there and can warn it of intruders."

"Which will agree with their legends and beliefs." The dragon nodded. "Impressively reasoned...except for one small flaw: How will you convince them that *you* know where the lair is?"

"I won't have to convince them."

"And why is that?"

Druadaen smiled. "Because you are going to show them the way."

The dragon reared back. "I am prepared to be either very amused or very angry."

Druadaen shrugged. "Before Ahearn and I sneak down the hill and sweep around to approach the plains from the west, you will slip out of this cave. Using the cover of the remaining darkness, and staying behind the contours of the hill, you shall glide north. Come morning when the settlers resume their march, you will soar high and remain visible for half an hour. They will surely see you...and watch as you fly to your reserve lair."

"That rather defeats the purpose of finding a way *not* to encounter them, wouldn't you say?"

"No, because even if we wind up traveling with the three riders S'ythreni has seen among the approaching settlers, we will not reach your reserve lair until late in the day. So they will not have been close enough to see that you did not go into it, but remained outside, hiding behind the crest of that hill."

The dragon nodded, understanding. "So come nightfall tomorrow, I may glide back here unseen, courting the cover of the intervening heights. Very clever. But there is one last problem. I know where my lair is, but you do not. How will you guide the murderous mob to a place you have not seen?"

"I won't be guiding them."

"Then who shall?"

Druadaen smiled. "Ahearn. Because you will send an image of it to his mind."

Ahearn stared at Druadaen wide-eyed. "I don't like *that* part at all."

The dragon looked like it might become nauseous. "Nor I. Which may be the greatest understatement I have uttered this century. Perhaps ever. However, Dunarran, either your toil among archives has been helpful or you are to be congratulated on your powers of induction, because your assumption is correct: just as I can detect what is in a mind, I can also send messages and images into it."

The dragon stood suddenly. "Very well. We shall undertake this plan. It is well considered, and quite considerate, besides. Which reminds me, there is something I planned to bring to your attention before you departed."

It moved its tail slightly. The very tip of it pushed aside a ruined shield, revealing a sword. It was very long and very straight, but what Druadaen noticed most was its almost hypnotic brilliance. As if the light it reflected first went deep into the mirrorlike metal before being sent back in a concentrated form. He'd never seen its like before.

Except...

Druadaen glanced down at the bracer on his wrist.

"Yes," said the dragon.

The bracer unwound itself, becoming the velene. The transformation was unrushed this time, and the creature was content to remain on his arm.

Druadaen heard the others gathering near him. They, too, were apparently mesmerized by the otherworldly blade. "What battle, with what hero, brought this into your, er, collection?"

The dragon barely moved as it spoke. "It is not mine. You will note that I keep it separate from all other objects herein."

"I see that."

"It is special."

"So," Ahearn quipped, "it isn't more of your rubbish, then?"

The flat stare the dragon turned upon him was infinitely more unnerving than any of its more animated expressions or colorful threats. The sudden close of the swordsman's mouth made a faint *pop*.

Druadaen forced himself to look up from the blade. "You still have not said anything about the battle whereby it came to be here. I presume you do not wish to speak about it?"

"I did not speak about a battle because no battle was involved."

Druadaen frowned. "So, did you find it in your travels?"

"Quite the opposite. The one who had it found me. After long travels of their own."

Elweyr's question sounded a bit too eager. "So you were able to ambush him, take it without a fight?"

"Or did you catch him trying to steal from you?" S'ythreni added.

A ripple of annoyance briefly clouded the dragon's otherwise emotionless gaze. "The one who brought the blade was neither a warrior nor a thief. Merely a traveler."

"Who sought you . . . to what end?" Druadaen asked.

"To bring me the sword."

"That's quite a gift," Ahearn commented broadly.

"I did not say it was a gift. I said it was brought to me."

"Why?" Druadaen asked, uncertain he'd get an answer to so direct a question.

"I did not know." The dragon's eyes met the velene's briefly, then rose to meet Druadaen's. "Until now." Its tail drew fully back from the sword.

"Are you giving it to me?"

"It is not mine to give."

Druadaen frowned, then remembered that Shaananca had used a similar phrase to describe . . .

The velene was looking up at him with its silver-statue eyes.

"But I may take it?"

"If you wish and if it is allowed."

Druadaen was tempted to ask *allowed by who or what?* but decided to skip another round of cryptic answers. He stepped forward, grasped the hilt, and lifted the sword.

And almost swung it up over his head. It was light, phenomenally so for its length, which was just under that of a true hand-and-a-half sword. The hilt was a similar compromise between the kind found on a longsword and its longer cousin. But on closer examination, the blade's most peculiar feature was what it lacked: maker's marks of any kind. No master's stamp, no guild sigil, not even a single letter or icon giving a hint as to its owner or origin. "Does it have a scabbard?" he wondered, realizing a moment later that he had spoken it aloud.

The dragon had stepped well away from him. "It did not arrive with one." It shook its head slightly. "Well, I'm glad *that's* over. Now, if we mean to follow this plan of yours, we should make haste.

"Dunarran, you and the steel-waver have at most two hours to ride far enough to the west so that the settlers will believe that you are arriving from that direction. The other three must make their way north and then east through the hills beyond this one until they reach a position from which they may observe and, ultimately, rejoin you. And I must make my way toward the Dragon's Talon, flying low and then waiting until the sun is high enough so that I may be seen flying among the peaks and then returning to my other lair. But before we part..."

He turned to look at Druadaen. Dragons' eyes were so different from humans—or any other animals'—that they were difficult to read. But they seemed...concerned?

"Dunarran," it said quietly, "I offer a word of personal perspective on an inquiry you have not been able to pursue...yet. Bear this in mind: the lands and seas of Arrdanc may not be as new—or unchanging—as short-lived races believe. This could become a considerable complication the further you pursue your admirable quest for the truth of the world."

Druadaen swallowed at the onerous phrase that the dragon dropped almost casually: "the truth of the world." It sounded, and felt, like seeing an anvil plummeting out of the clouds at his upturned face. "Thank you for that warning. That topic is at the core of my next inquiry, as soon as I return to Tlulanxu to investigate the history and origins of Saqqaru."

The dragon nodded slowly. "An intriguing subject. But, unless things have changed greatly, you will not find answers in dusty repositories of 'knowledge.'"

Druadaen frowned. "Truly? An esteemed Saqqari scholar repeatedly traveled to the Archive to seek information on related matters. He has requested me to visit him in his homeland. Perhaps there, I will learn more about the mysteries you mentioned regarding both lands and seas."

The dragon looked away. "I suppose you may find some of what you seek by visiting the libraries of great nations. But still, I counsel you to seek out those places where ancient truths are not a matter of record but living memory. Such as Mirroskye." The wyrm glanced at S'ythreni.

She shook her head. "I cannot help him. I...I am not entirely welcome there."

"A pity." The dragon's eyes returned to Druadaen's. "Then you have little choice but to seek others who, by one means or another, have recollections of such early times."

"And where would I begin searching for such persons?"

The dragon smiled. "Even if I knew, I would not deny you the exhilarating experience of discovering that for yourself."

"Well, perhaps my researches at the Archive will give clues as to how I might find them."

The dragon sighed, closed its eyes. "I do not wish to unduly influence you—we must follow our own paths through the Great Skein of Fate—but I would be remiss if I did not share this." His tone became not merely serious, but dire. "Mark me well, Druadaen: you must not return to Dunarra. Not yet."

Druadaen was puzzled and intrigued, but he shrugged. "And yet, I must. I am still an Outrider and I am duty-bound to report what I have learned in my travels."

"Did they not free you of any obligation to return in the near future?"

If ever, Druadaen emended. "Well, yes, but they could not have foreseen how much I have learned. And a small amount of additional research at the Archive could produce exactly the direction needed to determine the next step of my—"

"Human. If further answers were to be found in the Archive, you would already know them. As for reporting what you have learned, is doing so worth the risk of being unable to ask further questions?"

Druadaen frowned. "And why—or how—would that happen?"

The dragon shook its head sharply. "I do not know. And if I did, I could not say. I only know that it *could* happen. Almost anything can, when one delivers oneself into the hands of a greater power. And if you return home and find yourself prevented—or worse yet, prohibited—from continuing your quest, you will have a stark choice: obey or break with your homeland. That might be one of the prices you must pay along your journey toward the truth of the world."

There's that soul-withering phrase again. And maybe there is something to the dragon's warning. But for now, I must do my duty as I understand—and feel—it.

Still, it never hurt to gather a little more information, and the dragon might be willing to share a helpful destination if Druadaen signaled that he might consider it as an alternative to returning to Tlulanxu. "So, if I should not be seeking answers in the archives of Dunarra, where should I be?"

"On a ship bound for Shadowmere."

"In Far Amitryea? I just came from there."

"Life is nothing if not a font of perpetual ironies."

"And what," Ahearn asked impatiently, "would we find there that isn't better found here?"

The purple eyes snapped toward the swordsman. "Well, firstly, you won't find yourself face to face with an increasingly annoyed dragon."

Druadaen smiled. "A situation I will be sure to avoid. That said, I have resolved that peril must not be an impediment to my quest."

"Oh, there will be peril aplenty for you in Shadowmere, Dunarran. Just not the same *kind* of peril."

"What do you mean?"

"I mean what I said earlier: that you will have to find those answers and discern those dangers by traveling there. Which cannot start until you leave here. And that cannot happen until your friends have the information necessary to carry out your ploy."

The dragon rose and approached Ahearn and Elweyr. "I will show you where you need to go, unfold what you need to know," it told them somberly. "Meet my eyes. Do not look away, and do not resist." For a moment, neither the humans nor the great wyrm moved. Then it turned away and the two humans started, Elweyr much more violently than Ahearn.

"There," it said, "that is done. And it is time for us to part."

It started to move toward the mouth of the cave and the night sky beyond it, but Ahearn jumped after him. "Ah, before you take flight, I was wondering..."

The dragon turned, eyes and voice suggesting that its patience was very limited. "Yes?"

Ahearn struck his trademark "reasonable man" pose: hands out in appeal, tentative smile on his mouth, concerned frown on his brow, and a calculating look in his eye. "Now, Yer Wyrmship, since you consider your cave to be filled with, er, rubbish, and since you find it so foul and unsightly, I suspect we'd be willing to remove some." He started fitting his actions to his words. "By way of showing our appreciation for your toleration and hospitality, of course."

"Put that down. Yes, it is rubbish. But it is *my* rubbish."

Ahearn looked crestfallen.

"However..."

The swordsman looked up, hopeful.

"If you should happen to find anything outside, I lay no claim to that."

Ahearn's face returned to its prior mournful state. "I'm afraid there's not much call for dead, burnt trees."

"Is that all that's there? Hmm. Well, better luck next time, perhaps." The dragon stepped out into the night, nose high, as if smelling the wind. Then, with an irritated shake that ran the length of its body, gold and silver coins once again showered down from where they had become caught in his scales. As the great wyrm smoothed its macled hide, Druadaen heard Ahearn gasp in what sounded like shocked bliss infused with ecstasy.

The dragon gathered its thighs for a reprise of the first mighty leap with which it had launched into its earlier flight, then stopped, looked back at Druadaen. "Regarding your tale of what occurred at the river with the Kar Krathauans and Caottalurans. From what I know of your species' mantics, an attack so determined and carefully planned as that one invariably grows from deeper roots than mere vengeance. As your associates have conjectured. So walk carefully. I would be annoyed if you did not come back to pester me again. It has been...moderately diverting."

In a rush of movement too fast for Druadaen's eye to fully capture, the great wyrm took off into, and was consumed by, the darkness. They heard one flap of immense, leathery wings. Then it was gone, and the night was still.

An instant later, Ahearn rushed out and started scooping up the coins that had rained out from between the scales of the dragon's hide, murmuring gleefully to himself.

Umkhira's already-packed kit was slung over her left shoulder. "What now?"

Druadaen nodded at Elweyr. "What did the dragon show you?"

Elweyr was packing his own kit in an uncharacteristic rush. "We go north and follow behind the next bank of hills. We'll be watching for you from the crest of the one with the best view of the eastern sward. When you show up there, we'll ride to join you."

Ahearn called from his determined search of the area in front of the cave. "Gotta hand it to wyrm-scales; he gives adequate directions."

Elweyr stared balefully at his friend's back. "Yes. The dragon didn't leave much to the imagination."

"I think it would be interesting to have my mind touched by a dragon's," S'ythreni mused.

Elweyr stared over his shoulder at her. "Trust me," he said in a hollow voice, "you wouldn't enjoy the experience."

Wondering at the difference in the two men's reaction to having their minds in contact with the dragon's, Druadaen put his hands on his hips as he thought aloud. "One last thing to settle; where do we go after—if—we manage to draw off the settlers?"

"Do you mean to take the dragon's counsel?" Umkhira asked.

"You mean, not to return to Dunarra?" Druadaen shrugged. "If I had a clear path, any path, elsewhere, I would certainly consider it. But as it is, I have none. So I suppose—"

"The wyrm mentioned Mirroskye," S'ythreni muttered.

Druadaen frowned. "Yes, but you said we are not welcome there. And I know from Shaananca and others in the Consentium that the Iavarain of Mirroskye are not in the habit of inviting outsiders to visit."

"I've heard the same. For years," Ahearn called over.

S'ythreni's eyes were aimed straight ahead, but whatever they were seeing was not present in the dragon's cave. "There's another way."

"Tell us on the trail," snapped Elweyr, slinging his pack roughly over his shoulder. "We all have a lot of ground to cover. So let's get out of this damned place."

PART SIX

CONUNDRUM: HUMANS

Given how varied and long this journey has been, I had come to presume that no event, no outcome, could be so unique or unexpected that novelty alone would justify inclusion in this journal. But just when one believes a thing to be impossible, that is when fate reminds them of the hubris of such presumptions. Thus it was with my ruse of leading the settlers away from the dragon, because every part of the plan's execution defied what I have come to expect.

Which is to say, the plan worked without flaw.

The weather was excellent: clear and temperate, but not so warm that it wearied our mounts. With never more than a single moon in the cloudless sky, we had just enough light to ride from landmark to landmark, but not so much that we were at risk of being seen. Neither of our groups encountered any troublesome species, and an hour or so after the sun cleared the horizon, the dragon appeared flying high over the mountains, the occasional flap of its wings like a black flag waving in the middle of the light blue sky.

The settlers, whose numbers had grown overnight, had just arrived at the edge of the killing field and were debating whether they should go through or around it when Ahearn and I came galloping in from the west.

Ahearn told the tale of our having learned that this was the creature that slew his grandfather. He followed that poignant revelation with warm inquiries about their communities, striking a perfect balance between ignorance of their region with enthusiasm for learning more about it and them.

Those winning ways—what Ahearn called his "common touch"—quickly secured their trust (and, from the younger women who comprised just under half of the contingent, more than a few furtive, encouraging glances). I suppose he was just foreign enough to be intriguing rather than off-putting. He spoke a wild mix of Commerce, Vallishan pidgin, and Midlander. Taken together, his exchanges with the settlers were just broken enough to convincingly resemble the conversational efforts of a foreigner, create a plausible impediment to detailed questions, and yet clearly communicate our shared purpose: to kill the dragon.

All the while, the settlers kept wary eyes on the distant, soaring wyrm. Although they never said so openly, it was pitiably clear that they were very glad indeed that we had showed up—which, for Kar Krathauans, was the equivalent of weeping in relief.

When the dragon finally broke off from its swooping and gliding, Ahearn stood resolute and impassive as the settlers' fear increased in direct proportion to the growth of the creature's silhouette. However, after spending several eager minutes watching it approach, he cried in frustration when it veered off and headed for a hill far to the east. He pointed his sword in that direction and called upon any settlers who were so inclined to follow him to its apparent lair.

It was agreed that we would go ahead with two of their riders to attempt to locate the presumed cave, assess the approaches and the beast's alertness, and perhaps determine a plan of attack for the morrow. At no point did the settlers stop to wonder if their hide and worsted clothes and motley assortment of hunting spears, shortswords, and wood axes were sufficient for dragon hunting. While one could not help but admire their bravery, it also invited one to doubt their faculties.

By the time we reached the hill five hours later, stealthily climbed up its slopes, and crept into the wide cave, it was obvious that the dragon had been there but left. The riders cheered; the dragon had been chased off! But Ahearn's response was a grim shake of his head. "He'll be back," he intoned like Fate itself. "And I mean to stay and see this through." Alone? the settlers wondered. If need be, he replied.

A rider went back to communicate this to the approaching mob which spent the rest of the day walking to reach the foot of the hill. A few returned to the cave with the rider who'd borne the message to them all. But eventually, as the sun started sinking, the throng began to disintegrate, groups of two and three breaking off to make their way back west. Between the vindication of believing themselves to have scared off the great wyrm, and the lurking dread that it might return, the rest of the settlers departed after waving solemnly to Ahearn, the hero of the hour.

As the sky began to darken in the east, the riders who'd remained became restless. The four young settlers who'd joined us—all young men and women with impressive physiques but dull affect—seemed less worried. However, they were very attentive to the opinions and intents of the two riders, who were both leaders of respected steadings.

Ahearn congratulated them all on their resolve and courage, encouraged them to take a few handfuls of coins—and then stopped in mid-exhortation, listening intently. When asked, he said in hushed tones that he thought he'd heard the swoop and flapping of immense wings. He listened some more, announced that he'd *probably* been mistaken, and returned to chewing on the dried meat the settlers had pressed upon us.

The settlers never fully recovered from that quick pulse of panic and its abrupt reminder of their actual situation: if they did not leave soon, they would be spending the night in the lair of a dragon that was still at large. After overtly studying the looks on their faces, Ahearn stood and nodded approvingly at them. It was important to live so that they could fight again another day, he said somberly. He and his armsman (me) were trained and equipped for the business of hunting a dragon. But they all had families to look after, or start, and valor could demand no more than they had already shown themselves willing to do this day.

It was a bravura performance. Ahearn's mix of common sense and praise was all the excuse they needed to leave, casting regretful looks back at the two lone figures waving farewell from the high ledge of the lair. Within the hour, we had brought our horses into the cave, provisioned them, and eaten what I believed to be the day's-end meal.

But Ahearn's brisk completion of all those tasks had not been motivated by a desire to be ready to move before first light. Rather than preparing his sleeping roll, he began double-layering it into a large bag. His purpose became evident when he began scooping coins into it.

I expressed concern over whether the dragon had intended to include this cave when he had told Ahearn that he was welcome to anything outside his lair. Without a break in his labors, he assured me that the dragon had included an image which made his approval quite clear.

I could not tell if the lack of detail in that explanation was an attempt to evade the matter, or a byproduct of his monomaniacal focus on finding every coin. Either way, there was no proving what the dragon had or had not shown him. Besides, for the wyrm's own good, as well as ours, we would soon be far away, and it was very unlikely to return to its now-disclosed emergency refuge.

We were up well before dawn, leaving behind a cave without a single coin in it, as well as at least two dragon eggs that we never discovered. We made directly for the untamed sward to the east and were joined by the other three of our fellowship shortly after noon.

From there, we rode southeast for six days. Halfway through that journey, the country became less flat and was spotted with lakes, some quite large. The Kar Krathaun regional maps were extremely accurate and kept us admirably oriented and on course. On the seventh day, the hills which marked the southern limit of our ride appeared precisely where we expected.

Another day brought us around the southern end of those highlands and so, to the falls that marked the headwaters of the Quickrun River. We resolved ourself to several days of travel in Vallishar.

It took three days to reach the northernmost frontier of Tavnolithar, where we were able to negotiate a reasonable fee for passage downriver on a livestock barge. It proved both a noisy and noisome trip, but the speed of our progress and the relief after almost a full moonphase in the saddle kept us in good cheer.

The one awkward moment came on the first morning, when I approached S'ythreni about the reason we had settled upon Tavnolithar in the first place: that, according to her, a person or persons in its port capital of Herres offered the best chance of finding a way into Mirroskye. I asked if we would be taking ship from Herres to Eslêntecrë, the Iavarain preserve's only open port, and only city on the sea.

S'ythreni did not look up. "I hope so. But more importantly, you are going to Herres to meet someone."

"Who?" I wondered. "Do we need to send a request ahead?" I presumed it was a person of some importance.

"No. That will not be necessary. And 'we' are not going to meet him. Just you."

I may have frowned. "Is this person a friend of yours?"

S'ythreni's reaction was not one I had ever thought to see in her: embarrassment, possibly shame. "No," she replied eventually, "he is not my friend. But he is a person whom you may trust. And who is likely to help you."

"He lives in Herres?"

"No."

"Then how do you know we will find him there?"

She looked away. "Because I know."

I did not press her to say more, and I do not think she would have. However, from the earliest tales right up to accounts written during the First Consentium, there is an ill-defined—or at least undisclosed—affinity between trees and the Iavarain that dwell among them. Of particular interest are reports of messages being relayed with great speed between those who dwell in sizable forests. However, those accounts seemed to imply that this had only been observed between the wooded domains of the highest and oldest of the Iavarain. Specifically, the ones whose bloodlines were not merely ancient, but reached back to the Til'Uulamantre who ruled before the sundering of their race. Or so it is said.

Shortly after breakfast on the fifth day aboard the barge, the walls and taller towers of Herres peeked above the onrushing flow of the Quickrun. It is typical of many cities that had to be rebuilt after the retraction of the First Consentium: polyglot architecture with a wide variance among the materials and quality of the buildings. Its walls were quite well maintained, though: a probable consequence of being located only five leagues from the southern tip of its old rival Vallishar.

As soon as we had arranged for lodgings, S'ythreni disappeared to make contact with the mysterious individual she had mentioned. In the meantime, we resolved to sell what gear we had retained from the ambush.

We hadn't even finished revising our inventory when S'ythreni returned and informed me that the meeting was arranged. When? I asked. Right now, she answered and led me to an old but well-kept house several streets back from the wharves. It stood slightly apart from the other homes and shops that crowded around it, with a margin on all sides. The unleaded glass windows on the ground floor all boasted inset images of colored glass: a wave, a tree, a sun, a cloud, a distant bird, a porpoise, a horse. All were stylized to give the impression of the object in motion, rather than in detail.

I turned to ask S'ythreni if I was to approach on my own, but she was already gone. A voice calling my name drew my attention back to the now-open door and a young person standing beside it. He or she bade me enter with a gesture. I nodded my thanks as I did.

I discovered a male Iavan sitting at a small table near a window I had not noted from outside—probably because from without, it looked like a wooden panel. He smiled as it caught my attention. "You might be surprised how often that has proven useful."

"I can only imagine," I rejoined with a slight bow. "I am Druadaen, but you have already learned that through our mutual acquaintance, Alva S'ythreni." One of his eyebrows raised at my use of the formal honorific. "I, however, am unable to greet you by name, since she did not share it."

He nodded, gestured toward the only other seat at the table. "Please sit." When I had, he nodded more deeply: what some call a "seated bow." "I am called Tharêdæath."

I think—well, I *hope*—I kept my lips from reforming the name silently. One of the things that all branches of the Uulamanthi still share is a refusal to reuse names, which, if it was still true, meant that I was sitting in the presence of an Uulamantre whose deeds had figured significantly early in the First Consentium. I performed an even deeper version of a seated bow. "I am honored."

He chuckled. "You appeared to be surprised, more than anything else."

"I did not immediately recognize your name." Which was partially true. "I have only heard it—well, *read* it—in the context of your female rebirthing during the First Consentium: Tharêdæa."

He smiled. "As reported, you are indeed a scholar. And a Courier. And an Outrider." There was mischief in his eye. "Have I left anything out?"

"Possibly a remittance man, too," I admitted.

He laughed. "And a self-deprecating sense of humor as well." He produced a carafe of wine from a black sideboard. I hardly noticed the almost greenish tint of the vintage; the black wood held my eye. It was made of ironpith, the same material as S'ythreni's crossbow. All our recently gained wealth could not have paid for half of it.

"Wine?"

"Thank you, but I must decline," I answered, remembering at the last second that in a first meeting with Iavans, one avoided the word "no" when refusing any offer or other courtesy.

He smiled approvingly as he poured a small measure into his tall, thin glass. "You have made a study of my people. Or are our ways still so thoroughly taught in Dunarra?"

I shrugged. "I had the benefit of being educated in Tlulanxu, where there is no shortage of docents who are well versed in both our earliest history and that of our ancient allies."

"And who inspire young men to ask troublesome questions. Or so it seems."

Druadaen smiled. "I have them to thank for an excellent education. I have only myself to blame for the purposes to which I have put it."

He nodded, rolled the wineglass between his palms. "Tell me about those purposes."

Tharêdæath had an even keener interest in my researches than the dragon. At least half a dozen times he stopped me so I might explain some point in greater detail or expand upon the deductions and inductions which had led from one discovery to the next. By the time I had finished, the colored outlines painted on the floor by the window-images had moved from the far western end of his sitting room and were edging into the eastern half.

He took a sip of his wine, then laid that hand flat upon the table. "There is a swift Uershaeli ship waiting at the King's Wharf. My retinue and I will be taking passage eastward. Given your researches and peculiarly propitious arrival, I think you might be well served to join us." He must have seen the hopeful look in my eye. "It is not going to Mirroskye. However, I suspect that will ultimately be to your advantage."

"I trust your judgment in this, naturally. But I do not perceive the benefits you do."

He smiled. "It would be most disconcerting if you could. You have arrived at an auspicious time. Within the week, a Corrovani ship will find mooring in Herres' harbor, discharge two passengers on a skiff, and then depart. One of those passengers is an Uulamantre of my generation, lately a guest and advisor in the Citadel of the Urn Wardens at Araxor."

I remember becoming a bit light-headed: two Uulamantre whose lives reached back to the First Consentium, if not farther. "And the other passenger?" I remember murmuring.

"One of the Citadel's Greyblades."

When the imminent arrival of storied persons and famous orders of warriors start getting woven into one's casual chat with an ancient Uulamantre in his sitting room, there comes a moment when it is hard to believe that any of it is real. Or at least, real within the scope of one's own mundane existence. I abruptly felt outside myself, as though I was looking in upon the affairs of the great and the powerful or a scene from some tale of legend.

But then I was back behind my own eyes and nodding. "I was not aware that the Greyblades had endured as an order."

Tharêdæath shrugged. "Their heart and their name is the nation's, and vice versa. If one ceases to exist, it is likely the other will follow shortly. But all this is by way of underscoring why we may not go to Mirroskye, at least not at this time. Rather, we are responding to a summons from the Great Pool: to render aid determining the fate of a ship that was bound for Eslêntecrë. We know nothing else, but may be certain of this: if the matter was not grave, we would not be asked to sail to the other side of the continent."

"The other side of Ar Navir? Is that where the ship was lost?"

Tharêdæath's green eyes did not blink. "Eight miles out from the city you call Tlulanxu."

I remember that as the moment when I could no longer be surprised by whatever I might learn next. I remember him explaining that it was in fact an Iavan ship, which should have been invulnerable to mundane foes. Consequently, mancery or miracles were strongly suspected.

It also meant that someone or something of importance had been on that ship. Not because it was in Tlu'Lanthu, he explained (using the Uulamantre name for the city), but because the vessel was a-sea at all. Mirroskye sent fewer and fewer ships out upon the oceans because doing so invited contact, and contact was increasingly troublesome for the Iavarain: a tantalizing comment upon which he did not expand.

"So," I conjectured when he finished, "by proposing to bring me back to Tlulanxu, are you suggesting that my further endeavors would be best served by returning to the resources of the Archive's Reserved Collection?"

He shook his head. "No. I agree with your ancient friend in the mountains." That was a euphemism we had adopted for the dragon. "However, there is someone in Tlu'Lanthu who might make a brief—perhaps incognito—visit worthwhile. The Hidden Archivist."

I frowned. "The who?"

"The Hidden Archivist. Is that not your name for our curator who tends the ancient vaults?" Seeing the confusion in my face, he stopped. "I apologize, Druadaen. I have made a grave error and jeopardized you in doing so.

"When you suggested you might return to the Reserved Collection, I presumed you were privy to all of its secrets. And the presence of the Hidden Archivist is its greatest secret, about which I may not say more. Pray do not reveal to others what I have inadvertently revealed to you."

That only increased my confusion. "What can I possibly reveal, other than the term 'Hidden Archivist'?"

"Nothing, but that would be more than enough to cause considerable difficulties for all involved. At any rate, while I cannot presume to speak for him, I suspect he would be willing to speak to you. Intrigued, possibly. It is hard to say, with him." He stopped, mused, "And there may be an even more useful opportunity on our way there."

"I am amenable to whatever you suggest."

Something about my reply (maybe the speed and certitude with which I said it) made him smile and lean across the table, declaring plans like a Legion's Pretor. "Excellent. You must be ready to sail with us tonight since we cannot know when the Corrovani ship will arrive and we cannot delay our departure once it has."

"Honored Tharêdæath—"

"Tharêdæath is quite sufficient."

"Eh, very well, Tharêdæath: it is my keenest desire to join you, but I may not do so in good conscience unless there are enough berths for my companions, as well."

He waved a long, graceful hand. "Naturally. S'ythreni communicated not only the nature of your travels, but your fellow travelers. They are not merely allowed; they are very welcome."

"Thank you!" I started to rise. "I will approach the Uershaeli captain at once to pay our passage—"

His smile told me that I should stop talking. His hand waved me to sink back into my seat. I did both.

"Allow me to clarify; I have hired the ship for the duration of our journey. And it is you who are honoring us with your company, not the other way around. However, while we wait for the Corrovani vessel, it is best that you quit your lodgings promptly."

"Why?"

He frowned. "Your ancient friend in the mountains is quite correct: Sanslovans do not lavish resources on a single individual's act of vengeance. And even if they did, Kar Krathauans would not be party to such pettiness. Something else is afoot. I doubt either power is watching for you in Herres, but there is no reason to risk detection, particularly since there is ample space for all of you right here. I will have your friends summoned discreetly and their effects brought shortly after."

He called in his assistant (?) to take notes as he bade me describe the rest of my companions, the approximate total of each one's effects, the goods and mounts we had intended to sell and for what sums. He felt our prices were reasonable, but that we would have been hard put to get them since we were transients who obviously meant to leave in short order. He offered to purchase them from us at a rate of twelve silver for every ten we had meant to get from the city's merchants. I agreed immediately and he instructed his silent aide to have our payment ready by the evening. In gold. After months of relentless penury, it seemed that the avatars of fortune could not stop smiling upon us.

When all the arrangements were finished and Tharêdæath had sent his assistant to settle them, he poured another two fingers of wine and contemplated it. When he finally spoke, he did so in a tone of careful detachment. "If you are amenable, I would offer candid advice about your further researches. I would also suggest an unlooked-for opportunity to realize them."

I knew from his tone that this would be the conclusion of our conversation. I also discerned that he was setting aside his own reservations by broaching these topics: a signifier of both their importance and sensitivity. That is probably why I remember those last few minutes of our meeting with extraordinary precision. Or perhaps it's because I dream of them often, every second possessing the same crisp fidelity as the actual conversation.

"I agree with your ancient friend," Tharêdæath began. "You can no longer rely on books alone. Perhaps not at all, now. If you wish to proceed further, you must have direct access to memories of those times, not narratives constructed decades or even centuries afterward."

I smiled. "It sounds as though you heard the advice tendered by my ancient friend. Word for word."

If he heard the lighthearted irony of my comment, he neither acknowledged it nor replied in kind. "I am an Uulamantre," he answered with a shrug. "Our experience resonates with that of your ancient friend. We hold in memory what most of the world now considers legend, myth, or fairy tales for children. You are lucky to have made its acquaintance. Few beings live such long lives."

I nodded. "Meaning I am doubly lucky, for now I have met two of you."

This time, Tharêdæath smiled. "It is refreshing to talk with Dunarrans of your type."

"What type is that?"

"As you were in ages past. Before the burdens of empire weighed down the exuberance that shone from your young souls and illuminated the world. But that could not last. Even in the act of rising, the sun mutely proclaims that it will one day set."

"Of course, the sun *does* always rise again."

"True, but it is never exactly the same sun. Yours—Dunarra's— is no different. In succumbing to the arrogance of empire, and now the decrepitude of isolation, your nation's sun has passed its zenith. It does not matter that you call it a Consentium and that its governance does, in fact, conform to that label. That neither changes its place in the world nor how others see it: as an empire. But it is not beyond possibility that your people could rise anew. After all, it is the exception which makes a rule."

He studied the faintly green wine in his long, delicate glass and his tone became improbably casual, almost disinterested. "There is a place we shall pass on our way to your homeland. It strikes the eyes as a small archipelago of mesas. In fact, it is the remnant of a sizeable land; it was less than a continent yet more than an island. Even less of it has remained in lore. It is now merely an enigmatic reference in a few tomes, a name for which there is no longer a corresponding place." His eyes came to rest upon mine.

Encouraged, I asked, "And what is there?"

"Ruins. And in them, memories."

When I frowned at that puzzling turn of phrase, he laughed lightly. "Even the most soulful Dunarrans have a streak of literalism where they should keep a spark of poetry. I will be plain: there is a library in those ruins. A library almost completely untouched since the cataclysm which shattered that land."

"So the documents there are contemporary to the epoch most pertinent to my researches."

"Precisely. They have not been filtered and distorted by the ages. They are the day-to-day accounts and impressions of those who lived at that time, not self-important tracts and treatises."

"I suppose it is too much to hope," I ventured carefully, "that anyone would still know the approximate location of this library."

"It is indeed too much to hope," Tharêdæath agreed. "And yet, that too would be the exception that makes the rule...no?"

That was almost six weeks ago. We departed two days later and had fine weather, particularly once we entered the tropics. We were joined by another ship, this one recently arrived from Far Amitryea and about which I could learn nothing more; even the usually forthcoming Tharêdæath demurred sharing any details. Presuming he had any to share. It runs no standard and sends no messages. It never comes closer than a mile, but it never strays beyond two.

And today, just as the light was failing and the first moon appeared like a round ghost in the indigo sky, I caught sight of the islands of which Tharêdæath had spoken. They appeared above the horizon the way distant tablelands might above a plain: flat, squarish objects that rose up sharply from the water, their dusty sides bronzed by the setting sun behind us. And on one of the closest, I am told, an ancient library awaits us.

Whatever it might hold, I am filled with both anticipation and foreboding at the change it might bring to my researches. And even my life.

Including, quite possibly, the end of both.

CHAPTER FIFTY-FIVE

It was quite easy to navigate the archipelago that had once been the land of Imvish'al. The gaps between its various fractured parts were wide, and what remained was without banks or shores or even shallows. Shoals were few and far between.

The tops of the islands were several hundred yards above rolling swells and did not slope down to the water at all; they descended directly into it. Wherever the waves and currents were strongest and unrelenting, the once sheer sides had become concave, the brim of the land above now hanging over open water.

As Druadaen finished arranging the fit of his armor, Ahearn came to stand alongside him. "It's like looking at the remains of a child's puzzle," he mused as they waited for the skiff that would carry them to "Library," one of the few named islands in the archipelago.

Umkhira turned away from her somber study of the towering tan-ochre masses. "It is very strange. I have been watching for any sign that these island-buttes are made of unusually hard rock, but their sides are too regular for that. Also, they show layers of different kinds of stone."

Druadaen nodded, asked, "And what does that tell you, Umkhira?"

"It tells me that these objects are not simply what has been left behind after wind and water has worn at them. Because if so, the softer layers would be more eroded."

"You are quite correct, Lightstrider," said Tharêdæath as he emerged from the sterncastle. "Their peculiar shape is not the result of natural forces."

"So...*super*natural forces, then?" quipped Ahearn with a hint of seriousness at the end.

The ancient Uulamantre shrugged. "I may not say."

Ahearn's frustrated frown made it necessary for Druadaen to smother a grin. Using the phrase "I may not," Tharêdæath could have meant, "don't know" or "I am not allowed," and the Iavarain clearly had no intention of clarifying which he had intended.

S'ythreni was squinting at the side of Library. "There seems to be a set of flat rock outcroppings that follow upward all around its core, like a ragged spiral staircase." She lowered her eyes slightly as she glanced toward the Uulamantre. "Til'A'Thruadëre, I would ask: Have you knowledge of their origins?"

He smiled at her. "Be at your ease, Alva S'ythreni. I am not one to judge you, neither before nor now. You may speak less formally. But in the matter of those structures, I only have conjecture, not knowledge."

"Til'A'Thru—er, Tharêdæath, would you be willing to share those conjectures with your guests?"

He nodded slightly, staring at the islands. "From the first time I saw these islands—and I have only been here twice before—those climbing platforms were present. Since these islands have never known inhabitants, construction, or vegetation since the Cataclysm reduced Imvish'al to these fragments, those stepped platforms cannot be the product of mundane engineering.

"However, it is equally clear that they are not the result of natural forces. The other two named islands—Mastaba and Nursery—have similar structures. No others do. So I must conjecture that these were created by an immense, if crude, application of *manas*."

"So it *was* mancery," Ahearn breathed.

"No," Elweyr corrected quickly, with a nervous glance at the Uulamantre. "Not in the way you mean it."

Tharêdæath nodded. "This was not achieved by the casting of mantic cognates nor any form of dweomancy or even deistic miracles. It is conceivable—barely—that a broad array of such forces could be harnessed to create what we see before us, but then the shapes of the ledges and the islands themselves would have been more regular, more precise. These have the appearance of elemental transformations."

Elweyr goggled. "At *this* scale?"

Tharêdæath shrugged. "Many of the feats that now sound impossible were once living realities. We are speaking of the time when great dragons vied for power with nations, when chthonic direkynde and cryptigants still roamed, barely held in check." He nodded at the crude staircase. "Their powers were great but crude. Just as we see here." He stepped back from the gunwale and added, "I will tell the quartermaster to furnish you with climbing gear. Unless my eyes are becoming unreliable, I believe the path upward may not be as congenial as it looks from here."

"You climb pretty well," S'ythreni called from below. "For a human."

"A skill from my misspent youth," Druadaen chuckled down at her.

"I cannot picture that," she muttered.

"So you can't imagine me running from rooftop to rooftop?"

"No. I can't imagine you having anything vaguely like a 'misspent youth.'"

He didn't reply, in part because he had to focus on the tricky task of traversing a gap where one of the stone platforms had fallen away. But he also couldn't think of a valid rebuttal. *Was I really that boring, or was I just that cautious?* he wondered as he boosted from one handhold to the next, dislodging a few pebbles as he checked the seating of the piton he'd just placed.

"Hey! Watch what you're doing!" shouted Ahearn from even further below. A loud guttural grumble conveyed Umkhira's similar opinion of being beneath the tumbling chips of stone.

"Just about there," Druadaen shouted down and pulled himself up the rest of the way. Setting another piton quickly, he searched the sloping surface of the platform and found a startlingly convenient spot to tie off the guide rope and belaying lines. "All is secure," he shouted, glancing upward. The rest of the climb was comparatively simple: just navigating the giant-sized staircase to the top of the island-butte.

He spooled down the belaying lines and stood ready to assist the others. S'ythreni had stopped near where he'd secured them. "When were you going to mention this?" she asked.

"When the others are safely up here."

"Sensible," she conceded and stood with him, ready to assist.

But the others made the rest of the ascent safely, Ahearn being the last to clamber over the edge. "Well, I won't be disappointed if we don't have to do *that* again," he muttered, just before noticing that Elweyr and Umkhira were looking down at something in the seam between the platform and the sheer side of the rock column. He joined them, stared, turned back toward Druadaen. "The place you fixed this piton—that hole was already there, wasn't it?"

"Yes, but it had this in it." Druadaen held up a weathered bronze ring.

"So much for being the first ones here," the swordsman muttered sourly.

"Well," S'ythreni mused, "maybe that's today's 'disturbing surprise.'" She looked around the group. "There has to be at least one, right?"

Elweyr stared at her in something like pity and disgust. "I never thought I would have reason to say this...but you are revoltingly optimistic."

She smiled at him, then stuck her tongue out.

Druadaen looked up toward the lip of the tableland. "Either way, we can't know if there are more surprises until we get to the top. So let's hope for the best." But he kept his caveat to himself: *There's a first time for everything, I suppose.*

A skull glared at them as they came over the crest. It was resting in a fissure just a few yards beyond the lip, brown with age. The actual head had been smaller than any of theirs, but the shape was distinctly human.

"Well, that's reassuring," Elweyr muttered.

They found a few more ancient bones lying in other nearby gaps in the rock, along with a badly weathered bronze knife blade. Except for the tang, nothing remained of the hilt at all. It wasn't hard to imagine what had happened to it and the rest of the bones: the wind blowing atop the barren tableland had carried everything else over the side. The only exceptions were objects trapped in depressions so deep that even gales could not sweep them clean.

But Tharêdæath's assessment of the islands was correct: neither people nor vegetation had intruded since the sundering that created them. Library was flat, dusty, and featureless, except for a few low stone ridges and lumps some distance in from the edge. The other nearby island-mesas differed only in that their tops showed no such variations at all.

Leaning into the intermittent gusts, they made their way to Library's only landmark and discovered it to be the knee-height remains of a temple, worn down to the stereobate and a few wind-smoothed nubs of stone objects embedded around it.

"I think," Ahearn announced, "that the library may not be open today."

Druadaen tried to grin but the wind blew dust and grit into his teeth. "Tharêdæath mentioned ruins. Underground."

"And he was right," called Elweyr, who had stopped at one of the stone nubs. The size and shape reminded Druadaen of an outsized capstan. He knelt down and traced a finger along the seam where the rock met the ground. The wind blew new dust into the line he'd cleaned, but before it did, they saw that the stone had a metal rim and that a small amount of dust disap-peared down into the narrow seam between it and the ground.

"Odd way to get into a library," Ahearn muttered.

Elweyr shook his head. "This was a secret entrance." He glanced toward the almost vanished stone rectangle of the temple's base and smiled. "The library is under there."

"How can you be so certain?" asked Umkhira.

Druadaen smiled. "Before the modern age, many human nations were strict theocracies. The palimpsests of that time speak of scholars being exiled, imprisoned, even burned with their tomes and scrolls."

Ahearn smiled. "So where better to put a secret library than right beneath their arses. Oh that's rich, if true."

"Let's find out," said Elweyr, who rocked the stone gently, sensed where there was a bit of wobble, and pushed hard in that direction.

He almost fell into the hole that was revealed. The nub did not ease down into the ground; it swung rapidly out of the way, as if mounted on a loose, well-greased hinge. A dark set of spi-ral stairs descended into the darkness. "Glad we still have those bull's-eye lanterns," Elweyr muttered as they pulled him back up.

"And *my* eyes," S'ythreni said. "Tie a rope on me and stand aside."

✧   ✧   ✧

Twenty feet below the surface, the spiral staircase ended in a broad landing carved out of the surrounding rock. To one side, a much wider straight staircase continued down. On the other side was an alcove housing the secret entrance's mechanism—although that was a charitable term for it. It was a simple counterweight, actuated by an egg-shaped block of exaggerated proportions. When enough force was exerted, the change in balance caused it to roll, pulling the entry's stone cap with it.

Druadaen examined it, admiring the simplicity of the arrangement. "Ingenious," he said.

"Dangerous," S'ythreni countered. "That cursed stone flung itself away so quickly, Elweyr could have broken his neck."

Umkhira frowned. "So maybe it was crafted to kill intruders who did not know enough to lean away when it opened."

"I think there's another explanation," Druadaen said, pointing out the device's simple connections and counterweights. "This was designed to move something much heavier. So what has changed is the weight of the stone. The wind has probably worn it down to a fraction of its original size." He frowned. "But that means the actual entry would have been somewhat higher. It probably involved some kind of pedestal with a false bottom that could turn—"

"Druadaen?"

"Yes, Ahearn?"

"Maybe we should go find that library now."

CHAPTER FIFTY-SIX

Druadaen had just begun wondering if the journey to the bottom of the stairs might require several whole days when they came to the first landing. And the first skeletons. Or rather, what was left of them.

Elweyr passed the lantern to Druadaen, who sheathed what the others had started calling his "dragon-sword" and drew his shortsword instead. Once Elweyr had relaxed into a better posture from which to construct thaumates, he glanced at the remains. "Since the bodies were never removed, I'm guessing the invaders must have won."

Ahearn shouldered his sword as he kneeled to get a closer look. "I don't think there were any invaders. Their gear is all the same, more or less." He picked up a bronze shortsword with a wide, leaf-shaped blade. Its hilt was intact, although the leather wrapping on the grip crumbled at his first touch.

Elweyr frowned. "So maybe these were rebels and loyalists who killed each other during a coup?"

Ahearn shook his head. "I'd bet more than spare coin that what killed these poor bastards didn't use a weapon to do it: no sword marks on the bones. They're all in pieces. Splintered."

"Broken apart for the marrow?" Umkhira's tone was matter-of-fact.

Ahearn looked up. "No: by the force of the blow. Or, judging from the marks, the bite." He stood again, gesturing around them. "And see? They're all lying in a fan, just as they came down to the landing. Or backed up to the stairs maybe, because there are none on the down-side."

Umkhira nodded. "They were killed by enemies that came up from below."

Druadaen frowned. "Since there are no remains of the attackers, perhaps it was just one large enemy." He considered the dark maw where the staircase continued its descent and raised the bull's-eye cover: the narrow beam winked away, was replaced by a wide circle of light. He shook his head at Ahearn's irritated glance. "The beam was just as likely to give us away. It is more important now that all of us can see all our surroundings. Particularly since Umkhira's eyes are unlikely to see much contrast down here."

She shrugged. "Druadaen is correct; all things are the same temperature. And the river ambush taught us that we cannot rely on my eyes alone. We could miss many important details."

"You mean, like this?" Elweyr asked.

They turned to discover the thaumantic standing near the wall, looking at a vertically mounted crystal tube. He glanced back across the landing, pointed at a matching tube on the opposite wall. "I wonder what—?"

"Step away," snapped S'ythreni.

"Wha—?"

"Step away! There's light growing inside it!"

Ahearn squinted at the tubes. "I can't see anyth—oh!"

An extremely faint glow was now visible inside each tube, running from the top to the bottom.

"I started noticing them a while ago," S'ythreni said. She returned the stares of the others. "They just appeared to be a strange kind of cresset," she muttered. "Something that would protect a flame against wind or damp."

Druadaen studied the faint green glow. It was growing slowly, but also, very evenly. *I wonder...?* He glanced at Umkhira. "Is it getting warmer?"

She shook her head. "If so, I cannot see it."

Druadaen looked to Elweyr, who had raised his palm and was frowning. "No *manas*, either."

"So," Ahearn said, frowning. "If it's not flame, and it's not mancery—?"

"—then it's either a chemical that is reacting to the light. Or—"

"—or small animalcules, the kind that glow in the sea," S'ythreni interrupted, peering very closely at the tube. "It is filled with liquid. Maybe they *are* reacting to our light."

"Or," continued Druadaen, "maybe they are reacting to our movement. Elweyr got close to it just a few moments after I took the sleeve off the lantern. Either could have caused it to react."

"Assuming it's not reacting to something else," S'ythreni muttered darkly.

Ahearn stared at her. "Such as?"

"Food. By which I mean, us."

Elweyr sighed. "I think I liked you better as an optimist."

No one even smiled.

Druadaen and Ahearn exchanged glances. The swordsman shrugged, looked away. "Up to you."

Druadaen nodded. "From here, the decision must be up to each individual: go down or go back. I must continue. But whichever you choose, my high opinion of you will remain unaltered." He allowed himself a small grin. "Well, that is not entirely true. My opinion of you *will* change if you go back: I will know that you are eminently sane."

Smiles sprang up.

Ahearn rolled his eyes. "Godsblocks, will yeh just muzzle yerself and *lead*?"

The stairs seemed endless. As did the corpses.

The lower they went, the more crystal tubes started glowing to light their way, and the more landings they found littered with the bodies of those who had descended before.

The remains became steadily more substantial. The skeletons that predominated at first slowly gave way to desiccated corpses, some of which were largely intact. They were also increasingly varied in terms of their origins. One landing was filled with bodies dressed in crumbling furs, half of whom carried copper and even stone weapons. The very next held remains of several different species, all accoutred in fine gear, including one Iavan wearing perfectly preserved sheath armor. S'ythreni murmured her respects but increased her pace, impatient to reach the bottom of the stairs.

What they discovered there, almost an hour after beginning

their descent, was strangely anticlimactic: a single body, mummified by the dry air, leaning against the open half of a wide brazen portal. In one hand it held the jagged remains of a broken vial, whereas the other had ossified into a literal death grip around the hilt of a broadsword.

Druadaen asked Elweyr to light the second lantern and, once that was accomplished, slid the bull's-eye sleeve back into place on his own. He shone the beam into the dark beyond the portal.

A vast chamber, with broad-bellied pillars. From what little they could see, they and the walls had both been painted. In the case of the latter, there seemed to be designs, or possibly frescoes, layered between wide bands of color.

"Well," murmured Elweyr, "no bodies, at least."

"We haven't seen the whole room, yet," countered S'ythreni.

"Ah, *there's* yer natural optimism shinin' through, High-Ears," Ahearn whispered. But he made no move to cross the threshold. "Of course, there's no reason to be hasty." He held up a hand when Druadaen made to slip past him into the room. "That goes for you, too, mate. We've come this far; we can wait a few minutes while Elweyr uses a bit o' mancery to see more of what's inside."

But Elweyr was shaking his head. He pointed up at the portal's ornate lintel; sigils streamed along it like an arabesque of engraved serpents. "A warding barrier."

"Well, can't yeh get past it?"

Elweyr sounded as though his molars were clenched. "Not without knowing more about the constructs that are bound into it. I know the characters—well, some of them—from the surviving fragment of the earliest known thaumantic codex."

"How old?" Druadaen asked.

"Pre-First Consentium, pre-Ballashan. So, twenty-four hundred years. At least."

Druadaen found Ahearn's arm stretched out in front of him yet again. "All the more reason to be all the more careful," he said patiently, but firmly. "For all we know, that portal could do more than just keep Elweyr's mancery out. It could give us a lethal love tap if we try to cross it."

"Let's not debate this, Ahearn."

"Ah, then if we're not to discuss, let's remember who's the captain when we're making decisions of the moment, yeh? So it's my judgment that—"

He flinched as Druadaen's bracelet unfurled itself into the velene, already on the wing. It flitted through the portal into the darkness beyond.

"Now that's not fair!" Ahearn muttered, leaning into Druadaen's face.

Who smiled. "It wasn't my doing, but I think we can enter safely, now." He led the way.

There were no remains in the room, but Druadaen hardly noticed that. The size of a small arena, the frescoes on its longest, facing walls were divided into two narrative threads, each of which spanned multiple generations, possibly multiple centuries. Running parallel to those walls were two rows of the portly columns, bracketing a wide walkway that ran from the center of the smaller wall on their left to the center of its counterpart to the right. But it was what waited at the end of those two walkways that fixed Druadaen's attention.

In the center of the left wall was a set of narrow yet immensely tall doors. Druadaen could not read the flowing script that ran up one side of their marble frame and down the other, but the lintel clearly communicated the nature of the room beyond; it was a single slab of white marble carved in the shape of an open scroll, the bells at the ends of the two rods glinting gold in the lantern light. Surely they had found the library that gave the island its name.

But at the end of the walkway that led to the right-hand wall there was a much more enigmatic structure: a perfectly round, sigil-wreathed portal that opened unto darkness. And directly in front of it was a perfectly round pool of exactly the same dimensions, cut into what appeared to be a gigantic block of onyx that protruded just a few inches above the level of the floor, thereby providing a slightly raised rim.

"I do not like that," Umkhira almost growled when she saw the strange structure to the right.

As they approached it, they discovered that the pool was filled with an almost opaque amber liquid.

"I like *that* even less," Ahearn muttered, staring at the still surface. "Although I can't exactly say why."

Druadaen nodded. "I can. From extensive personal experience, I can tell you one thing about all that liquid."

"What's that?"

He turned and pointed. "It doesn't belong anywhere near books or scrolls." Seeing their long-suffering looks, he shook his head. "You misunderstand. My concern is not that it constitutes any immediate danger to the library. Rather, I am concerned that those who built this library placed it here *at all*. It was not merely illogical for them to put a reservoir so near their collection; it is disturbingly perverse."

The velene sped past his nose, swooped until it had his attention, and then glided straight to the library doors. Where it landed and sat. Patiently.

Druadaen nodded. "Let's get what we came for and then get back to the ship."

As with the secret entrance now far above them, the tall doors proved extremely easy to open, thanks to a clever counterweight system concealed within the walls. And if Tharêdæath had been mistaken in asserting that the ruins had never been entered before, his assertion proved to be correct about the library itself: it was undisturbed and pristine. Even the ladders to reach the uppermost shelves still stood ready, although they collapsed at first touch.

However, to call the storage space "shelves" was a misnomer. Rather, they were row upon row of stone gridworks. The square cubbies along the bottom were largest, those at the top the smallest, and just below each, three symbols had been incised into the rock. So, the room had at least ten thousand separate receptacles for scrolls. And almost all of them were full.

Elweyr's calculations matched Druadaen, leading him to assert that it would take the two of them weeks, maybe months, to track down mentions of Saqqaru. And although both of them had basic facility in a number of the ancient and dead languages which no doubt predominated in the collection, there were almost certainly others in which they had no skill or had never seen before. In short, the mantic concluded, they couldn't do more than sample a few hundred in the hope that they would be lucky to run across something that one or the other of them recognized as pertinent.

Although Druadaen had not expected so massive a collection, he had foreseen the problem of translation and held a thoroughly modern scroll out toward the mantic. "Here," he said, "use this."

"What is it?" Elweyr said, face screwing up as he scanned

down the unfamiliar words and, in some cases, unfamiliar character sets.

"The words for 'Saqqaru,' 'Cataclysm,' and two or three others in all the languages Tharêdæath and I knew which date back to the approximate time that Imvish'al was sundered. That includes predynastic Saqqari." He stared up at the stone gridworks surrounding them. "The code on each receptacle seems to progress as would numbers."

Elweyr glanced at the characters chiseled beneath each block in the nearest grid. He nodded. "So they had a directory of some kind. But unless we can find the directory—and read it—it does us no good."

Druadaen smiled and pointed to three nearby marble lecterns, gestured to others further away. "Unless I miss my guess, we'll find a copy of the main codex at all or most of them. Assuming at least one doesn't turn to dust the moment we touch it, we can scan the entries for the words on the list I just gave you."

Elweyr raised an eyebrow. "Well, the sooner we get to it, the sooner we'll have some idea of how long this is going to take. And then we'll have to find out if Tharêdæath can keep his ship waiting that long."

Which echoed Druadaen's greatest worry from the moment he'd seen the size of the library: whether their Iavan patron would ironically be the one who had to call a halt to the process of discovery he himself had enabled. Which simply reprised life's one indisputable lesson:

That Fate's favorite tool was irony.

CHAPTER FIFTY-SEVEN

"Hey, Philosopher," shouted Ahearn from the rim of the pool at the far end of the main chamber, "I think you'll want to see this."

Druadaen glanced at the promising scrolls two cubbies above him, sighed, and abandoned the precarious perch from which he had hoped to reach them. "What is it?" he shouted back as he began approaching down the walkway.

S'ythreni was standing beside Ahearn. "Something...strange."

Not reassured by the tone in her voice, Druadaen ran the rest of the way—and skidded to a stop when he saw what they were staring at.

The amber liquid in the pool was rising. Rapidly. And as it did, it became increasingly obvious that it was not anything like water; it had a viscosity almost half that of rapeseed oil. No wonder they hadn't been able to see the bottom of the pool. "When did this start?"

Ahearn shrugged. "Can't say for sure. It was very slow at first, so slow I didn't notice."

S'ythreni was staring down into the pool, squinting. "It began shortly after you and Elweyr opened the codex you found. At least, that was the first time I heard the gurgling."

"What gurgling?" asked Ahearn.

"The gurgling which I guess you *still* can't hear."

Druadaen saw the hint of incoming ripples where the liquid

entered through the portal in the wall. "Any better sense of where that leads?"

"Downward," S'ythreni said. "The ceiling of the tube starts sloping down after five yards. After thirty more, it disappears under the liquid." She wrinkled her nose at it.

"Do you detect an odor?" Druadaen asked.

She shook her head. "No, but that is what's strange. Water may not have a scent of its own, but it always carries one. Whether the brine of the sea or rain on the trees or the dank of a leaky cellar, you almost always know if there's water around because it spreads the smell of what it has touched. But this"—she shook her head again and took half a step away from the still-rising fluid—"nothing. Although the color is changing."

Druadaen saw it a moment later. "It's becoming more yellow. And more opaque."

Ahearn fingered the hilt of his sword. "So what do we do?"

Druadaen looked back at the library doors. They were solid, but hardly watertight. If the liquid kept rising, it would eventually spread all the way across the room and get under them.

S'ythreni looked at him. "Should we save what we can and leave?"

Druadaen put his hand to his head. "Even if we could, we don't know what to save, yet. That alone will probably take an hour or two. And I'm not sure if there's any way—"

The yellow liquid became level with the top of the onyx rim, edged out onto it...and stopped rising. A thick, distant gurgling followed a moment later.

"I heard *that*!" Ahearn exclaimed, drawing his sword.

S'ythreni laughed. "And what do you expect to do with a yard of steel?"

Umkhira looked from her post back at the main doors. "What is happening?"

"Unsure," S'ythreni shouted without turning around. "But I think..."

"Yes?" Druadaen and Ahearn chorused.

"It's starting to recede again. And the gurgling has resumed." She listened carefully. "But this time, it is the gurgling of liquid running out, not in."

"Well, that's a relief," said Ahearn.

Druadaen nodded but said, "Let's wait and see."

Ahearn had taken a more relaxed stance. "Well, at least the library is sa—"

A high, metallic peal cut at Druadaen's ears like a razor of sound. It was as if a silver bell had been hit so hard and so sharply that it rang and shattered in the same instant.

"What the hells—?" snarled S'ythreni—who flinched back as the velene flew past her to land on Druadaen's shoulder. The creature—object?—was noticeably warm.

"Is the velene all right?" shouted Elweyr from the doorway of the library.

"Why?"

"Because that sound—it was him!"

S'ythreni turned, stare at the rigid, almost pensive dragonette. "You mean, it screamed?"

"No, it...well, the sound just came out of it. From its whole body, I think," Elweyr replied as he began moving quickly toward the pool. Umkhira had already drifted halfway there but kept glancing over her shoulder, torn between standing guard near the stairs and helping her friends.

Ahearn leaned forward to check on the fluid that now resembled yellow syrup. "It's going down very quickly. I think in a minute or so, it will—*hey-a!*"

Ahearn jumped back as the syrup abruptly became thicker and, instead of draining toward the bottom of the reservoir, was sucked back out of it. The suddenly gelatinous mass disappeared down a vertical shaft at the back of the tube, making a slurping sound as it did. All the surfaces with which it had been in contact were completely dry.

But it had left something behind...or perhaps was simply revealing what had been there from the start:

A crude tan statue of a large, four-legged creature. It had the lean torso of a predator, but the head was still uneven and the tail—if it *was* a tail—was largely indistinguishable from the body. At best, it was an unfinished study, abandoned halfway to completion.

In the same moment that Druadaen got his first impression of it, the velene streamed down across him, from right shoulder to left hip, and looked up at him.

It had wrapped itself around the scabbard of his sword.

A rattle of sharp snaps echoed up from the onyx basin and Umkhira roared, pointing down into it.

The statue quaked, cracked, shook, and fault lines raced across its surface, fragments flying wherever they intersected. The entire surface began to shatter.

Except it wasn't the surface of a statue; it was a thin, brittle coating, spraying away from a violently flexing creature within it.

Its form was unlike anything that Druadaen had ever read about, dreamed, or imagined. The front of its body vaguely recalled the heavy limbs and claws of a bear, tapering into a torso with the same sleek, sturdy musculature of a great cat, but it was not derived from either of those species. Its fur was patchy on its apparently scabrous foreparts and upper spine, and its tail was surprisingly heavy, resembling ones he had seen—from a safe distance—on the supragant sloths of Solori.

But what held them all frozen for a moment was the head: it was a distorted, lopsided amalgam of scarred ape and unblemished toddler. But the eyes were alert, calculating, and—above all—maniacal. And without a blink, the beast was in motion.

Druadaen leaped backward, yanking his sword free as he did, damning himself for not having it out already. He recalled and dismissed his parrying dagger in the same instant: useless, against this opponent. Instead, he snugged his left hand upon the grip just beneath his right.

Ahearn got his bastard sword up in time to meet the beast's leap up out of the pool, smiling, holding it forth so the creature would wound itself upon the blade... but the point skipped aside. The monstrosity's foreparts were not scabrous after all, but plated like a pangolin, its irregular fur springing out from and obscuring the junctures between the segments.

As the velene swooped and darted around the creature, S'ythreni readied her crossbow. But the beast's tail came around, twisting, feinting, and then slashing—just as it unfolded a pair of opposed bone spikes.

S'ythreni dodged even as she fired, desperately bringing up the crossbow to block the heavy tail. It hit her ironpith weapon like a double-headed miner's pick as it discharged; a quarrel whined over the beast. The crossbow clattered away, still intact, but the string broke with a high-pitched screech. Thrown back by the blow, the aeosti turned her fall into a roll and came up with both shortswords drawn. Panting but with eyes narrowed, she was already looking for an opening.

Druadaen barely had time to swallow. In less than one second, the monstrosity had driven back two formidable foes, broken the weapon most likely to penetrate its armor, and had gained a foothold on the pool's onyx lip. And it was still in motion. So the very best tactic—

—would take too long to determine. Druadaen leapt toward it, bringing the sword's hilt above his shoulder while keeping the blade level and point forward.

The creature's reflexes were not merely daunting; they were terrifying. At the same moment its right paw recontacted the ground, its left whipped out at him—but not with a raking over-hand blow typical of animals. This was a hasty sweep: low and fast, long claws scything toward Druadaen's left calf.

He saw it and adjusted without thinking; his readied attack became a plunging, point-down guard that just barely managed to deflect the paw. And as it did, fragments flew up.

Both Druadaen and the creature started, staring at the falling chunks. The gleaming sword had clipped the ends of several of its armored plates and cut a deep groove into the thickest parts of others. On the hideous face, shock became terror which became redoubled fury—all in the space of half a second.

But that briefest pause was precisely what S'ythreni was watching for. She lunged toward the monstrosity's unplated haunches—and crashed into Umkhira who was charging in toward the same vulnerable spot, battle-axe raised high.

Both sprawled. S'ythreni's crouched posture sent her tumbling farther forward, closer to the creature. Swifter than thought, its tail snapped toward her, a thin rush of air trailing the spikes—but they glanced off Umkhira's shield, who dove to cover her aeosti comrade.

The velene swooped in at the monster's head. It noticed and jerked in that direction—in the very instant that the velene darted away.

The creature howled in frustration, its tail already swishing through a tight turn to make a return swing at the two women, but not before Ahearn and Druadaen charged it.

Eyes flicking toward the sword in the latter's hands, the beast sidestepped away from that mirror-bright threat; in that moment of distraction, its tail missed the two women, whirring a foot over their heads. It got up a paw in time to bat away Ahearn's two-handed cut, the forward momentum of which brought the swordsman perilously close to the monster.

Their faces barely a foot apart, its fast smile revealed two rows of hooked fangs, close kin to those Druadaen knew from the gaping maws of tiger sharks. The beast's neck cocked back and then snapped forward, jaws widening as they reached toward the swordsman's head.

Which was not there. The confusion on the hideous face became pain as Ahearn, who'd ducked forward and under the creature's jaw, brought his head up sharply, butting its chin with a percussive *crack*! It staggered back. So did Ahearn—just as Elweyr called for Druadaen to stand his ground.

The next moment, the mantic unleashed a thaumate; the beast's fur ignited, covered with small, dancing flames—which disappeared as if the universe itself had snuffed them out. Elweyr sagged and stumbled, cursing as he did.

As Druadaen angled in toward the flank of the rapidly recovering beast, he glimpsed several dire details. Its rear legs were no longer poised uncertainly on the lip of the pool. Umkhira and S'ythreni had jumped beyond the sweep of its tail but also beyond the reach of their weapons. And Ahearn was still recovering.

In that split-second assessment, the beast's eyes cleared and bored into Druadaen's.

He switched grip and gathered himself to leap forward against the now-advancing creature...

The velene darted past the creature's head, then spread its wings, turned, and was suddenly reverse-flapping away in the same moment it emitted another sharp pulse of sound: a piercing, painful cross between a ringing and a hum.

Druadaen resolved to ignore it as he engaged the creature but discovered that it had stopped and was writhing in agony. It staggered sideways as the velene hovered, as if centering itself to prepare another burst of sound...just before the tail swung around in a sudden, desperate swat.

One of the bone spikes connected. The impact snapped it off; the velene was catapulted away from the combat.

But in that unguarded instant, Druadaen had the opening for the two-handed thrust he'd been readying. It wouldn't be as powerful as a full swing from over his shoulder, but the creature's armor seemed more likely to deflect some or even most cutting attacks. Better to gamble that it was more susceptible to being pierced, particularly if hit at the juncture of two plates.

As Druadaen leaped forward, shoulder and arm muscles bunching, he caught a brief whiff of a completely unexpected odor: the almost chemical scent that immediately follows a lightning strike. Ignoring it, he focused on where he meant to drive in the point of his sword—

Which impossibly, but unmistakably, became slightly longer. And now tapered to a much narrower tip.

The stiletto-point slipped between the scales protecting the juncture of the creature's left leg and torso and effortlessly slid into the flesh beneath.

The creature jerked and yowled—more infant than ape—and turned sharply toward Druadaen, driving the blade in even deeper before that sudden spin slung his attacker sideways.

Druadaen clung desperately to the sword. As it came free of the ugly, maroon-leaking wound, he reached back with his legs, trying to find purchase, to stay on his feet to drive the blade home a second time.

But there was nothing under his feet, just empty air. Having been swung through a half circle, he came free of the creature just as he was passing over the pool.

An instant of confusion. Then an instant of reflex: old training of how best to fall—

But Druadaen hit the basin's onyx bottom before the reflex had completed. He felt something crack in his chest, lost vision for a moment, swam back to awareness—and realized his hands were empty. He tried to focus his eyes, fought against blackness, saw his sword lying against the side of the pool, but was distracted by movement in his returning peripheral vision.

On the onyx rim above him, the creature had staggered about to face him, every move wringing a gasp or shriek from it. Faltering at the edge, its eyes met Druadaen's and its face contorted with rage. And something very like longing.

Druadaen rolled to his knees, scrambled unsteadily toward his sword. The creature's powerful hindlegs bunched and released into a pounce down at him.

But a blur of motion hit the creature in its side. A battle-axe flashed and crunched into its lightly armored haunches, Umkhira's exultant war cry drowning out any sounds of surprise or agony the beast might have emitted. Slammed against the wall by the blow of the axe and then her body, it hit so hard that it bounced off and rolled to a stop near the opposite side of the basin. Umkhira flew back from her impact against the creature's armor plating and hit the floor of the pool with a suppressed groan.

Druadaen got one hand on his sword, swayed up to his feet, and discovered that the beast was already rising. Umkhira's battle-axe had cut a seam in the creature's scales and it was wheezing deeply, but its tail was already beginning to thrash and, skew-eyed, it began to track him uncertainly, warily.

Druadaen brought back his sword with his right hand, drew the parrying dagger with his left. If he could just deflect or even reduce one more blow, stay alive long enough to work around to the flank again—

The beast's eyes drifted back into synchrony and it smiled. It began to limp in sideways, circling to deny him the wounded flank as its tail's movements became more steady, more deliberate.

Druadaen realized that if he had to finish this fight on his own, time favored the creature. It's preternatural vitality, speed, and toughness were likely to prevail, even against the sword's startling capabilities. He drew a deep breath that told him he had indeed broken at least one rib, and then began circling as well, hoping he'd prove less injured and could turn the beast's flank before it could get much closer.

The creature evidently intuited the tactics behind the move and launched into a clumsy forward rush, tail drooping as its focus narrowed upon intercepting its target.

Druadaen saw he would no longer have an opportunity to attack the flank, switched stance so that the parrying dagger was slightly forward to deflect a first attack and hopefully create an opening that the sword could exploit. He put his weight on his back foot as the creature closed, saw its tail starting to flinch fitfully—just as a shadow flickered over both of them.

Druadaen glanced up.

Ahearn completed his leap down from the lip of the pool, both hands coming over his head to drive the point of his bastard sword straight down into the beast's unarmored lower back.

Blood flew up. The beast writhed, spun, threw the swordsman off into the nearest wall. Ahearn staggered to keep his feet, failed, slipped down to one knee, as the spasming beast dragged itself around to close with the newly vulnerable foe that had wounded it so badly, readying its tail for a vengeful, killing blow.

Until Druadaen, having used those two moments to gather his wits and regain his balance, took two fast leaps to close with the creature and drive his sword—which now grew *wider* than usual—into the gap he'd already opened in its armor.

Because the beast was fixated upon the attacker who'd left a bastard sword sticking up alongside its spine, it did not hear Druadaen's movement in time; it was still turning when the suddenly incandescent sword's point drove at it again. The point nicked and skipped off the inner margin of one of the armor plates, which guided it straight into the original wound.

The sword went in up to the hilt. Blood—violet, this time— gushed out, followed by a suffocating odor that reminded Druadaen of patchouli, cinnamon, and decay. The creature staggered, fighting to stay on its feet as it sent up a long, despairing wail in the voice of a small child. Then the cry constricted into a rattling gargle and the beast collapsed.

But it had not expired. Ahearn swayed to his feet as S'ythreni let down a rope and started down to check on Umkhira. Elweyr peered into the pit, sparing occasional glances back toward Umkhira's now empty rearguard post.

They slowly gathered around the dying abomination. Druadaen held his sword's now normal tip at its wrinkled and scarred neck. "If you move, you will die."

It growled and chewed at its lips before spitting out, "I'm dying anyway. So kill me. Kill me now, damn you! Why do you hesitate? Do it! End it!" When surprise at its vehement death wish stunned them into another moment's silence, it spat blood at them and tried to move its tail; it barely tremored. "Damn you all! Damn you for living! Damn you for a life without torment! I'll kill you! I swear it! I shall rend you limb from limb! I shall feast on your entrails. I shall—!" It coughed up a gout of blood. "Kill me," it wept.

"You shall get your wish soon enough, you bloody monster," Ahearn muttered through gritted teeth. He peered more closely at the peeling skin on its neck and loose, discolored plates on its flank. "Certainly before you get a chance to shed into a new skin, or body, or however the hell you restore yourself."

"Yes! Kill me now! Before the pain starts! I can't—not again! Too many times. Too many years—"

"Ever since you were made the sentinel of this library?" Druadaen prompted.

"Longer. Far longer than that." It groaned as older scales rattled, fell off.

"Not possible," Ahearn snapped. "Nothing can live that long."

S'ythreni's glance was disapproving. "And how can *you* be sure?"

Ahearn's retort was swift, even bitter. "Well, why should we believe *anything* it says? Besides, you've heard it rant; the beast is mad."

"I am no beast!" it frothed and screamed. "Or was not always. I am no longer sure. But when the skies fell and the moons rained down war, I was already old. Too old. Sleeping through changes. Each more horrible than the next." The creature's eyes refocused as it returned from whatever dark reverie had momentarily overtaken it; red-rimmed and bulging, one slipped sideways again, roving out of synchrony with the other. "Why do you stand and stare? You have me. Finish, brave heroes!" it spat through an agonized cackle. "Do what none could do before you!"

Druadaen shook his head. "I will not kill an adversary who cannot defend himself."

"Fool!" the child's voice screamed as the fanged mouth struggled to snap at him, teeth flying loose. "I will teach you—!"

Ahearn stepped in quickly and plunged his longsword into the wound Druadaen had inflicted. Repeatedly.

Druadaen rounded on him. "Damn you! Now we shall never know!"

"Know what?"

"What we came here to investigate: if Saqqaru has always existed or was added to the surface of Arrdanc at a later date. And how old the world *truly* is!"

Ahearn shrugged. "Druadaen, whatever this monstrosity might have seen through the ages, you couldn't trust its answers. And good luck sifting out truth from ravings like those. He was as mad as a snake in a rolling barrel."

Druadaen barely heard him, staring down at the body of a beast that, despite its malign madness, had lived through the times when Saqqaru was first recorded. Maybe had lived before it even existed.

As S'ythreni climbed up out of the basin to check on Elweyr,

Umkhira put a hand on Druadaen's shoulder. "Ahearn's final blows were necessary. There is no way to know how quickly it might have healed. Or what it might have turned into."

"Turned into?"

Umkhira shrugged, favoring her left arm. "Beastkynde can change shape when all three moons rise. S'ythreni's people are said to enter a tree with their old body but emerge with a new one. Insects transform within their cocoons. Are you so sure this creature could not have done something similar?"

Druadaen struggled to find a reasonable objection, but finally sighed and shook his head.

Umkhira nodded, stepped aside, and with a one-handed sweep of her axe, severed the monster's head. She picked it up. In response to their stares, she explained, "When fighting magical foes, it is best to be sure they will stay slain."

Before the echo of her axiom had died out, a deep groan welled up from the rear of the tube beyond the portal. Druadaen had heard a sound like that once before: when a mass of water had rushed into a stone conduit that could barely withstand the sudden surge in pressure. They turned to look up at the round opening above them.

Perched on the rim, S'ythreni squinted into it, then stepped back, eyes widening. "Get out of the pool. It's coming back."

"Trying to slurp up its dead pet," Ahearn snarled as he headed toward the rope, urging Umkhira before him.

"Or us," S'ythreni muttered.

Druadaen turned to follow...but the sword dragged in his hand as he did, as if something invisible was holding it fast.

"No time for observations and investigations, Philosopher," Ahearn cried back at him. "Get up the rope! Now!"

But the sword would not move. He brought his second hand to the hilt to tug on it, and as he turned at the waist to bring all his strength to bear, his torso moved slightly closer to the portal.

So did the sword.

"Druadaen!" cried Elweyr. "What are you waiting for?"

He shook his head. "It's not me; it's the sword." As if to prove he was telling the truth, the blade's deep-mirror surface took on a faint blue sheen.

"Drop it then!" Ahearn roared, halfway up the rope.

Druadaen shook his head. "I think..." He took a step up the

sloping bottom of the basin, coming closer to the portal until he could just barely see into it. The sword not only moved but seemed ready to go further.

"You're thinking?" Ahearn shouted. "*Now?*"

"About what?" Elweyr added, panicked.

"I think...I have to do this." Druadaen leaned forward, raising and extending the sword. Or was he following it?

"What the hells are you—?"

The gurgling became slower, almost sullen.

"It's coming," S'ythreni muttered from overhead.

Druadaen nodded...and watched a trickle of yellow slime trickle toward him out of the darkness.

He stretched the sword point toward it.

The trickle became a tendril, probed toward the blade, and just before touching it, yanked back as if scalded. With a thin slurp, it pulled back into the darkness. A moment later, there was a final gurgle; a great gulping sound, like a huge mass of water suddenly draining out of a plugged pipe.

"Now," he said with a smile at the sword in his hand, "I believe we can get what we came for."

"And then what?" asked S'ythreni. "Or have we finally finished your mad quest?"

"Not quite yet," Druadaen answered. "There's just one last visit I must make."

"What now?" she screeched. "To find more dragons or direkynde? Or maybe to go see one of the chthonic cryptigants that live in volcanos or beneath polar ice?"

"No, just a nice old man," he answered with a small smile. "Who lives in Saqqaru."

CHAPTER FIFTY-EIGHT

Druadaen put out a hand to steady Aji Kayo as they navigated a narrow and slippery path between stalagmites festooned with Saqqari warning chops. The elderly scholar was the one who knew the way to their destination, but knowledge did not protect him from the potential missteps of advanced age.

However, he not only navigated the tightest and trickiest spots sure-footedly, but he occasionally avoided them altogether with nimble hops.

"It is just ahead," he said reassuringly. "But this is a good place to stop."

"You wish to rest?" Druadaen asked solicitously.

"No. Do you?" the First Scholar retorted impishly. "Actually, this cave has places to sit. The cavern known as The Vengeance of the Gods does not." He lowered himself to a flat-topped stalagmite that resembled a decapitated mushroom. "Besides, this is a better place to talk. And since there are lanterns in here, a better place to read, as well." He waggled his wispy gray-and-white eyebrows at Druadaen conspiratorially. "And it is very private. Which I conjecture you knew, and which is why you proposed this particular outing instead of meeting in a more comfortable location. Such as near my hearth, furnished with ample wheat-wine."

"That would have been very enjoyable," Druadaen agreed, "but this is far more prudent."

"*Ai-ha!*" exclaimed the scholar. "A young man who speaks the word 'prudence' with the gravity of an old one? You frighten me, Outrider Druadaen; what has happened to you?" he taunted.

"I suppose I have matured since last we met."

"Is that what it is? Well, I do not think much of it! It makes you somber. And very dreary company!" He chuckled at Druadaen's small smile and rueful nod. "However, your message *was* unusually cryptic."

"I have become unusually cautious."

"So I perceive. No longer the eager young fellow I met in the Archive, then." He sighed. "Well, we should sit here or continue on. Which?"

Druadaen sat.

"So," muttered Kayo out of the side of his mouth, as if he might be overheard by the stolid rocks, "a clandestine meeting. So very dramatic."

"Probably unnecessary, but one can never tell."

Aji nodded. "Yes: I know something of the ship on which you arrived. It was originally destined for Tlulanxu, was it not?"

Druadaen smiled. "You are unsurprisingly well informed."

"And yet the master who hired that Uershaeli ship decided to come here, instead. No doubt incurring much greater costs doing so. Interesting."

It was a testimony to just how well informed Aji was that he knew the ship's itinerary and that it was not operating under the direction of its captain. "And you are probably also aware that it came up from the south."

"I believe I heard something to that effect," the scholar said with a small smile. "So tell me: What happened that you have come to Saqqaru instead of Dunarra?"

"Are you familiar," Druadaen began, "with a place known as Imvish'al?"

Aji's knowledge was evident in the question with which he replied. "Do you refer to the present-day archipelago or the ancient land? You have been there? You must tell me how that came to pass and what transpired!"

Which Druadaen did in considerable detail, often due to the unusual or incisive questions from the Saqqari First Scholar. At the end of the tale, he frowned. "And so you did not remove all the contents of the library?"

"We couldn't, although Tharêdæath gave it serious consideration. But then we received a message from Dunarra that redirected us."

"Here?"

"Yes, but only to provision ourselves for a longer journey."

"Ah," said Kayo, his face suddenly impassive. "Then this *does* concern the Hidden Archivist."

Druadaen stared before he muttered, "If this Hidden Archivist is such a secret, then how does everyone seem to know about him except for me?"

Aji smiled, covered a small chuckle with the back of his hand. "Hardly so, my young friend. But you must understand: that role has existed for millennia—since before Tharêdæath was born—and those who have held that office have often influenced crucial events. The capture of the current one is a matter of great significance."

"So I gathered. It's not every day that a ship receives new orders when it is in the middle of the ocean and has not seen any new vessels in weeks."

Kayo simply nodded.

"You do not seem surprised."

"Should I be? Or should you? It seems to me you are no longer a stranger to the powers and prerogatives at the disposal of those who make policy or are the embodiments of it."

Well, I guess that's true enough. "Since the Orchid Throne seems to rely on your counsel in similarly urgent matters, I can't help wonder if you have even more knowledge about our changed orders than I do. Or Tharêdæath, for that matter."

Kayo shook his head. "Knowledge? No. Conjecture? Yes." He shrugged. "Forces are being gathered to reclaim the Hidden Archivist. Ordinarily, that would have been done immediately, but I suspect it has taken this long to get reliable report of where he is being held...and by whom."

Druadaen had a sneaking suspicion that he knew even more than that, but to press would not only be rude, but pointless: Aji Kayo was a loyal servant of the Orchid Throne and would not divulge what he had been charged to keep secret. "If so, that leaves me in an awkward position. I am still an Outrider, but my friends owe nothing to the Consentium. Yet, if they do not come with us, then they are stuck on Saqqaru. And they will have to spend most of the coin they have won just to find passage back to Ar Navir, since it is unknown if Tharêdæath's ship will ultimately return here." *If it is still afloat, by that time.*

Aji waved a leathery hand as if to swat away those problems. "I am sure that something may be arranged for them. Now, let us return to a more pressing matter: How did you leave things at the library of Imvish'al?"

"As best we could. A small group of guards remained there. Key accounts and references on various topics were identified and removed for conveyance to Mirroskye. There was talk of sending an expedition from Mirroskye itself, but the Iavarain with us were not optimistic that the Council would take action. Then we received our new orders, and here we are."

Aji shook his head sadly. "Such a shame. Let us hope it does not end badly." He peered sideways at Druadaen. "Now, why was your request for a visit worded with such care, and why in a place so convenient to clandestine purposes? Could it have something to do with what you found on Imvish'al?"

Druadaen produced a small book from inside his coat. "The more I thought back upon our earlier meetings, the more I became certain that your researches have been similar to mine... but focused on your homeland. I also began to suspect that you came to see the same impossibilities, the same conundrums that I did. But by the time you wished to investigate them more deeply, you had already sworn your oath to the Orchid Throne. Which would also mean that your ability to travel—as often as you needed and wherever your investigations might lead—was extremely limited."

"And so?"

"And so, I think this may have been what you had hoped to find before you were compelled to work under such constraints." He passed the book to the old scholar. "It is not the original, but I copied it as faithfully as I could. And, speaking for the Council of Mirroskye, Tharêdæath has promised that those who wish to see the original, to establish its provenance for themselves and to check the accuracy of their copies, may do so at request."

"That is an unprecedented accommodation, among the Iavarain," he said with a deep nod. He opened the book, glanced at its contents, closed it again. "How did you come to know I sought exactly this?"

Druadaen shrugged. "I began by presuming that the Orchid Throne's records of Saqqaru's origins were either purged long ago or were sealed. And if they were sealed, that put you on the horns of a dilemma: whether you were seeking to find the truth, or had done so and wished to share it, you had to do so without breaking any oaths of silence or secrecy you might have made to the Throne. So you had to find the proof outside Saqqaru. That's why you visited the Archive Recondite so often and pored over the references on your own country.

"But because I read what you had—and often specifically consulted the very same references—I knew the limitations you had encountered. There was a great deal of tantalizing information available, but all of it was fragmentary, anecdotal, or inconclusive—such as the poems, and ships' logs, and traveler's journals that should have mentioned Saqqaru, but instead refer to this part of the ocean as a landless expanse.

"Then there are the navigation charts and guides that describe, in detail, carefully measured passages through these seaways but without ever encountering the land or people of Saqqaru—despite following courses which would have them sailing through hundreds of miles of plains and mountains. And although their nautical calculations could be challenged as 'backward,' their calendars seemed to bear them out. Their journeys from Mihal'j or Ar Navir simply could not have been made so swiftly had there been a landmass in the way.

"But all of those accounts were too scattered, too fragmentary, to be considered proof. So, I went in search of it." He glanced at the tome lying in Aji's hands.

The old man's eyes had either become rheumy or shiny. "You have observed and learned much, young Druadaen," he said. "I thank you for the book."

Druadaen touched a marker he had left in it. "I think you will find this section particularly gratifying."

Taking the hint, Aji opened the book, began to read, then glanced at his young friend. "And when did you learn to read ancient Saqqari?"

"I still don't. But I researched certain words and phrases, knew how to identify them."

Aji nodded, read for a long minute, then looked up. "There is much to read here. Would you be kind enough to summarize it for me?"

Druadaen nodded, pointed to the significant sections as he

explained. "With my friend Elweyr's help, we were able to read the Mihal'ji accounts pretty well. They seemed to be the predominant power upon Imvish'al and were great traders. This place was a logical midpoint for many of their journeys, particularly those where it would have been both safer and more profitable to take on fresh water and rations at such a convenient midpoint in the long sail to Solori and Khazhakt.

Druadaen looked Aji in the eyes. "There are hundreds of indexed and complete accounts by those traders, First Scholar. They recount their journeys, the goods they conveyed, the goods with which they returned, the smallest islands upon which they sheltered. There is never one mention of Saqqaru, but many, many log entries that recount in detail the measures taken to establish their course and position with precision: positions that would put them in the middle of this landmass. Which is why we may believe their plentiful maps that show this not only as open water, but with approximate depths and even well-charted fishing shoals.

"Ah," he exhaled, closing the book, "you have made an old man very happy. But also very fearful."

Druadaen frowned. "I understand why these findings make you happy, but... fearful?"

He nodded. "Yes, and I feel both for the same reason: because it confirms my suspicions. That pleases me very much. But the Orchid Throne will not welcome this."

"Even if it does *not* come from its own archives? And even if it is presented by you?"

"Particularly if it is presented by me. It is one thing for such things to be proven. It is another if the Empress's own First Scholar—whom she has declared the leading expert in our most ancient history—is the one to present the evidence and attest to its authenticity." Although no one was with them, he leaned close and murmured. "Circumspection is required in this matter. I shall not share these writings. For your own good, you must do the same."

Druadaen sighed. "It's a little too late for that, now." When Aji stared, he explained. "Just before meeting you here, I gave copies of this and the other references to the Second Courtier of the Orchard Throne's Penultimate Chamber."

Aji closed his eyes. "Youth," he sighed, "is so trusting." He patted Druadaen's long, strong hand with his small, wrinkled, and spotted one. "Perhaps there is a benefit in it. When a troubling artifact is surrendered so freely, so . . ."

"Ignorantly?"

Aji smiled. "If you like. But when so sensitive an item is remitted so readily, it cannot reasonably be seen as politically motivated. Rather, it is the sign of political ingenuousness." He shrugged. "It is rightly said that nothing suggests that an action was undertaken innocently as the actor's own ignorance of its consequences."

Druadaen shrugged. "I doubt I would have been allowed to keep the references, anyway."

"Of course not."

"But at least the copies I have made for Dunarra will always be available in the Archive Recondite."

"I am not sure they will be allowed there, either. But time will tell." He stood. "Come. Let us reflect upon these impossibilities you have proven while contemplating mute evidence of others."

Aji stopped and swept a hand at the walls of the immense chamber they had entered. "Behold: 'The Vengeance of the Gods.' Compelling, is it not?"

Druadaen could only nod. Although the Grotto of Stone Bones in the Under of the Gur Grehar had been impressive, this was astounding. Almost complete skeletons reared up from the ground or were frozen in the act of emerging from the rough walls. Creatures with skulls twice as high as a tall man stared at the ceiling, at each other, over their shoulders, and even at the entrance in which the young Dunarran and elderly Saqqari stood. Teeth the size of scimitars grinned in frozen anticipation of feasting on them or each other or whatever had been fleeing from the gigantic predators when they were trapped in stone eons ago.

They were surrounded by a horde of their smaller cousins. It was as if they had been swarming beneath and about the limbs of the larger ones when fate caught that action in a permanent still life. They ranged from the size of large aurochs to small, birdlike carnivores with long jaws and even longer legs. The petrified statuary extended all the way up the walls to the ceiling, where stalactites hung like the teeth in the upper jaw of a still greater beast, ready to swallow the entire scene in one bite.

The longest of them had deposited their mineral drippings upon many of the fossils directly beneath, thereby creating second, smaller stalactites that hung upon their jaws, tails, and spines like icicles of stone. It created a momentary impression, however impossible, that these skeletons had somehow been frozen while perversely animated in a parody of living.

Aji smiled up at Druadaen. "Even for those as talkative as we are, it has the power to leave one speechless."

Druadaen nodded. "And this is the battleground where these creatures were defeated by humans, with the aid of the gods?"

Aji nodded, pleased. "You remember the tale, then? Excellent. The legends say that these are the collected remains of many battles fought in this one place. Which must have been a marsh, as you can see from the ferns."

Druadaen had not noticed them, since they did not protrude from the wall. But now that he looked, the walls themselves held the solid remains and impressions of various tropical plants. "And were they also turned to stone by the gods?"

"So it would seem, although it remains an unanswered mystery how so many fronds might have given offense to deities. But do you see anything missing?"

"Well, human remains, obviously. But of course, the gods were on our side, so I am sure we had few losses." Druadaen smiled. "And besides, we were not the target of their ossifying mancery."

"Yes. I think you must be right about our unprecedented safety upon this battlefield. The primitive forerunners of our modern *qinshoqi*—temple-keepers, would be the closest translation—were the ones who, over generations, wielded the chisels that revealed this miracle. They say the lack of human remains is proof that the gods so love our kind that they did not suffer even one of us to die in the battles. But you may have noticed that it is not just our skeletons that are missing." Aji waited, explained when Druadaen did not follow his implication. "If you were to study every square inch of this chamber with great care, you would not find any broken weapons or tools. Not even a single flint spearpoint, nor the slightest fragment of other finished stone, let alone metal."

"And how do your *qinshoqi* explain that?"

"They assert that such items were not preserved because, like all things human, they were fallible and so, too fragile. That they have been crushed by the unrelenting mass of rock above, the rusting and eroding effects of water, or otherwise annihilated by the passing of the millennia."

Druadaen nodded, even as he stared at fine-boned, freestanding bird skeletons that could not possibly have outlasted a stone axe-head or metal implement. "And yet..."

"And yet." agreed Aji with a rueful smile. "Come, let us depart. I sometimes get a headache if I stay too long in this place."

Aji, blinking as they emerged into the daylight, asked, "I wonder: Did Tharêdæath make any remark upon your findings and your conjectures about Saqqaru?"

Druadaen shrugged. "Only to confirm that, to the best of his knowledge, no Iavarain histories refer to the Saqqari continent or people. It is not even mentioned in the collected tomes of the Iavan downfall."

Aji looked up with one eyebrow raised. "The *Costéglan Iavarain* is hardly an encyclopedic tract."

"No, but the scholarly commentary on it is extensive, and includes the equivalent of gazetteers. Although he has not read all of them personally, Tharêdæath does not recall any mention of a land with the geographic particulars of Saqqaru, nor any human culture or language that would be a logical antecedent of your own."

"Well," Aji grunted as they mounted the steep stairs that led away from the cave complex, "when you find the Hidden Archivist, you may no longer need to rely upon Tharêdæath's recollections. The person in that role must not only have read all the original sources, but could recreate most of them from memory, if required. And he has access to even older records of the Iavarain."

"In the Hidden Archive beneath Tlulanxu?"

"And elsewhere," Aji replied cryptically as they ascended the last few steps.

Ahearn was waiting for them at the top. He nodded, frowned, then bowed to Aji, who seemed simultaneously bemused and charmed. "I doubt you are here for me, Esteemed Warrior."

Ahearn bowed even more deeply. "An' it please you, I'm not." He turned to Druadaen. "New plans."

"Oh?"

"Two ships just docked, one running Dunarran colors. I've no knowledge of the other, but she's listing badly. And they bring news; we're no longer sailing off on Tharêdæath's shadowy mission."

Aji smiled. "So: it is already accomplished."

Ahearn stared at the wizened Saqqari, bowed again. "It's not often one such as me is in the presence of a sage who's also a soothsayer." He glanced at Druadaen. "He's got the right of it; whatever we were to help Tharêdæath do has already been done. But how yer scholar friend could know that in advance—"

Aji laughed. "No divination was required. It was a likely outcome." He turned to Druadaen. "At any rate, I am glad your travels brought you here and that you are no longer sailing into battle."

Druadaen smiled. "Yes, I could do with a little less danger, for a while."

But the smile left his face when Aji held up a very wrinkled index finger. "I did not say that, my young friend. I suspect you are now sailing to a different kind of danger."

Ahearn frowned. "Apologies, great sir, but I'm afraid you're mistaken in that prediction. We're bound back for Dunarra."

Aji smiled patiently. "Just as danger comes in many forms, it also lurks in many places." He turned to Druadaen. "May you take your next steps in safety... and with great care, my friend. Now you must excuse me; it is time for my nap."

CHAPTER FIFTY-NINE

As Druadaen started up the gangplank of the Dunarran square-rigger, he experienced a strange sensation; it was as if he'd never done so before. In his time as a Courier, he'd traveled on at least a dozen. But in those days, the sight of their distinctive shape, and the colors of the Consentium atop their mainmasts, always filled him with a sense of familiarity and safety. But this time, his reaction was arrestingly different: cautious, uncertain, even wary.

But as he stepped on to the ship's weather deck, he was struck speechless by a far greater surprise as a familiar voice said, "It's been a long, long time, lad. I wonder if you even remember me."

Druadaen turned toward the sterncastle and forgot to take another step, forgot where he was, even forgot why he was there.

Varcaxtan was standing just outside the coaming of the passage that led toward the officers' cabins at the rear of the ship. Physically, he had not changed greatly—not surprising, among Dunarrans—but there was a bit of gray in his hair and a few more crow's feet at the corners of his eyes. But those eyes were no longer the merry and interested ones he'd known as a boy; they were heavy, tired, even sad.

"Uncle Varcaxtan! What are you doing here? Where have you been? And what's wrong?" Without waiting for any answers, he plowed on, the long-suppressed surge of questions surprising even him. "And where did you go? I looked for you and for Indryllis as best I could. Everyone did. Shaananca did. Why didn't you come back to Tlulanxu? Why didn't you write? How could you—?"

Varcaxtan's head dropped, and he held up a hand. "Not now, lad. I'm sorry." He looked up; his eyes were liquid-bright. "In the end, the answer to all your questions is the same: orders and duty. And no, I can't explain right now. Not for a while, probably." He walked toward Druadaen with the gait of a reluctant executioner.

Druadaen resisted the sudden, irrational impulse to back away and flee down the gangplank. "What's wrong, Uncle Varcaxtan? Why are you on this ship?"

Another voice answered, from back near the coaming. It was less familiar, but Druadaen was sure he'd heard it before and peered around Varcaxtan.

Alcuin IV, wearing the small pin of a Pretor of Dunarra, was emerging from the dark of the sterncastle.

Standing before the two men, it was as if Druadaen's present was suddenly outnumbered by his past. Memories rising like floodwaters, he felt his worldly, more cynical self invert, become the anxious, callow youth whose hopes were outstripped only by his innocent idealism. To push that down, he snapped to attention as Alcuin approached.

But he hadn't even completed that rapid change of posture before the older man was waving it way. "Be at your ease. You must have passed our runner in the streets."

Druadaen made sure his voice was level, collected, calm. "Pretor, I was not aboard the Uershaeli ship when I received word of your arrival. One of my companions found and informed me. I came immediately."

Alcuin nodded, his eyes measuring. "You were with Aji Kayo, weren't you?"

Druadaen swallowed. *Does he read minds or farsee?* "I was, sir."

"Logical," the other man muttered to himself. "Then you have heard that the mission for which we—and you—were dispatched is already concluded."

"Yes, sir."

"And did Tharêdæath tell you the nature of the mission?"

"Well...he didn't mean to, sir."

Alcuin's eyes became harder, urgent. "Explain that, Outrider."

"We were becoming acquainted, just before sailing from Tavnolithar. I had reason to speak about my work at the Archive

Recondite, during which I made a reference to the Reserved Collection. He inferred that I had full knowledge of it."

"And so he mentioned the Hidden Archivist." Alcuin shook his head. "Damn. That makes matters more complicated."

"Sir?"

Alcuin stared at Druadaen for a long moment then glanced at Varcaxtan.

The big man shrugged. "He's his father's son, Alcuin. He'll figure it out soon enough."

Alcuin frowned at that answer, as if he had expected it but still didn't like it. His eyes returned to Druadaen's. "The Hidden Archivist was recovered a week ago from a stronghold off the coast of S'Dyxos. He has been conveyed safely to Dunarra—"

Druadaen was dismayed. "Sir?"

Alcuin closed his eyes, clearly frustrated at himself. "Yes, yes: that's at least five weeks by fast ship. So I am going to rephrase. And as far as you are concerned, this is the only thing I ever said on the matter: 'The Hidden Archivist is once again in Dunarran hands.'" He glanced at Varcaxtan who was smiling at him. "That's the first time you've smiled since The Nidus."

"Just listening to the lad...er, Outrider Druadaen...brings back memories." He smiled. "It was always a bit too easy to forget what should and shouldn't be said around him."

Alcuin suppressed his own smile. "I wouldn't know anything about that. I am ever the soul of discretion."

Druadaen cleared his throat. "Sir, while a Courier, I heard The Nidus mentioned, and I know it's on an island, but I don't know which island or where."

"Be glad you never had reason to learn those things, Outrider. The Nidus is on Zhedas Okkur and it is a very ancient citadel. It's always been, well, especially troublesome."

Druadaen had seen Varcaxtan's face crumple at the mention of the island. "What happened there, uncle?" He saw the man's eyes get bright again, and suddenly he knew. "Aunt Indryllis. Is she—?"

"We are uncertain of her condition," Alcuin interrupted sharply. "The end of our action in The Nidus was unexpectedly chaotic." He straightened. "But at this point, Outrider, it is no longer time to ask questions, but answer them."

Druadaen frowned at the forced transition to a sterner tone. "Yes, sir. What questions?"

"I'm not exactly sure, because I am not the one who wants to ask them. But there is one question I must have you answer before I am authorized to travel with you aboard this ship: Why did you attempt to contact the Hidden Archivist?"

What? "But...but, sir, I didn't."

"That is odd. And insufficient. Your name has been mentioned in the course of both locating and then recovering him."

"But by whom? And about what?"

"I will repeat myself once: now, *you* are answering the questions. Who have you spoken to about trying to contact the Hidden Archivist?"

"Sir, I never spoke about it because I never tried to contact him. I didn't know he existed! The only time such a subject arose was when Tharêdæath indicated that if the Hidden Archivist consented to it, he would arrange a meeting between us, pursuant to assisting my research."

"What research? Be specific and quick. And be assured: I have no intent on sharing your answer."

"Specific *and* quick? That will be difficult, sir, but I will attempt it."

Alcuin was not merely unsurprised at Druadaen's synopsis, but already seemed to be familiar with many of his investigations. However, his eyes narrowed and his questions came more rapidly when the linked topics of Saqqaru's mysterious origins and the ages of fossils and Arrdanc itself arose. Frowning, he nodded after hearing about the trip to The Vengeance of the Gods just hours earlier.

"Very well," he muttered. "That's enough. Well, for me, anyway. Your answers are promising, and presenting them in an official forum is the best way to clear the vague accusations being made against you."

Druadaen started. "Accusations against me? For doing what?"

Alcuin's jaw shifted disagreeably. "I cannot say."

Druadaen reflexively glanced at his uncle.

"You know better, lad. If the Pretor can't share more on the subject, then I certainly can't."

He nodded. "Can you at least tell me why you and Aunt Indryllis were on the rescue mission to The Nidus?" He glanced at Alcuin. "Did the Pretor ask for you especially?"

Varcaxtan shook his head. "Lad, I have been traveling with

Alcuin for years. Same with your Aunt Indryllis. We've done so almost since your parents ... well, from about the time you started your studies in Tlulanxu."

"As his advisors?"

"Well, that, too."

"As my protection," Alcuin said bluntly. "Against threats both mundane and mantic. I have no further questions to ask you. However, I have been enjoined to inform you that neither your uncle nor I shall have contact with you until we make port in Tlulanxu. This is to ensure that you have not had any further exposure to the concerns or questions that you will be asked to address upon our return.

"Now, return to the Uershaeli ship and fetch your gear. And your companions too if they wish to come along. We are sailing for home in the morning."

"Is it necessary that we change ships, sir? I have been told that Tharêdæath will be sailing in convoy with you to Tlulanxu."

Alcuin frowned and looked at the toes of his boots. "Don't make me insist, Druadaen."

It took Druadaen a moment to understand the Pretor's implication. "I ... I am to be taken into custody, then?"

"Not unless it becomes necessary. And as long as you are willing to travel on a Dunarran ship, we don't have to take that step."

Druadaen stood as straight as he could. "I will return with my belongings." But it wasn't until he'd reached the dock that he thought to shout up, "I will also bring those companions that elect to travel with me."

Although they'd be fools to do so, he thought as he made his way back to them.

CHAPTER SIXTY

The first three days at sea were so filled with sudden gusts of rain and confounding winds that Druadaen and his companions were ordered to remain below. Not that they would have been disposed to stretch their legs in the squalls that rolled over the ship unpredictably, but it did leave everyone but the two "book-worms"—he and Elweyr—both bored and tense.

However, the weather seemed to be relenting when they ate the third dinner of their voyage and then hastened to their bunks. The prospect of sleeping without being tossed out of them several times during the night was too welcome to put off.

For Druadaen, the current voyage had brought fairly normative dreams of his old home, probably because that was where they were bound. Or possibly, they were reminiscent ripples caused by the sudden reappearance of his uncle and the reminder of all the questions about his parents, their extended family, and their life that had never been answered.

In the middle of a dream which included bits of the discussion he'd overheard between Alcuin and Shaananca years ago, the scene suddenly changed. Shaananca was present once again, but Alcuin IV had been replaced by his grandfather Alcuin II, the Propretor Princeps himself. And the detail and immediacy of the experience told him that this wasn't a dream at all: it was another vision of a distant occurrence.

Behind Alcuin, the sun was just setting over Tlulanxu's unmistakable skyline. The Propretor turned away from the window and gazed at Shaananca. "Is there any possible connection?"

Shaananca was silent, then shrugged.

Alcuin II shook his head. "I am not trying to implicate the lad, you know. Or you. But the hieroxi... Well, they mean to find a common thread if one exists."

"Or if they can invent one which satisfies their limitless appetite for uncovering conspiracies."

Alcuin nodded impatiently. "Yes, but in this case, we have to consent to an investigatory forum, at least. If we refuse, they will have strong grounds to accuse us of acting out of favoritism."

"That would be absurd."

"Yes. You know that. I know that. I daresay some of them know it as well. But Druadaen's name has been connected with all three of the most blatant attacks on or near our borders, and all within the last twenty years. First the one in the Connæar Protectorate, then one right here in Tlulanxu's harbor and streets, and now the Hidden Archivist plucked from an Iavan ship within sight of our shores."

"It is ridiculous for them to even suggest that he—"

"Shaananca. It doesn't matter. His name is associated with all three attacks, and all carried out by Tsost-Dyxsos."

Shaananca stiffened. "There was never a final determination that they were the ones who attacked the farm."

"No, but you're the one who argued that the methods all pointed to S'Dyxoi. Or have you changed your assessment?"

Shaananca shook her head angrily.

Alcuin nodded sadly. "It's not fair to the lad, but life doesn't trouble itself with such moral niceties. And there's no way for us to stop the temples from making the most of his coincidental connection with the attacks."

Shaananca frowned. "Unless it's not a coincidence at all."

Alcuin leaned back. "Are you saying you think the lad *is* involved?"

"Of course not. But there's another possibility: that he's a means to an end."

Alcuin steepled his fingers and thought. "You mean that he's simply a convenient cat's-paw for the S'Dyxoi to increase the friction between us and the temples? Isn't that a bit too convenient?"

She shrugged. "The hieroxi may be right: that three times can't be coincidence. But the plot is more subtle: to give the temples a pretext to mount a politically divisive investigation."

Alcuin was nodding. "The Tsost-Dyxoi would like nothing better than to drive a wedge between us and our sacrists. But there's a missing piece: How do they make sure that the investigation occurs? They can't leave that to chance; they'd have to suborn—"

Shaananca started, then abruptly glanced around, as if she had detected something very close to where Druadaen's point of view was situated—

And as suddenly as the vision had begun, it was over. Druadaen discovered that, as on prior occasions, he was clutching his blankets close to his body, but this time, they were rank with the sudden sweat of terror.

His parents. The S'Dyxoi. The temples. The Propretoriate. The Hidden Archivist. Were all somehow connected in some strange and multi-sided intrigue? Or were none of them connected, making this no more than a surreal yet disastrous comedy of errors? Or, as was usually the case, was the truth someplace in between, and if so, how could he sort it out from all the false clues and misdirections?

Druadaen's mind not only began to race but started chasing in different directions, speculations and theories splitting and subdividing and multiplying until—

He leaped out of the bed, did not care what the weather was like, did not care that he was in a sleeping shift, did not care what Alcuin IV or anyone else might think if they saw him. He needed to get out of the claustrophobia of his bunk, of the compartment, of his own mind. He raced up the companionway.

He was breathing hard, but not from exertion, when he burst out on the deck—and discovered the sky above him littered with clear, bright stars. The ship pitched lightly as it moved through low risers, and two moons painted glittering paths upon the water which collided in a riot of multiple reflections.

Druadaen stopped, closed his eyes, drew in a deep breath—

And nearly coughed it out when a voice called, "Hey, Philosopher, you having bad dreams again?" In the light of both moons, he could make out Ahearn grinning at him from the fo'c'sle.

Other than a few glances from the midwatch, no one took particular notice as he made his way forward and up the short flight of stairs to the bow. Ahearn smiled at him all the way. "Well, aren't you a sight."

Druadaen smiled back, glad for the company, glad to have left the swirling uncertainties behind. "Anything to break the monotony."

One of Ahearn's straight black eyebrows climbed slightly higher. "You were *sleeping*, mate. Or were the dreams so monotonous that they woke you?"

I wish. "No. I just needed to get out of the cabin."

"And maybe out of yer dreams, too?"

"Maybe a bit of both. But what are you doing up here? You're a pretty sound sleeper, from what I've seen. And heard."

Ahearn feigned umbrage. "Is 'sound sleeper' your polite way of saying, 'sleeps like a rock and snores like a mill saw?' Because if so . . . well, I can't deny it, so I won't try." He smiled and leaned his elbows on the gunwale, looking west over the bow.

"Last time I saw that look on your face," Druadaen said, joining him at the railing, "we were leaving Dunarra."

"Aye, and that's what brought me up here. Well, truth be told, it's thoughts of that pony-sized beast I call my dog." His eyes wandered back to the moonlit western horizon. "I've got to make sure that he was delivered safely home. Not that I doubt Captain Firinne for a moment, but, well, our own lives show what becomes of careful plans, hey?"

Druadaen was struck by the deep seriousness of Ahearn's tone as well as his words. "You really do love that dog, don't you?"

"I do indeed," Ahearn breathed, eyes fixed on something far beyond the horizon. He seemed only partially aware of his immediate surroundings.

Druadaen glanced at him, suddenly realized what he had to say, to share. It was the last thing he wanted to bring up, to suggest. But he had to do it for Ahearn, and the others, because despite all odds, they had truly become his friends. "When we get to Dunarra," Druadaen said casually, "you and the rest should take passage someplace else. Maybe to Menara. So you can look in on Raun."

Ahearn looked sideways at him. "Now where's this malarkey comin' from?"

Druadaen leaned on his elbows, laced his fingers, looked out at the risers. "I will be, well, under investigation, I suppose you could say."

Ahearn half grinned. "Investigation for what? Reading too much?"

"No. Actually, I'm not sure, but if things get serious, well, treason."

"Treason?" Ahearn hissed, turning to stare at him. "You? Of all people? Godsblocks, what daft drivel could make anyone think that you—?"

"Ahearn. Listen now. I can't say much. Just that my investigations have... Well, either some powerful people are mistaken about what I've been studying, or I'm just a pawn in a much larger game. But whichever it is, the only safe course for you and the others is to go to Menara. Or further. Just don't be near me: this business is none of your concern."

"But it is, y'see," Ahearn said quietly with a small smile. "And it's not just because we're mates. And it's not just because there's no liars as dangerous as powerful ones. It's not even because we need to hope that, sometimes, justice might be done for you and me and the others and the whole wide world of scrapers and scrabblers after power and wealth. It's because of the innocents. For them more'n the rest." His eyes softened. "The ones who have naught but songs in their hearts and flowers in their hair." His eyes grew wet.

For no reason Druadaen could name, images of Ahearn flew past his mind's eye: the swordsman meticulously wrapping two out of every three coins in tight bricks; the cottage outside Menara; his description of the passing of the woman he'd loved: "Life. Death. Just the natural cycle of things"; and finally, his rageful readiness to attack a dragon in its own lair if its favorite target among humans was—

"A child," said Druadaen, wondering, nodding in both surprise and final understanding. "The cottage. You have a daughter there."

"Indeed I do," the swordsman confirmed in a voice of anguished pride.

"Then that is all the more reason why you must not tie your fate to mine. You have money now. You can stay and protect her, to be there as she grows up."

He wiped his eyes. "That's of no count. Aye, I have money, but it won't last forever. And when it's gone, then what am I to do? What am I to become, to be a good father to her? A farmer? A merchant? A grocer?" He scoffed bitterly. "Closest I come to a respectable trade is being a butcher, and I'm a damn messy one at that, eh?"

His jaw clenched tight; the muscles bunched and spasmed.

"This is all I know how to do; this sword is the only tool I've learned how to use. You saw how it was when you came along; I was scraping for money, talking as big as I could because my purse was as small as could be." He stopped suddenly.

"And then?"

"Well, then you show up and suddenly we have the attention of wizard aunts. We have a friend who thinks naught of rubbing elbows with Crown-lord Darauf of Teurodn and the like. And then, well, it stands to reason that with a mate like that, you'll never be entirely out of the money, yeh?

"But then...well, truth be told, it wasn't what you were searching for that made me stop and think. It looked like philosopher-madness, just as I said at the outset. But you weren't *mad*. You were handy with a sword, clever enough for a trained soldier, and most of all, you were true and never hasty. So I started wondering, well, if he's not mad after all, I wonder what it is that he's on about with all this esoteric codology about the world not working.

"And so I started watching and thinking about what you said you were seeking. And then you started finding it. And damned if it didn't make me wonder, too. Wonder if maybe this old world we're moving through isn't so much a hard-packed country road, but a bridge built over a bottomless swamp of uncertainties and mysteries. And what if some of that bridge's pilings are worm-eaten, or naught but lies? Well then, I reasoned, we're *all* at risk."

He shrugged. "That's no great never-mind for me, of course. After all, I accepted a life of danger and uncertainty, so a wee bit more hardly makes a difference. But"—and his eyes were suddenly shiny again—"but not for my little darling with flowers in her hair. Not her. I won't let her die because some cabal of gods and their priests and mancers keep us dancing and prancing on the surface of a world that's like to crumble under our feet."

He leaned straight into Druadaen's face. "So it's sticking with you, I am. Not just to keep her warm and fed, but to keep her safe. Because it's the answers you're after that will show me how best to protect her."

He leaned back and shrugged. "And besides, much as it pains me to say it, you're not the worst bloke I ever fell in with."

Druadaen laughed and jostled his elbow against the swordsman's.

"Ah, get on wit' yeh," the big man said, trying not to sniffle.

CHAPTER SIXTY-ONE

As the square-master made its final approach to the main wharf at Tlulanxu, Druadaen watched the city's skyline grow. He'd seen it from this perspective so many times as a homebound Courier, and he'd had many reactions to the sight: relief, comfort, pride, excitement, even a renewed wonder at its majesty and beauty. But this day, it evoked a new feeling: foreboding.

They docked at the very end of the longest pier but were not cleared to debark until an armed guard arrived. And it was not the watch or even the city guard; it was a section of Legiors. They came aboard and welcomed Alcuin and Varcaxtan and the others who had been with them at The Nidus. Half of the Legiors escorted them away. Druadaen's uncle turned to look for him, spotted him at the gunwale, was about to wave, but then reconsidered and nodded instead.

Shortly after, the second officer of the remaining Legiors came aboard and asked to speak to Druadaen and his "associates." His manner was not unfriendly but nor was it welcoming. He explained that Tlulanxu was being guarded more closely these days and that Druadaen's companions would be taken by skiff to the docks in the foreigners' quarter.

Druadaen interrupted, asked the officer to clarify: by foreigners' quarter, was he referring to the trade quarter? The officer answered in the affirmative, explaining that the terms were used interchangeably now. Druadaen and the group exchanged glances: when they had left, the term "foreigners' quarter" had only come out of the mouths of bigots and newly arrived persons who used it because it was a common label in other ports. And now, it was in Tlulanxu as well, apparently.

Druadaen asked if there was space for him in the Outrider's service hostel, but the second officer shook his head. Druadaen had already been assigned a private room at the Waiting House. He felt a chill move down his spine as he heard those words. The "Waiting House" was government and military slang, a shorter and somewhat sardonic reference to the House for Visitors Without Credentials. It was a clean and safe residence for persons claiming to have official business with the Consentium, but who had no standing with it or means of authenticating their ostensible bona fides. Typically, such persons spent a period of time there as their identities and business were verified: hence, the Waiting House.

But it was also the city's accommodations for credentialed foreigners who had been asked to remain in Tlulanxu pursuant to the resolution of an accusation against—or investigation concerning—them. Not quite house arrest, but still, a close cousin of it.

Druadaen asked if he was currently facing charges of some kind, or had been named in an investigation. The second officer had no knowledge of that. Druadaen then inquired about using the resources of the Archive Recondite. The second officer again had no direct knowledge, but informed him that it was regrettably closed. Druadaen asked to send a message to Shaananca, to inform her that he had arrived. The officer indicated that Shaananca was also currently in a private room at the Waiting House and, like him, would only be receiving official visitors.

Druadaen was preparing to ask about the possibility of sending written messages beyond the premises, but the second officer held up a palm. He patiently explained that he really had no other information regarding Druadaen's circumstances or restrictions and was in no position to speculate upon them. His only other relevant knowledge was the content of his orders: that he was to give Druadaen ample time to say his goodbyes, gather his belongings, and then depart with the remaining escort of Legiors. With that, the second officer nodded cordially and returned to the dock.

When he was gone, the others gathered around, offered subdued wishes of good luck and assurances that they would be waiting in the trade—well, "foreigners'"—quarter for as long as it took to get "this nonsense" sorted out.

Ahearn lingered behind, and once the others were out of earshot, he muttered, "Library closed, and yer auntie in a comfy cage next to yours?" He shook his head. "You know, I think I feel the brush of a spider's leg behind all this."

"The same spider whose web we tweaked in Vallishar?"

"Who knows? But if it's not, then this world is broken in another way." Ahearn answered Druadaen's quizzical look: "If it *isn't* the same spiderweb, then either Arrdanc is thick wit' 'em, or the gears which keep the world spinning are driven more by coincidences than causes."

Druadaen nodded. "You just might be right about that."

"About which?"

Druadaen shrugged. "Either. Both. There's no way to know which answer—if any—is the right one."

Ahearn shrugged back. "It's of a piece with how we're born and how we die: filled with uncertainty."

"Ahearn, you are beginning to sound like a philosopher."

"Bite your tongue and swallow it fer good measure!"

Druadaen laughed and, mindful that they might be watched, kept his tone and actions jovial as he said, "Take my sword with you. I left it atop your gear."

"What? Why?"

"Because I'm sure they'll impound it for the duration of this 'nonsense.' And even if I'm cleared, they might not give it back. Either way, I'd want you to have it."

"I suspect 'it' might have something to say about that." He scowled at Druadaen's uncertain frown. "Don't play the fool. We all saw what happened on Imvish'al, especially that little dance you did with it in the pool. That dragon knew what it was about when it put you and the blade together. And remember its words? He couldn't give it to you because it wasn't his to give." Ahearn glanced at the bracelet that was the velene's present form. "Same thing your magic aunt said about your silver beastie." He shook his head. "Don't know what all of them see in you, but I doubt I could change their minds."

Druadaen smiled, nodded. "Just don't tell anyone about the sword."

Ahearn blinked. "And just how stupid d'ya think I am? Of

course I won't!" His eyes and tone became serious. "Don't you worry; I'll keep it for you. As long as it takes."

In a capital where the rush and press of governing both a teeming city and an expansive nation combined to ensure that things never happened quickly, Druadaen rose the next day to discover four Legiors waiting outside his isolated room at the Waiting House. Politely, but firmly, they informed him that he was wanted at the Propretorium and hoped that noon would be convenient. Which was the polite Dunarran way of informing him that they would make sure he was present at the required time if they had to tie him hand and foot and carry him there bodily.

However, rather than being led to the Rotunda in which the Propretors met to deliberate and vote, his escorts steered him to one of the smaller meeting chambers housed in an attached building. As the door opened, and he faced the room, he discovered he recognized almost everyone inside from important public events during his days in the capital.

There were three Helper hieroxi present: Paramon of the temple of Unabasis, Sutaenë of Adrah, and Olcuissan of Amarseker. Alcuin IV was one of the two secular authorities in the chamber, the other being Wynclynran, Propretor and First Advisor for External Affairs, the Consentium's de facto senior intelligencer.

There was a sixth person he did not recognize, sitting on the same side of the table as the two secular members. She quickly discerned his uncertainty and introduced herself. "I am Seer Temmaê," she said with a sitting bow.

So, not just a representative of the Ar: a Seer. And not sitting with the temple leaders.

But before he could spare a thought on what that might signify, Hierarch Sutaenë folded her hands on the long table and nodded for him to come forward and stand at the small lectern across from them. Once there, she asked, "You are Druadaen, son of Tarthenex, yes?"

"Yes, Hierarch Sutaenë."

"And do you know why we have called you to meet with us?"

Druadaen frowned. "I have not been told what it involves. But I have reflected upon what it almost certainly does *not* involve."

"I am interested in hearing that," Paramon muttered.

At an approving nod from Sutaenë, Druadaen complied. "I have had no remit or orders from the Consentium since delivering a secure pouch to Talshane, the OEC station chief for Shadowmere, then in the Crimathan capital of Treve. So logically, I could not have failed to carry out orders since I have not been given any. Also, to my knowledge I did not violate my oath of service. If I had, the Consentium's military code would have brought a warrant against me, with charges specified, and any hearing such as this would be convened in a Legion headquarters. So I must presume that I have not been called here in regards to a military matter. Or have I overlooked something?"

"I can find no flaw with your conclusions," Sutaenë said with a nod. "Go on."

"Well, if the matter is not military, then it should be civil. But again, to my knowledge, I have committed no crimes. I reside fair confidence in that conjecture since, again, no charges have been brought against me and this is not a civil court. So it can't be that either, can it?" He waited for confirmation.

Sutaenë nodded. "Again, you are correct."

"Well then, it must have something to do with my questions."

"It may," Paramon agreed, leaning forward, "but you have left out a separate category of potential offenses: crimes against the state, some of which may have been committed before you joined the Outriders or even the Couriers."

Although he had a pretty fair idea of what was coming, Druadaen asked, "And what crime am I supposed to have committed against the Consentium?"

Sutaenë answered before Paramon could reply. "There is no specific crime being considered at this time. But you have been close or connected to three proven or suspected Tsost-Dyxos attacks on our territory. Some members of this board wished to hear your response to this strange circumstance."

Druadaen was suddenly glad for the vision of Shaananca and Alcuin II discussing this very matter, now three weeks past. He was not sure how he would have reacted had he been surprised—not to say ambushed—by the news that the S'Dyxoi might have been behind the attack on the farm. "My response is that all three attacks are surprising and deeply worrying. And in the first case, personally disturbing, if the attack that killed both my parents was indeed their doing."

Paramon leaned forward. "So, although your name figures in

all three reports, you still deny involvement in the planning or execution of these attacks?"

"Categorically." Druadaen stared at the hierarch of Unabasis, whose quick glance away indicated he'd understood the message behind the look: *I was* nine, *you cretin.* But Paramon's query had been useful to him, since it left no doubt that he was, as Druadaen had already suspected, the most hostile of his questioners.

"So," resumed Sutaenë, "let us turn to the questions—or rather, explorations—you have conducted on your own, Outrider Druadaen. Please describe them and explain your purpose for undertaking them."

Druadaen met her eyes. "Are you not already aware of them?"

Temmaê nodded. "We are. But they should be entered into the record. Besides, we have only the notes you gave to Captain Firinne to convey to the Archive Recondite. They are rich in observational detail but offer little comment on the impetus behind the investigations. Also, it is our understanding that you may have completed even more of them since."

"That is true, Seer Temmaê, but a sufficient answer to your question could prove...quite lengthy."

"We are aware of that," Sutaenë assured him. "Please proceed."

Which he did, adding his observations on the dragon to those of the Bent and the giants. At the end, he surveyed the faces arrayed before him. "However, I suspect it is my most recent investigation which was the catalyst for this hearing."

Paramon leaned forward again. "Oh? Why? If you wish to recant your findings, this is the time to do so."

Druadaen stared at him again. "Hierarch Paramon, how may I recant a position when I have not declared one? But I can answer your question about why I suspect my findings on Saqqaru are the issue of greatest concern to this forum.

"Most simply, the three investigations into contradictory phenomena in other species only imply inconsistencies in the world around us. But my findings on Saqqaru explicitly contradict the official history of that nation, as well as the accounts of Arrdanc's age and conformation that predominate among its many religions."

Sutaenë nodded slowly. "Yes. Tell us about those now."

"I shall synopsize, since I have already submitted my findings and sources to the Propretoriate Archive." He proceeded to share only the most salient facts and findings and concluded with a summary review of the precise and plentiful supporting evidence that had been found at Imvish'al.

Temmaê nodded her thanks when he was done and explained, "That was very helpful, as we had little time to read your extensive reports. However, I believe you cited another factor that strongly suggests Saqqaru appeared suddenly: that its language has no etymological overlap with any other on Arrdanc. And yet, that country's own earliest records reveal that, from that point forward, it was fully developed both commercially and culturally, possessed a lexicon that included place names for the other nations and cities of Arrdanc, and had a vocabulary consistent with a sophisticated understanding of sciences and engineering."

"The state of a language hardly constitutes empirical evidence," Paramon snorted.

Druadaen nodded. "I agree. That is why I did not include this element in my review. However, it is exactly what one would expect to discover if Saqqaru was not present on our world originally, but was then suddenly added with sufficient 'evidence' of its having always been there."

"Regardless of what is being asserted," Paramon persisted, turning away from Druadaen, "it is unconscionable that an impressionable young person should have had access to the documents which set him on this path. Those records should have been kept in the Reserved Collection."

"They were," Temmaê replied mildly.

Paramon rounded on Druadaen. "And so you violated the permissions of your position at the Archive?"

"No, I did not work in the Reserved Collection for many years. That occurred later, and then, only under special circumstance."

"What special circumstances are you referring to?"

"When I was given leave to work there, it was primarily to retrieve and then replace tracts required by elderly scholars who found the stairs too taxing. This did not require entering the collection itself, only depositing and picking up various references for the scholar. I was only allowed to enter the collection in later years."

Alcuin jumped in before Paramon could respond. "The decision to permit him to do so arose from a recommendation put forth by the secular authority that oversees the administration of the entire Archive: Senior Archivist Shaananca."

"Who should be held to answer for her disastrously capricious decision." Paramon turned toward Druadaen. "You may thank her unconscionable—and suspicious—dereliction of duty for your present unhappy circumstances, young Outrider."

"Actually," Alcuin objected mildly, "the final decision on that proposition rested with my grandfather."

Sutaenë's eyes widened as she looked sideways at him. "What did you say?"

"Senior Archivist Shaananca did not act autonomously in this matter. Because it was unprecedented, she put her recommendation before the highest secular authority: Propretor Princeps Alcuin II."

"And he permitted it," Paramon said, sounding both disgusted and angry.

"Obviously." Alcuin IV's smile was chillingly mirthless. "Perhaps I should summon him to these proceedings? To explain himself?"

Paramon seemed to be considering that offer when Sutaenë leaned forward and stated, "I am sure it will not be necessary to review all the recommendations and permissions that pertain to this matter."

Temmaê spread one hand upon the table before her. "I am not sure that I agree. It seems that there is still such resistance to Outrider Druadaen's later report on Saqqaru that now the focus has shifted to whether his own, earliest researches in the Reserved Collection were lawful. I propose that we settle both matters at once."

"And how would you propose to do that?" Sutaenë asked.

"By speaking to a person who has spoken with the Hidden Archivist, who has empowered him to act as his representative before this forum. I refer to Tharêdæath of Mirroskye."

Sutaenë frowned. "This matter concerns Dunarra, not the Iavarain."

"A point of order," Alcuin IV put in. "The Reserved Collection was established in conjunction with the Great Pool of Mirroskye, in part to provide a means of controlled access to the Hidden Archivist. Who, by the terms of that agreement, must be an appointee of the Great Pool, and who must be apprised of, and confirm, all applications to the Reserved Collection for obvious security reasons."

"An outdated agreement that is a vestige of a dead alliance," Paramon muttered.

"Perhaps you would wish to raise that topic with Tharêdæath."

"Perhaps I might, but I don't see him here."

Temmaê smiled. "That can be remedied." She turned to Sutaenë. "Tharêdæath is waiting in the corridor outside to answer any and all questions pertaining to these various matters."

Sutaenë stared at her. "Why was I not informed?"

Temmaê's smile did not change. "Since these proceedings are, as Outrider Druadaen correctly pointed out, unofficial, it seemed unduly formal to present a list of potential speakers. Just as it was apparently deemed unnecessary to ensure that the Outrider was given advance notice of the suspicions connecting the Tsost-Dyxos to his parents' deaths."

Gnarled Wynclynran leaned over to look at Sutaenë. "If you want the most credible source with the most complete information on the Reserved Collection, then insofar as Senior Archivist Shaananca is unavailable in the Waiting House, you will want to speak with the Hidden Archivist's designated spokesperson."

Sutaenë glanced down the table at the other hieroxi. Only Paramon scowled his disapproval. "Against my better judgment, I will allow Tharêdæath to speak—for the sake of this forum's unity."

Sutaenë gestured to the Legiors posted by the door, and they ushered in the Uulamantre.

Tharêdæath looked as relaxed and composed as when Druadaen had chatted with him in his sitting room in Herres, but his eyes belied that demeanor; they were quick, assessing.

"Welcome, esteemed Tharêdæath," Sutaenë began, leaving out the proper Iavan honorific that he was due as an Uulamantre. "You are familiar with our inquiry, I believe?"

"I am honored to speak before you and am familiar with the inquiry. I presume you wish me to attest to what I know of the evidence Outrider Druadaen has unearthed in relation to the origins of Saqqaru?"

"We do, Til'A'Tharêdæath," Alcuin answered, the honorific earning a small nod and smaller smile from the Uulamantre. "Speak at your leisure."

"I shall be brief, which I trust shall not be heard as being terse. In short, Outrider Druadaen has proven independently what the Uulamantre have always known: that before the Cataclysm that followed the events recounted in *Costéglan Iavarain*, there was no continent of Saqqaru. And if its people colonized it from some other region on Arrdanc, then we have no record of their prior existence nor of their migration. And I must point out that before the Sundering, my race sailed all four corners of the world and made—and kept—detailed records on the other races we encountered."

"Are you claiming you could not have overlooked any?"

"No, Hierarch Sutaenë. The longer one lives, the more one avoids using the word 'impossible.' But it would be very, very unlikely for us to have overlooked such a profoundly different culture that would also had to have significant seafaring capabilities to effect a migration to the new landmass.

"However, its original absence from the surface of this world is indisputable. I do not have the Hidden Archivist's complete recall of the sources, so cannot chant them for you. However, if you are interested, he has indicated that he will ensure that an embassy of your scholars would be welcomed in Mirroskye, where they would be permitted access to our archives.

"The Hidden Archivist has also asked me to convey that, between his long personal knowledge of Shaananca and having overheard comments by his captors at The Nidus, he rejects any suggestions or suspicions that she might have been in collusion with, or even unwittingly manipulated by, them. On the contrary, they considered Senior Archivist Shaananca a singular threat to their plans."

"Which were what?" Paramon asked, leaning forward quickly.

"It is not my place to say," the Uulamantre said, lowering his eyes slightly. "Besides, I believe that as the First Advisor for External Affairs, Propretor Wynclynran would have at least as much information on that matter as I do. I may only say that the Hidden Archivist swears on his kin and his tree that Shaananca is not to be suspected of any wrongdoing."

"And Outrider Druadaen?" asked Olcuissan impassively.

"He did not say."

"Because he did not know?"

"I suspect it is because he refused to dignify such a theory by deigning to respond to it."

Sutaenë and Paramon both bristled. Druadaen resisted the urge to bite his lip. There it was: the infamous Iavarain proclivity for responding to specious comments with serene but biting disdain.

Paramon did not fail to exploit Tharêdæath's slip in decorum. "I wondered how long it would take our esteemed guest to curl a lip at his barbaric hosts. Even though we are supposed to accept him in lieu of the actual authority on such matters." He crossed his arms. "I am not disposed to accept the word of anyone but the Hidden Archivist himself."

Wynclynran looked down the table at him with dead eyes. "Hierarch, you are certainly aware that the Hidden Archivist cannot emerge from hiding, ever. And certainly not after being seized by the Tsost-Dyxos."

"I am aware of all of that. But that does not bear upon whether I deem the input of an intermediary reliable enough for admission as evidence."

Olcuissan's voice was crisp. "As you have already been reminded, this is not a trial."

"No, but it should be."

"Enough," Tharêdæath said quietly, but with such firmness that the room became silent. "I have come at the behest of various members of this forum. However, I have been questioned as though I am a suspect, rather than a friend."

"I presume you have a point to make?" Paramon speculated with faux diffidence.

Druadaen glanced at Sutaenë. So did Alcuin, Wynclynran, and Olcuissan, waiting for Sutaenë to censure, or at least mildly rebuke, Paramon.

But instead, she said, "Perhaps you find our courtesy strained because you claim to have known the 'truth' about Saqqaru all along. Assuming, that is, that your account of its origin is any more accurate than the ones brought to us by this Outrider."

The room was utterly silent. Druadaen suspected it was because, like him, they were still wondering if they had heard correctly: that the senior leader of the largest single temple in the Helper pantheon—Adrah—had just implied an august emissary from Mirroskye warranted brusque treatment because his people had not conveyed the information they had on Saqqaru's origins. Information that, it was suggested, was either the product of mistake or mendacity.

Alcuin recovered from his surprise first. "Til'A'Tharêdæath—"

But the Uulamantre held up a long-fingered hand. "No, my friend. I cannot let this pass. Hierarch Sutaenë, you know the twinned history of our peoples since the Cataclysm. You know that the Iavarain do not insist on helping where their help is not wanted. Or where it is received with doubt and resentment, as has been the increasing reaction of your human temples. With some notable exceptions," he added, glancing at Olcuissan. "We have accommodated your fears and restrictions. We have allowed ourselves to be muzzled so that our words would not be at odds with the cosmology and creation accounts promulgated by your deities.

"But there comes a point where our input becomes pointless if your restrictions leave us unable to share salient facts, or alert you to dangers, that live in our memories but not in yours. Yet some of your hieroxi have asserted that it is only those memories and knowledge that make it acceptable to 'tolerate' creedless beings like ourselves. We have found the inherent contradiction baffling, to say the least.

"But now, it seems you no longer value our memories at all because you no longer believe them." He leaned slightly toward Sutaenë, his eyes narrowed, questioning.

Sutaenë was visibly sweating as she forced herself to say, "There is considerable dispute within my temple, and others, over such harsh opinions of the Iavarain. But in the matter of the origins of Saqqaru—and therefore, the world—there is no room for debate. Our gods tell us one thing; your memories and records claim another. Our duty as consecrants is as clear as the creedlands we walk every night."

Tharêdæath nodded sadly. "We repeatedly advised your forebears on the inevitability of this very conundrum and how it might affect their temples. In time, we predicted, the truth of the world would emerge, even if we agreed to remain silent." He shrugged. "We were ignored."

"They were fools to even listen to your godless fables!" Paramon shouted. "My temple is done with their ways. And with you. And so are the others that I represent. We will not have you tree-birthed perversities steering us from the shadows. Not any longer!"

Tharêdæath straightened and shook his head. "We are at an end, then."

"Til'A'Tharêdæath," Alcuin said, standing, "this is neither the will nor the word of the Dunarran people. This is—"

"This is," the Uulamantre interrupted sadly, "the holy writ of your temples, which have the ear of your people. I am sorry, my friend, but we must take our leave. And the Hidden Archivist shall be departing with us. No, do not object: this possibility was foreseen by the Great Pool. I am bidden to inform you that as of this moment, the covenants that have bound our peoples are deemed undone."

Sutaenë stood too. "Til'A'Tharêdæath," she said, finally using the proper honorific, "surely there must be a way to resolve your dissatisfaction with our alliance. Surely we can persuade you to—"

But Tharêdæath silenced her with a slow shake of his head. "It is your own intransigence which has brought this to pass. It lies within your scope—and only yours—to correct it. For it is not we who have changed; it is you." He bowed, smiled sadly at Alcuin, then Druadaen, and then left without a backward glance.

CHAPTER SIXTY-TWO

The door to the council room closed. Both Alcuin and Sutaenë sat heavily.

Druadaen watched as Paramon assessed the stunned faces in the room and, eyes bright, recaptured the initiative by moving the inquiry into a new domain of contention. "Outrider, I have a question about the notes you sent back to the Archive Recondite with Captain Firinne. Specifically, it is about a phrase you used in several places. You write that 'the world is broken.' Tell me, what do you mean by that?"

Between contempt for the hierarch's obvious scheming, and the ruin it had just wrought before his eyes, Druadaen was not mindful enough to moderate his tone or his words. "How is it *not* broken? How is it that, every ten years, the Bent reproduce into yet another Horde? How do giants even move, let alone exist? How do dragons' wings not tear apart when holding a multi-ton creature aloft? How is it that a world only ten millennia old has fossils that take much longer to form? And how is it that a continent and a people appear out of nowhere?"

Paramon shrugged. "You suspect inconsistencies, witness and measure them, and conclude that our world is broken, rather than seeing them as evidence of miracles." His tone was so suddenly calm that Druadaen knew a trap was coming. "So, it seems that whatever you presume lies behind these 'contradictions,' it is not the power of the gods. Which means you clearly do not believe in them."

Druadaen did not have to feign a short surprised laugh. "Not believe in the gods? Why, what else *but* acts of gods could explain such impossibilities?"

"Well, if you *do* believe in gods, then you are disputing their wisdom and the accounts of creation they have revealed to their consecrants. In short, you are a heretic."

Druadaen had to keep his suddenly resurgent anger in check. "How can I even *be* a heretic when no god would have me?" He was suddenly grateful for his old, and oft-repeated, training to become an epiphane. "I was taught that the creedlands only exist because the gods are equal as well as different. And because of that, a person can only be accused of heresy within the confines of their own creed." He shook his head. "I don't have one."

Paramon's impatience returned in a flash of heated annoyance. "Still, how can you say the world they made is broken, when you admit that the gods have the power to sustain it with their miracles?"

Druadaen shrugged. "Firstly, I do not know that they created the world. All I know is that temples assert it is what their gods told *them*. But if that is true, then I can only conclude that the gods have little regard for the physical properties and rules that both order and govern their creation. On the contrary, they alter and frustrate its natural laws at every turn."

Temmaê's voice was calm, possibly intrigued. "But why would they do such a thing?"

Druadaen nodded. "That question is the root of all my others. Because if the gods made an orderly world only to keep breaking the rules that are the source of that order, then they have, by their own standards, created an intrinsically broken world."

Sutaenë lifted her chin. "Which is simply one of the ways they strengthen our faith: by leaving such challenges with which we must grapple."

"Sutaenë, I mean no disrespect, but is that truly a worthwhile test of faith when violations of the natural laws created by those gods are explained away, denied, and even suppressed by their anointed?"

"We suppress nothing!" exclaimed Paramon.

"Then what do you call this forum? Why do so many of the

Consentium's most powerful leaders deem it necessary to summon a single, unremarkable Outrider before them to argue such matters?" Druadaen risked a shrug. "If you had full confidence in your cosmology, and that exceptions to the natural order are simply a test of faith, then you would not hide them. Logically, questions would be embraced as the path whereby belief is expanded, not endangered."

Olcuissan shook her head, frowning. "You may not be a heretic, possibly not even a nonbeliever, but if not, then your contempt for the gods is profound. And ill-advised."

Druadaen shook his head. "I cannot have contempt for entities of which I have no personal knowledge. I simply assert that the many contradictions of natural law—extending even unto the origins of our world—are neither adequately addressed nor answered by the gods' own account of creation. If that account is, in fact, accurate."

Sutaenë bristled. "And you say you are not a heretic, suggesting that the words of the gods are false?"

"Hierarch Sutaenë, I fear you mistake my meaning. I freely admit I have no idea what the gods have or have not said. Rather, I am posing a different question: Were the gods the source of those accounts, or were they written by nervous hieroxi who noticed the same apparent inconsistencies I have and resolved to explain them away or bury them?"

Paramon's rage had him spraying spittle. "You call us liars!"

"Not at all," Druadaen responded mildly. "I am simply pointing out a very basic truth: that not all humans are truthful. Not even those that the gods choose to anoint as their servants."

Sutaenë's frown was ominous. "You believe that gods fail to detect such flawed souls during epiphanesis and then consecration? Or that they would fail to correct such misconduct?"

Druadaen met her damning eyes. "Do gods know our future actions? Do they meet their followers in the creedland to correct their errors in belief or deed? On the first matter, I am told the gods have always been silent. On the second, I have never heard of a god speaking to a follower as they dreamwalk." He paused, studied the silent hieroxi. "But perhaps one of you has experienced otherwise?"

He was answered by utter silence and utter stillness, except for a slow, small grin on Temmaê's face.

Until Sutaenë—tears starting into her wide, desperate eyes—shouted, "Who are you, to question millennia of faith? This is why consecrants keep such matters to ourselves: look at where your cursed questions have brought us, and what they have wrought! Mirroskye and the Consentium parting ways; it is worse than my worst fears of what could arise from this forum. This is what Tsost-Dyxos wants! Us bickering, our oldest allies walking out the doors that they first built and later bequeathed to us."

Paramon took that as his cue. "Do you see what you have done, you impudent pup? You are ruining what thousands of years could not!"

"Then it wasn't very solid to begin with," Druadaen said with a sigh. "I am but one inconsequential person asking peculiar questions to which almost no one listened. Until they became troublesome. But rather than ignore or tolerate or encourage them, you summoned me here with great urgency." He shook his head. "It is not my nonbelief or even my investigations that concern you; it is the fear of what might happen if others begin asking the same questions I have."

Druadaen shrugged. "One person does not have the power to topple a temple...unless it has become so dry and brittle that, with a single push, it is ready to collapse under its own weight."

No one at the table spoke until Alcuin rose. "Thank you for your forthright statements, Outrider. Please wait outside with the escort."

There was no way to keep track of the passing time in the corridor. The many buildings of the Propretorium were designed to be citadels of last refuge as well, so their casement windows admitted little sun on the best of days. But this one was still overcast. Of course.

Druadaen wondered if they were deciding whether to release him, ask him more questions, or arguing over his fate—whatever that might mean in the context of such a strange and unofficial forum as this one. He had almost accepted that he had no reasonable reason for anticipating any outcome more than any other when the door opened and one of the guards asked Druadaen to return.

The faces behind the long table were impassive. Senior officials every one, they had all developed the ability to remain utterly expressionless. They continued doing so until he had once again come to stand behind the small lectern facing them.

Sutaenë stood, tilted her chin a little higher before she spoke. "Druadaen, son of Tarthenex. Your questions, investigations, and opinions clearly demonstrate that you reject the authority of the temples of the Helper pantheon, as well as the theology and cosmology that is their foundation, and for which the acts of living gods stand as daily proof. Indeed, you have turned your back upon all creeds. So now they must turn their backs upon you."

You mean, a second *time?* he wanted to ask, but didn't.

"Accordingly," she continued, "insofar as you do not recognize the powers or prerogatives of Dunarra's temples, nor profess allegiance to or membership in any of them, you must be deemed a person who is unwilling to ensure their welfare when acting in the name of the Consentium. As such, we are formally petitioning the secular authorities to immediately suspend your status and rights as an Outrider, as well as any other official position or capacity with which you have been entrusted. This measure is adopted pending your final and irrevocable dismissal from national service."

Druadaen managed not to blink in surprise. Clearly, this had been a forum in name only; having become a bone of contention between Dunarra's religious and secular authorities, his own fate hung in the balance.

As Sutaenë sat and Alcuin stood, he wondered just how ferocious this fight was going to get.

Alcuin cleared his throat. "It is the opinion of the representatives of the Propretoriate here present that Outrider Druadaen has committed no offense against the Consentium or any other power. Furthermore, we reassert that he has the same rights as any citizen, including full freedom regarding his religious practice and affiliation, including nonbelief."

It was a reassuring start, but there was something creeping into Alcuin's tone, something too much like . . . regret?

"However, insofar as our society is made stable by the harmonious synergy of both secular and divine power, and insofar as the particular activities of Outrider Druadaen would cause especial and profound strife between those two institutions, the Propretoriate is, effective immediately, resolved to release you from service. With great regret."

Druadaen managed not to sway but could barely keep track of the flowing words as the shock moved through him.

"Since this matter is not being resolved in a court or other official hearing, you may contest it. However, I must warn you that the Propretoriate does not encourage nor welcome a challenge to this decision and would look unfavorably upon it. The secular powers of Dunarra cannot safely reject or ignore the deepest concerns of the divine, and we have agreed to this resolution as a singular accommodation to their singular level of concern.

"We do, however, encourage you to pursue any other profession you may choose within Dunarra. Your various commanders, as well as the Propretoriate representatives here present, shall be pleased to support those pursuits with letters of recommendation. You will be recorded as having served the Consentium with honor, high merit, and in a fashion befitting of an exemplary citizen."

Paramon allowed a smile to creep up the corners of his mouth. "About that citizenship."

Alcuin, who had been halfway into his seat, frowned, stood again. "What about it?"

"I am afraid," the hierarch explained, "that he was never a citizen."

Alcuin's frown was as intense and dangerous and worried as his voice. "What do you mean?" But it was Temmaê's reaction which turned Druadaen's stomach hard and cold: she closed her eyes and put her fingertips to her smooth forehead.

Druadaen didn't know how, but he was suddenly quite sure that his was a lost cause.

"Well," explained Paramon, "when the Outrider's name came up in connection with all three Tsost-Dyxos attacks, we discovered that his parents were not, in fact, Dunarran. It was not by chance that they dwelt in Connæar, although it seems they never swore fealty to her king, either. Which means they also lacked status as citizens of that protectorate. So their son was, and still is, as unattached as they were."

"But...but I have served the Consentium as a citizen!" Druadaen blurted out before he was even aware he was going to do so.

"Under false pretenses," amended Paramon.

"But I did not know!"

"That is a moot point. Your service does not make you a citizen, particularly retroactively." Paramon turned and smiled broadly at

Alcuin. "Did you not wonder why we so quickly abandoned our demands that he be banished? Or worse?" The hierarch shrugged, turned away from Alcuin's silent, fuming stare. "Now, there is not even a need to formally banish you, young sir. We merely demand that the secular authorities promptly enforce what they should have long ago; revoke what was always your *provisional* status as a citizen of Dunarra."

Druadaen straightened. "Your authority is religious, not secular. You cannot dictate matters of citizenship!"

Paramon looked at him, almost amused. "Can't we?"

Druadaen looked to Alcuin—and in that moment, and in Alcuin's anguished, rageful expression he read a crushing truth that he had never thought to encounter in Dunarra: that even here, justice, rights, and promises are all dispensable when the fate of an individual is the price to be paid for the unity of a nation.

Druadaen felt a chill run out from his shoulders and down his spine. "So, is it the temples that rule in Dunarra, now?" he asked the room. Then he stared at Alcuin. "And are priests now autocrats, *presumed* to have the support of what is supposed to be a voting citizenry? Am I the only one who sees the paradox— not to say 'contradiction'—in this?" He stepped toward Alcuin.

He heard the escort moving behind him.

Alcuin waved them to stop. "I am sorry, Druadaen. This is my fault. I was unaware of the details regarding your parents."

"And apparently," Paramon said, "young Outriders are not the only ones who can conduct detailed research. Just as comparatively young secular leaders are not the only ones who can exert influence beyond the normal limits of their office."

"I'll apply for citizenship," Druadaen muttered. "Certainly I can—"

"Certainly you cannot," Paramon almost gloated as Sutaenë stared at her colleague in frank disgust. "There is a law against it, in these specific circumstances."

Druadaen frowned, fought against the feeling that his head was starting to spin. "What is he talking about?"

Olcuissan looked straight forward as he explained. "It is an obscure code that dates to the end of the First Consentium. When Dunarra retracted, thousands of people who'd worked with it, or served it as military auxiliaries, begged to become citizens. The numbers were too great. So an ordinance was passed that excluded prior service as a factor in considering requests for citizenship."

"Well," Druadaen muttered, casting about for a solution. "I can make my request without reference to my prior service. I can still apply. Just as I am."

"You need persons to speak for you, young former Outrider," Paramon pointed out. "And if anyone should happen to make a personal recommendation against your application—well, I'm told that makes the outcome very uncertain and very, *very* lengthy." Paramon smiled. "But do try! I'm sure you'll be rejected in no more than five years' time. Well, perhaps seven."

Peripherally seeing Alcuin's head sag, Druadaen knew that Paramon was neither lying nor exaggerating. "Where . . . where shall I go?" he wondered aloud.

"Not our business," Paramon said, "and you must depart the Waiting House within the day, now that your status has been determined. You came on a ship? Good. You probably haven't unpacked yet, so with any luck you can be on one tonight. Or sleep in the foreigners' quarter. Or the streets."

Paramon stood, every other eye in the room burning into him. If he noticed, he gave no sign. Still in high spirits, he said, "Well, Sutaenë, do call an end to this dreadful forum! I'm late for lunch."

EPILOGUE:

THE LAST LESSON

Druadaen entered the foreigners' quarter through the dockside gate and discovered all four of his companions lounging on their packs at the foot of the pier. One look at them and he knew: *They've heard already.*

"Well," S'ythreni sighed, "it took you long enough." But her smile was almost gentle.

Umkhira spat in the direction of the inner city. "They disgrace themselves. They do not deserve you."

Elweyr shrugged. "I'm just glad they didn't lock you up for good."

Ahearn's face conveyed a strange mix of emotions; his eyes were sad, but his smile was genuine. "Well, are you ready to go?"

Druadaen had never needed to sit to gather his thoughts, but now he did. "I'm not sure I'm ready to *walk*." Smiles sprung up in response.

Ahearn sat beside him. "Now, to my way of thinking, the biggest problem with countries and kingdoms is that, well, they're just too big. Take this day for example. Man comes home, havin' done great service to his nation and even its allies, never asking fer a pence in return. And what does he get? Why, kicked in the teeth, then in the bollocks, and then to the curb. All because high and mighty lords and ladies are having a 'difference of opinions' about whose ass should get bussed first, eh?"

"Well," Druadaen mumbled, "it is a little more serious than that."

"Ah, well, let's leave off 'serious' for now, yeh, mate? You've always got plenty o' that commodity. But right now, I'll presume upon your patience to take just a few more liberties.

"As I was saying, the bigger the place, the shorter its memory and the smaller its heart. And while this Dunarra of yours is better than most, well, it's bigger than most, too, i'n't it? So it only stands to reason that you'll always give more than you'll get back, you'll always show it more loyalty than it shows you, and you'll always hurt to leave it more than it's sad to see you go. So—to coin a phrase, Philosopher—take a page from our book. We're small and we'll get roughed up and probably die faster and be forgotten sooner than most, but while we live... Well, we know who we are, what we're about, and that our mates have our back as we have theirs. And now that you're loose of the shackles of this place, you're free to be what you should have been from the very start.

"And what's that?"

"Why, you're one of *us* now! And that, my friend, should be country enough for any man."

"I suppose it is," Druadaen said through a smile that surprised him. "And I suppose we should—"

"Lad," said a familiar voice, "someone wants a word with you."

Druadaen turned and stood quickly. It was Varcaxtan, and he had a strangely disheveled and wiry man in tow. "Uncle Varcaxtan, what are you doing here?" He saw the look in the gentle green eyes. "Oh. I see you've heard, too."

"*Heard*? Alcuin just about tore a hole through the wall when he came back." Varcaxtan shook his head. "He tried to get you off the hook, lad. But the temples, they just weren't having it. They weren't going to be happy until they had you out. But we'd best leave all that for later; we haven't much time for this friend of mine to say his piece."

Druadaen and the others stared at the prematurely old, even wizened man standing before them in a daze or a stupor. Or even an episode of open-eyed sleepwalking.

"Er..." Druadaen began, "I am pleased to meet you...?"

The man's face did not become animated, but his voice and mouth were suddenly quite lively. "Well, I never did share my name and I have no intention of doing so under these circumstances.

And speaking of circumstances, I thought I made it very clear that you were not to return to Tlulanxu. But there you are anyway. It is so frustrating, trying to help humans; you give them perfectly reasonable advice and they ignore it. And why shouldn't they? After all, I've only lived a century for every year they've—"

"Dragon?" gasped Druadaen.

"Well, of course!"

"But...what...? I mean how—?"

"There you go again, babbling question words without subject, verb or predicate. What did they teach you in school, human? No: don't answer that. You'll probably give me the syllabus of every class you attended after you were out of diapers. Possibly those that came before.

"Now pay attention. We do not have very long. This is very wearying for me, particularly when the body I enter is as, eh, compromised as this one."

"*Aa-hai!*" Umkhira exclaimed. "It is true? Dragons can possess the bodies of fools?"

"Well, not exactly a fool, Lightstrider. If Varcaxtan hasn't related this poor fellow's circumstances, he used to be a sail handler on one of your ships. Quite proficient. But bad weather and a worse misstep and he fell to the deck. Barely survived."

"And not much in the way of thought left," Varcaxtan muttered. "He was a good fellow, too."

"At any rate, his mind is accepting of the arrangement. This is the only way he may move around and see the world outside the house of his oldest daughter—who very much welcomes these reprieves from her care of him. Now, I presume I've answered all your pestiferous questions, so we shall get on with my reason for being here at all."

The wizened man spasmed, quaked, and was quiescent again.

"Hello?" Druadaen said, when no further speech emerged from the slack mouth.

Then the lips writhed and the same voice emerged, but with an entirely different cadence and accent. "Hello, Druadaen. I am sorry that I cannot be there to see you off yet again, but I am still being 'entertained' in The Waiting House." The laugh that followed was musical and high.

"Shaananca?"

"Yes, my boy."

Elweyr leaned back. Ahearn's eyes were wide. Umkhira traced a warding sign in the air before her.

"I am so very sorry for what happened today. I feel I may have been responsible."

"What do you mean?"

"There isn't the time for that now. Only enough time to tell you this: recall your father's words, Druadaen. About what you might achieve and who you might become. Always be ready to follow that path. Without doubt, without hesitation."

As soon as Druadaen pushed past the strange sensation of speaking earnestly to Shaananca through a blank-eyed invalid, he asked, "What are you suggesting or foretelling?" He laughed. "That I might yet be a general or a Propretor somewhere else?"

"Shaananca" smiled back at him. "That, too, may be in your future."

"But my father said—"

"Your father said many things. And you were a young boy when you heard them. But you did the most important thing you could at that age: you remembered and cherished his words. Now you are old enough to begin exploring what they might mean."

Druadaen shook his head. "Shaananca, I'm sorry. I don't really understand what you're trying to tell me."

"I'm telling you that your father saw something in you before the rest of us did. It is why you have become such an extraordinary Outrider."

"Yes...so extraordinary that I have been dismissed." The snickers behind him didn't feel derisive; they felt...well, they felt like home.

Shaananca wasn't joining in for the laugh, however; her voice was deadly serious. "Being banished is often what happens to those few who have the skill, integrity, and perhaps fate to find information that is not merely new, but that challenges what we think we know. Your father saw that potential in you. Only later did I discover how correct his perception was." She paused. "This may be hard to hear right now, and perhaps hard to believe in this moment, but it is fortunate for us that you are on this path that leads you *away* from Dunarra."

"Fortunate in what way?"

"Fortunate in that you are still free to find the truth. It is a great gift, even if it causes turmoil and pain."

"It most certainly causes those," he agreed.

"You have learned that better than most ever do. But should you ever waver in your resolve, remember this: while there is no mancery that can show us the outcomes of our present deeds, there is never any profit in turning one's back on the truth. Doing so almost always inflicts terrible costs, sooner or later. So keep asking your questions, Druadaen, son of Tarthenex and Mressenë. We depend on it."

"'We'?" he repeated. But the invalid's face and mouth were slack once again. He glanced at his uncle. "Does the dragon do this frequently?"

"No more than I must, I assure you," the dragon's "voice" answered.

Druadaen shook his head, was surprised to find himself laughing. "How on all the moons do you and my uncle know each other? How did you meet?"

"It was he who brought me the sword."

"Him? He's the traveler?"

"Did I not just say that?"

Druadaen hardly noticed the dragon's barbed reply. "Uncle, who gave you the sword?"

Varcaxtan thought for a moment. "No reason not to say, I suppose. Alcuin II."

"The Propretor Princeps?" Druadaen realized the entire group had now pressed close in behind him, hanging on every word. "Why did he want me to have it?"

"Well, firstly, he wasn't the Propretor Princeps back in those days. And you weren't even a glimmer in your parents' eyes, yet. At least I don't think so."

"Was it Alcuin's? Where did it come from? Who made it?"

"Lad," Varcaxtan muttered, "I didn't even know what it was I was carrying."

The "dragon" chuckled. "He was quite delightfully ignorant when he arrived. The very epitome of human haplessness. Extremely entertaining."

"Hush, you ill-tempered old wyrm, or I'll—"

"You'll what?"

"I'll tell them about the time you found yourself in the mind of a Wolfkynde, it changed, and you couldn't get out."

"Please don't," the dragon sighed.

"It was rutting season," Varcaxtan whispered behind his palm.

"I heard that!" the dragon barked.

"You were supposed to."

"A likely story. Now, enough of Varcaxtan's tall tales, exaggerations, and outright lies. I received another message for you, Outrider, just before arriving here."

"Aye, that was strange," Varcaxtan agreed.

"It was indeed. I have lived long enough that I thought I was running out of new experiences, but wherever this Dunarran's existence touches mine, it seems novelty erupts like mushrooms after spring rain."

"What was so unusual about it?" Elweyr asked eagerly from over Druadaen's shoulder.

"Ah, the thaumantic. Acceptable to hear your voice. Albeit barely. But on the matter of this contact: it was as if the person I met was under the influence of another mind."

"You mean, while you were occupying this invalid, you encountered *another* occupied person?"

"That is precisely what I mean. I find the mere fact that I could be so easily located unnerving, almost as much as the message itself."

"What was it? Whom from?" Druadaen asked.

By way of answer, the dragon's voice became strangely detached, almost as if he were being possessed as he repeated it. "Convey this to Outrider Druadaen of Dunarra. He is guaranteed enough wealth to recompense him for his journey here, and a reasonable amount more. My mistress desires that Druadaen should come and discuss matters of mutual interest."

There was a pause and the invalid shuddered, blinking and flinching as if in a fast-moving dream.

"The wyrm was asking questions on your behalf, at this point," his uncle whispered.

Then the dragon's dronelike recounting of the messenger's words resumed. "I assure you, the promise of coin is quite genuine. The discussion is not upon just any topic, just as the invitation does not come from just any person. The Lady of the Mirror would have words with you in her tower in Shadowmere, across the great ocean sea in Far Amitryea. And no, she does not propose to be Outrider Druadaen's patron. She has two needs only. Firstly, that he commences travel immediately to speak with her. Secondly, that his present group remains with him at least until he has met with the Lady."

The invalid went silent, then the dragon's own "voice" came out. "Intriguing, I'd say."

"I agree. But why did she want my companions to come along? Does she have need of them, too?"

"No, but she needs them to ensure *your* safety until you reach her tower." The dragon sighed. "*Now* will you go to Shadowmere as I advised?"

"Well, yes, but that's a group decision." Druadaen glanced over his shoulder and found the group nodding eagerly; promise of coin had that effect on them. "But how did the Lady know to find you? And how in the hells do you know Shaananca? And why—?"

The "dragon's" eyes closed in weary exasperation. "Stop. Please. I am growing tired. One more question. Then I must withdraw."

Druadaen thought, realized that what he needed was not a fact, but a conjecture, one that only the dragon's singularly informed perspective might provide. "Why do you think the Lady of the Mirror is contacting me?"

"My, you are starting to ask better questions. Perhaps there is hope for you after all. However, rather than reply with an unavoidably narrow speculation that might prove moot within five seconds of meeting her, you may be better served by several concrete observations about her, since those will prove useful no matter why she has summoned you. And they will also alert you to the immense scope of what that meeting may portend.

"Both legend and report indicate that a meeting with the Lady is a fateful event with many possible outcomes, all of which have one thing in common: the lives of those who meet her are forever changed. Some go mad; some become hermits; some ride forth incognito on quests they will not disclose; some devote their lives to study and reflection; some return to their simple roots; and some never return at all. But if there is any way that one might reasonably hope to behold the truth of the world—past, present, and possible futures—it would be to pay a visit to the Lady of the Mirror."

The invalid began to sag. "I must rest. Varcaxtan, please escort this poor fellow home, if you please." And with that, the invalid leaned heavily against Varcaxtan's shoulder, barely standing upright on his own.

"Here you go," his uncle murmured to him. "I've got you. We'll just make our way back, now." He glanced at Druadaen. "By the way, after Alcuin told me about this morning's outcome, I made some inquiries around port. Turns out that the Uershaeli ship that Tharêdæath hired for passage to Saqqaru and then here is making for her home port on the morrow. I took the liberty of strolling by to see where she was going after that. Turns out she is set to refit and make her other long run of the year: to Far Amitryea. And so, of course, Shadowmere will be one of her ports of call."

"Where is she berthed?"

His uncle smiled and pointed just over their shoulders. "Just one along the pier. Any closer and it would bite you."

Druadaen frowned, thinking this was too good to be true. "But how many open bunks do they have?"

"Well, I didn't get an exact count," Varcaxtan answered, "but I know they've got enough for six."

Druadaen frowned more deeply. "But there are only five of us."

"No, we're six. I'm joining you. Since you've an invite to the Lady, that's where I must go, too."

Druadaen's confusion about his determination to meet the Lady cleared in the same instant that his heart jumped, ever so slightly. "So you think Indryllis is alive?"

His uncle frowned. "Honestly, it's not likely, but if the Lady can find the dragon to send you a message when he's moving around in another body, and not an hour after you were sent packing, well then, I figure she's the best chance I have of finding out if my darling is alive, where she might be, and how I might get her back. Now, I'll get my friend back to his family and return with my kit as soon as I'm able. Probably just a few hours, but no later than dawn."

Druadaen thought for a moment. "It sounds like you've had good luck dealing with the Uershaeli captain, Uncle Varcaxtan."

"I'd say we get on, yes."

"Well, do you think you could convince him to make a slight detour before heading back?"

"Depends. Where to?"

"Menara." Druadaen glanced at Ahearn. "I think some of my friends have business ashore."

Ahearn started, then smiled as broadly as Druadaen had

ever seen. His uncle noticed the exchange, allowed a little grin of his own. "I'll talk to the captain. I'm sure something can be worked out." He started helping the withered sailor back toward the dockside gate, leaned his head back with a broad smile. "Now, don't leave without me, lad!"

"Wouldn't dream of it," Druadaen shouted, smiling back. He nodded to himself, then turned to the others. "Back to sea for us, then. Which means we have much to do and little time in which to do it. We've got to book passage, stow our gear, buy spares and rations and alchemical reagents and more."

Rather than move, the other four just looked at him. Smiling.

"Stop staring and start moving," Druadaen muttered. "We have to step lively if we mean to sail for Shadowmere with the morning tide."